MW01503242

Forever LOVE

USA TODAY & WSJ BESTSELLING AUTHOR

SIOBHAN DAVIS

Printed by Amazon

This paperback edition © August 2022

ISBN-13: 9798843879082

Editor: Kelly Hartigan (XterraWeb) editing.xterraweb.com

Duet cover design by Shannon Passmore of Shanoff Designs

Duet cover photography by Regina Wamba

Formatted by Ciara Turley using Vellum

When FOREVER Changes

Forever Love
BOOK 1

USA TODAY BESTSELLING AUTHOR

SIOBHAN DAVIS

Gabby

Looking back, I should have seen the signs. Perhaps I did, but I subconsciously chose to ignore them.

From the time I was ten, when I first met Dylan, I knew he was my forever guy. Back then, I couldn't put words to what I was feeling, but, as the years progressed, I came to recognize it for what it was—soul-deep love. The kind only very few people ever get to experience.

Dylan was more than just my best friend, my childhood sweetheart, my lover. He was my soul mate. We were carved from the same whole—destined to be together forever.

Until he changed.

And I believed I was no longer good enough.

Until he shattered me so completely, it felt like I ceased to exist.

And I'd never experienced such heart-crushing pain.

Until he leveled me a second time, and I truly wanted to die.

But I had to stay strong because I wasn't alone in this cruel twist of fate.

I look to the sky, pleading with the stars, begging someone to tell me what I should do because I don't know how to deal with this. I don't know how to cope when my forever has changed, and I can't help wondering if I had seen the signs earlier, if I'd pushed him, would it have been enough to save us?

Or had fate already decided to alter our forever?

Dedication

In memory of Justin (Jay) Thomas

Note from the Author

This book contains sensitive subject matter that might pose potential triggers for some readers. I cannot be more descriptive without spoiling the story. If you are concerned about a specific trigger, please email me: siobhan@siobhandavis.com

Due to mature content and themes, this book is not suitable for anyone under the age of eighteen.

Chapter One
Gabby

Start of sophomore year in college

"A bunch of us are heading to the frat party later. Want to come with?" Myndi asks as we make our way out of the building on Friday after our last class of the day.

"Thanks for the invite, but I've already got plans."

She smiles knowingly at me, her green eyes twinkling. "Let me guess? With a certain hot, rich, tech nerd who worships the ground you walk on?"

I grin. "Yep. It's our four-year anniversary, so Dylan is taking me out to dinner to celebrate."

"Aw, he's so romantic. You've definitely got yourself a good one, Gabby."

"I know. I'm really lucky to have found my person. I can't ever imagine my life without him in it."

Sticking her fingers in her mouth, she makes a gagging sound. Late afternoon sun glints off the red undertones in her hair, highlighting her natural beauty. Myndi's genuine personality and laid-back manner completes the perfect package. Travis was a damn fool for cheating on her. But it's most definitely his loss.

My bestie has had no shortage of offers since we returned to campus from summer break a couple weeks ago.

"Too cheesy?" I'm still grinning as I say it. Nothing can put a dent in my good mood today. Not even the mammoth assignment Prof Brown just handed us.

"Definitely, but you own that, girl, and feel proud! Dylan's the catch of the century, and if you weren't my bestest friend in the entire universe, I might feel jealous."

I loop my arm in hers as we walk through campus. Glorious sunshine beats down on us, and it feels good to be alive. "Your Prince Charming is out there too, waiting to be claimed." I had thought Travis might be the one, but after the shit he pulled, it's clear I was mistaken. "I still can't believe Travis cheated on you with that skank. He was so devoted last year."

My bestie shrugs, but she can't disguise the flash of hurt glimmering in her eyes. "Neither can I, but I guess I never really knew him at all. Everything he said to me was a bare-faced lie."

"Let's schedule a girl's night for next week," I suggest. "Just you and me. We can grab dinner and a movie or hang out at my place. I'll kick Dylan out for the night."

Myndi and I met our first week of freshman year, and we've been pretty much joined at the hip since then. We're both studying nursing, so we spend every day together, and when she started dating Travis last year, double dates became a regular occurrence.

Travis and Dylan were close, until Travis did the unthinkable over the summer and Myndi kicked him to the curb. Now, Dylan refuses to return Travis's calls, and I admire his loyalty to my friend—as if I need additional reasons to adore my long-term boyfriend and childhood sweetheart.

"That'd be great, but I don't want to kick Dylan out of his own condo. We'll just ban him to the bedroom and commandeer the living room."

"Sounds like a plan."

A shrill whistle pierces my eardrums, and I look up as my name is called. My brother, Ryan, waves from across the street. He's in his running gear, and, judging by the hair plastered to his forehead, I'm guessing he's on the return route of his daily jog. He sprints across the road with a certain look on his face. One I've seen way too many times to count.

"Good evening, ladies," he says, all but ignoring me as he grins seductively at my friend. Very slowly, he peruses the length of her body, licking his lips and folding his muscular arms across his torso. Myndi's chest visibly heaves as she returns the eye-fuck, and I know it's time to stop this train wreck from happening.

I punch Ryan in the arm.

Hard.

"Ow!" Rubbing his arm, he scowls at me. "What the fuck was that for?"

"Quit with the sleazy 'come fuck me' looks. Myndi is my best friend so that means she's off limits to the likes of you." I prod my finger in his solid chest to drill my point home. It's not the first time I've had to issue a warning. He's been after her since last year. Although he'd never make a move on any girl in a relationship, now that Myndi and Travis are no more, he seems to have made it a mission to get her underneath him.

As much as I love my brother, and I truly *adore* him, he's a complete manwhore, leaving a trail of broken hearts all over campus. If I thought his intentions were serious, and that Myndi was into it, I wouldn't stand in their way, but I don't want to see her hurt. And I don't want things to become awkward. Even though Ryan, Slater, and their crew are seniors, we still hang with them a lot, and if Ryan treated Myndi like one of his "girls," things would definitely get messy.

"You're lucky you're my favorite sister," he grumbles, shoving my finger away.

I purse my lips and narrow my eyes. "I'm your *only* sister."

"Exactly." He smirks, and I roll my eyes.

"Myndi has just had a bad breakup and the last thing she needs is Mr. One-night Stand hitting on her."

He slams a hand over his chest, feigning upset. "You slay me, little sis. Such cruel words."

"Don't even try to deny it. There's a running roll call of your conquests on the wall in the girls' restroom." A sour taste fills my mouth. "That is something I should never have to see." I'm not confirming it's a list of the hottest guys on campus with each girl rating their skills on a scale of one to ten. Or the fact he and Slater are more than holding their own at the top of the list. Ugh. A sister does not need to know this stuff.

He puffs out his chest, and his lips curl up at the corners. "Can't help it if the ladies love what I'm offering." He shoots us a smug grin. "It's all in the James' genes. You'd know it if you hadn't attached yourself to Woods when you were still in diapers."

I smack his chest this time. "I was fifteen when Dylan and I first started going out. Asshat."

"Does Woods know you get off on beating up defenseless men?" He grabs his chin between his thumb and forefinger. "Or is that the standard he's used to?"

I fist my hands into knots, working hard to quell the urge to thump him again. "Ugh. You are so freaking annoying. Thank God, it's your last year here."

Quick as a flash, he grabs me into a headlock, messing up my hair. "Don't be mean, Tornado. You know you'll miss your favorite brother."

Ryan started calling me Tornado when I was about five after my propensity to race around the place, blowing in and out of rooms like a tornado. I've always had an abundance of restless energy, and it's why you'll rarely find me lounging around doing nothing. I like to keep active. The only exception is sleep. I love my bed and enjoy sleeping late, but once I'm up and out in the world, I'm always on the go.

I aim a punch toward his gut, but he snatches my wrist and effortlessly lifts me up, throwing me over his shoulder. I hate being the smallest in my family and the fact all three of my brothers use that to their advantage when it suits them.

"Put me down, Randy Ryan," I yell, balling my hands into fists and pummeling his back. Ryan hates that name, and I love throwing it out to piss him off. The girls in high school gave him the label, and it stuck, much to his disgust. Especially when Sexy Slater rubbed his much cooler nickname in his face. My brother's best friend was a permanent fixture around our house growing up, so I've spent years listening to them winding one another up. Slater's practically a surrogate James.

Especially in the last year.

A pang of sorrow slams into me, but Ryan derails my emotions when he swats my butt, dragging me back into the moment. "Hitting is not nice, Gabby. Mom and Dad would be so disappointed to realize their little baby girl is a wannabe Katie Taylor."

"Neither is screwing girls, making them fall in love with you, and then ignoring them, but you don't see me running to the folks like a big blabbermouth." I wriggle aggressively in his hold, and he relents, finally letting me down. I move to punch him in the gut again, but I'm only messing around. When he holds his hands up in a defensive stanch, I grab his face and smack a loud kiss on his cheek instead. "Love you, little big bro."

I'm the youngest in our family, and Ryan is the youngest of my big brothers, and we're the closest in age so, naturally, we formed the closest bond. When I was a kid, I used to call him little big bro, and it's kinda stuck over the years.

He slings his arm around my shoulder, kissing my temple. "Love you too, little sis. Always."

"You two are legit crazy," Myndi says, and I hear the amusement in her tone. "How the hell did anyone survive living in a house with the two of you?"

"We mostly just ignored them," a familiar deep masculine voice says from behind. I brush knotty strands of blonde hair back off my face and grin at my pseudo-brother.

"Sup, bruh?" Ryan greets Slater with a loud slap on the shoulder.

"I'm heading to Lil Bob for a workout before the party tonight."

My eyes drift over Slater, noticing the new tatt on his left arm and the rippling biceps stretching tight under his formfitting shirt. Slater has always enjoyed working out, but since his Mom passed six months ago, he's become a little obsessed. He's a permanent fixture at the sports facility the students have christened "Lil Bob." I guess it's part of his coping mechanism, and I'll never criticize him for that. Just thinking about his mom brings tears to my eyes, so I can only imagine how he must feel.

Noticing my lingering gaze, he arches a brow, and I blurt the first words to land in my brain. "You cut your lovely hair."

His lips curl up at one corner. "Not since the last time we met. Your observational skills suck, Belle."

Slater is the only one to call me that. I was obsessed with *Beauty and the Beast* when I was little, and Slater used to tease me saying I wanted to be Belle for access to the library. But he was only partly right. I did daydream about being Belle, but I was no different than any young girl my age, and I wanted to be her for the *prince*. Not the books! Anyway, the name stuck, and Slater has called me Belle ever since. Ryan prefers Tornado, Mom insists on using my full name, and Dad always calls me Buttercup. Most everyone else calls me Gabby. Dylan and I have pet names for one another, chosen when we were kids before either of us fully realized what we would become.

Some girls might hate being known by so many names, but it's always made me feel special.

I stick out my tongue, and Slater laughs.

"I swear your haircut must have its own Twitter profile by now," Ryan supplies, mock scowling. "If I see one more tweet about how hot Slater Evans is with his buzz cut, I'm gonna puke." He punches Slate in the shoulder. "It's good to know at least one girl is immune to your charms."

Myndi is watching all the back and forth with amusement, and I half-expect her to whip out a bucket of popcorn and settle in to watch the show.

Reaching up on tiptoes, I run my hand over Slater's shaved head. "Wow, it's so soft." He flashes me a blinding grin, showcasing his perfectly white, perfectly straight teeth. "Maybe I can convince Dylan to follow in your footsteps." Slater's smile fades, and his Adam's apple jumps in his throat.

"Dylan would look so hot with that haircut," Myndi agrees.

"I'm gonna head," Slater says, eyeballing Ryan. "See you back at the house." He gives me and Myndi a quick wave. "Catch you later."

"You coming to the party?" Ryan asks, his gaze bouncing between me and Myndi.

"I'll be there," she confirms with a smile, and they share a look. I have a feeling that train wreck is gonna happen whether I stage an intervention or not.

"I'm not sure. I don't know if Dylan has something planned for after dinner."

Myndi smirks, her mind clearly gone to the gutter, and Ryan frowns a little. Guess he doesn't like the idea of his sister having sex any more than I like thinking about him and his hordes of female admirers.

I kiss Ryan on the cheek before looping my arm through Myndi's again. "I'll text you later," I say, starting to walk away. "Have fun and stay safe!" I practically have to drag Myndi away, watching with resignation as she glances over her shoulder, shooting him a final drawn-out look. "You like him."

Her smile disappears, and she chews on the corner of her lip in an obvious tell.

"It's okay if you do," I rush to reassure her. I've never understood the apparent taboo of getting with your friend's brother or vice versa. It's not like there's any shared DNA or blood relation, so who cares?

You should be free to love who you love without barriers.

"You're both adults, and you can do what you want. I just don't want you to get hurt, and Ryan's not exactly boyfriend material."

"I know that, and I'm not looking for a replacement boyfriend. I want to focus on my studies this year, and boys will only get in the way, but that doesn't mean I can't have fun. I don't want my vajayjay to shrivel up and die from lack of use."

I grin. "That would never happen around here, and you should do what feels right. I'm a judgment free zone, but you've got to promise it won't come between us. If Ryan fucks things up, I don't want it to affect our friendship because you mean too much to me."

She squeezes my arm. "I would never let anything come between us. Especially not the weaker sex."

We both burst out laughing at our own private joke, and as we make our way through campus, I hope she's right.

Chapter Two

"**Y**ou look beautiful, baby," Dylan says when I emerge from our bedroom, ready for a night of celebration. I'm wearing the black lace dress he loves and my black and gold strappy sandals. I've curled my hair into soft waves, and it hangs to my shoulders. I've kept my makeup minimal, knowing he prefers the more natural look. Plus, I'm too lazy to spend ages in front of the mirror, primping and preening. Au naturel suits me just fine.

"And sexy as hell," he adds, stalking toward me like a man on a mission.

I back up, raising my palms out in front of me. "We don't have time," I protest when he flattens my back to the wall, bending down to kiss that sensitive spot under my ear.

"I'll be quick," he murmurs, pressing a trail of hot kisses along my neck while his hand slides up the inside of my thigh.

"You're insatiable lately." We've had a healthy sex life since we popped one another's cherry when we were seventeen, but Dylan has been acting like a sex-obsessed addict the last month, and he can hardly keep his hands to himself.

Not that I'm in any way complaining, you understand.

Tilting my head back, I readily grant him more access to my neck.

"You turn me on so much, Gabby. It's like the longer we're together, the more I want you."

For a geeky tech nerd, he sure is a diehard romantic with a special affinity for words. I cup his smooth cheeks, staring into his clear hazel eyes. "I love you, Dylan. More with every passing day."

His lips meld to mine, and I angle my head, kissing him deeper as an ache starts throbbing down below. Dylan shoves my dress up to my waist and cups me through my panties. "I love you, Dimples, and you're mine. All mine. Now and forever."

I don't need any convincing.

For the longest time, I've known I was his. Only ever his.

Sliding my panties aside, he slips two fingers inside me, curling and twisting them at the right angle to hit the perfect spot. My hands fist in his messy brown hair as he drops to his knees, tugging my panties down my legs and burying his face in the apex of my thighs. Dylan could ask me to agree to anything while he's eating me out, and I'd be powerless to resist. He knows exactly how to work me into a quivering mess, and I love how enthusiastic he is.

I spread my legs wider, moaning as he licks up and down my slit before suctioning on the swollen bundle of nerves and sucking hard. It takes me all of three minutes to shout out my release, his name tumbling from my lips like a prayer.

Then he's inside me, thrusting frantically, pushing all the way in and hitting every sensitive nerve ending. I love how amazing it feels when we're joined like this. It's as if he was created purely to drive me to distraction. To turn me crazy with lust and love.

I loop one leg around his hip, and he digs his fingers into the flesh at my waist as he slams into me, harder and harder. Dragging my dress down one shoulder, he roughly yanks my bra down, lowering his head and pulling my taut nipple into his hot, wet mouth. I grip him tighter, my pussy clenching and unclenching around him as I sense him getting close. He grabs my bare ass, fondling my cheeks, while thrusting relentlessly into me, fucking me with everything he's got.

My breath is coming out in exaggerated spurts, and I'm barreling toward a second release. Then Dylan is roaring my name, spilling his hot cum deep inside me, and that sends me over the edge again.

Our joint ragged breathing is the only sound in the room as we both come down from our high. With tenderness, Dylan releases my leg, carefully placing it on the ground. Then he grabs some tissues and cleans me up before snatching my lace thong off the floor and helping me back into it. I smooth my dress down, fixing my bra and the shoulder of my dress.

Dylan leans down, softly pressing his mouth to mine. "Happy anniversary, Dimples."

I circle my arms around his neck, smiling at his childhood nickname for me. "Happy anniversary, Freckles." I brush my fingers across the smattering of freckles along his nose and cheeks.

Reaching behind, he pulls out a long black box from his back pocket. "For you." He hands it to me, maintaining eye contact. "I hope you like it. I drove the sales clerk insane with my indecisiveness."

I quirk a brow, surprised. Dylan is one of the most decisive people I know. And a huge planner. I'm shocked he hadn't already perused their website and picked out what he wanted before he visited the store. But he's been busy with his robotics project lately and a little stressed and distracted.

I peck his lips gently. "I will like it because you chose it for me, but you already gave me flowers and you're taking me to dinner, so there really was no need to buy me a gift."

He kisses my cheek. "At least I know you're not with me for my money," he teases.

"No. That'd be the earth-shattering sex."

"I knew you were just after me for my body." He gestures at himself, and I can't contain my grin. Dylan is lean and strong, and I love every inch of him, but he's a long way from the ripped look a lot of guys on campus are sporting these days.

But I wouldn't change him for the world.

I love absolutely everything about him.

"And your brilliant mind. Don't forget that too," I purr, tapping a finger against his temple. And it's true. Dylan's intelligence and genius brain are the biggest turn-ons.

"Don't keep me in suspense." He jerks his head at the box still lying unopened in my hand. "Open it."

When I pry the lid open, a shocked gasp leaks out of my mouth. "Jesus, Dylan. This is too much." The glittering choker-style necklace sparkles and glistens under the full glare of the living room lights. I know the tiniest diamond can cost a fortune, so the sheer size of the diamonds and rubies in this necklace indicates exactly how expensive it is.

"I'm good for it, and I wanted to spoil you." He shoots me that infamous lopsided grin of his that always melts my heart and dampens my panties.

Holding my hair to one side, I turn around as he moves to close it around my neck. "I know you are, but I don't need extravagant gifts to prove you love me."

And we don't do this. We agreed a long time ago not to let the money go to our heads.

Dylan has been a multi-millionaire since he sold his licensing app to Microsoft when he was fifteen, but he's never been extravagant with his wealth.

Apart from purchasing this condo for us to live in while we study at UD, and moving his mom into a house in my parents' neighborhood, he isn't known for splashing the cash. He still drives his dad's old truck, preferring to get it repaired every time it breaks down rather than purchasing a shiny, new SUV or flashy sports car. And I love him even more for it.

So that's why this has thrown me. But I don't want to appear ungrateful either.

He steers me to the long mirror in the hall, wrapping his arms around my waist from behind as I stare, slack-jawed, at my reflection in the mirror. Resting his chin on my shoulder, he captures my eyes in the mirror, and there's no mistaking the love radiating from his gaze. "You look even more stunning now." I run my fingers along the exquisite diamonds and rubies, speechless for once in my life. He places a gentle kiss on my cheek. "You deserve the world, Dimples, and I intend to give it to you."

I spin around in his embrace, resting my hands on his shoulders. "You already have, Dylan." Tears glisten in my eyes as I stare into his beautiful, expressive face. "Every day with you is a blessing and a gift, and I love this life we share."

"To us." Dylan clinks his glass against mine, and I sip the nonalcoholic champagne while gracing him with a wide smile.

"To the future." We toast again, before setting our glasses down and linking hands across the table, smiling at each other like lovesick fools. It's been like this since we admitted our feelings at fifteen and took our friendship to a whole new level.

I have never so much as looked at another guy since that day.

Dylan is all I see.

All I'll ever see.

"Mom wants us to come for dinner on Sunday," he says, just as the waitress brings our desserts. "We don't have any plans, right?"

I pause with my spoon halfway to my mouth, frowning a little. "We already promised my folks we'd drop by, remember? It's exactly six months since Slate's mom passed on Sunday, and they're hosting a family dinner. They don't want him to be alone on the day."

He rubs a spot between his brows. "Shit. Can't believe I forgot that."

"It's no biggie," I say, diving into my chocolate fondant. "I'll call

Mom and tell her to add another place. Tell your mom to come over at three."

The frat house is crammed to the rafters when we arrive an hour later. Music thumps out of loudspeakers, and a lively crowd is dancing in the main living space. Laughter trickles in from the back-yard, and we make our way through the kitchen and outside. Dylan grabs a couple of red cups on our way, and we sip the warm beer as we maneuver through the crowd, looking for familiar faces.

A shrill whistle pierces the air, and I jerk my head in that direction. Ryan shoots a hand up, and I tug on Dylan's arm, ushering him to the far end of the yard where my brother and Slater are holding court with a bunch of their buddies and a gaggle of fawning girls. Slater gets up from his chair the instant we arrive, offering it to me. When Dylan sinks into it, Slater glares at him. "It's for Belle, douche."

Dylan grips my hips, pulling me down onto his lap. "And *my woman* is seated. Problem solved." He pushes my hair aside and starts nibbling on my earlobe. Slater narrows his eyes but doesn't retaliate.

Over the years, Dylan and Slater have grown more antagonistic toward one another, especially recently, and I have no idea why. There's only two years between us and Ryan and Slater, but when we were ten—when Dylan and I first met—the guys were twelve turning thirteen and they thought they were so mature. They made it their mission to tease the crap out of us any time they could, and they loved to pick on Dylan because his bestie was a girl and he had an unusual obsession with computers.

Dylan was already a tech whiz by the time I met him, and he had an unnatural level of technical intelligence that was rare. It was no huge surprise when the app he developed came to the attention of the big tech giants and they entered a bidding war to acquire the rights.

Dylan and I had only formally become boyfriend and girlfriend around the same time. Everyone embraced our relationship, having always known our friendship was headed in that direction—Slater being the exception. It's not that he's come out and said it, but I always get the impression he thinks Dylan isn't good enough for me.

Which is ridiculous, because, if anything, it's the other way around.

"You made it!" Myndi drops down onto the ground alongside us, crossing her legs and smiling up at me. Another couple of girls from our nursing group joins us, and we chat casually while the boys trade insults behind us, laughing and joking loudly. Dylan is chatting with Ryan, running his hands through my hair while they talk.

"I need to pee," I say, climbing to my feet.

"I'll grab us some fresh drinks." Dylan rises to join me. Taking my hand, he brings me back into the house. He pecks my lips and swats my butt as I leave him in the kitchen.

There's a long line for the bathroom, so I pull out my cell, checking social media while I wait. The line moves at a snail's pace, and I cross my legs, urging my bursting bladder to hold tight for another few minutes. I lean against the wall beside one of the bedrooms while absently flicking through Instagram. The door to the bedroom is slightly ajar, and conversation trickles out to greet me.

"I'm calling bullshit on that. Dylan Woods is completely devoted to his girlfriend, and everyone knows it," a female says, piquing my interest. Pretending to be engrossed in my cell, I move a little closer to the door.

"I'm telling the fucking truth," another girl retorts, clearly pissed. "Why the hell would I make it up?"

"Maybe because you're still sour over the fact he's continuously rejected your advances and you want to try and save face."

I'm used to girls hitting on my man. He's a bit of a celebrity around these parts since the news broke of the teenage-prodigy-cum-multi-millionaire. The local paper also made a big deal when he turned down Yale to attend the University of Delaware. Most commentators speculated it was because I'd chosen to attend here, but they don't know the real reason. I would've happily moved with Dylan to any part of the country, but he didn't want to leave his Mom.

Since his dad died in a car accident when Dylan was six, he's been a rock for Heather and there's no way he'll ever leave her. Dylan's dad was the love of Heather's life, and she swears she'll never marry again. She won't even date. Dylan is the only man in her life, and she's happy to keep it that way.

If I didn't love Heather like a second mother, I might feel resentful of their close bond, but that is the furthest from the truth.

"You're a complete bitch," the girl snaps. "I'm not making this up."

"If you're trying to cause issues in his relationship, it won't work. He's crazy about her, and you should leave them alone. You're such a jealous bitch."

I have to smother the laugh waiting to rip free of my mouth. I don't know who that girl is, but I already freaking love her.

Girls hit on Dylan a lot, but I'm rarely jealous. We've been together a long time, and I trust him implicitly. I know he'd never do anything to jeopardize what we have, so this conversation is more amusing than anything.

"Screw you, Ana. I know what he said, and he was clearly aroused when he said it. He couldn't hide the bulge in his pants."

I roll my eyes, not even pretending that I'm not eavesdropping any more.

"If he wanted to suck your tits so badly, why didn't he?" the other girl challenges again. "I mean, you expect us to believe that Dylan fucking Woods, tech genius and the sweetest, most notoriously faithful guy on campus, said that to your face and then just walked away?" She scoffs. "I'm not buying it. You're delusional."

I could seriously kiss that girl. And she's voiced my sentiments exactly. Dylan is the *last* guy to say something crude to any girl. Yes, he has a bit of a dirty mouth in the bedroom, but that's only with me.

"The only reason he walked away is because it's his anniversary today and he was bringing his girlfriend out to dinner. He took my number and said he'd call or text me."

All the blood suddenly leaches from my face, and my heart starts beating erratically in my chest. *How the hell does she know that?* The line moves again, and I push off the wall, part of me grateful I can no longer hear the rest of the conversation and another part of me desperate to see what she says next.

I chew on the inside of my cheek as I contemplate all I overheard. Forcing a sudden bout of nausea aside, I think about this logically. She could have found out about our anniversary any number of ways. She could have overheard a conversation Dylan had with someone about today and our dinner plans. Hell, she could even have been eavesdropping when I told Myndi earlier this evening.

That's got to be it.

Because there's no way Dylan would ever say something so lewd to another girl, and there's no way he would ever take another girl's number.

As I make my way back outside, I shove all thoughts of that horrid woman aside, determined she's not going to ruin this special night.

Chapter Three

I wake on Saturday morning, a little achy, and my lips curl into a smile as I remember all the ways in which Dylan showed me how much he loved me last night. I got a full-body workout, and about four hours sleep, max, but I'm not complaining. Dylan is getting more and more adventurous in bed, and I'm loving it. Not that it was ever underwhelming, but when you've been a couple for as long as we have, it can tend to slip into a familiar pattern. I'm not sure what's brought it on, but I'm embracing this new sexier version of my man.

"Rise and shine, Dimples," the man of the moment says, entering our bedroom carrying a tray. He's only wearing boxers, and his hair is all messy, but he looks totally gorgeous. And completely fuckable. He grins as he approaches the side of the bed. "You've got to stop looking at me like that, Dimples, or I won't be able to restrain myself."

My eyes dart to his crotch of their own accord, and I spot the tell-tale tenting in his boxers. "Who says I want you to show restraint?" Arching a brow, I lick my lips and sit up, letting the covers pool at my waist, exposing my bare chest. He curses, gently placing the tray on my lap.

"You need to eat food first, and then you can eat me." He grins suggestively, and my lady parts swoon.

"What a tempting proposition." I lean forward, capturing his lips in a brief kiss. "Thank you for making me breakfast."

Taking my wrist, he raises it to his lips, placing a feather-soft kiss there. "It's my pleasure. I love taking care of you."

"You do such a good job of it too." It's the truth. Every weekend morning, Dylan is up early to cook me breakfast. On the nights where I have late classes or I'm at Lil Bob doing yoga or running the indoor track, he is always outside waiting to escort me home. When it rains, he leaves an umbrella by the door before he leaves. When my period hits, and I'm in agony, he administers pain pills, back and stomach massages, and readily goes to the pharmacy for tampons if I've run out, all while making sure I'm eating and getting plenty of fluids. On girls' nights out, he insists on driving me there and back, and he never has any issue with dropping any of the other girls home either. There are countless other examples I could give to prove my point.

I lucked out the day I met Dylan Woods.

There is absolutely no denying that.

It's no wonder so many girls are lusting after my guy, but most don't know him, and all they see are dollar signs in their eyes. If girls knew the truth about how amazing he is, there would be stampedes to my door.

That's not to say he's perfect. Because he isn't. No one is. He can be moody, cranky, and obsessive when he's working on some new tech project. He has the worst taste in clothing, stays up way too late playing video games, and we'd live in a pigsty if I didn't clean up his mess, but his strengths far outweigh his shortcomings.

Case in point.

He pecks me on the lips before lifting the fork and placing it in my hand. "Eat, babe. I'm gonna grab a quick shower, and then I'll be back." He winks, and I can't help swatting his butt as he saunters away. He shoots me a sexy look over his shoulder before disappearing into our en suite bath. The water turns on as I'm shoveling forkfuls of fluffy scrambled egg into my mouth. The bacon is crispy and well-done. The coffee strong and black. Just how I like it.

I've only just finished eating when he strolls back into the bedroom, wearing a skimpy towel around his hips. Beads of water slide down his chest, trickling into the promised land below. His hair is damp and slicked back, highlighting the exquisite bone structure of his face. Placing the tray on the bedside table, I kneel up, beckoning him with my fingers. "Come here, stud. I want to show you my appreciation."

He crawls over the bed toward me, grinning. "What did you have in mind?" He props up on his side, facing me.

"Let me show you." I flash him a cheeky wink as I tug at the towel, freeing his impressively hard cock. Wrapping my hand around the base of his dick, I start stroking him slowly. His eyes darken as he watches me, and warmth pools low in my belly.

"I need to touch you." He taps on my legs, and I readjust my position, placing my head at his cock and my feet against the headrest of the bed. He parts my folds with both hands and leans in, swiping his hot tongue up and down my slit. I moan loudly before bringing my face in line with his cock, taking him deep into my mouth.

We pleasure one another, and he comes first, spilling his salty load down the back of my throat. Then he lies down flat on his back, pulling me on top of him so my thighs are straddling his face. Keeping a tight grip on my hips, he devours my pussy with his tongue, alternating between dipping inside me and swirling his wicked tongue around my clit.

His fingers move from my hips to my ass, exploring and probing. When his thumb presses into my puckered hole, I gasp, writhing on top of him like a woman possessed. He's never touched me there before although we have discussed it in the recent past. He pushes his thumb in farther while his tongue works overtime on my clit. I detonate on his face as a powerful orgasm rocks through me, and he stays with me, through wave after wave, until I roll off him, collapsing face-first onto the bed.

He curls into my side, pressing delicate kisses all over my naked back. "How was that for you, baby?"

I can scarcely lift my head up, and he chuckles, running his fingers up and down my spine, brushing the cheeks of my ass.

"So good," I mumble into the pillow. "I'm still seeing stars."

He chuckles again, focusing his attention on my ass as he fondles me. "I want to take you here," he whispers, running his fingers through the crack of my ass. "I'm so hard thinking about it."

I flip around to face him, eyeing him carefully. There isn't much I would deny him, but I'm not sure about that. He already knows this. I cup his face. "You know I'm not ready for that yet."

He lies down beside me, tweaking my nose. "I would never force you, Gabby, but I could tell you liked that."

My pussy and ass tighten at his words. "I did but having your cock in there is a whole other ballgame, pun intended."

He grins. "How about some gentle exploration? We can take our time, and if you still don't want to go there, then that's completely fine."

That is something else I love about Dylan. He's always willing to find some middle ground. Open to compromise. "I can live with that."

"Awesome." He kisses me sweetly. "I'm heading to the library to meet Chase and a couple of the others to work on our robotics project, but I thought we could grab a movie later, if you like?"

I snuggle into him, pressing my cheek to his chest. "I'd love that." We hug for a few minutes before Dylan slides out of the bed to get dressed.

I watch him, inwardly chuckling at the garish red-and-green-patterned shirt he pulls on over a yellow T-shirt. It's like he got dressed in the dark, or he's colorblind, which I know he isn't. I've long since given up trying to influence his style, and it's part of what makes him so unique. And such a dork. But he's *my* dork, and I wouldn't change him for the world.

Shoving his feet into his battered Chucks, he threads his fingers through his hair, grabs his keys and wallet, and dips down to kiss me.

Oh, to be ready in thirty seconds flat. Boys have no idea how easy they have it.

"See you later, beautiful. Have a good day. Love you."

"Love you too," I say, mid-yawn, stretching languorously in the bed. Deciding to take a quick nap before I head out to meet Myndi for lunch, I close my eyes and thank God again for bringing Dylan into my life.

The following afternoon, we set out early for the ninety-minute drive back home. I want to get to my house before everyone arrives so I can help Mom with the food prep. We drive with the truck windows half down, and a balmy breeze blows strands of hair all over my face.

Dylan fiddles with the radio, finally settling on a station playing back-to-back songs from the last decade, and we shoot the breeze as we listen.

My eyes automatically lock on his when *our* song starts playing. Reaching over the console, he takes my hand, bringing it to his lips for a kiss. My heart swells with an outpouring of emotion as I let my mind wander back in time.

The front door slams, and I jump up, racing down the stairs, desperate to hear the news. Dad grins at me, hanging up his jacket and placing his briefcase on the hall table. "Where's Dylan?" I ask in a breathless voice.

"I dropped him home on the way. He's expecting you, and, given the circumstances, I think we can let you stay out past your normal curfew."

I squeal. "So, it went well?"

"Better than well," Dad says as Mom ventures into the hall, hearing his words.

"You struck a deal?" she says, smiling.

"Yep." Dad looks pleased as punch. "We ended up fielding several offers from all the top tech firms." Mom snuggles under Dad's arm, and he presses a kiss to the top of her head. "Dylan chose to sell to Microsoft because he believed that was a better fit even though their offer wasn't the top one."

Pride laces Dad's tone, and it makes me unbelievably happy. Dad has been like a surrogate dad to Dylan since he came into my life, and my family has welcomed my bestie with open arms, in the same way they welcomed Slater Evans into the fold. When Dylan asked Dad to act as his attorney on this deal, he didn't hesitate to accept.

Dad reaches out, cupping my face. "That boy is whip smart, and he has a good heart. You chose well, baby girl, and your mother and I want you to know that we approve."

"Wow, steady on, Dad. We're just friends." Although I really wish it was more, but Dylan doesn't look at me like that. I think I've always been in love with him, but it wasn't till I turned thirteen, got my period, grew boobs, and experienced a surge of hormones that I started really looking at my bestie with different eyes.

"If you say so," he teases, and he and Mom share a knowing look.

I roll my eyes. "So, what time can I stay out until?"

"Ten thirty, and not a minute later, young lady," Mom replies.

I have my hand on the door handle when Daddy calls out. "Be careful riding your bike, and stick to the sidewalk."

I roll my eyes again. "Dad, it's only four blocks away, and I know how to stay safe."

"No harm in reminding you, Buttercup." He grabs me into a hug. "I don't want anything bad to happen to my little girl."

I wonder what he'd think if he knew his little girl is having regular dirty dreams about her best friend and waking up in a pool of sweat, aching and throbbing down below.

Throwing my bike down on the grass, I bound up the steps to

Dylan's quaint two-bedroom house. I yank the door open and call out as I step foot inside. Heather, Dylan's mom, pops her head through the kitchen door. "He's in the living room, sweetie."

"Thanks, Heather."

"I've just ordered pizza and ice cream. Hope you're hungry."

"Ravenous," I lie. I'm stuffed to the gills after dinner, but I'll happily force down some pizza and ice cream in celebration of Dylan's big achievement.

I open the door to the living room, and Dylan is standing with his back to me, facing the fireplace.

MTV is on, and the haunting melody of Rihanna's "Stay" sends shivers up my spine. It's currently my absolute favorite song in the whole wide world, having knocked Taylor Swift's "Love Story" off the top spot, and that's no mean feat.

Softly, I close the door and walk toward him. "Dad told me the good news." I come up to his side. "I'm so proud of you." I tug on his arm, and he looks down on me. Dylan has shot up to over six feet these past few months, and I feel like a midget beside him with my five feet six inches.

He doesn't speak. He just stares at me strangely, and butterflies scatter in my chest when his gaze drops to my lips. Something indecipherable electrifies the tiny gap between us, and my mouth is suddenly dry. He reaches up, winding his fingers through my hair and arching my head back. His darkened eyes probe mine, and my heart is careening around my chest like a Formula One car. I gulp nervously as he leans in, and then his mouth is on mine and he's kissing me like I'm the air he needs to breathe.

I can hardly believe it.

I've dreamed of this moment for years.

In all my imaginations, it never felt as amazing as this. His lips glide across mine like they were meant to fit perfectly with my mouth. When his tongue prods at the seam of my lips, I open willingly for him, moaning when his tongue meets mine and his arms clasp firmly around my back. He holds me flush to his body as he kisses me relentlessly, and I wonder how we're both still able to breathe.

We only break apart when the doorbell rings, announcing the pizza has arrived.

We stare at one another. His cheeks are flushed, his eyes alive and bright, his lips swollen from my kisses.

"I love you, Dimples," he says, holding my gaze confidently. "I love you so very much, and I know I could never live without you."

"You love me?" I whisper, and I know I'm rocking the whole "deer in the headlights" look. "Like really love me?"

He chuckles, brushing his thumb against my lower lip. "What other way is there to love someone?" he teases.

"There are lots of different ways to experience love, Dylan." I purse my lips and send him a chastising look. "You know what I'm asking, but I'll spell it out. Do you love me just as a friend or as something more?"

"Do friends kiss other friends like that?" He winks.

"I don't really know. You're the only true friend I have."

He wraps his arms around me as Heather hollers for us to come to the kitchen. "I've been in love with you from the minute I first laid eyes on you, Dimples." My heart feels like it's going to erupt from my chest. "I love you like I will never love any other girl. There has only ever been you for me. I would literally lie down and die for you, beautiful."

I glare at him, slapping his chest, and he stares incredulously at me. I'm guessing that's not the reaction he was hoping for when he declared undying love. "Why the hell didn't you say something sooner?!" I demand, thinking of all the years of frustration I've endured believing my love was unrequited.

His expression turns serious. "I wanted to have something concrete to offer you. And I wanted to make sure the timing was right for both of us. Today's deal has secured our future, and it means I can make all our dreams come true." He swipes his nose against mine, and his breath is warm on my cheek. "I love you, Gabrielle Eloise James. I loved you yesterday. I love you right now. I'll love you tomorrow and every single day after until the day I die."

Tears pool in my eyes. "I love you too, Dylan. So very much. And I've wanted to tell you for ages, but I was afraid of ruining our friendship."

"Stay" continues to play in the background, on a loop, because he knows it's currently my favorite song and it's clear he planned this.

Dylan brushes his lips softly against mine. "That could never happen. We are one and the same, Gabby, and nothing or no one will ever come between us."

"You really mean that?"

He nods. "I believe in us one hundred percent. It's you and me, babe. We're meant to be together."

I smile over my tears, and my heart is throwing the party of all parties in my chest. I feel like pinching myself to ensure this moment is real.

He gently cups my face, as the last lines of Rihanna's song play in the background. He brushes his lips against mine again. "So, what do you say, Dimples? Will you stay forever mine?"

Chapter Four

"I still remember that day as clearly as if it was yesterday," Dylan says, dragging me back to the present. Every time that song plays, we are both transported back to that day. "I can still feel our first kiss." He touches his lips, and the look of adoration on his face as he too reminisces melts me into a puddle of goo. Stretching across the console, I kiss him softly, my heart consumed with love for this boy.

"Me too, babe, and my lips tingle every time I think of it." My heart is fit to burst. "You made me the happiest girl alive that day."

"Ditto, beautiful. I still can't believe I got this lucky. You're more than any guy could ever hope for."

Tears glisten in my eyes, and I squeeze his hand. I'm too choked up to respond, but he gets it, and we don't talk as we listen to the rest of the words. They get me, right in the feels, like every other time I've heard this song. With a dreamy smile on my face, I stare at Dylan while he drives, and I can tell he's equally as moved as me.

"You still want it for our first dance?" he asks, when the song ends.

"Without a shadow of doubt."

From that moment on, we've had everything mapped out. Once we crossed that point, and admitted our feelings, we've enjoyed planning our lives together. We're getting engaged as soon as we graduate, and we've already decided we only want a short engagement. I'm definitely one of those girls who has her wedding day all organized, down to the song we'll dance our first dance to and the type of cake we're going to have—red velvet with cream cheese frosting, if you'd like to know.

I don't care that it's not considered cool to get married young anymore.

When you've found your soul mate, there's no reason to wait.

We love each other, and there will never be anyone else for either of us.

There has never been any truth more assured.

And I've blossomed these last four years with the knowledge that Dylan loves me as completely and irrevocably as I love him.

His love has given me the confidence to surge forward in my life, and I'm blessed that I've never had to face any difficulties or deal with any obstacles. I know I'm very fortunate. That I have amazing parents, brothers I love, a career I'm looking forward to pursuing, and the love of my life by my side. We're especially fortunate that we have the funds to make our dreams come true. The Microsoft payout secured our future, and Dylan's exceptional genius means it's only the tip of the iceberg.

I don't think life gets much better than this. I never take it for granted, offering up thanks regularly to God for giving me this amazing life.

Little did I realize how everything would soon shatter, tearing my world apart.

"Let me look at you," Mom says as we enter the kitchen, holding me at arm's length as she casts her eyes over me. "You look thinner." She narrows her eyes to slits.

"I haven't lost weight since you saw me last week." I roll my eyes. "You say this every time I come home." My fast metabolism combined with my love of running and yoga and good genes means I maintain a slim figure even if I eat like a horse most of the time. I'm sure one of these days it'll catch up with me, and I'll wake up the size of an elephant, but, for now, I'm happy to continue in denial.

"Is she eating enough?" Mom asks Dylan, ignoring me.

"She eats more than I do, Lucy. Stop worrying. I'm taking care of our girl." He gives her a quick hug as Dad opens the back door.

"Well, if it isn't love's young dream." His booming voice echoes around the large kitchen. "Hey, Buttercup." He reaches for me, enveloping me in his strong arms. "How's my little girl?"

"I'm good, Daddy. Crazy busy with coursework already, but it's all good."

"Wow," Mom says, finally noticing the new adornment around my neck. "That is a beautiful necklace."

I sling my arm around Dylan's waist, and he pulls me in close to his side, kissing the top of my head. "Dylan got it for me for our anniversary," I confirm.

Dad squeezes Dylan's shoulder. "Make sure you add that to your homeowner's insurance policy, son." Always so practical, just like my beau.

"Already taken care of, Paul."

"Good man." Dad beams at him like a proud father.

The front door slams with a loud bang and footsteps approach. Ryan steps into the room with a customary smirk on his face. He's wearing low-hanging jeans, a faded Linkin Park shirt, and Old Skool Vans. His blond hair is a little on the long side at the moment, falling over his forehead, and his blue eyes twinkle with mischief. It's no wonder the girls on campus drop their panties for him without hesitation. "Don't all rush me at once," he quips, holding out his arms.

Mom sinks into his arms, tenderly embracing her youngest son. After they hug it out, she gives him the once-over too. "Do any of you kids eat?" she murmurs, scowling at his lean but well-defined torso.

"Does ingesting beer count?" Ryan retorts, smirking.

"How the hell are you, son?" Dad gives him a firm man-hug.

"I'm straight fire, old man."

"Care to repeat that in English?" Dad requests.

I laugh, moving toward my brother. "Put him out of his misery."

"Dad, I'm good. Chill." Ryan jerks his head at Dylan. "Sup, asshat?"

"Whatever, douche," Dylan replies with a grin, as they trade the usual insults.

"Language, Ryan," Mom says, stirring a pot on the stove. "We'll have young impressionable children here today, and I don't need Dean or Annie getting on my case about your cursing."

"Reprimand Dylan too," Ryan says, pouting.

"What, are you like two again?" I tease.

"I'm opposed to favoritism in all its forms. Dylan cussed too but Mom's given him a pass 'cause he's clearly her favorite."

"For the love of all things holy, Ryan. When will you ever grow up?" Mom exclaims before turning to Dylan. "The swear jar applies to everyone today. You included, Dylan."

"Yes, ma'am." Dylan grins at her.

Ryan grabs me into his arms, squeezing me half to death. "Missed ya, Tornado."

"You only saw me on Friday, Randy Ryan."

He ignores my use of his loathsome pet name. "That was two whole days ago. Can't go twenty-four hours without my little Tornado fix."

"You're so full of shit."

"Gabrielle!" Mom screeches so loud I have to stick my fingers in my ears.

"For fuck's sake, Ma, chill out. I think the whole neighborhood just heard you," Caleb says, walking in with his arm wrapped around his fiancée, Terri.

I fling myself at my middle brother, hugging him fiercely. "It's so good to see you. I really missed you both." I grin at my soon-to-be sister-in-law, hugging her too.

Even though there are six years between us, Caleb and I got on really well growing up. He's the most laid-back of my three brothers, and he was always my go-to guy if I needed to figure something out in my head.

While I'm closest to Ryan, and we spend the most time together, I've always had a real soft spot for Caleb. He and Terri teach at the local high school, and they're getting married next year. They went traveling during summer break, and I was already back at UD by the time they returned, so this is the first time I've seen them in months. Although we've kept in contact via FaceTime, it's no substitute for the real deal.

I take a step back and glance at my brother. He's tall, like Dad, Ryan, and Dean, and he has the same blue eyes we all have, but he has the darkest skin and the darkest hair of all of us. Add a tan to the mix, and my brother is looking as hot as ever. "Look at you," I say. "All tanned and gorgeous. Traveling obviously suits you."

"We had a fabulous time," Terri supplies. "I would highly recommend it."

"You look gorgeous too, Ter. I'll bet you were hit on left and right."

She laughs and Caleb scowls. "Don't mention the war," she murmurs under her breath, grinning.

"Girl talk, later," I say, pointing between us.

"Where's your other half?" I hear Dad say to Ryan.

"Dropped him off at the house. He wanted to check on it and grab some of his stuff," Ryan says.

"Slater shouldn't be worrying about the house," Mom cuts in. "Your dad goes over every week to check on it and to mow the lawn. And we have a gardener coming in once a month to maintain the backyard." Slater's mom was an avid gardener, and their backyard, although small, is testament to her considerable green thumb and her remarkable skill.

Dylan wraps his arms around me from behind, resting his chin on my shoulder. He knows how much Janine's death still affects me, and it's like he has a hotwire to my emotional state. That he knows how sad I am right now.

We spent a lot of time with Slater and his mom over the years, and it saddens me so much that she was taken early. She had a tough life, and it doesn't seem fair. To her or the only son she left behind. We are pretty much all Slater has by way of family now, and I know he's been struggling since her passing and that Ryan's really worried about him.

"I think he just wanted some alone time, Ma," Ryan adds. "Today's been hard for him."

Silence engulfs the room, only broken by the pitter-patter of little feet approaching. Dean and Annie's twin two-year-old daughters burst into the kitchen. "Gramma! Gramma! We broz cake!"

Mom wipes her hands on her apron and crouches down in front of her only grandchildren. Tia shoves a box at her. Mom kisses her cheek. "Thank you, sweetheart!" Then Mom kisses Mia on the cheek. "And you too, sweet girl." Dad swoops in then, pulling Tia up into his arms and throwing her into the air.

She squeals in delight. "Again, Gramps. Again!"

"Oh my God, Paul, please don't do that," Annie, my brother's wife says, bustling into the kitchen, looking stressed. "You'll give me a coronary."

Annie has been with my brother Dean since they were sixteen, and they married when they were twenty-four. The girls came along two years later.

Annie can be high-maintenance at times, and she has a tendency to overreact to things. Dean and Annie had one of those on-again, off-again relationships, and no one in the family ever expected them to end up married with kids, but they seem happy. On the outside at least. *Because who the hell knows what really goes on behind closed doors?*

"Dad, put her down or she's liable to puke on you," Dean says, materializing in the now-crowded kitchen. "When we weren't looking, she demolished a couple of cupcakes in the car on the way here so her tummy's a bit icky."

Dad puts her down so fast it's a wonder he didn't give himself whiplash. I snort out a laugh, feeling Dylan's chest rumbling with silent laughter behind me.

Mia starts tugging on Annie's leg. "Me need go potty."

Annie rubs a tense spot between her brows, looking even more hassled. Ryan and I share a look. "I'll take her," I suggest, holding out my hand. "Come on, Minnie Mia. Auntie Gabby will take you to the bathroom." She grabs onto my hand willingly, grinning up at me, and my heart melts. I adore my two nieces even if they are a complete handful at times.

I bring her to the bathroom, trying desperately to decipher her endless stream of chatter, but I can only make out the odd few words. It's actually amazing how advanced their vocab is for their ages, even if a specialist interpreter would come in handy sometimes.

The doorbell chimes as we reach the bottom of the stairs, and I haul Mia into my arms before opening the door.

Slater stands there with his hands shoved in his pockets and his shoulders slouched. I take one look at his forlorn face, and a sharp ache spreads across my chest. "Go back to the kitchen, Mia. There's a good girl." I steer her in the right direction, and she toddles off. Straightening up, I refocus on the broken man still standing on the porch. Pulling the door closed, I step out beside him. "How are you holding up?" I peer up at him.

He kicks at imaginary dirt with the toe of his boot, shrugging. I take his hand and pull him over to the love seat, forcing him to sit down. I drop down beside him. "Have you spoken to anyone yet?"

He shakes his head. "I can't, Belle. I can't force myself to open up to a stranger." Slater was a complete mess the first month after his mom passed, and we were all so worried about him. I suggested he visit a therapist, and he said he'd consider it, but then he showed up on campus for the last few weeks of spring semester and threw himself back into college life, and he seemed more like himself. I thought maybe he'd sought help and it was working.

"Well, then talk to a friend." I know Ryan has tried talking to him, but he clams up. "If you can't talk to Ryan, you can always talk to me. I won't judge or ever share anything you confide in me."

"Thanks, Belle. I know you wouldn't, but I just..." He trails off, hanging his head.

I link my fingers through his and squeeze his hand. "Don't bottle things up. It's not healthy. Find someone you can talk to. Please." I lower my voice. "I know how much you loved her, and it's okay to give in to your grief. You need to let it out."

His chest heaves, and a sob emits from his mouth. Tears prick the backs of my eyes. To see a big, sturdy guy like Slater so vulnerable is heartbreaking. I slide my arm around his broad shoulders, and he leans into me.

"It's so fucking unfair," he hisses. "She worked so hard all her life to make sure I had the best opportunity in life, and then she gets cancer and dies within three months." He looks into my eyes. "What kind of God would do that? To her? To me?" His voice is choked, and I'm struggling to maintain my composure. "She was only starting to live her life again. For the first time, I was going to be able to take care of her. To repay her for everything she's sacrificed for me, and that was taken from me too. I ... I—"

"Dimples, you out here?" Dylan shouts, interrupting whatever Slater was about to say.

Slater scoots over to the other side of the love seat as if I'm diseased. Dylan steps outside and looks over at us, freezing on the spot. Slater hastily brushes his tears aside, getting up and eyeballing my boyfriend suspiciously. "Dylan." He brushes past him, avoiding further eye contact before disappearing into the house.

"What's going on?" Worry lines crease Dylan's forehead as he drops down beside me.

I rest my head on his shoulder. "Slate's struggling, and I was trying to get him to open up."

Air whooshes out of his mouth, and he relaxes back in the seat. "I feel for the guy. I genuinely do, but he's not your responsibility, babe."

Something about that seriously pisses me off. "He's my friend, Dylan, and I'm trying to help," I snap. "He needs to talk to someone, and he can't, or won't, talk to Ryan."

"Hey." He grips my face, forcing me to look at him. "I know that, and it's one of the things I love about you. You're loyal to a fault, and I know you want to help, but I just meant maybe he needs to speak to a professional."

My anger floats away. "He seems reluctant."

"Gabrielle!" Mom's high-pitched voice reaches me from the kitchen, and I stand.

"I better get in there and help before she blows a gasket."

"Or burns the meat," Dylan jokes, having sat through many of Mom's overcooked efforts over the years.

"Yes, there's that." I stretch up on tiptoes and kiss him. "Is your mom still coming?"

He frowns. "What do you mean?"

"When we discussed this on Friday, I told you to call your mom and invite her. Didn't you do it?"

He pulls at his lips as he considers it. "Shit. I forgot."

"Well, you better call her now. Tell her to come over, if she wants to. We have more than enough, and Mom already assumes she's coming."

I'm shaking my head as I leave him on the porch to call his mom. I don't know why he's such a scatterbrain at the minute. I think this robotics project has him more stressed out than usual.

I help Mom in the kitchen while everyone else mingles outside. Dylan comes back in, stating Heather isn't coming. Apparently, she made plans with her yoga crowd when her son failed to confirm if we were dropping by today or not.

Once we are seated outside, with heaped plates in front of us, Dad shushes everyone and gives a little speech. We all look up at him, and he scans the table before clearing his throat. "Looking around the table today, at the faces of all those I love and hold dear to me, is a reminder of how precious and fragile life is. Every one of you means the world to me and Lucy, and we want you to know you are cherished and loved."

He clamps his hand on Slater's shoulder. "It's been six months since we tragically lost Janine. An angel taken from our world way too soon. She was a special lady. An amazing mother and a fantastic friend." Tears roll down my face, and as I look around the table, I see I'm not the only one. Most everyone has tears in their eyes. Even the guys.

Dad focuses on Slater. "We know you're hurting, son, and I wish I could take your pain away. I hope you know you'll always have a place at this table and in our home. We love you, and we're here for you."

Slater's jaw is rigidly tight, and he's struggling to hold things together. However, he summons courage, placing his hand on Dad's shoulder. "Thank you, Paul. That means a lot to me. You all mean a lot to me, and I could not have gotten through this without your support."

"We'll always have your back, man. Always," Ryan says.

Slater nods, offering a weak smile.

"Today, we honor Janine in the best way we know how," Dad continues, his voice dripping in emotion. "By sharing a meal, enjoying our family time, and with as much laughter as we can manage. So, I'll ask you to raise your glasses to the sky," he says, and we all oblige. Even Mia and Tia raise their plastic cups, on their best behavior as if some inner sense has told them it's important to be solemn and quiet. "And toast the wonderful woman we all miss. To Janine."

"To Janine." We speak uniformly, chinking our glasses and toasting Slater's beautiful angel in the sky.

After dessert, we move to the gazebo area, taking up spots on the couches as we watch the girls race around the garden playing. Conversation has flowed smoothly, but it's more understated than usual. Slater has been unbelievably quiet, and my heart aches for him.

"Tornado," Ryan says, claiming my attention. "We're heading to the graveyard now if you want to come."

"I don't see the point," Dylan says before I've had time to reply affirmatively.

I sit up straighter, twisting around to look at him with a puzzled look on my face. "What point?"

"The point of visiting a graveyard. It's not like the person is still there or anything. It's just a bunch of decaying bones in a box in the ground."

There's a collective sharp intake of breath, and I stare at my boyfriend as if he's grown ten heads. "Dylan! Don't be so insensitive."

"What?" He shrugs like it's no biggie. "I'm just saying what everyone thinks."

Slater stands, hands balled at his sides, a muscle ticking in his jaw. "Thanks for your sympathy, douche."

He storms off. Ryan glares at Dylan. "What the fuck, man?"

Dylan just shrugs again, and Ryan sends me a weird look before chasing after his friend.

"You need to apologize to him." I work hard to keep the anger from my voice.

"For what?" Dylan shouts, throwing his hands in the air. "Speaking the truth?"

I jump up. "For being an insensitive asshole! The guy only lost his mother six months ago! She was the only parent he's ever known, and he was devoted to her! And you may be a *Bible*-bashing atheist, but Janine was deeply religious, and if going to the graveyard helps Slate, then we should support him."

"Why?" He shrugs. "What's he to me?"

I need to leave before I truly say something I regret. "I don't know what the hell has gotten into you, Dylan, because I know this isn't you, but you Goddamned will apologize to Slate. It's the least you can do."

There's a deathly hush in the gazebo as everyone listens with bated breath. Dylan and I are usually a drama-free zone, so this is most unusual, and I'm sensing no one really knows what to do—whether to intervene or let it run its course.

"You don't tell me what to do. You're my girlfriend, not my fucking mother."

I, honest to goodness, feel like punching my boyfriend in his tactless mouth. I can't believe the words coming out of his mouth or the nerve of him to say it in front of everyone. I thought he had more respect for me and for my parents. I'm not sure what Dad sees on my face, but he stands, placing a hand on my elbow. "Buttercup."

"Dad. Don't." I shuck out of his hold. "I'm going after Slate." I look at Dylan, seeing how he'll react.

"What? I'm not stopping you." He feigns indifference, but his nostrils flare, and he's a bit red in the face, so I'm not buying it for a second.

Ignoring the sharp stab of pain that shoots through my heart, I grab my purse and take off without uttering another word.

Chapter Five

Taking Mom's car, I catch up to the guys at the cemetery. Ryan and Slater are sitting down in front of Janine's grave with their knees bent and matching solemn expressions. I drop down beside Slater, resting my head on his shoulder. "Did you do that?" he asks in a strained voice, pointing at the neat flowerbed.

Lifting my head, I nod. "Mom and I came here last weekend. The flowerbed was a bit neglected, so we tidied it up and bedded some new plants."

With tenderness in his eyes, he leans in and kisses my cheek. "Thank you, Belle." His voice is barely louder than a whisper, and tears glisten in his eyes. Ryan looks helplessly at me behind his back.

"It's no problem. I know how much enjoyment your mom got from gardening, and I think she'd like it."

He squeezes my hand. I want to say something. To apologize for Dylan's insensitivity, but I don't want to get into it here. It feels disrespectful. We sit there, not speaking for ages, until Slater quietly asks us to give him some time alone with his mom. Ryan and I amble back to the parking lot.

"What the fuck was that all about back at the house?" he asks while we lean against the side of Slater's SUV.

"Fucked if I know. I can't believe Dylan said something so crass. And in front of everyone too."

"It's weird. I've never known Dylan to act like that." He turns around so he's facing me. "Did something happen between him and Slate?"

My brow puckers. "Like what?"

He shrugs. "I don't know, but the last couple times we've all been together, I've sensed some serious tension between them."

"That's not really anything new. They've never been close."

"It's more than that. I just thought Dylan might've said something to you."

"He hasn't, but you can bet after that outburst I'm going to ask."

"Ask who what?" Slater inquires, rounding the front of the car.

I blurt out the first thing I can think of. "Myndi. What she sees in this guy." I poke my finger in Ryan's chest, smirking. A split second later, my eyes pop wide when he flushes a little. I push off the car, straightening up as I scrutinize his face. "Hang on here a second! Did something happen between you two?"

He rubs the back of his neck, looking a little sheepish. "Did you not speak to her today?"

I shake my head. "She called when I was in the kitchen helping Mom serve up dinner, and I didn't have time to answer. What's going on?"

His lips pull into a smug grin, and I slap his chest. "You. Did. Not!"

"Jeez, baby sis. Why are you so aggressive all the time? I think you need to get laid more often. Work out some of that anger."

"I get laid at least once a day, thank you very much."

Both Slater and Ryan pale. "Now I seriously want to ram my fist in Dylan's face," my brother says.

"Join the club," Slater mumbles, and my good humor fades.

I touch his arm. "I'm so sorry for what Dylan said. He was way out of line, and I know he didn't mean it."

Slater snorts. "Oh, I think he meant it all right." Opening the driver-side door, he hauls his ass into the car before I can respond. Ryan sends me an "I told you so" look before sliding into the passenger seat beside him. I tap on Slater's window, and he rolls it down. "And you shouldn't be apologizing on his behalf," he adds before I can get a word in. "It's not your fault your boyfriend's a fucking douche."

Whoa. "Okay. Enough." I cross my arms and eyeball Slater. "What exactly is going on? Did something happen with you and Dylan 'cause you're both snarking at one another all the time and I'm getting sick of it."

"Ask your boyfriend," he grumbles, turning the key in the ignition.

"I'm asking you."

He shakes his head. "You need to ask Dylan."

His voice brokers no argument, so I give up protesting. "Fine. I will." A conflicted look washes over his face, and an uneasy feeling settles in my gut, but I force it aside for now. "I have something for you. Well, it's for your mom's garden, actually. Could I meet you back at the house?"

His eyes probe mine. "I was going to head back to the city, but we can make a quick detour at the house."

"Okay, cool. I'll meet you guys there."

I trail them to Slater's house and park behind his SUV in the driveway. I'm glad I thought to take the shrub from Dylan's truck before I left my parents' house. My cell pings from inside my bag, and I take it out as a message pops up from my boyfriend. I swipe my finger along the screen and read his text.

I'm really sorry Dimples. Please come back.

I'm still furious with him, so he can stew a little longer. Tossing my cell back in my bag, I grab the pot and shimmy out of the car. As I walk toward the guys, Slater's eyes dart from the plant in my hand to my face. "I thought we could plant a tree in the backyard in memory of your mom," I explain.

As he stares at me, unnamed emotion shimmers in his eyes. His Adam's apple bobs in his throat. His chocolate-brown eyes darken, and his gaze drills into me, as if he's trying to worm his way inside. A strange fluttery feeling takes up residence in my chest. I want to look away, because the intensity on his face is making me slightly uncomfortable, but it's as if my eyes are glued to his. Without a word, he takes the pot from me, silently handing it to my brother. Then he pulls me into his embrace, wrapping his strong, muscular arms around me.

Slater has hugged me before.

Countless times.

But this feels different. Different for us. And different from any hug I've ever had before. Warmth rolls off him in waves, crashing into me, turning my limbs floppy. I hold onto his waist to steady myself, and my mouth turns dry. My eyes meet Ryan's over Slater's shoulder, and he's deep in thought as he watches us.

Snapping out of whatever haze I'm in, I extract myself from Slater, clearing my throat. "We'd better get started before nightfall descends. Unless you'd rather plant it alone?"

Slater's cheeks are a little flushed, and he won't meet my eyes as he speaks. "No. Let's all do it together."

I move to walk away, but he gently takes my hand. "Thank you for this, Belle. It's extremely thoughtful. It means a lot." His voice cracks a little. "Mom would love it. She loved you so much."

Tears instantly well in my eyes. "I loved her too."

Another moment passes between us. Then he wets his lips, looking a little nervous. "But, the thing is, I don't know if I'm going to keep the house, so maybe we should keep it in the pot until I decide."

"I'm pretty sure we can dig it up and replant it if we need to."

His shoulders relax a little. "Okay, that's good."

My eyes probe his. "I don't mean to pry, but I'm a little surprised you're considering letting the house go. I assumed you'd want to keep it. To live in it again after you graduate."

Right now, Ryan and Slater live in a four-bed brownstone ten minutes from campus with two other seniors. It's only three blocks from the condo I share with Dylan.

"I'm still undecided," he admits, looking between me and Ryan. "Part of me can't bear to part with this house, and the idea of some stranger living in it doesn't sit right with me either. Mom worked her butt off for this house, and I see her in all the little touches, but that's also part of the problem. It kills me being here without her, and I don't know if I could live here again on my own."

"You won't always be on your own."

He shrugs. "Maybe. Maybe not."

Spoken like a true commitment-phobe.

Slater and Ryan had girlfriends during junior year of high school, but it didn't last long. Since they moved to UD, they've gained quite the rep as party-loving bad boys with a predilection for casual hookups and one-night stands. To my knowledge, neither of them has had a relationship in years, but I'm well aware I'm not privy to the ins and outs of their sex lives. They are not unique in their outlook. Plenty of guys come to college to sow their wild oats and only settle down once they leave and join the real world.

Which only makes me even more grateful for Dylan and the love we share.

"You won't be alone forever," I tell him confidently, because Slater is a great guy and a great catch, and one day, some lucky girl is going to capture his heart and turn his world on its axis. "You might feel differently about the house then." He shoves his hands in his pockets, shrugging again. "Unless you need to make a call on it now, I think you should hold tight for the moment. You're still grieving, and you might make a decision and then come to regret it. Don't rush into anything."

Surprisingly, he reaches out, cupping one side of my face. "How do you always know the perfect thing to say? You're so smart and compassionate." His voice lowers, and he peers deep into my eyes. "Don't ever change, Belle. For no one."

A strange sensation sweeps through me.

It's difficult to describe.

It feels a lot like falling, yet I'm soaring at the same time.

Slater rubs his thumb across my cheek, eliciting a fiery trail of tingles I feel all the way to my toes. My heart starts beating to a new rhythm, and my chest inflates as inexplicable emotion twists my stomach into knots.

Okay, I'm officially weirded out. Things have just skyrocketed into unchartered territory, and my body is as confused as my head with the visceral reaction to Slater's soft touch and reverential words. His eyes pierce mine intensely again, and this odd vibe between us alternates somewhere between strange, freaky, and familiar.

Something real passes between us in this moment, and I veer between elation and guilt.

Ryan comes to the rescue this time, finally breaking whatever spell we're under. In a deliberate move, he pulls me away from Slater, circling his arm around my shoulder and tucking me in close to his side. "Come on. Let's go plant this pretty before it's dark."

So, we do. With everyone ignoring what just transpired.

Choosing a spot in the backyard is challenging because Janine has most every inch of ground already planted, but we find a spot beside a crab apple tree which is perfect. Not exposed to the elements, but not completely sheltered either.

All three of us are quiet as we bed the star magnolia plant. When we're done, we stand and admire our teamwork. We're in a line, with our arms draped around one another, while we take a moment alone with our thoughts. We may not have a green thumb like Janine did, but, for virtual first-timers, I think we did an admirable job.

A cough from behind startles all of us. Turning around, I'm surprised to see Dylan standing on the top step, looking out of his comfort zone. "Sorry for barging in, but the front door was unlocked." He glances at me and then eyeballs Slater. "I was hoping to have a word in private with you." Ryan and I exchange a loaded look, but we step away, leaving the guys to talk.

Dylan squeezes my hand as I brush past him, and I squeeze back. It means a lot to me that he's made the effort to come here and put this right. That's more like the Dylan I know and love.

I switch the Keurig on while Ryan pulls up a chair in the kitchen. We don't talk for a couple minutes. It's only when I've slid a mug of coffee to Ryan that he engages me in conversation. He looks a little awkward, like he's struggling to find the right words.

I could help him out, but where would the fun be in that? So, I let him squirm for a couple minutes.

"Is everything okay with you and Dylan?" he blurts. "I mean, I don't want any details or anything, but if there's trouble in paradise, you can talk to me."

I smirk. Can't help it. "You really want to talk boys?" I quirk a brow. "Have you changed personality overnight?" I point between us. "We don't do this. It's not our thing." It's the one unspoken rule between us, and virtually the only topic that's off limits.

"You're my fucking sister, Tornado. Of course, it's our thing. I'm here for you, no matter what's going on in your life."

The pissed look on his face sobers me up. I reach across the table and take his hand. "Hey. I was only joking, and I know I can always talk to you, but you don't need to worry, everything's fine between me and Dylan." I smile at him. "He's still my forever guy."

"You sure about that?"

Alarm bells ding in my head. "Of course, I'm sure! I've been hopelessly in love with Dylan for years. He's my person. That'll never change."

"You were so fucking young when you got with him. Don't you ever feel like you're missing out?"

Now he's really starting to piss me off. "If you're referring to the fact I'll be riding the one cock for life, then no, I don't feel like I'm missing out."

"Fuck's sake, Gabby. Do you have to be so crude? It's not very ladylike."

I flip him the bird. "In case you've forgotten, I grew up with three brothers. Crude is practically our middle name. And I've overheard my fair share of your conversations, which are usually way more graphic than my statement, so spare me the ladylike bull unless you want to officially cement your sexist status."

He sighs, scrubbing a hand over his chin. "This wasn't the way I wanted this conversation to go, and I don't want to argue with you. I love you, baby sis, and I just want you to know I'm here for you. Always. I'll always have your back."

My bad mood evaporates with his sincere words. My brothers are genuinely the best. Sure, they gave me shit when I was younger, but I have always felt protected and cherished, and there isn't anything they won't do for me, or vice versa. I know I'm lucky, especially where Ryan's concerned, because we really are a pretty tight unit.

From the minute I arrived on campus last year, Ryan has looked out for me and actively included me in his life, which a lot of brothers wouldn't do. And I had Dylan, so it's not like it was even necessary, but that's just the way my brother rolls.

People often ask me if I miss not having a sister, but I can honestly say it's never bothered me because I have three awesome brothers who I've always been able to confide in. And, with Ryan, we're as close as any two siblings could be.

So, no, I do not feel like I've missed out.

I go around the table and hug my brother. "I love you too, little big bro. Sorry for overreacting. I know you care, and I appreciate how you're always looking out for me, but you don't need to worry. Dylan and I are solid."

Chapter Six

After dropping Mom's car home and saying goodbye to the rest of my family, we set off back to the city. Dylan hasn't said one word to me since we left Slater's house, and I can't stand the tense silence anymore. "Do you want to tell me what's going on with you?" I ask, as he takes the exit onto the highway.

"What do you mean?" He looks briefly at me before refocusing on the road.

"That outburst was most unlike you, and I've noticed you and Slate snapping at one another a lot lately. If something is going on, I'd like to know."

A shuddering breath leaves his lips, and when he glances at me, he looks extremely nervous.

A heavy weight presses down on my chest, and nausea swims up my throat. "What?" I whisper. "What is it?"

He drags his lower lip between his teeth and worry lines form on his brow.

"Dylan. You're scaring me. What's going on?"

He sighs. "Let me pull over and I'll explain." Spotting the sign for a gas station up ahead, he pulls off the highway and drives to the place, bringing the truck to a standstill in a vacant parking space. He grips the steering wheel tight, and my heart is hammering against my rib cage as anxiety starts running rampant inside me.

Unbuckling his seat belt, he turns to face me. "You know I love you to the moon and back and that I'd never do anything to intentionally hurt you, right?"

Oh God. That sounds like the start of a confession if ever I heard one. My vocal cords refuse to work, so I can only nod. Wiping my suddenly sweaty palms down the front of my dress, I try to prepare my heart. I have no idea what Dylan is going to say, only that I'm not going to like it.

"I was going to tell you this the minute we got home. Swear." Little drops of moisture cling to his hairline, making me even more anxious. I nod again, seeing the truth in his eyes. "You remember the night we arrived back at the condo after summer break when I went out with Chase and the guys?"

"Yeah," I croak, knotting my hands in my lap.

"We went to the club, and I had a few too many beers."

The instant remorseful look on his face causes a sharp ache to spear me straight through the heart. I think I know what he's about to say, and it's going to kill me. Tears leak out of my eyes, and he notices.

He cups my face and his expression is fierce. "No, no, no. It's not what you're thinking, baby. I haven't cheated on you."

His words do little to reassure me. "Then what is it because I feel like I'm having a coronary."

He yanks my face to his and smashes his lips against mine. His kiss is frantic and urgent, but I can't kiss him back. Not until I know what this is about. I pull back, hating the hurt look that flashes across his face. "Just tell me what you did, Dylan. Please." More tears spring forth, and I'm powerless to stop the flow.

"A group of girls joined us later in the night, and one of them got a bit clingy with me."

A sob bursts free, and the ache in my chest transforms, scalding me from the inside. "Baby, I didn't touch her. I swear to you, but I was a little too slow removing her wandering hands."

"What exactly does that mean?"

He drags a hand through his hair, and a pained expression crosses his face. "She was running her hands up and down my chest. I was trashed, and I didn't notice at first. It was only when she grabbed my crotch and started stroking my cock that I realized what was happening."

Bile floods my mouth, and I want to scream at him for letting any girl put her hands on him, but I force my words back down, waiting to hear all of it.

"Slater appeared at our table then. I hadn't seen him come in, but, apparently, he'd seen me. He saw her hand on my cock, added two plus two, and came up with fifty. I told the girl to go, and then Slater and I got into it. He refused to believe me, and I told him to fuck off and mind his own business. He told me to tell you and threatened that he would if I didn't man up." His eyes scan my face. "That's what we've been arguing about. Every time I see him, he asks if I've told you."

"Why didn't you tell me?"

"Because I was fucking afraid to. Afraid you wouldn't believe me. Afraid to upset you. I fucked up, but she meant nothing to me, and it went no further. All night, I was talking nonstop about you. She knew I had a girlfriend. I think she was just trashed and horny, and I was conveniently there."

I give him a "do ya think I'm stupid" look. "Don't insult my fucking intelligence, Dylan. I've seen what these girls try to do. As soon as they find out who you are, they see you as a meal ticket. They all want a ride on your cock, and, you know, I've never really given it much thought because I trust you and I have faith in what we have but this..."

I shake my head, trailing off because I'm afraid of saying something I can't take back. Memories of the conversation I overheard at the party, unhelpfully, surge to the forefront of my mind, confusing matters further. "Did you tell some girl you wanted to suck her tits and take her number last Friday?"

"What?" His brows climb to his hairline. "No! Of course not! Where the fuck did that come from?"

"I ... never mind. Forget it." I'm letting my imagination run wild. I grip his face, staring directly into his eyes. "I want you to promise me that you've told me the truth and that nothing happened."

He looks me dead on. "I love you, Gabby. Only ever you. I swear it's the truth. Nothing happened with that girl or any girl. You're the only one I want."

That was the first of many lies.

Chapter Seven

When I return after using the restroom, Dylan is hunched over the side of the truck, vomiting. A pile of puke rests at his feet. "Crap, Dylan. Are you okay?"

"Water," he croaks, holding up a hand to keep me back.

"Okay. I'll get some stuff, but let's move you to the restroom first." I help him to the men's room, depositing him there while I go into the store. When I reemerge, he's back behind the wheel, cradling his head in his hands.

I haul myself up into the passenger seat and close the door. "Here." I hand him a bottle of water. When he lifts his head, his pallor is ashen, and little beads of sweat dot his brow. I place my palm over his forehead. "Shit, you're hot."

"Straight fire," he teases, and I can't help grinning.

"You can't drive in this condition. Let's swap seats."

We switch around, and I force him to drink a full bottle of water before we leave. He dabs at his mouth and his brow with the tissues I bought, his complexion getting paler and paler as we eat up the miles.

Wincing, he cradles his head in his hands, rocking back and forth in the seat.

"Do you need me to pull over?" I ask.

"Keep driving," he murmurs. "Need bed."

It's a wonder I don't pick up a ticket for speeding with the way I drive us home. I get Dylan out of the car, into the elevator, and into our apartment. He's leaning on me the whole time, and I'm struggling to hold him up, but we somehow manage. I strip him down to his boxers and help him into bed. "Need my medication," he whispers, clutching his head.

"Shit. You have another migraine?" Dylan suffered terrible migraines when he was a teenager, but he was symptom free for a few years until he started suffering again a couple months ago.

"Feels like my head's exploding."

"I'll be right back." I run to the bathroom and grab his pills, fetching a fresh glass of water from the kitchen and helping him to take the medication. I place a cold cloth over his hot forehead and pull the covers up over him. "Try and sleep, baby." I press a kiss to his cheek and switch off the bedside lamp and the overhead lights, plunging the room into darkness.

"Gabby," he calls out as I tiptoe out of the room.

"Yes?"

"I love you to death. You know that, right?"

"I do, and I love you too." I might be pissed at him for getting trashed and leaving himself vulnerable to that gold digger, but I know he loves me, and I'm not going to deny that I love him too. That slut is not going to come between us, but God help her if I ever get my hands on her.

He sits up, but I can't make out his features in the dark. "Don't ever leave me, babe. I would die without you."

"Forever, Freckles."

"Forever, Dimples."

I only manage to grab Myndi for a private chat on Monday after classes end. Forcing her to come for coffee with me, before her shift in the diner starts, I demand answers. She sits at a table, scrolling on her phone, while I place our orders. Handing her a paper cup, I slide into the seat across from her. "Okay, hit me. What's the dealio with you and Ryan?"

"What's he said?"

"Pretty much nothing, but he was grinning like the cat that got the canary, so I know something happened."

She beams at me, drifting off into her own little bubble. Rolling my eyes, I click my fingers in her face. "Jesus, you've gone all moon face on me too. Just spit it out before I start drawing my own conclusions."

"I called you yesterday to tell you, but you never picked up."

"Sorry. We were out with the folks. It was an anniversary dinner for Slate's mom. I was going to call you back, but then we had some drama, and then Dylan was sick on the way home, so I never got a chance to return your call."

"Is Dylan okay?"

I nod. "It's his migraines again. He was feeling better this morning, but he still skipped classes to stay home."

"Ugh, migraines are the worst." Myndi removes the lid and blows on her latte.

"I can't believe they've come back. They plagued him for years when we were growing up."

"It could be all the looking at screens. Has he had his eyes tested?"

"That was my first thought when they reappeared, and, yes, he's been tested, and his eyesight is perfect. The doctor has said a lot of people who experience migraines end up with a recurring condition. There's not a hell of a lot he can do really, but I'm sure the stress of his robotics project isn't helping either." I take a sip of my black coffee, inhaling the bitter aroma as I drink. "Anyway, enough deflecting. What happened with my brother?"

"He came into the diner Saturday night as my shift was ending and asked me to go to a party with him. I declined, because I was exhausted and pretty much dead on my feet, so he suggested we go back to his place with some takeout and a movie." She blushes, and I arch a brow.

"And?" I prompt.

"We made out for a bit, but it was all quite innocent. At some point, I fell asleep. Woke up on the couch with your brother draped around me. Panicked like fuck and hightailed it out of there. Spent the morning pacing my dorm, trying to remember if anything else happened."

"You fucked him?"

"No!" Her eyes widen. "I didn't, but I was freaking out because I couldn't remember if I did or not. Anyway, I was debating calling you, and then Ryan showed up, freaking out because I left without waking him. He reassured me we didn't have sex and asked me out again." She scrunches up her nose. "I said yes, and we're going out to dinner Wednesday night. Hope you don't mind."

"Are you sure you want to go there?"

She bites her lower lip. "I know what I'm getting into, Gabby. I'm under no illusion, but I like him. He makes me laugh. And no one has ever kissed me like he did. Oh my God, he—"

"Ugh." I put my palm right up in her face. "Nuh-uh. Sharing is *not* caring in this instance. There are certain things I do not want to know about any of my brothers. Like how they kiss or what they're like in bed, so you'll have to censure your comments while you're dating him."

She giggles. "Sure. I think I can manage that." The wide smile on her face concerns me, but Myndi's a big girl, and it's not my place to interfere. "Are you sure you're okay with this?" she asks, deep worry lines creasing her brow.

"I love you, and I love my brother. If anything serious was to develop between you, I would be ecstatic. Genuinely. But you know what he's like, so please just guard your heart."

When Forever Changes

When I return to the condo later that night, Dylan rushes to greet me, wrapping his arms around me and holding me tight. I hug him back, and a deep sense of contentment courses through me. "How are you feeling?" I ask after a bit, easing back to examine his face. Color has returned to his cheeks, and he's smiling.

"All good. Migraine's gone."

I press my lips to his. "Thank God. I hate seeing you in so much pain."

Delicious aromas tickle my nostrils, and I pick my head up. "What am I smelling?"

He kisses me softly. "I made dinner. Hope you're hungry."

"Is the Pope Catholic?" I joke.

He steers me to the dining table. The lights are dimmed, and two candles flicker softly atop the table. A bottle of wine is chilling in a bucket, and he pours me a glass. "Dinner will be about twenty minutes, so I thought you might like to have a bath first?"

"That sounds perfect," I murmur, savoring the delicious, crisp, cold white wine as it glides down my throat.

Taking my hand, he leads me to the bathroom. Steam, and the scent of jasmine, rises from the already full tub. Rose petals float across the surface of the water, and romantic music plays in the background. Dylan places my glass of wine down on the edge of the tub and starts removing my cardigan. "You're spoiling me," I murmur as he trails a fine line of kisses over my exposed shoulder.

"You deserve it, and I like spoiling you." He pops the buttons on the back of my dress, and it slinks to the floor. I kick it aside, standing in front of the tub, with my back to my boyfriend, in only my lace thong and bra. "Thank you for looking after me last night, and I'm sorry about the club and for not telling you sooner."

"I want to forget it, but that bitch better hope I never run into her."

He bites down on my shoulder, and I wince at the unexpected

sting. "I love it when you get all territorial and feisty." Peeling the straps of my bra down my arms, he unclasps it and tosses it aside. I lean back against him, and his hands creep around to my front, trailing up my stomach. He cups my breasts, kneading them softly. "I love your tits," he whispers, nibbling on the lobe of my ear. "I wish I could join you, but I need to check on dinner."

He grinds his hard-on against my ass, and a moan slips out of my mouth. "I don't mind if it's overdone. I'm used to burnt dinners," I rasp.

He chuckles, rubbing his crotch against the crack of my ass while his fingers tweak my nipples. Lust stirs low in my belly. "Tempting as that is, I want tonight to be special."

"Every night with you is special."

He turns me around, and the look of adoration on his face gets me right in the feels. "I love you, Gabby. I love you so very much." He presses his forehead to mine. "And I really am so sorry about that girl in the club. I promise it will never happen again."

I sweep hair back off his face. "Dylan, it's okay. I forgive you, and I trust you."

He fuses our lips together, kissing me passionately, igniting every nerve ending in my body. I press my semi-naked body against his, needing him to fill me. "I need you," I whisper over his mouth.

"And you shall have me." He pulls back, grinning. "After we eat." I pout, and he laughs before his eyes darken with lust. "Take off your thong," he commands. "I want to see all of you."

Licking my lips, I shimmy the barely there lace down my legs and perch on the edge of the tub, opening my legs. "See how much I need you?" I tease, opening my legs wider.

The bulge in his sweatpants mushrooms, and there's no ignoring his obvious arousal. "Fuck. Me."

"Yes, please." I'm not above begging.

He holds my chin, tilting my face up, and bites my lip. The sharp sting sends shockwaves of lust whipping through me, and I grab his ass, pressing myself into his hard-on. "Baby, please."

His eyes are black pools of desire as he stares at me. "Get in the tub, drink your wine, and pleasure yourself, but you're not allowed to come."

Everything south of my belly button tightens and tingles. "Fuck, that's hot."

His answering smile is pleased. "Wear a sexy dress, but nothing else. I want easy access." Leaning in, he kisses me sweetly. "Love you to bits, Dimples."

"Love you too, stud." I swat him on the ass as he departs the room. "Even if you are leaving me wanting."

"Not for long, baby," he promises with a seductive grin before closing the door.

I love this new, more domineering side of Dylan's personality and the added excitement it's brought to our bedroom activities. But, in this moment, as I stroke myself to the brink of release but hold back, like he's asked, I kinda want to knee him in the junk too.

Dinner is delectable, and I polish off every morsel, which is a miracle because I'm panting with desire and squirming in my seat the entire time. Dylan runs his hands up and down my legs and the insides of my thighs as we eat, teasing me until I'm a writhing hot mess on the chair.

Once the table is cleared, he lifts me up onto it, pulling me out to the edge, and proceeds to remove my dress. When I'm completely bare to him, he lowers me back, spreading my legs and devouring me with his tongue and his fingers. I orgasm in record time, and then he carries me to the bedroom.

"Lie on your stomach," he instructs, and I oblige. Warm liquid drops onto my back, and then Dylan is massaging every part of me with firm hands. I'm like a quivery mass of Jell-O on the bed as he skillfully caresses every inch of my body. When he's finished, he nudges my legs up until I'm kneeling, plunging two fingers inside me. He pumps his fingers in and out of me fast, and I'm spiraling toward bliss again. Then he slams into me without warning, and I cry out as he fills me up. He fucks me hard and fast, and I'm ascending a peak when he pushes his thumb into my ass, pressing it in as far as it will go. I buck like a wild animal, climaxing again a few seconds later. Dylan roars as his orgasm hits, pumping his hot seed inside me.

While we used condoms when we first started sleeping together —even though I was already on the pill—we decided to forgo them after the first time we went bareback. Neither of us have ever slept with anyone else, and we don't plan to. I've been on the pill for years, and I love the feel of him buried deep inside me with no barrier. Fucking with condoms is no comparison.

"Jesus, Dylan. That was incredible."

He drops down beside me, pulling me into his side. "Every time with you is incredible. You were made for me, Gabby. We fit together in every conceivable way."

I fall asleep, cocooned in his arms, feeling cherished and loved.

Chapter Eight

The rest of the week passes in a blur of coursework and late nights at the library. I go for a run with Ryan on Thursday night, and I quiz him on his intentions toward Myndi in the coffee place after. "I like her. A lot," he tells me. "And I promise I'll treat her good. Contrary to my rep, I treat every girl with respect. I tell every single one of them my intentions before we do anything."

I stare incredulously at him. "So, what? You say I'm just gonna fuck you and leave you?"

He thumps me on the arm. "Always so crude." I flip up my middle finger, and he chuckles, slinging his arm over my shoulders. Ryan is the most affectionate of my brothers, and he's going to make some girl extremely happy one day. Whenever he decides to stop fucking around and settle down that is.

"To answer your question, I make sure every girl understands it's a one-time thing and there'll be no seconds."

"But none of them appear to get that." Honestly, the number of girls chasing after Ryan at any one time is ridiculous.

"Multiple orgasms tend to nuke a few brain cells or they

purposely choose to forget." He shrugs, and I spit coffee all over the table.

"TMI, Ryan. Jesus." I shudder. "Unless you want me to share intimate details, and I'll tell you—"

He clamps his hand over my mouth. "Most definitely not. I like Dylan. Don't give me reasons to hate him."

"So." I drum my fingers on top of the table. "What are your intentions toward Myndi? And I'll take the censored reply, please."

He smirks. "I haven't met any girl in years that I've liked enough to want to take it slow. To get to know her better. But I do with her. I can't tell you what's going to come of it, if anything, but I will promise you to treat her right, and I'll do my utmost not to hurt her."

"Fair enough. I appreciate that. She's my best friend, and I don't want anything to get awkward between all of us."

"Speaking of. Did you talk to Dylan about the shit with Slate?"

I nod, trying to ignore the knots coiling in my gut. I believe Dylan, but the thoughts of any girl with her hands all over him sour my stomach. I'm trying to push it from my mind, to forget it like I promised Dylan I would, but, for some reason, I keep dwelling on it. "I did, and it's all cool."

It's obvious Slater didn't tell Ryan, because Dylan's face is still intact. I owe Slater big time for that. While there isn't much I keep from my brother, I don't want him knowing as it'll only cause more hassle so I'm deliberately downplaying it. But my brother is an astute fucker, and he stares me out of it, waiting for me to spill my guts. I school my features into a blasé smile, and, after a tense face-off, he finally backs down. "Okay, that's good. Hopefully, everyone can play nice from now on."

I'm coming out of the pharmacy the next evening when I see them.

Dylan is across the road, leaning against the wall, smiling as he talks to a tall girl with long dark hair. I don't recognize her, and I don't like the way she's leering at my man. My instinct is to charge across the road with all guns blazing which is most unlike me. I'm not usually jealous. Deciding to hold back, I plaster myself to the side of the building, hiding in the shadows as I watch them.

Dylan throws back his head, laughing heartily at whatever she said, and butterflies scatter in my chest. My pulse is racing, and my heart is thumping wildly. I clasp the paper bag to my front, swallowing the lump of fear wedged in my throat. The girl thrusts her ample cleavage out and places her hand on his chest. My breath falters. He looks down at where her hand rests and then lower, his gaze clearly raking over the swell of her breasts in the low-cut top she's wearing.

A whimper escapes my mouth, and tears sting the back of my eyes.

Dylan lifts his head and says something to her, and then she moves her other hand up the left side of his chest, and I see red.

Screw this shit. I can't watch another second and not do anything about it.

I race across the street like a woman possessed. Dylan notices me approaching out of the corner of his eye, and his whole body tenses. Quickly, he removes her hands and takes a step back. He says something to her, and she jerks her head to the side as my foot hits the sidewalk.

"What the fuck is going on here?" I spit out, glaring at my boyfriend.

"Calm down, Gabby." Dylan pulls me into his side, but I push him off. "This is Bianca. She's a computer science major too."

I take one look at her curvy body poured into the tight top and barely there jean skirt and snort. "And I'm fucking Santa Claus." While I know you shouldn't judge a book by its cover, I'll chop off a tit if that brainless bimbo is actually a tech head.

"Really?" she replies, cocking her head to the side. "Is he a good lay?" She laughs at her own stupid joke, and I'd have a quick comeback ready if I wasn't currently completely freaking out on the inside. I never got a look at the girls discussing Dylan in the bedroom at that party last week, but I would never forget the girl's raspy voice.

I'd bet my life it's the same girl—the one who told her friends that Dylan said he wanted to suck her tits and asked for her number.

I think I'm going to throw up, but I refuse to let this bitch see, so I compose my features into a neutral expression, ignoring her and focusing on Dylan. "Can we leave now?"

"Of course. See you later, Bianca."

"So nice meeting you..." she trails off, tapping her finger on her chin and looking introspective. "Sorry, I'm just trying to remember if Dylan mentioned you, but nope. He never said a word."

Dylan stiffens. "Don't be a bitch, Bianca. You know exactly who Gabby is."

Noticing his expression, she quickly backtracks. "Of course. Your girlfriend knows I was only joking."

All sense of composure leaves me. Clenching my hands into fists, I step up to her, uncaring that she towers over me in height and in her heels. "Stay away from my boyfriend, you fucking skank," I snarl.

"Gabby!" Now it's Dylan's turn to be disgusted with *me*. He pulls me back. "She didn't mean it."

"Yes, I did." I glare at her. "Screw off and leave us alone."

"See you in class, McStudly," she purrs, blowing him a kiss, and my claws come out. I lunge at her, but Dylan senses my reaction, and he tightens his hold on me, hauling me down the road in the opposite direction.

She totters away with a smug grin on her face.

My sudden flare of rage switches direction. I shove at Dylan. "Let me go."

"Not until you calm the fuck down."

"Let me go or I'll scream."

"Now you're just being childish."

"I don't care. I don't want you touching me. I want you nowhere near me."

"You're completely overreacting, Gabby. She's a friend from class, that's all."

I harrumph. "Do I look like I'm stupid?" I peer up at him, and he looks like butter wouldn't melt in his mouth. "I saw you! I was watching from across the street."

"And what did you see?" He sneers, letting me go and crossing his arms defiantly across his chest.

"She pushed her tits into you, and you were ogling them like you wanted to lick them."

He laughs.

He actually laughs.

I see red again and lift my leg to knee him in the balls, but he stops me. "Quit that shit, Gabby. You are being completely unreasonable. I admit I looked. She has a great rack, and they were in my face. But there's no crime in looking."

"There is when she's pressed up against you, feeling you up, and inching her way toward your mouth!"

"You're such a hypocrite, Gabby."

"What the hell are you talking about? I never so much as *look* at another guy. Why the hell would I want to?"

"Don't lie. I see the way you look at him," he spits.

I'm genuinely confused. "Look at who?"

"Slater fucking Evans."

My eyes pop wide. "Are you kidding me right now? Slate is like a *brother* to me!"

He pokes his finger into my chest, pinning me with a ruthlessly cold glare. "I'm calling bullshit on that," he yells, causing the couple in front of us to look over their shoulders.

I thrust his finger away, stepping back from the harsh glint in his eyes. In this moment, I do not know the man standing in front of me.

Even in the heat of an argument, Dylan has never raised his voice or glared at me like this.

Not once in all the years we've known one another.

I lower my voice and plaster a smile on my face, purely for the couple's benefit. They have stopped walking, and now they're looking at me with concern in their eyes. I nearly give myself lockjaw I'm smiling so hard. With one final glance between me and Dylan, they resume walking, and the smile drops off my face.

At least all the forced smiling has calmed me down a little. "I have never looked at Slater with any kind of interest, so whatever you think you've seen, you're mistaken, and I sure as hell haven't flirted with him or told him I want to suck his tits!"

He rolls his eyes. "This again? At least think of something original if you're going to throw crap at me."

"I know you said it, and I know it was her." I hate how my voice breaks.

"You're making a big deal out of absolutely nothing."

I square my shoulders and pin him with a serious look. "I want you to look me in the eyes and tell me nothing is going on with Bianca."

He moves in closer until his face is right up against mine. He eyeballs me without flinching or any emotion on his face and says, "Nothing is going on with Bianca. Absolutely nothing."

My heart plummets to my toes, and tears stab the back of my eyes. I can almost physically feel my heart splintering behind my rib cage. I shove the bag with his migraine medication at his chest. "Liar."

Then I turn and run.

Chapter Nine

I'm still sobbing by the time I reach Myndi's dorm. Just as I round the corner of her building, I spot her and Ryan leaving. They have their arms wrapped around each other, and they're swooning at one another with matching lovesick expressions. They don't even notice me as they head out on foot in the opposite direction. I know if I called after them they'd readily forgo their plans to comfort me. But I don't want to ruin their night. And I don't want Ryan to see me like this. He'd probably put Dylan in the hospital if he saw the state I'm in.

So, I take a risk and go back to the condo. It's empty, and that does little to reassure me. *What if he went after her?* Images of Dylan sucking on Bianca's tits torture me as I change into my running gear. I can't believe he lied so competently to my face. But he clearly forgets how well I know him. Dylan has a bunch of tells I'm familiar with, and that's how I know he's not telling the truth. Heartfelt pain consumes me, and I burst into tears as I drop onto the ground.

After a little while, I give myself a pep talk, drying my eyes and refusing to drown in a sea of tears while he's out doing who knows what.

I decide to use the indoor running track tonight even though it's still mild enough to run outdoors. I'm terrified in case I bump into Dylan and that cow and fearful I'll be up on a murder charge if I do. No, I need time to think everything through, when I'm less emotional, before deciding on my next step.

I run lap after lap, pushing my limbs to the limit, but even the burn in the back of my calves does nothing to quell the tsunami of emotions contorting my insides into knots. So, I head to the gym and start pummeling my fists into the punching bag. I have no clue what I'm doing, but I just go at it, venting all my pent-up frustration and pain.

"Shit, what did the bag ever do to you?" Slater says, materializing at my side.

I'm almost out of breath as I answer him, and my knuckles throb, but I'm relishing the pain. "I'm imagining it's Dylan's head," I hiss.

Slater shoots me a sympathetic look as he moves around, holding the bag for me. "He told you."

I gulp, nodding tersely.

"I'm sorry."

Little does he realize that's not the reason I'm upset, but I don't want to get into it with him. Or anyone for that matter. I just want to rage silently at the world with my fists. "I don't want to talk about it."

"No problem." Slater starts giving me tips, helping to improve my punch and my aim, and we stay like that for about twenty minutes.

He insists on driving me home as it's completely dark out now. Pulling up in front of our building, he kills the engine and twists around to face me, the leather squelching in the process. "Are you okay?"

I shrug. "I don't know. I'm too mad right now to figure anything out."

"If you need a place to crash, you can come to our place. Take my room and I'll sleep on the couch."

"No, I..."

Do I need a place to crash?

That thought hadn't even crossed my mind. I've never ever thought about what would happen if Dylan and I split up, because that's never been on the cards. I don't even know if it is now. I don't know what exactly has gone on with Bianca. Maybe it's nothing more than what I've learned. As much as that hurts to admit, and as tempted as I am to tell him to fuck off, I'm not throwing away my relationship over a skank who won't leave my boyfriend alone. I haven't invested all this time to walk away at the first big hurdle.

Whatever this is, we'll work through it.

We have to.

Because the alternative doesn't bear thinking about.

"Belle." Slater slides his hand up my arm, eliciting a rake of little shivers.

I jerk my arm back, confused over my physical reaction to him lately. Screw Dylan for planting stupid thoughts in my head.

"I'm okay. I don't need a place to stay, but thanks for offering."

He opens and shuts his mouth in about ten seconds flat, obviously wanting to say more but thinking better of it. "Thank you for the ride." I hop out. Before I close the door, I add, "I'd appreciate it if you kept tonight between us. I don't want Ryan to worry about me. This thing with Dylan will blow over. Every couple has their share of arguments."

He slants me a look of disbelief, and a muscle pops in his jaw. "Whatever you want," he says, through gritted teeth. Restarting the engine, he white knuckles the steering wheel as I shut the door, and then he tears off out of there.

Dylan is sitting on the couch in the dark when I return. I'm tempted to ignore him, but pretending everything is okay will not make the issue disappear. His eyes follow me as I take a seat opposite him. The air is fraught with tension. I cradle my head in my hands, struggling to find the right words. My heart is shattering, and my resolve is weakening. I reach over and flick on the lamp, blinking as my eyes adjust to the light. Tears glisten in my eyes as I look at my boyfriend. The harsh glare from earlier is gone, replaced with a look that is part terror and part remorse.

Tears roll down my cheeks, and I hate what this is doing to me. I cannot even remember the last time I cried before this week. "I know you lied to me," I whisper, swiping angrily at the hot tears coursing like a waterfall down my face. "Am I not enough for you anymore, Dylan?"

"Oh my God, no, Gabby." He drops to his knees in front of me, looking up with anguished eyes. "Of course, you're enough. More than enough." Tentatively, he drops his head into my lap, and my fingers move of their own accord, threading through the dark strands of his hair. We sit like that for several minutes, the air heavy with all that's left unsaid.

"Are you breaking up with me?" I whisper after a bit.

He sits down beside me, pressing his forehead to mine. "No, baby. No, no, no. That is the last thing I want. I love you. I swear it."

My sobs fill the room, and I hate that I can't stop crying, but I don't know how to deal with the flurry of conflicting emotions battering me from all sides. "I need you to tell me the truth, Dylan. Did you say that to Bianca? Did you take her number, and have you been texting her?"

The look of shame on his face confirms it, and I completely break down, sobbing uncontrollably. He tries to wrap his arms around me, but I scoot away from him, curling my knees into my chest as I cry.

"I'm so sorry, Gabby. It meant nothing. It means nothing."

"Like the girl with her hand on your dick meant nothing?" I spit.

He hangs his head, and his chest heaves. "I don't want anyone but you. I mean it." He moves closer on the couch. "I love you, Gabby. I have loved you practically my whole life. You're my entire world."

"Why, Dylan? Why did you say that to Bianca, and why are you texting her?"

His eyes plead with me. "I don't know why I said it. It just popped out of my mouth, and I don't know why I took her number or texted her back when she texted me."

I bare my teeth at him. "What a stinking pile of shit, Dylan! Of course, you know why you did it! Because you thought she'd let you suck her tits and she'll probably let you fuck her ass too? Is that what this is? You've been harping on about that for weeks, knowing I'm not comfortable with it. Have you found someone who is?"

He claws a hand through his hair, gulping. "Fuck no! I swear to you, Gabby, it's like my brain disengages sometimes, and I blurt stuff that's in my head without thinking."

I swipe the tears from under my eyes. "What a convenient excuse," I hiss. "But at least now you've admitted it's what you've been thinking." I stand, not wanting to be in his presence a second longer. "I feel like I don't even know you anymore, because the boy I fell in love with would never have treated me like this and then blatantly lied about it." I step around the couch. "I'm going to take a shower, and I'd really like it if you're gone when I come out."

A muscle ticks in his jaw. "I'm not going anywhere, Gabby. I know I fucked up, but I'm not walking away from here or from you. I know I've hurt you, and I'm so unbelievably sorry about that, but I'm not giving you up."

"Fine. Then I'll leave." I stomp away, and he races after me.

He tugs on my elbow, hauling me up against him. "You're not leaving."

"I'd like to see you try to stop me."

He circles his arms around my waist, and I attempt to wriggle out of his hold. "You have every right to be mad at me. I don't blame you in the slightest. And I know you need time to calm down. Take whatever time you need, but you are not moving out, Gabby. I love you. I love you. I love you." Tears pour down his face. "I'm so sorry. I promise it will never happen again. I will never hurt you like that ever again. Please, baby." He rests his head on top of my hair, and all the fight leaves me.

I slump against him, clinging to him pitifully. "What's happening to us?" I whimper as tears prick my eyes again.

"It's going to be okay, baby. We're going to be okay." He kisses my forehead. "Once you still love me and I love you, it will be all right."

Except everyone knows that sometimes love just isn't enough.

Chapter Ten

I sleep on the couch, much to Dylan's dismay. But I can't lie beside him in bed pretending everything's okay when it isn't. I toss and turn most of the night, my brain refusing to switch off. I don't know if that's normal.

If the piercing pain in my chest is normal.

Because Dylan's never done anything to incite such reactions in me before. I want to believe him when he says he loves me, because I see the truth in his eyes, but I don't understand how he can say that and then blatantly flirt with other women and text that cow behind my back.

And it's not just the flirting.

His cold, sneering behavior outside the pharmacy hurt me just as much. He let me walk off knowing full and well I was upset, and he didn't attempt to come after me. I'm too afraid to ask him where he went, so I didn't ask, and he didn't offer it up. That is one of the questions that plagues me into the early hours of the night.

The next thing I know, I'm being shaken awaken. "Gabby! Gabby!"

I sit up, yawning, and brush knotty strands of hair back off my face. I squint at Dylan, trying to focus my blurry eyes. "Where's the fire?" I ask in a sleepy tone.

"Where's my black checkered shirt? I've looked everywhere, and I can't find it."

"I don't know. It's either in your closet, in with the laundry, or the ironing pile."

"I've looked there! It's not there," he snaps. "What the fuck did you do with it? You know that's one of my favorite shirts."

I narrow my eyes to slits. "Don't take that tone with me. It's got to be there somewhere. Look again."

"It's. Not. Fucking. There," he yells, and I flinch at the aggression on his face and in his voice.

I throw my hands up. "Well, then go buy a new one!"

"I want to wear it now," he says through gritted teeth. He yanks the covers off me. "Go look for it. Now."

"I'm not your damn servant. Go look for it yourself."

His nostrils flare. "This is all your fucking fault! It's your responsibility to find it!" he yells, and I'm done.

"I am not talking to you when you're like this. When you decide to grow up and act like an adult, come talk to me. Until then, leave me the hell alone." I hop up, shove past him, and lock myself in the bathroom.

I angrily strip my sleep shorts and tank off, my hands balling into fists at my side. I'm enraged and tempted to run back out there and kick him in the junk.

How dare he speak to me like that!

He knows damn well that we share the household chores. If the stupid shirt is lost somewhere, it could just as easily be his fault. And I really don't get what the big deal is anyway. Dylan has hundreds of shirts! Why is he so worked up over this one? The apartment door slams violently just as I'm stepping into the shower.

I tilt my face up to the warm water as steam fills the cubicle. I don't understand where Dylan's hot and cold attitude is coming from, but if he thinks I'm going to put up with that shit, he can think again.

Resting my head against the glass, I contemplate what the heck is going on, wondering where the hell my sweet, mild-mannered man has disappeared to. If this is what the stress of his current project is doing to him, I'd rather he can it in favor of something less taxing.

Needing a distraction, I head to the mall and buy a new dress for tonight.

We're all meeting at the club where Slater works later to celebrate Myndi's twentieth birthday. The owner knows we're friends of Slater's, so he won't serve us alcohol, but he turns a blind eye if he sees us with a beer in hand. He's told Slater on the QT that he'll deny all knowledge if the cops arrive and bust us. It's handy that Ryan, Slater, and most of their group are already twenty-one and they can get the drinks in.

Dylan hasn't returned by the time I get back. I make dinner, leaving his on a plate covered with saran wrap, and then I go to get ready.

I'm dressed and doing my makeup when he arrives home. I sense him standing behind me in the doorway, but I purposely ignore him.

He pads toward me, and I stiffen. "Gabby. I'm really sorry."

"That's all you seem to be saying these days," I retort, refusing to look at him.

"I know." He sounds sad, and my every instinct is to turn around and cheer him up, but I can't continue to let him get away with this behavior. He can't think this is acceptable to me—because it isn't.

I won't be treated like this.

"Here." He thrusts a bunch of white lilies at me. "Peace offering."

I inhale the scent I love so much before setting the flowers down on the dresser. I turn to face him. "Thank you for the flowers, but that's not going to make everything right."

He sinks onto the edge of the bed, burying his head in his hands. "I know that too." His voice is laced with resignation.

Silence engulfs the room for a bit, and then he lifts his head, and his eyes rake over me. "You look beautiful, Dimples."

"Thanks."

God, I hate how awkward and formal and upsetting this is. But I don't know how to fix this. If it's even in my power to do that.

"Shit." He bolts upright. "It's Myndi's birthday thing. I completely forgot."

I give him a curt nod, and he glances at his watch. "Give me a few minutes to grab a shower and change, and then we'll call an Uber."

I clear my throat. I've already given this a lot of thought today. "I'm going by myself."

"What? No!" He stands right in front of me. "I'll be on my best behavior. Promise." Right now, I see the lost little boy I fell in love with as a kid, and it would be as easy as breathing to just give in to him, but I can't.

"It's not just about that." I gulp painfully because this is going to hurt me too. "I don't want you to come with me. I'm still too angry and upset, and I don't want to end up fighting and ruining Myndi's night."

He reaches out to touch me, and I instinctively move back. He flinches and hurt splashes across his face.

I don't think I've ever shrunk from his touch before.

His eyes probe mine, and I'm struggling not to give in to the tears building at the back of my eyes, but I'm determined to be stronger. To deal with this like a grown-up and not to fall apart at every turn.

"You really want to go alone?"

I nod.

He hangs his head, and his shoulders heave. I feel like the biggest bitch, but I've got to remind myself I haven't done anything wrong. He's the one changing. Not me.

Slowly, he lifts his head, and the furious look in his eyes drains the color from my face. I clasp a hand over my chest, gulping back panic. Dylan has always been prone to mood swings, but I've never seen him flip so quickly from one extreme to another. "I know why you're doing this," he spits. "It's so you can be alone with *him*!"

Not this again. "It's got nothing to do with Slate, if that's who you're implying. I find your suggestion offensive and hurtful. I haven't done anything to make you doubt me."

Unlike you. I think it, but I don't say it. I don't want to leave here all upset and ruin the night. Myndi is my best friend, and I want to celebrate her birthday with her.

"That's not really true though, is it?"

"What exactly are you accusing me of?" I demand, placing my hands on my hips.

Locking his hands behind his head, he blows air out of his mouth. "Nothing. Nothing. Forget I said anything." When he steps toward me again, the naked aggression is gone from his face. "Please let me come with you. A few drinks and some dancing is just what we need to put us back on track." He moves to cup my face and I let him. "Let me make it up to you. I promise I'll treat you like a princess all night. I love you, baby. Please don't push me away."

I shake my head, and I can barely speak over the lump in my throat. "No," I whisper. "If you love me, you'll let me go by myself because it's what I want."

His hand drops away, and he's quiet for a bit. "Okay. If that's what you want."

"It is."

He nods and leaves the room. My lip wobbles, and my hand is shaking as I finish my makeup. I don't know why it feels like I've done something wrong when I haven't.

Grabbing my purse and a light jacket, I step out of the bedroom and into the main living space. "I called an Uber," Dylan says from his position on the couch. "It's waiting outside for you."

"Thanks."

I walk toward the door with a sick, twisty sensation churning in my stomach.

"Gabby. Wait." He races to my side, leaning in to kiss me on the cheek. "Have a good night and tell Myndi I said happy birthday. Make sure someone walks you out later, and don't wander off by yourself."

"I will."

He pulls me into a gentle hug, and I'm fighting tears again. It's official: I'm a complete basket case. He pecks my lips sweetly. "I love you. Stay safe."

I feel like a complete bitch as I walk away from him, and I almost change my mind, but something tells me not to.

The others are at the table Slater reserved when I arrive. Ryan and Myndi are eating the face off one another with no consideration for their other guests. Another couple of girls are there from our class with their boyfriends, along with Slater and two of his buddies. Slater usually works Saturdays, so he must have gotten the night off.

"Saved you a seat," Slater says, patting the empty space beside him. "We can squeeze in and make room for Dylan," he adds with a grimace, looking over my shoulder for my boyfriend.

"Dylan's not coming."

"He's not?" Myndi asks, finally surfacing for air.

"He's got another migraine," I lie, feeling bad about it but not wanting to say anything to my bestie tonight about the shit going on in my life.

"That's too bad," Ryan says. "You should've told me, and we would've swung by to pick you up."

"Dylan got me an Uber. It was no biggie."

"I'm driving, so I'll drop you home later," Slater says.

"Cool. Thanks."

"Right? What's your poison? You want a Cosmo or a beer or that Godawful sweet crap you like," he asks.

"I think I'll have the Godawful sweet crap. I need the sugar rush."

"It's your teeth," he says, sliding out past me. "One sickly sweet fruity drink coming up."

I chat with the others and give Myndi her birthday present while Slater is at the bar. Myndi rushes around the table, squealing and hugging me, in between drooling over the Michael Kors purse I bought her.

Slater returns with a tray full of drinks and we all relax, chatting, laughing, and drinking. I'm trying to enjoy myself, but it's like there's this thunderous cloud looming over my head, ready to erupt at any second. I don't usually drink too much, but I'm deliberately knocking them back tonight because I want to feel a happy buzz and forget.

It doesn't take long to feel the effects and then I'm dragging Myndi and the girls up to the dance floor where we work up a sweat. Out of the corner of my eye, I spy a group of girls swarming our table, moving in on the guys. Myndi notices too, but she doesn't make any attempt to go back there, watching to see how Ryan reacts.

My brother expertly deflects each and every advance, and Myndi's smile is so wide it might split her face. A sour taste fills my mouth as I watch a girl in a barely there red dress plaster herself to Slater. She's sitting in his lap with her arms on his chest, licking the side of his neck. His hand is on the exposed part of her back, and he's making swirling motions with his fingers as he talks to his buddy. The girl doesn't seem to care he's paying her scant regard, continuing to paw at him with her mouth and her hands.

"Ahem." Myndi draws my attention away, and my cheeks flush red. She pulls me over to the side of the dance floor. "You don't seem yourself tonight. What's going on with you?"

"Nothing. I'm fine."

Pursing her lips, she scrutinizes me with a slight frown. "You sure?"

I vigorously nod my head. I will tell my bestie everything that's going down, just not tonight. I don't want anything putting a dampener on her birthday night. "I don't know why he does it," I say, jerking my head in Slater's direction in a deliberate attempt to manipulate the direction of the conversation. "I don't know how anyone can just randomly sleep with strangers."

"That's because you've only ever been in love with the one guy. It's not actually that difficult. It's just sex. A way to let off steam. It's quite easy to remain detached and just enjoy the act for what it is."

"I don't think I could do it," I say, my eyes wandering to the table again of their own volition. I hurriedly disguise my reaction when my

gaze locks on Slater's. The girl is still in his lap, except she's straddling him now and pressing kisses all over his face.

But he isn't looking at her.

He's eyeballing me.

With an intense, smoldering look on his face that skyrockets my
pulse into orbit.

I quickly look away. "Let's keep dancing," I implore, holding
Myndi's hand and tugging her back out onto the dance floor. I force
my eyes frontward and ignore all temptation to look over at our table.
After a few minutes, I find my rhythm again, and all errant thoughts
flee my mind.

When the music shifts, slowing down, I suddenly find myself
deserted on the dance floor as the girls melt into the arms of their
guys. A pressing weight settles on my chest, making breathing difficult. Dylan would ordinarily be here, pulling me into his arms and
holding me tight against his body. Potent longing consumes me, and I
sorely regret telling him he couldn't come tonight. I already miss him.

A hand lands on my elbow and I startle. "Hey, it's only me,"
Slater says, extending his hand. "Dance with me?"

I eye his hand warily. It isn't the first time I've slow danced with
Slater, but somehow, this feels different. I should say no, but my head
bobs in agreement instead, and he takes my hand in his warm,
callused one, leading me over to the far side of the floor, away from
the others.

He pulls me into his embrace, heating me upon contact. Tentatively, I place my arms around his neck, trying to keep an appropriate
distance between us. For some reason, I'm acutely aware of every
rippling muscle in his chest and abs and how defined his biceps are.
Noticing how warm and alluring his eyes are, as if it's the first time
I've realized this. And how did I never spot how full and kissable his
lips are.

My thoughts veer into new confusing territory, and I don't understand this odd reaction to my brother's best friend. A guy I've known
for years and only seen as an extension of my brother.

Heat seems to roll off him in waves, knocking into me and rendering me senseless. We're swaying from side to side without speaking, and an undercurrent zips between us, charging the air. A fine line of sweat trickles down the back of my neck, and my mouth is dry. I'm wondering why I felt it was a good idea to do this when it feels fraught with tension.

"Relax, Belle," Slater says, recognizing how uncomfortable I am. "I won't bite." He grins wickedly. "Unless you want me to."

My lips curve up at the corners. "Stop that. I'm not one of your groupies. Your lines don't work on me, mister." I glance over my shoulder briefly, but I can't see our table from here. "Speaking of groupies, what happened to the latest cling-on, and shouldn't you be dancing with her?"

"Shelby knows the score, and if I wanted to dance with *her,* she'd be up here with me."

"Why do you do it?" I blurt. "Why do you screw all those girls?"

He smirks, arching a brow. "I think it's pretty obvious." He tweaks my nose, and I swat his hand away.

"Don't you get sick of it? Don't you feel lonely?"

He shrugs. "I'm usually too busy to feel lonely, and girlfriends are more trouble than they're worth. I'm happy the way I am. Besides, I don't hook up that much anymore."

I'm calling bullshit on that, but I'm not going to challenge him now. Not when I'm buzzing and acting weird around him.

"Does Dylan really have a migraine?" he asks, losing the cheeky smile and fixing me with a penetrating look.

"No," I whisper, averting my eyes. "I just needed some space to clear my head."

He tilts my chin up with his finger. "I need you to answer something for me."

"Okay." Trepidation is evident in my tone.

"What did Dylan tell you about the night I saw him?"

My eyes dart all over his face. "Why does it matter? He told me about that girl, and I'm trying to forget about it."

"Just humor me." He tucks my hair behind one of my ears, sending shivers down my spine.

Slater is a stubborn fucker at the best of times, so I know he won't let this drop. Might as well just tell him what he already knows. "He told me this girl was coming on to him and she grabbed his crotch, but he stopped it from going any further."

His Adam's apple jumps in his throat, and a flash of anger whips across his face. He cusses, closing his eyes briefly, and immense fear is like a vise grip around my heart as realization dawns. My heart thrashes against my rib cage, and blood thrums in my ears. "That's not what happened, is it?" I whisper, hating how my voice breaks.

Slowly, Slater shakes his head. "No, sweetheart. That's not how it went down."

Chapter Eleven

"Tell me. Please." My heart is pounding, and nausea pools at the back of my throat, but I'm not going to shy away from this. I need the truth. If Dylan won't give it to me, I'll seek it wherever I can.

Slater's features soften, and he pulls me a little closer to him, circling his arms more firmly around my back. "Belle, this is going to hurt, but I told him if he didn't tell you then I would. I've given him every chance to come clean, but he's left me with no choice. I won't ... I can't stand by and watch him do this to you."

"Please just tell me what really happened," I beseech, not sure how much more anxiety my heart can withstand.

"I went up to his table because he was all over some other girl."

The first rupture penetrates my heart.

"They were making out like crazy, and I was furious with him, but it was much worse when I got to the table." Tears are already streaming down my face. Slater kisses my forehead. "God, Belle. I hate to be the one telling you this, but you need to know."

"Go on," I rasp, just needing to get all the breaking over and done with.

He hugs me tight and then eases back, looking me directly in the face as he rips my heart to shreds. "She was giving him a handjob under the table, and he didn't seem to care that they weren't being very discreet."

"No!" I gasp. "Dylan wouldn't do something like that!"

"Belle." His voice is soft as he cups my face. "Do you think I'd lie to your face? This is *me*." His eyes examine mine as silent tears continue to fall. "Do you think I'd ever want to hurt you like this? I care about you. Deeply. You know me. You know I wouldn't make this up."

"I ... I know but ... but Dylan wouldn't do that to me! Especially not in public."

A pained expression is etched on his face, and a second rupture tears my heart straight down the middle. A strangled sound rips from my throat, and Slater gathers me into his arms, holding me tight against him and lowering my head to his shoulder. I sob into his shirt as he holds me, my mind a mess of warring emotions. "I'm so sorry, Belle." He rubs his hand up and down my spine.

"Why would he do this to me? To us?" I cry.

"I don't understand it either. I know that's not Dylan's usual M.O. I was shocked as fuck. He's the last guy I'd expect to do something like this."

"Get your fucking hands off her!" I'm forcibly ripped from Slater's arms as Dylan pulls me into him. Hastily smoothing my thumbs under my eyes, I bat my tears away and stare at the rage-filled expression on Dylan's face. His nostrils flare as he pulls me behind him.

"Let me go," I demand, trying to shuck out of his hold.

"Don't, Gabby," Dylan says in a clipped voice, indicating he's as pissed at me as he is at Slater. As if *I've* done something wrong.

And that does it.

I snap.

Yanking my arm away, I place myself in front of him with Slater at my back. "Tell me what really happened with that girl in the club."

"I already told you what happened," he hisses, glowering at Slater over my shoulder.

"I want the truth this time."

Ignoring me, Dylan growls at Slater. "What the fuck did you tell her?"

"I gave her the truth, not the pack of lies you fed her."

"Fuck you, you interfering asshole!"

Before I have time to second-guess his reaction, Dylan flies around me, thrusting his fist out and grazing Slater on the side of his jaw. Slater's a big guy though, and he barely flinches. Dylan is also unsteady on his feet and swaying a little. I take a proper look at my boyfriend, noticing his flushed skin and bloodshot eyes, and I can tell he's totally smashed.

The crowd around us has stepped back a little, and I feel the weight of several pairs of eyes on us.

"Do that again and I'll hit you back," Slater warns. But it's like Dylan has lost all sense. He throws himself at Slater like a madman, landing another punch on his face, this time on his nose. Blood spurts from Slater's nose, and whatever restraint he had is gone. He hits Dylan, square in the face, and his head whips back. I clamp a hand over my mouth, frozen in place as I watch the two of them go at it. They throw jabs and punches at one another while the crowd forms a circle around us, whooping and hollering.

"What the actual fuck?" Ryan shouts, appearing at my side and looking from me to the two guys with an incredulous look on his face.

"Do something," I plead, just as a couple of bouncers approach, pulling the guys apart.

"Move aside, Miss." A gruff voice says from behind me, and I step aside as two cops materialize.

Shit. Someone called it in, and they obviously had a cruiser close by.

"Fuck." Ryan sighs, scrubbing a hand over his stubbly chin as we watch Slater and Dylan being cuffed and read their rights.

"Call Dad," I tell him, finally breaking out of my dumbstruck-alcohol-influenced haze.

"I love you," Dylan yells over his shoulder at me, wrestling with the cop as he steers him through the crowd.

"I'll fix this," Ryan tells Slater as he's led away by another cop, his eyes latched onto mine.

Ryan slings his arm around my shoulders as we follow my boyfriend and his best friend, watching as they are removed from the club and put into the back of a police cruiser. Ryan, Myndi, and I take a cab to the station, and Ryan calls our dad on the way, quickly explaining what happened. He agrees to meet us there.

"What the hell is going on, Gabby?" Ryan asks me from the front passenger seat, after a few minutes of tense silence. "And don't tell me nothing. Those two have been at each other's throats for weeks now. I know this is somehow connected to you, so, for the love of God, please just fucking tell me."

So I do. I tell them both the whole sordid tale, leaving nothing out this time. I must be all cried out because I don't shed a single tear as I tell them what Slater told me tonight.

"Oh my God, Gabby. I'm so sorry," Myndi says, wrapping her arms around me. "I wish you had told me."

"I didn't want to ruin your night."

She hugs me to her. "You wouldn't have. At least now I understand why you've been so preoccupied lately and why you looked so sad tonight."

"I'm going to fucking kill him," Ryan seethes. "I'll be having a few choice words with my best buddy too. He should've told me this."

"Don't do that. Don't take it out on Slate. He was trying to do the right thing, and it's not his fault."

"He still should've told me. I'm your brother. It's my job to protect you. Not his."

"I'm not a little kid anymore, Ryan. I'm an adult, and I'm responsible for myself. I don't expect my brother to ride to the rescue all the time. It's my relationship and my responsibility to sort it out."

94

"Please don't tell me you're going to stay with him after this?" He pins disbelieving eyes on me.

"I don't know what I'm going to do," I truthfully admit. Knotting my hands in my lap, I sigh. "I mean, this is Dylan, Ryan. *Dylan.*"

"I don't care what's come before, Gabby. He doesn't get to disrespect you like that. Especially not with the history you guys have."

"I know." My voice is meek, resigned. "But you've got to let me deal with this. I know you want to protect me, and I love you so much for that, but you've got to step away and let me handle this. I'm not going to let Dylan treat me like this. Mom and Dad have brought me up to have more self-respect than that."

That seems to appease him for now.

We hang around in the waiting area of the police station for Dad to arrive. Neither Slater or Dylan are anywhere in visible sight.

Dad turns up an hour later, and he goes straight to the desk, completing some paperwork and handing over his credentials. He takes a seat beside me while the officer at the desk goes to talk to the officers in charge of the case. "You want to tell me what happened, Buttercup?"

I give him an abbreviated, censored version and he listens attentively, without interrupting. When a tall man with salt and pepper hair arrives, he gets up, going over to greet him. Then he returns, standing in front of me with the man. "This is David," he tells me. "He's an attorney colleague of mine. I can't represent both Slater and Dylan as it'd be a conflict of interest, so David will take one of them on." Dad sits back down, taking my hands in his. "You need to tell me who you wish me to represent."

"Slater." Both Ryan and I say it at the same time.

"You sure, Buttercup?" Dad asks.

I nod. "Dylan can easily afford to pay the legal fees. Slater needs you more."

Dad nods, patting my hand. "We'll try to make this go away, provided they both agree not to press charges, and provided the police are willing to waive charges too." He smooths a hand over my hair. "This could take hours, and it's already late. You should go home."

"I'm not going anywhere, Dad." Seeing the determination on my face, he doesn't even attempt to argue.

Ryan manages to convince Myndi to go home. He goes outside to put her into a taxi, and then he returns, pulling my head down on his lap. "Sleep." He drapes his jacket over my upper body. "I'll wake you when there's news."

I close my eyes, sure I won't be able to sleep at a time like this, but I guess the emotional exhaustion has taken more of a toll than I thought, and the next thing I know, I'm being woken up. I sit up, groggily stretching, and a loud yawn escapes my lips. Ryan growls at the base of his throat, holding me close to him.

"Gabby?" Dylan's voice sounds uncertain. I flinch, and a sharp ache pierces my chest cavity as everything comes rushing back at me. Raising my eyes, I meet his worried gaze. His hair is sticking up all over the place, and his eyes are still bloodshot and red-rimmed. Bruising shadows paint the area under his eyes, and he looks exhausted and worn out. "I'm so sorry."

Ryan growls again, and I don't need to look at his face to know he's shooting daggers at my boyfriend.

"Can we go home and talk?" Dylan asks, refusing to look at anyone but me.

I stand, clearing my throat. "Let's talk outside." Wordlessly, Ryan drapes his jacket around my shoulders, pressing a kiss to the top of my head. Dad appears then with Slater in tow. Slater purposely ignores Dylan, looking straight ahead. A muscle pops in his jaw, and tension percolates the air. I pass my father and touch his arm. "Can you stay for a few minutes, Daddy?"

"I'm going nowhere, Buttercup."

Dylan opens the door for me, and I step out into the early morning, grateful I have Ryan's jacket to ward off the slight chill in the air. We descend the steps and I turn left. Leaning my back against the wall, I wrap my arms around myself and stare at my boyfriend. "Why do you keep lying to me?"

Shoving his hands in the pockets of his jeans, he gulps nervously. "Because I'm scared of losing you."

"It's true, isn't it? What Slate told me."

Dylan nods with his eyes downcast.

The pain is instant, intense and all consuming. "Why, Dylan?"

"I wish I could tell you, but I don't know." He takes a step toward me, and I recoil, not wanting him to come any closer. If I'd slapped him, he wouldn't look as hurt. "I just ... sometimes I'm like a different person, and I can't control it ... the impulse to seize the moment, and I just stop thinking and go for it." Tears glisten in his eyes. "And then I snap out of it and I realize what I've done, and I hate myself. I *hate* myself for doing this to you, but I can't seem to stop."

Emotion clogs my throat, and I can't even form words. Tears spill down my cheeks. "You don't love me anymore."

"No, baby. That's the thing. I do. I love you so much, and I hate hurting you." He cups my face. "Please believe me."

"How can I when you're ripping my heart apart?" I sob. "I don't understand, Dylan. Everything was perfect when we came back to campus, and now everything has turned to shit." My heart bleeds and I wish I could turn back the clock. To a time when my love was enough for him and we were amazing together.

He presses his forehead to mine, and we're both crying now. The pain in my chest is so severe it feels like I'm having a heart attack. I sidestep him, needing to put distance between us. I'm tired and emotionally drained, and I can't think straight when I'm like this.

"I'm going to go home with my dad. I need some space." He reaches for me again, but I step back. "Don't, Dylan." I shake my head, tears clouding my vision again. "Don't make it worse."

He scrunches fistfuls of his hair, kicking at the side of the wall. "I know I've no right to ask you this, but please don't give up on us. Don't give up on me. I love you, Gabby. I love you so much."

"I wish I could believe that."

"It's the truth! I swear it."

Thing is, I can see the truth resonating in his eyes, but how can he say he loves me and then go and do all this other stuff with different girls behind my back? Either he's deluding himself or he's a better liar than I've given him credit for.

"I want to believe that, Dylan, but..." I trail off, unable to do this now. "Just give me some space."

Reluctantly, he nods. "If that's what you need, but please come home tomorrow. Let's talk some more. I know we can work through this. We've been through too much together to lose what we have."

"I'll be home tomorrow night," I agree. Stepping around him, I start climbing the steps.

"Please remember I love you." Dylan says this as my dad, Slater, Ryan, and his attorney friend step outside. Slater sends Dylan a look of disgust mixed with disappointment, and Ryan folds his arms, narrowing his eyes at Dylan.

"Just go," I say, turning to face him.

"I'm sorry, Gabby. More than you can ever know." Then he slopes off with his shoulders hunched and his hands inserted in his pockets.

I wet my dry lips. "I'm coming back with you, Daddy."

Dad pulls me into his arms. "No problem, Buttercup. Your momma's already waiting up for you."

"Are you okay?" Slater asks, concern shining in his eyes.

"I don't know," I honestly answer. "I'm sorry you got dragged into this. I know you were only looking out for me."

"Forget about it," he says. "Just take care of yourself."

I offer him a weak smile. Ryan pulls me out of Dad's arms, hugging me to him. The scent of his familiar cologne is comforting. "You want me to come with?"

I shake my head. "Thanks, but I just need to be on my own with my thoughts."

"Well, I'm here if you need anything."

"*We're* here," Slater cuts in. "We'd both do anything for you, Belle."

Tears prick my eyes. "I know and thank you." I shuck out of Ryan's arms, stretch up on my tiptoes, and kiss Slater's cheek.

"Come on, Buttercup," Dad says, nestling me under his arm. "Let's get you home."

Chapter Twelve

Mom has a veritable breakfast feast waiting for me when I arrive home, but I can barely stomach more than a few mouthfuls. "Sorry, it's delicious, but I..."

"It's okay, honey." She kisses my temple. "I understand. Why don't you grab a few hours' sleep, and maybe we can talk then?"

I nod, letting Mom help me into bed like I'm a little kid again. She pulls the covers up under my chin, tucking my hair behind my ears. "I don't know what's happened, Gabby, but I know you're hurting, and I hate to see my little girl in pain. Sleep and we'll try to figure this out then."

"Thanks, Mom." I sit up and hug the shit out of her. It's like I've regressed in time, and I just want my mom to kiss me and make it better. To promise everything will be okay and she'll look after me.

When I wake, it's after three p.m., and dim rays of sunlight are peeking through the gap in the curtains. I shower and get changed, grateful I keep supplies and some clothes at home.

Dad is mowing the front lawn as I come down the stairs, and I smile at the familiar sight. Dad is a creature of habit, and he always mows the lawn on Sunday afternoons. Mom is pottering around the kitchen, singing along to the radio, and the normalcy of it all brings a faint smile to my face. "Can I help?" I ask, and she startles.

"Oh my gosh, honey, you gave me a fright. I didn't hear you come in." Switching off the radio, she steps in front of me, inspecting my face. "How are you feeling?"

I shrug, and she encases me in her arms, rubbing my back and instantly making me feel better. "Dinner won't be till five, but I'll heat up some soup for you. Go and take a seat at the table."

She sets a piping hot bowl of homemade pea soup in front of me a few minutes later, and I inhale the sweet, minty steam with a contented sigh. I wolf down the soup while she sips on her coffee, staring absently out the window into the backyard. When I'm finished, she leans over, taking my hands in hers. "Do you want to talk about it, honey? It might help to get it all off your chest."

I don't talk for ages, but Mom has the patience of a saint, and she waits me out. "It hurts, Mom," I say, holding my hand over my heart. "It hurts so much." Tears sting my eyes.

"What did he do?" she gently asks. In a trembling voice, I tell her everything, holding nothing back. Her face drops and her expression turns sad. "Oh honey, I'm so sorry to hear that."

"He says he still loves me, but how can he love me and do that? I would never do that to him."

She sighs, rubbing soothing circles on the back of my hand. "I was fearful something like this might happen," she admits, and I quirk a brow.

"You knew he'd cheat?"

She shakes her head, and waves of thick, glossy blonde hair, so like my own, fall around her face. "No, but you were both so young when you fell in love, and it was so intense. You were completely wrapped up in one another in a way that belied your years."

"I've loved him from the minute I met him," I admit, "and he felt the same even if we took years to confess that to one another. I have always known this wasn't puppy love or a fleeting feeling. I've always known he was meant for me and I was meant for him, but now it feels like I don't know anything anymore, and I don't know what to do. I haven't planned for this."

"No one plans for the speed bumps, honey, and that's just life."

"I can't stay with him if he's going to cheat on me, but then it feels like I'm giving up. Throwing away everything we have and everything we have planned, and that doesn't feel right either."

"Maybe you just need some time apart."

"I've thought of that too, but what if that's it? And we never get back together? I don't know if I can bear to lose him."

She moves her chair in closer to me. "If your love is meant to be, you'll find your way back to one another." She caresses my cheek. "You know we love Dylan like a son, right?" I nod. "I hate he's hurt you, but we all know that boy, and he wouldn't intentionally set out to do this. I'd stake my life on it. That doesn't mean I condone it or that I'm not furious with him, because I am, but maybe he's being honest when he tells you he doesn't know why he's done this."

She presses a tender kiss to my forehead. "You're adults now, but you're both still growing and developing and finding your place in the world. Sometimes feelings change even when we don't want them to. Or a sense of restlessness sets in. Maybe Dylan needs to experience the world without you to realize you are his forever love."

"I don't need to do that to know that he's mine!" I protest, not liking where she's going with this.

"Perhaps *you* don't, but you're not the one struggling with your feelings. He is."

I stare out the window, heartsick at the fact Mom could be right. "What if I lose him Mom? What if I let him go and he doesn't realize that? What if he meets someone else?"

She forces my gaze to hers. "If that happens, then it's not meant to be." My lower lip wobbles. "I don't want to upset you, honey, but I think you need to consider the possibility that maybe Dylan *isn't* the one for you after all. Maybe there's a greater love waiting in store for you." I chew on the inside of my mouth, tears cascading down my cheeks. I hate that I'm a hot mess. That I can't even think about the prospect of not having Dylan in my life without falling apart. I know I need to be stronger than this, but right now, I can't summon the strength I need.

Mom wets her lips. "I've never told you, or any of your brothers, this before, out of respect for your father, but I think you need to hear this now."

My curiosity is piqued, and my tears automatically dry up.

"I'll let him know later that I've told you this because there are no secrets between us." She clasps my hands, and a faraway look ghosts over her face. "I was a lot like you growing up. Most of my friends were boys, and my best friend was a boy who lived four houses up. Mickey was in my life from the time I was a toddler, and we were joined at the hip, a lot like you and Dylan were once you met. I loved him so completely, and he loved me in return. We were fourteen when we became boyfriend and girlfriend, and we were even more inseparable then. We had our whole lives all mapped out, but we didn't anticipate fate coming between us. Mickey gained a full ride to play ball at the University of Southern California, and the plan was for me to join him, but I didn't get a scholarship, and my parents couldn't afford to send me there, so we had no choice but to attend different colleges. He was going to give it all up to come to UD with me, but I wouldn't hear of it. He had too much talent, and it was too great of an opportunity to pass up. Our relationship was solid, and this was only a temporary setback, or so I thought."

A shuddering breath passes through her lips. "I still remember how much I missed him at first. How much it hurt. Like a limb had been forcibly ripped from my body." She smiles sadly. "We talked every day, and we met up any chance we could get, but it was hard." Her eyes light up. "Then I met your father on campus. It was the start of my sophomore year and his senior year. And it was like fireworks exploded when our eyes met. I knew instantly he was important, and your father told me after he felt the same."

"Oh my God." I lean forward on my knees, mesmerized. "What happened with Mickey?"

"I was tortured for months. I told your father I was in a long-term relationship, and he said he respected that, but he didn't give up pursuing me. We became really good friends. I knew it was wrong, because I felt the connection between us, and I knew I was falling for him, but I couldn't stop it, even if I'd wanted to, and I didn't."

She looks up at the ceiling, exhaling loudly. Then she drops her head and eyeballs me. "I never believed it was possible to love two men at the same time, but it's what happened. When you think about it," she muses, "it's not really that unbelievable. Why is it society accepts we can love multiple siblings at the same time, love both parents at once, have several friends we love, and yet, it's not deemed acceptable or believable to love two men, or more, in a romantic way at the same time?"

"I don't know," I say, my brow puckering. "I've never really thought about it, but when you put it like that, it seems totally plausible."

She nods. "Well, that's the situation I found myself in. In love with two amazing men, but I could only choose one to spend my life with." An anguished look appears on her face. "I wouldn't wish that decision on my worst enemy," she whispers. "I was so conflicted, and I knew someone was going to end up hurt. I kept both of them at arm's length for months, unsure what to do, and then my mom said something profound to me." She squeezes my hand. "She told me to imagine they died and see which one I could live without."

"Geez. I always knew Grandma Hudson was nuts, but that's a bit extreme."

Mom laughs. "There were no gray areas with your grandma. She didn't shy away from speaking her mind. They were two qualities I admired in my mother." Mom looks nostalgic. It's been eight years since Grandma passed, and I know she still misses her like crazy. "And she was right. I gave it serious thought, and I realized that I couldn't live without your father in my life."

"Wow."

"I know." She bobs her head. "I felt so sure it would be Mickey.

Because we had been together for years. We knew each other inside and out. We thought we had it all worked out."

"But you didn't," I answer for her.

"No." Her eyes well up. "I never cheated on him, but when it came to the point where I wanted to progress things with your father, and I knew he was the one, I had to pull on my big girl panties and break things off with Mickey. I hated telling him. Hated breaking his heart. It was the singular most awful conversation of my life, but he's gone on to great success in his sporting career, and he's married with two kids. That helped me to get over the protracted sense of guilt I always carried with me."

"How do you feel about him now?" I risk asking.

"I'm not betraying your father by telling you this because it's something he already knows. I cut Mickey Delaney out of my life thirty years ago, but he still owns a piece of my heart. He always will. In the same way I know I still hold a piece of his."

Her words wrap around my own tormented heart, and intense emotion compresses my chest. I never knew this about my mother. This is the first, and I suspect the last, time she will speak to me about her first love. There are some similarities in our situations, which is a little freaky, but there are lots of unspoken messages in what she has said too.

Silence engulfs us for a bit, and I can only imagine how difficult this trip down memory lane is for Mom, even though I know she loves my dad to bits.

My parents are the perfect example of a wonderful, supportive, loving marriage, and I've never doubted their love. My parents are hugely demonstrative with one another, and we grew up surrounded by affection and always knowing how much we were loved. I know how lucky I am to have had that. So many of my school friends came from broken or dysfunctional homes, and, even at a young age, I came to appreciate the love and respect my parents showed for one another and our family life.

Mom clears her throat, squeezing my hands tight. "We're very proud of you, Gabby. You're a sweet girl, and you have the biggest heart. Dad and I both know you will be successful in life no matter what you decide. We will always support you, because you're our daughter and we love you unconditionally."

"I love you too, Mom," I croak. My family is big on the "I love yous," and we're known for our open affection, but this is deeper, and her words are exactly what I need to hear in this moment.

"So, don't think this is me telling you what to do. You need to make your own choices in life, and you're more than equipped to do it. We won't judge—we'll support. But I want you to consider the possibility that maybe there is someone else out there for you. Maybe there's someone else out there for Dylan. Maybe you were meant to have this intense first love, but it was not meant to be your forever love. It doesn't negate what you two have shared. It doesn't extinguish the love you will always have in your heart for him."

She pauses for a minute, composing the right words. "Or maybe you two just need some time apart to evaluate your relationship. Maybe you *are* destined to be together and everything will work itself out. Just promise me one thing. Promise me that whatever you decide, you will ensure you are making the right choices for *you*." Her eyes bore into mine, and I nod. "Trust and respect are vital in any relationship. If you don't have that with Dylan anymore, then you don't have a future. But you still have a past with him. Don't let what happens from this point on tarnish those memories because they are a big part of who you are."

A lone tear sneaks out of my eye. Mom's words slay me. But I need to hear them.

"You may not have a future, but you will always have that past. Don't let anything or anyone take away those happy memories of your first love."

Chapter Thirteen

My brother Caleb drops me home later that night. He knows what's happened, and he offers to listen, but I can't talk about it anymore, and I'm grateful he lets it go, using the quiet time to try and organize my thoughts. Mom's advice has been playing on a continual loop in my head, but I'm still undecided.

Dylan mutes the TV and rises to greet me when I arrive back at the condo. With his messy hair, swollen eyes, and scruffy chin, he looks as bad as I feel. We face one another, staring for a few moments, both of us struggling to find the right words. And then we move, like magnets, drawn to one another at the exact same moment in time. We fall into each other's arms, and we stand there, hugging, just hugging, for a long time. The familiarity of his scent, his body heat, and his touch is equally comforting and painful at the same time. I break away first, not altogether surprised to discover fresh tears covering my face.

I think I've cried a river today.

More than I've ever cried in the space of a day before.

"I'm sorry," Dylan croaks.

"I know you are."

"Don't leave me." The anguish in his voice slices through me, constricting my lungs, making breathing difficult.

I choke on a sob. "I can't talk or think about this anymore tonight, Dylan. I just want to sleep. Can we agree to meet back here tomorrow evening, and we'll talk it through then."

He cups my face. "If that's what you want."

I nod, moving toward the couch and grabbing the sheets and pillows I left there from Friday night.

"I'll sleep out here. You take the bed."

"It's okay. I don't mind."

"Gabby, take the bed," he snaps, and I flinch.

Tears well in his eyes. "I'm sorry. I didn't mean to say it like that."

My chest visibly rises and falls as I look at him, wondering where the man I love has disappeared to. This short-tempered, lying, cheating version is a pale imitation of the real Dylan.

Suddenly, I'm overcome with sadness.

For *him*.

I walk out of the room without uttering another word, and I get ready for bed in a kind of daze. Snuggling under the covers, I breathe in Dylan's scent, curling my body around his pillow, wishing I could go back to a time when everything was perfect.

But I know I can't.

Dylan is already gone by the time I get up the next morning, and I'm grateful. Although I had a restless night's sleep, I'm in a clearer state of mind today, and I know what I need to do.

Myndi sticks to my side like glue during the day, especially after I tell her what I have decided. I speak with Ryan, and he readily agrees.

By the time Dylan arrives back to our apartment, nerves have set in, and I'm on edge. Which is stupid, because I'm not the one in the wrong. It's not my actions that are forcing me down this path.

I make coffees and we sit down at the dining table, across from one another. Dylan looks at me with forlorn eyes, and his knee taps up and down. Summoning courage, I clear my throat and start speaking. "You have really hurt me, Dylan. In a way I never, ever imagined you could or would. I know, deep down, this is not who you are, but I can't stand by and watch you shatter my self-confidence and destroy what we have, so I'm going to move out for a while. I think we need some time apart to reconsider our relationship."

"No, Gabby, please. Don't do this. I need you." He reaches across the table for my hand.

"And I need to do this." I snatch my hand back. "I love you, Dylan. I love you so much it hurts. Doing this is killing me as much as it's killing you, but I won't be one of those girls who turns a blind eye, and I won't live in denial. I expect my boyfriend to be one hundred percent committed and loyal to me. Without exception."

I finish my coffee and stand. "I suggest you take the time apart to think about whether you can offer me that. If you can't, then we're finished for good." My voice cracks on the last sentence, and the composure I've worked so hard to maintain crumples. Looking away, I sob, and that pain in my heart intensifies.

Dylan is crying too, and he looks miserable as he gets up and comes to me. He pulls me into his arms, and I go to him, resting my head on his shoulder and holding him tight as we both cry. "I love you, Gabby. I love you to the ends of time. I'm sorry I've done this to us, and I'm going to do everything to make things right again."

I lift my head, sniffling. "I really hope you mean that, Dylan, and that you stick to it."

"I will, baby. I will." He kisses me, and I let him. His kiss is fierce and desperate and a silent plea all at the same time.

The doorbell chimes, and I tear my lips away, drying my tears on the sleeve of my shirt. "That's Ryan. He's here for my things." I open the door and let my brother in.

"You okay?" he asks, carefully inspecting my tear-stained face.

"Yeah. My stuff is in the bedroom." He kisses the top of my head, glaring menacingly at Dylan before walking out of the room.

Dylan says nothing, watching as Ryan takes my two cases and the small box from our bedroom. I haven't packed up all my stuff, just enough for a couple weeks. "I'll follow you down," I tell Ryan as he loiters in the doorway, waiting for me. "I just want to say goodbye to Dylan."

"If you're not out in five minutes, I'll be back," he warns, glowering at my boyfriend before he leaves.

Veins pop in Dylan's arms as he balls his hands into fists, and a muscle ticks in his jaw. I'm instantly on guard. "Where are you moving to, Gabby?" he barks.

"I'm staying with Ryan."

"Over my dead fucking body are you staying there!"

I plant my hands on my hips. "Excuse me? He's my *brother,* and I'll stay there if I like. You don't get to dictate this, or anything, right now."

Dylan's hard, angry façade slips, replaced with one of sheer panic. He moves toward me. "Baby, please. You can stay here, and I'll go stay in a hotel. Just don't go there."

I shake my head. "This is *your* condo, Dylan. You own it. I'm not kicking you out of your own place, and I'm not staying here. Not when things are up in the air with us. It wouldn't feel right." I need to be away from all reminders of Dylan if I'm to figure out what my head and my heart want. Staying here, where we've been so happy, where there are constant reminders of Dylan, would only make things worse.

He starts pacing, and I can almost see his mind churning. "We're not breaking up, right? This isn't what this is. We're just taking some time out, right?"

He looks to me for confirmation, and I nod. "For now."

Agony is etched across his face, but I won't retract my words. I don't know what lies in wait for us around the corner, and I won't give him false hope. I don't know if I can get over his betrayal. It doesn't matter that he hasn't physically slept with another girl—to the best of my knowledge—because making out with someone who isn't me is still a betrayal. The fact he let some slut give him a handjob in public disgusts and sickens me every time I think about it.

"If Slater so much as looks at you funny, I will kill him," he seethes.

I exhale slowly, counting to ten in my head. "For the last time, Dylan, nothing is going on with Slate, and you really have a nerve making demands on me after what you've done. Don't piss me off."

"Baby, he wants you."

I laugh. "You are being ridiculous, and I'm not having this conversation again. I think it's best if we don't contact one another. I'll touch base with you in a couple of weeks, and we can see how we're feeling then," I suggest, grabbing my jacket and my purse.

"Gabby!" Dylan rushes to my side, pulling me into his embrace. "Please don't give up on us. I'm begging you. Please remember how much I love you and everything that we've planned."

"I won't, Dylan, but I can say the same to you. Don't do anything else to destroy us. Use this time to try and figure out if I'm truly who you want."

"I already know that, Gabby." He clings to me. "Please change your mind. Stay here and we can figure things out. Leaving is like you've already decided to give up on us."

That really annoys me. I shuck out of his arms, working hard to quell my anger. "Don't you get it? If I stay here, nothing will change. I'm doing this because I love you and because it's the best way of salvaging our relationship. Don't make me regret this, Dylan, because there won't be another chance."

Chapter Fourteen

"**Y**ou can take my room," Ryan says, opening the door to the brownstone he shares with Slater, Austin, and Michael. "Michael had to go home on short notice; his dad isn't well, so I'll bunk in his room for now."

"You sure? I honestly don't mind sleeping on the couch. You know me—I can sleep just about anywhere."

Dropping my bags on the floor in the hall, he messes up my hair. "Oh, I know, Tornado. I still remember that time you fell asleep, headfirst, into your dinner." He chuckles.

"I was three, asshat." I shoulder bump him.

"It was so cute, in a gross kind of way."

"Yeah, Mom was still picking bits of carrot out of my hair the next day." I smile at the memory.

Ryan slings his arm around my shoulders, smacking a loud kiss off my cheek. "Fun times, little sis." He steers me into the kitchen, and I giggle at the sight that awaits me. Slater is standing in front of the stove, wearing a wide grin and an apron that reads "Can I suggest the sausage?" with a picture of a hand with the index finger pointing downward.

"Hey, Belle." His warm brown eyes meet mine. "Hope you're hungry. I made Mom's chicken potpie and peach cobbler for dessert."

My tummy rumbles in appreciation and the guys laugh. "I think that's your answer," I joke, "and it's not like I'd ever turn my favorite food down."

"Good, because I've made way too much food for the three of us."

"Isn't Austin joining us?" Ryan inquires, rummaging in the refrigerator. "Beer?" he asks, looking at me, and I nod.

"Nah. He's working an extra shift tonight. Won't be home till late."

I get to work setting the table, sipping on my beer as I go. "It's not like it'll go to waste. I know how much food you two put away."

"We're growing boys, Tornado. What do you expect?"

"Nothing less, Randy Ryan."

He scowls. "Gabby."

"Ryan." I smirk in his direction as Slater shakes his head, quietly chuckling.

"I might need to set some new house rules."

"Oh, this I gotta hear." Slater takes the pie out of the oven and starts slicing it into sections.

"One," Ryan starts, "Randy Ryan is banned. It's on the list of words that deserve to die a thousand deaths. I do not want to hear those annoying words leaving your lips while you're here."

"Well, then you have to agree to refrain from calling me Tornado. Fair's fair."

He shakes his head, rounding the table and pulling my chair out for me. "You don't get to dictate, Tornado. Our house, our rules."

"Defend my honor," I beseech Slater as he slides a loaded plate in front of me.

Gently placing his hands on my shoulders, he pins Ryan with a serious look. "Your sister is right, and I'm all about equality. While Belle is living here, she has an equal say in all things."

I reach up, squeezing his hand. A tingle of electricity dances over my skin from the slight contact, and I pull my hand back as if it's contaminated. My cheeks heat as I pick up my silverware and dig in.

"Why do you get to use a nickname and I don't?" Ryan inquires, wolfing into his food.

Slater slides into a seat across from me. "Because I'm me, and you're just Randy Ryan. Now shut up about stupid house rules and eat." He stabs his fork in Ryan's direction, and we all laugh.

The rest of dinner passes pleasantly with the boys ribbing one another in between demolishing the entire potpie and all the dessert. So much for having too much food. I try to force Slater into the living room after dinner, so I can clean up, but he's having none of it. Ryan has gone upstairs to get changed. He's taking Myndi to a movie, so that leaves Slater and me on clean-up duty.

We work silently and efficiently, rinsing and loading plates and glasses into the dishwasher. I'm acutely aware of his presence and how the muscles in his arms flex and roll as he bends and straightens. When the back of his shirt lifts, exposing a strip of toned, tan skin, my stomach does a strange, twisty motion and my body overheats. Silently slapping myself upside the head, I tell myself to get a grip. This is Slater. My pseudo-brother. I don't know why I'm feeling weird around him lately.

I could blame Dylan for putting notions in my head, but, if I'm honest, it commenced before he started hurling ridiculous insinuations at me.

I'm wiping down the countertop while Slater is sipping from a bottle of water, watching me, and I'm aware of his dedicated attention. My mouth feels suddenly dry, and all the tiny hairs on the back of my neck lift. "You doing okay?" he asks quietly after a bit.

Throwing the cloth in the sink, I shrug. "I'm taking it one day at a time."

"For what it's worth, he's a fucking idiot."

"Thanks, but I really don't want to talk about Dylan. I'm trying to clear my head so I can think straight, and going over everything won't help my agenda."

He steps in closer to me, tilting my chin up with his finger. Heat floods my body, and I lose the ability to breathe. His eyes shimmer with emotion when he speaks. "Don't sell yourself short, Belle. Any guy that has you in his life is a lucky sonofabitch. You deserve to be treated like an angel. Anything less just won't cut it. You hear me?"

I can only nod, because his touch and the intensity of the way he's looking at me has rendered my vocal cords ineffective. My eyes flit to his lips, and I wonder what it would be like to kiss him.

I jerk away from him, my cheeks flaring at the inappropriateness of my thoughts. "I, ah, I get it." I look down at the floor, mumbling. "I should go unpack."

"Sure. Let me know if you need anything."

I race up the stairs, even more confused and tormented than I was earlier. Ryan has already deposited my bags in his room and cleared out half of his closet, but the rest of the room is a mess, and I set about stripping and redressing the bed in my own bed linen and tidying up the room. Ryan pops his head in while I'm on my cleaning-ninja buzz, offering again to take me with him on his date, but I shoo him away. I don't want to feel like a fifth wheel, and I don't want to be envious or jealous of my best friend. Ryan and Myndi have really clicked, and I'm genuinely happy for them. I don't want to rain on their parade. Ryan needs the love of a good woman, and if it'll stop him from screwing his way through campus, then I'm even more in favor of the relationship.

After I've dusted and wiped clean every disgusting surface, emptied the trash cans, and vacuumed the floor, I unpack my things and hang them up. Changing out of my clothes into a lace-trimmed camisole, I flop down on the bed, plug in my earphones, and select my favorite Kelly Clarkson album. Her brand of angsty, edgy music and emotional lyrics are exactly what I'm in the mood for now.

I must have fallen asleep because I wake hours later in darkness, music still playing in a loop on my cell. Stifling a yawn, I remove my earphones and swing my legs out of the bed. I slip out into the corridor to use the bathroom. The hallway is eerily quiet, and there isn't a sound from the house.

I scrub my face, clean my teeth, and take a pee. Opening the door, I scream when confronted, unexpectedly, by Slater. "Oh fuck. You scared the crap out of me."

"Sorry," he says, failing to hide a smirk that looks in no way apologetic. "I just wanted to make sure you were okay. I knocked on your door earlier, but you didn't answer."

"I fell asleep listening to music, and I'm fine. Stop worrying. Please. I'm not going to fall apart."

"That's virtually an impossibility." His eyes start wandering. "I'll never not care about you." An electrical charge sizzles in the air, and my nipples harden in response. I realize I'm only in a flimsy cami and my lace thong about the same time Slater does.

His eyes darken, and he visibly stiffens as he rakes his gaze up my bare legs, lingering on my tits for a fraction too long. I clutch the side of the door, feeling a little woozy. He scrubs a hand over his prickly jaw. "You better not parade around Austin dressed like that or Ryan will blow a fucking gasket," he grits out, his deep voice heavy with tension.

"I thought everyone was asleep," I murmur, "and point noted. Now, if you'll excuse me?" I arch a brow, waiting for him to move aside.

He watches me through hooded eyes as he silently steps sideways.

"Night, Slate. Sleep tight and don't let the bed bugs bite." I walk away, trying my best to keep my tone jovial, to dispel the frisson of desire flickering between us.

"Night, sweet Belle." His voice is soft, and I feel his heated stare ogling my bare ass cheeks as I slink back into my room. The instant the door is closed, I flatten myself against it, silently counting to ten, in an effort to regulate my breathing.

I don't know what the hell is going on with me right now.

Only I'm beginning to wonder if Dylan wasn't right. Maybe coming here *was* a mistake.

Chapter Fifteen

I don't see much of Slater the rest of the week or the week after. Between classes and work, he's not home much, and I'm grateful. Whatever it is I'm feeling toward him can't get in the way of figuring out what I need to do about Dylan. Dylan has messaged me every single day, at least a couple of times, despite my request for a blanket no-contact policy. I don't respond, even if I'm sorely tempted.

I miss him. I miss him so much, and I feel lost without him. But I'm also coming to a few new realizations. Things I'm uncomfortable admitting even to myself. Ryan manages to drag it out of me on Friday night as we're going for a run around campus.

"You're a million miles away, Tornado," he says, stopping at a bench to take a breather. "I don't think you heard a word I just said."

I drop onto the bench, rooting in my bag. "I didn't, sorry. My head's all over the place."

Ryan guzzles from his water bottle, and we drink in silence. "A problem shared—"

"Is a problem halved," I finish for him. It's Mom's favorite saying, and she always uses it when she wants to get us to open up about something.

I finish my drink, stuffing the empty bottle back in my bag. "Let's jog back and talk." We set off for home at a slower pace. "I guess everything that's happened with Dylan has forced me to take a long hard look at myself and my life, and there's plenty I don't like."

"Like what?"

"I didn't realize how reliant I'd become on him and how much of my own identity I've lost in our relationship. I ... I—" I slam to a halt, and Ryan stops running too. "I feel like I don't even know who I am anymore. How to be without him, and that's not right. Not healthy."

"Let's walk the rest of the way," Ryan suggests, and I fall into step beside him. "Until recently, I've had no issue with Dylan, but I've always felt your commitment to one another bordered on the unhealthy at times. You were so hot and heavy, and I hated how you deferred to him on certain things. How you were happy to let him make the decisions, even if I knew it's not what you really wanted to do."

"Has everyone noticed?"

He shrugs. "I don't know. It's not like we all sit around dissecting your relationship. Dylan's a good guy, and we had no reason not to trust him with you. But I've always felt you're different with him, and that's made me uncomfortable sometimes."

"Is it a bad thing?"

"I honestly don't know, and it's not like I've given it huge thought. You were happy, and he treated you right. That was all that mattered, but now..." He trails off, but he doesn't need to elaborate. I get his point.

"I've come to the same realization myself, and I don't like it. If we stay together, and I still haven't decided if that's what I want, but, if we do, it's not going to be like it's always been. I'm going to make changes. Starting with getting a job."

"Yeah?" Ryan lifts a brow.

"Yeah." I say it with confidence. "And then I'm saving up for my own car. I need to be more independent."

"How do you think Dylan will react?"

"He won't like it, and he'll tell me it's unnecessary, that he has plenty of money. But that isn't the point. I have tons of money in my bank account, but it's not mine. I haven't earned it, and I don't want to sponge off him. I want to earn my own money and buy my own things. I should never have fallen into the habit of just letting him pay for everything. It's not right. I've sat on my high horse and criticized every girl that's hit on him for being a gold digger when I'm really not any better."

Ryan takes hold of my arm, forcing me to a stop again. "Hang on here a sec. You are *not* a money-grabbing whore. You've loved him for years, before he had any money. Just because you've accepted his generosity and let him pay for things does not mean you're a gold digger."

"Maybe not, but I don't want to rely on him to fund me. I want to be more independent, and I want to have more interests in my spare time that are mine. Not tagging along with whatever he wants to do."

"Good for you, little sis." Ryan presses a kiss to the top of my head. "But don't beat yourself up too much. You've always been really selfless. Happy to go along with other people's plans and always the first to offer to help. That doesn't make you a bad person, neither does wanting to do stuff for yourself now."

"Thanks, little big bro." I wrap my arm around his waist. "And thanks for always being here for me. I appreciate you, even if I don't always show it."

Ryan insists that I come with him and Myndi to the club later, and I don't put up too much of a protest. Austin is there along with a few of Ryan's buddies. Slater is working behind the bar tonight, and he sends over a beer for Ryan and a couple of fruity drinks for me and Myndi before we've even had time to order them. I blow him a kiss in thanks, and he grins.

"So, Gabby," Austin says, sliding in closer to me until our thighs are brushing. "How are you enjoying your new abode?" He gives me his full attention, his blue eyes pinning mine in place.

"It's cool, although I didn't think I'd be in the house alone so much. You guys are hardly ever there."

"We're all busy. Senior year is a bitch, and I've been pulling extra shifts lately. Saving up for repairs on my Harley."

"You have a bike?" I inquire, taking a sip of my drink.

"Yep, but she's been out of action for a while. The parts I need are outside my budget. Hence the double shifts." He waggles his brows and clinks his glass against mine. "But I should have her fixed up in the next couple weeks. I'd love to take you out on it sometime."

"I'd like that. I've always imagined riding on the back of a bike, dressed all in leather, with my hair streaming behind me, throwing caution to the wind," I answer truthfully.

I'd shamelessly tried to convince Dylan to buy a bike before, but he was having none of it. He spent about fifteen minutes giving me this big lecture on the dangers of motorcycles, spewing a load of road stats like an encyclopedia, and all sexy images disappeared from my brain.

"Well, fuck me," Austin says, moving his arm around my shoulder. "That's like my favorite wet dream, right there."

"Pfft. As if you haven't lived that dream a thousand times over, I'm sure," I scoff. Austin is almost as legendary for his manwhore ways as the now-reformed Ryan and new, tamer Slater.

"Not with anyone as sexy as you." He winks, holding me a little too tight for comfort.

"Powers!" Ryan hollers over the table at Austin. "Keep your fucking filthy hands off my little sister."

Austin holds up his palms, protesting innocence with an angelic face. "Just making small talk, bruh. No need to get your panties in a bunch."

"Powers?" I inquire, removing Austin's arm from my shoulder and scooting away from him a little. I'm choosing to ignore my brother's timely intervention. While I'm grateful, he has to stop babying me too. Everyone has been sheltering me, and it's time I learned to stand on my own two feet. I'm more than capable when left to my own devices.

"Your brother thinks he's a comedian," Austin deadpans. "Austin Powers? Man of mystery? Legendary womanizing party whore?"

I giggle. "Now I get it. That's one of Ryan's better ones," I tease.

"Of course, you'd say that. You Jameses are as thick as thieves."

"That we are, but I wouldn't have it any other way."

Austin leans in close, pressing his mouth to my ear. "I envy you that, you know. I—"

"Thought you were meeting Nadine?" Slater barks, appearing at our table and shooting daggers at Austin.

Austin surveys Slater for a moment before stretching his arm across the back of the booth behind me. He smirks at his roomie. "It was a casual arrangement, and I'm discovering the scenery in here is much more alluring tonight."

Slater purses his lips, exuding tension.

I slide out of the booth, not wanting to get in the middle of whatever is going on between them. "I'm going to the restroom."

"Wait a minute," Slater says, ignoring Austin and focusing on me. "I came over to speak to you. Ryan mentioned you were looking for a job, and we're hiring. My boss can talk to you now if you're interested."

My eyes light up as if it's Christmas morning. "I'm interested. Definitely."

He smiles. "Okay, go to the restroom, and then come find me, and I'll bring you to him."

A half hour later I walk back to our table with the biggest grin on my face. I sit down beside Ryan and Myndi. "I got the job. I start tomorrow night."

"Congrats, babe." Myndi shoves my brother out of the way so she can hug me.

"I'm proud of you." Ryan kisses my forehead.

"Welcome aboard, Belle," Slater says, looming over me. "This one's on the house." He hands me a champagne cocktail. "Anyone asks, it's nonalcoholic." His lips kick up, and he sends me a cheeky wink.

I stretch up and kiss his cheek. "Thanks. Can I get a ride with you to work tomorrow?"

"Of course. You know you don't even have to ask." Bending down, he whispers in my ear, "I love the idea of you working with me."

Shivers cascade down my spine, confusing the hell out of me. "Me too." I look into his eyes and get momentarily lost.

A throat clearing snaps me out of it. "I expect you to watch out for my little sis, bro," Ryan says. "If anything happens to her, and I mean, *anything*, with *anyone,* I'm holding you responsible."

"Ryan!" I hiss. "Cut that shit out. I can look after myself."

"Nothing will happen to Belle while I'm around, so stop being an ass. You know you don't even have to go there."

"Don't I?" Ryan cocks his head to the side, eyeballing Slater intensely.

Slater looks seriously pissed, and the boys drill piercing stares at one another as Myndi and I look between them, wondering what the hell is going on.

"Cool, brother." Ryan nods. "Once you understand the score."

"I got it," Slater snaps before spinning on his heel and stalking back to the bar.

I slap Ryan in the chest. "What is with you?"

"Just looking out for you."

"You remember our conversation earlier? That goes for you, Caleb, and Dean too. You all have to stop jumping in to protect me. You need to let me handle this, and, quite frankly, I'm pissed that everyone seems to think I can't deal by myself."

Ryan straightens up, pulling at the collar of his shirt. "It's not the same thing."

"No?"

He scratches the back of his head, looking contemplative. "No, it's not. I'm just trying to protect you, not control your every move and thought."

"Now you're being mean. That's not what Dylan does."

"You're right. I'm sorry, and I don't want to fight. Not when we should be celebrating your new job and newfound independence."

"I'll drink to that," Myndi says, offering up her glass.

I leave at five p.m. the following day with Slater for my first shift. "Are you nervous?" he asks, as he drives us to the club.

"What gave me away?" I laugh, trying to rein in the butterflies running amok in my chest.

"Oh, I don't know." He glances over at me, grinning. "It could be the way you haven't stopped jerking your knee, or the way you're knotting your hands in your lap, or the worry etched on your gorgeous face."

"You think my face is gorgeous?" I blurt, instantly wanting to find a hole to crawl into.

"Abso-fucking-lutely, and don't pretend like you don't know it. You'd have to be blind to not see how every head turns when you walk into a room."

Now I stare at him like he's just sprouted horns out of his head. "That is such an exaggeration. I know I'm pretty, but I'm hardly in that kind of league."

He mutters under his breath before swinging his SUV into an empty spot outside the club. When he cuts the engine, he turns to face me. Cautiously, he reaches out, cupping my cheek. "That's exactly what I'm talking about." His warm breath oozes over my face, raising goose bumps along my bare arms. "The most beautiful women are those who are completely unaware of the power they possess. Those who don't fake it or obsess over their looks. Those who just are. Women whose inner beauty outshines what's on the outside."

"Like your mom," I say, conjuring up an image of her gorgeous dark features and remembering her selfless heart. She sacrificed so much for her son, and it was that innate goodness that shone through, overriding her natural beauty.

"Like Mom." He rubs his thumb across my cheek. "Like you," he adds, staring at me with glassy eyes. My pulse thuds wildly in my neck as he continues to stare at me, peering deep into my eyes, and something shifts in the space between us. His thumb continues caressing my cheek, and a new layer of butterflies scatters in my chest. The longer he looks at me and the more he touches me, the more conflicted he looks and the more confused I feel.

"You're so beautiful," he whispers after a couple tense minutes. When he moves his face in closer to mine, my heart races a hundred miles an hour as if it's about to take flight from my chest. My mouth is dry and my panties the complete opposite. "And so inherently good." His eyes lower to my mouth, and I think I've actually stopped breathing.

Is he thinking about kissing me?

And why is that getting me all worked up?

A loud rap on the window breaks us apart, ruining the moment. Startled, I jump, and my heart does crazy loops behind my rib cage. Slater lowers his window halfway down. "Hey, Shel."

A pretty girl I recognize beams at Slater. She's the girl who was draped around him a couple weeks ago when we were at the club celebrating Myndi's birthday. I'd noticed her while I was out on the dance floor. She smiles adoringly at him, like he's the center of the entire universe, purposely ignoring me. "You coming in?"

"Sure." Slater presses his back into the seat, angling his head in my direction. "Shelby, meet Gabby. She's starting tonight."

If looks could kill, I'd be ten feet under with the heated glare she sends my way. But she hides it well, disguising the venomous expression before Slater notices. "Sweet. Nice to meet you."

"Thanks, and same here," I coolly reply, wondering what her beef is with me. It's not like I even know the girl, but I've seen her sniffing around Slater on more than a couple of occasions, and I know her type.

We walk into the venue together, and Slater leads me to the staff area. It's a large square room with a bunch of comfy couches, a long rectangular dining table and accompanying benches, and two doors off to the side. "Here." Slater hands me a shirt. "This should fit." He appraises first me and then the shirt. "Boss likes 'em on the tight side," he semi-apologizes, and I shrug.

"It's no biggie."

I follow friendly Shelby into the female changing room and proceed to get changed. She ignores me, and I don't feel inclined to strike up a conversation either, so I do my best to forget she exists.

Shucking out of my jeans and shirt, I pull on the denim cut-offs I brought with me and slip the branded T-shirt over my head. It's a very snug fit. The material clings to my generous D-cup breasts and stops short of my waist, showcasing a wide strip of my stomach. I have a feeling Ryan is going to blow a fuse when he gets a look at me, but he'll just have to deal. This is the standard uniform for all female waiting staff, so he shouldn't be too surprised.

Stuffing my clothes in my bag, I scoop my hair back off my face, smoothing it into a neat ponytail.

"A word of advice," Shelby says, suddenly cutting through the quiet room. "Stay away from Slater." I turn to face her. "He's mine."

Keeping my spine straight, I hold my nerve as we face off. "I don't know what you think you know, but it's not like that. Slate's one of my best friends, and I have a boyfriend."

She snorts. "You might want to have a word with your *boyfriend* about that."

My heckles are instantly raised. "What do you mean by that?"

"I don't think he got the memo," she says in a condescending tone, and a now-familiar anxious feeling floods my chest, constricting my air supply. I haven't heard from Dylan the last three days, but I had texted him earlier asking if we could meet tomorrow to talk, and he had responded enthusiastically. Not for the first time, I wonder what exactly he's been doing during our separation.

My mind is deviating in all different directions now, and that fluttery panicky feeling has overtaken me again. I've worked so hard to keep a logical head these past twelve days, and now I'm spiraling into a downward circle. Shelby smirks, as if she knows where my head has gone, and that helps me regain control. I'm not going to allow some spiteful bitch to plant ideas in my head.

Ignoring her, I push out into the main staff area where Slater is waiting for me. "What's wrong?" He immediately notices my altered expression.

"Nothing." I force a wide smile on my face. "Just nervous."

He eyeballs Shelby circumspectly when she reappears in the room. "There's no need to be nervous, Belle." He rubs a hand up and down my back. "I'll be training you, and I've made sure I'm working every night you're scheduled for the rest of the month." I can almost feel the daggers embedding in my back.

I stick by Slater's side as he shows me how to work the register and explains how things operate out on the floor. The club is actually more of a bar-slash-club, opening at five daily for happy hour and food and then it offers customers late-night drinks and dancing. Slater talks me through the different menus, clarifying how to process orders for food and drink. I shadow him as he serves drinks behind the bar, watching how he expertly juggles a multitude of different orders at once. Then he sends me out on the floor with another waitress—thankfully Emma is much friendlier than Shelby—and I watch her take orders on a couple tables before venturing on my own.

The club is already busy even though it's still early. Before I know it, a couple more hours have passed, and I'm delighted that I'm comfortably holding my own. While I've never worked in a bar or club before, the experience I had from the diner when I was fifteen is coming in handy.

A few guys are a bit handsy, but I'm able to deal with them, and it helps to know Slater has my back. Every time I look around, I instantly meet his eyes, like he's perfectly attuned to my presence.

"Here," Shelby says, roughly shoving a tray at me. "It's time for my break. Serve this to table fourteen."

She walks away without waiting for my response, and I flip my finger up at her retreating form. "Very naughty, Belle," Slater whispers in my ear as he makes his way back to the bar, chuckling.

I'm still smiling as I walk to the table to distribute the drinks, but it doesn't last long. My legs turn weak and my hands turn to butter when I spot Dylan sitting at an adjoining table with Bianca straddling his lap. He doesn't notice me because he's too busy devouring her mouth and groping her ass.

The tray crashes to the floor, glass shattering and splintering as drinks go flying everywhere.

Tears spill down my cheeks as Dylan finally notices me, tearing his mouth away from Bianca's at the sound of the commotion.

The look of horror on his face is almost comical. Hurriedly, he shoves Bianca off his lap, sliding out of the booth and calling my name.

But I don't wait to hear what he has to say, spinning around and elbowing my way through the crowd.

Chapter Sixteen

I don't get very far, running headfirst into a solid wall of muscle. Slater's arms don't hesitate, and he wraps me up in his embrace. "It's okay, Belle. I got you."

"Please, Slate. Get me out of here. I can't talk to him."

"Get your sleazy hands off my girlfriend!" Dylan demands from behind me, and I hug Slater tighter, squeezing my eyes shut, not wanting to look into the face of the man I thought represented my forever.

"I hardly think you're in a position to make demands," Slater growls, tightening his grip on me.

"Gabby, please, talk to me," Dylan pleads.

Sniffling, I pull my big girl panties on and turn around to face him, keeping Slater's arms around me for support. I hastily swipe at my damp eyes, determined to hang on to my dignity. In the background, I spot Emma and another waitress cleaning up the mess I made.

It hurts looking at Dylan.

It hurts so damn much.

Especially when that bitch Bianca circles her arm around his waist from behind. Dylan shucks her off, shouting at her to leave. She shoots me a filthy look as she skulks back to the table, like this is all my fault. "Gabby, I'm sorry, but I've been missing you so much and—"

Slater snorts, cutting Dylan off. Dylan's hands ball into fists at his side, and he glares at Slater like he wishes he'd drop off the face of the Earth. "Fuck off, asshole. This is nothing to do with you," Dylan spits out, jabbing his finger in the air. He's slurring his words, and his eyes are unfocused, his pupils darting all over the place. I'm wondering if he took something other than alcohol, but that'd be so out of character for him.

"The hell it isn't. Just give me an excuse, dickhead. I'm primed and ready for round two." The challenge is evident in Slater's glacial tone and expression.

"Don't," I say quietly, looking up at him. "Don't fight him. I don't want you getting into any more trouble."

This time it's Dylan's turn to snort in disbelief. "Him? What about *me*?"

"What about you?" I shout, swallowing the lump of betrayal clogging my throat.

"You fuck off for two weeks," he slurs, swaying on his feet. "To live with him!" His nostrils flare. "You won't answer any of my texts or calls, and now you're taking his side?"

Anger sluices through my veins, and I wriggle out of Slater's embrace. I put my face in Dylan's, wondering how a face I love so much can now look so hateful. "Firstly, I moved out to give you time to think about our relationship. I didn't 'fuck off.' I asked you to give me some space because I was hurting. Your actions hurt me, you fucker!"

I jab my finger in his chest. "But you couldn't even do that." A layer of calm determination washes over me, masking the multitude of emotions I'm feeling under the surface. "I'll make this really easy for you now. We are done. Finished for good. I never thought you'd be capable of such deception, but it just goes to prove how little I really know you." Tears prick my eyes, but I manage to keep them at bay. "I'll stop by the condo tomorrow to pick up the rest of my stuff. I'll drop my key on the counter before I leave."

"No, Gabby. No." He grabs my arm, digging his fingers into my flesh. "You're not leaving me. I won't allow it."

"You don't have a say anymore. I'm done with this bullshit. I loved you, Dylan. I loved you so completely, but I love myself more, and I'm not going to stay with someone who cheats behind my back, who says one thing and does the other. I don't even want to be your friend. I want nothing to do with you going forward. Don't wait for me after class. Don't call or text. And don't come here expecting me to speak to you. As of now, you are dead to me. Now get your fucking hand off me."

When he doesn't move a muscle, Slater takes his arm, pushing him away and gathering me safely under the crook of his arm. A couple of bouncers materialize at his side. "Throw him out," Slater instructs them, pointing at Dylan. "And the whore too." He jerks his head at Bianca who has wheedled her way back to Dylan's side. "Tell the guys at the door they're both banned."

"Fuck you!" Dylan hisses at Slater before turning his venom on me. "And fuck you too! You cunts deserve one another." One of the bouncers takes Dylan by the elbow, dragging him toward the exit. "Bianca is worth ten of you, Dimples. And she loves it up the ass!" he hollers, ensuring no one in the vicinity misses it. Lancing pain attacks me on all sides, and despite my conviction, tears spill out of my eyes, rolling down my face.

Dylan has just laid bare the true extent of his betrayal, and I'm destroyed. Huge, wracking sobs erupt from my mouth, and Slater pulls me back into his arms, whispering assurances in my ear as I fall apart. He pulls us over to a quiet corner, away from prying eyes. Dylan is cursing and shouting as he's hauled outside, and I'm grateful the music is playing, drowning out most of his insults.

When I lift my head up, a few minutes later, Shelby's spiteful smile is the first thing I see. "You did that on purpose," I say, pulling myself together.

She fakes a look of concern. "I tried to warn you earlier, and you wouldn't listen. You needed to see for yourself. That's not the first time they've been in here."

"Stop stirring shit," Slater reprimands. "That's the first time I've seen him in here with her," he tells me, looking deep into my eyes. "If it wasn't, you would've heard about it."

"They usually come in when you're not around. You weren't supposed to be working tonight, remember?" Shelby says. "But you switched your shifts around to accommodate *her*." She spits the word out like it physically pains her to say it.

"Yeah, and I'll be doing the same going forward." Slater pins Shelby with a dark look. "Stay out of this, Shel. It doesn't concern you, and if I find out you'd anything to do with them being here tonight, you can kiss your job goodbye."

Shelby harrumphs, shrugging. "Yeah, I don't think so." She slinks up to him, not making any effort to lower her voice. "You're not the only one I'm fucking around here."

"Get lost, Shel." Slater's aggravation is crystal clear. "And stay the hell away from me and Belle."

Shelby snarls at me before flouncing away, flipping us the finger as she goes.

"I'm not sleeping with her," Slater rushes to confirm, rubbing the back of his neck and looking awkward as hell. "It was one time, a while back."

I shuck out of his arms. "None of my business what you do to whom, and I better get back to work. You can dock my pay for the drinks." I attempt to shuffle off, to help the girls who are still cleaning up the floor, when Slater takes my arm, stalling me.

"You don't have to stay. I'll square it with the boss man, and I'll take my break early to drop you home."

I fold my arms across my chest and shake my head. "No way. I'm not going home on my first night. I'll finish my shift."

"Belle."

"No." I fix him with a resolved expression. "I'm finishing my shift, and then you can drive me home."

I have zero clue how I manage to temporarily paper over the cracks in my heart and complete my shift, but I do. I even manage to deflect the ever-growing line of handsy guys trying to cop a feel. When you're dating someone who's a minor celebrity on campus, it seems everyone knows the exact moment when you're back on the market again. Slater spends half his night throwing lecherous assholes out of the club for hitting on me.

We don't talk as he drives home. I close my eyes, resting my head against the window, hoping that my physical exhaustion will mean I can sleep, because I so need to crawl into bed and forget this night ever happened.

"Night, Slater. Thanks for the ride," I say the instant we step foot inside the house. I am halfway up the stairs when he stops me with his words.

"Will you be okay?"

I grip the handrail tight as the tenuous control on my emotions starts to slip.

"If you need me, I'm here for you," he adds.

His obvious concern prods at the iron cage I've tried unsuccessfully to build around my heart. "No, Slate. I'm not okay, but I will be, and thank you, but I just want to be alone."

He comes up the stairs, tentatively wrapping his arms around me from behind. "He doesn't deserve you, and you *will* be fine. Come get me if you need me during the night."

I sniffle and nod, twisting around to look up at him as a thought passes through my mind. "Please don't say anything to Ryan."

He sighs heavily. "Don't ask me to lie to him. I already feel like shit for concealing the other stuff from him in the first place."

My stomach sours at the reminder. "I'm not asking you to lie. Just let *me* explain to Ryan when he gets back in the morning. And I'd rather we didn't mention any of the things Dylan was shouting as he was dragged out. I'm really not in the mood to repeat them."

A thunderous look creeps over Slater's face. "He's lucky I didn't beat him senseless."

"I'm glad you didn't. He's not worth getting into trouble over. If he wants to fuck around, that's his business."

"He's a fool."

I really can't go there now. "Night, Slater. Sleep tight."

"You too, Belle."

My resolve crumbles the instant I shut the door to the bedroom, and I sink to the floor, sobbing as I let myself feel everything I've been holding in all night.

I want to get this all out.

To purge it from my system so I can move on like Dylan so clearly has.

I crawl from the floor, climbing up onto the bed and curling on my side. Burying my head in my pillow, I attempt to muffle my cries, grateful that Ryan and Austin are both away tonight. It's humiliating enough without having multiple witnesses.

The door creaks open and shut a few minutes later, and the bed dips behind me. Sobs continue to wrack my body, gut-wrenching and agonizing, and it's as if someone died. To me, it feels like an actual death, and I'm not just mourning the loss of Dylan but the loss of a future I thought I had all mapped out. I cry harder when Slater pulls me against him with my back to his chest. His arms encircle me, and he holds me tight as I howl in torment. "Let it all out, Belle. I've got you."

I'm sure I'll be really embarrassed over this in the morning, but right now, I don't give a shit. I can't control the expulsion, and it needs to happen to release me from this inner hell. Slater doesn't say anything else. He just holds me close, and I cling to him as I slowly let go of my past.

At some point, I cried myself to sleep. When I wake the next morning, Slater is softly snoring behind me. We are still in the same position. Fully clothed, on the outside of my bed, with him spooning me from behind. He's like a furnace, and I'm sweating under my clothes, but I'm in no hurry to move, enjoying the security of his embrace.

A throat clearing alerts me to my brother's presence. My eyes fly to the door, and Ryan is there, lounging against the wall, gaze narrowed as he watches us.

"Morning," I croak, wincing at how hoarse my voice sounds.

"What the hell's going on, Gabby? Why is Slate in your bed?"

"Technically, he's not," I say, unsuccessfully attempting to extricate myself from his grip. "He's on *top* of my bed."

At that moment, Slater, very unhelpfully, decides to nuzzle into my neck. A satisfied moan slips from his lips, and he blatantly inhales, rubbing his nose in my hair. "Mmm, you smell good," he murmurs in a sleep-laced tone, pressing his morning wood against my ass. I can't stop the whimper that escapes my mouth in time, and Ryan turns a very unflattering shade of red. If his jaw clenches any tighter, he'll give himself lockjaw.

"This is not what it looks like," I rush to assure him before he loses it. "Nothing happened, so there's no need to go apeshit on Slate."

"Someone better start explaining," Ryan grumbles, and Slater stills behind me, slowly coming to.

"Ryan, dude. Stop freaking out," Slater says after a tense minute of silence, his voice drenched with sleep. "I was only consoling Belle. That's it. No need to look at me like you want to rip my head from my body."

"That's not the only part of your anatomy I'd like to dismantle right now," my brother growls, slanting thunderous looks in Slater's direction.

"Seriously, chill, bro." Slater scoots away from me, and I instantly feel cold. I lie flat on my back as he swings his legs out the other side of the bed. Resting his elbows on his knees, he yawns. Thank God, he's wearing a tank and sweats and that he's hiding the evidence of his arousal until he's gotten himself under control. The last thing I need is Ryan jumping to conclusions.

"Why did you need consoling?" Ryan asks, focusing on me again. "Has something happened?"

Tears automatically pool in my eyes, and I hate that I'm so weak and how my tear ducts seem to have a direct hotline to my emotions.

Ryan sits on the edge of the bed and takes my hand, lacing his fingers through mine. "I'll kill Dylan. I fucking will. What'd he do now?"

"I'll let you two talk," Slater says, getting up and moving around the bed. He lingers in the doorway, glancing over at me with a tender look on his face. "You'll get over this, Belle, and you'll see that it's not the end of the world. You still have your whole life ahead of you."

He doesn't wait for me to reply, leaving the room and pulling the door shut behind him.

"Scoot over," Ryan says, toeing off his shoes, and I move into the vacant, warm spot Slater just left behind. "Now tell me everything, and don't even attempt to leave anything out."

Chapter Seventeen

I told my brother everything, and now I'm trying to talk him off the ledge. He's hellbent on going over to Dylan's and knocking the shit out of him. It's only when Myndi arrives that he finally calms down. "Go for a run with Slate, and work it out of your system," she tells him, pushing him out of my room. "And don't go near Dylan. You have to respect Gabby's wishes."

"Promise me, little big bro." My eyes narrow as I give him my "I mean business" look.

He huffs out a defeated sigh. "Fine, but all bets are off if I happen to cross paths with the cheating slimeball."

"Ryan."

"Fine, fine." He lifts his hands in surrender. "Have it your way. I'll go run it off, and when I come back, Slate and I will come with you to get the rest of your stuff."

"Thank you."

Ryan bends down, pressing a kiss to my forehead. "He doesn't deserve you, and Slate's right—you'll bounce back. It's his loss, not yours."

Myndi shoves him out of the door, none too gently, pecking his lips briefly, before jumping on the bed and hugging me. "I was in the coffee place and heard some girls gossiping about what went down last night. I came straight here. You should've called me."

"It was late, and I doubt I could've composed myself long enough to call you."

"Oh, babe, I'm so sorry."

"I just can't believe he cheated on me. After all the years we've been together and everything we had planned."

"I can relate a little. While my situation was different, it didn't hurt any less. But I was only with Travis ten months, so I can only imagine how much pain you're in."

"Fuck, it hurts like a bitch, Myndi. I've never hurt so badly before."

"The guys are right," she says, smoothing my hair behind my ears. "It'll get better, and you'll move on, even if it doesn't feel like it now." She smiles at me. "Look how happy I am now, and I'm almost grateful to Travis because his actions have led me to Ryan, and he makes me so unbelievably happy."

"I'm really pleased for you, Myndi, genuinely I am, but I'm giving guys a wide berth. I have no interest in dating anyone."

We chat for a while longer, and I'm feeling slightly better as I head into the bathroom. I take a leisurely shower while Myndi waits downstairs.

When I step into the kitchen, she's busy at the stove cooking bacon and eggs. "Take a seat," she suggests, talking over her shoulder, while waving a spatula around. "This is just ready."

My tummy rumbles appreciatively even if I don't much feel like eating.

She slides a plate to me, and we eat in silence. After forcing a few mouthfuls down, I push my food away, and get up to refill both our mugs.

"I didn't have much of an appetite those first few days either," Myndi supplies. "But you need to try and keep your strength up."

I hand her a fresh cup of coffee, plonking my butt in the seat again. "I'll try. I don't want to let this derail me. It's killing me inside, but no amount of tears will change the situation. I just have to put it behind me, chalk it up to experience, and move forward on my own."

The front door opens, and the boys come into the kitchen a few seconds later. They are both in running shorts and tops, sweat coating their faces and clinging to their hair.

"Ugh!" I pinch the bridge of my nose. "You guys stink to the high heavens."

"Giz a hug, little sis," Ryan says, approaching me with his arms wide-open and a stupid grin on his face.

"You couldn't pay me to hug you, either of you, right now," I semi-joke.

"What about you, babe?" Ryan says, diverting his attention to my bestie. "Any hugs for your man?"

"I'm with your sister," Myndi deadpans, swatting him away with her hands. "There is nothing you could bribe me with that would make me touch you right now."

A mischievous twinkle glints in Ryan's eye. "Not even a repeat of this morning?" He winks, and Myndi's cheeks turn fire-engine red. "You fucking loved what I did with my—"

I clamp my hand over his mouth, stalling his sentence. "Oh God, I just threw up in my mouth. Do not go there. Like ever. Unless you want me to return the favor someday, if I ever decide I'm brave enough to let another man into my life."

Myndi shoots me a sympathetic look. "Gabby, you'll be back in the saddle before you know it."

"There's no rush," Ryan cuts in. "Gabby hasn't been single since the dark ages. Some time alone is just what she needs."

"Thanks, Dr. Phil, but the only one making decisions about my life around here from now on will be me."

"Go shower, babe," Myndi says, pushing Ryan toward the door. "Please, before we puke."

Slater is guzzling a bottle of water while smirking at the conversation. "That goes for you too," I say, eyeballing him. "Go, before you permanently contaminate the air supply."

"I thought girls liked their men all sweaty." He waggles his brows suggestively.

"Sex-induced sweat is different," I agree, and now it's Ryan's turn to look ill. I can't help pushing it. "And such a fucking turn-on." I deliberately lick my lips, and Slater's grin cracks wide.

"Don't even attempt to add to that," Ryan says, pointing his finger at me. "I do not need to hear about my sister's sex life."

"Well, I don't have one anymore, so I guess that's lucky for you." I gulp back the hot coffee as a sharp ache stabs me in the heart.

I see Myndi mouth "Just go" to my brother, and both guys leave the room. She slides her hand across the table, squeezing mine. "You're doing great, Gabs. And you're going to be fine. You have all of us and we'll get you through this."

An hour later, the four of us pull up outside Dylan's building. Wiping my sweaty palms down the front of my jeans, I give myself a silent pep talk, telling myself I can do this. With a bit of luck, he won't even be in and we can get in and out quickly.

"You don't have to do this," Ryan says, poking his head through the gap from the backseat. "The three of us can go in there and do a snatch and grab."

I curl my fingers around the door handle. "I appreciate the sentiment, but I'm not going to hide in the car like a coward. I'm not going to let him see how much this hurts." I open the door. "C'mon. Let's get this over and done with."

Slater locks his SUV and moves to my side, slinging his arm around my shoulders in a show of solidarity. Ryan and Myndi are holding hands, and Ryan is narrowing his eyes in Slater's direction again. Just as we reach the entrance to the building, a tall, leggy brunette steps outside, twisting my insides into knots.

"Ignore her," Slater says through gritted teeth. Myndi hisses and glares at Bianca. It takes every ounce of self-control to walk past the bitch without commenting, but I won't give her the satisfaction of knowing how devastated I truly am.

"I already cleared out the closet and the en suite to make room for my stuff," Bianca hollers from behind me. "Your crap is in boxes in the hall. Don't forget to leave your key before you go." The gloating smugness in her tone irritates the hell out of me, and I want to claw my fingernails down her face and punch her in her lady parts, but I choose the moral high ground and ignore her instead. She's clearly trying to get a reaction out of me, and I won't sink to her level.

"Ignore the slut," Ryan says, shooting daggers at her. "I know her face from the frat scene. She's done the rounds, and she won't last long. She doesn't have it in her to sleep exclusively with one guy."

Despite how much I hate Bianca, I can't let my brother's sexist comment go without commenting. "Knock it off, Randy. You and Slater pulled this shit all the time."

He slants me an incredulous look. "Now you're fucking defending her?"

"No," I say, punching the code into the keypad on the wall. "She is a fucking skank for going after my boyfriend, but she's free to sleep with whomever she likes, and she shouldn't get labeled a whore when men get to do it all the time and they give each other pats on the back. I hate double standards."

Slater's jaw is tense as he storms through the door to the elevator bank, jabbing the button like it's done him a personal injury. "What's up with him?" I murmur to Ryan.

He shrugs. "Fucked if I know. He's moodier than you with PMS." I thump my brother hard in the upper arm. "Holy hell, Tornado. That fucking hurt."

"Good. You deserve it for that comment. You know damn well the torture I go through every month."

He tugs on my elbow, holding me back. Myndi decides to give us some privacy, moving to stand beside Slater as they wait for the elevator to descend. "What do you mean? You still go through that?"

I'd kinda forgotten that my brother hadn't been around a couple years. I nod. "Yep. I thought it'd get better after I had the laparoscopy and they removed the lesions on my ovaries, but it's gotten bad again the past few months. I've seen my Ob-Gyn, and she says I might need to have the procedure again. She's put me on a different type of pill, but it's not working; my cycle's as erratic as ever, and I'm still experiencing bouts of pain."

"You should've said."

I swallow over the lump in my throat. "Dylan looked after me, and it's not something I like to publicize or dwell on."

I've had painful periods since I was fifteen, but I was only diagnosed with endometriosis when I was eighteen. After the op to remove a cluster of chocolate cysts that had formed on my ovaries, I had a few pain-free months before mild symptoms started again.

My periods have always been erratic, and it's only when I collapse, feeling nauseous, sweaty, and crippled with cramps that I know Mother Nature is about to make an unwelcome visit.

My last period was so bad I collapsed in a toilet cubicle in the bathroom of McDowell Hall for at least an hour. It was our first day back, and I was crippled. Doubled over in the worst pain imaginable, and I couldn't move an inch. I had to message Myndi from my position on the floor—the cold tile was a balm to my heated skin—and ask her to call Dylan. He scooped me up off the floor and carried me out to his truck, and then I spent the next three days in a heap in bed, alternating between throwing up and the worst case of diarrhea known to mankind. And let's not forget the ten-day-long heavy bleeding or the extreme fatigue that knocked me off my feet.

I've been meaning to go back for an appointment, but I've been busy with coursework, and I haven't had any symptoms since, so I'm kinda hoping there's been some divine intervention and the problem has miraculously resolved itself.

Talk about wishful thinking.

The elevator arrives, and I loop my arm through Ryan's, steering him forward. Once we are inside, Slater punches the button, and the doors close. Ryan pulls me into his side, pressing a kiss to my temple. "Promise you'll call me if you need help with that in future."

"I will." I look up at him. "I won't have any choice." When I get a bad attack, it's debilitating, and I can't cope without help. Dylan was always so compassionate and caring, fussing over me and helping me through it.

Maybe that's why, when we step into the condo, I rush to his side the minute I see him on his knees in the living area, rocking back and forth with his head in his hands. I crouch over him. "How bad is it?"

"Bad," he whimpers, still clutching his head. Screw that fucking bitch for just walking out of here and leaving him like this.

"Have you taken your medication?"

"No," he pants.

I straighten up. "Can you guys start moving my stuff while I get his pain pills."

Slater and Myndi gravitate to the boxes littering the hallway, while Ryan crosses his arms, fixing me with a stern look. "He's not your responsibility, Gabby. Let his new girlfriend look after him."

His words cut a new line through my fragile heart.

"Don't have a new girlfriend," Dylan pants out.

"Fuck buddy, whore, relationship wrecker," Ryan adds. "Don't give a shit what label you give that skank."

"It's not like that."

Slater stomps over with a box in his arms, glowering at Dylan even though he can't see him because he still has his head in his hands. "Yeah, dude? So how the hell did her clothes get in your closet, and who shoved all Belle's stuff haphazardly into these boxes, breaking shit in the process?"

Slowly, Dylan lifts his head, squinting and cowering from the overhead lights. "I didn't tell her she could do that." He turns his bloodshot eyes on me. "I swear I didn't ask her to move in. She's *not* moving in." He clutches the back of the couch, struggling to his feet. "This is all a big misunderstanding, Gabby. Ask them to go and I'll explain."

I shake my head, concern transforming to anger. "I can't believe the nerve of you to stand in front of me and claim this is a big misunderstanding. I saw you!" I scream, and he winces. "I saw you all over her. Tell me, was she the first or just the first of many?"

"Belle." Slater softly cautions me, and he's right.

It doesn't matter anymore.

What's done is done.

I grab fistfuls of my hair. "Ugh! I'm not doing this. We are over, Dylan. I'm moving out, and I never want to speak to you again." I turn my eyes on Ryan and Slater. "Please just move my stuff to the car."

I stalk to the kitchen, grab a glass of water and his pills, and return to Dylan. "Take these and go lie down. And you really need to go back to the doctor."

Anxiety is a heavy weight on my chest as I make my way to the bedroom to check the bitch boxed up all my stuff. One look at the crumpled sheets has my resolve wavering, but I fight tears and focus on the task at hand, pulling out drawers and tipping the last few personal items into the box I brought with me. I check the bathroom, grabbing my toiletries and adding them to the rest of my stuff. Against my better judgment, I wet a cloth and step back into the bedroom.

Dylan is lying facedown on the bed, still clutching his head in his hands. He has drawn the drapes, and the room is in darkness. "Here's a cold cloth." I place it on his bedside table.

His hand snakes out, encircling my wrist. "I'm so sorry, Gabby. More than you could possibly know. I swear I didn't mean for this to happen."

"Don't, Dylan. Don't make it worse. You have devastated me and ruined us. There's no going back, so just let it go. Let me go." Tears roll silently down my face as I walk to the door, vowing this is the last time I cry over that man. I turn around to look over him one final time. "I really loved you, Dylan. You had my whole heart. I hope she was worth it."

Drying my eyes, I lift my shoulders and walk out of the room, and his life, with my head held high.

Chapter Eighteen

The mood in the car is subdued, so I plug my cell into the stereo system and press shuffle on the music app. Music fills the awkward silence, and I hum along as some of my favorite songs play. My mouth turns dry when "Love Story" by Taylor Swift comes on, and my lower lip wobbles as so many memories associated with that song spring forth in my mind. I sense Slater glancing at me, but I avoid making eye contact because I can't guarantee I won't burst into tears.

I was ten going on eleven when that song was released, but I instantly fell in love with the all-consuming romance of the lyrics and the melody. The dark-haired hottie in the video didn't hurt either, and it's the first time I remember having a serious crush on any guy. I'd met Dylan a few months previously, and we became instant besties. He loved teasing me all the time about my obsession. Especially when Caleb taught me how to play it on my guitar, and I drove my family insane strumming it nonstop.

My lips tug up at the corners when Ryan starts belting out the words, ending the tense atmosphere. Then Slater joins in, and I can't help singing along, smiling as we all start singing louder to be heard.

Soon it becomes a competition, and we're all practically shouting while Myndi's gaze bounces between us like we've all gone batshit crazy.

All good humor fades as Taylor sings the last line, and a sob escapes my lips before I can stop it. Slater reaches across the console, squeezing my hand, helping to keep the tears at bay. I smile at him through blurry eyes, grateful for his understanding and his lack of judgment.

"Is someone going to explain what just happened," Myndi asks, "because it feels like I just wandered into auditions for a spoof version of *Pitch Perfect*."

I'm sniffling as I twist around to face my bestie. "That's one of my all-time favorite love songs, and it was released just after I met Dylan. I learned how to play it on the guitar—"

"Don't remind me," Ryan cuts in. "We had to tie her up and tape her mouth to put an end to the torture. Remember, Evans?"

Slater smiles at me. "I thought it was super cute."

Ryan makes a gagging sound, and we all laugh.

"You remember that time I begged you to let me and Dylan come camping with you?" I ask my brother, as I'm confronted with more memories attached to that song.

"You mean that time you *blackmailed* me into convincing Mom and Dad to let you come with us?"

I snort. "I didn't blackmail you. I just used my considerable powers of persuasion."

Ryan scoffs, turning to face Myndi. "She found out I'd smoked some weed, and she told me, point blank, that if I didn't persuade the rents to let her come she'd tell them I was smoking dope and doing tons of other shit they wouldn't approve of."

"I even went and got photographic proof when he refused at first," I snicker.

"You were always very resourceful, Belle." Slater grins.

"I grew up surrounded by boys. Some of their shit was bound to rub off on me," I explain with a shrug.

"What happened with the camping?" Myndi urges me to continue.

"The instant the tents were set up, these two"—I point at Slater and Ryan—"started fucking around with the girls they brought, so Dylan and I took off on a hike before I became traumatized for life." I send a glare at the boys.

"Don't ask to hang with the big boys if you can't handle it," Ryan shoots back.

"I was *fifteen*, and I should *not* have had to hear that." I shiver all over as the screams and shouts coming from Mabel White's mouth replay in full volume in my head. "The mistake I made was not doing the same when you were in earshot. Would've loved to see how you handled it then, Ryan."

He purses his lips, wagging his finger at me.

"Anyway, Dylan and I found a private spot to make out..." I blush at the memory of giving each other oral sex for the first time in the small cave we found tucked into the side of the mountain.

"Ahem." My brother clears his throat. "Move it along before I ask Slate to turn the car around and go back and beat Dylan to a pulp."

"We kinda lost track of time, and it was dark when we started making our way back," I tell Myndi. "Neither of us had realized how far we'd walked. I could hardly see, and I tripped over a rock and sprained my ankle." Emotion clogs my throat. "Dylan had to carry me for miles back to camp. He was well over six feet by then, but he was skinny as fuck, and I know it must have killed him, but he never complained. Not once."

My voice cracks a little, and I pause for a second to gather myself. "To distract me from the pain, he sang this song the whole way up the mountain." Tears roll down my cheeks, and Ryan squeezes my shoulder.

"Ryan was drunk," Slater continues the story, instinctively knowing I can't go on, "and I was the only sober one with a driver's license, so I drove Belle to the hospital. Dylan passed out on the backseat, totally exhausted."

He looks adoringly at me. "You were so brave. I knew you were in pain, but you wouldn't cry. I let you play that damn song on a loop the whole hour it took to get to the nearest hospital." He chuckles.

"And you held my hand while the doctor bandaged me up." I smile weakly at him, wondering why, in all the times I thought about that night, I never remembered how concerned he was and how well he looked after me. He never left my side, carrying me back to the car and giving me his camp bed because it was more comfortable than the one I brought. "Did I even thank you?"

He shrugs. "You didn't need to, Belle. It's not like it was a chore."

Our eyes lock, and something passes between us. It's a fleeting acknowledgment of something I've felt before. Something brewing these last few weeks. Or maybe it's been longer, and I've just never noticed. Without pausing to think about it, I lean over the console and place a soft kiss on his cheek. "Thank you," I whisper, almost keeling over in shock when a blush creeps up his neck. For the first time, I wonder if I'm not the only one experiencing strange reactions.

Ryan clears his throat again, and we snap out of it. That's the end of the reminiscing though, and we're all quiet the rest of the trip.

Ryan remains in my room when the last of the boxes is deposited. "Have you thought about what you want to do?"

I shrug, flopping down on the bed. "I guess I need to start looking for a place to live."

"I took a call from Michael last night. His dad isn't good, and he isn't coming back for a while. He wants to stay there and help his mom look after him. He's deferred this semester, and he asked me to rent out his room, so you can stay here if you like."

"Won't that cramp your style?"

He ruffles my hair. "Nah. I'm at Myndi's half the time, and you've seen how little the guys are here."

"Won't they mind a girl moving in?"

"I honestly don't think either Powers or Evans will care. I'm pretty sure they love having you here. The house is spotless, and your cooking expertise is definitely appreciated. But, if it makes you feel better, I'll run it by both of them tonight."

"And you're sure you're okay with this? Most brothers wouldn't want their little sister moving in."

Leaning over, he presses a kiss to my forehead. "I'm not most brothers, and I want you here. If I didn't, I wouldn't offer."

I push up to my knees and hug my brother. "Thank you. I love you."

He squeezes me tight. "I love you too, and I'd do anything for you. You never have to doubt that."

"I know." I'm so lucky I have three brothers—four if you count Slater—who would literally kill for me if I asked.

Ryan sits on the edge of my bed, and I pull my knees into my chest. "Okay, cool. Ask them, and if they agree, at least it gives me some breathing space to find my own place for next semester."

"That's if Michael even comes back. I have a feeling he'll be gone longer than one semester."

"That sucks about his dad. Tell him I'm thinking of him."

"It's a shitty situation."

"I dread the day when we have to face something similar." A shiver works its way through me.

"It's something I avoid thinking about, and at least our parents are still young and healthy."

"Can't help thinking about it though."

He sighs. "I know, and I feel for Michael. He's super close to his dad. This will hit him hard."

"I don't doubt it, and I know what he's going through," Slater says, popping his head through the open doorway. "Wouldn't wish it on my worst enemy."

"I know, dude." Ryan's expression is sympathetic as he stands. "But he's strong like you. He'll get through it." Ryan claps him on the back as he walks out.

"You got a sec, Belle?"

"For you? Always."

That brings a contented smile to his face. Tellingly, he closes the door and props his butt against the edge of the desk. "I need to get something off my chest."

Butterflies nestle in my tummy, and I'm suddenly on edge. "Okay."

"You seem to be under a misconception about me, and I don't like it."

My eyes pop wide as I'm taken aback. "If I've offended you in some way, I'm sorry."

He crosses his ankles. "It bothers me that you think I'm some raving manwhore when I'm not. I'll admit I was a little crazy for a while senior year of high school and I probably overdid it freshman year of college, but tales of my conquests have been greatly exaggerated around campus. I've been with a lot less girls than you think."

"Sorry if I've been judgmental. I honestly didn't mean to be, but you and Ryan always seemed to have different girls with you, and it's not like either of you have ever really had a proper relationship."

"I want that, Belle, but there's only one girl I've ever desired that with, and she wasn't available."

My heart skips a beat. "What girl?"

"The only girl who's ever mattered. The one I've tried so hard to forget, but she's ruined me for all others."

"Do I know her?" I whisper, wondering why I'm internally debating whether it could be me. I shove that ludicrous assumption aside.

As if.

He peers deep into my eyes, and the moment turns intense again. His gorgeous eyes smolder with emotions I can't decipher. My heart is pounding behind my rib cage, and my gaze moves to his lips without any conscious thought. *I wonder what it would be like to kiss him? To have those large hands explore my body?* I'm betting Slater goes all out to please the woman he's with, and, suddenly, I'm hugely curious to experience that.

I jump up off the bed, heart thumping wildly. An ache throbs down below, and I'm confused as fuck. I shouldn't be thinking of Slater like that. Of any guy like that. I've just come out of a relationship and my heart is broken.

But if that's the case, why is it presently soaring at the thought of something happening between Slater and me?

Chapter Nineteen

I shove Slater out of my room after that on the pretense I needed to unpack, but really it was to conduct an internal examination. To question whether I've finally lost the plot. I reach the conclusion it's the stress of the breakup making me think crazy thoughts.

Because there's no way Slater feels like that about me. I'd know if he did. Apart from that blush earlier, he's never given me any indication proving otherwise.

The school week is long and arduous, not helped by the fact Dylan refuses to give up. He calls and texts all the time, and a bunch of lilies arrives daily with pleading notes for forgiveness.

I'm sitting in the living room with my cell on the couch beside me and a large glass of white wine pressed to my lips, wondering if I can go through with this.

"Whatcha doing?" Myndi asks, wandering into the living room a couple minutes later.

"Be there in a sec, babe," Ryan hollers down the stairs as Myndi sinks onto the couch beside me.

"Dylan won't stop texting and calling, and he's freaking out over the fact I returned all his money."

"I didn't know you did that."

I take a big gulp of wine. "Yep. It's official. I'm single, heartsick, and completely broke."

"How do you feel about the money?" she asks, not needing to inquire into my state of mind over my newly single status.

"Fan-fucking-tastic, actually. Freeing. I should never have accepted his money to start off with."

"He was your forever guy. Of course, you should have."

"Well, I'm not letting myself rely so much on a guy ever again."

"Good for you, babe, but that still doesn't explain why you're sitting here looking all tortured and drowning in a bottle."

"I'm debating whether to block his number," I admit, taking another healthy mouthful of wine.

"Oh. I see."

"It makes it final, and there's a part of me resisting, but I don't see that I have much choice. I can't move on if he won't let up with the messages. I need it to stop."

"Just do it, sis," Ryan says, stepping into the room. He leans down and kisses Myndi on the mouth. "Hey, baby. You look absolutely beautiful." Myndi swoons, and it's obvious to everyone that these two are falling deep.

I smile at my brother. I've never seen this side of him before although I always knew he had it in him.

Dylan used to look at me like that until he decided I wasn't enough for him. Until he chose to cheat on me rather than being truthful and breaking things off before he started sticking his dick in random pussy.

Any nostalgia I was feeling withers and dies. Hurt lances me on all sides, and a big lump forms at the back of my throat while tears sting my eyes.

And that decides it for me. Picking up my cell, I draw a deep breath and block Dylan's number, hating how my hand shakes and my heart cries with the action.

***

At work Friday night, Shelby makes no attempt to disguise the venomous looks she slants my way. I'm trying to ignore her, but I feel her eyes following me around the room, and it's not so easy to shake her off.

"Ignore her," Emma says, coming up behind me as I'm leaving a table with their order. "She's a jealous, spiteful bitch, and no one likes her. Except for the boss, but that's only because she's spreading her legs for him. Tramp."

"I don't get what I did to piss her off. It's like she hated me before she even met me."

We reach the counter and place our drink orders with Slater. He winks at me, expertly filling various drinks while taking more orders from customers at the bar. Emma leans in close to my ear. "She wants Slater, but he only has eyes for you."

I gawp at her, wondering if I need my ears checked. "That's ... that's ... preposterous!" I splutter. "He's like one of my brothers!" I wince as I say it, realizing I've been using that excuse for a long time. If I really searched my heart and my soul, I'd see he's not like that. Not at all. But I'm not ready to face up to that truth just yet. If I ever will be.

Emma inspects my face, her expression turning soft. "You didn't know, did you?"

My cheeks heat up. "He doesn't have those kind of feelings for me."

"Honey." She leans in closer so he can't hear. "He's incapable of hiding it. It's so obvious, and I don't even know either of you that well, but I have eyes in my head, and I'm telling you Slater Evans has the hots for you."

I shake my head, not wanting to believe it.

"What's more, I think you might be feeling it too."

Emma's words lie dormant in my mind the next couple of weeks as I settle into a new routine. The guys are like passing ships in the night, and it's rare that we're all in the house at the same time. Ryan and Myndi are practically glued at the hip now, so I still see a lot of my brother, and I see Slater at work, of course, but I've been purposely keeping a distance between us, unsure how to deal with the fact he might have feelings for me. I focus on my studies, and when I'm not working, I'm usually in the library or out running. I go home on Sundays, but that only makes me sadder because everything reminds me of Dylan.

I'm trying so hard to be strong, and it's a little easier now he isn't able to call or message me, but it's not that easy to let go of the past. To forget the guy who has meant everything to me. To move on from a future that won't ever come to fruition. I manage to keep it together during the day, but at night, my memories return to haunt me, and I sob into my pillow every night.

When Ryan is here, which is only half the time, he usually slips into bed with me in the middle of the night, holding me and making it better. But I can't rely on my brother to get me through this. I've accepted the reality of my new situation, but try telling that to my heart, because it's still pining for the only boy I've ever loved.

I return to the brownstone Sunday night with my guitar in tow. I kinda lost interest in it a couple of years ago, but now, more than anytime recently, music has become my solace. I'm sitting on my bed, attempting to play the latest Shawn Lucas hit when there's a knock on my door. "Come in," I holler, setting my guitar aside.

Slater opens the door and lounges against the doorway. "Don't stop on my account. That sounded good."

I snort. "Don't lie. That was horrid, and you know it."

"It wasn't that bad."

"You're going straight to hell for all the white lies," I tease.

He pushes off the doorframe, strolling toward me, and my heart starts fluttering. He sits down beside me, and the citrusy scent of his cologne swirls around me like a blanket. Butterflies dance in my chest, and when he runs a hand through his hair, my eyes follow the movement in greedy fascination. He's growing his hair out again, and I like it. I can imagine grabbing fistfuls of his hair as we ... I halt that thought, shocked at how easily my mind went there.

"You're just a little out of practice," he adds, and my eyes blink rapidly while my pulse thrums wildly. Until I remember he's talking about the guitar and not my abandoned, lonely vagina.

I blush, and he smiles funnily at me.

I rub the back of my neck. "I know. I can't even remember the last time I picked up my guitar."

His grin turns wicked. "Should I warn Ryan to bring his earmuffs out of the attic?"

I thump him in the shoulder. "I was never *that* bad."

"I'm only messing with ya. You know you're good."

"Not as good as Caleb."

"But Caleb lives and breathes music. You went through phases."

"True. I liked it but not enough to keep it up." I purse my lips, looking down at my guitar. "I'm not even sure why I brought it back here, to be honest."

"I think it's good you're rediscovering yourself." He reaches out, tugging on a stray strand of hair that has fallen loose from my ponytail.

My heart stutters in my chest, and our gazes lock. "You think I lost myself?" I ask, my voice cracking a little.

His eyes search mine, for what I'm not sure. Tentatively, he raises his hand, cupping one side of my face. I swear I stop breathing. Butterflies are racing a marathon inside my chest, and my heart feels ready to erupt from my rib cage.

"I think you know you did," he whispers, staring at my mouth.

My chest visibly heaves, and his eyes drop lower on my body. My nipples instantly pebble, and I'm praying he can't see through my thin sweater and cotton bra.

When he lifts his eyes, meeting mine again, I have to smother a gasp. His pupils are dilated, his dark gaze swallowing me whole. My core pulses, and my hands feel clammy, so I wipe them on the side of the bed, never taking my eyes from his.

His Adam's apple bobs in his throat, and he leans in a little closer. My heart is going crazy, jumping around my chest like fireworks on the Fourth of July. His hand tightens on my face, and he brushes his thumb across my cheek, eliciting a trail of shivery tingles. My tongue darts out, and I wet my lips. His eyes track the movement, and he scoots in closer beside me, grasping the other side of my face and tilting my head up slightly. He looks at my mouth again, and inner conflict flares in his eyes for a brief second, but then it's gone again, and he's lowering his head, lining his mouth up with mine.

Oh my God.

He's going to kiss me.

Slater Evans is going to kiss me.

And I'm going to let him.

I close my eyes as he moves to bridge the last gap between us.

A massive thud on the window scares the living daylights out of me, and I shriek. I open my eyes instantly. Slater's expression is a mixture of confusion, frustration, and relief. Another thud hits the window, and we both stand. "What the hell is going on?" Slater stalks to the window and lifts the blind.

He cusses under his breath, and I walk toward him. "What is it?"

"See for yourself." He grips the window ledge tight, a muscle clenching in his jaw.

I peek around him, struggling to believe my eyes.

Dylan is outside, throwing stones at my window. From the way he's staggering about, I can tell he's drunk.

The sight of him hits me hard, and I close my eyes, silently begging him to leave. I'm never going to get past this if he won't let me go.

Another stone hits the window, and I open my eyes. Slater looks like he wants to pummel Dylan into the ground. He's shouting now, but we can't hear him through the window.

"Shit." I rub at my temples. "I'd better go down to him before the neighbors call the cops."

Slater turns to me, gripping my shoulders. "Belle." His voice is choked, his expression tormented. "I ... I ..."

Thunk. The stones just keep on coming, and I know I have to face him even if it's the last thing I feel like doing.

I shuck out of Slater's hold, shooting him an apologetic look. "I need to go. We'll talk later. I promise."

Chapter Twenty

"**D**ylan, what are you doing here?" I stand in the open doorway, wrapping my arms around myself as I stare at my ex.

"We need to talk, Dimples," he slurs, staggering all over the place as he walks toward me.

I rear back from the toxic fumes pouring off him in waves. "You're smashed, and you shouldn't be here."

He makes a grab for me, but I sidestep him, avoiding his reach. "Please, baby. Please, come back home. I miss you."

Sighing, I count to ten and draw upon patience that is in limited supply. "That's not gonna happen. There is nothing you can do or say to undo the damage. Please just stop trying."

He slouches against the wall, pinning bloodshot, pained eyes on me. "I made a mistake. Why can't you forgive me?"

That supply of patience is growing thinner by the second. "I'm not doing this again with you, Dylan. You chose to cheat on me behind my back and lie to my face. There is no getting over that, so just quit this ... whatever this is. I'm not changing my mind."

His eyes dart behind me, instantly darkening. Slater gently places his hand on my lower back. I know it's a show of support, but I asked him to stay upstairs for a good reason. Dylan's lips twist into a snarl. "Oh, I see how it is," he spits out. "You stand there all high and mighty pretending like I'm the only one at fault, when you're nothing but a lying whore."

I plant my hands on my hips and glare at him. "Excuse me?"

"You're fucking *him*! How is that any different than what I did?" His words hurt, but it's hard to take him seriously when he's slurring and swaying and completely trashed. I'm not going to argue with him when he's like this.

"I haven't been with anyone during our relationship or since it broke down, and that's the last I'm saying on the subject." I move to close the door. "Go home, Dylan."

He shoves his foot in the door, stopping the motion. Snatching my arm, he yanks me out of the house. "I'm not leaving without you." He starts dragging me down the path, his fingers digging into my arm. "This has gone on long enough."

"Stop it!" I try to wrestle out of his grip, but he has an iron-strong grasp for someone so drunk. "You're hurting me."

Strong hands rip me away from Dylan, and Slater plants me behind him, shielding me with his body. I grab hold of his shirt, burying my face in the cotton, thankful he's here. "I will only say this once, Woods. You ever touch Belle without her permission again and I will fucking end you. Don't care if I go to prison for it. Stay the hell away from her."

"She isn't yours!" Dylan roars, shoving Slater, and we both stumble backward.

"I'm not yours either," I shout back, losing control of my tenuous emotions. "And you made that choice, not me!"

"Stop your lying bullshit!"

"You have ten seconds to get the fuck off our property or I'm calling the cops," Slater says, extracting his cell from his back pocket.

Dylan sneers. "Call them. See if I care."

I wrap my hand around Slater's wrist, stalling him. "Don't. Please. I don't want to involve the cops."

I step in front of Slater, trying to appeal to Dylan one last time. "If you ever loved me, Dylan, you will let me go. Please. Just let it go."

"So that's it, huh?" He glares at me with so much hatred in his eyes, and I can't understand what I've done to deserve it. "You're a fucking cunt! I fucking knew you'd trade me in for him!"

My mouth hangs open in shock. I can't believe he's just said what he's said. It feels like I've never known him at all. The Dylan I know would never be so crude and demeaning.

Slater's entire body goes rigid, and I know he's working hard to restrain himself, but Dylan is pushing his buttons on purpose. "What did you just call her?"

"You heard me!" Dylan hisses, swaying unsteadily on his feet. "She's a cunt! You're a cunt! You're both fucking cunts." He yells so loud it's a wonder the whole street hasn't heard him.

A car door slams, and I look up in time to see Ryan racing across the front lawn. "What the actual fuck is going on here?" he demands to know, his gaze bouncing between us.

"And here's another pair of cunts," Dylan unhelpfully adds. "Let's just call this the House of Cunts. I'll even get a sign made."

"He is fucking wasted." Ryan looks disgusted, shaking his head in dismay. Myndi appears at his side, and he pulls her in protectively to his body.

"Thanks for pointing that out, Captain Obvious." I rub at the tense spot between my brows.

"I see you got yourself a new cunt, Ryan." Dylan eyes Myndi up and down. "I always thought she had a nice rack, but not in Gabby's league. Gabby's tits are fucking awesome. Man, I miss sucking your tits, babe."

I drop my head, embarrassed and appalled. Ryan looks like he's seriously contemplating murder.

"I've had enough of this," Slater says, crossing his arms and leveling a thunderous look at Dylan. "You have ten seconds to get out of here or I'll make you, and, trust me, right now I'm sorely tempted to smash my fist in your mouth until you shut the fuck up."

Dylan drops down on his butt, bringing his knees to his chest and grinning up at us. "You know what? I think I might stay here tonight." He picks a stone out of his pocket, tossing it up and down in his hand.

"The hell you are," Ryan grabs him by the shoulders, attempting to pull him up.

Dylan lashes out, seizing Ryan by the shirt and yanking him down to the ground. Ryan takes a tumble, cursing as he shoves Dylan off. There is no strength in Dylan's grip thanks to his inebriated state, but that doesn't stop him from trying. He swings his fist in my brother's direction, but Ryan easily dodges his efforts, clutching his wrists tightly and holding them together. "Dylan. Cut this crap out, and get your sorry ass home. You're not helping your cause here in any way."

"Your sister's a cunt. She's a fucking cunt!"

A muscle ticks in Ryan's jaw, but he holds it together well. "So you've said, and, no, she isn't, but I'm not in the mood for a pissing contest when you're wasted, and we've given the neighbors enough of a show." He hauls Dylan to his feet. "I'm taking you home." He tugs on Dylan's elbow as he glances over his shoulder at Myndi. "Go inside and wait. I won't be long."

"Ugh." Dylan wobbles precariously on his feet, clutching his stomach. "I don't feel too hot."

"Yeah, buddy." Ryan shakes his head. "I'll bet." He gets Dylan in the car without much protest. "See you in a while," he tells us before hopping behind the wheel and speeding away.

"Wow," Myndi says as all three of us stare blankly at the retreating car. "If I didn't know better, I'd say aliens have abducted Dylan Woods and sent an imposter back to Earth in his body."

"An obnoxious asshole of an imposter," Slater supplies, absentmindedly taking my hand in his. "And you didn't hear the worst of it. He's completely out of his mind."

We walk slowly back into the house, gravitating en masse toward the kitchen.

Myndi makes a beeline for the coffee pot, while Slater opens the refrigerator. "Beer or wine?" he asks, looking over his shoulder at me.

"Actually," I say, opening the overhead cupboard, "I need something stronger after that." I remove the bottle of vodka I stashed there last week and pour myself a shot, relishing the burn as it glides down my throat.

We don't talk much after that. We transfer to the living room and put Netflix on, but I'm not paying attention, my mind churning a hundred miles a minute. I throw my head back on the couch and close my eyes. Slater's big hand lands on my shoulder, and he gives me a solidarity squeeze. It's the most natural thing in the world to lean my head on his shoulder and seek out his comfort. It's something I've done countless times, but it feels different now after what transpired upstairs.

That day in the car outside the club, I suspected Slater was going to kiss me, but I convinced myself afterward that I was exaggerating. But there's no way I'm mistaken this time. He *was* going to kiss me upstairs before Dylan turned up and ruined everything. And I really wanted him to.

What the hell is up with that?

Before I can quiz myself any further, Ryan returns, flopping down on the small couch beside Myndi.

"Thanks for doing that," I say, because I know it took a lot for Ryan to act reasonably with all the crap spewing from Dylan's mouth.

"I only did it for you. I fought the urge to beat sense into his stupid ass the whole trip." He scrubs a hand over his chin. "What the fucking hell is wrong with that dude? He's like Jekyll and Hyde or something."

I worry my lip between my teeth, deciding to voice my recently-realized fears. I clear my throat. "I'm actually wondering the same thing. What if there is something wrong with him?" I sit up straighter, propping my elbows on my knees and cradling my head in my hands. "I didn't see it when I was living with him, but it's more apparent now. I think he's sick."

Ryan sits beside me, taking my hands in his much larger ones. "Gabby. I know you want to believe there's some big explanation for this, but I think the truth is much simpler. Dylan's just finally let all the glory go to his head. He thinks he's King Dick now, and he's got a taste for the player lifestyle and he likes it."

"It's no surprise he's struggling to let you go too, but he can't have it both ways," Myndi adds.

"But what if that isn't it? What if he is sick? What if that's why he's acting so weird?"

"Belle, he's not acting weird. He's just being a giant bag of dicks," Slater states.

"I know you want to see the good in everyone, Gabs. That you want to find an explanation for why Dylan has done what he's done, but it's exactly how it appears. He'd rather get wasted and fuck around than stay committed anymore."

I look down at my lap, my chest heaving, hating the look of pity on Ryan's face.

"I'm sorry if that hurts, but you can't let what happened tonight set you back. You're moving on, and you need to let him go too. He made his decision, and he's not your responsibility any longer."

I nibble on my lips as a whole host of emotions plays havoc with my heart and my head. Maybe they're right. Perhaps I'm plucking at straws. Trying to find some excuse for his behavior, when there isn't any excuse that makes this all right. I lift my chin. "Yeah, you're probably right."

"You know we are," Slater replies softly. "And, you're not going to like this either, but I seriously think you need to consider a temporary restraining order."

My eyes pop wide. "I'm not in any danger from Dylan!"

Slater gently takes hold of my arm, rubbing his thumb along the slight discoloration forming on the underside of my arm. "No?" He arches a brow. "Then what's this?"

I say nothing. It's not like I can deny Dylan gave me that bruise when he tried to drag me from the house.

"I think Slate could be right," Ryan says, his face darkening as he glances at my bruised skin. "I know you don't want to, but if he touches you again Gabby, you'll have no choice. If you won't do it, I'll go straight to Dad. That shit is not acceptable." He blows air out of his mouth, shaking his head sadly. "I warned him in the car, but I don't know if I got through to him."

"Okay." I hold up my palms. "I promise if anything happens I'll seriously consider it. For now, can we please switch the subject because I'm sick of talking about it."

I approach the apartment block the following evening, after classes have ended for the week, with a healthy dose of apprehension. Ryan and Slater would string me up if they knew I was here, but I can't let this go until I've at least broached the subject with Dylan. It changes nothing about the demise of our relationship, but now that the idea has taken root in my head, I won't rest easy until I've shared my concerns with him.

I know I don't owe him anything, but we've been a huge part of each other's lives, and it doesn't feel right to ignore my gut.

My heart is in my mouth as I knock on Dylan's door, waiting for him to answer. The door swings open, and Dylan stares at me as if I'm an apparition. His lips are swollen, and his hair is all messed up. It's a look I know well, and bile floods my mouth. "Who is it, honey?" Bianca calls from inside the condo. A spike of pain shoots through my heart, but I hold my ground, determined to say what I need to say.

"No one!" Dylan shouts back, grinning maliciously at me. "I'll be back in a sec." He pulls the door closed behind him, forcing me back out into the hall. "What do you want?" he snaps.

"I, ah, I was hoping we could talk for a few minutes. Someplace private."

He smirks. "You want to come inside?" He quirks a brow. "Be my guest." He pushes the door open, stepping aside to let me enter.

Discussing this in front of Bianca was *not* what I had in mind, but I can't bow out now without looking weak. I step into the kitchen, wetting my dry lips and willing my heart rate to calm the hell down.

"What's that bitch doing here?" Bianca demands, storming into the kitchen and putting herself all up in my face.

"I'm not here to cause trouble. I just wanted to talk to Dylan."

"You're not his girlfriend anymore." She grabs my elbow in the exact same place Dylan did last night. "And you're not welcome here. Get out."

She tries to drag me away, but I resist, holding onto the kitchen counter for dear life. "Dylan, please. Just let me say what I came to say, and I'll go then."

Dylan shrugs. "If Bee doesn't want you here, then you have to leave."

"What?" My face falls. "You're letting her kick me out?" I lose my grip on the counter, and Bianca grabs both my arms, manhandling me toward the door. "Does the nine years we've known each other count for nothing?"

"You tell me!" he snarls, anger contorting his face unpleasantly. Out of the corner of my eye, I spot Bianca flinching a little. "I tried to speak to you last night, and you had your brother physically haul me away. How is this any different?"

"What?" Bianca stops trying to force me out the door, glaring at Dylan. "You went over to her place?" I wince at her high-pitched tone.

"Shut the fuck up, Bee. It's none of your business." Her face turns puce with rage, but she bites her tongue and resumes her attempts to shove me outside.

"It's different because I'm not drunk or hurling insults at your face!"

"I don't care. You made your point last night, and I got the message loud and clear."

"Dylan, I'm worried about you. I—"

He lunges at me, yanking me out of Bianca's arms, and shakes me. Everything shuts down inside me at the murderous look in his eyes.

Ryan was right. Dylan *is* dangerous. Unpredictable and out of control.

I was stupid to come here.

Stupid to think I could reason with him.

Stupid to care.

"You don't have the right to worry about me anymore." He pushes me out the door and this time I willingly go. "You're nothing but a cheap whore. Go home and fuck Evans because you'll never get to fuck me again." With one last shove, he throws me out into the corridor, slamming the door in my face.

I walk down the hallway and into the elevator on autopilot. I'm shook up, trembling all over, and I'm mad. So freaking mad. How dare he treat me like that! How dare he let that bitch treat me like that!

My hands are shaking as I remove my cell and punch the button. Dad picks up on the third ring. "Buttercup. Is everything okay?"

"No, Daddy, it isn't. I need your help. I need to get a restraining order against Dylan."

Chapter Twenty-One

"I need to get laid," I tell Myndi the next morning when we gather in the kitchen for breakfast. Ryan, Austin, and Slater have already gone out on a run, so it's just the two of us.

"And when did you decide this?" she asks while I pour myself a cup of coffee.

"Last night after I went to see Dylan to share my concerns and he and his girlfriend threw me out of the condo like I was scum of the Earth."

She spits her coffee all over the table. "They did what?"

I nod, taking a big glug out of my drink "Yep. It's official. Dylan Woods *is* a giant bag of dicks."

"Ryan and Slater are going to freak when they hear you went there."

"Only if they find out." I waggle my brows, and she grins.

"These lips are sealed." She makes a zipping motion with her fingers.

"Anyway, Ryan will be pleased. I filed for a restraining order because Dylan actually scared me last night."

She frowns. "In what way?" I sit down and tell her the whole story. Leaning her elbows on the table, she frowns some more. "What if you are right, Gabby, and he *is* sick? Because it just seems like he's getting crazier and crazier."

I shrug, pouring the last remnants of my coffee down the sink. "Not my problem. I tried to talk to him, and he didn't want to know."

"And now you wanna get laid?"

"Yep. He actually did me a huge favor last night. I'm not upset anymore. I'm just mad. Mad that I wasted so much time on someone so unworthy. And I'm not wasting a second longer. I need to get back in the saddle to finally rid myself of all thoughts of Dylan Woods. I know it's cliché, but it's been said that the best way to get over someone is to get under someone else, and there's got to be some truth to it. I've never had a one-night stand, and I intend to rectify that. Pronto." I grin at her. "I need you to be my wingwoman."

"Name the time and place, and I'll be there," she readily agrees.

"Tonight, at the club."

"Wow. You're definitely not wasting any time."

I jump up onto the counter, crossing my legs. "No time like the present, and there's no one to stop me. I'm free as a bird." I giggle for added effect.

"Aren't you working tonight?"

"I took the night off because I was going to head home for the full weekend, but I already called Mom and told her I changed my mind. I'll just go home tomorrow like I usually do."

Myndi gets up and walks over to me, hopping up onto the counter alongside me. "Cool, but I need to ask you something, and don't bite my head off." Her eyes drill into me. "What about Slate?" she softly inquires.

I send her a funny look. "What about him?"

She tilts her head, examining my face. "Do you really not see it?"

I squirm a little, averting my eyes as I feign nonchalance. "See what?"

"How much he's in love with you."

178

I try to laugh it off, shoulder checking her. "Don't be silly. Of course, he isn't, and I wish everyone would stop saying it."

"Who else has noticed?"

I chew on the inside of my mouth before admitting it. "Emma at work appears to be under the same illusion you are."

"It's not an illusion. Babe, it's as obvious as the nose on my face."

"Not to me or Ryan it isn't," I semi-lie.

"Hmm." She purses her lips, looking lost in thought. "I can't figure out if Ryan is as unobservant as you or if he knows and he's trying to pretend he doesn't. How do you think he'd feel about it if you and Slate got together?"

"I honestly don't know, and it's not something I've given a lot of thought to." Truth.

"But have you thought of him like that?"

I decide to come clean. "Actually, there's something you don't know." I wince as I look her straight in the eye. "Don't kill me, but Slate's been on the verge of kissing me twice, the most recent being Thursday night, only Dylan showed up and thwarted his plans."

She thumps me in the arm, but I grin and bear it. I deserve it. "I can't believe you held out on me!"

"It wasn't intentional," I admit. "I'm trying to deny it ever happened, and speaking about it makes it too real."

"Slate is a great guy, Gabby. He's smart, funny, hot as sin, and he worships the ground you walk on. It would hardly be a hardship, and I think you two would be so good together."

"That's not what I mean." I swivel around, crossing one leg over my knee. "I think I ..." I squeeze my eyes shut and draw a brave breath. I can't believe I'm going to admit this out loud. "I think I have feelings for him," I whisper.

"Hey." She touches my cheek, and I open my eyes. "It's not a crime to acknowledge that."

"It is when I'm a hot mess, Mind."

"You're not a hot mess. You're just getting over something huge, and you're still healing."

"And that's exactly why I shouldn't start anything with Slate, if that's even what he wants. Maybe he just wants to fuck me."

Myndi thumps me on the arm again. "Now you're being mean. Slate would never look at you as just a quick fuck, and you know it."

I sigh. "I know that deep down which is why I can't even consider him an option now. It's too complicated and I can only handle so much heartache. I think I've already reached my quota for this year."

She slings her arm around my shoulder. "What you need is to have some good, unadulterated fun. Everyone knows you have to kiss a few frogs before you meet Prince Charming. I'm living proof of that."

"Oh God." I face palm. "I've created a monster." I roll my eyes. "A pair of monsters, because my brother is as lovesick as you!"

"Aw. I so love hearing that!" She goes all googly-eyed, and I can't help smiling.

"I think you and Ryan have just claimed the 'love's young dream' tag in my house, and I'm happy to pass the mantle over." I squeeze her tight. "But as much as I love my brother, he's not coming tonight." I fix her with a stern expression. "He'll ruin all my fun. You know how protective he is."

"I do, and I agree. Hos before bros." We knuckle touch, grinning. "I take my duty as your wingwoman extremely seriously, which is why we need to start getting ready now."

"Now?" I glance at the clock on the wall. "It's not even eleven!"

"Girl, have I taught you nothing this past year?" She pulls me down off the counter with her. "If you're doing this, you want to go *all* out."

"I have no clue what I've set myself up for, do I?"

"None. But it's going to be so fun."

We return to the house five hours later, completely pampered and raring to go. "What the hell did you do to your hair?" Ryan asks, skipping down the stairs as soon as he hears the door opening and shutting.

Self-consciously, I run my fingers through my hair, checking my reflection in the mirror in case the newly added pink strands have turned illuminous green or something on the way home. "You don't like it?"

He scrutinizes my hair on all sides. "No, I do. It looks really good on you. I'm just surprised is all."

"It was time for a change, and it's on trend."

"You look hot," he says, planting a kiss on top of my head. "You both do." He turns and pecks Myndi on the lips. "I think you'll need a chaperone tonight, and I volunteer as tribute."

"Nice try, but no." I wag my finger in his face. "You are *not* going to rain on my parade tonight."

"Moi?" He feigns innocence. "As if."

"Give it up, babe," Myndi says, patting his ass. "Have a guys' night with Slate."

"Slate's working."

"Crap, I forgot that," I murmur. "He better not ruin my fun either."

"The more I hear about this girls' night, the less I like the sound of it," he grumbles.

I mess up his hair. "Oh, chill out. It's not like I'm going to be doing anything you didn't do when you were young, free, and single," I tease as I start to walk up the stairs.

"Yeah, that's exactly what I'm afraid of."

"You are *not* wearing that out of the house!" Ryan bellows when I come down wearing my new, sexy outfit.

"What's wrong with it?" I inquire, running my hands over the tight-fitting, strapless black and pink minidress.

"I've seen you wear more to the beach, Gabby!" he splutters, and I titter.

"Oh my God. You're turning into Dean. I never thought I'd see the day." In a lot of ways, my eldest brother was more like my dad growing up. There's nine years between us, and he was like the clothing police when I was a teen, regularly freaking out when I was trying to sneak out wearing something I shouldn't. I run my fingers through my soft curls as I look in the mirror, tossing my hair over my shoulder and grinning at my reflection. I look good, and I don't mind admitting it. I'm going to own it tonight!

"Hang on, now," Ryan says. "Let's not go too crazy. Dean has the biggest rod shoved up his ass, and I've only recently acquired a teeny-tiny one." He pinches his fingers together as he scans over my bare legs and six-inch stilettos. "At least you have inbuilt weapons if anyone steps out of line," he jokes.

"That's the spirit." I smack a loud kiss off his cheek, lowering my voice as I tease him. "Just hang onto that thought when you get a look at your girl."

Myndi appears at the top of the stairs, as if on cue.

"No way, babe." Ryan goes to meet her halfway, profusely shaking his head. "There is no way I'm letting you go out by yourself looking that fucking hot." His eyes are out on stalks as he runs one hand up her outer thigh.

I cough loudly. "Sibling alert! No groping while I'm around."

Ryan plants a light kiss on Myndi's lips. "I really want to kiss the shit out of you right now but not with all that sticky stuff on your mouth."

"Rain check, babe." Myndi brushes past him, winking mischievously. "And that's a promise." She swats him on the butt.

"Can you stop feeling my brother up for a second, and let me know if I look okay?"

"You're straight fire, babe." Myndi kisses my cheek. "You'll be fighting them off in droves."

"Not helping," Ryan mumbles, grabbing his keys. "C'mon, let's go before I change my mind and lock both of you in the house."

The club is jumping when we arrive, but it's always crazy busy on Saturday nights, so it's not unusual. I have to fight my way to the bar, shoving copious girls aside to get to Slater. He's busy fixing drinks and concentrating, his head down. "Hey, Slate," I holler, leaning over the counter to catch his attention.

He lifts his chin up, a smile spreading across his mouth until he locks eyes with me. His jaw slackens as his gaze rakes over me, taking in the hair, the low-cut dress, and the professional face of makeup I'm wearing.

The outside world fades into the background while I swoon under the intensity of his expression. He can't take his eyes off me, and he's ignoring the customers shouting for his attention. A crackle of electricity swirls around us, and there's no way I can deny the attraction between us, not when it's practically slapping me in the face. His Adam's apple bobs in his throat, and his voice is coarse when he speaks. "Wow, Belle. You look stunning. You're the hottest girl in here by a mile."

Someone scoffs behind me, and I can't help blushing. I pretty much melt at his words before I give myself a stern talking to. I'm here to flirt, kiss some boys, and maybe find someone to screw later. I'm determined to stick to my plan, and mooning over Slater isn't on the agenda.

"Thank you. Does that compliment earn me a couple of fruity specials under the counter?" I cheekily ask, my brows nudging up.

His lips kick up. "For you. Of course!"

"Slater!" Shelby hisses, barging her way through the throngs at the bar. "Quit with the flirting and start filling orders. Some of my customers are complaining."

He grabs her tray, pinning her with a deadly look as he sets drinks on it. "Your orders have been sitting here waiting. Watch your fucking tone. I don't report to you."

"Don't piss me off, Slater. Or need I remind you how close I am to Donny."

She's so lame—tossing the boss's name around in a veiled threat. Everyone knows Slater is a damn fine bartender, and he's worked here way longer than Shelby. If anyone's taking a hike, it'll be her. But she seems to have missed that memo.

"Slut," she hisses, none too discreetly, as she passes by me with her tray. I laugh it off because no one is spoiling my good mood tonight.

Slater passes me two drinks. "Enjoy and be careful out there. It's packed tonight, and the crowd is rowdy."

I stretch up and kiss his cheek. "Thanks, and I'll be fine."

When I return to where I left Myndi, standing over in a less-crowded corner, the rest of our gang is there. We waste little time getting into the party spirit. A few drinks later and I'm buzzing as we force our way onto the teeming dance floor.

I'm glad for my mini dress now, because the heat is stifling, and my hair is already sticking to the back of my neck. We dance our little asses off while I keep an eye on the crowd, checking out hotties. A few guys flirt with me, but none of them are giving me tingles, so I make my excuses after a couple dances, returning to my friends.

A short while later, a firm hand lands on my hip, and a warm body presses against me from behind. "Hey, gorgeous." His voice is deep, his breath warm on my neck, and I shiver a little. "I've been watching you move, and I had to come and dance with you. Please tell me you're here alone."

"Maybe I am. Maybe I'm not." I decide to play coy as we subtly start moving against one another.

He trails a finger up my arm, and shivers skate over my skin. "If you were mine, I'd never let you loose on the dance floor by yourself." He spins me around so I'm facing him, smiling at me like he's just won the lottery. "I'd be a complete obsessive freak, keeping you by my side all night."

He's gorgeous. The epitome of tall, dark, and handsome with his chiseled, stubbly jawline, piercing green eyes, and sultry dark hair. "So, you're one of those possessive alpha types?" I tease.

"Most definitely." He drops his hands to my hips, forcing my body to move in sync with his.

"And does that admission usually work for you?"

He laughs, and it's a deep, full-bellied rumble that does funny things to my body.

"I generally don't have to try that hard."

"Wow," I admit as the music slows down. "Healthy ego right there."

He pulls my arms up, placing my hands around his neck. "Nothing wrong with being confident, is there?" He grins, hauling me closer against his body, and we start to slow dance.

"A little confidence is sexy. An overabundance just spells douche."

He laughs again. "We'll have to agree to disagree," he murmurs, flattening his hand against my lower back. "You look a million dollars by the way. And I'm Jack."

"Gabby. And thank you. You're not so bad yourself."

"Don't kill yourself with the compliments, doll."

Now it's my turn to laugh. "No point in making it too easy for you."

"So, what's your deal, Gabby. I know there's got to be a reason why someone like you hasn't been snapped up already."

"Maybe I have a third boob or a sixth toe. Perhaps I've got a flatulence issue or I'm one of those creepy cling-ons, you know girls who latch onto you and refuse to let go?" I joke.

"You're really selling it to me here."

I giggle. "You know I'm kidding. I recently broke up with someone after four years, so I'm just looking to let off a little steam." I shrug like it's no biggie. Like this isn't the first time I've ever been in this situation. Like I'm used to picking up random guys in clubs.

"What an idiot." He leans down, pressing a kiss just under my ear. "But his loss is definitely my gain."

"There you go with the overconfidence thing again."

"So that's not you palming my ass or rubbing your sexy little body against me?" He lifts a brow in amusement when I look around his body, and, sure enough, that *is* my hand squeezing his pert ass cheeks.

"I have no idea how that happened. Zero." I smother my smile.

"Sure, you don't, doll." He winks. "Just like you'll pretend this didn't happen either." Before I can quiz him, he closes his mouth over mine, claiming my lips confidently and expertly, and I sink into his kiss, giving it my all. He tastes like beer and peppermint, and his lips are soft but insistent. I don't resist when he runs the tip of his tongue around the seam of my lips, looking for an invite. I open to him, allowing his tongue to explore my mouth as I tighten my grip on his neck. With one hand on my waist, he grinds against me, while his other hand creeps up my back, holding me in place at the neck. He deepens the kiss, angling my head and devouring my mouth, and my mind is made up. Jack is perfect hookup material. I can tell he's done this a lot, and I doubt he'll have any expectations beyond one night, and that suits me perfectly.

We dance for what seems like hours, chatting and drinking, and I'm really enjoying myself. Myndi checks in with me regularly, giving me a subtle thumbs-up. Every so often, I feel Slater's eyes on me, boring a hole into the back of my skull, but I deliberately ignore him. I know he won't approve and that he's probably a little pissed, but I need to do this for me. To finally put Dylan behind me.

Jack is a senior, like Ryan and Slater, so the drinks keep coming, and soon, I'm more than a little tipsy. But it's a happy buzz, and I feel in control of myself.

"God, you taste so good. Feel so amazing," he mumbles against my ear while his hand moves lower, caressing my ass. I moan, grabbing both his hands and planting them firmly on my butt. The alcohol has definitely lowered my inhibitions, and I'm more than a little horny. I lick my lips as he digs his hands into my ass, eliciting another lustful groan. His pupils dilate, and he looks at me like he wants to eat me whole, and I'd happily let him. "What do you say we get out of here and take the party somewhere more private?" he suggests, grazing his nose along the column of my neck.

I lean back a little, examining his flushed face and lust-filled eyes. "How do I know you're not a mass murderer or a serial rapist?"

His expression turns serious. "I promise you're safe with me, but if you like, you can send my number to one of your friends." He pulls his cell and driver's license out of his pocket. "Take a pic of my ID so your friends know where you are and how to get me if I harm a single hair on your head."

I take his cell, snap a pic of his ID, and send it to Myndi before handing it back to him. "Thank you." I wipe my suddenly clammy hands on the side of my dress. "I haven't done this before. Had a one-night stand, I mean."

"Well, then I'm flattered to be your first." He takes my wrist, planting a soft kiss on my flesh. "I promise you'll have a night to remember."

I loop my arm through his, sending a text to Myndi from my own cell, letting her know I'm leaving. "I'm going to hold you to that."

He puffs out his chest. "I have faith I'll rise to the challenge."

I giggle at his innuendo as he leads us off the dance floor. I'm swaying a little, but I'm pinning that on my heels rather than the alcohol consumption.

We've just made it to the door when Slater shoves his way in front of us, doing a great impression of an angry Mike Tyson. "Where the hell do you think you're going, Belle?"

Chapter Twenty-Two

"**S**late. Come on." My eyes plead with him to drop the big brother routine.

"You're drunk, Belle."

I cross my arms over my chest, stumbling a little. "No, I'm not."

"Evans, butt out," Jack says, his voice low and carrying a warning.

"Do you know who she is? Is that why you're doing this?" Slate demands.

I frown. "Wait? What?" I ask, sober enough to feel embarrassed when a loud hiccup erupts from my mouth.

"I know she's gorgeous and gagging for my cock," Jack retorts, grabbing my hand. "That's all I care about."

"I know your rep," Slater replies. "But I didn't think even you'd stoop so low as to take advantage of a girl when she's drunk and clearly incapable of making a sound decision."

"What's the matter, Evans? You want to fuck her and she gave you the brush off? Or have you already dipped your wick and she's not interested in round two?" He prods his finger in Slater's chest. "Guess what, I don't give a fuck. She's coming home with me, and I'm going to show her a good time."

Slater ignores him, focusing on me. "Don't do this, Belle. I don't trust him with you, and I don't want you to end up doing something you'll regret."

Jack pulls me into his side, squeezing my waist. "C'mon, doll. Ignore this fuckwit. Let's go."

I rub at my eyes, smudging my eye makeup in the process. I may be drunk, but I'm not stupid. I'm not liking the vibes I'm getting from Jack anymore, and even though I know Slater doesn't want me going home with any guy, I don't think he'd deliberately interfere without good reason. I try to shuck out of Jack's embrace, but he's holding me too tight. "You know what, Jack. I've changed my mind." I have a feeling I'm slurring my words, hating that I am.

Jack abruptly lets me go, and if it wasn't for Slater's fast reactions, I'd have fallen flat on my face. "Your loss, doll." He shrugs before landing an intentionally hurtful parting blow. "Drunken sluts are in plentiful supply around here, and it won't take long to find a replacement." The ugly sneer on his face takes me aback. Gone is the charismatic charmer, and I've never felt more gullible. "No wonder Woods traded you in for Banging Bianca. She knows how to give a guy a good time." He pushes past, sending me a disparaging look as he makes his way back toward the dance floor.

While Slater has been holding onto me, he's been having a quiet word with one of the bouncers. Jack is suddenly hauled back and thrown out of the club, cursing at the top of his lungs, threatening Slater with all manner of abuse.

I stumble on my heels, and Slater sighs as he steadies me. "What am I going to do with you?"

Fuck me? I mentally punt kick that unhelpful little voice in my head, hoping I didn't express that sentiment out loud.

The look of amusement on Slater's face doesn't appease my bruised ego, and I scowl at him. "You don't have to do anything with me. I'm not your responsibility." I push out of his embrace, teetering precariously on my heels, but I manage to steady myself unaided this time. "I'm going back to my friends."

"Belle." He reaches out, gently taking my elbow. "I was only trying to lighten the mood, but I'm sorry if I offended you. Jack is bad news, and you would have regretted it."

"Because he's a player?" I ask, planting my hands on my hips. "News flash! I knew that! And it suited me perfectly because I'm not looking to get into another relationship. I just wanted to fuck Dylan out of my system."

Shock splays across his face, mixed with anger and some other emotion I can't decipher. "You're not that girl, Belle, and you shouldn't start now."

"Don't tell me what I should and shouldn't do." I remove his hand from my arm. "And you're a hypocrite. It's okay for you to fuck anything with a pulse, but when Jack does it, he's bad news."

His nostrils flare, and I think I might have pushed him too far. "That's not fair."

I prod him in the chest. "You know what else isn't fair? You cock-blocking me! Butt out. It's none of your business." I attempt to stomp off, but I'm struggling to maintain my balance as I head back to my friends. I'm more drunk than I realized.

"I thought you'd left?" Myndi says, coming toward me with her jacket on.

"Slate put an end to that." I pout. She smiles, opening her mouth to defend him, no doubt, but I cut her off. "Don't even attempt to say it. I just want to get back out there and see if I can salvage this night before it's a complete write-off."

She winces. "Babe, I'm sorry. I thought you were gone, and I called Ryan. He'll be here in a few minutes."

I close my eyes, and the room spins. Reaching out, I grab onto Myndi. "Whoa."

"Maybe you should call it a night?" she quietly suggests. "There'll be other nights."

"Yeah. I think you're right. My head doesn't feel too hot, and I've got the spinnies. Let's just go home."

Ryan laughs when he sees me, shaking his head as he picks me up like I weigh nothing, carrying me to the car. "Someone's going to have a sore head in the morning."

"Someone has a sore head now," I mumble, groaning as alcohol sloshes uneasily in my stomach. "Ugh. Why did I drink so much?" I lie down in the backseat, closing my eyes as Ryan starts the engine.

I wake up as I'm gently lifted up and out of the car. "Shh," my brother says, cradling me close to him. "Sleep it off. We'll take care of you."

He deposits me in my room, and Myndi helps me get my dress off. Then she rubs a facial wipe over my skin, removing the remnants of makeup, before pulling a loose shirt over my head. I'm tucked up in bed when Ryan returns with a bottle of water and two pain pills. I dutifully swallow them, draining the bottle of water before I pass out.

I wake a few hours later with my tongue practically glued to the top of my mouth. A dull ache spreads across my forehead, and my tummy feels tender, but at least I don't feel as bad as I did when I first left the club. Desperately needing hydration, I get up and mosey downstairs, yawning.

I open the refrigerator, pulling out a couple bottles of chilled water, and turn around, shrieking at the unexpected sight of Slater standing in the shadows, watching me, with his arms folded over his broad chest. The two bottles slip out of my hands, dropping to the floor. "Shit, Slate. You scared the crap out of me."

"Sorry, I didn't mean to startle you. I only got in a short while ago."

My head is throbbing, and I just want to go back to bed and forget this whole humiliating night. "I'm just gonna head back to bed." I pad across the cool tile floor.

"Wait a sec," he calls out when I reach the door.

I turn around, leaning against the doorframe. "What?"

He walks toward me stealthily, and my heart rate accelerates. "You need to understand something. Jack has a habit of picking up beautiful girls, charming the panties off them, and persuading them to make a video of their night together. Then he shows it to all his buddies, and they ridicule the girls behind their backs. I didn't want that to happen to you, Belle, and I'm only telling you this so you know he's not a good guy. Ask Ryan if you don't believe me."

"Seriously?" My face falls. How did I misjudge his character so badly? I mean, I knew he was a player and it would only be a one-time thing, but he seemed like a decent guy.

He nods. "I'm sorry."

I shake my head. "No, I'm the one who should be apologizing for the things I said, and I knew you were only looking out for me, but I was drunk and..." I trail off, unwilling to articulate the rest of my thoughts. I've already made enough of a spectacle of myself in front of Slate tonight.

"And?" he gently prompts.

My legs wobble, threatening to go out from under me. "Ugh. I really need to sit down."

Wordlessly, he takes my hand and guides me into the living room, pulling me down beside him on the couch. He turns to face me, and his leg brushes against mine, sending fiery tingles up and down my body. My face grows hot, and I look away.

"Belle," he whispers. "What's going on?"

I tip my chin up slowly, meeting his warm brown eyes. All I see is concern and compassion in his gaze, and I remind myself this is Slater. I've never had any trouble talking to him before, and I know he won't judge me. "I've never been with anyone but Dylan," I start explaining, "and I just wanted to hook up with some random guy and do the deed and finally start forgetting about him, but I couldn't even do that right." I harrumph. "I'm so naïve, and they're just lining up to take advantage of me."

"You know I won't let that happen, and not every guy is a douche." He cups my face. "You'll find someone amazing, Belle. Someone who sets your world on fire. Someone who appreciates how beautiful and special and intelligent and caring you are, and he'll be the luckiest bastard because he'll get to spend the rest of his life with you in it."

He has no idea how badly I needed to hear those things right now. How low I've really sunk since all the shit went down with Dylan. How battered my self-confidence is.

So, I really can't help what I do next.

Maybe it's the alcohol still buzzing in my veins. Or his heartfelt words shatter my lingering denial. Or I'm finally opening my eyes and seeing what has always been right in front of me—*who* has always been in front of me.

Whatever it is, I don't stop to question it, I just act on my feelings, jumping onto Slater's lap and planting my mouth on his. His lips are soft and plump, like crushed velvet, and his familiar citrusy scent swirls around me, providing comfort and reassurance. He doesn't kiss me back, at first, but I persevere, circling my arms around his neck and angling my head, deepening the kiss in the process. Then his lips are gliding against mine, and his hands are on the move, flattening against my lower back, drawing me in closer.

I run my fingers up his neck, dragging my nails through his hair, and he moans into my mouth. My body is alive, thrumming with need, and my head is swimming in awe. I can't believe I'm kissing Slater, and it feels like the most natural thing in the world. He's igniting an inferno inside me, cranking my lust to new, undiscovered heights.

All from a kiss.

Imagine what sex with him would be like. I grind my hips against his as the thought lands in my mind, and he stills underneath me, his lips freezing in place.

He rips his mouth from mine, and I stare at him in confusion. "Why'd you stop?" I pant, still running my fingers through the hair at the base of his neck.

Reaching up, he takes my hands and carefully lifts me off him. "This is wrong, Belle." He pins me with a pained expression, rubbing a hand over his jaw. "We shouldn't have done that."

I'm mortified, and my cheeks flare red. Oh my God. I've totally misread the situation, and I basically forced him into kissing me when he didn't want to. My heart hurts at his words, and I can't even look him in the face. "I'm sorry," I mumble, climbing to my feet, still avoiding looking at him. "It's totally my fault. Just forget it happened."

"Belle." He calls out to me as I run out of the living room, but this time, I don't stop, racing up the stairs and disappearing into the safety of my bedroom.

As I crawl under the covers, deeply humiliated, contemplating how the hell I'll ever face Slater again, I wonder why I keep getting everything so wrong, questioning if I'm a terrible judge of character, because I don't seem capable of making the right decisions lately, especially when it comes to the men in my life.

Chapter Twenty-Three

I become adept at avoiding Slater over the course of the next week, which I know is the chicken's way out, but I can't face another rejection so close after the last one. I'm hoping if enough time passes he'll just forget about it and we can resume our easy friendship like it never happened. I'm too embarrassed to even tell Myndi about it, so I just throw myself into my classes and my studies, and when Emma calls with some emergency Friday lunchtime, I agree to cover her shift at the club later that night, knowing Slater won't be there.

The club is busy, and I'm exhausted by the time I get home. Muted sounds of music and the hum of conversation accost my ears as I step foot inside the house. I poke my head through the living room door, my gaze roaming over the crowded space. "Hey, Gabby!" Austin waves his hands at me, summoning me inside.

I push past people until I reach him. "I didn't know we were having a party." I peer out the window into the backyard. A bunch of people are hanging out there, lounging on the deck, squatting on the grass, and huddled around the fire pit.

He slings his arm over my shoulder, pulling me into his side. "It was a spur of the moment thing." He smacks a kiss off my cheek before turning me around and introducing me to the guys he's with. "This is my new, gorgeous housemate, Gabby."

I warm at his compliment, smiling up at him. He smiles back, and it lights up his whole face. With his shoulder-length sandy-blond hair, piercing blue eyes, and tatted arms, Austin is quite the looker. But something tells me he knows it too.

A couple of his friends give me the once-over, not even attempting to disguise their interest. I'm flattered but not really in the mood to flirt. "Want a beer?" Austin asks, pulling a cold one from the ice bucket on the table beside him.

"Sure." I wrap my hand around the bottle, popping the lid. "It was a long shift."

"How are you enjoying working at the club?" he inquires, slipping his hand from my shoulder down my back.

"I like it. Shelby's a prize bitch, but apart from her, everyone is really nice to work with and I'm settling in."

"Don't let Evans hear you dissing his girl."

"She's not his girl," I protest, and he quirks a brow as he brings his beer to his mouth.

"Whatever you say."

His comment pisses me off. "I'm going to get changed into something more comfortable." I shuck out of his embrace. "I'll catch you later."

He pulls me back, nudging my hair aside and whispering in my ear. "I'll be right here waiting, gorgeous." He presses a kiss to my neck, flicking his tongue over my sensitive skin so I'm left in no doubt of his intentions. "Hurry back to me." He pats my ass before releasing me.

"Wow. Are you always this forward?"

"When I see something I want, you betcha."

I shake my head, laughing. "I admire your honesty, but it's not going to happen. We're roomies and we need to keep it strictly platonic."

"Ah, babe, you're no fun." He grins mischievously, pulling me into his chest and circling his arms around my back. "We can be sneaky," he whispers, "so the others will never know."

I laugh again, pushing out of his arms. "You're incorrigible."

"I like to call it determined."

I wave at him as I walk off. "See you later, Powers!"

I maneuver around the couples kissing on the stairs, offering up a silent prayer that no one is fucking around in my bed. When I reach my bedroom, I rest my ear against the door, listening for any moans or whimpers. Detecting none, I cautiously open the door and stick my head inside, relieved to find it empty.

I take a quick shower, careful not to get my hair wet, and then I dress in my black skinny jeans, a sparkly black top, and my ballet flats. A slick of lip gloss and a thick coating of mascara completes my party look, and I head back downstairs. I figure now is a great time to catch Slater and clear the air without having to spend too much time with him or making it obvious that I've been avoiding him on purpose. I'm assuming he and Ryan are around somewhere, so I bypass the living room and head straight for the kitchen.

A couple of guys and girls are laughing over by the refrigerator, but it's the sight of Shelby kissing Slater, her body practically super-glued to his that has me running out of the kitchen like there's a rocket up my ass. He calls out after me, but I'm way too fired up to stop.

He fucking lied to me! He told me there was nothing going on with her, that he wasn't interested, and now she's draped over him like a silk sheet.

My judgment is obviously completely skewed. How could I have thought he'd any interest in me when he's clearly still interested in her? The fact he rejected me last week and now he's in there with her only adds fuel to the fire.

Screw this.

Slater might not be interested in me, but I know someone who made his interest very clear. And, right now, I'm hurt and needy, and

I want someone to take me in their arms and at least pretend like they're into me. Psychologists would have a field day with me right now, but I don't care.

I storm into the living room, making a beeline for Austin. He's laughing at something one of his friends is saying so he doesn't notice me stalking toward him like a hunter stalking her prey. Not until I'm right in front of him, grabbing him by the shirt and pulling him into me. My lips crash down on his, and, as anticipated, he doesn't let me down, wrapping his arms firmly around my back and plundering my mouth with the same urgency. Anger pumps through my veins, supercharging my determination, and I grab onto him tighter, pressing myself into him, welcoming the feel of his growing erection nudging against my lower stomach.

Boy can Austin kiss. His lips are on fire as they move against mine with skill, and I'm going with the flow, indulging the freedom that comes from kissing a hot guy I find attractive and knowing nothing more will come of it. He slides one hand up my back, gripping my neck firmly and forcing my head to the side so he can ravish my mouth even more. His tongue swirls around my mouth, and he grinds his hips into mine, growling at the back of his throat when I squeeze his ass.

I'm ripped off him so fast I have to blink a couple times to figure out what just happened.

"What the actual fuck, man?" Austin stares at a furious Slater as if he wants to tear him limb from limb.

"I told you to keep your hands off her!" Slater hisses, and I snap out of whatever daze I'm in.

"Fuck off, Slate." I maneuver around him, curling into Austin's side. "You have no right to tell anyone anything in relation to me. Shoo!" I flap my hands in his face. "Your skank is waiting for you in the kitchen."

"She's not my anything."

"Spoken like a true manwhore," I sneer, as Austin slips his arm around my waist.

Slater's fists ball up at his sides, and he closes his eyes momentarily. When he opens them again, he looks conflicted. "It's not what it looks like." He drags a hand through his hair. "Look, can we go somewhere to talk?"

"I'm busy right now," I say, taking hold of Austin's hand and pulling him out through the room.

"Belle, stop." Slater tugs on my elbow. "You don't want to do this."

I shove him away. "Stop cockblocking me!" I hiss. "I'm capable of making my own decisions, and I'll do what I want. Do *whom* I want!" Okay, I'm acting like a spoiled, immature bitch. I know I am, but I'm hurt and mad over what I witnessed in the kitchen and what I perceive to be double standards.

I drag Austin out into the hallway with me. He's starting to look a little uncomfortable, but I'm not giving him an easy out. He was into this until Slater interrupted us, and I know he would be happy to take this to my bedroom, so I'm not giving him the opportunity to back out.

I start climbing the stairs, pulling Austin with me. "Um, Gabby."

"Don't say it!" I snap, glowering at him over my shoulder. Slater is standing at the bottom of the stairs, looking up at me with furious eyes. I have to work hard to resist flipping him the bird.

Man, I'm really releasing my inner child tonight.

I wonder if heartache negates the logical, rational part of the brain, because I know I'm acting irrationally, but I refuse to change course either.

I pull Austin into my room, slamming the door shut and pushing him down on the bed. Before he can argue, I pounce on him, straddling his hips and pulling my top off so I'm only in my jeans and bra.

"Gabby, wait, look, I..." He shoots me an apologetic expression as he gently takes my hands, holding me back.

I want to kill Slater. I think I could throttle him with my bare hands for ending this before it even started. "Great, you're rejecting me too. Super."

My humiliation is complete.

Scrambling off his lap, I perch on the edge of the bed with my head in my hands. Now, I'll have two housemates to avoid. I'll have to move out and find somewhere else to live.

"Look at me." Austin forces me to look up. "You're fucking gorgeous, and I want you, I do." He lowers his head to his crotch and then looks up at me with a lopsided grin. "It's not like I can deny what you do to me."

"So, let's do this." I cup his face. "I know you don't want anything beyond a hookup, and that's just perfect for me. I'm not looking for anything more either. Slate's just being an asshole."

Austin sighs. "C'mon. We both know he's not an asshole." He presses a kiss to my forehead and stands. "If anyone's an asshole, it's me, because I see how he looks at you." He runs his fingers through my hair as he stands in front of me. "I want to fuck you, Gabby, but not at the expense of our friendship or the friendship I share with Evans. I won't get in the middle of whatever is going on between you two."

"Nothing's going on between us," I say, grabbing his hips and looking up at him with what I hope is a seductive look.

The door to my room bursts open, and Slater storms inside like an out of control tsunami. He takes one look at the setup, adds two plus two, and comes up with ten. He lunges at Austin, but Austin is fast, and he steps to the side before Slater makes contact.

Which means Slater lands on top of me with a loud roar, and I'm bearing the full extent of his rage.

Austin takes that as his cue, winking and giving me a thumbs-up signal before slipping out of the room and closing the door behind him.

"Get off me, you big oaf!" I shove at Slater's shoulders, urging him to move while trying to ignore the way my traitorous body is responding to the fact he's lying on top of me, strategically positioned in all the right places. His face is pressed into my collarbone, offering him a nice view of the girls, barely covered in the flimsy black lace bra I'm wearing.

He seems to realize this at the same time, and he jumps up off me as if I'm contaminated. Another splinter of hurt rips through the weak organ in my chest.

"Now get out!" Tears prick my eyes as I rise, pointing at the door. "Just get out."

"I'm not leaving until we discuss this."

"I don't want to talk to you, and this is my room, so get out."

"I didn't kiss Shelby, and I wasn't lying when I said I'd no interest in her."

I slant an incredulous look his way. "I saw it with my own two eyes!" I yell, jumping up. "Don't try and make out like I'm crazy! I know what I saw."

He takes a step closer to me. "I didn't invite her here. She came with a bunch of other people and tried to latch onto me, but I told her bluntly to keep the fuck away from me. What you saw was her following me into the kitchen and jumping on me."

I harrumph, shaking my head. "My God, you're such a fucking liar! You were kissing her!"

"She. Was. Kissing. Me!" he roars. "For the love of God, why are you so fucking stubborn!"

"Oh, maybe because you keep lying to me?" I plant my hands on my hips and let anger flow through me like a steamroller. "Or maybe it's because you rejected me last week, yet you have no issue letting that skank climb you like a fucking monkey!"

He grabs onto his hair, and a strangled sound slips out of his mouth. "You are the most infuriating woman I know." Quick as a flash, he stalks to my side, grabbing my face in his large hands. He's not exactly gentle, and his eyes are flaring with heated emotion. "Are you that clueless, Belle? Or do you really think I'm such an asshole?"

"I don't think it. I know it."

"You are draining every last ounce of my patience," he growls, wrapping his hand around my head.

"Sorry I continue to be such a disappointment to you!"

"Belle." He sighs. "How can you be so blind?" He shakes his head, drawing our faces closer until there's no more than a couple inches between us. "I'm not interested in Shelby! She cornered me and took advantage for a split second. I swear that's all that happened."

I shrug. "It doesn't matter. I don't care. Kiss who you like. Fuck who you like. Just leave me out of it."

"I want to bang your head against the wall and eradicate all stubbornness and stupidity from your brain."

"Wow, I didn't realize you hated me that much."

His eyes darken, and he stares at me with a myriad of different emotions washing over his face. His chest heaves. A muscle pops in and out of his jaw. He gulps as his eyes flit to my mouth, his Adam's apple bobbing in his throat. The hand at the back of my head reels me in closer until we're only a hairsbreadth away from one another.

I stop breathing. My heart thumps behind my rib cage, and heat spirals through me.

He closes his eyes for a split second. When he opens them again, I gasp at the lust-drenched look radiating from the back of his eyes. "Fuck it!" His breath is warm as it ghosts over my face, and I sway on my feet, intoxicated, excited, and confused at the same time.

Decision made, he slams his lips down on mine, kissing me like I've never been kissed before. It's as if I'm the last woman on Earth and his survival depends on this kiss. He moves me over to the wall with obvious urgency, never once breaking our lip lock. He pushes me up against it, pressing his body flush against mine. I'm on fire, my body tingling all over. Stars explode in my mind, and I'm moaning into his mouth, clutching at his back, my hands greedy as they start exploring his hot body.

His hands are on the move too, trailing up the sides of my body, brushing against my breasts. My breath stutters, and an ache builds in my core. When he grabs my leg, yanking it up and around his waist, I rock against him, needing the friction to ease the throbbing down below.

He grinds his hips into mine, emitting a primal moan from the back of his throat. Liquid desire coils low in my belly, and I'm rocking against him like a woman possessed, needy and completely out of control.

He's aggressive, channeling all his frustration into every sweep of his lips and every thrust of his body, and I'm matching him head-on. I'm still so freaking angry, and I'm attacking his mouth with every pent-up feeling inside me. My hands slip under his shirt, and I drag my nails up and down his back, eliciting more heady grunts from his mouth. My body is alive, thrumming with a craving so intense it will take countless hours to sate my appetite. I bite down on his lower lip, sure I've drawn blood, but that only increases the pressure of his lips on mine and the tightening of his grip on the back of my head.

Without warning, he tears his lips from mine, pinning me with a look that is a combination of anger, frustration, sheer lust, potent helplessness, and something much, much deeper.

"Hate you, Belle? Are you fucking insane?" He presses his forehead to mine, and both our chests heave up and down. His breathing is ragged. My pulse throbs wildly in my neck. I'm a strange mix of aroused aggressiveness, and I can't decide if I want to throw him on the bed and have my wicked way or slap the shit out of him.

I feel like doing neither with the words that come out of his mouth next.

He steps back, and the pained expression on his face hurts me almost as much as his previous rejection. "I don't hate you, Belle." His voice is quieter, more composed. "I could never hate you. Not when I love you so fucking much."

Chapter Twenty-Four
Slater

S mooth, Slater, real fucking smooth. Ugh! I run a hand back and forth over my head, silently berating myself. I've loved that girl from the sidelines for years, and never, ever did I envision blurting it out just like that. After I'd just attacked her mouth and her body in a rage of lust and anger. And, as if that wasn't cowardly enough, then I ran. Hightailed it out of there before she even had time to process it, let alone respond.

So much for having self-control and waiting for the right moment to reveal my feelings.

Ryan will string me up by my balls if he ever hears about this.

One of the reasons I've stayed away from Belle is her brother—my best friend, the guy who's always been there for me, especially in the last year. I'm not sure he'd be all that thrilled about me and his sister getting together, but that hasn't stopped my imagination from going into overdrive since Belle broke up with Dylan.

A part of me feels huge guilt because I regularly wished for it to happen. When she was with him, he was all she saw. No one else existed outside their little love bubble. I wanted to hate him so badly, but, until lately, he never gave me any reason to. He treated her like a princess, worshiped the ground she walked on, and she literally had stars in her eyes every time he stepped into the room.

I longed for her to look at me like that.

But I was invisible.

Her brother's best friend. Someone to share a laugh and a joke with. That's not to say we aren't close, because we are, but I was always firmly relegated to the friend zone. Now, I might finally have an opportunity to do something about that, and I'm screwing everything up.

The last thing Belle needs right now is me professing love and then fleeing. She's not ready to hear it yet, and I hope I haven't ruined it. I haven't waited all these years to throw it away the first chance I get.

No. I can be patient.

I can wait for her to get into the right headspace. To realize I've been here this whole time. Loving her from afar. Silently hoping and praying that someday our time would come.

Ryan raps on the door. Three quick staccato raps. His signature. He doesn't wait for a reply before poking his head through the doorway. "What the hell was all that screaming and shouting about?" He's wearing his dark, serious look. The one that usually spells trouble.

"Nothing for you to worry about," I lie.

"Uh-huh." He narrows his eyes at me. "I think we need to talk."

I sigh, nodding reluctantly. If he heard our shouting, he's probably got a good inkling of what's going on. I don't like concealing things from him, and I've kept this secret from my best bud a long time. Maybe it's time to lay it all on the line. I've probably wrecked my chances with Belle anyway, so even if he wants to kick my ass, it'll be short-lived once he realizes there's nothing to be pissed at me for.

"Have at it." I swing my chair around as he shuts the door and drops down on the bed.

"What's going on with you and Gabby?" He doesn't mince his words, and it's one of the qualities I've always admired in Ryan. If he's pissed, you know it immediately. He's not afraid to put it all out there.

I rub a hand across the back of my neck, wondering how to start this conversation.

"I'm not a fucking idiot," he adds. "You think I haven't noticed how you look at her?"

I sit up straighter in my chair. That surprises the hell out of me. Not just because I thought I'd been careful to guard my feelings when I'm around her, but more that he figured it out and hasn't said anything before now.

"Nothing is going on. I swear." And that's no word of a lie. Belle and I aren't anything. Not yet.

Ryan's having none of it. "Do you love her?" His expression is deadly serious, his eyes drilling into me.

I swallow over the lump in my throat, nodding. "Yeah, yeah, I love her."

"For how long?"

I shrug. It's not like I was keeping count. "Since I realized what that word truly meant."

"Does she know?"

I wince, scrubbing a hand over my stubbly jawline. "I might've accidentally blurted it out just now."

His look is one of surprised amusement. "Your timing sucks."

Air whooshes out of my mouth. "Tell me about it. I promised myself I'd wait, but it feels like I'm always fucking waiting."

"You know you're like a brother to me, and I'd do anything to see you happy, but I gotta speak my mind, and you're not who I'd pick for my little sister."

I had a feeling he might not like this, but to hear it spelled out so bluntly actually hurts. "Wow. Don't fucking sugarcoat it or anything."

"Dude, you've been around the block. A lot."

My hands clench at my side, and a muscle ticks in my jaw. "Only because I was doing everything to forget her. To try and find the same connection with any other girl, but it never happened. I didn't feel a thing for any of those girls. They were faceless, nameless fucks. Nothing more. Why the hell do you think I haven't been in a relationship since that one time in high school?"

He arches a brow. "Because of Gabby?" I nod. "Shit, dude. You've had these feelings for her for years?"

"Yeah, and I'm not kidding. I really love her. I've been done with screwing around for a while. You know that. That's not who I am."

"Aw, look, I know. I know you're solid." He sighs, and he has the decency to look a little ashamed. "But this is my sister."

"You think I don't know that? That I wouldn't take care of her the way she deserves to be cared for?"

"I know you would, but you don't have the best track record."

"Sex is just sex," I say. "I've never let myself get close to any girl. Feel any level of intimacy, because I..."

Fuck it. I don't think I can say it.

Ryan and I have had some deep and meaningful conversations from time to time, but it's not the norm. While he single-handedly got me through the aftermath of my mother's death, we don't tend to get into heavy shit when we're talking about women, and I'm not sure I can start now. Not when his sister is the object of my obsessive affection.

"Because you were saving that for Gabby," he astutely surmises. I nod, and he looks deep in thought. He leans forward on his elbows, propping his chin in his hands. "You know I always wondered if she'd actually end up with Dylan."

"You were probably the only one. To everyone else, it was a foregone conclusion."

"I didn't have any issue with him until recently, and I genuinely liked the guy. He's practically family, and he adored my sister and treated her well, but I didn't like how she changed sometimes when she was around him, and I wondered if they'd go the distance."

"Will anyone ever measure up for Gabby?" I toss it out there, still a little wounded over his earlier statement.

He eyeballs me intently. "Look, bruh. All I want is to see her happy. If that's with you, then I won't stand in your way. Hell, it'd be cool to think that someday we might officially be brothers." He grins. "But if you hurt her, I'll chop your balls off and feed them to the piranhas in my parents' fish tank."

"I would never hurt her. Never."

"I know you wouldn't mean to. Doesn't mean it won't happen. Relationships aren't easy, and you and me, buddy, are complete novices," he says, pointing between us.

"You and Myndi seem to be doing okay."

"Yeah, but I'm fucking clueless, and I've seen enough of relationships to know they're never plain sailing. Look at Dean and Annie. They are a fucking nightmare. Always arguing and blanking each other for days at a time. Even Caleb and Terri have had their ups and downs."

"But you had the best example growing up. Your parents are solid."

"Yeah." He looks at the floor.

"You really like Myndi, don't you?"

He nods, smiling. "I've never met anyone I wanted to tie myself to, until Myndi. I've turned into one of those dudes we used to joke about—pussy-whipped and proud." He grins wickedly. "That's the new me."

"Don't fuck it up."

"Right back at ya."

I lean back in the chair. "You're forgetting one very important thing. Belle and I aren't together."

"If it's meant to be, it'll happen."

I smirk. "Listen to you, getting all philosophical and shit."

He grins again. "I'm trying, dude. Wait till you see. My sister will have you wrapped around her little finger before long, and you'll even forget you've got a set of balls."

"I would gladly welcome the day," I honestly admit.

"Fuck! You're pussy-whipped already."

We have a good ole laugh at that. But then the laughter fades, and Ryan gets all serious again. "There's just one more thing I gotta say, and then I'll butt out. She's been through a lot lately. You know that. I think it'd do her good to be on her own for a while. You've had the whole college experience. She hasn't."

"You better not be saying what I think you're saying!" I grind my teeth to the molars.

"Knock that shit off, bruh. Of course not! But she needs to let loose. To find herself. I'm not sure getting into another serious relationship so soon is a good idea."

"You think I don't know that?" I claw a hand through my hair. "I told you I'm trying to be patient. My earlier slipup was just that. Besides, Belle should be the one to decide. Not you or me."

"Agreed, and I'll support her no matter what. But it goes for you too, man. You've been through hell this year, and your head still ain't right. Maybe it's not your time yet."

"I have considered that, but she ... she makes everything feel right. When she bought that tree..." I choke up and I have to pause for a breath. "Belle gets me. There's always been this connection between us even if I'm the only one who's felt it."

He slowly bobs his head. "When you know, you know."

I nod agreeably, and it's a profound moment. We're both quiet for a bit, and then his lips kick up. "Now I'm off to beat my chest and pound my woman, because all this pussy talk is threatening my manhood and scaring the shit outta me."

I grin, unable to resist pushing his buttons a little. "Lucky you. I guess I'll just have to beat one out in the shower and try not to imagine it's your sister on her—"

"I'll fucking knock your ass through that wall if you continue that sentence," he yells, only half-joking.

"I'd like to see you try." I flex my biceps on purpose.

"Is that a challenge?"

"You want it to be?"

He grabs hold of my shirt, pretending to go for it. "That's it. You.

Me. Outside now." He can't keep the grin off his face as he lets me go, slapping a hand over my back. I'm laughing, feeling lighter than I have in ages, grateful my best bud knows and that we're going to be okay. We're more than okay.

We're right back exactly where we started.

Chapter Twenty-Five
Gabby

I don't get much sleep after Slater leaves. My body and mind are all keyed up, and it's too difficult to switch off. I trace a finger along my lips, remembering the heat of his kisses. I slide a hand down over my belly, recalling how amazing it felt when he pressed up against me, thrusting his impressive hard-on into me, dry fucking me against the wall with no apology.

My hand slips under the band of my panties, and I touch myself, climaxing in seconds as images of Slater roll through my mind. I'd like to say it's brought welcome relief, but it's only a temporary release.

I want him.

I want his cock inside me, rocking me into oblivion.

I want him so badly I could scream.

But my thoughts aren't that simply packaged, because along with the intense longing is immense guilt and a healthy dose of confusion. He told me he loved me and then he bolted out of the room quicker than a horse bolting from the starting gate. Was it because the thought terrified him or he said something he felt could be misconstrued? And if it's true, how long has he felt like this? And is it the same as what I'm feeling? I know I'm attracted to him, and I know I have feelings for him too, but I can't figure it out. And why the hell does it feel like I'm betraying Dylan by even thinking these thoughts?

Ugh. I bury my head in the pillow, groaning. I'm going to give myself a headache going over and over it.

After a couple hours tossing and turning, I get up. It's early morning anyway, and I might as well get moving. I decide to take the bus home, rather than waiting for Ryan to surface.

Mom and Dad are in the sunroom reading the papers when I arrive at the house.

"You're very early, Buttercup," Dad says, getting up and enveloping me in his arms.

"I couldn't sleep so I took the bus."

"You look tired," Mom says, pulling me out of Dad's embrace and wrapping her arms around me. "Why don't you go upstairs and try to get some sleep?"

"Nah. I'm up now. I think I'll just hang out here with you and read."

We spend a pleasant few hours in silence, reading and drinking copious coffees. It's peaceful and relaxing and just what the doctor ordered.

I get up to help Mom prepare dinner just after midday. We work efficiently and quietly, side by side, until she decides to test the waters. "Do you want to tell me what's on your mind?" she asks, looking over at me briefly while chopping the carrots.

"Who says I've got something on my mind?"

"You show up here exhausted, with a frown on your face, and you looked up from your Kindle every five minutes staring off into space. I'm betting you can't even tell me what that book is about."

She's right. I can't. The words just floated in one ear and out the other. My brain refused to switch off, going around and around in circles. "I hate that I'm like an open book, pardon the pun."

Mom puts the knife down and turns to me. "That's one of my favorite things about you. And you know a problem shared—"

"Is a problem halved." I roll my eyes as my lips tug up of their own accord. "We need to find you some new clichés."

She laughs, pinning my hair behind my ear. "Why look for new ones when the old ones are absolutely perfect as they are."

"Slate kissed me!" I blurt, bursting with the need to tell someone.

"Ah." She smiles. "And how was it?"

I blush a little. "It was … epic. The best kiss of my life."

"I wondered how long it would take him to reveal himself."

I put my knife down and stare at her with wide eyes. "What?" I splutter.

"Slater has never said one word to me, but I guessed a long time ago that he was in love with you. His eyes follow you when he thinks no one is looking, and he's always the first to offer to help if you need anything. That boy would walk over hot coals for you. I'd bet money on it." She smiles nostalgically. "It was the night of junior prom when I first noticed. He couldn't take his eyes off you."

"I didn't notice."

"You only had eyes for Dylan," Mom softly replies.

Guilt jumps up and slaps me. "I feel like I've betrayed him," I whisper. "Which is stupid because he's the one who betrayed me."

"Your feelings are never stupid, honey. And you can't force yourself to feel a certain way. You're loyal through and through, so I'm not surprised to hear you feel like that, but at least you can acknowledge it."

"I'm not sure it helps."

"You just need time to let those wounds heal. You gave years of your life to Dylan. He's not someone you can get over in a few short weeks."

"You should have been a psychologist," I admit truthfully. "I always feel better after I talk with you."

She pulls me into a hug. "That's what mothers are for."

"I definitely lucked out in the Mom department." I kiss her cheek. "I love you."

She hugs me tighter before pressing a kiss to my forehead. "It's easy to be your mother, Gabby. You make it so easy to love you." She pats my back and lets me go. "Let's continue working while we talk," Mom says, picking up her knife again. "Or I won't have dinner ready by the time Ryan, Slater, and Myndi arrive."

My heart thuds behind my rib cage in a mix of exhilaration and fear. "You didn't tell me he was coming for dinner!"

She chuckles. "Gabby, relax." She rubs a hand around my back in a soothing gesture. "When Ryan said he was coming home today, I told him to ask Slater and Myndi. It won't be any different from the thousands of other times he's joined us for Sunday lunch."

Eh, yeah, it will. Because this is the first time I'll be remembering how good it feels to touch him and how hot his kisses make me. And let's not even mention how I got myself off in record time this morning just thinking of him doing naughty things to my body. A warmth spreads up over my chest, creeping onto my neck.

Mom tilts her head to the side, eyeing me with new curiosity. "I don't want any details, but did this kiss lead to other things?"

My cheeks flare up. I'm comfortable talking with Mom about most things. Except details of my sex life. I draw the line at that. "No! It wasn't like that," I lie, because it most definitely was heading in that direction until he put a stop to it.

"Well, then there's nothing to worry about. This is Slater. Everything will be fine."

"I don't know about that. He kissed me, blurted out that he loved me, and then bolted out the door. I have no idea what's going on in his head or what he's really thinking."

"Oh, honey, don't waste your time trying to figure out the inner workings of the male brain. You'll just give yourself a headache."

I burst out laughing. "So that's how you and Dad have managed to last this long," I tease.

"That's one of my many insights," she jokes, wiggling her brows. "Just hit me up any time you want more tips," she quips, nudging my hip.

We put the potatoes and carrots into pots and put the meat in the oven. Then we grab some coffee and sit down at the table. "So, I know how Slater feels about you, but how do you feel about him?" she inquires, sipping from her cup.

"I'm not sure." I worry my lip between my teeth. "I mean, there's definitely an attraction, and we already have a close friendship. My feelings toward him are stronger than I realized, but I can't put a name to it. And my head is still a mess over Dylan. I'm not really sure what I want."

"That's all completely understandable. Have you told Slater any of this?"

I shake my head. "I didn't see him before I left."

"Well, if you want my advice, you should tell him what you just told me. Clear the air so there's no awkwardness, and let him know where he stands so he doesn't get hurt. That boy has been through a lot this year."

"I know, Mom, and I don't want to do anything to hurt him or jeopardize our friendship."

She stands, messing up the top of my hair. "Talk to him, and everything will work out the way it's meant to."

I'm half-expecting Slater to be a no-show, so I'm a little surprised when he rocks up to the house with Ryan and Myndi a couple hours later. I hug Ryan and Myndi but deliberately hang back with Slater, unsure of myself and where I stand with him.

"Hi, Belle." His smile is borderline shy as he shoves his hands in his pockets, rocking back on his heels.

"Hi, Slate." My voice is more high-pitched than usual, and I'm sure everyone can detect the anxiety in my tone. My palms are sweaty, and I discreetly rub them down the front of my jeans, all the while my heart is jackhammering in my chest. It's been years since I've felt this antsy and excited around a boy.

"Myndi, go say hi to Paul while Ryan helps me set the table," Mom suggests, steering them out of the room while subtly winking in my direction.

I pull on my big girl's panties and plaster a smile on my face as I look at Slater. "We need to talk." We both speak the same words at the same time, cracking up at the awkwardness of the moment, but it helps to ease the tension.

"Do you want to sit on the front porch? It's probably our only chance at privacy."

"Sure."

I'm conscious of his attentive gaze watching my every step as we walk through the house and out the front door. I sit down on the love seat, folding my hands in my lap.

He sits alongside me, careful to keep a little room between our bodies. I can't decide if I'm relieved or disappointed.

He reaches out, taking my hands in his. "I'm sorry for running out on you last night like that."

"It's okay. You don't need to explain."

"I think I do." His voice is softer, and I tip my chin up, staring into his handsome, earnest face.

"Did you mean it?"

"Yes." He peers deep into my eyes. "I do love you although I had no intention of telling you that yet."

"Why?" I can guess, but I'd rather hear him say it.

"You're not ready, Belle." He reaches up, stroking my cheek.

"I feel something for you too, but I'm not sure what," I admit honestly.

His eyes sparkle, and his mouth pulls into a smile. "That's completely okay, and I don't mind being patient while you work things out in your head."

"I'm sorry for how I've been treating you. I'm a bit of a hot mess right now, and I know I've been acting crazy and irrationally, but sometimes, I wonder if I even know who I am anymore."

"You don't need to apologize. I know how much Dylan hurt you. I have murderous thoughts about the guy most nights, so I can only imagine the kind of turmoil you're in, but don't doubt yourself, Belle. You're the same sweet, fun-loving girl you've always been. You don't need Dylan to confirm that. You're still you, Belle. Never question that."

"Why haven't I seen how utterly amazing you are?" I ask the question out loud even though it's more of an internal one. "I mean, I've always known you were amazing but not in this way."

"Dylan was your whole world."

"Yes, he was."

"Which is another reason why I can wait." His eyes are completely serious as they bore into mine. He lowers his tone a little. "I don't want to be your rebound guy." He pauses momentarily. "I want to be your forever guy."

Tears prick my eyes. "You really mean that." It's more of a statement than a question because I see the conviction on his face and hear it resonating in his words.

"I've loved you for a long time, Belle. I wanted to believe our time would come, but, to be honest, I never really believed it would. I thought I'd missed my chance."

My eyes probe his, and I grip his hand more tightly. "I'm not sure how to respond to that," I whisper.

His thumb starts tracing little circles on the back of my hand. "That's okay. You don't need to say anything now. I've learned how to be patient. I can be patient a while longer." His eyes twinkle with mirth. "Although, after last night, I think I've realized my patience has its limits."

My cheeks heat, and he chuckles. "Last night was hot." I grin. "Kissing you was ... wow."

"Just wow?" he inquires with an arrogant swagger, palming one side of my face.

"What, you want a medal?"

He shoots me a lopsided grin. "A gold one would be nice."

"Dude, I can't lie, as much as I want to tease you about it. If I'm dishing out medals, only platinum will do. You totally owned that kiss."

He throws back his head, laughing, before pinning me with a heated stare. "God, I really want to kiss the shit out of you right now."

I quirk a brow. "Ahem, Mr. 'I have patience.'"

He sighs. "I know, you just make it so hard to resist. I don't know if you realize exactly how beautiful you are. Your heart, mind, and soul are every bit as beautiful as your gorgeous exterior, and I've spent years trying to resist temptation."

I'm not sure what expression he sees on my face, but it's enough to make him backtrack. I guess my shock and confusion is transparent, considering I'm an open book and all, and that helps rein him in.

"But I mean what I say. You're one of my best friends, and I don't want that to change even if nothing ever happens between us. No matter what, your friendship is so important to me."

"I'm glad you feel like that, because your friendship means the world to me too." Briefly, I press my lips to his. "And I'm excited about the possibilities for us in the future, but I need to get my head on straight first. I don't want to hurt you or mess anything up."

He lifts my hand to his mouth, planting a soft kiss on my skin. "I'm glad we're on the same page, and I'm really glad we had this conversation. I don't want anything to be awkward for us or any of the others."

"Which is why we should also keep this to ourselves for now."

His eyes scrunch up and he purses his lips. "It might be a little late for that."

"Ah, crap. You told Ryan, didn't you?" I sit up straighter as a thought occurs to me. "Or has he always known?"

He shakes his head. "No. The only person who knew about my feelings for you was my mom." Both our expressions turn sad. "She gave us her blessing," he whispers, and my heart thumps frantically. "But we don't have to talk about that now," he quickly adds, no doubt spotting the abject terror on my face. "Ryan heard us arguing last night and put me on the spot. I had to tell him, but he'd pretty much figured it out for himself."

"I hope he wasn't mad at you, because if he said anything mean, I'm going in there now to kick him in the junk."

Laughter rumbles through his chest. "No, my little ninja. No junk-kicking is required. He was actually cool about it although he did promise to feed my balls to the piranhas if I hurt you."

I wince. "Ouch. He doesn't mess around." My parents' obsession with their red-bellied piranhas is so weird. They look innocuous floating in the tank until they open their mouths, snapping their jagged teeth. As a kid, they used to give me nightmares, but I never told my parents because I knew they would've gotten rid of the tank, and I didn't want to take that away from them.

"When it comes to you, Ryan never has."

"I know. He's amazing, just don't tell him I said that!"

"Don't worry. That dude's ego is big enough without me adding to it." He touches my cheek, ensuring I have his full attention. "You know I would never intentionally hurt you, Belle."

"Of course."

"But you're not the only one who's a bit of a mess right now, and I don't want to start anything with you until I know I can be the man you deserve. I don't want to push you into something you're not ready for and then let you down."

"You could never let me down, Slate." I thread my fingers through his hair. "That's a virtual impossibility."

Mom calls us from inside the house, and we stand. "I'd like to think that's true, but I don't want to take any chances with you." He pulls me into a tentative hug. "Because you mean everything to me, Gabby. Absolutely everything."

"I want you to become everything to me too." It's the most sincere response I can give him.

"I can wait for that."

I look up at him, still wrapped around him. "So, how do we do this?"

"Let's hang out as friends, like we always do, and just see what happens."

I nod, even as I wonder how I'm going to keep my hands off him now I know how amazing it is to be kissed and touched by him. "I'm down with that plan." I stretch up on tiptoes, planting a light kiss on his cheek. "Thank you, Slate. For always looking after me when I don't even know how to do that myself sometimes."

Chapter Twenty-Six

I sleep soundly that night for the first time in weeks, and as I step foot on campus Monday morning, there's a new spring in my step. The week flies by in a hive of activity. Things are relaxed between Slater and me although I can't pretend that things are exactly back to normal. Every opportunity we get, we're sharing sly looks and smiles, and our usual bantering has elevated a few notches to full-on flirting. But without the pressure of expectation or any feelings of guilt, it's amazingly blissful, and I'm practically floating around the place on a cloud.

I cleared things up with Austin too, telling him Slater and I have feelings for one another but we're taking things real slow. He was cool about the whole thing, and even Ryan wasn't too concerned when we had a little heart to heart. Dylan hasn't come near me, and the couple of times I've bumped into him around campus, we've both pretended not to see the other. While it hurts, it doesn't hurt as much as it used to.

So, life is good, and for the first time in weeks, I'm smiling again.

Mom and Dad are gone away for a romantic weekend so Ryan,

Myndi, Slater, and I decide to forgo heading home on Sunday, agreeing to spend the day together.

Slater drives us to the nearest state park for a hike. It's only a forty-minute journey, but I nod off with the swaying motion of the car, and it's not long before he's swinging into the parking lot and killing the engine.

I'm yawning as I slip out of the back seat. "You should've said you were tired, and we could have set out later," Slater says, helping me into my jacket.

"I'm fine. I think all these late shifts are just finally catching up to me."

"I can always ask Donny to schedule you off earlier. You don't have to stay till closing every shift, but you might have to change nights. At least you could avoid Shelby that way."

"I'm not running away from that psycho bitch," I hiss. "I can handle her."

"Didn't quite look like that last night," he says, removing the bags and locking the SUV.

"The only reason I didn't retaliate when she deliberately knocked into me was because I have some class, and I'm a professional, even if it was embarrassing to be cleaning up another tray of ruined drinks so soon after the last one."

Myndi loops her arm through Ryan's, and they set out with us following on their heels.

"I'm sorry she's being a bitch," he says, pulling a beanie over his head. My inner tigress rears her head, and saliva pools in my mouth. Slater looks fucking hot in that hat, and I'm thinking all manner of forbidden thoughts, but I force them aside, because we've agreed to tread carefully, and I don't think jumping his bones less than a week after making a deal conveys a willingness to take it slow.

"Don't apologize for something you aren't responsible for. It's not your fault she's a complete psycho."

"I don't know why Donny keeps her around. She's a shitty waitress, and no one likes her."

226

I nudge him in the ribs. "Don't pretend like you don't know. She's told everyone she's banging him."

We head out on one of the shorter routes, quickly building a steady pace.

"Except I don't think she is," Slater replies. "I think it was just a one-time thing and she's using it to keep everyone in line. She knows no one will complain about her if they think she has Donny wrapped around her little finger." He rubs his hands together, blowing on them. "Fuck, it's cold."

It *is* pretty cold today so we've all wrapped up accordingly, bringing our rainproof jackets incase the heavens open. "If the world is cold, make it your business to build fires," we both say in unison, repeating one of Mom's favorite phrases, breaking out laughing at the fact that we've gone there again.

"Sad." Ryan turns around in front of us, shaking his head. He's wearing a faux solemn expression. "So sad."

"I think it's cute," Myndi, says smiling at me.

I flip them both the middle finger. "And that's what I think. Move on. Nothing to see here, folks."

Myndi giggles, snuggling in to Ryan's side, and I have a fleeting urge to do the same with Slater. The thought takes me aback, so I ignore it. We continue walking, chatting casually as a group. Myndi and I packed a picnic, which the guys currently have safely secured in their backpacks, and I'm scouting the area for an ideal spot to stop. I'm suddenly ravenous and in desperate need of a drink. Slater removes two bottles of water from his bag, handing one to me. I stare at him like he just hung the moon. "How did you know I was thirsty?"

"It might have something to do with the fact your tongue is lolling out the side of your mouth like a dog in heat," my brother supplies.

"If anyone resembles a dog in heat, it's you, brother dearest. If you don't stop pawing at my best friend, I might have to resort to drastic measures. Like binding your balls or shoving your dick in a blender."

Both guys wince.

"Don't even fucking joke about something like that, Tornado." Ryan shudders, and I laugh.

"Pussies!" I snicker.

"Watch your language, Gabrielle." My brother does an amazing impression of Mom.

"Watch your wandering hands, Randy Ryan," I retort, eyeballing his palm which is currently manhandling my friend's pert derriere.

"My girlfriend is sexy as hell." He shrugs, sending me a smug look. "It's hardly my fault if I can't keep my hands off her."

I roll my eyes, and we press on ahead. The paths are gravelly, and I'm glad I wore my hiking boots. Every time, I slip up, Slater is by my side, helping to steady me. After a while, he decides it's safest to hold my hand, and I don't mount any protest. His hand is warm and solid in mine, fitting perfectly.

I've worked up a sweat, and I unzip my jacket to cool off as we decide to stop at an empty picnic area. The tables are sheltered under a blanket of trees which helps offset the light drizzle now falling from the sky.

Myndi and I unpack the sandwiches, wraps, fruit, and cookies we brought, and we all dig in.

"This reminds me of the time we all went hiking at Cape Henlopen, remember?"

"The time dufus here fell off his bike and broke his leg?" Slater says, nudging Ryan.

"Yay, what a happy memory to bring up," Ryan deadpans.

"It is a happy memory up to that point. We stayed in those cabins for the weekend, and we went swimming, and biking, and fishing, and Mom made peanut butter and jelly sandwiches too."

"You have some memory, Gabby," Ryan says. "I barely remember what I ate yesterday, let alone on a weekend trip six years ago."

"It's weird what things trigger memories," I muse. "Or the minor details that imprint in one's mind."

"You wore a pink ribbon in your hair that weekend," Slater

quietly says, tugging on the end of my ponytail. "The color was almost identical to these pink strands in your hair."

I turn to face him, as Ryan splutters, "Dude, you have it so bad."

"I don't even remember that," I admit, smiling shyly at him.

"You'd just gotten those pink acid denim Vans, and you wouldn't take them off even to sleep." He chuckles. "Remember, your Mom tried to untie them when you were asleep, and you woke up and gave her hell!"

I reach under the table and give Slater's hand a gentle squeeze.

"Oh shit!" Ryan laughs. "I totally remember that."

"Unfortunately, I remember it too." I shake my head. "I had zero style if I thought those sneakers were cool."

"I had a pair too," Myndi says, "and I remember sleeping with them on my pillow for a week."

"Girls." Ryan rolls his eyes.

"Hey, be nice." Myndi elbows him in the ribs. "Unless you're planning on sleeping alone tonight."

I gather up the empty wrappers, hurrying to the trash can before I hear something I don't want to hear. Slater comes up behind me with the rest of the trash. He leans in close to my ear. "You were the prettiest girl I'd ever seen with that ribbon in your hair. I watched how the wind blew little strands of your hair across your face as we cycled, and I remember feeling jealous, because they got to be close to you and I couldn't."

I turn around and look up at him, conscious of how close we're standing together. "You were thinking those thoughts even then?"

He chases a few stray strands of my hair, tucking them back into my ponytail. "I think I've always had those thoughts of you, Belle, but I never properly understood what they meant." His eyes bore into mine, and I could easily drown in the seductive, chocolatey depths. I've never noticed before, but Slater has impossibly long lashes for a guy. They are thick and dark, and they frame his beautiful eyes perfectly. Electricity ripples in the air, and my body is already responding to him. It's as if once I opened my mind and my heart to the possibility of an us that the floodgates have opened, and I'm over-whelmed with all these wonderful new sensations whenever I'm around him.

It's an exhilarating feeling—falling and soaring at the same time.

Planting my hands lightly on his chest, I clear my throat, working hard to keep my voice from shaking. "If you keep this up, I'll be the one breaching those patience limits you've set."

"You're making me feel so many things, Belle."

"I know. I'm feeling it too."

His answering smile is dazzling. "I have wished for this for so long I'm almost afraid to open my eyes every morning in case I'm dreaming."

I place my hand on his cheek. "Feel that?" I whisper. "It's real."

"Ahem." My brother clears his throat, pinning us with a knowing look. Myndi swats the back of Ryan's head, cursing under her breath. "We should continue before the rain starts coming down in buckets."

The moment is gone, and we smile at one another as we resume walking. This time, Slater takes my hand immediately, and he doesn't let go until we're back at the car.

I nod off again on the journey home, feeling tuckered out after the five-mile trek in the brisk air.

"Thank you for taking us," Myndi tells him when we arrive back at the house. I'm rubbing sleep from my eyes as I climb out of the car, yawning.

"You're welcome. It was fun." His eyes flit to mine. "We should definitely do it again."

Ryan opens the front door, and Myndi follows him inside the house. I place my hand on Slater's arm, stalling him. I wet my dry lips. "You wore your beloved Converse, a pair of skinny jeans, and a gray and red Hollister sweater that trip. You freaked out when your new Nike ballcap blew off your head during the bike ride, and you jumped off, racing down the path after it."

I smile as the memory replays in my mind. "You knew your mom had saved up to buy it, and you were terrified of going home and telling her you lost it, so you made sure you didn't. You also slipped me an additional cookie under the table when no one was looking, and I know it was you who left that shell from the beach by my bedside table."

Slater's mouth is hanging open, and he looks like he's seen a ghost.

I stretch up on tiptoe and whisper in his ear. "It seems you weren't the only one thinking those kind of thoughts back then. You weren't the only one struggling to understand what they meant."

When it comes to Slater, I'm remembering a whole host of things I had forgotten. Or maybe I deliberately pushed them away, because I was falling for Dylan at the same time.

I rock back on my heels, and my voice comes out loud and strong. "I might not have understood it back then, but I'm beginning to now." I rub my thumb across his lips. "I don't think what I'm feeling now is something new." I peer into his eyes. "I think I'm resurrecting feelings I buried because I either didn't want to or couldn't work out what they meant when I was only a kid."

I press my mouth to his briefly, pulling back before it develops. "But I'm not a kid anymore, and I'm beginning to get a clearer picture." I can't keep the smile off my face as I take in his awestruck expression. "Prepare yourself, Slater Evans, because I think a tornado's about to blow into your life and tilt your world upside down."

Chapter Twenty-Seven

I get up earlier than usual the next morning, deciding to cook Mom's infamous blueberry muffins before I go to class. Slater and Ryan are just returning from a run as I'm preparing to leave the house. Ryan's nostrils twitch. "Is that what I think it is?" He sniffs the air.

I pinch the sides of my nose as I speak, trying not to gag over the sweaty stench clogging my lungs. "Yup! I made blueberry muffins. They're cooling on a rack in the kitchen."

Ryan smacks a slobbery kiss on my cheek. "Inviting you to live here was a genius idea."

I push him away. "Ugh, you need to get your stinky ass in the shower, quick smart."

He chuckles, sidestepping me and making his way toward the kitchen.

"See you later." I toss a quick wave at Slater as I dart outside the door before I hurl.

After classes end for the day, I attend yoga in Lil Bob with Myndi, stopping to register for guitar lessons on the spur of the moment when I spot the small sign on the bulletin board. I stay late at the library the following night, completing an assignment that's due on Friday, and I work an extra shift at the club Wednesday night, so I don't see much of my housemates until Thursday night when I end up cooking dinner for everyone with Slater.

Slater's a fantastic cook, and Janine taught him all her recipes. He makes her magical meatloaf while I bake cobbler for dessert. We work well together, and there's no shortage of flirty looks and witty banter exchanged.

"Dinner's up!" I holler from the kitchen, and Austin, Myndi, and Ryan come bounding into the room.

"Oh my God. This meatloaf is orgasmic!" Myndi exclaims, moaning over a mouthful of the sumptuous baked dish.

"If you keep that moaning up, the meatloaf won't be the only orgasmic thing in this room," Ryan teases.

I throw a bread roll at his head. "That's disgusting. We're trying to eat."

"Just keeping it real, Tornado."

Austin looks up from his cell, his eyes catching mine. "A few of us are going to the new *Fast and Furious* movie tonight. You want to come?"

I'm pretty sure he means all of us, but the fact he was looking directly at me when he posed the question has Slater growling and shooting him menacing looks.

Austin cracks up laughing. "Man, you are so easy to wind up. I mean all of us, asshat." He thumps him in the arm. Pressing his mouth to my ear, he smirks at Slater as he whispers, "He so needs to get laid. Do the guy a favor and help him out."

Now it's my turn to whack *him* in the arm.

Slater's eyes narrow to slits as he glares at Austin, but Austin just cracks up laughing again.

"I think a movie sounds great," I cut in, defusing the situation before the guys end up in a fist fight or wrestling around on the floor. "I love the *Fast and Furious* franchise, but I really miss Paul Walker. It's just not the same without him."

"Gabby had this massive crush on Paul Walker when she was like twelve or thirteen," Ryan explains for Austin and Myndi's benefit.

"Oh, girl," Myndi says, looking wistful. "I'm with you. He was so talented and so dreamy. It was unbelievably sad when he died. I don't mind admitting I cried."

"I can't watch *Fast and Furious Seven* without crying," I admit, "especially at the end with that Wiz Khalifa song."

"Oh, gosh, yes!" Myndi agrees, nodding. "I cry every time "See you Again" comes on the radio."

"Don't worry, Gabby," Austin says with a mischievous twinkle in his eyes. "I'll be right there if you need a shoulder to cry on."

"Dude, you are just begging for a fist in the face." Ryan smirks.

Slater gets up, cool as you like, pressing his hands down on Austin's shoulders. "If Belle is crying on anyone's shoulder, it'll be mine."

The possessive quality to his tone would have feminist groups up in arms, but it makes my heart sing in a way it hasn't for a long time. "Damn straight," I say, grinning at him like an idiot.

He pulls me up from my chair, bundling me into his arms, and I go willingly. Resting my head on his chest, I close my eyes, inhaling his scent and his warmth and the safety his arms bring. He presses a kiss atop my head while holding me close. The others quietly clear the table around us, but we don't budge position, continuing to hold one another close. If I could, I would stay locked in his arms forever.

Slater and I are spending more and more time together, and we're settling into an easygoing routine. We both work Friday and Saturday night at the club. I was expecting it to be a lot quieter because of the approaching holiday, and the fact plenty of students have already gone home for Thanksgiving break, but it's actually crazy busy, and we're both exhausted by the time Sunday rolls around.

Myndi and Ryan are visiting her parents for a few days, so we spend Sunday lounging about the house in our pajamas, stuffing our faces with chips and pizza while we watch back-to-back movies on the couch lying beside one another.

Slater is constantly touching me—running his hands up and down my arms, threading his fingers through my hair, or brushing his lips against my cheek. I snuggle against him with my back to his front, siphoning his warmth and his comfort, and it's the most relaxed I've been in weeks.

We don't kiss or touch intimately although we continue to share heated looks, and I'm starting to question why we're holding back when it's obvious we both want to go there.

Slater drives us home to Lewes Tuesday lunchtime. Although Mom has invited him to stay at our house, he's decided to go to his own place. "Are you sure you don't want to stay here?" I inquire one final time as I stand on the front porch of my house.

"Yeah." He scrubs a hand over his chin. "I think it's time I finally cleared out Mom's closet."

"You want some help?"

His face brightens. "Would you?"

I nod. "Of course, but if it's something you want to do alone, that's completely fine too."

He props his butt against the railing, crossing his feet at the ankles. "I'm dreading it, to be honest, but I can't put it off any longer. She's been gone eight months. It's time." Reaching out, he twirls a lock of my hair around his finger. "I'd love some help. Thank you."

I cup one side of his face, wanting to kiss him so badly, but I don't want to cross the boundaries we've set either. "Let me spend a couple of hours with the oldies, and then I'll come over."

"I'll come back for you. It'll be dark by then, and I don't want you walking by yourself."

Just then, my brother Dean's car pulls up to the curb, and he gets out, opening the back door to unbuckle the girls from their car seats. "Hey, Dean." I skip down the steps, walking toward my brother.

"Ga-bee!!" Mia shrieks, bouncing in her chair when she spots me.

Dean pulls me into a one-armed hug. "Hey, sis." His voice lacks his usual enthusiasm.

"Any chance you could drop me over to Slate's later?" I ask while removing Mia from her seat. She wraps her little arms around my neck, and her legs go around my waist. I snuggle her close, peppering her face with tons of tiny kisses. She giggles and squirms in my arms.

"No problem." He bumps his fist against Slater's. "Hey, man. What's up?"

"Nothing much."

Tia crawls out of the car, making a beeline for Slater. She tugs on his leg. "Up! Up!" she demands with her arms raised.

Slater chuckles, grabbing her up and onto his shoulders. She squeals, and Mia starts wriggling in my arms again. "Me wanna do that, Auntie Gabby!"

Dean swoops into action, taking his daughter and planting her squarely on his shoulders. "Let's leave the heavy lifting to the men."

He winks at me, but I'm not amused. I have a string of choice words ready on the tip of my tongue, but I hold back, purely because my nieces don't need to be privy to such cussing. "Your daughters are your only saving grace right now, Dean James, but if I hear such a sexist remark coming out of your mouth again, I will not be responsible for my actions."

"Christ. Now you sound like Annie!" he snaps. "It was only a Goddamned joke, or have you lost your sense of humor too?" He storms off up the path without waiting for my reply.

"Sh—Sugar," I quickly recover, looking at Slater. "Someone's in a foul mood."

"Yeah," he agrees, keeping a firm hold on Tia's legs as she bounces around on his shoulders. "And that's unusual for Dean."

Slater is right. Dean is usually laid-back and nonconfrontational, so I wonder exactly what's eating my brother.

Slater leaves after depositing Tia in the kitchen and saying a quick hello to my parents. I spend a couple hours playing dolls and jigsaws with the girls before Dean announces it's time to leave. He

237

has spent the best part of his visit holed up with Mom in the kitchen, but he doesn't look any less troubled as we walk the girls outside. I strap Mia in her seat while he secures Tia, and then I plonk my butt in the passenger seat. "Thanks for the ride," I say, as he glides out onto the road.

"It's on the way so it's no biggie." He clears his throat, looking briefly at me. "I'm sorry for snapping at you earlier. I'm not in the best mood, and I didn't mean to take it out on you."

"It's fine, and I've already forgotten it." I glance at my big brother, noticing the fine lines crinkling the corners of his eyes and the down-turn of his mouth. "If there's anything I can help with, you know you only need to ask."

He pats my hand. "Thanks, Gabby, but I don't want to burden you with my problems." He subtly motions at the girls. "And I can't talk with little ears."

"I understand, but just know I'm here for you if you need me."

He pulls up in front of Slater's house, killing the engine. "I really appreciate that." He kisses me on the cheek. "I'm proud of you, little sis."

I arch a brow. "You are?"

"Yeah." He nods. "I admire how you've dealt with your breakup. I know it can't be easy, but you're just getting on with it."

I shrug. "I'm learning that life doesn't always follow a set plan, and no one else is going to forge a new path for me. I miss Dylan, I really do, but he made his choice, and I've got to accept that. I could sit here and wallow in my grief, blame him for eternity, or criticize myself for all the things I could've done differently, but I'd rather learn from it and move forward. Letting it destroy me would all be on me, not him. It's up to me to choose how I react to the curveball thrown at me."

He breaks into a smile. "You sound so like Mom, and I'm even prouder now."

"Are you going to be okay?" I inquire, because I'm worried about my brother. Anyone can see he's carrying the weight of the world on his shoulders, and he's obviously stressed. If I had to guess, I'd say things aren't going so well with him and Annie. I hope I'm wrong. I really do, but the last few times I've been around them, the tension has been off the charts.

He sighs, looking out the window. "I hope so."

The door to Slater's house opens, and he's standing on the small porch, waving. The girls jump up and down in the back, pleading with Dean to let them go inside.

"That's my cue to leave." I kiss his cheek. "Call me anytime. I'm free to babysit while I'm home if you and Annie need some time to yourselves."

"Actually, that might not be a bad idea." He looks reflective. "I'll text you."

I blow kisses to the girls and get out of the car.

"Is everything okay?" Slater asks when I reach the porch.

"Something's going on with Dean, and I'm concerned."

He ushers me inside, helping to take my coat off. "I'm sorry to hear that. Problems with Annie?"

"He hasn't said, but I think so."

"Hopefully they'll work it out." He shoos me into the living room. A blast of heat blankets me the second I step foot in the room. A roaring fire blazes in the hearth, adding to the homey vibes. "You didn't eat, right?" he asks, starting to back out of the room.

"No." Not since I demolished half the leftover chicken potpie for lunch, but that was a few hours ago.

"I made burritos and I thought we could eat in here. The house is still warming up, and this is the coziest room."

"You didn't have to do that, but thanks. That sounds perfect."

We watch TV as we eat, chatting comfortably like we've done hundreds of times in this very room, and I realize how naturally relaxed I am in Slater's company. He knows me so well, and vice versa, and being with each other like this is as easy as breathing. But that simmering electricity is there in the background, humming and purring, and it's getting harder and harder to deny how I feel around him. To ignore how hard my heart beats when he smiles at me. To avoid staring at those cute little dimples in his cheeks when he laughs. To forgo the urge to grab hold of his rippling biceps and explore every inch of his magnificent body. To refuse the almost overwhelming need to crush my lips to his.

Considering I've never looked at Slater as anything but a friend—until recently—I'd expected to feel awkward knowing he's secretly harbored feelings for me while I've been trying to figure out exactly how my feelings toward him have changed. But it's not awkward in the slightest.

Perhaps it's testament to the strength of our friendship. Or the potency of the attraction between us. But imagining Slater as something more than just a friend seems like a natural extension of our relationship, and it's not uncomfortable. Like, at all, and that realization has shocked me. If anything, I'm eager to experience a different side of Slater.

Over the next couple hours, we go through Janine's closet, folding up clothes for the local charity place and boxing up some of her personal possessions that Slater wants to keep. It's not as sad as I thought it'd be, and we exchange stories about his mom into the early hours.

Slater insists on driving me home when he spots me yawning, and a little part of me is disappointed he didn't ask me to stay, but I don't voice it.

He's told me he wants to take things slow, and I agreed.

But as I crawl into bed, my body craving his touch, I wonder why the hell we're waiting.

Chapter Twenty-Eight

The following day, I join Mom and a couple of her friends for lunch, and we bump into Heather, Dylan's mom, on our way out of the café. I haven't seen her since Dylan and I broke up although I had thought of phoning her but ultimately decided it was just best to leave it. She pulls me into a warm hug. "Gabby, it's so good to see you." She kisses me on the cheek before exchanging greetings with Mom. "You too, Lucy."

"We'll miss you tomorrow," Mom tells her with raw honesty. Dylan and Heather have come to Thanksgiving at our house every year for the past seven years, so tomorrow will be a new first.

"We'll miss you too." She clasps hold of my hand. "I don't know exactly what happened between you and Dylan, and I've picked up the phone to call you a million times, but I didn't want you to feel I was interfering." She pauses, composing her words. "My son's an idiot." Her firm tone takes me by surprise, along with her words. Heather idolizes Dylan, and they have such a close relationship. "And Bianca won't last. I've only met her once, but I can see she's all wrong for Dylan."

Her words burn a hole in my chest, and I hate that I still care.

So much for my fighting talk yesterday.

It's just I've seen Dylan around campus with different girls, and I assumed Bianca was no longer on the scene. If he's brought her to meet his mother, it's more serious than I thought. I'm shallow enough to admit it hurts that he's picked someone like her over me. It's the ultimate slap in the face. But I don't want Heather to know that, so I plaster a fake smile on my face. "It's not any of my business anymore, and I wish Dylan well. He's free to date whomever he wants."

She bites down on her lip, looking a little unsure. "I don't like who he is when she's around, and I know she's just a flash in the pan." She squeezes my hand. "I don't think you should give up on him. He'll come to his senses."

"No offense, Heather, but I won't be a consolation prize or some weak girl who lets a guy walk all over her." I'm not sure if she's aware her son cheated on me behind my back, and I'm not going to be the one to tell her, so I'm skirting around the issue. "I wish things had turned out differently, but they didn't, and there's no going back. At least not for me."

A look of utter sadness ghosts over her face. "I'm sorry. It wasn't fair to put that on you, and you're right to be strong, because you're a wonderful girl, and you deserve to be treated with the utmost respect. I just hate that my son has let the best thing that's ever happened to him walk out of his life." She shakes her head. "I don't understand it."

"If things are meant to be, they'll find a way back to one another," Mom cuts in, looping her arm through mine and starting to steer me away.

"It was good seeing you, Heather. Happy Thanksgiving." Mom guides me to the parking lot as we both wave, and I'm grateful she intervened. That was more difficult than I envisioned it would be.

It's only as we're in the car on the ride home that I realize I should've mentioned my concerns about Dylan's health, but I was too busy trying to get away from her to remember that niggling voice that still loiters in the back of my mind.

Slater comes babysitting with me that night. Annie is decidedly frosty as she lists out a ream of instructions. You'd swear I never babysat my nieces before, but I smile agreeably while subtly digging my nails into my thighs.

"Wow, she's so fucking uptight," Slater admits in a whisper after Dean and Annie have left for dinner.

"She's always been a bit highly strung, but lately she seems really tense and bad-tempered. We've never been close, not in the way I am with Terri, but I feel for her. I know it can't be easy being at home with the girls all day, but Dean's a great dad, and he seems hands-on from the minute he arrives home from work."

"Maybe he's slacking in the bedroom department, and he needs to up his game."

I whack Slater across the back of the head. "Sex is not always the problem or the answer."

He shoots me a wicked grin. "Maybe not, but it sure helps relieve stress."

"Auntie Gabby?" a sleepy voice calls, and I look up to see Mia at the top of the stairs. "Can you and Slater read us a story?"

According to Annie, they've already had their bedtime story, and she told me to send them back to bed if they got up, but I hardly get to see my nieces, and, in my opinion, you can never have enough bedtime stories. I look to Slater.

He shrugs. "I'm cool with it."

We go up to the girls' bedroom, and I lie down beside Mia while Slate half-lies beside Tia. His legs are way too long for her kiddie-sized bed, so he has to sit up straighter and bend his knees to fit. We take it in turns reading stories and I have to stifle a giggle when Slater puts on different voices as he reads the various parts in the book. After twenty minutes, both girls are fast asleep, and we tiptoe out of the room, returning downstairs.

It takes about a half hour to agree on a movie, and that's only because I won rock, paper, scissors and got my own way. We settle down to watch a romantic movie about a girl who falls in love with her twin's boyfriend. Slater is muttering obscenities under his breath after only ten minutes, and I pinch his thigh, telling him to shush.

He's only just returned to the living room with a bucket of popcorn when the front door bursts open and Annie races into the hall, sobbing. Slater never closed the living room door after him, so we watch uncomfortably as the scene plays out. Dean runs in after his wife, pleading with her as she flies up the stairs with mascara-streaked cheeks. "Annie, please. That's not what I meant."

"I hate you!" she flings back at him. "I regret the day I ever set eyes on you!"

I quietly toe my shoes on as Slater shoves his feet back into his boots.

"Annie, please." Dean attempts to cajole his wife as a high-heeled shoe comes soaring down the stairs at him.

My eyes pop wide, matching Slater's startled expression.

Dean ducks at the last minute, narrowly avoiding a stiletto heel in the groin. He audibly sighs. "We need to at least try to discuss this like civilized adults. Please, Annie. Think of the girls."

"Screw you, Dean. I hate you, and I want you out of this house. Pack a bag and leave!" she hisses.

We get up, and I lace my hand in Slater's, clinging to his side as we inch out of the room. It's clear they need their privacy, and we should go.

Annie disappears and a door slams upstairs a couple seconds later. It's a wonder the girls haven't woken with all the noise. We venture out to the hallway, and my heart aches at the sight of my brother with his eyes closed and his forehead pressed to the wall. His shoulders are slumped, and he looks defeated.

"Dean? What can I do to help?" I don't bother asking him if he's okay, because he's clearly not.

Slowly, he lifts his head, and I'm startled to see tears glistening in his eyes. I've never seen my older brother cry. Never. I rush to his side, without hesitation, wrapping my arms around him in a fierce hug.

He leans into me, hugging me back equally as fiercely, his head resting on top of mine.

"I'll wait outside," Slater whispers, placing his hand lightly on my back as he passes.

"What's going on, Dean?" I whisper, forcing his head up so I can look him in the eye.

"I brought up the subject of divorce," he chokes out. "But I didn't even get to say half of what I wanted to say before she erupted, like usual."

Tears stab my eyes. "Oh no. I'm so sorry."

"Yeah, me too."

"Is that what you want?"

"No, not really, but I can't keep going on like this. Pretending everything's fine when it isn't. I don't want my daughters raised in a house that isn't full of love. Maybe if I was like Annie, and I hadn't grown up knowing what it was like to be loved and cherished, I might find this environment normal, but we got the best example, Gabby. Is it wrong to want that for my own kids?"

"Of course, it isn't. I'm no expert, but when I imagine being married with kids, I imagine an environment similar to what we had growing up. That's not to say it was picture perfect, because we both know it wasn't, but I want to bring all the best parts of our upbringing into my own family, and I expect my husband to do the same so we're keeping both our families' traditions alive while creating our own new version."

I used to daydream about the day when Dylan and I would be married with kids. He was young when his dad died, and he missed him terribly. I know Dylan will make a great father because he'll give his kids everything he didn't have.

"You've always had such a wise head on your shoulders," Dean says, hugging me again. "And I don't want to shatter your illusions, but marriage is damn hard. Raising kids is hard. If you don't have a solid unit to start with, you're already on the back foot. I think that's why I failed."

"You didn't fail, Dean, and this isn't a solo effort. It requires two to make a relationship work."

"Annie has tried, Gabby. I don't want you to think less of her, because we've both tried to fix things, but it's just not working."

"What about couples counseling?"

"We've been attending sessions for the last year, but we're just going around in circles." He straightens up, holding me at arm's length. "I shouldn't be burdening you with this. You've got your own shit going on."

"I don't mind, Dean. That's what family is for."

"I'm so grateful for mine, but if you want my advice, it's to live life to the fullest while you're young. Have fun before you tie yourself down with responsibility. Do what feels right and instinctual. Don't let anyone tell you how you should feel or what you want. Know your own mind, and be strong enough to follow it."

He brushes hair back off my face. "I'm not going to say I regret anything because that would be like denying my daughters, and I live for those two gorgeous girls, but I haven't always made the right choices *for me*. Learn from my mistakes. Take control of your own destiny, and don't let anyone else tell you how to live your life."

I'm still mulling over Dean's words as Slater drives me home. "Can we go for a walk on the beach?" I ask, not wanting to return to the house until the obvious upset is gone from my face. If I walk inside like this, Mom and Dad will instantly know something's wrong and I'll spill my guts. I figure Mom is already somewhat clued in, but it's not my place to say anything, and I know my brother, and he wouldn't want Mom and Dad to know what went down tonight.

"Sure thing." He makes a U-turn, heading in the direction of the beach.

It's pretty cold down by the shore, and I'm glad I brought my heavy coat, but I've no tie for my hair, and it's already blowing all over my face.

"Here." Slater tugs his beanie down over my head, carefully tucking my hair underneath. "You need this more than me."

"Thanks." I thread my fingers through his as we start walking. Apart from a lone figure with a dog walking up ahead, there isn't another soul in sight. It's not exactly ideal beach-walking weather, but the chilly air is exactly what's needed to dispel my sad thoughts.

"That was pretty sucky, huh?" he says as we walk.

"Yeah, it was. I feel so bad for all of them."

"Yeah. Me, too."

"I think they're going to divorce."

"Ah, shit, really?" He looks genuinely upset for them.

"It's looking that way."

He squeezes my hand. "I'm real sorry to hear that."

We walk in comfortable silence to the far end of the beach and then turn around and start walking back. My thoughts are fixated on Dean and what this will mean going forward. A blast of cold air barrels into us, and I shiver. Slater pulls me into his side, trying to shelter me from the worst of it. "Can I ask you something?" I inquire after a bit.

"Shoot."

"How badly did you miss not having your Dad around growing up?" Slater has never known his dad, and, for years, his mom told him his dad was dead. When he was thirteen, he discovered his dad wasn't dead at all. That he was alive and well and fully aware he had a son he'd never met. Turns out, he was a well-known politician, married with a family of his own. His public image was that of a dedicated family man, and it was one he'd carefully cultivated over the years. He wasn't prepared to risk that by acknowledging an illegitimate child.

I remember that day so clearly. Slater showed up at our house in floods of tears, clutching a crumpled letter in his hand. It seems his mom had been writing to his dad frequently begging him to take an active interest in his child's life. She was only twenty when she met him and fell head over heels in love. She didn't know he was already married with a pregnant wife until it was too late. She was pregnant with Slater by then. The guy begged her to have an abortion, and when she refused, he threatened her and then cut her out of his life.

That must've been so difficult for Janine. I can understand why she tried to shelter the truth from Slater, but it devastated him when he finally found out. I can't imagine what that discovery must've been like or how deep the wounds run. Knowing your father didn't want you and that he treated your mother with so much disrespect was bad enough but then to learn you have half-brothers and half-sisters you didn't know about must've seriously messed with his head.

Slater doesn't talk about it. At least not to me, so I know my probing question has thrown him for a loop. He's quietly contemplative for a few minutes, and I'm just about to tell him to forget I asked when he steers me over to a large rock. We sit down, and he keeps his arm slung around me, warming me with his body heat. "When I was younger, I had moments where I hated not having a father in my life, but mostly I was fine." He rubs his hand up and down my arm. "When I discovered my father was alive and learned how he'd abandoned my mom, I was so freaking angry at first. At him and her, but I got over the initial shock, and I forgave Mom for not telling me the truth. I was glad he wasn't a part of our lives. My feelings haven't changed."

"Have you ever met him?"

"Once." His jaw is rigid, his tone cold. "He turned up at the house the day after Mom's funeral telling me how sorry he was and offering me a big, fat check."

My mouth drops open. "You never said."

"I only told Ryan. I was too fucking mad and upset to even think about it." He kicks a loose stone at his feet, and we both watch as it sails toward the water. "I tore up the check and told him to fuck off and never come back. I haven't seen or heard from him since."

"What an asshole."

"My sentiments exactly. I didn't need him when I was growing up, and I sure as shit don't need him now."

"Well, it's his loss." I cradle his face in my hands. "He missed out on the opportunity to love one of the best men I know."

He stares deep into my eyes as he presses his forehead to mine. "Thank you, Belle." We stay like that for a few minutes, and despite the plummeting temps, I'm warm all the way through. After a while, he straightens up, looking deep in thought again. He brushes some wispy, stray strands of my hair back under the beanie, staring at me with a serious expression. "Going back to your original question, I don't feel like I missed anything. Mom was amazing, and I had Ryan and you and your family, and your dad has always been there for me if I needed some manly advice."

He chuckles, as if he's remembering something funny, and now I'm wondering what kind of conversations they might've had over the years. "If you're thinking what I think you're thinking, you shouldn't worry. Dean will still be an active presence in the girls' lives even if he and Annie divorce. The girls won't miss out. Some might say it's better than living in a house full of arguments and tension."

That's pretty much what Dean said earlier.

"It's still sad though."

"Yeah, but life will go on, and it doesn't have to be the end of the world. You're proof of that. Sometimes life throws us curveballs we're not expecting, and it ends up being the best thing ever."

It's not a like for like comparison, but I get his meaning. "If you'd asked me six months ago what I'd do if Dylan and I ever broke up, I would've told you I'd fall to pieces and never recover."

"And now?" He rubs his thumb along my lower lip.

"Now I know it's not the end of the world and there are other possibilities." I reach up, trailing my fingers through his hair. "I know we said we'd wait, Slate, but I'm really struggling to understand why we agreed to such a stupid plan."

A grin tugs up the corners of his mouth. "I've had similar thoughts lately."

My heart soars at his words. "The future is uncertain, whether we wait a day, a week, a month, or a year to be together. I say we grasp life by the collar and go for it." I circle my arms around his neck. "I like you a lot, Slate. I know we won't deliberately hurt one another in the same way I know if it doesn't work out that our friendship will be okay." Provided he doesn't do a one-eighty like Dylan. I press a soft kiss to his mouth. "I just want to be with you. We're spending all this time together anyway, and all that's missing is sex."

His eyes darken almost instantly, and he pulls me up onto his lap. "I'm not gonna lie; I've had the worst case of blue balls for months." He grins. "I definitely want to take our relationship to the next level, but are you sure, Belle? Are you really sure you want this with me?"

I bob my head vigorously. "I am, Slate. I want to experience this with you. I don't know what's going to happen, but I trust you to look after my body and my heart. Do you trust me?"

"Unequivocally."

"Want to throw any other fancy words around?" I tease.

He laughs, tweaking my nose. "You're too cute."

My eyes zone in on his lips, and I'm dying to kiss him. I need to taste him again. To feel his heated touch all over my body. "So, are we doing this?"

"We're doing this." The smile that graces his mouth is so wide it threatens to split his face.

"And no hiding," I add, pressing my chest into his. "If we're doing this, we're not pretending we aren't together."

"Absolutely not." He winds his large hand around the nape of my neck, reeling me in closer. "I want to shout from the rooftops that you're finally mine."

"I like the sound of that," I whisper, as his mouth draws near.

"Good, because now that I've got you, I've no intention of ever letting you go." His mouth descends on mine, and though I want to kiss the shit out of him, I don't want to get carried away here. I jump up, grabbing his hand and pulling him to his feet instead of prolonging the kiss. His expression is a mix of confusion and fear. "That's it?"

I press my body against his, grinning up at him. "Slate, if I let you kiss me here, I won't be able to stop at just that. We need to go back to your place and do this properly. Like in a bed. Or on the couch." I shrug, pinning him with a suggestive look. "Or against the wall or on the kitchen counter. I really don't care where as long as it's private and we're alone."

"Well, why didn't you say so in the first place?" He scoops me up into his arms and starts running. I'm giggling as he races with naked urgency toward his car.

Before he starts the engine, he stretches over the console, capturing my lips in a searing hot kiss that seems to go on forever. When we break apart, I'm sweating underneath my chunky coat. "That's a promise of what's to come." He turns the key, and the engine purrs to life. "And I hope you got lots of sleep last night, Belle, because you won't be doing much sleeping tonight."

Chapter Twenty-Nine

Our lips collide, and we're greedily tearing at one another's clothes the instant we step foot in the house. We stumble along the hallway and up the stairs, kissing and laughing and depositing articles of clothing as we go. When we reach the top of the stairs, Slater throws me over his shoulder, racing the few feet to his bedroom. He kicks the door open with his foot, and then he's flinging me down on the bed, pulling my boots and socks off and dragging my jeans down my legs. I'm in my bra and panties, my gaze raking over him, and my heart is hammering behind my rib cage, my chest heaving while I drink in every delectable inch of his potently masculine body.

His shirt is off, exposing oodles of smooth, tan skin and the tattoos covering his arms and magnificent chest. I sit up and lean forward, trailing my tongue up the center of his stomach, over his rock-hard abs, and the defined contours of his chest. His cock jerks behind his jeans, and I palm his impressive hard-on, rubbing his erection through the denim. He's long and thick, and saliva floods my mouth at the thought of tasting him. Wasting no time, I pop the buttons on his jeans and yank them down his legs.

He's not wearing any underwear, and his cock springs free, standing proudly to attention, with a lick of precum already coating the top. I flick my tongue at the sticky head, lapping it up, and Slater curses, gently placing his hands on my shoulders to keep himself steady. I can't believe I'm doing this with Slate or how much the sight of him, and the thought of him, turns me on. Nothing about this moment could ever feel wrong. I sit up on my knees, taking his length into my mouth while I wrap a hand around his base, stroking him in slow, firm movements. I suck him deep, moaning at the delicious salty taste of his warm, velvety soft flesh.

One of his hands slips down my back, and he unclasps my bra, quickly tossing it aside. He plays with my nipples, alternating between them as he rolls the hardened peaks between his thumb and forefinger. Then he cups my left boob, kneading it roughly while thrusting more aggressively into my mouth.

"Fuck, Belle. That feels so good, but I don't want to come in your mouth." He pulls back, removes his jeans fully, and throws them on chair. I lick my lips at the sight of him standing before me with his sculptured body, big cock, and the lust-drenched look on his face. "Lie back on the pillows," he commands, and I scoot back up the bed.

He crawls over me slowly, his tongue darting out and licking my sensitive flesh as he makes his way up my body. With his hands and his mouth, he explores me fully, but he leaves my panties on, trailing a line of hot kisses up my stomach and over my breasts. He nuzzles my neck and gently bites my earlobe before hungrily claiming my mouth. His kiss consumes me, and I'm lost in a sea of sensation. He probes my mouth with his skillful tongue, extracting all manner of moans and groans from me. When he leans his hard body flush against mine, my hips buck up like they have a mind of their own, and I'm writhing underneath him, whimpering as blissful tremors course through my body.

All I can think about is him filling me. Claiming me and making me his. I want it more than I've ever wanted anything.

His mouth is unrelenting as he ravishes my lips, his tongue

brushing against mine as he grinds his erection into my sweet spot. When I can't take it anymore, I move my mouth aside, biting down hard on his shoulder. It's a mix of pleasure and frustration and all-consuming need. "Please, Slate. Please. I need you to touch me. I'm going crazy."

"I *am* touching you," he teases, moving his hand down to fondle my breast.

I growl out a warning, and he chuckles. "Touch my pussy, Slate. Please." I grind against him, desperate for friction, needing to feel him pressing against me down there.

"Impatient as ever, Belle." He chuckles, dragging his mouth across my hot flesh as he glides lower and lower.

"You call it impatient, I call it horny as fuck," I pant, squirming when his tongue delves into my belly button.

His laugh is louder, and it rumbles through his body. He scrapes his stubbly chin along the inside of my thighs, and I emit a frustrated scream. An urgent tug, a sharp rip, and a wave of cool air confirms my panties are no more. I sink into the bed in grateful relief when he swipes a finger along my slit. "Is this what you need, baby?" he teases, running the tip of his finger along my pussy.

"Slater!" I bury my face in the pillow, stifling my frustrated screams.

Then he finally takes pity on me, pushing two fingers inside me, frantically pumping them in and out as I ride his hand without shame. "Yes! More! Harder and faster."

"So demanding." He chuckles, thrusting his fingers faster and curling them just right. Then his mouth is on the sensitized bundle of nerves at my apex, and he's sucking hard.

I shatter into a million glorious pieces. Fireworks detonate behind my eyelids, and the most delicious tremors rip through me, contorting my body like an expert gymnast. My back arches off the bed, and I'm bucking and pulsing against his hand as the most intense orgasm sends me into a blissful realm.

He nudges my legs apart, and I open my eyes as he kneels in front of me, opening a condom wrapper with his teeth. "That was the hottest fucking thing I've ever seen, Belle, and I've never been this hard in my life. I need to bury myself inside you so deep that you forget who you are and where you are. I want it so you don't even remember your fucking name."

Heat floods to my core at his promising words. "Get inside me already." I'm salivating like a dog in heat.

He suits up and positions his cock at my entrance. Then he thrusts inside me in one fast, hard jab, and I cry out as he fills me and fills me, and I forget where I end and he begins. There is no Belle or Slater in this. Just us. One connection. One heartbeat. One soul.

Leaning down over me, he holds himself still inside me. His lips brush against mine briefly. Sweetly. Tenderly. Once, twice, three times. "Please tell me you feel this, Belle. That this isn't all me."

I know he's not just talking about the feel of his thick cock wedged in my tight heat.

Bringing my hand up to his chest, I lay my palm over the point where his heart beats wildly. "It's not just you," I whisper. "I'm feeling this too, Slate. I'm feeling so much."

He kisses me more urgently this time, but it's still slower than the way he was devouring my mouth previously. "Nothing has ever felt like this because my whole life I've been waiting for you," he says against my lips.

I grab his face in my hands. "Make love to me, Slate. Show me what we've both been waiting for."

He circles his hips and starts a slow thrusting motion, in and out, taking his time and savoring every second.

I feel him everywhere.

Invading my body.

Filling my heart.

Capturing my mind.

Completing my soul.

I wrap my legs around his waist, resting my ankles on his ass, pulling him in tighter to me but urging him to keep the pace slow, wanting to feel every pulse of his cock, every jerk of his hips, every heady feeling as his length slicks up and down my inner walls, changing me forever.

Our hands slowly explore every inch of glistening skin. Our mouths worship one another. It's exquisitely beautiful, and the sensations building inside me are out of this world. There is no other way to describe it. My climax is mounting, and the moans slipping from my mouth are growing louder and more insistent.

He slides his hand down between us, pressing his thumb on my swollen clit, rubbing it in circles that undo me.

"I'm going to come again. Oh God!" I moan, digging my ankles into the flesh of his ass, now urging him to go faster. He doesn't let me down, picking up his pace, pulling out and slamming back in as his thumb presses down harder on my clit. Lowering his head, he suctions his mouth around my nipple, sucking hard, and I explode again, shouting his name over and over as my body floats higher and higher, riding wave after wave of incredible pleasure. He pulls my legs up higher until they're resting on his shoulders, and then he's slamming into me, pounding my body with a look of wild determination on his face. When he roars out his release, I feel his cock pulsing inside me, his body jerking as he gives me everything, holding nothing back.

We collapse on our backs, both perspiring and panting, with our arms and legs still entangled. He crushes me to his side, pressing a fierce kiss to my temple, and I curl myself around his sweat-slickened torso.

We don't speak for several minutes. We just hold one another, and it's one of the most intimate moments of my life. It's definitely a "pinch me" moment, something so unbelievably awesome that I require concrete proof that it's real and I'm not dreaming.

I prop up one elbow, pushing knotty strands of my hair back off my face. "Did that just happen?" I rasp, still struggling to get my breathing under control.

He caresses my cheek, and the look on his face blows my breath

257

away. His eyes are full of so much love, his face displaying every emotion he feels from awe to disbelief to deep-seated conviction. "Yes, my love." My heart rejoices at his words. "I love you, Belle. I love you so fucking much."

"I love you too, Slate." Tears gather in my eyes at the admission because my heart is so full, and it's so unexpected, and it's like this just crept up on me without me noticing. "How I never realized it before now I don't know," I truthfully admit. "But it's true. I do love you." I press my mouth to his. "So, so much."

"All I care about is where we are now and where we're going." He pulls my head down to his again, kissing me thoroughly. "And the fact we're both finally in the same place."

I rest my head on his chest, and he reels me in close, wrapping his arms snugly around me. I'm in heaven in his embrace, and nothing has ever felt so right. "I love you, Belle. Only ever you. For now and forever."

Chapter Thirty

I text Mom to let her know I'm staying at Slater's, and then we spend the majority of the night getting intimately acquainted with every freckle, every scar, and every nuance of each other's bodies. Slater finds creative ways to elevate my pleasure to new heights, and I'm greedy for his touch and his kisses, and we literally can't keep our hands off one another. We finally fall asleep in the early hours of the morning, only for Slater to wake me up a few hours later, easing gently into my body again.

Each time is as magical as the last, and if it wasn't for Thanksgiving, I doubt anything or anyone would be able to pry me from this bed today.

My cell vibrates with a message from Mom, and I reluctantly throw the covers off, swinging my legs out the side. "I need to get home and showered so I can help Mom with the prep."

Slater circles his arm around my waist, hauling me back into him. "Shower here," he says, nipping at my earlobe. "And then I'll drive you home."

"If 'shower here' is code for let's have shower sex then I'll never make it home on time."

"I can't help it if I can't keep my hands off you," he whispers, nuzzling his nose into my neck and lowering a hand to cup my tit.

I turn around, pushing him down flat on the bed, and straddle him. "You're insatiable."

"Only when it comes to you."

I lean down, kissing him passionately. "I love getting to know this sexy, romantic side of you, but I really have to go. I can't let Mom down, and, besides, we still have two more days here before we have to return to Newark. We still have plenty of time to fuck our brains out."

He tweaks my nose. "You're such a naughty girl, Belle, but I fucking love it."

I send him a saucy wink. "I aim to please."

"I'm a lucky man." He gives my ass cheeks a squeeze. "And I know I'm a greedy sonofabitch, but I'm not going to apologize. Not when it comes to you. I've been dreaming of this for years."

A goofy smile breaks out on my face. "You do know Ryan is going to enjoy jerking you around when he sees us together? You might want to tone it down a little."

He rubs his thumb along my lower lip. "I couldn't give a flying fuck, babe." He pecks my lips. "I'm not holding back. I can handle whatever that dipshit throws my way."

I press a soft kiss to his lips. "Thank you." I peer deep into his eyes. "Thank you for loving me and putting a smile back on my face again."

"You're welcome, and you know I'd do anything for you, Belle. *Anything.*" He gently holds my face in his hands, gazing adoringly at me and my heart swoons.

I force myself to get up and dressed, because the more Slater spouts endearments, the less I want to leave our little haven. I make coffee and toast while he grabs a quick shower, and we leave as soon as we've eaten. My heart is singing a symphony as he drives me home, and I'm bursting with happiness.

We kiss up a storm in his car outside my house, steaming up the windows in the process. Every time we attempt to separate, to go into the house, we end up grabbing onto one another again, our mouths meshing together as if they were never meant to be apart.

A loud rap on the window finally succeeds in ending our unplanned make-out session. Slater lowers the window, and Ryan pokes his head through with a shit-eating grin spread over his face.

"That was borderline pornographic and weirdly arousing." He half-smirks, half-grimaces. "I saw Old Man Jensen's curtains twitching. Ten bucks says he's got his cock in hand, jerking off right this very second."

"You are a disgusting pig," I tell him. "And we were only kissing."

"You had your tongue so far down his mouth you were practically making love to his tonsils," my brother retorts.

Myndi appears behind Ryan, swatting him across the back of the head. "This from the guy who was trying to convince me to blow him while he was driving."

"Ugh, jeez, Myndi!" Now it's my turn to grimace. "I seriously did not need to know that." A shudder works its way through me.

"At least your poor eyes weren't tortured. I'll never recover." Ryan pulls back from the window, shaking his head in faux distress, but his expression is playful.

"Dude, I swear you were a chick in a previous lifetime," Slate says, getting out. "You are more dramatic than any girl I know." He rounds the car and opens my door, offering me his hand.

I'm grinning at him like a lovesick fool as I take his hand and stand. I'm thankful I have my back to my brother, because I can only imagine the cheesy comment. "Thank you!" I press a kiss to Slater's cheek. "I've been saying that for years, but no one believes me."

"I was there too," Slate agrees, sliding his arm over my shoulder. "And I can confirm it's true. There's no male or female on this Earth more dramatic than this dude right here." He pokes a finger in Ryan's chest.

Myndi wraps her arms around Ryan. "I love your drama-llama," she says, like a bona-fide suck-up, stretching up to kiss him.

"Lucky you found the only girl on the planet happy to put up with your shit," Slate teases, as we walk up the steps to the house.

"I'm one in a million, and my girl knows she landed the catch of the century." Ryan flips Slater the bird.

"Glad to see your ego is still astronomical, little big bro."

"Nothing would put a dent in that ego," Dean says, materializing in the doorway. "And there's nothing wrong with a hefty dose of self-confidence." He reaches out, grabbing Ryan into a hug. "Good to see you, man."

Dean looks like shit. His skin is pale, his chin unshaven, and bruising shadows darken the skin under his bloodshot eyes. His shirt is so crumpled I'm guessing he probably slept in it. I shuck out of Slater's arm and hug my older brother. "How are you?"

He circles his arm around me, walking toward the kitchen. "I've been better, but I'm holding it together."

"What happened?"

His entire body is rigid against me. "Annie kicked me out, and she took the girls to her mom's today. She's refusing to answer any of my calls. I think I'll have no choice but to start legal proceedings. She's not going to keep me from my daughters."

I squeeze his side. "I'm sure she won't do that. She's just hurting right now."

He presses a kiss to the top of my head. "I hope you're right, but these things have a habit of turning nasty."

As a junior attorney in the same firm as our dad, Dean has handled several divorce proceedings on behalf of clients, so he knows what he's talking about.

He stops me at the door to the kitchen, holding me at arm's length. Ryan and Myndi have gone upstairs to dump their bags, so it's only Dean, Slater, and me in the hall. Dean glances at Slater, his eyes narrowing ever so slightly. "Considering my sister never came home last night, and she currently reeks of sex, I'm guessing we need to have a conversation."

My eyes go out on stalks. "Oh my God!" I slap his chest. "Stop embarrassing me!" I hiss. "I'm a grown woman. I don't need your permission or approval to have sex."

"Relax, Gabs." He turns me around, giving me a gently nudge. "Go shower before Mom and Dad notice. I promise I won't hurt him." He cocks his head to the side, fighting a smirk. "Well, not too much."

"It's cool, Belle." Slater wraps his hand around the back of my head. "Take a shower while I talk to your overbearing big brother." He pecks my lips briefly. "But don't take too long." He swats my ass as I walk away, and I don't know whether he's incredibly brave or ridiculously stupid to taunt Dean like that.

When I arrive back downstairs a half hour later, freshly showered and changed, I'm grateful to find things relatively peaceful. I pop my head in the game room first, strolling to Slater's side and examining his face. "What?" he asks.

"Just checking for any signs of injury." My eyes trek up and down his body, and my tongue darts out, wetting my lips as heat coils low in my belly. Hot damn. Slater is the definition of sex on a stick, and it's going to take colossal effort to keep my hands off him today.

"Keep looking at him like that, Tornado, and I'll have no choice but to inflict bodily harm," Ryan says, lining up his pool cue to take his shot.

"Bite me."

"Don't fucking tempt me."

"Leave them alone," Dad says, trying, and failing, to smother his delight when Ryan messes up his shot. "Any guy who puts that kinda smile on my Buttercup's face gets my seal of approval."

"Thank you, Daddy!" I blow him a kiss.

"But all bets are off if you do anything to wipe it off again," Dad warns, sending Slater a look Dirty Harry would be proud of.

"Jeez, tough crowd," Slater mumbles, only half-joking.

"Ignore them," I say, wrapping myself around him. "I plan to." I smile up at him, and my heart soars when he pins me with that same adoring look from earlier. Someone, Ryan, I think, makes a gagging sound, but we don't pay him any attention. Slater encircles his arms around me, and my entire body relaxes against his embrace. Butterflies scatter in my chest, and a fluttery feeling lands in my stomach as we continue looking at one another. It's as if we're the only two people in the world, and we're all each other needs. It's been a long time since I've felt this kind of feeling, and it's both new and familiar at the same time, and it fills me with warmth and joy.

"I love you," he says, not even attempting to lower his voice for the audience. He gets extra brownie points for his confidence.

"I love you too," I reply, equally assured, stretching on my tiptoes to kiss him. We don't prolong it—no sense in pushing all the overprotective men in the room to breaking point—but I practically float on air as I walk out of the room. From the corner of my eye, I spot my brothers and my dad smiling, and it pleases me no end to know we have their approval even if they're hellbent on making Slater work for it.

I join Myndi and Mom in the kitchen, and we sing along to the radio as we prepare our Thanksgiving dinner. When I confirm Slater and I are now together, Mom draws me into the biggest hug, whispering she hopes I'm happy and that she wishes us the best. Myndi is already busy planning tons of double dates, and I'm on cloud nine as I move into the formal dining room to set the table.

Strong arms slip around my waist from behind, and a contented sigh leaks from my lips. "Missed you," Slater whispers, nudging my hair aside so he can plant a kiss on my neck. A shiver coasts along my spine, and I feel his kiss all the way to the tips of my toes.

"What the hell did I miss?" Caleb asks from the open doorway, with an amused grin on his face.

We both lift our heads up. "I've already been subjected to the Spanish Inquisition," Slater drawls, keeping a firm hold on me. "Ask your dad and your brothers to fill you in."

"Ah, it's like that." Caleb's face brightens. "You've got bigger balls than me, dude."

"I happen to think your sister is worth it, so bring it. I can handle it."

Caleb steps toward us, grabbing Slate into a man-hug. "It's about time you made a move. Good for you."

Terri comes into the room, practically glowing. "What's going on?"

"Slate and Gabby finally got their act together," Caleb tells his fiancée, pulling me into a hug. "I'm happy for you," he whispers in my ear. "But if he hurts you, I'll string him up by his balls."

My laughter is muffled against his chest. "You'll have to beat Ryan to it. He's promised to feed his balls to the piranhas."

"Congrats, guys. That's great news," Terri says, nudging Caleb out of the way so she can hug me.

Dinner is a rather boisterous affair, as usual, with everyone trying to talk over everyone else and tons of ribbing and teasing, but there's a dark cloud hovering over the occasion with the notable absence of Annie and the girls. Dean is trying his best to enter the spirit of things, but I notice he only toys with his food while he's knocking back the whiskeys like they're going out of fashion. But no one calls him out on it, because we can tell how much he's suffering.

Slater and I hold hands under the table every chance we get, and I'm as giddy as a teenager in the first flush of love. He's constantly sneaking sly glances at me, and I'm as bad. I'm sure we look like a pair of lovesick teenagers, but I honestly couldn't care less. I love the way Slater makes me feel, and I still can't get over the fact I've fallen for my brother's best friend, one of *my* best friends, a guy who has always been there right under my nose if I'd only bothered to look.

I don't miss the looks we're picking up around the table either, but I can tell everyone is genuinely pleased for us. I doubt you'd find any girl happier than me anywhere on the planet right now.

Caleb and Terri are in a huddle, whispering, glancing around the table every so often. "What's that all about?" Ryan murmurs into my ear.

I shrug. "Haven't a clue."

A couple minutes later, Caleb clears his throat. "Um, Terri and I have some news."

Everyone mutes, giving them our full attention. My brother circles his arm around his fiancée, and he's bursting with pride as he says, "Terri's pregnant. We're expecting a baby."

The room erupts as everyone offers heartfelt congratulations. This news is the only thing all day to bring a genuine smile to Dean's face, and I can tell how delighted he is for them.

"Congratulations!" I hug Terri carefully. "That is the best news ever! Do you know how far along you are?"

"Twelve weeks. We've known for a little while, but we wanted to wait until we'd passed this first milestone, and had our first ultrasound, before we said anything, just in case." I hug her a little tighter, understanding what she's alluding too. Terri was pregnant a year ago, but they lost the baby at the ten-week stage, and it devastated everyone, so I can understand why they felt the need to hold back this time.

I glance at her flat stomach. "Wow, you'd never know you're growing my niece or nephew in there; you look amazing. The first thought I had when you stepped through the door was that you were glowing."

She beams at me. "Thank you, and I'm feeling great. No sickness or anything. I've been a little more tired than normal but that's it."

"I'm so happy for you." My eyes shine with tears. "For both of you," I say, pulling Caleb into our embrace. "You are going to make awesome parents."

"And we're happy for you too, Gabby," Caleb replies. "Slater is a good guy."

"You two look so good together," Terri adds. "You deserve every bit of happiness. I wish you guys all the luck in the world."

Chapter Thirty-One

It's been two weeks since Thanksgiving, and I'm still floating on a cloud, completely and utterly one hundred percent madly in love with Slater Evans.

Life has a funny way of surprising the shit out of me, in the most incredible way.

But I should've known it wouldn't be all plain sailing.

We are in the midst of exams, and both of us are studying like crazy, so we're cramming in as much together time as we can. We split our days between the dining hall and the library, only returning to the house when we're both beat.

It's one such evening, and Slater and I have just taken a well-earned break. We're walking hand in hand through campus, in the direction of the coffee place, when we come across a small crowd, clustered in a circle, in the middle of the road.

"What's going on?" I muse, chewing on the corner of my mouth.

"Let's find out." Slater leads me over to the crowd, and we edge our way through.

"Dylan!" I cry out, squeezing through a few girls to make my way to my ex. He's lying on the ground, his body jerking and thrashing about, his limbs flailing uncontrollably. "Oh my God!" I drop to my knees, and my stomach lurches violently as his eyes roll back in his head and drool dribbles out of his mouth. I try to remember what I know of seizures, forcing myself to remain calm. "Did anyone call nine-one-one?" I shout.

"I did." A girl with mousy-brown hair and glasses steps forward.

"How long has he been like this?" I ask her as Slater crouches down alongside me.

"It happened just as I was coming out of the coffee shop," she explains, glancing at her watch, "so, about two minutes."

"We need to get him on his side." Together, we move him, and Slater stays kneeling behind him, helping to keep him propped up. Strangled sounds are coming out of Dylan's mouth while his body continues to spasm.

"Dylan. It's Gabby, can you hear me? An ambulance is on its way."

He grunts, and I take that as acknowledgment that he knows I'm here. "Just hang tight," I say, my voice choking on the words. I wish I could hold him through it, but I know the worst thing you can do when someone is having a seizure is to try to hold them down.

"There's nothing to see here," Slater hollers at the growing crowd. "Go home and give the guy some privacy." The shuffling of feet behind me confirms at least some are leaving. The blare of sirens echoes in the distance, and I will the ambulance to hurry up.

After a few minutes, the spasming slows down, and then it stops altogether. Dylan's body is spent, and he visibly deflates, but I shake my head when Slater moves to lie him flat on his back. "We should keep him on his side until the paramedics arrive." The sirens were silenced a few seconds ago, and from the screeching of tires, I know the ambulance has arrived.

"Dylan?" I study his face. "Do you think you're going to be sick?" Froth is bubbling in his mouth, and I'm concerned. His eyes are more lucid when he stares at me, but he can't, or won't, speak. "I'm just going to check your airways are clear," I say before gently opening his mouth and running my finger around, loosening the well of saliva pooling there. Then I unbutton the top few buttons of his shirt, allowing him to breathe more easily.

Blatant fear radiates from his gaze as he reaches out, shakily clasping my wrist.

"Excuse me, miss," a male voice says from behind. "I need you to step aside."

"Don't leave me," Dylan rasps, still clinging loosely to my wrist.

"I'm not going anywhere," I promise.

Slater and I step aside to allow the paramedics access to Dylan. The girl with the glasses is still here, and she looks really upset. "Thank you for calling an ambulance," I tell her. "Can I get your name and number? I'm sure Dylan will want to thank you."

"I've never seen anything like that before," she says, her voice trembling.

I put my arm around her. "Neither have I. It was scary as shit." She nods, looking like she might burst into tears at any second.

One of the paramedics pulls me to one side, asking me a bunch of questions which I do my best to answer. I can only see the ends of Dylan's legs because the other two paramedics are crouched over him, hiding him from view.

When the paramedic goes back to the ambulance, Slater comes up behind me, wrapping his arms around my waist. "Are you okay, Belle?"

I stare absently at him. "Define okay."

"Did that ever happen before?"

I shake my head. "Never." I twist around so I'm looking at him. "Dylan has never had a seizure as long as I've known him, but I can't account for the last couple months."

The paramedics strap Dylan to a gurney and wheel him toward the ambulance. The crowd has dwindled, but a few assholes remain, filming the events on their cell phones. Fucking parasites. Slater lets go of me, grabbing one of the douches and whipping his cell out of his hand. "Have you no decency? The guy just had a seizure! Do you think he wants this uploaded to social media?" He deletes the recording, thrusting the cell back at the guy while I take a pic of the other jerks.

"My father is an attorney," I tell them, "and I just snapped all your faces. If anyone posts anything online, you can expect to get served."

"You should go, Belle," Slater says, gesturing at the ambulance.

"Thank you." I hug him tight. "Will you follow me to the hospital?"

"Of course. I'll be there as soon as I can."

I peck his lips briefly. "Can you call Heather? She needs to know. I'll message you her number."

"I'll contact her. Go before they leave without you."

I run toward the ambulance, calling out to the guy currently closing the rear doors. He stops, and we exchange a few words before he lets me into the back.

Dylan is still strapped to the cot and hooked up to a machine. I sit down beside him, taking his hand. It's a little weird seeing him after all these weeks of no contact, but I'm glad we happened to be there, because the thought of anything happening to him sends a dagger clear through my heart.

"You're here," he whispers, clasping my hand a little tighter. Beads of sweat dot his pale brow, and his eyes are still a little unfocused.

I nod, forcing a soft smile on my face. "I promised, and it's not like I could leave you like that."

"Thanks, Dimples." His eyes fill with tears, and my heart falters in my chest.

Old fears resurface, and I can't help thinking that my gut instinct was right—that there's something terribly wrong with Dylan. The whole trip I'm silently praying that I'm wrong, but I'm absolutely terrified that I'm about to be proven right.

I'm pacing the hallway in the hospital when Slater arrives. The instant he pulls me into his arms, I burst into floods of tears. "What's happened?" His eyes drill into mine, and there's no mistaking the alarm etched on his face.

"Nothing, well, I mean, I don't know," I sniff, clutching a handful of his shirt. "He talked a little in the ambulance, and then he fell asleep. They whisked him away the minute we arrived, and they won't tell me anything because I'm not family."

"Heather is on her way. Your parents are driving her."

Ryan and Myndi turn up a few minutes later, and we relocate to the waiting room. Slater keeps his arms around me the entire time, and I cling to him as worry for Dylan eats away at me. My parents arrive about an hour after that. "Heather is outside talking to the doctor right now," Dad supplies, sitting down across from me. "What exactly happened?"

I tell him how it went down, and just as I've finished speaking, the door opens, and Heather enters the room. I stand, going to her immediately. She grabs me into a hug, and her body trembles against me. "Thank you for being there for him," she whispers, releasing me, and taking one of my hands in hers.

"It's lucky we happened to be walking past," I say, glancing over my shoulder at Slater.

"Thank you too, Slater." She smiles weakly at him.

"I'm glad I could help. Is he going to be okay?" Slater asks.

"The doctors want to keep him in for a day or two to run some tests. They need to determine what caused the seizure."

"You should tell them about his migraines too. They were more frequent in the—"

"What the hell is she doing here!?" a high-pitched voice shrieks, cutting me off mid-sentence.

Bianca storms into the room, glaring at me like she wishes I was dead.

"Bianca." Heather touches her arm, attempting to placate her. "Gabby and Slater were the ones who brought Dylan here."

"That doesn't explain why she's still here," she snaps, sending venom-filled glances my way.

"I've known Dylan since I was ten years old, and I have every right to be here. More of a right than you." Every muscle in my body is locked tight, and I'm in no mood for putting up with her catty shit. Slater comes up behind me, placing his hand on my lower back.

"I'm his girlfriend, and I don't want you here." She pouts like a toddler getting ready to throw a temper tantrum.

"Tough shit, and I don't answer to you."

Tension bleeds into the air as we face off, and I have to quell the urge to swing my fist in her face. I don't think I've every truly hated anyone before, but I'm pretty sure I hate Bianca. She got her way. She coaxed Dylan out of my arms, and he's no longer mine, so what difference does it make if I'm sitting here?

"If you won't leave, I'll get the staff to throw you out," she threatens.

I very much doubt she'd be able to do that, and it's not like having girlfriend status gives her any weight around here, so I'm tempted to tell her to shove her threat up her ass and stick it where the sun doesn't shine. But Heather looks really upset, and that's the only reason I back down.

"I don't want to cause a scene," I tell Heather, ignoring Bianca completely. "So, I'll leave, but I'm doing this for you and Dylan. Can you text me updates as you receive them?"

"Of course." Her expression is one of complete gratitude.

"Let's go." I take hold of Slater's hand. "I'll talk to you later, Mom and Dad," I say as Ryan and Myndi rise.

"We'll come with," Ryan says, glowering at Bianca. "Let's leave Banging Bianca to look after her boyfriend. I'm sure she'll make an excellent caretaker." His tone is thick with sarcasm, and I could happily kiss him for coming to my defense. Bianca digs her nails into her palms, and I can tell she'd love to have a go at Ryan, but she doesn't want to risk upsetting Heather further.

The four of us walk outside, and I only release the breath I'd been holding in the corridor.

"Jealous bitch," Myndi fumes. "She's clearly worried if she feels you're still a threat."

"She's right to be worried," Ryan adds. "I've spotted Dylan around campus the last few weeks with plenty of girls who aren't Bianca. I highly doubt she's even his girlfriend."

"Can we stop talking about her? She puts me in such a foul mood."

Slater presses a kiss to my temple as we wait outside the elevator.

"Gabby!"

I turn at the sound of Heather's voice, watching as she runs toward me.

"Gabby, I'm so sorry about that." Unhappiness is transparent on her face. "If anyone is leaving, it should be that rude young woman, but she's Dylan's girlfriend, and I'm not sure he'd want me to do that."

It hurts that Heather can't stick up for me even if throwing Bianca out might upset Dylan. But I won't add to her woes, and she's clearly beside herself with worry, so I can afford to push my hurt under the carpet and be the bigger person. "It's fine, Heather. I understand. Just make sure Dylan knows I was here and that I'm worried about him."

"I'll ensure he knows. Thank you again."

She scurries back to the waiting room, and we make our way out of the hospital in silence.

Chapter Thirty-Two

Heather is true to her word, texting me regular updates from the hospital over the course of the next two days. My parents got to speak to Dylan the first night, and they confirmed he seemed okay, and he was asking for me. Slater and I haven't talked much about it, and I'm trying to focus on getting through my exams and not worrying too much, but it's challenging because I can't shake the awful thought that something is seriously wrong.

"I feel guilty for worrying about Dylan, like it's cheating on Slate to even be thinking of my ex," I tell Myndi on Friday night. We're having a girls' night out with some of our classmates to celebrate the end of our exams.

"If it was anyone but those two guys, I'd probably say I understand. However, Slater knows your history with Dylan, and he was worried about him that day too. I think he'd worry if you *weren't* concerned about your ex."

"Hmm, that's probably true," I say, sipping my soda. "He was amazing when it was all going down. Helping me with Dylan and insisting I go in the ambulance with him."

"Slater's an amazing guy, Gabby." She slurps her cocktail through a straw, and I momentarily reconsider my choice of beverage, but I'm just not in the mood for alcohol tonight. Since the night I got trashed and almost made a huge mistake with that asshole Jack, I've stuck to soda anytime I've gone out. I prefer to have a clear head so I don't risk making any more stupid decisions, and I haven't really felt like drinking anyway.

"He is. He's the best."

"And there it is," Myndi deadpans. "The dreamy look of love."

I chink my glass against hers. "It takes one to know one," I tease back.

"Amen to that sister. We did good, Gabby. Real good."

"I know, and I'm deliriously happy with Slate, but I'd be lying if I said I wasn't crazy concerned about Dylan. It's not like I can just switch off my feelings. We might not be together, but I don't want anything to happen to him."

"I'm sure if it was anything serious, you'd have found out by now," she reassures me.

Slater and I hang around Newark for another few days, working some extra shifts at the club, before we pack up and head home for the holidays.

We've decided to stay at Slater's place, but we'll sleep over at my parents' house Christmas Eve and Christmas Day night. In the meantime, I'm looking forward to the time alone—especially the ability to have wild, noisy, monkey sex whenever we want and wherever we want.

Sex with Slater is my new addiction, and it's just as well I'm flexible from yoga because the positions he gets me into demand extreme flexibility and stamina. While we've been going at it like rabbits the last few weeks, neither of us have been able to fully let go back at the house because we're conscious of my brother and Austin and the paper-thin walls.

So, yeah, I'm going to enjoy this break, and I'm planning to make the most of it, including taking the time to find out what's going on with my ex. I've all but decided I'm going to drop by Dylan's house to find out what's going on when he texts me from his mom's phone, confirming he has meningitis and he's being kept in the hospital for observation and treatment. When I offer to come visit, he confirms there's a strict no-visitor policy in place. He tells me not to worry and wishes me Merry Christmas, and I get the distinct impression he just doesn't want or need me around.

"Penny for your thoughts," Slate says, coming into the living room and throwing his coat and scarf down on the couch. I shriek when he places his cold hands on my cheeks, hopping up and knocking him off the arm of the chair. He chuckles, pushing himself up from the floor.

"Shit, your hands are like icicles."

"It's fucking freezing out there. I think it might snow this year."

"Oh, I'd love it if it did," I say in a whimsical voice. "I love the snow."

"I know you do." He draws me into his body, tweaking my nose. "Remember the time we tried to build an igloo in your backyard?"

I giggle. "We were such idiots. There was only about four inches of snow on the ground, barely enough to make a snowman let alone attempt an igloo."

"Remember Dylan printed out that 'how to make an igloo' guide he downloaded from Google and he got real mad at the three of us because we kept trying to skip some of the steps."

"Yeah, he's a bit anal like that at times." My smile fades a little. "I hope he's okay."

Slater sinks into the chair, pulling me down onto his lap. "I thought you said he doesn't have a serious strain of meningitis and that he'll recover?"

I rest my head on his chest, listening to the steady beat of his heart. "Yeah, but I can't help worrying."

He rubs his hand up and down my spine. "He'll be fine."

I look up at him. "You're right, and I'm sorry. It's not fair to keep mentioning my ex."

"It's a bit of an unusual situation, and you and me both know Dylan is much more than just your ex. He was your best friend growing up. I'm trying to remember that and not get too jealous."

"You have nothing to be jealous of." I move around in his lap until I'm straddling him. I lean down and brush my mouth against his. "I'm with you now. I love you, and you've made me unbelievably happy. That's not going to change, but I can't pretend that I don't care about Dylan or worry about him. Maybe I shouldn't, because what he did to me was horrible, but I can't force myself to feel a certain way."

"I wouldn't want you to." He smooths a hand over my hair. "I might be jealous, but I also don't want you to change. Dylan was a huge part of your life. I know how big your heart is and that you won't ever completely turn your back on him. I know you'll always care about him, especially when he's unwell." He grazes his thumb along my cheek. "You wouldn't be you if you didn't feel like that. Don't worry about me, I can process my own selfish thoughts."

I kiss the shit out of him after that speech, pouring every emotion into it. When I pull back, both our cheeks are flushed, our lips swollen. "I don't know what I did to deserve you, but I'm going to offer thanks to God every single day." Tears prick my eyes. "Jeez, Slate, you couldn't be any more perfect, and I fucking love the shit out of you. Trust me, you have nothing to fear, nothing to be jealous of. I'm all yours."

"Prove it." His eyes twinkle mischievously.

"Challenge accepted." I slide off his body, whipping my sweater dress and leggings off in record time. Slater's pupils dilate as he watches me through hooded eyes. His hands are locked behind his head, and his lazy sprawl belies the heat in his gaze. Keeping my eyes locked on his, I unclip my bra and fling it aside. Then I shimmy my lace thong down my legs, standing in front of him completely naked.

His erection is straining against the denim of his dark-stained jeans as I lean over him, popping the button and dragging them down his legs. "Do you ever wear underwear?" I inquire, amusement coloring my tone while I remove his jeans and socks.

"Around you? Never. Easy access, babe." He smirks, and I swat his hand away as he reaches out to cup my breasts. "No touching until I tell you you can."

"Fuck. I love it when you turn all dominatrix."

I lift the hem of his shirt, and he helps me pull it up and over his head. I stand in between his legs, drinking him in from the top of his head to the tips of his toes. His hard-on stands proud against his stomach, the tip of his cock already glistening with precum. No matter how many times we fuck, he's always aroused and ready for action at the drop of a hat.

I crawl over him, keeping my body aloft as I bend down and capture his mouth in mine. Our tongues duel fiercely, and he slaps my ass firmly. I moan into his mouth as liquid drips from my pussy. "Touch me," I command in a breathy voice, and he instantly dips two fingers into my wet heat. I push down on his fingers as he nips at my nipples with his teeth, gently biting the puckered tips. I grind against his hand, already dying for him.

"Fuck, Belle. You're always so wet for me."

"You turn me on so much, Slate. And I can't wait any longer. I need you." I take hold of his wrist, pulling his fingers out of my body, and then I position myself over his throbbing length, lowering onto his cock until I'm fully seated. I don't move for a moment, enjoying the fullness of his body in mine and the intimacy of our connection.

His hands glide up my thighs and skate over my stomach. He fondles my tits, rolling and pinching my nipples, sending darts of desire shooting to my core. I start moving, leisurely at first, up and down, and circling my hips. A groan leaves his lips, and the hands on my tits grow more urgent. He rocks his hips up, pushing into me as I press down, and I moan as pleasurable tremors invade my body, heating me all over.

"Come here," he says, pulling me down to him so he can devour my mouth. We rock gently against one another as we kiss, and his fingers trace a path up and down my spine. I'm squirming against him, on fire all over, and craving everything he's offering. "I love you," he whispers.

"I love you too," I murmur against his mouth.

"Show me how much, baby. Ride me hard."

I don't need any more encouragement. Sitting up, I lift and slam back down, going harder and faster, picking up speed and thrusting my hips forward, so his cock is angling perfectly inside me, hitting my sweet spot. Slater grabs one of my hips and starts thrusting up into me, while his other hand moves lower and his thumb starts rubbing my clit. We're both moaning, bucking our hips and riding harder and faster, until my orgasm creeps up on me out of nowhere, and I shatter on top of him, milking his cock, clenching and pulsing as my release rockets through me.

Lightning fast, he flips us around, pulling out as my back hits the chair. He strokes himself over my stomach, and streams of hot semen shoot over my slick skin. He empties his load on top of me, roaring my name as his orgasm reaches a peak. Then he collapses on top of me, uncaring about the sticky present he just gave me, and I wrap my legs and arms around him, just holding him to me. His face is pressed against my chest, and I kiss the top of his head, threading my fingers through his hair. He hasn't cut it since returning to UD, and I love it longer like this, curling around his ears and the back of his neck.

"Fuck, that was incredible," he says after a bit as I continue to run my fingers through his hair.

"Every time with you is incredible," I truthfully reply.

"Way to stroke a guy's ego," he jokes.

"In your case, it's true."

I protest when he gets up, extending his hand toward me. He

chuckles. "We need to shower, babe, and I promise I'll make it worth your while."

His cock is already hard again, and I lick my lips, reaching for it as he pulls me to my feet. "Show me what you've got, stud," I say, caressing him slowly. "And maybe *I'll* make it worth *your* while."

He throws me over his shoulder and smacks my ass. "Now you're asking for it, and you know I never back down from a challenge."

He spends the rest of the night proving that to me.

Christmas comes and goes, and we only have a few more days left here before we return to college. Snow made an appearance, as Slater predicted, and I enjoyed being confined to Slater's house, watching TV and making love in front of a roaring fire, enjoying one another's company and each other's bodies. But the last couple of days I've been feeling unwell. It's hard to describe, but I've been experiencing these weird stomach cramps, and Slater was insistent I go to the doctor, so I'm currently standing outside the doctor's office, in complete shock after leaving my appointment.

My mind is whirling a million miles an hour, and I'm trying to put some structure to my thoughts before I walk to the restaurant to meet Slater. We've barely left his house the whole vacation, and, as the snow has now cleared, he was adamant he was taking me out for an early dinner.

I start walking in the direction of the restaurant, but I'm locked in my mind the entire time, wondering how this happened and how the hell I'm supposed to break this kind of news. Before I know it, I look up, and I've arrived at the new little Italian place we've heard so much about. I don't even remember the journey here, and, as I push through the door into the welcoming warmth, I'm still in a daze, still no wiser as to how to tell Slater my news.

The waitress escorts me to a small booth tucked into the corner of the restaurant. As it's early, it's not busy, and there are only a couple of other tables filled. Slater stands, pressing a kiss to my lips and helping me out of my coat. The waitress looks on with evident envy on her face.

"What can I get you to drink?" I vaguely hear her ask.

"Belle? Baby?" Slater's brow puckers in concern. "Do you want a sparkling water or a soda?"

"I, uh, I'll have a sparkling water. Thanks," I mumble, sliding into the seat beside my boyfriend.

"What is it?" he asks the minute the waitress is out of earshot. "You're scaring the hell out of me right now."

I gulp over the wedge of emotion in my throat, turning to face him. He takes my hands in his. "Shit, Belle. You're trembling. What's going on?"

Tears well in my eyes, and I'm almost choked with emotion, but, somehow, I manage to blurt the words out. "I'm pregnant, Slater. We're having a baby."

Chapter Thirty-Three
Slater

T he words greet my ears, and all the air leaves my lungs. My jaw slackens, and I stare at my beautiful Belle, looking up at me with so much love and fear on her face. Tears spill out of her eyes and down her cheeks, and that breaks me out of whatever shocked daze I'm in. "You're pregnant? When? I mean how?" She giggles, and the sound is like music to my ears. It also helps to ease the strain. I tenderly cup her cheek, peering into her beautiful, shiny, big, blue eyes. My heart is beating a million miles a minute. "Obviously, I know how." My lips tug up into a suggestive smile. "We've been fucking like wild animals any chance we get, but I thought you said you couldn't get pregnant?"

Her chest heaves, and she opens her mouth to speak when the waitress reappears with Belle's water. I order our food, picking out the first things that catch my eye on the menu, along with another round of drinks for both of us. As soon as she leaves, Belle starts filling me in. "My Ob-Gyn said it would be extremely difficult to get pregnant with my condition, not that I *couldn't* get pregnant," she clarifies. "I know we had unprotected sex a few times, but I thought it was fine because I haven't had a period for months and you always pulled out."

"Except for that one time." I arch a brow. There was this one time, a few weeks ago, when I wasn't sure if I'd pulled out quick enough, but Belle wasn't worried, so I never gave it a second thought.

"Yeah, I'm guessing that's when I conceived although we won't know until I have an ultrasound. Because I haven't had periods in months, we can't work out my dates that way, so the doc booked me in for an emergency ultrasound tomorrow in the hospital."

"At the risk of sounding like a dumb jock, if you haven't had periods, how did you get pregnant?"

She folds her hands in her lap. "I don't fully understand it, but I was obviously still ovulating." She frowns a little. "My Ob-Gyn prescribed some new birth control pills which were supposed to help regulate my periods, and I'm guessing that had something to do with it."

A beat of silence descends. My mind is fucking blown. This has come completely out of left field. Belle looks me straight in the eye. "Please tell me what you're thinking. I know this is a huge shock, but are you happy or unhappy?"

I pull her to me, pressing my lips to her forehead. Her delicate, floral scent swirls around me, grounding me like always. It's hard to speak over the lump in my throat, but I try. "I love you, Belle. You know that. As far as I'm concerned, you're the only one for me. Was I planning on having kids with you right now? *No*, but that doesn't mean I'm unhappy. I'm *not* unhappy. I'm fucking delirious, gone, because I'm so fucking overjoyed at the thought of my baby growing inside you right now." As the words leave my mouth, I bathe in the absoluteness of them.

I place my hand over the teeny-tiny little stomach she's sporting. I hadn't even paid it any attention. We've been holed up at my place, eating and fucking for weeks, so a little weight gain made complete sense. I'm surprised when moisture stabs my eyes. "I'm over the moon, babe, and I promise to be with you every step of the way, holding your hand and supporting you. And when our son or daughter arrives, I am going to be the best damned father ever."

Although I'm equally terrified, and a whole host of fears are waiting in the wings, ready to attack my euphoria, I damp them down. So what if I didn't grow up with my father in my life? I've had enough good examples to learn from. The fact my dad wasn't around only makes me more determined to be there for my child. To give him or her everything I never had.

Belle is openly crying now, and I reel her into my arms. "Shush, it's okay. Everything's going to be okay. I'm with you. You've got me. You've got all of me."

She swipes at her tears, easing back to look at me. "I'm not scared, Slate. Well," she sniffles, "I mean, I am, because giving birth and being responsible for a tiny human is freaking scary as shit, but these tears are happy tears." She kisses me softly. "I love you, and I already love our baby." She rubs a hand over her stomach. "It might not have been planned, but a baby is a blessing from God, and I have no regrets."

I barely remember eating our meal or driving us home, but I'm fully aware as I make sweet love to my pregnant girlfriend that night, and every touch, every thrust, every kiss, and every caress is magnified a hundred times at the thought of my seed developing in her belly. I didn't think it was possible to feel this much love, but as I watch Belle's chest rise and fall in sleep, I think I might burst at the seams.

I know, looking at her, that she is my life, my future, my family.

As soon as the timing is right, I intend to propose to her. If I have my way, we'll be married before the baby arrives, but I'll let Belle decide what she wants to do.

As I wrap my arms around my sleeping beauty, I take a moment to memorize this night and to cherish this precious gift she's given me. As I drift off to sleep, I realize what a lucky bastard I am.

Belle's knee taps up and down as we wait in the reception area to be called for her ultrasound. I place my hand on her thigh to stall the movement. "Relax, babe. Everything's going to be fine."

She drains the last cup of water like a pro. She's been told to drink water and not to pee until after the ultrasound. "I can't help worrying." She bites on the corner of her mouth. "You know what happened to Terri and Caleb last year, and she said the doctors told her a lot of women miscarry the first time. What if something's wrong? I have been having those weird cramps? What if it means there's a problem?"

I wrap my arms around her, kissing her head. "You need to keep calm. Stress can't be good for the baby, and I'm sure everything is fine. The doctor told you the heartbeat was healthy and strong, right?" She nods, having told me yesterday that the doctor put some device to her stomach and she'd heard the heartbeat. I was devastated to have missed it, but I'm hoping today's ultrasound will more than make up for it.

"Gabrielle James?" A woman in a clinical blue shirt and pants calls Belle's name out at the top of the room, and we stand. Belle clings to me, and her expression is a mix of excitement and fear. "Follow me," the woman says with a warm smile when we reach her. She pushes through a set of double doors, and we follow her along a corridor and into a small room. She instructs Belle to get changed into a gown, confirming the doctor will be along shortly.

I clutch Belle's hand as she lies on the cot, waiting for the doctor to arrive. "Do you want a boy or girl?" I ask, partly by way of distraction.

"I don't mind once the baby is healthy," she instantly replies, confirming she's already thought about this, "but the thoughts of a little boy just like you has my ovaries dancing a happy dance."

I reach over and kiss her. "I'm imagining a little girl with those gorgeous blonde curls you had as a kid and that cute, toothy smile that always melted my heart, and now I'm feeling all warm and fuzzy inside."

She beams at me. "Maybe it's twins, and we'll both get our wish!"

My eyes pop wide. "Steady on there, Belle, I'm not sure we're ready for two just yet!"

Her body shakes with laughter as the door opens, and an elderly gentlemen with a mop of salt and pepper hair approaches the bed. He has bushy gray eyebrows and a thick gray mustache. The same lady from before slips into the room as the doctor introduces himself. "So, are you ready to meet your baby for the first time?" he inquires with a genuine smile.

"Definitely," Belle says excitedly.

"You're the daddy?" he asks, and I smile.

"Yep, that's me." I squeeze Belle's hand, my heart bursting with pride.

"You estimate you're about five or six weeks pregnant?" He's scanning her chart. "Is that correct?"

"Yes." Her eyes sparkle with excitement.

"Okay, let me just have a feel of your stomach first." He pushes her gown up to just under her bra and starts probing her belly. A frown puckers his brow, and Belle's face pales. I squeeze her hand, trying to ignore the alarm bells echoing distantly in my ears. Please, God, let there be nothing wrong.

He removes his hands, sending her a reassuring smile. "This will feel cold, so prepare yourself." He squirts a gel-like substance all over her stomach, and, to give Belle credit, she barely flinches.

That's my girl.

The nurse turns on the machine, and the screen is blank at first. The doctor trails a hand-held scanner over Belle's tummy, rubbing the gel all over her skin. All of a sudden, a loud *whoosh-whoosh* sound fills the room. "That's your baby's heartbeat," the doc confirms as an image loads on the screen. I'm no expert, but it sounds steady and strong, thumping rhythmically as Belle and I stare at one another in amazement. The most profound sensation presses down on my chest as I listen to our unborn child's heart beating powerfully, and I'm struggling to hold it together. I've never heard anything so amazing.

"I'm sure your doctor confirmed this is just a basic ultrasound, but you can book in for a 3D ultrasound once we process your paperwork, and you'll be amazed at how clear the image is."

The screen loads in front of us, and I lean forward, squinting as I try to distinguish what I'm seeing.

The doctor runs the scanner back and forth a little over Belle's stomach until the picture is clearer. "Look, Belle." I can't contain my excitement as I point at the image. "I can see his head and his arms and legs."

"So, it's a he now, is it?" she grins, her eyes glued to the screen, gripping my hand even tighter.

"It's amazing." I sound like a pussy, all choked up and emotional, but I couldn't give two shits. All I can think is that Belle and I made that little human in there, and it's the most miraculous thing I've ever seen, ever heard.

"I felt that!" Belle exclaims as the baby turns on the screen. "Oh my God!" Her eyes pop wide. "That's what I've been feeling! It was the baby moving! They weren't weird cramps at all." Her shoulders relax as a layer of stress lifts from her.

"Yes, and your pregnancy is much more advanced than you thought," the doctor says, still rubbing the monitor over her belly as he examines the baby on the screen.

All the blood drains from my face.

"What ... what do you mean?" Belle asks quietly, her face pale like mine.

"Judging from the development of the fetus, I am estimating your pregnancy at sixteen or seventeen weeks. It's usual for mothers to start feeling the baby move and kick at this stage."

He is saying other stuff, but I've zoned out. Blood is thrumming in my ears, and my vision is blurring in and out. My heart is torn to shreds, eviscerated, as reality sinks in. Disappointment and grief sweep over me, and my chest aches painfully as all-too-familiar feelings threaten to drown me.

I feel this loss as acutely as I felt the loss of my mother.

I don't need to be a genius to do the math.

I'm not the father of Gabby's baby.

Dylan Woods is.

Chapter Thirty-Four

Gabby

The doctor is most likely telling me important stuff, but I'm not listening to a word. I'm watching Slater's world crash down around him as he reaches the obvious conclusion. The same one I reached the instant the doctor confirmed my pregnancy is more advanced than I thought.

Slater isn't my baby daddy. Dylan is.

My heart pounds wildly, and I'm betting my blood pressure is off the charts. My head is a hot mess. I don't know what to think. How to process this life-altering curveball. Slater was so happy. Happier than I can ever remember him being. And now he looks like his world has just ended.

"Slate." My voice is hoarse, and I can barely get the word out over the raw pain in my throat. He hops up out of his chair, extracting his hand from mine. He sways a little on his feet, and his eyes are jumping wildly all over the place. "I'm sorry," I whisper, tears trickling down my face. "I didn't know."

I remember my Ob-Gyn told me to use additional contraceptive measures when she first switched out my pill, but I thought she was just being overly cautious because she'd previously told me I would most likely have difficulty conceiving thanks to my endometriosis. I didn't take it as seriously as I should have. And then I caught that bug going around campus and spent a couple days worshiping the porcelain gods. I never even considered how it would affect my birth control.

If I'd had more than twenty-four hours to process my pregnancy, I might have thought more carefully about when I most likely conceived, and I might have been able to better prepare Slate.

But, honestly, it never crossed my mind that he might not be the father.

The doctor and nurse are exchanging puzzled expressions.

"I can't, Belle. I just..." He doesn't finish his sentence, racing from the room before anyone can stop him.

My lower lip wobbles as I struggle to keep the tears at bay. It feels like my heart is rupturing behind my chest cavity.

"Is everything okay, Ms. James?" the doctor asks in a gentle tone. I can only shake my head. He sends me a sympathetic smile while he wipes my stomach with a paper towel. "We're done here for today. I'll email the results to your doctor, and you should meet with her to discuss your prenatal care."

He shares another look with the nurse before bidding me goodbye and walking out of the room. There's nothing like a pregnant woman on the verge of an epic meltdown to send a man running for the hills.

The nurse helps me sit up. "Is there anything I can do to help?"

"No," I whisper. "But thanks."

"Do you need me to call a taxi for you?"

I shake my head. "No, I'm good." Even if Slater has left without me, I can call my own taxi or call Mom to come and get me.

"Okay, well take your time getting dressed. This room isn't in use the rest of the day, and if you change your mind, if you need anything, just go to the reception desk and ask for Mary."

"Thank you, Mary." I offer up my best smile. Both her and the doctor were very kind, helping to settle my earlier nerves.

She leaves the room, and I get dressed like a zombie. My tears have subsided, giving way to shocked numbness. I sit down on the chair Slater vacated, burying my head in my hands. *How the hell could I have been pregnant this whole time and not know?* Thinking back, now I understand why I was so teary when all that shit was going down with Dylan. It was pregnancy hormones, and I didn't even know. But, apart from being weepy and more emotional than usual, and a few bouts where I slept for unusually long periods, I have felt completely fine. I've had no vomiting or nausea and no other symptoms. Lack of periods was nothing new for me either.

A horrific thought surfaces in my mind. I drank alcohol on several occasions in the early stages of this pregnancy, and I know that isn't a good thing. I run out to the reception desk and ask for Mary.

I'm biting my nails to the bone as I wait for her to return. I babble out my concerns the instant she arrives, frantically knotting and unknotting my hands as I pace the room.

"Relax, Gabrielle. While alcohol consumption isn't advised in pregnancy, especially in the early stages, there is no risk to your baby unless you were drinking regularly and to excess." She forces me back down into the chair. "Everything looks perfectly normal on the ultrasound, so there is nothing for you to worry about."

"Thank you, and I'm sorry if I overreacted."

"Not at all." She smiles at me. "It's natural to have concerns." She hands me a large envelope. "I've gathered all the information we have on pregnancy. Start taking your vitamins straightaway, eat healthily, get plenty of rest and sleep, and don't forget to exercise regularly. Then attend your appointments, and everything will be fine."

Her words are hugely reassuring, and I'm calmer as I walk out with her. I'm disappointed that Slater isn't in the waiting room. Not that I blame him. I can't even begin to imagine how upset he is.

I'm upset for him too.

I'm just not sure how I feel myself.

It seems wrong to admit I'm upset that the little family scenario I'd visualized with him will not become reality, because that's like admitting I wish the baby was his and not Dylan's, and I can't bring myself to say that either.

I'm lost in thought as I walk out through the hospital. Mom's words from a couple months ago reemerge in my mind.

I love Slater. I know I do. I love him very much.

This doesn't change that.

But I still love Dylan too.

Not in the same way—I can't love him like that when he's hurt me so badly, but I used to daydream about having Dylan's baby, and now I am. *So how can I say I'm upset about it?*

And how ironic is it that I find myself caught between two men I love, just like my mom.

I exit the hospital, taking a seat at the nearest bench as I try to figure out my thoughts.

This is a clusterfuck of epic proportions.

I don't know what to do. Where I go from here.

There is only one thing I am sure of—this baby is my sole priority. No matter how devastated my heart is, I have to stay calm and remain strong for my unborn child. Stress isn't good for the baby, and I've already missed out on the first sixteen weeks of my pregnancy, so I owe it to my child, and to myself, to put both of us first.

Whatever mess I've made of my love life will have to take a back seat.

I get up, still feeling heartsick, and upset for Slater, but feeling more settled at the same time, because at least I have a focus.

But I need to make plans so that I'm prepared when this baby comes into the world.

First things first—I need to have a conversation with Dylan.

I'm waiting in line at the taxi stand when Slater pulls up to the curb. He kills the engine, gets out of the SUV, and comes around to my side. "I'm sorry for walking out like that. I'll take you home."

"It's okay, I understand." My heart aches at the sorrowful expression on his face.

He opens the passenger door and helps me inside before sliding behind the wheel. He adjusts the heating, turns off the radio, and then eases the SUV out into the evening traffic.

A horrible, awkward tension lingers in the space between us, and I hate it.

"I'm so sorry, Slate. I swear I thought this baby was yours," I blurt, and I can't get these words out fast enough. "It never even crossed my mind that it could be Dylan's, and I had no idea I was pregnant when I first started sleeping with you." He says nothing, white knuckling the steering wheel while a muscle pops in and out of his jaw. "Please say something."

"What do you want me to say, Belle?" His voice is clipped. "You've managed to turn my world upside down twice in the space of twenty-four hours." His voice cracks at the end. Looking in the mirror, he signals and pulls over to the shoulder, putting the car in neutral. He doesn't look at me when he speaks. "I wanted this baby so badly," he whispers. "I already loved it. The only other time I've felt this much joy lately is when you agreed to be mine." He rests his head on the wheel. "And now I've lost both of you."

I can't offer words of comfort because there are none. I want to tell him I'm still his and that we can work this out between the three of us, but I need time to think it through, to decipher what I'm feeling, to try to work out what I want. And I can't make any promises to Slater until Dylan knows.

I can't tell anyone else until I tell him. I've already sent him a couple of texts asking to meet, but he hasn't replied so far.

"I need time to process everything," I tell him. "My head is a mess, and, for my baby's sake, I need to try and keep it together."

He nods slowly, staring out the window, still avoiding looking at me. "Of course, and I don't want anything to jeopardize our ... your ... baby's welfare."

Fuck, that hurt me every bit as much as it hurt him.

He restarts the engine. There isn't much more we can say. It's a shitty situation, but I won't say I regret being in this position because this baby already means the world to me.

"Where do you want to go?" he asks.

"I need to go back to your place to pack up my stuff, and could you drop me at Mom's then?"

He nods, and his Adam's apple bobs in his throat. "Sure."

We don't speak after that. It's too painful. When we get back to his house, he leaves me to pack my stuff alone, and then he drives me to Mom's. We sit in the car for a couple of minutes, both lost in thought, staring blankly out the window. Ryan hovers on the porch, somehow sensing we need to be left alone. I messaged him before we left Slater's house asking for a ride.

"You should go," Slater says.

"No matter what happens from here on, please don't forget how much I love you."

Finally, he turns to look me in the eye. I hate the devastation I see there. Hate that I can't take the man I love in my arms and make things better. "And I love you, but it seems our time is already up."

"Don't, Slate. Nothing is decided."

"Belle." His voice softens, and he reaches out, palming my cheek. I lean into him, needing his touch. "I love you enough to know I need to let you go."

A single tear slips out of the corner of my eye, rolling down my face. I can't respond, because my throat has virtually closed, clogged with so much pain it feels like I'm dying. If it was possible to experience death while still breathing, then I'm feeling it. A sob bursts free of my mouth, and it's taking every molecule of willpower not to throw myself at him and beg him not to leave. But I can't do that to him. I can't be selfish.

"Don't cry, sweetheart. I'll be okay. You need to think of what's best for you and the baby." He gulps, and I can see how hard he's working to keep a neutral expression on his face. "That baby needs his father, Belle. I wish to God it had been me, but it's not, and I'll have to find a way of dealing with it. You need to at least give Dylan the choice."

"I love you so much. I'll always love you." I lose the fight, and tears pump out of my eyes, gushing like Niagara Falls.

Slater doesn't hesitate, pulling me into his arms and holding me tight. "Believe me, I know." He kisses me softly, just once, but it's everything. "You were the best thing to ever happen to me, Belle. Loving you has been a pleasure and an honor."

Choking sobs consume me, and it feels as if they've been birthed straight from my anguished soul. "I need to go," I cry. I can't handle this searing pain in my chest anymore. And I feel guilty for the thoughts spinning through my mind. For the voice screaming in my ear telling me to fight for him, not to let him do this, that he's all my heart wants. But I can't give a voice to that inner shouting.

Slater deserves better, and if I love him, I should let him go too.

"Goodbye, Slate." I grab my bag and get out of the car, not looking back despite the temptation to do so when he revs the engine and the car tears off away from the curb.

Ryan is racing toward me with fury on his face. "I will fucking beat him to within an inch of his life!" he yells. "What the hell did he do to you?" I'm sobbing so hard I can't even explain. "Gabby, what did he do? Are you hurt?"

I shake my head. "No." I swipe at the moisture under my eyes. "Slate hasn't hurt me."

He scrubs a hand over his jaw, the tension not easing. "I don't understand then. What's going on?"

"I can't tell you yet, Ryan. I need you to drive me to Heather's."

He jerks back, and his eyes narrow suspiciously. "Please don't tell me you've broken up with Slate to go back to that cheating asshole?"

I shake my head again. "It's not like that."

"Then what is it?"

"I need you to trust me. Just drive me over, wait outside, and then I'll tell you what's going on."

He sighs heavily, flipping the car key over and over in his hand. "I hope you know what you're doing, Gabby. Come on."

Chapter Thirty-Five

I approach Dylan's front door with a hefty amount of anxiety pressing down on my chest and a fine coating of sweat on my clammy hands. My mouth is as dry as the Sahara Desert. Squeezing my eyes closed, I silently coax my pounding heart into quieting down. I raise my hand to knock, when the sound of raised voices filters out through a gap in the door. It's ajar and I peek in, immediately spotting the broken vase lying in smithereens on the hardwood floor. I push the door open and step foot inside, about to open my mouth and announce myself when conversation reaches my ears, and I clam up.

"Gabby deserves to know!" Heather cries out, and I momentarily stop breathing.

I creep along the hallway, tiptoeing around the shattered glass, inching closer to the kitchen door.

"I can't, Mom. I just can't. I've hurt her enough already."

"She'll understand, son, and she'd want to know. She'd want to be here with you."

"No! I don't want her knowing!"

"But, Dylan, I really thi—"

"Goddamn it, Mom! This is my decision to make, not yours!"

Blood is racing through my veins, and my stomach is tied up in knots. Giant goose bumps have sprouted on my arms, and all the tiny hairs on the back of my neck are standing to attention. I have a terrible feeling about this.

"Dylan, that girl has loved you her whole life! You can't shut her out of this!"

"Mom, please!"

Dylan sounds on the verge of tears. I should make my presence known, but my feet are rooted to the floor, and I couldn't move right now even if I wanted to.

"You think this is easy for me?" he shouts in a strangled tone. "You think this is what I want!? I'm not telling her *because* I love her. I love her so fucking much it hurts." He gasps, and the air is thick with tension. "I'm protecting her from further heartache in the best way I know how." Dylan sounds utterly defeated, and I'm scared out of my mind. *What could he possibly be hiding from me? And how much more can I take?* I rub a hand over my stomach, drawing comfort from the motion.

"You're taking away her right to choose!" Heather's pleading tone gives way to sobs. "And that's not right. She'll never forgive you for this." Heather is inconsolable. "I'm begging you, please call her. Tell her to come over, and then be honest with her."

I've heard enough. My head and my heart can't withstand any more. I step into the kitchen, swallowing the bile coating my mouth. "Be honest with me about what?" I ask as they both turn to face me.

Dylan stumbles back, gripping the side of the counter to steady himself. He looks ghastly. He was stick thin the last time I saw him, more gaunt than I'd ever seen him, and while he seems to have filled out a little, he doesn't look well, at all. His eyeballs are bloodshot and sunken, and his skin is an unhealthy shade of gray. His eyes are red-rimmed, and he has at least a weeks' worth of stubble on his chin and jawline.

Heather looks distraught. Her eyes are swollen, her skin flushed and blotchy from crying.

They both stare at me as if I'm a ghost.

"What are you keeping from me, Dylan? What's going on?"

"You shouldn't have come here, Gabby." He gulps, taking a step back.

I halt my forward trajectory. "Are you still contagious?" I should've thought of that before coming here. I can't risk picking up meningitis. Dylan shakes his head, and I release the breath I'd been holding. "But you're clearly still sick." He slowly nods, and all sense of relief flitters away. Certain things slot into place. "You didn't have meningitis, did you?" I quietly ask.

He shakes his head.

"Go sit in the living room," Heather suggests. "I'll bring in coffee and cookies."

"Sure, Mom, because coffee and cookies will make everything better." His bitter tone matches the sour expression on his face.

"I know this isn't you talking," she softly says. "Just go in the room and sit down. You're wearing yourself out, and Gabby looks like she needs a seat."

Dylan looks at me with the saddest expression I've ever seen. "I wish you hadn't come here, Dimples, but I'm really glad you did because underneath it all, I'm a selfish prick."

"Dylan. Please." Heather shoots me a helpless look.

"Come on, Freckles." I loop my arm through his. "Something tells me both of us need to be sitting down for this."

"You look beautiful," he tells me as we sit down beside one another on the couch.

"Thank you. I'd like to say you look the same but—"

"I look like shit," he finishes for me.

"Well, I would've been a little more eloquent, but, yeah, I've definitely seen you looking better."

He turns toward me, and I gaze upon a face I have loved for years. Gone are his sickly features, and he's just the boy who claimed my heart when I was a kid. "Before I start, can I please just hold you?" he asks. "Because I've missed you so fucking much."

I desperately need a hug too. It's been one hell of a day, and I know it's only going to get worse. I slip off my coat and lean into him, resting my head on his shoulder as his arms encircle me. "I never stopped loving you, Gabby, you need to know that," he whispers in my ear. "I'm so unbelievably sorry for what I've put you through. I wish I could turn back the clock and undo everything. You are the last person I ever wanted to hurt."

I squeeze my eyes closed and just breathe him in. Instinctually, I know whatever he has to tell me is going to destroy me all over again, and I just want to savor this moment. To remember all the times he held me like this and how good it felt.

"There are so many reasons to be angry these days," he continues in a low voice, "but that's the one that gets me the most."

I sit up straighter, resting my hands lightly on his chest. Tears gather in my eyes again. Pregnancy hormones are no joke. "Dylan, I can't bear this a second longer. Please tell me what's going on."

"I wanted to spare you this, because I've put you through hell already, but I can't pretend to be upset that you're here when I'm not." His lower lip wobbles. "I'm trying to be strong for Mom, but I'm failing miserably. I've never needed you as much as I do right now."

"I'm here, Dylan." I lower my hands, taking his callused palms in mine. "And I'm not going anywhere, but you need to tell me the truth before I throw up all over your floor because the anticipation is making me ill."

His eyes turn glassy as he peers into my face. "There's no easy way to say this, babe. I can't hide this anymore, and I can't sugarcoat it."

My heart is jackhammering behind my rib cage, and I'm urging him to get it off his chest. "Just tell me, Dylan. Tell me."

"I lied when I said I had meningitis. I told you that to keep you away from me and from the truth, because it's much worse than that."

"Your headaches," I whisper.

He nods. "I should've gone back to the doctor when you suggested it, but I knew, deep down, I knew something was very wrong, and I wanted to deny it. I think some part of me already knew it was too late."

"Dylan," I sob, tears cascading down my face now. "You're scaring the hell out of me."

He holds my face in his shaky hands. "I have a brain tumor, Gabby. Inoperable, terminal brain cancer. The doctors estimate I have four to six months left to live."

Chapter Thirty-Six

"No, Dylan! No!" My lungs tighten, my airways constrict, and I'm gasping, desperately trying to draw enough oxygen to breathe. "You can't die! You can't!" I fling my arms around him, clinging tightly to him as sobs wrack my body. My desolate cries are the only sound in the room, and if I thought I was in pain before, it pales in comparison to the heart-wrenching pain shredding my insides into itty-bitty pieces.

"I'm so sorry, baby. I wish I could offer you hope, but it'd only be a lie. There isn't anything that can be done." My sobs pick up in earnest, and I bury my face in his neck, inhaling his familiar scent while silently screaming in my head. He presses a kiss on top of my hair, hugging me tightly, and we cling to one another as Heather quietly slips in and out of the room, depositing a tray on the coffee table before she leaves. "It feels all kinds of wrong to offer up excuses," he says, stroking my hair, "but the tumor is the reason why I changed. Why my life is an even bigger mess."

I lean back, staring at him through blurry eyes. "It altered your personality," I say as it all clicks into place. "I should've realized." I bite down, hard, on my lower lip. "That day I came to your place, the day Bianca threw me outside"—he winces, and torment radiates from the backs of his eyes—"I was trying to tell you I was concerned. I didn't notice when I was living with you, but after time apart, I began to think there was a possibility that something was wrong. But I should've realized earlier. I'm a nursing student, for flip's sake. I should've known you would never do those things to me without there being something behind it." I drop my head to his shoulder again, and my voice is muffled by his shirt. "I'm so sorry I failed you."

He grips my shoulders, forcing me to look at him. "No, Gabby. I won't let you blame yourself. This is *not* your fault. Do you hear me?"

"I should've made another appointment for you and insisted you get another opinion when your migraines came back in earnest. I was your girlfriend, and I should've known that version of you wasn't you."

He grips the sides of my face, inspecting my tear-sodden eyes. "I will not allow you to take responsibility for this. You didn't know, and why would you have thought it was anything different? You know I've had migraines on and off for years. Besides, even if you had somehow convinced me to go for more tests, it was already too late. I've had this tumor for longer than a couple months, Gabby. Although the symptoms were only noticeable recently, my neurologist said there was probably changes to my immune system that went undetected for much longer than that. There isn't anything you or I could've done to prevent this, so please stop blaming yourself."

"We should seek out a different opinion. You have money, surely there are other surgeons who could operate to remove the tumor or some new radical treatment you can try? There's got to be options."

"I've been to three different specialists, Dimples, and they all concur. It's too late to save me. The tumor is pressing on the frontal lobe, and it's too risky to attempt to remove it. It's a glioblastoma grade four tumor, and it's growing aggressively."

"This doesn't seem real," I whisper, as a strange kind of numbness seeps into my bones. "Why you, Dylan? You have your whole life ahead of you. This isn't fair."

"Believe me, I know. I've spent the last few weeks so fucking angry. As if it isn't bad enough that I'm dying, this illness has robbed me of my identity, caused me to lash out and hurt the people I love, to transform into an asshole I hate."

He runs his thumb along my cheek. "I'm on steroid medication now which helps reduce the personality effects, but I still react out of character at times. And I've been warned that the medication may leave me vulnerable to anxiety and emotional mood swings. If you're going to be around me, you need to prepare yourself for that."

"What do you mean, *if* I'm going to be around? Of course, I'll be here! Where the hell else would I be?"

He hugs me again. "You've no idea how grateful I am to hear you say that, but you need to think about this, Gabby, because it's not going to be pleasant."

I shuck out of his arms, more than a little irritated. "I don't need to think about it, Dylan. I'll be here with you for however long you have left, and I can't believe you were going to take that choice away from me!"

"I was trying to protect you."

"Your mom was right. I would never have forgiven you if you'd gone ahead with it."

"Then it's just as well you barged your way in here and forced my hand." He grins.

I slump on the couch as the emotional weight of today does a number on me. I'm exhausted, both mentally and physically, and I have yet to break the baby news to him. "I still can't believe this. It's surreal. I keep hoping I'm going to wake up and discover it's just been a horrible nightmare."

He sighs, dropping back on the couch beside me. We both stare up at the ceiling. "I know. I'm not sure it's even properly sunk in with me yet. Some days, I wish I'd never had that seizure. That I lived in ignorance until my dying breath."

"Don't say that." I twist my head to the side so I'm looking at him. "That would be a horrible way to go."

"Babe, my death is not going to be easy. The doctors have explained how I'll deteriorate, and it's going to be fucking awful by the end. I don't want that for me or you or Mom."

I thread my fingers in his. "We don't need to think about that now. We should just take it one day at a time and fill each day with as many happy memories as we can."

"There she is," he whispers, lifting our conjoined hands to his mouth. "There's my beautiful, optimistic fighter." He presses a kiss to my knuckles. "That's the best thing you can do for me, Gabby. Help me to forget. I don't want to spend whatever time I have left being all morbid and shit because I might as well shoot myself now if that's the case. I just want to enjoy the time I have left. With you."

I smile at him through fresh tears. "I can do that. *We* can do that."

"Good. Now we best drink our coffee before it goes cold. Momma Woods is pretty fierce these days." He sits up straighter, scooting to the edge of the couch, and pouring coffee into two cups.

I add a dribble of cream and absently nibble on a cookie as I mull over everything. Dylan is reflective too, but the silence isn't uncomfortable, because there is no way two people as close as Dylan and I are could ever experience awkward silence. It's like I said to him, this whole situation is surreal. On the one hand, being back in this house, drinking coffee with Dylan, seems so normal it's almost refreshing, but, on the other hand, it seems weird that the world still carries on as usual after delivering such a bombshell. After the initial shock and tears have subsided, I'm in a bit of a numbed aware state, and it feels odd to be almost pretending like the big C doesn't exist.

And I still haven't worked out how to broach the baby subject. I'm tempted to put it off for another day, but I can't take even a single day for granted anymore. I came here to tell Dylan he's going to be a daddy, and I'm not leaving until I do.

I'm sure I'll want to rage at the world once my emotions return with a vengeance, but it's like my body and my mind are working in sync, understanding I can't cope with the pressure of everything that's shaken me like a violent thunder storm today.

I finish my cookie and put my coffee down. "Dylan, I came here today because I had something to tell you too."

Worry lines crease his brow. "Okay." He draws the word out, and I sense the fear building inside him. He puts his cup down and gives me his full attention.

"This was already going to be a shock, but, after what you've told me, it's going to be an extremely emotional thing to hear, but I can't sugarcoat this either."

"Rip the Band-Aid, Gabby. I can handle it."

I wet my dry lips and draw a brave breath. "I'm pregnant, Dylan, and the baby is yours."

"He fucking knocked you up!" Ryan roars, storming into the room with his fists clenched before Dylan can even respond.

I jump up, holding out a hand to stop him. "I told you to wait in the car, so what the hell are you doing here?!!"

"Eavesdropping is obviously a James family trait," Dylan says, standing and pulling me away from Ryan.

"This is why you were crying and why Slate isn't returning my calls," Ryan surmises. Understanding ghosts over his face. "Aw, shit, man. He knows, and he thought it was his, didn't he?"

I have no idea if Dylan knew Slater and I were officially together, but I'm not going to lie. "We both did," I confirm, nodding at my brother. "Slate came with me to the ultrasound, and he was devastated when the doctor confirmed I was much further along than I thought."

"I can't believe this," Dylan says, looking shell-shocked as he sinks to the floor, taking me with him. I'm on his lap with my legs off to one side. I rest my head on top of his as he lowers his hand to my belly, rubbing the small bump. "*My* baby, *our* baby, is growing inside you?" An awestruck expression adds much-needed color to his face. I nod. He kisses me, and I let him. It's a soft, tender kiss that doesn't last more than five seconds. When he pulls back, tears cloud his eyes. "I imagined this moment so many times but never like this." His voice is swimming in emotion. "I didn't want it to be like this."

"What a fuckup you've made of your life, asshole," Ryan unhelpfully cuts in. "If you think you're going to abandon Gabby and leave her to deal with this alone while you shack up with that slut Bianca or fuck your way through every skank on campus, you have another think coming."

Ryan obviously hadn't been eavesdropping long enough. "Sit down and shut up," I tell my brother, pointing at a chair. When he opens his mouth to retaliate, I pin him with one of my special death glares. "There is stuff you don't know, so before you say one more word, sit down so I can explain."

He perches on the arm of the couch, narrowing his eyes suspiciously at both of us. "So, explain."

"I have terminal brain cancer," Dylan bluntly says.

Ryan's eyes almost bug out of his head. "What?"

Dylan slings his arm around my waist, holding me firmly against him. "The tumor is pressing on the part of my brain which controls my moods and inhibitions, among other things. It altered my personality in a way I couldn't control. For months, it felt like there was a different person inside me. I'd react, say and do things, without thinking, hurting others in the process, and then I'd snap out of it and hate myself for it. It was kind of a relief to finally have an explanation although it doesn't make up for all the hurt I've caused."

Ryan looks floored, plopping down onto the chair. "Shit, man. I don't know what to say."

"There isn't much to say. I'm dying, and all I can hope and pray for now is that I live long enough to see my child born."

That statement cracks through whatever hazy wall I've been sheltering behind, and I burst out crying again. Dylan cradles me to his chest, holding me tight as I sob.

No one speaks, because there's nothing anyone can say to take away this pain, or the realization that my child is going to grow up without a father.

Dylan will die knowing he's leaving his son or daughter behind without the privilege of ever getting to know and love him.

Chapter Thirty-Seven

The next couple days are some of the most harrowing I've ever experienced. I called a family meeting at our house, and Heather and Dylan came with me. Together, we told my family the news about Dylan's cancer and my pregnancy.

Copious tears were shed.

Frequent hugs were doled out.

Numerous whiskeys were drunk. I had to stick to water, and it was one of the few times in my life where I desperately wished I could ingest alcohol until I passed out. At least I had a partner in crime—Terri was abstaining too. We've discovered we are due to give birth only nine days apart. My child will have a ready-made playmate in his or her new cousin. It brings some small degree of comfort to know my future sister-in-law is pregnant alongside me.

I'm stumbling through life at the moment like I'm walking through fog. But I'm trying to hold it together for the sake of my baby, and for Dylan. But it's hard. Because I remember how difficult it was for Slater those last few weeks when his mom was dying, and I know exactly what's lying in store for us down the line. However, every day I give myself a little pep talk, reminding myself that dwelling on that now will not change the outcome. All it will do is ruin whatever time we have left. So, I'm choosing to push it aside. I will handle that bridge when we come to it. For now, I'm going to do everything in my power to forget about that. To just take each day as it comes. If Dylan can maintain his composure, and not fall apart with everything going on, then I owe it to him to be strong.

In a weird role reversal, I'm spending every waking minute with Dylan and every night tossing and turning in bed worrying about Slate. No one has seen or heard from him since the night he dropped me off, and I'm hugely concerned. Both Ryan and I have left tons of voicemails and sent hundreds of texts and messages, but he hasn't reached out to either one of us. Ryan has checked with some of their buddies and stopped by Slater's place, and he even traveled back to the house in Newark in the hopes of finding him there, but he's vanished without a trace.

"When are you returning to UD?" Dylan asks me later that night when we are back at his place, watching a movie. Heather has returned to work, teaching her yoga classes, happy that I'm here to keep an eye on her son. I think she's been afraid to leave the house in case anything happens to him while she's gone.

I pull my knees into my chest, preparing to tell him what I've decided. "I'm not going back. I've decided to take a leave of absence for the moment. I already emailed my advisor to put things in motion."

He pauses the TV, twisting around so he's facing me. "I don't want you to put your life on hold for me."

"I'm not." I shake my head. "I'm just prioritizing the things that are important in my life right now. That means you and the baby. I can go back to college any time."

I lift the framed ultrasound pic off the coffee table, smiling at the image of the tiny human growing inside me. Mom surprised me this morning with the cute frame, and I'm so appreciative for my parents' support. My brothers too. While everyone is upset over Dylan's prognosis, they are overjoyed at the prospect of another James' grandbaby.

When Forever Changes

My heart is so full of love for this child, and it was instantaneous, like I got smacked in the face with a giant love bubble the moment I found out I was expecting. I haven't the first clue about being a mom, and while it's scary, especially with the realization that I'll be parenting him or her on my own, excitement is the overriding emotion. Even though I only have a small bump, I can't stop rubbing it. It's like my hands are superglued to my stomach.

As if he knows I'm thinking about him, the baby levels a swift kick to my left side, and my hand instantly moves to that spot on my tummy. "Even the baby agrees," I say, smiling at Dylan. "Quick, come here and feel." I lift my top, exposing my little baby bump as Dylan kneels on the carpet before me. I take his hand and place it in the spot where the baby just kicked. "Give it a minute, and hopefully, he'll kick again."

Dylan's palm is clammy and a little cold on my skin, reminding me that he's ill. "I don't want you to miss out on anything."

Because you're going to miss out on pretty much everything else.

I think it, but I don't articulate it, because I'm abiding by Dylan's wishes and trying to act as normally as possible. I'm trying not to think about his illness and how he's not going to be with me to experience every milestone in our baby's life. It makes me incredibly sad, but I shove those thoughts aside. I don't have much time left with Dylan, and I'm determined to do everything I can to make it the happiest time it can possibly be, given the circumstances. "This is your experience as much as it's mine."

The baby rewards us with another confident kick, and the look on Dylan's face is priceless. Tears prick his eyes. "Wow, that was a strong kick. I think our boy's going to be sporty. He must get that from your side of the family because we both know how completely uncoordinated I am," he jokes.

"Hopefully, he, or *she*, will be the best of both of us." I've taken to calling the baby "he" because I hate calling it "it," but we've both decided we want to learn the sex, so, hopefully, at my next ultrasound we'll find out whether it's a boy or a girl.

"If it's a girl, I hope she looks like you." Dylan plants a soft kiss to my stomach. "You hear that, little one? I hope you got your momma's good looks and her charming personality."

"I hope our baby inherits your quirky sense of humor and your intelligence," I say, running my fingers through his hair. He presses his cheek to my stomach even though the baby has settled down again. "If our kid has even a tenth of your intelligence, he'll conquer the world."

Dylan lifts his head off my stomach, moving closer to me. Winding his hand around the back of my neck, he pulls my face toward his, making his intention crystal clear. As much as it hurts me to do this, I turn my face to the side so his kiss lands on my cheek instead of my mouth.

Unspoken words settle in the space between us.

His eyes bore into mine, and his gaze skims over my face. He's trying to mask his hurt, but I know him well enough to see it. "I know I've no right to ask this, but I'm not going to hold anything back either. Where do we stand, Gabby? What is this between us?"

I rub a tense spot between my brows, before patting the empty space beside me. "Come sit with me." He climbs off his knees and sits down on the couch, leaving a little gap between us. "I'm going to be brutally honest with you, even though this will hurt, but I don't want there to be any lies or mistruths or discomfort between us."

"Is it Slater?" he asks, and I can see he's bracing himself for my reply.

"Yes, and no." I tuck my hair behind my ears and level him with an earnest look. "Slater and I have been dating these past couple months, and it was serious between us."

"Was?"

"Slater let me go when we discovered the baby was yours. He was trying to do the right thing, because he knows..." I have to stop, because I just can't say this to Dylan. I can't put words to what we both already know and hate.

"What it's like to grow up without a father." Dylan goes there.

"As I do, and it's the last thing I would wish for my child," he whispers, hanging his head. I scurry to his side, resting my head on his shoulder.

Silence engulfs us.

"Do you love him?" he asks after a bit.

"Yes."

There's a pregnant pause. "I don't need to ask if he loves you because I know he does. I suspect Slater Evans has loved you as long as I have."

I don't confirm or deny it, and silence descends again. Fear rolls off Dylan in waves, and, because I know him inside and out, I can tell what's on his mind. "Ask me," I whisper.

He clears his throat, taking my hand and holding it tight. "Do you still love me?" he whispers.

"Most definitely yes," I reply immediately, and his whole body relaxes. "And I've forgiven you for what you put me through, but it doesn't mean I've forgotten all the ways in which you hurt me." I lift my head so I'm eyeballing him. "I know now you couldn't help your urges. I understand it wasn't you. I know you would never intentionally set out to cheat, but it doesn't change the fact that you did. It doesn't obliterate the pain and the hurt I still feel inside every time I think of it. And I can't get past that enough to pick up where we left off in our relationship." I look down at my lap. "I'm sorry."

"Hey," he tips my chin up with one finger. "Don't be sorry. None of this is your fault."

"It's not yours either."

"It doesn't make any difference. We are where we are, and I respect you, Gabby. So much. You can't help how you feel. How I've made you feel. I wish you didn't feel like that, but you can't force it. And don't feel guilty about Slater. I pushed you into his arms."

"Slater is the other reason I can't be your girlfriend. I have strong feelings for him too, and it just wouldn't feel right."

Air whooshes out of his mouth, and he looks so unbelievably sad that I briefly reconsider. *Am I cruel to deny this to him when he's dying? Can't I push the hurt and betrayal aside, long enough to give him his girlfriend back for however long he has left? Am I selfish to put my own feelings before his?*

"I understand. I don't like it, but I'll respect your wishes." Dylan pulls our conjoined hands up to his chest, right over the place where his heart still beats strongly. "I know what's going through your mind now. I know how utterly selfless you are, and that you're beating yourself up inside for not falling back into my arms. But I don't want you to pretend anything with me. That isn't what I want at all, so don't feel guilty or selfish."

I hate the sense of relief powering through me at his words, but I appreciate his honesty. "Thank you." I debate whether I should ask the next question, but I don't want to spend the next few months on edge wondering if she's going to show up any time. "Speaking of girlfriends, what about Bianca?"

"Bianca was never my girlfriend, and she wasn't living with me despite what she led you to believe. That day you showed up to collect your stuff, I genuinely had no idea she'd replaced your clothes with her own shit. As soon as I got over my migraine, I made her take all her stuff back to her dorm."

"But you *were* with her."

"Yes, but it was only ever sex." I knew he was sleeping with her, but, God, that admission still hurts so damn much. He, at least, has the decency to look ashamed. "I'm not proud of my actions, Dimples, but I can't undo them, unfortunately." He rubs soothing circles on the back of my hand. "You don't need to worry about Bianca. I took care of it in the hospital. I don't even know why she was still around, because I treated her pretty terribly too. I was furious when I heard what she'd done, how she'd spoken to you, and I ripped Mom a new one for not standing up to her."

"Heather was upset and afraid for you, Dylan. I knew if it was any other circumstance, she would have."

"Well, that's not something that will ever happen again. Bianca is gone, and I'm here now, and no one will be speaking to you like that again."

"Thanks, Freckles." I return my head to his shoulder. "It'll just be like old times. When we were besties."

"Except now we're besties with a baby on the way," he adds, pressing a hand to my lower belly. I can hear the smile in his voice. "Not that you'd know by looking at you. You're still tiny, Gabby. I don't know where that baby is hiding."

"Don't jinx me. Now you've voiced that, I'll bet I blow up like an elephant. You'll wake up, and I'll be waddling all over the place."

"I wouldn't care," he says, pressing a kiss to the top of my head. "You'd still be the most gorgeous pregnant woman ever."

"Dylan," I whisper, circling my arm around his waist.

"Yeah, Dimples."

"I love you."

He hugs me fiercely. "I love you too, Gabby. You and Junior. Even when I'm no longer of this world, I will still love you both so much."

Chapter Thirty-Eight
Slater

"Jesus H, man. Where the fuck have you been?" Ryan grabs me into a hug the minute I step foot inside the house.

"Went to the cabin to clear my head." It was Paul's suggestion, and it was a good one. I called Gabby's dad after I dropped her off that day to explain why I wouldn't be around for a while. The Jameses are like family to me, and I didn't want to drop off the face of the earth with no word. While I didn't divulge Gabby's secret, I told him we'd had to end things and it would hurt too much to be around her.

Paul's such a good man. He didn't pry. He just told me how sorry he was to hear that, and he offered me the use of his cabin, promising he wouldn't tell anyone I was there.

I've always loved the solitude of that place, and we spent many happy times in that cabin over the years, so I jumped at the chance and took off immediately.

"Did it work?" Ryan asks, dragging me out of my mind.

"A little," I lie. The solitude was actually the reason I came back. I was going out of my fucking mind imagining Gabby curled up in bed beside Dylan every night. Mentally, I cursed myself for telling her I was letting her go. I thought I was doing the right thing. Making it easy for her to go back to him. To build a family with the guy she always dreamed of building one with.

But I was a fucking fool not to fight for her.

"Dude, I've been trying to reach you, because there's shit you don't know. Stuff you need to hear." He motions for me to follow him into the kitchen. I drop my bags on the floor in the hall and follow him.

He pours me a whiskey straight, and I arch a brow. "Far be it from me to turn good whiskey down, but isn't it a little early?"

"Not for this conversation it isn't."

I take the drink and pull out a stool.

"I want to ask you one thing first." Ryan leans forward on his elbows. "I know about the baby, but what I don't know is why you walked away so easily."

I growl, throwing the whiskey down the back of my throat in one go. "There was nothing easy about walking away from your sister. It was the hardest fucking thing I've ever done, but I did it for her. Because I love her enough to set her free."

"Fuck, you're a better man than me, Evans. I don't think I couldn've done the same thing."

"I wouldn't be so sure about that. I've spent the past week berating myself for handing her back to him. My own experiences clouded my judgment, and my head was, *is*, all over the place." I rub a hand over my aching chest. "I thought that baby was mine, and I was so fucking happy."

"I'm so sorry, dude. I really am."

"I know Belle still loves him, and I didn't want to be responsible for depriving a child of his father, but what I failed to realize, in the heat of the moment, was that Dylan doesn't have to be with Belle to be that kid's dad. I was a stupid fucker to let her go without at least discussing it, and I'll spend the rest of my life paying for my mistake."

Ryan stares at me strangely, and I have no clue what's going through the dude's head. The stool scrapes as he rises, going to the cupboard and retrieving the bottle of whiskey. He sets it down on the counter between us. "You're going to need another one of those."

I scrutinize his face but he's still giving nothing away. "What don't I know?"

"Shit, man. I hardly know where to start." He scrubs his hands down his face, looking like he's aged overnight.

I try to brace myself for whatever hell he's about to unleash. I don't speak for the next few minutes as he fills me in on everything I missed. When he's finished telling me, I pour both of us another whiskey, and we down them without saying a word. I bury my head in my hands, drawing deep breaths. "Fuck. That's ... shit, I have no words." I crick my neck from side to side, attempting to loosen the kinks but my shoulders are locked tight, rigid with stress and shock. "How is Belle coping?"

"She's putting on a brave face, but I know it's killing her."

"Tell me what I should do."

He holds up his palms. "Dude, don't look to me for that. I can't tell you what to do, and, honestly, I can't see that there's anything you or anyone can do to help make this better."

I drag myself through the next two weeks, going about my business as I need to, but there's a massive void in my life. I fucking miss the shit out of Belle. It's as if someone has reached into my chest and squeezed my heart so tight it's barely functioning. My life is empty without her, and I don't know how I'm ever expected to get over it. I've even resorted to sleeping in Belle's bed some nights, because the sheets still smell like her and I need to feel close to her. After some lengthy internal debate, I sent her a text the day after I returned to UD, telling her how sorry I was to hear about Dylan and offering my support as a friend.

But she never replied, and I didn't message her again.

Ryan confirmed she's not returning to college, and I should be grateful that I won't have to see her and Dylan together, but I miss her so Goddamned much I honestly think I'd prefer if they were here even if it would devastate my heart repeatedly to see them parading around campus as a couple again. Even work brings me no measure of joy, because every time I look up, I expect to see Belle flirting with a customer or flashing those baby blues at me.

I'm sitting in the living room in the dark, nursing a bottle of whiskey, when Myndi returns after her shift at the diner. She spends so many nights here now she should just officially move in. I'm expecting Ryan to broach the subject with Austin and me sooner rather than later. Not that I'd have any objections. Myndi's cool and low drama, so I'd have zero issue with her becoming a permanent fixture around here.

I lean my head back against the couch, wishing I could erase this shitty day and start over. I stormed out on my shift earlier tonight after I got into a humdinger of an argument with that bitch Shelby. She was throwing hurtful accusations around about Belle, and I lost my shit with her. Almost hit a girl. Donny could tell I was close to breaking point, so he told me to get the fuck out of there and I didn't need to be told twice.

"Whatcha doing sitting here in the dark?" Myndi asks, propping her hip against the open doorway.

"Drowning my sorrows in a bottle of Jack," I reply, waving the bottle at her.

"Can anyone join this pity party or is it a solo effort?"

I grin. "You're welcome to join me, but don't you want to cuddle up to your man in bed?"

She kicks off her shoes and drops down into the reclining chair. "Ryan is presently snoring his head off upstairs, and I believe I'll need at least a couple shots of whiskey to knock me the fuck out. Otherwise, I'm liable to murder him in his sleep." I can just detect the sweet smile she throws my way in the dark room. "You're actually doing your best friend a favor by letting me join you."

"Well, when you put it like that." I stand. "I'll grab you a glass from the kitchen." When I return a couple minutes later, Myndi is stretched out in the chair with her legs kicked out in front of her.

"I could marry this chair and live happily ever after just stretched out like this for the rest of my life," she purrs contentedly.

"I think your boyfriend might have a word to say about that," I tease pouring her a decent shot of J.D.

"I can make room for Ryan, provided he keeps the snoring to a minimum."

"Good luck with that plan." I chink my glass against hers, welcoming the burn as the whiskey glides down my throat. "I can't remember a time Ryan didn't snore, even when we were younger, and it was uncommon for kids to snore like that. It's why I used to sneak into Belle's room in the middle of the night."

Myndi snorts. "Yeah, I'll bet that was the reason." She lowers her voice an octave. "Creeper."

I bark out a laugh. "I'm sure the way I used to stare at her while she was sleeping could be viewed as creepy, but I never looked at it like that."

"You just loved her," Myndi softly adds.

"Yeah." I down the rest of the whiskey and pour another. My hand shakes a little and my vision is unfocused, but I want to get completely shitfaced so I can fall asleep and dream of nothing.

"I'm sorry you're hurting. That you're all hurting."

"At least she has him. All I have is this half-empty bottle, a huge helping of regret, and a massive dose of the green-eyed monster." I gulp back the whiskey like it's water. "And I know how that makes me sound. I'm a fucking horrible person to be jealous of a guy that's dying. I mean, Christ." I put my glass down, dragging my hands through my hair. "I don't wish that on him, on anyone, and I am genuinely so fucking sorry for the guy, but I also hate his fucking guts because he has everything I've ever wanted so, even though he's dying, he's still the luckiest fuck on the planet."

"That's a lot of fucks in the one sentence."

"The situation warrants it."

"Damn straight." She raises the chair and puts her glass down, sitting more upright. "But here's the thing, Slate. Gabby isn't with Dylan, at least not like that."

I frown. "What do you mean?"

"She's not sleeping with him, Slate. She's not his girlfriend. She is there as his best friend and the mother of his baby, but that's as far as their relationship goes, so you can stop torturing yourself over that at least."

"Why? Why the hell isn't she with him?"

"Only Gabby can answer you that." She stands, draining the last few drops from her glass. "But, if you want my advice, don't give up on her. If you love her, just hang tight."

I'm walking out of class the following afternoon when Ryan messages me to let me know Belle is coming to the house to collect the rest of her stuff. He warns me Dylan will be with her and that he'll let me know when they're gone. Perhaps he's right. Maybe I should steer clear. But I'm racing across campus to my SUV before I've even consciously decided to show up.

Dylan is coming down the stairs with a paper box in his arms when I burst through the open front door. His eyes lock on mine, and he stops mid-step. He doesn't look great. Dude looks a little bloated, and you can tell from his eyes that he's seriously unwell. I clear my throat. "You need a hand?"

He resumes walking. "Nah. I've got this."

I shove my hands into my pockets, rocking back on my heels as he descends the stairs.

To say it's awkward would be putting it mildly.

I step aside to let him pass. "Dylan." He stops in the doorway, glancing over his shoulder at me. "I was really sorry to hear the news."

He turns around, putting the box on the ground, and a sneer pulls up the corners of his mouth. "Were you? Or did you throw a party knowing I'll be dead soon and you can move back in on my territory?!"

"Dylan!" Belle appears at the top of the stairs, glowing like an angel despite the look of horror on her face. "That was really inappropriate," she quietly says as she comes down the stairs. "And very unfair."

A myriad of emotions treks over his face, and he looks like he's trapped in some internal dilemma. After a minute, he sighs. "Shit, sorry, man. I take it back."

I'm not sure what's going on here, but I accept his apology. "Thanks, and it's already forgotten."

"This is the last one," Ryan says, traipsing down the stairs with another box in his arms. He doesn't look in the slightest bit surprised to see me.

Belle moves away from the stairs, and she's standing so close to me I can smell her delicate floral scent, and my heart aches painfully.

"I'll wait for you in the car," Dylan tells her, looking quickly at me. "Take all the time you need."

She smiles at him. "Thanks, D."

Ryan puts his box down and pulls Belle into a giant hug. "I'm going to miss you so much, but I promise I'll drop by every Sunday, and if you need anything, at any time, I'm only a phone call away."

Belle sniffs, hugging him tight. "Thanks, little big bro. You're the best."

"I love you, Tornado." He presses a kiss to the top of her head. "Nothing is too much trouble for you."

Tears glisten in her eyes when she pulls away. "Damn pregnancy hormones," she jokes, swiping her damp skin.

Ryan pats her stomach, and my eyes drift to the growing bump. It's only been three weeks since I've seen her, but she looks noticeably pregnant now. My stomach is tied up in knots.

"Take care of my niece or nephew," Ryan says, kissing her on the cheek. He gives my shoulder a squeeze. "I'm heading back to class. Later."

I nod, watching as he picks up the box and leaves, closing the door over behind him.

Belle clears her throat. "Dylan didn't mean it. He blurts out stuff without being fully aware of what he's saying. His neurologist suggested we point it out to him when he's being inappropriate so he can try to become more self-aware." Her tongue darts out, wetting her lips, and my eyes follow the movement like the greedy, selfish bastard I am. "It's not as bad as it was," she says, continuing to defend him. "because he's on steroids and other meds to help control the side effects." That explains his bloated appearance. Poor guy.

"It's fine. You don't have to explain. Ryan filled me in."

She shuffles awkwardly on her feet, and I can't think of anything to say, which is ridiculous, because Belle and I have never had any difficulty communicating.

"How have you been?" she asks in a gentle tone.

"I'm okay," I lie. "I'm so sorry, Belle. I couldn't believe it when Ryan told me."

Her face falls. "Yeah, it's horrible, but I'm trying my best to stay strong for Dylan." Her hands gravitate to her belly, and she rubs them over her bump.

"You look really beautiful. Pregnancy suits you."

"Thank you." Her features soften. "I miss you," she whispers.

Fuck. I want to pull her into my arms so badly it's physically paining me to keep my hands in my pockets. "I miss you too. So much."

Tension is thick in the air as we stare at one another. Belle has always been beautiful, but she's absolutely stunning right now even with the veil of sadness hanging over her.

"I shouldn't have pushed you away," I truthfully admit. "I thought I was doing the right thing but—"

"Please, don't, Slate." Her face contorts, and I can see her pain, and feel it as acutely as mine.

"Let me help, you, Belle. Even if it's only as a friend. You shouldn't have to go through this alone. I know what it's like to care for someone who is dying, and you need all the support you can get. You were there for me with Mom. Let me do this for you."

"I'm not alone, Slate. Everyone is rallying around, and while Dylan is tired and feeling a little sick from the chemo and radiation, he's actually not too bad, and we go out and do stuff most days."

"Are you back together with him?" Man, I'm such a selfish ass. I swore I wasn't going to ask her that. I look at the ground. "Forget I said that. It's none of my business."

She moves in front of me, gently taking my arm and pulling my hand out of my pocket. She threads her fingers through mine, and that one gesture is everything. "Look at me," she whispers. I tip my head up, hating to see so much torment on her face. "I'm not sleeping with Dylan. I'm supporting him as his best friend and the mother of his child, and he knows that's all I can offer him."

I hate how my heart skips to a new beat. How hope replaces the blood flowing through my veins. How my soul rejoices at her words. How I hold my breath in expectation of her next sentence.

"But I can't be with you either, Slate."

Everything euphoric withers and dies. All hope leaves me instantaneously.

"It doesn't mean I don't love you, because I love you so much it kills me to say this, but I can't let my feelings get in the way of what I need to do. I have to prioritize Dylan and my baby, and I hate that it means I have to shut you out, because you don't deserve that, but I can't just be your friend. Not when you are so much more than that. Not when it's taking every ounce of self-control I possess to stop myself from kissing you right now."

Screw this shit. I can't stand here, watching the woman I love in utter agony, and not try to do something. I take her into my arms, holding her tight. Her body trembles underneath me, but she doesn't fight this, circling her arms around my waist and hugging me back.

"I don't want to make things difficult for you, Belle, so I'll stay away," I whisper. I almost choke as the words leave my mouth, because it'll kill me to walk away from her, but I can't be selfish. She's going through hell, and I won't add to it. "But it doesn't mean you won't be in my thoughts and on my mind twenty-four-seven. It doesn't mean I won't be there for you if you ask me to. It means I respect your wishes and I don't want to add to your agony. It means I can be patient and that I'm going to wait for you. It means I love you more than life itself and I will do whatever is necessary to help ease this burden on you."

Squeezing my eyes closed, I press a kiss to the top of her head, committing the feel of her in my arms to memory. "Take care of Dylan, but don't forget to take care of yourself too."

Then I release her, walking upstairs without a backward glance, letting her leave, not knowing when, or if, I'll ever see her again.

Chapter Thirty-Nine
Gabby

The next couple of months fly past far too quickly. Even though each passing week brings me closer and closer to meeting my child, it also reduces the time I have left with Dylan. Although he'd previously told the neurologist and oncologist that he didn't want chemoradiation, he changed his mind the instant he found out about the baby.

"Come in, Dylan," Dr. Stevens says, opening his door and extending his hand. Dylan wobbles a little on his feet as he gets up, but I know better than to try to help. Dylan hates that Heather and I have to do so much for him. Hates the loss of independence. Since he started chemotherapy and radiation, he has been tired and nauseous, and some days he only has enough energy to move from his bed to the couch and back again.

"Hello, Gabby." Dr. Stevens shakes my hand, offering me his usual warm smile. "You are positively blooming."

"Thank you." I return his smile before taking a seat beside Dylan in front of the desk. My hands rest on top of my bump, rubbing my swollen belly as if on autopilot.

"Did I tell you we're having a boy?" Dylan says, his tone radiating with pride as he puts his hand on top of mine.

"You mentioned at your last appointment that you were going in for an ultrasound." The doctor sits down on the other side of the desk. "That's fantastic news. Congratulations."

"Thank you."

"So, how have you been?" he asks, eyeballing Dylan.

"The same, pretty much. Some days are better than others."

The doctor's expression turns more serious, and he straightens up in his chair. I've come to recognize his little tells, and he's gearing up to tell us something we won't like. Bile floods my mouth, and I cling to Dylan's hand. "I think we can call a halt to the chemo and radiation, and that should give you some relief from the symptoms."

"Why?" I inquire.

He shoots us a sympathetic look. "I'm afraid the treatment isn't working. It's not slowing the growth of the tumor. It's just too aggressive."

I close my eyes, inhaling and exhaling deeply and silently counting to ten in my head. It's the only way I'll hold the tears at bay.

"Is there anything else we can try?" Dylan quietly asks, slinging his arm around my shoulder.

"I'm going to change some of your meds, and alter some of the doses, but, apart from that, I'm afraid there isn't much more we can do. I'm sorry."

I open my eyes, and Dylan is nodding. "Okay, thanks."

The doctor runs through the changes to his medication, and I take out my notepad, writing it all down. I've found, from experience, that I don't always remember everything the specialists tell us. It's been so overwhelming, and all these new words and procedures are foreign to me, so now I write it all down. And when Dylan is asleep at night, I pore over my iPad, lapping up every bit of information I can find. My dad always says knowledge is power, and I've found that to be true with Dylan's situation. The more informed I am, the more I can ask the type of questions that need to be asked.

When the appointment is finished, we walk to the door hand in hand.

"Gabby, before you leave." Dr. Stevens rounds the desk with a leaflet in his hand. "I thought this might be of interest to you. It's a support group for caregivers." His compassionate eyes probe mine. "I know how devoted you are to Dylan, but it's important you take care of yourself too. You and the baby."

"You think I don't know that!" Dylan snaps. "I'm looking after her the best I can."

I smooth the creases in his brow with my thumbs. "Freckles, you're doing it again. The doctor wasn't personally criticizing you, he was just reminding me to take care of myself and the baby."

A muscle clenches in Dylan's jaw, and he curls and uncurls his fists at his side. When he has himself under control, the rage on his face fades. "Sorry, Doc."

"Nothing to be sorry for. Take care of yourselves, and I'll see you at the next appointment."

We walk out to the car in silence. The prognosis weighs like a ten-ton truck on my mind, but it's my job to cheer Dylan up, so I push my own gloomy thoughts aside, turning to him once we are both seated. "Do you feel up to going somewhere this afternoon? Just the two of us?"

His chest heaves, and he looks out the window without replying. Disappointment settles over me, but I plant a smile on my face as I turn the engine on and pull out of the hospital parking lot.

Dylan had to relent and purchase a new vehicle because his dad's old truck isn't the most reliable. Between his cancer and my pregnancy, we can't afford to take any risks, so he bought a brand spanking new Ford Expedition. He insisted on putting it in my name, but I didn't argue. Like I didn't protest when he installed the baby seat, bought the most expensive baby furniture on the market, and hired an interior designer to transform one of the spare bedrooms in his Mom's house into a nursery. I know he wants to have everything in place, to make sure we're prepared and I'm looked after, and you won't hear me complaining. Fact is, watching his enthusiasm while we shopped online for everything brought a smile to my face. I need to see evidence of the old Dylan to remind myself that he's still the same man I love at times when he lashes out. Although his outbursts are few and far between, it's still horrible to bear witness to.

Cancer is an evil disease, irrespective of where it invades your body, but brain cancer is its own special brand of evil, because it steals personalities before it steals lives. It's like a double assault with a deadly weapon, and it's so brutally unfair.

"Yeah, let's do that," Dylan says, cutting through my thoughts. "I'd like to do something together."

My smile returns, and there's a new little pep in my heart. "Any special requests?"

"How about we rent bikes and go for a ride and picnic in the park? We haven't done that in years."

"Excellent idea! Provided I can fit this ginormous bump behind the wheel." I wink at him.

"You're not ginormous. You're still as gorgeous as ever." He leans over the console, pressing a kiss to my cheek.

"And you're still a complete charmer."

"I'm only telling the truth. Companies should be snapping you up to promote their pregnancy products. Sales would go through the roof."

"You know you're biased, right?" I arch a brow, glancing at him quickly.

"You know you're delusional, right?"

I throw back my head laughing. "All right, I'll give you that one."

Heather shoots me a concerned look when we arrive back at the house and tell her our plans, but I send her a reassuring one in return. I won't let anything happen to Dylan while he's with me. I understand her concerns. I'm the same every time I'm not with him.

My family has been amazingly supportive. Mom drops by most days for coffee and a chat. Some days she drags me out for a walk, insisting I take a break. Other days, she drags Heather out for lunch with the girls, so she has some time away from her caregiving duties. Dad drops by every weekend to mow Heather's lawn and do any odd jobs around the house. My brothers take turns stopping by to watch a movie or grab a pizza or to just gossip about stuff going on around town, doing anything and everything they can to keep things normal for Dylan.

Consequently, I'm forced out of the house at least one night a week. Either Terri insists I go to some prenatal class with her or Myndi shows up to drag me to a movie, or Dean takes me and the girls out for an early dinner, but my family is insistent that I get some alone time for myself. Dylan encourages me to go, and I do it, but I can't relax. Every second I'm away from him, I'm worrying that something will happen while I'm gone.

So, I understand Heather's concern, especially since she's upset over the report from the doctor. But that's exactly why we need to do this. Dylan needs a distraction, and, if I'm honest, I do too.

Heather chats with her son in the living room while I make sandwiches, chop fruit, and pack some crackers and chips for Dylan along with some bottles of water and juice. I load them into my backpack, and then we set off on foot, walking the couple of miles to the park. It's still quite cold this time of year, and the sky is overcast, but no rain is predicted, so I feel confident we can risk it.

Dylan rents a couple of bikes from the bike hut outside the park. I can't help laughing at the bike he rents for me. It reminds me of the bike my Grandma Hudson used to own with a basket up front and a tinkling bell. "Mock me all you want," he says, taking my bag and putting it into the basket. "But you'll thank me when your shoulders and back aren't aching from carrying that thing."

"It's thoughtful and sweet," I say, hugging him. "Thank you."

Playful squeals fill the air as we cycle past the children's playground. "Remember how we used to hang out here in the evenings during summer break," Dylan says, smiling as he watches the kids shrieking gleefully on the swings and hollering as they race down the slide.

For a couple years, when we were thirteen and fourteen, all the kids from our class used to hang out in the park in the evening. Sherilyn Kane used to bring her docking station and hook us up with some tunes. We thought we were so cool. I smile as I take a trip down memory lane.

"I remember you pushing me on the swing so hard I fell off, landing face-first in the dirt, and my skirt blew up around my waist, exposing my panties to Michael Lyons and Jeremy Manning."

"Don't remind me," he scoffs. "I was so concerned about you that I didn't see those pervs creeping over you."

"Dylan, Michael and Jeremy drooled over any female with a pulse." I shake my head, laughing, as we pedal away from the playground. "They didn't discriminate, and I was nothing special."

"You were to me. It's why I gave both of them black eyes two weeks later when we returned to school and they were telling everyone about seeing your pink panties with the purple butterflies, except they left out the circumstances, wanting everyone to read more into it."

I stop cycling, putting one foot to the ground. "You never told me that was you!"

"I might've had some help from Ryan and Slater, but it was my idea." He looks pleased as punch. "They never breathed a word about you again."

"Wow." I grin at him, and we resume cycling. "Any other secrets you're hiding from me?"

He looks deep in thought. "You remember the first time I took you to a Shawn Lucas show?"

I nod eagerly. "As if I could ever forget. I cried when the tickets sold out in less than twenty minutes and I hadn't managed to secure any. Then you surprised me with VIP tickets, and I nearly told you I was in love with you right there and then." Dylan took me to my first Shawn Lucas concert a couple months before he landed his Microsoft deal and before we got together as a couple. I've always wondered how he afforded it, because money was tight in their household until he hit the big time with his app.

"You almost burst my eardrums with your screaming." He grins at me. "Man, you have a fine set of lungs on you, Gabby."

I laugh. "I don't think I've ever been more excited."

"Oh, I can think of a few other occasions," Dylan teases as we cycle into the woodland area of the park. "Like all the other times I took you to his show."

From that point on, Dylan made sure he secured tickets every time Shawn Lucas played in town. Last year, he even got backstage passes, and I nearly had a coronary getting to meet the man himself. I've loved Shawn's music since he first appeared on the scene, but his last album was simply phenomenal, and I can't wait for his new world tour to kick off so I can see him performing "Midnight Dancer" live on stage. He wrote it for his girlfriend, Dakota, and it's the most romantic song I've ever heard. His emotion literally bleeds through every word and you can tell he poured his heart and soul into the song. She's a lucky girl. Not only is Shawn super-hot and super talented, he was also super nice when I met him, going out of his way to help me relax and not calling me out for my embarrassing fangirl gushing.

"And now you've got that dreamy look on your face like you do every time you think of Shawn Lucas." He rolls his eyes, pretending to be hurt, but I know it's all an act.

"You helped perpetuate the crush," I tease. "You don't get to complain after the fact! But what does this have to do with you keeping secrets?"

"Remember I told you my Xbox broke?" I nod, frowning. "It didn't. I sold it to Matty Johnson to get the money for the tickets."

"No way, Dylan! You loved that Xbox, and your mom had saved up all year to buy you the newest console the previous Christmas." My heart swells with love at the realization of his sacrifice. "I can't believe you did that. That Xbox meant everything to you."

"You meant more, and it was worth it to see the look on your face at the show."

"You're amazing, Dylan. I didn't think you had the power to surprise me anymore, but you keep doing it."

"I'm sure I missed out on several boyfriend of the year awards for taking you to that show year after year. You've no idea how painful it was for me," he says, deliberately downplaying it.

He draws to a stop at the picnic area, getting off his bike and leaning it against one of the tables. Then he helps me off mine, taking the bag and my hand and pushing me gently down on the bench. "I know you secretly have a thing for him too. Fess up. I'm pretty sure I have documentary evidence of you screaming and singing along too," I tease.

For a second, he looks terrified until he realizes I'm joking. "Shit, you nearly gave me heart failure. If such a recording exists, you have to promise to destroy it. I don't want my son witnessing that shit."

"You know I'm messing with you." I shoulder check him, grinning. "I was far too busy fantasizing about Shawn to even think to record you."

"Ouch. Now she tells me," he quips, helping me unload the food and drinks. "Way to bruise a guy's ego."

I hug him quick. "Aw, you know Shawn doesn't hold a candle to you, Freckles. I only had eyes for you."

He smiles, but it's sad, and I know what he's thinking. I press my lips to his softly and briefly. "I love you, Dylan. I always have, and I always will. Forever and ever." Tears well in my eyes, and I attempt to brush them aside, because I don't ever want Dylan to know how hard it is to remain upbeat all the time. I don't want him to see how devastated I truly am underneath my sunny façade.

He presses his forehead to mine. "Did I love you enough, Gabby? Did I show you how much you mean to me? Did I tell you how you occupy my every waking thought? How much you brighten up my life just by being in it?" A sob leaves his mouth, and I wrap my arms more firmly around him. "Do you know how much I love you for giving me this precious gift?" His hands slip under my coat, landing on my enlarged belly. "Do you understand how much it means that you've given up everything to stay with me as I live out my final days?" He looks me straight in the eyes. "I have days where I'm so consumed with rage I want to punch the wall until I bleed, but then I remember all the good things in my life. Especially you, and I can't hold on to the anger."

He removes his hands from my belly, cupping my face. "I love you so much for giving me that, too. For helping to ease this burden, and I'm so sorry that I can't give you the future we talked about but I'm going to do everything in my power to make sure you're cared for after I'm gone."

"You already have, and I don't want you wasting your energy worrying about stuff. I just want to enjoy this time we have left together."

"If there's any positive to come out of today, at least it means I should feel better now I'm no longer suffering the side effects of the chemo and radiation." Fierce determination washes over his face. "I know there will come a time when I won't have much energy, and I won't be as mobile, and my movements will be restricted. But, until then, I want to fill each day with as much happiness as we can squeeze in." He places a soft kiss on my forehead. "So, what do you say, baby? How about making some new happy memories you can share with our son?"

Chapter Forty
Slater

It's been almost four months since I last saw Belle, and if I thought it'd get better, I was clearly mistaken. I miss her now as much as I missed her at the start. Maybe more so. By my calculation, she's about thirty-four weeks pregnant at this stage, and I can't help wondering what she looks like now and how she's feeling. Is she nervous or excited now the birth is drawing nearer?

Ryan told me the baby is a boy and that her pregnancy is going well. The Jameses have all rallied around her, as I knew they would. When Mom was dying, they were there for me. Every. Single. Day. Lucy brought a home-cooked meal every evening, and Belle and Ryan took it in turns dropping by at night. Caleb and Dean were there to relieve me of caretaking duties so I could get out of the house once in a while.

There's no way I would've gotten through it without their love and support, and I'm not even their own flesh and blood. So, I know they're doing everything for Belle, ensuring she's looking after herself and insisting she takes breaks from the house.

I stopped going to Sunday dinner because Belle and Dylan are there most weeks, and I promised her I would make this easy for her by staying away, so I've stuck to my word despite the daily struggle.

I've picked up my cell to call her more times than I can count. And I know I'm driving Ryan demented asking about her all the time. But I can't just switch my emotions off.

I've thrown myself into my studies, and as finals approach, I'm feeling confident that I'll get the grades I need to secure the job of my dreams.

I've attended three interviews with Excelsior Engineering in the past couple months, and they extended a provisional offer last week. Everything hinges on my finals, but, provided I keep my cool on that day, it should be in the bag. Most of my classmates would chop off their left nut for this job, so the fact I'm contemplating turning them down seems crazy. But I don't want to make any decision that might adversely affect Belle. Even though I'm not with her, and there's no guarantee I ever will be, in the back of my mind, I'm hesitant to go through with it, in case I blow things permanently with her. Which *is* nuts, because I can't put my life on hold either.

For now, I'll follow through with the process, and I don't have to make a decision until I have my final grade, so there's plenty of time to think it all through.

As I park outside Dylan's house, I wonder if she'll be here. You could've knocked me over with a feather when Dylan called, asking to meet me. He didn't give any indication of why he wants to talk, but I don't have to be a rocket scientist to figure this is something to do with the girl we both love.

"Slater, how nice to see you," Heather says, enclosing me in a hug the second she opens the door. "How are you feeling about your finals?"

"I've worked hard, so I'm feeling confident, provided I don't mess up on the day."

"I'm sure you'll do great. Your momma would be so proud."

"Thanks, Heather." I clear my throat. "How are you doing?"

Her smile falters a little. "Some days are better than others, you know."

"Yeah. It's not easy watching someone you love deteriorate before your eyes. I fucking hate cancer. Excuse my language, but I can't mention that word without getting mad."

"I'm with you. It's hard to believe in a God when things like this happen. First my husband, and now my only son." Tears pool in her eyes, and I react instinctively, hugging her gently. She sniffles, clinging to me, and I remember how much a hug meant when I was at home caring for Mom when she was dying. "At least I'll have my little grandson in my arms soon, and it's about the only thing keeping me going right now." She eases out of my arms with a sad smile. "Thanks, I needed that."

"You're welcome. If there's anything else I can do, you only have to ask."

"I know that, son." She pats my arm again. "Today hasn't been a great day. He's up in his room, and he's expecting you."

I swallow my nerves, forcing the words out. "Okay. Is, ah, is Belle here?" Jeez, I'm about as obvious as the nose on my face.

"No, honey. Dylan sent her off for the afternoon because he wanted to speak to you alone."

I nod, trying to disguise my disappointment. "Sure. Which room is it?"

"It's the second door on the left when you reach the top of the stairs."

I take the stairs two at a time, suddenly apprehensive. But I'm here now so I might as well see it through. I knock on the door and an unknown female voice tells me to come in.

I'm completely unprepared for what I see.

Dylan is on a standard-issue hospital bed, propped up on a bunch of pillows, attached to a drip. A woman in scrubs, a nurse, I assume, is helping him take his meds. He looks ghastly. He's bald, pale, and he's no longer sporting the bloated look I remember. His skin hangs from his bones. Ryan said he wasn't doing great the last couple weeks, but this is still a shock. He's deteriorated much quicker than I expected.

For his sake, and Belle's, I hope he can hold on long enough to see his son born.

"I can wait outside." I move back toward the door to give him privacy.

"No, stay," he croaks, his voice sounding dry and raspy. "We're just done here."

"Okay, Dylan." The nurse holds her thumb and forefinger to his wrist before scribbling something on a chart. "You're good for now. Press the button if you need me."

"Thanks, Rowena." He gestures at a chair by his bed. "Sit, Slater." I plonk my ass in the chair as Rowena closes the door. "Thanks for agreeing to meet me. I wasn't sure you'd come."

"I'll admit I'm curious, but I figured this was to do with Belle, and I think the world of that girl so ... I'm here."

"You guessed correctly." He eyeballs me with a clarity that seems to belie his condition. "Gabby has six weeks until her due date, but I doubt I'll be in a position to attend the delivery. I want you to take my place."

He just puts it right out there.

You could hear a pin drop in the room, and I know I'm gawking at him in utter shock. Never in a million years did I think Dylan Woods would ask me that. "I would be there for her in a heartbeat, you know that, but I don't think that's your call or mine to make. That should be Belle's decision."

"Agreed. But if you and I are on the same wavelength, it'll make it easier to persuade her."

"She specifically asked me to stay away, and I'm trying to abide by her wishes."

"We both know why Gabby asked that of you. She knows being around me might dredge up difficult memories for you, and ... she doesn't want to hurt me by letting me see how much she's in love with you."

My mouth drops open, and he chuckles. But his laughter quickly turns into a spluttering, coughing fit. I reach for the button to call the nurse, but he swats my hand away, pointing at the jug of water by his bed. I pour him a glass, adding a straw, and hold it to his mouth while he sips from it. When the coughing has stopped, he pushes it away, and I replace it on the bedside table before reclaiming my seat.

"Thanks. Not being able to do stuff for myself fucking sucks."

"I remember what it was like for my mom. She hated the loss of independence too."

"I'm sorry I wasn't more sympathetic back then. I felt threatened by you, and that stopped me from going to the house with Gabby."

"It's water under the bridge now, Woods."

"I always feared it, you know," he says, looking me square in the face. "I knew you were in love with her too, and I worried I'd mess up and lose her to you. It seems my fears weren't in vain."

"From what I've been told, that wasn't your fault."

He shrugs. "Not that it matters anymore, and I didn't ask you here to rake over the past."

"What is it you want from me, Dylan?"

His chest heaves, and his eyes well up. He takes a minute to speak. "I want you to take care of my family after I'm gone." My mouth dries up. "I know you love Gabby as much as I do, and I trust you to take care of her. To take care of my son."

"But you hate me," I blurt.

He smirks. "You were trying to take away the only girl I've ever loved. I hated you for that, but I didn't hate you per se." He runs his tongue over his dry lips. "Man, I'd kill for a shot of whiskey right now."

"If I'd known, I could've smuggled some in with me."

He grins. "If Gabby or Mom found out they'd string you up by your balls. They restrict all my fun these days."

"Only because they love you."

"I know. But back to business. I know you're a good guy, Evans. And you know what it's like to grow up without a father. I don't want that for my son. I want my son to have a father and a loving family. I want him to have siblings, because we both know how lonely it can be as on only child. We're lucky, because we both had the Jameses in our lives, but it's still a solitary existence."

"I don't know what to say." To say I'm shell-shocked is putting it mildly. "And I can't force myself on Gabby if I'm not who she wants."

"Stop being a fucking martyr!" he snaps, coughing profusely again. I stand, but he gestures at me to sit back down, so I do. When the coughing fit ends, he continues. "She loves you. You love her. And you're the only person I trust with my girl and my son. Yes, she might take some convincing when the time comes but I trust you to do the right thing." His breath wheezes out of his chest, and the strangled sound is hard to listen to. "Of course, if you don't love her and you don't want a family with her, that changes things." He drills a challenging look at me.

"You don't have to doubt either of those things. I love Belle with my whole heart. She's the only woman I've ever loved. The only woman I ever will. It would be an honor to raise your son and share my life with both of them."

"Well, that's settled then."

I crank out a laugh. "This has got to be one of the weirdest conversations I've ever had."

"You're telling me." His expression turns solemn again. "I hate that it's come to this, but burying my head in the sand won't change anything. So, I'm doing everything I can now to make sure my family is looked after when I'm gone."

"If there's anything else I can help you with, you only have to ask."

"You mean that sincerely."

"I do."

He nods, eyeballing me the entire time. "Just get her through this, Slater. Help her move on."

"I will do my very best."

"Thanks, man."

"You don't have to thank me. And you don't need to worry about them. I promise I will take care of them."

Chapter Forty-One
Gabby

We had one semi-blissful month after our day in the park before Dylan's condition took a turn for the worst. During that one-month reprieve, we lived life to the fullest. Taking day trips to local places Dylan had always wanted to visit. Visiting the arcade and playing pool and video games. Meeting up with friends at the bowling alley. Vising the waterfall and walking some of the smaller trails at the state park. Catching some of the latest movies and going for pizza at Dylan's favorite pizza place afterward. We even took a painting class together for a few weeks, giving up when we realized we were both talentless with a paintbrush and wasting our time.

Our nights were filled playing board games, reminiscing over old photos, recalling old vacations, and regaling one another with funny stories we remember from our shared childhood. When I explained I had started playing guitar again, Dylan insisted I play for him every night. I thought playing all our old songs and revisiting all our old memories would kill me inside, but it's actually been strangely comforting.

"We need to talk." Dylan pins me with a lethal look as he holds my cell out to me, a new message open on the screen, and I immediately know what he wants to discuss. Damn it. I shouldn't have left it on the coffee table for him to see.

"It's not a big deal. I'll just block that number like I did the last three she sent me texts from."

"The hell it isn't," Dylan spits. "She's been messaging me too, and this has got to stop."

"I'm guessing Banging Bianca isn't sending *you* threatening messages though."

He sighs, smoothing a hand over his bald head. "I thought I dealt with her in the hospital, but she's persistent. And now this." He points at my cell. "That's completely unacceptable, and I'm putting an end to it right now."

Dylan's way of dealing with his crazy psycho bitch of an ex is to ask her to come to the house to meet him. Go figure.

She arrives on time the following afternoon, looking shell-shocked to see me sitting beside Dylan when Heather shows her into the living room. "What's *she* doing here?" she huffs, planting her hands on her hips.

"Gabby lives here, and I asked her to sit in on this conversation."

She glares at me, but I keep a neutral expression schooled on my face. When her eyes drop to my obviously pregnant belly, her mouth hangs open, and she's momentarily silenced. It doesn't last long, however.

"I'm not talking with her here," she pouts, as if she has any say in this.

"Unless you want me to call the cops and tell them you've been harassing both of us, you will sit your ass down. Right now." Thank God, Dylan's having one of his better days today, because he needs to be firing on all cylinders to deal with this cow. His tone brokers no argument, and after another bit of posturing, she finally sits down on the couch across from us. "I'm going to talk, and you're going to listen, and then you will get the fuck out of my house, when I tell you to go."

Her nostrils flare and a muscle ticks in her jaw. She knots her hands in her lap and glares at Dylan now.

"I tried to be nice about this in the hospital, but you seem to have a big issue with listening to what people tell you, so you leave me no choice but to spell it out." Dylan clasps my hand. A scowl appears on Bianca's face. "I spent the whole of freshman year ignoring your advances for a reason." My eyes pop wide as I stare at Dylan when he makes that admission. That's news to me; although, having seen how Bianca operates, I can't say I'm overly surprised at her actions. I'm just shocked that Dylan never mentioned anything to me.

"I had no interest in you. Zero. Zilch. You only managed to get your way this time because I was too fucking sick to know I was being manipulated. If I was of sound mind, I would never have touched you. Gabby is the only woman I've ever loved and desired, and that hasn't changed. What we had meant nothing to me. Nothing."

Bianca sucks in her cheeks as if she's swallowed something sour.

"You preyed on me when I was most vulnerable, and you lied and twisted things to hurt Gabby as much as you could, and I will never forgive you for that." He pauses for a moment, considering his next words carefully. "I know I didn't always treat you right, and even though it was a part of my illness, and I have little time for how you treated Gabby, I am sorry for anything I said or did that caused offense."

She snorts, and it's not a good look on her.

"But this shit has got to stop." He points at my cell. "This is the only time I will give you a heads-up. Stop texting me and stop texting Gabby." He places his hands on my swollen stomach. "Gabby is pregnant with my baby, and she's under enough stress as it is."

"You expect me to care about this ... why?"

"Wow. You really are a cold-hearted bitch." I sit on my hands to avoid the urge to lunge at her.

"I'll report you for harassment and obtain a restraining order if you continue," Dylan supplies. "I'm sure you don't want that on your record."

She sits up straighter, thrusting her shoulders and her chest out. "Write me a check and I'll go away." She drills him with a smug look. "You can erase me from your life in two minutes. You'll never have to hear from me again."

"How much?" Dylan asks the same time I say. "No fucking way."

"What?" I stare at Dylan like he's insane. "You've got to be kidding me."

He leans in to my ear. "Please trust me on this. I know how to handle her."

I grind my teeth to the molars, shooting daggers at the superior look on that bitches face.

"Fifty K will cover it."

I bite down so hard on the inside of my mouth I taste blood.

"Five," Dylan pushes back, and they end up settling on fifteen. It infuriates me that he has to pay her off but I bite my tongue and let him handle this, even if it's killing me to stay quiet.

Dylan writes the check and gives it to the gloating cow. "You won't be able to cash that until you sign the paperwork my attorney sends you," he tells her. "So, don't do anything stupid in the meantime."

"I've got what I wanted, and I won't jeopardize it." She gives the check a big kiss, and I want to wipe that victorious look off her face so bad. "See you around, Dylan." She rakes her gaze over him quickly. "Or not," she adds, without a shred of remorse, and I lose hold of my emotions.

Climbing to my feet, I growl as I lunge at her, but Dylan gets to me first. He has to physically hold me back as I thrash about, dying to wring her damn neck. I have never hated anyone as much as I hate this girl. This was all a game to her. Some warped kind of "get rich quick" scheme, and I'm enraged at her flippant disregard of Dylan and what he is enduring. "Get the fuck out, you gold-digging slut!" I shout as Heather appears in the doorway.

"You heard the lady," Heather says, looking every bit as angry as I am. "Get out of my house, and never come back. You're not welcome."

Dylan encloses his arms around me, rubbing a hand up and down my back while Heather escorts her outside. "Calm down, Dimples. It's pointless getting worked up over her."

"I can't believe you paid her off! We could've taken out restraining orders."

He tips my chin up. "Yes, but that wouldn't have stopped her. She'd have found other ways to torment us. This way, she's gone for good." He smooths his thumbs along my furrowed brow. "Don't be mad, Dimples. This was the best way I could protect you and our son. She's out of our lives now, and that was worth every cent."

Four days after the Bianca meeting, Dylan had another seizure, a more serious one this time, and he ended up hospitalized for a few days. His medical team told us to prepare ourselves and confirmed time is running out.

Even though I'm furious with God, and questioning whether he even exists, I still pray every night. Begging him to keep Dylan alive long enough to meet our son.

Dylan threads his fingers through my hair as I'm curled up beside him in bed. It's hard for him to get downstairs now, so I spend the majority of my time in his room these days.

For a while, we were sharing a bed again at night. Nothing sexual happened, because Dylan has respected my wishes and it's at the point where he wouldn't have the stamina anyway. Apart from the odd few kisses, and the fact Dylan is dying, we are basically back where we started—as close as two friends can be. Sleeping beside him has been comforting for both of us. I'm less anxious knowing he's close, and he gets to sleep with his arms around my expanding belly. Every night, without fail, he speaks to my belly, talking to our son with so much love and adoration in his voice it chokes me up. And every morning, the first words out of his mouth are "Good morning, beautiful, and how's my precious son today?" He says this while showering kisses on my belly, and it's hard to keep my emotions in check.

I'm so grateful I made the decision to defer college and move in here. I wouldn't have missed these last few months with Dylan for anything. And I'm glad my pregnancy has been plain sailing. While I'm suffering a little heartburn right now, and sleeping is quite uncomfortable, I really have very little to complain about.

"I've been thinking about names," Dylan says, breaking through my reverie.

It's only four weeks until my due date, and we haven't agreed on a name yet. It's hard sometimes to focus on baby stuff when Dylan's condition takes up most of our time. Now that Rowena is here, we have more time to discuss the important stuff.

Dylan insisted on hiring a nurse when he began to need help with bathing and using the toilet. He refused to let me or Heather assist him and I understand it. He wants to hold onto his dignity for as long as he can, and it's easier to let a stranger help with those things.

I cried myself to sleep the night we had that conversation, cursing God and cursing cancer. I've so much hatred, anger, and frustration locked up inside me that I worry I'm going to self-combust one of these days.

"What were you thinking?" I ask, lightly resting my hand on his bony chest.

"What about Billy Paul Woods?"

My throat swells, and it's difficult to speak. "I love it," I croak, after a bit. "Naming him after both our dads is perfect."

"Are you sure, Dimples? Don't agree just because I'm dying."

That makes me angry. "Don't you dare say that to me! I would never concede on something so important unless I was in complete agreement. You can't say that to me, Dylan. Not ever. Because I'm trying so fucking hard to be strong for you and that, that ... you saying that breaks my heart." Tears fill my eyes, and I can't work out if they are angry or sad tears. Probably a bit of both.

"I'm sorry." He holds me closer. Well, as close as we can get with my monster belly in the way. "It was uncalled for." He presses a weak kiss to my cheek. "You're one of the strongest people I know, but I'm worried you're bottling all your feelings up inside. We need to face facts, Gabby. I'm dying, and we both know I don't have long left."

"I don't want to be selfish, Dylan. I can't admit what I'm feeling."

"You can tell me, babe. I guarantee everything you're feeling I'm feeling too."

As soon as he gives me permission, the floodgates open. "I hate that you're leaving me and I'm so angry. At you. At God. At life."

"I was angry too, but it's a pointless emotion. It won't give me back my life, and I don't want to waste the time I have left. I'm so grateful I got to spend these last few months with you."

I draw a shuddering breath. "Well, you're clearly a much better person than me, because I hate God for giving me such little time with you. I've researched it, and some patients with GBM survive for years! You have only had it a few months. It's not fair."

"I know, babe. It isn't fair, but there's nothing we can do to alter it." He leans his head on mine. "What else?"

"I'm scared you won't be around to see our son being born." My voice shakes, because this is my biggest fear right now. "I want you to meet Billy. To get to hold him. Even if it's only one time."

"Fuck, Gabby, I'm terrified of missing out on that. I promise you I'm going to hold on. I'm going to meet our son. Trust me. I will hold Billy in my arms, even if it's with my dying breath."

I wrap my arms around him, burying my face in his neck, hoping to ward off the tears threatening to fall. "I trust you, Dylan, and I know you'll keep your promise."

"I'd like you to do something for me," he whispers.

I look up through damp eyes. "Anything. I'll do anything for you."

"I want you to let Slater attend the rest of your appointments, and I want him to support you through the delivery."

I blink several times, resisting the urge to tug at my earlobes, sure I must have heard that wrong. "What?"

"Don't get mad, but I've spoken to Slater about this, and he's happy to be there for you, if you'll let him."

I'm shocked into absolute silence. Both that the boys were talking behind my back and that they seem to have reached some kind of agreement. I don't know how to feel about it. I'm a third mad, a third happy, and a third confused.

"I know this might seem strange," Dylan continues. "But he loves you, and I trust him to take care of you. We both know I can't be there for you, and I don't want you to do it alone, Gabby. Let Slater do this. Let him hold your hand and help you through it."

I tell Dylan I need a day to think about it, and I force Myndi to come to the house the next day for lunch, because I need to bounce it off someone. To run through the pros and cons. She confirms Slater asks about me all the time, and she encourages me to go for it. After some further internal debate, I agree, even if I'm scared of doing it too.

Letting Slater adopt some kind of pseudo-father role is dangerous because I don't want to raise his hopes only for me to let him down again. He deserves so much more than I can offer him right now. I cannot even consider what my future holds, beyond making plans to care for my child.

Slater shows up on Thursday to drive me to my appointment, and I'm as nervous as a ninth grader starting high school when I see his SUV pull up to the curb outside. "That's my ride," I tell Dylan, stepping away from the window.

He smiles. "Relax, Dimples. It's only Slater."

"I'm not nervous," I lie, bending down to kiss his forehead.

"Message me the minute you come out."

"I will. See you soon." I blow him a kiss as I close his bedroom door.

Slater is talking with Heather when I waddle downstairs. He stops talking mid-flow when he spots me. We stare at one another, and I feel my cheeks turning hot as his gaze rakes over me. It's been months since I've seen him, and he's still as jaw-droppingly gorgeous as ever. My heart thumps ecstatically, and my body is dancing a tango, both clearly forgetting the memo: the one that says he's no longer mine to swoon over. I give himself a quick talking to and smile at him. "I know, I look like a hippopotamus squeezed into this dress, but most of my maternity clothes are way too tight, and I simply refuse to waste money buying more when it's so close to my due date."

Slater's lips kick up, and my pulse races. "You're cute when you're babbling."

I roll my eyes, and Heather smiles, leaning in to kiss my cheek. "Good luck at your appointment, and text me the second you get out."

"I've already promised your son the very same thing. Don't worry. I will."

Slater takes my bag without asking, placing his hand on my lower back and urging me forward. "Don't worry, Heather. I'll look after our girl."

Warmth from his hand heats me on contact, and my body tingles in anticipation. It's been so long since my lady parts have had any action I tremble at the slightest touch.

At least, that's the excuse I tell myself.

"For the record," he says, as soon as we are outside, "you're the most beautiful pregnant woman I've ever seen."

"That's only because you haven't seen that many," I instantly retort.

He laughs while helping me down the steps. "A rephrasing is clearly in order." He turns me around so we're facing one another. "You're beautiful, Belle, even more so with that beautiful new life growing inside you. Never doubt that."

My lower lip wobbles as pregnancy hormones strike again.

"Damn, Slate. You can't say stuff like that to me. Not when I'm all hormonal and I cry at the drop of a hat these days. I even cried watching *The Bachelorette* the other night, and that's just plain embarrassing."

"Don't worry, your secret is safe with me," he quips, unlocking his SUV. "I'm not going to lie. If you look beautiful, I'm gonna tell you you're beautiful. It's as simple as that." He helps me into my seat, before running around the car and sliding behind the wheel.

"Thank you for doing this."

"It's my pleasure. I meant it when I said I wanted to help, and this is in no way a hardship." He maneuvers the car out on the road.

"Well, I appreciate it. I nearly keeled over when Dylan told me you two had spoken. What I wouldn't give to have been a fly on the wall for that conversation."

"I was pretty shocked myself, but I'm glad he reached out to me even if you didn't." He glances briefly at me as he takes the next junction, heading toward the highway.

"You know why I didn't, Slate." I pin earnest eyes on him.

"I do, and it's fine, Belle. I'm just glad to be here now."

The next couple weeks roll by, bringing us closer and closer to the two big impending events. It's hard to get excited about the birth when Dylan goes downhill with every passing day. Heather cries herself to sleep every night, and her anguished sobbing destroys me, but I can't cry. I'm in this kind of hazy bubble, where I'm aware of the ticking clock but it's like it's not real. I know it's a form of denial, but I'm doing whatever I can to survive.

This particular night is a huge test in self-control. Dylan has been throwing up relentlessly even though there's barely any contents in his stomach to expel. And he's angry and aggressive even though he's weak. I felt the need to intervene when I heard things being thrown around the room.

When Forever Changes

Rowena was on the verge of tears when I forced her to take a break. Now I'm sitting beside Dylan, listening to him rasp and curse and scream while sweat rolls down his face and bile dribbles from his mouth. Every time I try to blot the sweat from his brow or wipe the vomit from his chin, he swats my hand away. "Get out, Gabby! Just get out!" he yells. "I want to be fucking alone."

"I'm not leaving you alone."

"I fucking want you to leave me alone," he roars with more strength than I'd expect. His body may be failing him, but that old Dylan Woods tenaciousness still lingers in his tissues.

"Well, tough, because I'm not going anywhere."

"I want Rowena."

I push my hurt aside. "Rowena needs a break, Dylan. She'll be back soon, and then I'll leave."

"You don't understand." Sobs wrack his thin frame. "I hate that you have to see me like this." His chest convulses as tears deluge his face. "I don't want you to remember me like this."

I can't stop my own tears from falling. "I know, baby. I know, but don't push me away. I love you, and I will always remember you the way you were before you got sick. You don't need to doubt that."

"I don't want to die, Gabby," he sobs, and my fragile heart cracks a little more. Dylan hasn't ever admitted this so bluntly. He's been so strong and so accepting, and it's difficult to hear this. But he let me vent before, and he needs to get this out. "I don't want to leave you. I don't want to miss out on my son growing up. I fucking hate this!"

I rest my head on his chest, sobbing along with him. "I know, Dylan. I don't want you to go either." He rests his quivering hand on my back, and we cry together. My heart is so full of anguish it almost feels like I'm dying too.

Gradually, our sobs subside, and we just lie there like that, holding one another, both consumed with agonized thoughts.

"I'm sorry, Gabby. That was selfish of me."

I look up at him through tear-stained eyes. "Don't apologize. Don't ever apologize for how you're feeling."

"It's weak, and I don't want to add to your load. I already know how hard this is for you and Mom."

"Dylan. Expressing your innermost thoughts isn't weak. You are the most incredible man I've known. The way you've carried yourself throughout this is nothing short of inspirational. But you're only human, and it's not wrong to feel like this, and you shouldn't be afraid to offload on me. I love you." I take his hand and press a kiss to his palm. "I love you enough to handle it."

"I'm so lucky to have had you in my life, Gabby. I hope you know that. Loving you has been the very best part of my existence. I know our son will grow up loved and cherished by an amazing mother, and that helps me deal with this."

"I promise I won't let him down. I will do my very best by him, and I'll make sure he knows who his daddy is too. He may not have the chance to get to know you in person, but he *will* know how amazing you are."

"I have every faith in you, babe." He pats the empty space beside him. "Come lie with me. I promise I'm done shouting and throwing things."

I lie down beside him, and his hands gravitate to my belly. "There is something important we haven't discussed, and I think it's time." I probe his eyes. "You know I stopped believing in God the night my dad died," he starts explaining, and I nod. While I wouldn't quite call Dylan an atheist, I know he's struggled with his beliefs for years. Heather turned to her faith after her husband died, while Dylan chose the opposite path. "And I sure as fuck don't believe in him now. If it was up to me, I wouldn't have a funeral or be buried. I was tempted to leave instructions in my will telling you to throw a big party instead, but I can't do that to Mom." He stops to draw a breath. Talking for long periods tires him out all too quickly.

I run my hand over his smooth skull while he gathers his strength. He likes me doing that or so he says. He closes his eyes briefly, and a little contented sigh slips out of his mouth. After a couple minutes, he opens his eyes, smiling. "I love you," he whispers.

"I love you too."

He takes my wrist, bringing it to his mouth and planting a soft kiss on it. "I've made arrangements for my funeral and burial. It's all taken care of you, so you won't need to worry. My attorney, David Weston, has all the details. I decided it doesn't really matter what I believe or what I want. Funerals aren't for the dead. They're for the living."

"I'm sure that will be of huge comfort to your mom."

"I hope so, because it's mainly her I'm doing it for." He rests his forehead on mine. "I know it's not easy for us to sleep beside one another anymore, but stay with me tonight?"

I look into his eyes, and all I see is the boy I grew up loving. I can look behind the pallid skin and the sunken eyes that have lost their sparkle and see the boy who twirled me for hours on the dance floor at prom. The guy who carried me for miles uphill the night I sprained my ankle. The man who made sweet love to me all night long the first night we got the keys to his condo. And there are a whole host of other memories lying in the back of my mind as I look at him.

"I don't want to be anywhere else," I say, snuggling into him and closing my eyes.

Chapter Forty-Two

The following evening, my water breaks, and it hits me that this is finally happening. I'm sitting on the chair in Dylan's room, waiting for Slater to get here, trying to keep my panic contained. I'm not due for another eighteen days, and I'm worried something is wrong.

"Come here, baby," Dylan rasps, removing the oxygen mask from his mouth momentarily. He pats the space alongside him, and I perch my fleshy ass on the corner of the bed. "Does it hurt?"

"Not much," I semi-lie. I've experienced far worse pain with my endometriosis, but I know these achy waves rolling through me have the potential to reach epically painful proportions.

"How far apart are your contractions?"

"About every twenty minutes."

"Okay, so that means you're still in early labor." Dylan ingested books on pregnancy and parenting the first couple months after we found out, so it's no surprise he's well informed. "There's plenty of time to get to the hospital, and Slater just messaged me to say he's only ten minutes away."

"I hate that I ruined his night. I should've just gotten Mom and Dad to bring me."

"You'd have ruined his night if you *didn't* call him. You know that." He's probably right. "Are you nervous?" he adds.

"Yeah, but I'm excited too." And relieved. Or at least I will be once everything is okay. I know it's not inconceivable to go early, and we've gone beyond the point where it's risky, so I'm sure it'll be okay. I'm wondering if Billy knows his daddy doesn't have long left. If he's as eager to meet him as Dylan is and he's just decided to arrive a little early.

"Me too." It's hard to tell what Dylan's feeling by his face anymore, but there's a light in his eyes I haven't seen in weeks.

I take his hands, placing them on my stomach. "Do you feel that?"

"Whoa! Yeah."

I take deep breaths as another contraction rolls through me. "It's getting stronger." I glance at the time, so I can keep track, and update my OB once we arrive at the hospital.

"It's really happening, Dimples." He rubs my belly again. "I can't wait to meet him."

"Slater is here, Gabby," Heather says, popping her head in the door. "And your mom just rang to confirm they are en route to the hospital."

"Thanks, Heather." I'm sure she would've loved to be there too, but there's no way she'll leave Dylan, and I don't want her to either. I know Rowena is here, but he needs a loved one here in case anything happens.

That is the absolute worst thought to pop into my mind in this moment, and I rush to shake it away. Tears spill down my cheeks as I lean forward to kiss Dylan goodbye. "Bye, baby. Don't go anywhere while I'm gone."

He lifts a shaky hand to my face, caressing my cheek. "I'll be right here waiting."

"I'll FaceTime you the minute I'm holding him in my arms," I promise, drying my tears and giving him a reassuring smile. "Love you, Freckles." I brush my mouth against his cracked lips one final time.

"Love you, Dimples," he replies before I make my way downstairs.

"I'm sorry for cutting your night short," I tell Slater when I'm strapped into the car and we're on our way.

"Are you shitting me, Belle?" He looks a little bit mad. "I only went out because we were celebrating the end of finals and I won't see a lot of those guys again, but I was drinking soda all night in case something happened." The anger fades from his face, and he reaches across the console, squeezing my hand. "Trust me, there is nowhere else I would rather be." His voice carries a layer of elation that helps settle my nerves.

"I'll end up giving birth in the back seat if you continue *Driving Miss Daisy*," I joke ten minutes later when we've barely advanced more than a few miles.

"I'd prefer to get you to the hospital safely, Belle. Unless you're telling me your contractions are coming more regularly now?"

"Nope. It's still every fifteen to twenty minutes."

"So that means you're only a couple centimeters dilated, right?"

I gawk at him like he's just grown an extra head or two. He chuckles. "I asked Dylan to send me some of those books he was reading. I wanted to be prepared. And I soaked up everything during the prenatal classes, unlike someone I could mention." He purses his lips, smirking at me.

"Hey, it's not my fault I dozed off the last couple times. The instructor's dulcet tones lulled me to sleep."

"You seem very calm."

"Don't believe everything you see. I'm a freaking hot mess on the inside. I accidentally turned on this show the other day and the woman was giving birth. I swear she screamed so loud she damaged my eardrums even through the TV. It scared the shit out of me. How horrific must the pain be to shriek like a banshee during labor?"

He reaches over, squeezing my hand. "They probably told her they'd double the cash if she dramatized it for the viewers."

I snort. "Maybe. Or maybe it's just that painful."

"You can always change your mind on the epidural," he suggests, finally taking the exit for the hospital.

"I'd really like to do it without, but I guess we'll have to see."

Slater takes control once we arrive at the hospital, checking in with reception and wrapping his arm around my shoulder, keeping me close, as we ride the elevator to the maternity ward. They instantly hook me up to a fetal monitor, confirming everything is fine. Baby Woods has just decided to come into this world early after all. We both breathe a sigh of relief, and Slater kisses the top of my head. "Thank fuck. I'd be lying if I said I wasn't a little worried on the way here."

"I know," I say, lacing my fingers through his. "I was too." I chew on my bottom lip. "Do you think Billy knows his daddy doesn't have long left and he decided to arrive early, so he gets a chance to meet him?"

"If Billy has some of your compassion and selflessness and some of Dylan's genius brain, then I totally think he's made that call." He raises our conjoined hands, pressing a kiss to the back of my hand.

"I know it's going to get crazy once my family is let in, so I just want to say this now. Thank you so much for doing this with me. I know you've had a lot on your plate lately, especially with finals, and I appreciate you giving up your time to come to my appointments and classes."

"Like I told Dylan, you don't need to thank me. I'm happy to be here." He pulls his chair in closer, and it looks like he's conducting some form of internal debate. "Actually, that doesn't even come close to conveying how fucking ecstatic I am to be a part of this. I love you, Belle, and that's never going to change. And I loved Billy from the second I found out about him. It doesn't matter that he's not my flesh and blood. I love this kid because he's a part of you, and I already know he's going to be as precious and special as you are, so there's no

362

way I would miss out on this." He wipes his thumbs under my damp eyes. "I'm *honored* you chose me to do this with you. I know you could've asked your mom or Myndi, and I'll always be grateful you asked me to share this magical experience with you."

"Slate, my God." I can scarcely talk over the lump of emotion in my throat. "Come here. I need to hug you."

He wraps his arms around me, and I rest my head on his shoulder, acknowledging how lucky I am to have this man's unwavering support.

My parents enter the suite just then, and we break apart. "Oh honey." Mom kisses my cheek. "Look how beautiful you are. Doesn't she look beautiful, Paul?" She glances at my dad over her shoulder.

"Hey, Buttercup." He kisses my forehead. "Mom's right. You're beautiful, like always. How are you feeling?"

"I'm okay. The OB confirmed I'm only three centimeters dilated, so this could take some time. At least Dylan organized this private suite in advance, and there's plenty of room for everyone to hang out." I swing my legs off the side of the bed, and Slater helps me down onto the ground. I toe my slippers on as he helps me into my robe. "We're going to go for a walk. She said that would help."

Slater offers me his arm, and I loop mine through his. Then we set off, bumping into Ryan, Myndi, and Dean on the way out the door. After we've exchanged greetings and hugs, Slater guides me out into the corridor, and we spend an hour pacing the hallways, shooting the shit to pass the time and help distract me. When Caleb calls, Slater finds a bench and helps me sit down as I talk to my brother. He can't be here as Terri is presently sleeping and he doesn't want to leave her side. She's due to give birth in a matter of days so she could go at any time. I reassure him it's fine and that I look forward to seeing them once I'm back home.

We resume walking after that, but the contractions are coming much faster now, and I have to stop every so often, clutching onto Slater as I pant and gasp my way through them. When they become too much, Slater insists on bringing me back to the suite.

He summons my OB and kicks my family out to the waiting area as soon as she arrives. He's busy tapping away on his cell while the doctor examines me. Slater has been messaging Dylan nonstop, every step of the way, taking tons of pics and sending regular updates. I've even spoken to him a couple brief times. I want Dylan to feel as connected to this moment as possible.

"Everything looks good, Gabby," the OB says. "You're almost there. Hit the button when you feel the urge to push and I'll be back." Then she leaves me alone with Slater, and my family rushes back into the room, excitement lighting up all their faces.

"You're looking a little red in the face there, Tornado," Ryan jokes after a particularly intense contraction. "It can't be that painful or women wouldn't be pushing peanuts out of their vajayjays every second of every day." He winks, attempting to smother his laughter.

Dean shakes his head. "You're an idiot."

"A stupid, sexist idiot," Myndi adds, rolling her eyes.

My head falls back on the pillow, and I'm panting and sweating with all the exertion. "Punch him for me, please?" I beg Slater, clutching tightly to his hand.

"Right." Mom claps her hands. "I think it's time we gave Gabby her privacy. She needs to maintain her strength, and she can't do that with all of us here." She leans in to kiss me. "Good luck, darling. You're a natural."

"Aaghh!" I scream as intense pain takes hold of me, washing over my stomach in waves of searing agony. Holy shit. I thought the cramping and pain from endometriosis was bad, but this takes the cake. Ryan races out the door faster than Usain Bolt on skates, and tears of laughter sneak out of the corner of my eyes.

Slater snorts, squeezing my hand.

"We're right outside, Buttercup." Dad pats the top of my head. "And we're so proud of you."

"Annie screamed the place down giving birth," Dean says when it's his time to kiss me. "It's completely normal. And she cussed like a sailor!" His smile is sad. "You're doing amazing, Gabby, and I can't wait to meet Billy." He slaps Slater on the shoulder. "Take care of my sister and my nephew."

"Oh, Gabby." Myndi is crying tears of joy. "Thank you for having me here. This is one of the most incredible things I've ever been a part of." She hugs me while I grit my teeth, riding out another contraction. "Knock it out of the park, sister." She waves before slipping out of the room, and I collapse against the pillow.

"Oh, thank fuck! I thought they'd never leave and I ... Aaghhh!!" I scream bloody murder, and a string of expletives rips from my mouth. Slater rubs my shoulders, offering assurances, but I can hardly hear him over the pain. Another wave hits me, and I pant furiously, mentally coaching myself to get a grip. Ryan was right about one thing. Plenty of women do this every day, a lot without pain relief, and if they're strong enough to withstand it, then so am I. "Fuck, Slate." I whimper, squeezing his hand so tight I'm probably stopping the blood flow. "This hurts so fucking much."

"You've got this, Belle," he says, propping me up with more pillows and popping an ice cube into my mouth. He wipes my sweaty brow. "Remember your breathing." He joins me in inhaling and exhaling, and the look of concentration on his face is extreme. If I wasn't in so much freaking pain, I'd probably find it funny. "Remind me." I pant. "Why I said no to an epidural?"

"Because you're a sadist?" he jokes.

"Clearly." I pant before screaming so loud it's a wonder the window didn't shatter. "Push the button, Slate."

"Are you—"

"Push the fucking button!" I yell as pressure bears down on me. "Holy shit!"

The doctor rushes into the room, conducts one final examination, and then gives me a thumbs-up. I giggle at the absurdity of the gesture in the situation, but it helps relax me a smidgeon. "Next time you feel like pushing, go for it."

She guides me through each step. "Good job, Gabby. His head is out." Slater looks down to where it's all happening as the nurse immediately suctions Billy's mouth, clearing his airways.

"Oh, Belle. He's so beautiful. He has a mass of dark hair." Slater's words drip with awe.

I grind my teeth and push as another contraction hits, and a shrill cry pierces the air. Tears pump out of my eyes as my little boy exercises his lungs. How can such a tiny human emit such loud cries?

An intense burst of pain eclipses my joy, momentarily, and then I feel his body slide through my channel. It's the weirdest and most amazing sensation. It's almost instant relief, and I collapse against Slater, exhausted and exhilarated.

"It's a beautiful baby boy," the doctor confirms, and I strain my neck to see over the flabby mountain that was once my flat belly. "Would you like to cut the cord?" she asks Slater.

I look up at him, and my heart melts. Slater is quietly crying, his face full of wonder, and I fall in love with him all over again. "Can I?" he whispers, looking at me with intense longing.

I nod, because I don't trust myself to speak. Slater cups my face and presses a firm kiss to my lips before moving to the end of the bed. I watch him snip the cord with tears rolling down my face. He smiles adoringly at Billy, and the look of love on his face is unmistakable.

Slater stands watch while the nurse checks his vitals, cleans him up, and then brings him to me. She lays him flat on my chest, skin to skin, and I can hardly see over the tears flowing from my eyes like a river. "Welcome to the world, Billy," I whisper, kissing the top of his head. "I'm your mom, and I love you so much." His tiny body feels warm and soft against my skin and I'm instantly head over heels in love. I lay my hands on his tiny back, marveling at his perfectly formed fingers and toes. He whimpers, nudging his head against my breast, his plump little mouth opening and closing. I've already made a decision to not breastfeed at first. It's not that I don't want to, because I do, but I want to spend as much time with Dylan and my son as possible, and it's easier to rely on pre-made formula for the time being.

"I love you," Slater tells me, pressing a passionate kiss to my lips. "He's so beautiful, Belle." He places his hand carefully on top of his head. "He's so small." I can hear the marvel in his tone.

Slater snaps a pic and sends it to Dylan. Then he opens his Face-Time app and calls him, holding the cell out for me. The instant Dylan connects to the call, Billy emits an anguished cry, and I shunt up in the bed, cradling him in my arms. "Shush, little man. We'll feed you soon. You've got to say hi to your daddy first." I take his little hand and wiggle it at the screen.

Tears are rolling down Dylan's face. "Look at him, Dimples. Look at the perfect little boy we made together."

I can't stop the tears from streaming down my face either, but this time they're happy tears. "He has your hair."

"And your blue eyes," Dylan adds. Actually, his eyes are a darker shade of blue than mine, but the doctor said it might take a few weeks or even months for his natural eye color to come through.

"He's perfect." I smile at Dylan. "We created a perfect little human, and I already love him so much."

"Hurry home, babe," Dylan says, his voice breaking as he starts coughing. He pulls the oxygen mask onto his mouth, and his head falls back on the pillow. He's exhausted and clearly fighting sleep.

"I'll be there as soon as I can. Sleep, my love, and we'll see you soon." I blow him a kiss, nodding at Slater, and he ends the call just as Rowena and Heather reappear in Dylan's room.

It's a timely reminder that I need to get back to him asap.

Chapter Forty-Three

S later runs out to the hallway to tell my family the good news, and then he returns, helping to dress Billy before settling in the chair to feed him his first bottle. My son has a fine pair of lungs on him, and I'm sure my family can hear his cries out in the hallway. The instant Slater puts the nipple in his mouth, his lips suction over the tip, sucking greedily. Slater and I lock eyes, smiling as we exchange similar emotions. It's a profound moment, and he looks so natural cradling my son in his bulky, tatted-up arms. My heart tugs, continuing to thump wildly as I watch Slater feeding Billy while the doctor stitches me up. After, the nurse helps me into a fresh nightgown, and then she cleans the bed. I'm propped up in the cot, watching Slater cradling my son in his arms, softly humming to him while he sleeps, with tears welling in my eyes. Billy emits a little contented sigh, and my heart surges with love. It's a beautiful, beautiful moment, but my heart is split in two.

Slater places my sleeping son in my arms, pressing a kiss to my temple. "He's beautiful, Belle. Just like his mom. That was the most incredible experience of my life. Thank you for sharing it with me."

He gently caresses my cheek. "You were born to be a mom." He walks away before I can respond, opening the door to my family.

They fall in love with Billy instantly, taking turns holding my sleeping beauty and cooing over him. I'm so happy they're here, but I'm itching to bring my baby home to his daddy. Although an early release has been prearranged—something else Dylan thought to organize—I still need to wait a couple hours for the all clear.

There are times when being wealthy comes in handy. Not only did Dylan hire the best OB in the state and organize this private suite, he also hired a maternity nurse to look after me at home, and he's paid a fortune to secure the OB for home visits too.

As I'm driving home with Slater and my son a few hours later, I silently pray. Begging God to give us as much time together as a family as possible before taking Dylan from us.

Heather has tears in her eyes, and her arms wide-open, the instant we walk through the door. Unbuckling Billy from his carrier seat, I carefully hand him to Grandma. She dots little kisses all over his face, whispering how precious he is and how much she loves him.

"How are you doing?" Slater whispers, circling his arm around my waist when I sway on my feet.

"I'm okay. Sore and tired but it's fine."

"How would you feel about me staying here for a couple days? I could help mind Billy while you rest."

"I can't ask you to do that, Slate."

"You're not asking. I'm offering." He peers into my eyes. "It's not like I have much else to do. I've already given my notice at the club, and most of my stuff is boxed up at the house. I can ask Austin or Ryan to deliver them to Mom's house for me."

"I feel like I've already asked too much of you."

"Belle. You know how I feel about both of you." He lowers his mouth to my ear. "I want to be here with you. If you send me away, I'm just going to wallow in misery. Let me help take care of you while you take care of Dylan."

"You're a good man, Slater Evans." I press a kiss to his cheek before turning to Heather. "I'd like Billy to meet his daddy now." She nestles my precious boy back in my arms, and I walk upstairs with Slater protecting me from behind. Outside Dylan's room, he squeezes my shoulder and presses a kiss to Billy's soft cheek before going back downstairs.

Dylan is sleeping when I step inside the room. Rowena looks up with a great big smile on her face. "Oh, Gabby. He's a little beauty." She touches his cheek, beaming at him. "He looks so much like Dylan."

"I know. Except for the eyes, he's the image of his daddy, and I couldn't be happier about it."

"Dylan tried to stay awake, but he was drained; however, he gave me strict instructions to wake him once you arrived."

"I'll do it, thanks, Rowena."

She quietly slips out of the room, and I move over to the bed, sitting down beside a sleeping Dylan. I'd like to say he looks at peace while he's asleep, but his face is contorted in pain, even in slumber, and I hate how much he's hurting.

It's selfish to pray to God to prolong Dylan's life when he's in so much pain.

I should be begging God to take him as painlessly as possible.

"Dylan, baby." I press a kiss to his mouth. "Wake up, Freckles. I have someone here who wants to meet you."

Dylan stirs slowly, grimacing as he gradually opens his eyes. I lie down, placing Billy in between us. "Say hello to your son."

Dylan's eyes instantly flood with tears, and he reaches out, running the tip of his finger down our baby's cheek. Billy murmurs, but he doesn't wake. "Oh, Gabby. Look at him." His voice is laden with emotion.

"I know, right?" I press a kiss to the top of my baby's head, reaching my arm over to hug Dylan. "We made a beautiful baby, Dylan. And he's so much like you."

Dylan places a shaky kiss on Billy's forehead, closing his eyes and inhaling. I wish he could smell that gorgeous baby smell, but his senses aren't what they used to be, another side effect he's had to deal with lately. "And he's okay, Gabby? He's perfectly healthy?"

"He's absolutely perfect, Dylan. Passed all the checks with flying colors. He's even a good weight for a preemie."

"I was so scared I wouldn't make it to this day," he admits. "I'm glad I didn't miss this." He watches Billy's tiny chest rising and falling with awe and adoration on his face. "It helps, you know," he whispers, curling his finger through Billy's small hand. "At least I'm not leaving you totally alone. That there's this part of me left to comfort you and Mom."

"He already brings me so much joy, and while nothing can compensate for your loss, I know he'll help me get through it."

"I want you to move forward with your life, Gabby. To find love again. I don't want you to be sad, Dimples." Dylan takes my hand, linking our fingers and resting them over Billy's stomach. "I know you will be at first, but promise me you'll try to remember all the amazing times we had together rather than focusing on the time we didn't have." His breathing becomes labored, and he pauses for a bit. "I would rather go out like this having loved you for nine years than live a long, healthy life without you in it." He raises our joined hands to his lips, kissing my fingers. "Thank you, Gabby. For filling my life with love and happiness and for giving me this most precious gift." His breath is wheezy, and he's clearly struggling, so I reach over for the oxygen mask and fit it over his mouth.

"It's been my absolute pleasure to share my life with you, Dylan. You've shown me how amazing it is to love and be loved, and, for as long as I live, I will never forget you. Billy and I will love you forever." The heaviness pressing down on my chest almost makes it impossible to go on, but I do it for him. "Now, sleep, Freckles. We'll be right here when you wake up."

Billy wakes me a few hours later, emitting noisy, hungry little cries. Before I can even rub the sleep from my eyes, Slater is there, kneeling by the bed. "I can feed him if you want to go back to sleep," he whispers, already reaching for Billy.

"Are you sure?" I ask through a yawn.

"Positive. I'll bring him back when he's done." He casts a concerned look in Dylan's direction.

"Thank you, Slate."

I'm asleep before my head even hits the pillow.

The next morning, the house is a hive of activity. The photographer arrives to take some family photos, and I should be amazed Dylan organized it at such short notice, but I've seen him in action these past few months, and he's been on a mission. It's the same photographer we used to take our maternity shots, but that time, Dylan had been mobile, and we'd gone to his studio. This time, he has to work around the poor lighting in Dylan's bedroom, but I don't care how they turn out, because they're the only family photos we will have, so they'll be precious to me anyway.

Dylan's in a lot of pain today. I can tell by the way he winces with even the slightest movement, but he refuses his usual morphine shot, saying he wants to be fully conscious every second he has left with his son. I hold Dylan while he feeds his son a bottle, keeping my arms propped underneath his the entire time. He struggles to keep his eyes open, falling asleep before his son does. I lay Billy down beside his dad, snapping more pics as I sit in the chair by his bed. Heather sits across from me, and we share knowing looks. We both know the end is close, but neither one of us can admit that out loud.

Slater takes over when Billy wakes, changing his diaper and taking him out for a walk in his new stroller. Then Mom arrives, insisting on making lunch and practically force-feeding myself and Heather. We refuse to leave Dylan's side, so she carries everything up on a tray.

Terri and Caleb arrive in the late afternoon, and I race down the stairs to say a quick hello before returning to Dylan. I'm terrified to leave his side for even a minute.

My maternity nurse arrives, and she runs a few checks on me and Billy. She cautions me to get some sleep, telling me my body needs rest and good nutrition, but I zone her out. There's no way I'm going to sleep while Dylan is at death's door. I doze a little in the chair, but I can't fully fall asleep, and that's the way I prefer it.

Dylan moans a lot in his sleep, and it's heartbreaking. I can't bear to see him in so much pain. I tell Rowena to give him the morphine, and he drifts into a more peaceful sleep. When he wakes a few hours later, he's lost the ability to speak. Every time he opens his mouth, no sound comes out, and my heart aches for him. Tears leak out of his eyes, and I wonder how much more indignity he can take.

I beg God to take him.

To spare him any more pain.

I don't want this for him.

I hate to see the man I love like a shell of his former self.

I'm happy he got to hold his son in his arms. That he got to kiss him and tell him he loves him. That we got some family photos taken and I'll have something to show our son when he's older.

Over the last few hours, everyone comes in to say their goodbyes. I'm numb as I sit in a corner watching it happen. The only time I leave Dylan's room is to go to the bathroom. The next time I take a bathroom break, Slater is waiting for me outside when I emerge. "Billy's fed and bathed and fast asleep in his crib."

"Thank you for taking such good care of him."

"Your mom and the maternity nurse helped too. Turns out changing diapers isn't as easy as it looks." That pulls a tiny smile from my mouth. "And don't even get me started on how difficult it was to figure out the stroller. I'm an engineering major, and it still took me at least an hour to fit it together. It only worked because I had to enlist your brother's help in the end."

I full-on laugh at that. "Damn. I would've paid good money to see that."

Slater cups my face, looking at me softly and sweetly in a way I don't deserve. Tears leak out of my eyes unbidden, and I mash my lips together to trap the anguished sobs threatening to emerge.

"Come here," he says, opening his arms, and I fold into his embrace without hesitation. "You're going to get through this, Gabby." He rubs a hand up and down my spine. "It won't be easy, but you have so many people who love you and want to help. Including me."

"I know." I press my head to his chest and close my eyes. "I just want this to be over for him because I hate seeing him in so much pain."

"That's the worst. I felt like that with Mom."

I hold Slater tighter. "I couldn't have gotten through this last month without you. Thank you."

"I'm here for you, Belle. Always."

Reluctantly, I pull out of Slater's embrace after a couple of minutes. "I better head back. I don't think he has long." Silent tears cascade down my face.

"I'm so sorry, Belle."

I swipe at my eyes, removing all trace of my tears. "I know you are."

Smiling sadly, I turn around without another word and walk back into Dylan's bedroom.

Chapter Forty-Four

Dylan died in his sleep during the night. It was peaceful in the end, and I'm grateful for small mercies. Heather and I were by his side, each of us holding his hand. Heather sobs. Huge, wracking, gut-wrenching sobs that shake her whole body. Her head is on Dylan's chest, and her hand is still laced in his. Rowena removes all the tubes from Dylan's body with tears streaming down her face.

I don't cry even though the pain in my heart is indescribable. I'm incapable of releasing my tears. Perhaps I'm in shock. Or I'm storing them up for the right time to let loose. I just stare at him in the bed wondering how it came to this. Cursing God for taking all my hopes and dreams away. Screaming at him in my head for stealing the boy I've always seen as my forever.

Can you go on living when your heart is irrefutably broken beyond repair?

Will I find the strength to be both mother and father to the son Dylan left behind?

How can I move forward when all I want to do is go back? To

return to a time when we were so in love and tangled up in one another.

My mind churns painfully as I stare at the lifeless body of my love.

My family comes into the room. They've been here all night, and they already said their goodbyes, so I know this is for me and Heather. They surround me as Heather says a few prayers. Slater sits down beside me, taking my other hand in his. He has the baby monitor in his free hand, and I glance at the screen, grateful my son is sleeping soundly and that he isn't a witness to this. Then Caleb arrives with two guitars, extending one to me, but I shake my head. I can't play. Not now. Maybe not ever. I'll always associate it with Dylan, and, right now, it's far too upsetting.

Caleb plays some of Dylan's favorite songs while my mom lights candles and incense around the room. "Dylan would really like this," I say in a voice barely louder than a whisper. The singing, the candles, and the love of family. The prayers, not so much, but, like he said, this part is for the living. Although, I like the thought that maybe his spirit still lingers in the room, watching over proceedings.

Myndi and Ryan stand behind me, each placing a hand on my shoulder. Mom and Dad sit on either side of Heather, comforting her while sending waves of love in my direction. Caleb sings his heart out for Dylan. A heavily pregnant Terri sits at his feet, rubbing her belly and clinging to her fiancé's leg. Dean swipes tears away when he thinks I'm not looking.

I'm surrounded by love, by people who would do anything for me, but their support and love can't extinguish my heartache. I shiver, feeling unbearably cold on the inside, and this deep void, this cavernous hole, in my heart aches with the knowledge I lost a part of myself too today.

When Forever Changes

The next few days are incredibly difficult, and my son is the only thing keeping me sane, tethering me to this existence. The pain isn't as overwhelming when I'm holding him in my arms. I cling to him like a life preserver, and I'm hugely selfish, resisting giving him to anyone but Heather and Slater.

I can't sleep, because every time I close my eyes, I see Dylan's tormented face and hear his ragged breathing, as he clung to the last vestiges of life. I argue with the maternity nurse when she suggests I take some sleeping pills. Then I argue with Slater after I fire her. He begs me not to do this. Tells me I need to take care of myself if I want to take care of Billy. I relent, apologize, and ask her to come back.

The funeral service is tomorrow, and I'm dreading it. Which is why I'm up at four a.m. nursing a bottle of vodka on the couch. I fed Billy an hour ago so that should buy me a few hours of solitude to drink in peace.

"I guess it's a good thing you're not breastfeeding yet," Slater says, yawning as he strolls into the room. He's only in low-hanging sweats, and the sight of his naked torso stirs something in me, but I ignore it and the lustful thought that enters my mind.

I'm disgusted with myself.

My boyfriend, my best friend, and the father of my child isn't even in his grave yet and I'm having immoral thoughts about another man.

"I don't need a lecture," I snap, unfairly venting at Slater.

"I wasn't criticizing," he softly confirms, sitting down on the couch beside me.

"I know." I sigh. "I'm sorry. In case you hadn't noticed, I'm not the best company these days."

"You're grieving. I understand."

"Am I?" I swig straight from the vodka bottle. "Is that what this empty, numb feeling is?"

"If I could absorb your pain, I would. I would do anything to spare you this."

I swig from the bottle again. "Mr. Smirnoff is doing a pretty good job right now."

Slater looks like he wants to say something, but he wisely stays quiet. "Want some?" I offer him the bottle.

"Why the hell not." His fingers brush against mine, sending ripples of electricity shooting through me. I squeeze my eyes shut, hating myself for my reaction to him. While it's understandable—because Slater and I had something good and it didn't end because those feelings ceased—it's still wrong.

We take turns drinking in silence, and my head is starting to cloud over.

"I spent the entire two weeks after Mom's funeral either drunk or drinking," he admits.

"Did it help?"

"I thought it did, at the time, but it only prolonged the agony. Everything I worked so hard to avoid was still there when I came out of my alcoholic coma."

"I just need this one night. To try and blot it out, because I don't know if I can get through tomorrow otherwise."

"I'm here for you. You can lean on me."

"I can't offer you anything, Slate. We can't pick up where we left off," I blurt. "I'm empty inside," I say, even though it's not fully true.

"The only thing I'm asking for is the ability to support you and Billy. You're still one of my best friends, and I'm not doing anything I wouldn't do for any other friend in the same situation. I don't expect anything in return."

I should tell him no because that's not a fair bargain, and, deep down, I suspect he's hoping for more of something I can't give him. But those aren't the words that leave my mouth. "Hold me, please?"

"You never have to beg, Belle," he replies, hauling me over and into his lap. He takes the open bottle from my hand, placing it on the table, and then he wraps his big, warm, strong arms around me. I rest my head on his shoulder, feeling less alone as my eyes drift shut.

I don't remember falling asleep, but when I wake, I'm lying on the couch with a blanket wrapped over my front and Slater curled around me from behind.

"I thought you could use some coffee," Heather says, holding it out to me as she eyeballs Slater and the bottle of vodka suspiciously.

"This isn't what it looks like," I rush to reassure her. "I mean the vodka is, but nothing happened with Slater. I just got drunk and fell asleep."

"You don't have to explain anything to me, Gabby. But you do need to hurry if we're going to make it to church on time."

"Shit." I glance at the clock on the wall. "I missed Billy's seven a.m. feed."

"It's okay. I gave him his bottle, and he's napping in his bouncer now."

Guilt washes over me, and I vow that's the last time I'm turning to alcohol. I can't afford to blur the pain with vodka because I have responsibilities. Billy is my entire world now, and I won't let him down. Not when I'm the only parent he has left and he's relying on me.

***

The funeral is every bit as horrendous as I expected it to be. Heather disapproved of my plan to bring Billy with me, but she doesn't get to make that call, so I overruled her. She doesn't realize how much I need to hold my baby in my arms to survive this day.

Halfway through the service, Billy starts crying and nothing settles him. Mom offers to take him outside, but I physically can't part with him, so I leave myself. Slater goes with me, and I'm grateful for his hand on my shoulder as we walk back up the aisle. Every person we pass is a blubbering mess. Even grown men cry as they watch me trying to soothe my son during his father's funeral.

I cling to Slater and Billy at the graveside, ignoring the funny looks sent my way. They can judge all they like. I don't care. I can't watch as they lower Dylan's casket into the ground. While my eye ducts remain tear free, the same can't be said for the messy organ in my chest. My heart has ruptured. It's ripped into a million jagged pieces, weeping inside the rib cage it's hiding behind.

It's even worse back at Heather's. People accost me on all sides, offering condolences, tearing up as they smile at Billy, telling me how much he looks like his daddy. Slater doesn't leave my side, but that's in part due to the fact I won't let him. I'm terrified to be left alone. I can't deal with my own emotions, so how the hell am I expected to deal with everyone else's?

"Here," Ryan says, approaching with two glasses. "You both look like you could use a stiff drink."

Slater takes the tumbler of whiskey, but I shake my head. "I drank my fill of vodka last night, and I'm not touching another drop of alcohol. I neglected my son this morning, and I won't make the same mistake again."

"Don't be so hard on yourself, Tornado. No one blames you for having a much-needed drink or taking some time for yourself. You only gave birth a few days ago and you've had no time to rest."

"I'm okay."

"No, little sis, you're not." He folds me into his arms, resting his cheek on my hair. "But you will be."

The next month passes by in a blur. I throw myself into motherhood, trying to deflect the myriad of emotions plaguing me in the aftermath of Dylan's death, but it's not easy.

I attend the reading of Dylan's will at his attorney's office with Heather and my family. I guess I no longer have to wonder what he was doing all those nights he squirrelled himself away in his room, claiming he needed some alone time.

I walk out of his attorney's office in a shocked daze. Dad circles his arm around my back. "You hanging in there, Buttercup?"

"Barely," I truthfully admit. "How the hell did Dylan manage to do all that behind my back while he was battling such a terrible disease?"

Dylan bought Billy and me a house. He also established a trust fund for his son and left me more money than I know what to do with. He made a considerable donation to a local cancer charity and established a company with his friends—the ones he was working on his hush-hush robotics project with. He's patented everything and set it up so both me and Billy have a twenty percent shareholding in the company.

Chase was at the meeting, at Dylan's request, and he explained everything, outlining their ambitious plans. With a top investor already onboard, it's looking like Dylan has helped his friends build a company with enormous potential, leaving a legacy and a potential future role for his son.

He also ensured Heather is well provided for, and he left something for every member of my family. He even included Slater in his will.

"Dylan was always a planner. I'm not shocked he went to such lengths to ensure his family is provided for. That man loved you with his whole heart, Buttercup. I knew he wouldn't let you down."

I cling to the box I'm carrying. "He did all this too, without me even suspecting. He's still managing to surprise me." I briefly inspected the contents in David's office before we left, and I'm still in shock. There are two bundles of cards in the box. One set is for Billy. The other is addressed to me. Dylan has written birthday cards for every significant milestone in both our lives. There are also five photo albums chronicling our relationship with tons of handwritten notes accompanying the pics. Now I understand why we spent so many nights reminiscing over the past. While Dylan's memory was sketchy thanks to the fucking cancer, mine was intact, and I loved reminding him of some of our best stories.

Dylan didn't just want to ensure his son knew who he was, he wanted him to know how epic our romance was, so our son understood he was born from a very special kind of love. I only glanced at the first few pages of one of the albums before I had to put it aside. The pain was instantaneous and intense.

As I place the box in the corner of my room, I know it will torment me every time I look at it. However, I know there are some challenges I'm not strong enough to face yet.

Chapter Forty-Five

Another month passes, and nothing much has changed, except I'm now fitting into all my old clothes and Billy's eyes are a lighter blue, mirroring mine. He's also giving everyone these massive, cute smiles, and while I didn't think it was possible to love him any more than I already do, every day he proves me wrong. He's getting bigger, and his progress is on point according to his most recent developmental check.

"Please, Belle," Slater begs me over the phone. "You wouldn't come out to celebrate with the guys so please do this one thing for me. It's only dinner, and it'll do you good to get out of the house."

"I get out of the house every day, Slate. I take Billy on long walks, and we visit the park and regularly go swimming. He has playdates with his cousin Ryder, and I'm constantly around at Mom's. I've even joined a local mom and baby group." I pack my days with activity, investing all my energy in my child.

Mom tried to talk to me about it.

She knows what I'm doing.

That I'm filling every second in the hope it'll distract me from the gaping hole in my heart. That I'm tiring myself out so that when I pop one of my sleeping pills at night I won't have any nightmares or remember that Dylan is no longer here. She wants me to speak to a grief counselor, but, so far, I'm resisting. I'm not ready to deal with all my confusing emotions, and I'm happy to spend my days with my son, pouring all my energy and effort into being the best mom I can.

So, it's ironic that Slate is calling me out on that.

"You're an amazing mother, Belle. Don't think I'm criticizing. I'm so proud of you for prioritizing his needs and not letting the pain distract you from caring for your son. But you need to prioritize yourself too. You have tons of babysitters and all I'm asking for is one night. One dinner between two old friends. Don't you want to help me celebrate my graduation?"

"You're guilting me into this?"

"If that's what it'll take, then hell yeah."

I sigh down the phone. "Ugh. You don't play fair, but okay. Fine, I'll let you take me to dinner."

"Wow, try to curb your enthusiasm, will ya?"

"What do you expect when you're virtually blackmailing me into going out with you."

"Ouch. Way to kick a guy when he's down."

I'm being unfair. I know that. Slate has demonstrated the patience of a saint these past couple months. His unflappable devotion to me and Billy hasn't gone unnoticed, but I can't give him what I suspect he wants. He hasn't broached the subject with me, but I see the way he looks at me, the way he looks at Billy, and I know, if I asked him, he'd move heaven and earth to be a family with us.

But I can't get over the sense of betrayal I feel whenever I'm around Slater and he stokes my desire into orbit. It's why I've been trying to push him away recently. Making excuses and avoiding him whenever I can.

He deserves to find someone without baggage. Someone who can love him unconditionally. Someone who isn't a broken mess on the inside.

Slater has just graduated top of his class, and he has a tempting offer from one of the best engineering companies in the country. His star is rising, and no one deserves it more than he does, but I sense his hesitation. He doesn't want to leave me and Billy behind. He hasn't voiced that sentiment, but Ryan has dropped enough hints for me to draw my own conclusion.

Slate has just been offered his dream job, and there is no way I'm letting him pass the opportunity up because of me.

"Now, this isn't so bad, is it?" Slate asks, grinning at me over the table.

I tap a finger on my chin, pretending to consider it. "I'd give the restaurant ten out of ten, the company a six."

"Ouch. You sure know how to wound a guy's ego." He cuts a piece of his steak slowly and precisely. "Except I know you, and you're full of crap."

I bark out a laugh. "Wow, I think this job offer has really gone to your head. You're definitely giving Ryan a run for his money in the arrogance stakes."

He holds his fork out to me. "I'm going to pretend you didn't just insult me and let you try this because it's out of this world."

I open my mouth and let him feed me even though it makes me hugely uncomfortable. A loud moan escapes my mouth as the juicy flavors burst on my tongue. "Damn, that's good."

Slate gulps, shifting on his chair, and his eyes turn heated. "I've been assured they have awesome steakhouses in Iowa too."

"You'll be all set."

He places his knife and fork down, piercing me with a serious look. "Come with me, Belle. I want you and Billy by my side."

Acid churns in my gut, and I swallow over the monster-sized ball lodged in my throat. "Slate, we're not even together. It wouldn't be right."

He leans his elbows on the table, and the movement stretches his shirt tight across his impressive biceps, and I can't help a momentary

387

drool. It's arm porn at it's very best, and I'd challenge any female with a pulse not to stare. He notices my attention, and his lips curve up. "You only have to say the word, and we can rectify that. You know I still love you."

"Stop," I whisper, looking down at the table. "You know I can't."

"Can't or won't?" His inquiring tone is gentle.

"Both." I risk a glance at him, and I can see him carefully choosing his next words.

"This is only going to add weight to your arrogance theory, but I know you still love me, Belle. I know you want me as much as I want you." He wets his lips, reaching his hand across the table for mine. Warmth filters up my arm from his touch. "I also know you aren't ready to confront that fact, and I completely get it. You loved Dylan too, and I understand you're suffering, so I would never force this on you."

"So, then you know why I can't move to Iowa with you."

"I'm not putting any labels on it, Belle. I love you and I love Billy, and I want you both with me, so I can take care of you."

"It's not your responsibility to take care of us, and I don't know what was said between you and Dylan, but you don't owe me or him anything."

"You think this is a burden?" His tone is a little harsher. "Or that I'm saying this purely because of some promise I made to Dylan?" His eyes blaze. "I'm asking you this because I love you! Both of you, and I can't bear the thought of being hundreds of miles away from you." He pulls his hand back, rubbing his tense jaw. "I just want to be with you, Belle. I don't want to lose you."

"Slate. I can't give you what you want. What you need." I shake my head. "I'm sorry."

"I promise I'll be patient. I won't force you into anything until you're ready to take that step. Just, don't give up on us. I know we can be so good together. I know we can be a family."

"You have your whole life ahead of you, and I can't hold you back."

"If you come with me, you won't be."

"Are you sure about that? Have you properly thought this through? You'll be in a new city, at a new job, making new friends and contacts, and the last thing you'll need is to be saddled with a woman who isn't even your girlfriend and someone else's kid. We'll only tie you down, and you'll end up resenting us."

If I'd slapped him, he wouldn't look as hurt.

"I can't believe you've just said that. Is that really what you think of me? You think I'd rather be going out every night, getting wasted and fucking random girls, than coming home to you and Billy?"

"I don't think it'd start out like that. I think you mean well, but, in time, it would all feel like a chore, an unnecessary burden. Especially when you're getting nothing out of it. Because I can't promise you a Goddamned thing, Slate. I'm broken. I'm devastated, and I still haven't properly grieved. You'll grow tired of waiting for me and jerking off instead of having sex. Eventually all the girls throwing themselves at you will start to look desirable. When I can't give you what you want, and you get fed up of waiting, and you start screwing around, where would that leave me and my son? Billy is my sole priority, and I can't take any risks. He's too important to me."

I know Slater would *never* do that. Not in a million years. I hate lying to him, hate hurting him like this, but I won't let him sacrifice his future for me.

"Wow. I never realized you had such a low opinion of me." He clicks his fingers, gesturing at the waiter for the check. "I came here tonight to ask the woman I love to share my life. To tell her that no measure of time waiting will be too much. That I understand she's mourning, and I, of all people, know what that's like. That you can't put a timetable on grief. I was going to tell her I'll wait until she's ready to ask her to marry me, because I know when she agrees it'll be the happiest day of my life because I'll not only be gaining a wife, I'll be gaining a son too."

The waiter places the check on the table and walks away. Slater withdraws some bills from his wallet, slamming them down on the table as he stands. "But I guess the joke's on me, because you've already figured out who I am and what I want, and you've clearly already given up on us."

Shame burns a new hole in my heart as I watch the agony spread across his face. I can only hope that, in the long-term, he'll find it in his heart to forgive me. When he has this amazing life, and he meets some lucky woman, maybe he'll realize I was right, and understand I pushed him away because I love him too much to ruin his future. I can't give Slater my whole heart, my undivided attention, while I'm still mourning Dylan. The guilt and the hurt won't let me. Slater deserves better than me. He may not know it, but I do. Slater deserves to be loved wholly and completely and a girl with half a heart can't offer him that.

———

My cruel words worked, and, one week later, Slater moves to Iowa and out of our lives without any further contact.

That night, for the first night in almost ten weeks, I cry.

I sob my heart out, drenching the pillow with my tears.

I finally cry rivers for Dylan.

I grieve the loss that my son will carry with him throughout his entire life.

I mourn that beautiful, precious future I had all planned out as a kid.

And I shed tears for the only other man I've ever loved or am ever likely to. The one I pushed away in a misguided attempt to protect both our fragile hearts.

Chapter Forty-Six

Two Years Later

"I'll see you next week, Gabby," Cassandra says as we leave class together. "Oh, and don't forget that podcast next Tuesday. I already registered your interest, and you should've received an email with a link to join the session."

"Thanks, Cassie. You're the best." I grab her into a quick hug. "I think I owe you a drink or ten at this stage."

"I'll hold you to that next time we go out!"

We wave, heading in opposite directions. Cassie is off to meet her boyfriend for dinner, and I need to drop by the grocery store before going home. I'm glad I only have classes one night a week and that I can do the rest of my study online. I hate being away from Billy for any length of time, especially at night.

I drive the five blocks to the grocery store and race inside, eager to grab what I need and head home.

I'm standing in front of the cereal aisle, jumping up in a feeble attempt to reach the Cheerios on the top shelf when all the tiny hairs lift on the back of my neck.

I sense his presence before he speaks. "Need a hand, Belle?"

His deep voice sends shivers down my spine, and his citrusy scent conjures up a million happy memories of leisurely mornings and lazy afternoons wrapped around one another in bed. I promptly drop the four-pack of beans I'm holding on my foot, yelping as my face heats up. "Shit! Slate. You scared the hell out of me."

He bends down to retrieve the cans, and I sneak a peek at him. His hair is longer on top but clipped neatly around his ears, and where it meets the nape of his neck, but it's still as thick, dark, and silky as I remember. He's wearing a blue dress shirt and charcoal-gray pants that mold to his shapely ass. He straightens up, and I flush an even deeper shade of red when he notices my staring. His lips twitch as he places the beans in my shopping cart, and I take a proper look at him.

He's wearing his hair in a slicked-back style that is more mature and professional looking than the way he used to wear it in college. It only serves to highlight his gorgeous face. His skin is radiant and tanned, and he's sporting a neatly trimmed layer of stubble on his chin and cheeks. His rich brown eyes glisten with health, and his mouth is pulled into a smile as he stares back at me. Gosh, he's gotten even better looking over the last two years, or maybe that's just my mind playing tricks, because, hella, Slater Evans is a damn fine sight for sore eyes.

His eyes latch on mine, and I forget to breathe. My heart dances a tango in my chest, and my pulse is beating wildly out of control. God, I've missed this man. So, so much. Not a day has passed since we parted when he hasn't been in my thoughts and on my mind.

He chuckles. "You look shocked to see me."

"Ugh, that's 'cause I am." I arch my brows.

He frowns. "Didn't Ryan tell you I was back in town?"

"Nope, but things are a little strained between us at the minute."

"Cause of what happened with Myndi?" he correctly guesses.

"Yeah. He broke her heart and now she's taken a job overseas." Not that I'm laying all the blame at Ryan's door. Relationships are two-way streets, and Myndi was the one who actually broke up with him. While she won't divulge the specifics, she said she had no choice because of something Ryan did. It's heartbreaking because I know she still loves him, and she was secretly hoping he'd chase her, but he seems to have given up on them. Last week, I tried to get him to open up about her, but he told me, point blank, that he doesn't want to talk about it and to let it drop.

"Hey, do you have time to grab a coffee? I'd love to catch up," he asks.

"Sure." I can't keep the smile off my face. "Let me shoot Mom a message and make sure she's okay to babysit a while longer." I tap away on my phone, and Mom replies straightaway. When I look up, I catch him checking me out, and my lady parts dance a happy dance. "I'm good, but I still need to finish my shopping."

Slater grabs a box of Cheerios from the top shelf, handing them to me. "I presume this is what you were looking for?"

"Yeah. I've passed my addiction on to my son, and now he goes through bowlfuls of the stuff."

"How's Billy?" Slater walks with me as I grab a few other items and toss them in my cart.

"He's awesome. He's the sweetest little boy ever."

"Well, he does have you for a mom, so..." He pauses for a beat before smiling. "Anyway, I'm glad everything worked out for you." A layer of sadness washes over his face, and the easygoing atmosphere turns a little tense.

"So, uh, how long are you back for?"

He stares into my eyes, and it's intense. "I'm back for good, Belle."

I suck in a sharp breath and stop walking. "How come? What happened with your great job?" While I don't ask Ryan for updates on Slater that often, because it still hurts to think of him, I cave every now and then. I know he's done well for himself in Iowa, gaining three promotions in two years and quickly moving up the ranks.

"The job's still great. Look, it's a bit of a long story, so why don't we save it for over coffee?"

We pay for our items at separate registers, and then we offload our bags in our respective cars and head to the café across the street. Slater insists on placing our orders, so I take a seat by the window, trying to caution my overexcited heart to stop overreacting. Just because he's back doesn't mean anything is different. He doesn't seem to hate my guts, for which I'm grateful, but that doesn't mean I'm forgiven or that he's nurturing any lingering thoughts of me or an "us."

"Here you go." He hands me my latte, taking the seat across from me. His long legs brush against mine under the table, and my overly enthusiastic long-neglected hormones go crazy at the fleeting contact.

It's official.

I'm completely pathetic.

And most definitely still hung up on Slater Evans.

He opens the lid of his coffee, closing his eyes as he inhales the bitter, chocolatey notes. "Man, I've missed this."

"Don't they have good coffee in Iowa?" I ask, taking a sip of my drink.

"They do, but coffee never tastes as good as it does back home."

"True. So, tell me. What's happening with your job?"

He leans back a little, and the way his gaze rakes over me sends delicious tremors of desire ricocheting through me. "The company I work for is setting up a new office in Wilmington, and they asked me to manage it. It was too good of an offer to turn down and ... I've missed home."

"Wow. Congratulations. Ryan told me you were doing amazing things, and I'm so happy for you. I always knew you'd be successful."

"Thanks, Belle." A faint blush stains his cheeks, and it's so cute. "What about you? Did you return to your nursing studies?"

"No. Ryan didn't tell you?" I ask him the same question he asked me back in the store.

He shakes his head, clearly debating whether to explain himself.

"I asked Ryan not to talk about you." He pauses, and his Adam's apple bobs in his throat. "It hurt too much."

His admission is like a dagger through the heart. "I'm so sorry, Slate." My voice is soft. "The last thing I wanted to do was hurt you, but I wasn't in a good place back then, and I—"

"It's fine, Belle. Forget about it. It's in the past, and I'd prefer to leave it there."

Cue a second dagger straight through my remorseful heart. "Oh, okay." I look down at the table as I sip my coffee, trying to push the pang of disappointment aside.

"You're a full-time mom then?"

I tip my chin up. "Mostly, but I'm studying for an online degree in alternative medicine, and I attend acupuncture classes once a week. It's why I was in town tonight."

"That's great, Belle, and I can totally see you doing that."

I shrug. "I was sad to leave nursing behind, but I don't want a job with such erratic hours. This way, once I'm qualified, I can set up a practice and dictate my own hours. I want to be there for Billy as much as I can." The other factor in my decision was my reluctance to return to UD. I didn't want to be confronted with the ghosts of my past at every turn. It was time to make a clean break. To forge a different path in life.

His cell pings, and he extracts it from his pocket, checking a new message. "I'm sorry, Belle, but I've got to go, something's come up." He sends me an apologetic smile, and I mask my disappointment with a fake nonchalant smile.

"No problem, I should get back to Billy anyway."

"Do you have any recent pics on your phone?"

My smile is genuine this time. "Do I what?" I laugh, swiping my finger across the screen of my iPhone. "Here. These ones were taken at the park yesterday."

I hand him my cell and he flips through the photos, his smile growing wider and wider. "He's gotten so big, and he looks happy and contented." He lingers over the photo of Billy and me. We're both wearing goofy smiles for the camera, tucked in close together with our arms wrapped around one another. "You both do."

He hands the phone back to me and stands. I slip it in my purse and grab my coffee. "Yeah, it's taken a while, and a lot of therapy, but, I'm good."

We walk out together. "I worried about you a lot after I left."

"You did?" I look up at him as we reach my car.

He nods. "Whoever coined that phrase 'out of sight, out of mind' was a lying asshole."

"Don't let Mom hear you saying that," I joke. I'm back in that nervous-excited space again. He chuckles, and I unlock my car. "Well, um, thanks for the coffee, and maybe I'll see you around sometime." I'm rambling and purposely avoiding looking at him.

"Belle." His hand lands on my arm, and my skin tingles all the way to my toes. "I'm glad you're in a better place. That you and Billy are doing good. That's all I ever wanted for you."

Tears prick my eyes. Slater Evans was always far too good for me. "Are *you* happy?" I blurt, twisting around and looking up at him.

"Yeah." He nods. "Mostly." His eyes flick to my lips, and butterflies scatter in my chest. Electricity crackles in the space between us, and he jerks back as if slapped. "I'm sorry to cut and run like this. How about a rain check?"

My head bobs vigorously. Way to play it cool, Gabby. "Why don't you come to my house for dinner on Sunday? We'll all be there. I'm sure everyone would love to see you. You can meet Ryder, Caleb and Terri's son, and Dean's new girlfriend Alice."

When I pushed Slater away two years ago, I didn't stop to consider everything he stood to lose. I took away the only family he's ever known, and I've never forgiven myself for that. Sure, Ryan keeps in regular contact with him and he's spent plenty of weekends in Iowa, and my parents visited him last year. I also know Mom mails him cards on his birthday and holidays and that she's begged him to come home for Thanksgiving and Christmas. Just like I know he only turns her down because of me.

There were so many occasions where I went to pick up the phone or drop him an email, to tell him I was sorry, that I didn't mean those hurtful things I said, that, in my warped mind, I convinced myself I was doing the right thing, but I always stopped myself from following through, afraid I'd only make things worse.

Maybe now he's back, I can finally fix it so he doesn't feel uncomfortable coming back into the fold.

He's been quiet while I've been babbling internally and externally.

"Please say you'll come," I practically beg. "Everyone misses you."

Especially me.

He shoves his hands in his pockets, looking like he's weighing up the pros and cons. When the lines on his forehead smooth out, I know he's made his decision, and I release the breath I'd been holding. "Okay, that sounds cool. Thanks, Belle."

My heart soars skyward, and I work hard to keep my squeal of delight locked up inside. "Great. I'll message you the address. Come at three!"

Chapter Forty-Seven

"Relax, Buttercup, you're giving me heart palpitations with all that jumping around," my dad says, smiling at me in amusement as I race around the kitchen checking everything.

"I just want everything to be perfect," I reply, lowering the heat under the green beans. "This is the first time we've all been together in two years. I want it to be special."

"And it will be special, because of the people around the table. Who cares if you burn the carrots or chargrill the meat until it's barely edible? We've never let your mom's cooking stop us from having a good time."

"I heard that, Paul!" Mom hollers from the dining room where she's setting the table with help from Mia and Tia. Caleb, Dean, and Ryan are playing ball in the backyard with Ryder and Billy while Alice and Terri are enjoying a cold glass of white wine on the deck, chatting up a storm as they watch the big kids play with the little ones.

Dad chuckles, topping off my wine glass and patting me on the back. "I know why you're nervous, sweetheart, and you don't have any reason to be. Slater doesn't hold grudges. He's already proven that if he agreed to come here today."

"Sometimes I hate how close you and mom are. I told her all that stuff in confidence," I grumble.

"And I have kept your confidence," Mom says, coming into the kitchen with my nieces in tow. "Girls, why don't you take Grandpa outside and play with your cousins?"

The girls need little encouragement. Even though Dean's ex-wife Annie insists on dressing them like little princesses, they are quite the tomboys these days.

Dad kisses me on the cheek. "Your mom doesn't need to say anything for me to understand certain things, sweetheart. I just want you to be happy, because you deserve all the happiness in the world."

I throw my arms around him. "Thanks, Dad." He blows me a kiss before stepping outside.

"Sit down for a sec." Mom takes me by the hand, pushing me into a chair at the table. She hands me my glass of wine and sits down with her own. "I'm delighted Slater is moving back, for a variety of reasons, especially because it gives you a chance to make amends. It hurts me that you're beating yourself up over what happened. Your actions may have been misguided, but you did it out of love. I'm sure once you explain Slater will understand and forgive you." She takes a sip of her wine.

"But?" I prompt, knowing there's one coming.

"But I don't want you to get your hopes up. He's been gone over two years, and you told him to forget you. What if he has?"

My heart falters in my chest. It's not like I haven't considered this in the days since we ran into each other, and it would probably serve me right. "Do you know something I don't?" I gasp, slapping a hand over my chest. "Oh, God, he was with someone when you visited last year, wasn't he?"

She vigorously shakes her head. "No, there was no one on the scene then. I asked him outright." She smirks a little. "But that doesn't mean he isn't in a relationship now. I just think you need to prepare yourself, Gabrielle. While it would make me incredibly happy to see you two together again, you have to consider it may not happen. I don't want to see you hurt. Not when you've worked so hard to process your feelings since Dylan died."

"You're right, Mom. I have been getting a little carried away. I just wish I had reacted differently when he asked me to move to Iowa with him." Now that my head is less fuzzy, my perspective is completely altered. I've realized just how much I love Slater, how much I've always loved him without even knowing, and the thought I pushed one of the great loves of my life away has been eating me up inside.

"Baby, you were hanging by a thread back then, and I happen to believe you made the right call. There is no guarantee if you'd moved there that it would've worked out. Remember everything you went through after he left."

I nod, getting up. "I know. Well, a really smart woman once told me if it's meant to be it will happen. And if it doesn't, I'll just have to deal with the consequences of my decision."

"That's my girl." Mom stands, coming around the table and pulling me into her arms. "I have a good feeling about this, but take your time. There's no rush."

The doorbell chimes, and I knock my glass of wine all over the table. "Shit! Goddamn it." I grab a cloth from the counter, hurriedly mopping it up.

"Breathe, Gabrielle." Mom's laughing as she walks out to the hall to let Slater in.

I remember to whip my apron off in time, smoothing a hand down my pretty pink dress as Slater walks into the kitchen looking like he just stepped off the pages of *GQ*. He's wearing a fitted black shirt rolled up to the sleeves with a few buttons open on top, offering a glimpse at his impressive chest. Dark denim hugs his legs in all the right places, and he's wearing the latest Vans on his feet. He still has the same neat layer of facial hair and the slicked-back locks, and he looks ruggedly handsome and good enough to eat. I'm salivating, and my panties are already damp.

God, I seriously need to get laid.

"Ahem." Mom clears her throat, giving me a pointed look.

Yep, definitely need to get laid unless I want to keep embarrassing myself in front of Slater.

"The house is gorgeous, Belle. Dylan chose well." As soon as the words leave his lips, I see him wishing he could backtrack.

"Yes, he did," I rush to reassure him, smiling so he knows I'm not upset.

While it was so hard to talk about Dylan in the months after he died, I don't shy away from mentioning him anymore.

It still hurts.

It will *always* hurt, but to stop speaking about him is like denying he ever existed, and I want to remember him, because he brightened my world and helped shape me into the woman I am today. I owe Dylan so much, and my life is fuller for having had him in it. My grief counselor has helped me enormously in coming to terms with everything, and I also want to ensure that Billy grows up knowing who his daddy was.

So I want Slater to relax. To understand it's not a faux pas to bring up his name. "And, true to form, he thought of everything," I continue. "We have a game room, a home gym, a home theater, an indoor pool, and a children's playground and basketball court in the backyard."

Slater looks relieved. "I wouldn't have expected any less." He clears his throat. "These are for you." He hands me a massive, expensive-looking bunch of flowers and a bottle of wine. If I ever needed proof of how distracting he is, the fact I didn't even notice he was holding gifts when he arrived confirms it.

"Thank you. They're beautiful." I bury my nose in the blooms, inhaling deeply. "What can I get you to drink? We have pretty much everything."

"I'll take a beer," he says, as Ryan steps into the kitchen from outside.

"If it isn't my *main man*." He walks up to his best bud, and they do the whole man-hug-slap-on-the-back thing. "It's so good to see you, bruh."

"It's good to be here."

The backdoor bursts open and Ryder and Billy come racing in. "Mom!" Billy shouts, as if I'm miles away instead of standing right in front of him. "We need a dwink. We're thirrty."

Slater chuckles.

"Sure thing." I crouch down to my son and my nephew. "Who's winning?"

"Me!" they both say at once, and we all laugh.

"More importantly, who's having the most fun?" I ask.

"Me! Me!" They both jump up and down, and their exuberance warms me from the inside out.

Mom grabs some chilled bottles of water for the boys while I scoop Billy up into my arms. His little legs and arms go around me automatically, and I hug him close, burying my nose in his hair. Billy's always so affectionate, and I never take it for granted, cherishing every precious moment.

"I love you, Mommy," he says, planting a slobbery kiss on my cheek.

My heart melts, like it does every single time he says it. "I love you too, little munchkin." I tweak his nose. "So, so much."

The expression on Slater's face, and the unshed tears in his eyes, almost undoes me. It's a look of absolute joy mixed with extreme sadness, and I know I'm responsible for putting it there. "Hey, buddy. I want you to meet someone really special." I walk to Slater's side, sliding Billy to my hip. "This is our friend Slater. Will you say hi to him?"

Billy's arm flies out, and he extends his hand for a shake. It's so adorable and the first time he's done this. My heart swells to bursting.

Slater shakes his hand, and his large palm swallows Billy's much smaller one. "I'm Billy. You be my fwend?"

"I'd love that, buddy." Slater's voice rattles with emotion.

"You play bahketball?" Billy's eye's pop wide when Slater nods. "Oh, yay." He wriggles out of my arms and I let him down. "C'mon!" He grabs Slater's hand without hesitation, dragging him toward the door.

My heart is in my mouth as I watch them together, and I'm so overcome with emotion I have to look away before anyone spots the tears in my eyes. At some point, when the time is right, I want Billy to know Slater was there when he was born and how profoundly affected he was by the experience. I still well up every time I remember the tears of joy he shed. It's a moment that will forever bind the three of us together.

"What about me?" I hear Ryan ask as they walk outside, the pout evident in his mock-surly tone.

"Oh, sweet child. You've got it bad." Mom caresses my damp cheek, smiling softly.

"I do. I have it bad. God, that was so sweet." There's no point denying it. "I'll never forgive myself if I've messed it up forever. We were so good together, and it felt so right. The timing sucked, is all."

"Start by being his friend again, and then see where it leads," she advises.

Slater returns to the kitchen twenty minutes later, full of praise for Billy. "Oh, Belle, he's amazing. Always smiling and laughing and he has so much to say!" he gushes.

"He takes after Gabrielle," Mom confirms. "She had an incredible vocabulary at age two as well."

"You should be so proud, Belle. He's a real credit to you."

He has no idea how much it means to hear that. "Thank you, but it's pretty much all down to Billy. He's always been so good and so sweet despite how much my family tries to spoil him rotten."

"I can see how easy that'd be."

My smile is so wide it threatens to split my face. The look of adoration and pure, unconditional love on Slater's face for my child makes me want to fling myself into his arms and tell him I'm still crazy about him, but I manage to restrain myself somehow.

"Can I help with anything?" he asks, resting his hip against the counter.

"Could you drain the beans?"

He rolls his sleeves up higher, and I greedily follow the movement until I remind myself I'm supposed to be channeling friendship and restraint.

"I'll organize the drinks and let everyone know we're almost ready," Mom supplies, slipping outside with a knowing wink.

"How long have you lived here?" Slate asks as he takes the pot with the green beans to the sink.

"A little over a year. I couldn't even bring myself to check out the house the first six months after Dylan died," I honestly reply. "I have a great grief counselor and she helped me work through some stuff. When I finally came here, I fell in love with the house straightaway, but I wasn't ready to move in by myself yet."

"Did you stay at Heather's?" he inquires, straining the water off the beans and tossing them back in the pot.

"I moved back to my parents' place a little while after you left. I didn't want to do that to Heather, but there were too many memories in that house, and it wasn't healthy for me there. She was a little pissed, but she understood, and she got over it. I make sure she sees Billy every day."

"I thought she might be here today."

"She usually is, but she's on a cruise with some of her friends in the Caribbean right now."

The others pile into the house then, and dinner gets underway. It's just like old times, and the atmosphere is relaxed. Thankfully, I didn't burn anything, so the food is good too. Everyone bombards Slater with questions about his life in Iowa and how he feels about coming back home. I don't contribute much to the conversation, but I hang off his every word, basking in the glow from his presence. Every so often, our eyes meet across the table, and there's no denying the chemistry we still share. It's as palpable as if it was a living, breathing thing.

He's always the first to break eye contact though, and I wish I had a hotline to his mind, so I could hear what he's thinking. To know if there's any chance of salvaging our love.

Terri and Alice insist on cleaning up, and they cajole their men into helping too. My parents take the kids back out to the yard so it's only Ryan, Slater, and me left at the table. "Would you like a tour?" I suggest, angling for an opportunity to talk to Slater alone.

"I'd love a tour." He stands, offering me his hand and helping me up. The feel of his warm palm against mine sends a flurry of memories to the forefront of my mind. When we were together, it was often the little gestures that meant so much to me. Like holding hands, or cuddling up against him on the couch, or waking up beside him. "Lead the way," he says, dragging me back to the present.

"You coming, Ryan?"

He arches a brow. "I thought I was persona non grata?"

I round the table and wrap my arms around my brother. I'm not one to bear grudges for long, and I hate this tension between us. "I'm sorry for butting into stuff that's none of my business. I'm just disappointed for both of you, but I don't want to argue with you over it."

"You know, better than anyone, that sometimes love just isn't enough." He's talking to me but eyeballing Slater as he speaks.

"Yeah," I murmur. "Sorry for trying to force you to talk to her when you clearly don't want to."

He holds me close, pressing a kiss to the top of my head. "It's okay. I know you meant well, but you've got to let it go. It's over, and you should work on retaining your relationship with your best friend instead of trying to fix her love life."

"You're right."

"You hear that, Evans?" he quips, and I roll my eyes. "I think you need to say that again, Tornado, so I can record this momentous moment."

"Jerkface." I shuck out of his embrace, grinning.

"Love the bones of you, Gabby." He squeezes me one more time. "Let's never fall out again."

"Agreed, and I love you too."

"I'm going to help the others in the kitchen," he says, backing toward the door. "Enjoy your *tour*." He enunciates the word as if it's code for something else, something dirty, and my cheeks inflame.

Slater chuckles. "I've missed your brother even if he needs a slap at times."

"You're preaching to the converted," I joke, gesturing for him to follow me. I take him upstairs first and we keep the conversation light and nonconfrontational as I show him around. Then we come back downstairs, and I take him to the gym, game room, theater, and swimming pool. Our final stop is the living room. It's our personal, private space and the one room I'm nervous to show him.

"That's a fabulous picture," he says, instantly walking to the large printout of Dylan and me. It's the most dominant feature in the room, taking center stage over the marble fireplace. It's my favorite photo from my maternity shoot. I'm sitting cross-legged on the floor, and Dylan is kneeling in front of me, kissing my swollen belly. The ruby and diamond choker around my neck is as dazzling as the day Dylan gave it to me. I remember that shoot with so much fondness, and I'm glad Dylan thought to organize it.

"I think so too. I really wanted to display one of the family ones we had taken the day after Billy came home, but they are too upsetting, and I don't want to remember Dylan like that."

He nods his head in agreement. "I didn't take any photos of Mom when she was dying for that very reason. I want to remember how she looked before she was ill and keep those memories alive."

"I have the album kept up for Billy, and he can make the call when he's old enough to deal with it."

"He mentioned Dylan outside, so he clearly knows who he is."

I wrap my arms around myself. "I talk to him all the time about his dad. I promised Dylan, but even if I hadn't, I would still talk about him. I want Billy to grow up knowing how amazing his father was and that he would've done anything to be here with him."

A pang of guilt flashes across Slater's face, but it's gone so fast I'm not sure if I imagined it. "Dylan would be very proud of you, Belle."

I smile up at him. "I hope so." I wring my hands, trying to work up the courage to say what I need to say. It's harder than I thought, but I force myself to go there. "Slate?"

"Yeah?" His eyes drill into me.

"I miss your friendship, and I was hoping, now you're back, that we could spend some time together. Get reacquainted."

His face twists into a mild grimace, and my stomach dips, but I keep a placid expression on my face. "I miss your friendship too, and I'd like that, but I'm going to be very busy with work so..."

He doesn't finish his sentence, but he doesn't need to. I don't blame Slater for being wary, and, this time, it's my turn to put everything on the line for him. "I understand, but maybe when you have some downtime, you can text me and we can go out or you can come here for dinner or I can come to your place. I'd love to see what you've done with the house."

Over dinner, Slater explained he was renovating his Mom's house, and it sounds like a big project. I'm so glad he decided to keep it and not sell it like he was considering at one time.

His eyes scope mine out, and I wish I could wind back the clock and remove the enduring sadness that radiates from him like a flashing beacon. "It's still a work in progress, but maybe I can show you sometime." His response is very noncommittal and I sense that's on purpose. He averts his eyes, and I try to dampen the hurt forming in my chest.

"Great. Just message me during the week and we can make plans."

Except I don't hear from Slater at all that week, or the week after, and my fingernails are basically chewed to the bone at this stage. I've tried to put myself in his shoes, to understand what's going on in his head, but I'm not sure if he's keeping his distance because he's still hurting, because he's genuinely busy, or because he's just no longer interested in being in my life.

I've done a lot of soul searching these past couple weeks, and I believe if I'm to have any chance of a relationship with Slater that I've got to do all the hard work this time.

Slater helped get me through a dark period in my life, and he did it selflessly even though he was hurting himself in the process. But he still didn't give up, waiting patiently in the wings for the timing to be right. I was the one who fucked it all up by throwing him away, like it was easy to discard him, like he didn't mean everything to me, so it's up to me to rectify this.

It was only in pushing him away, and in dealing with the aftermath of Dylan's death, that I truly understood what Slater means to me. In recent months, I'd been formulating a plan to go to him and beg for forgiveness and a second chance. Now, he's virtually on my doorstep, so what the hell am I doing sitting around wallowing in self-pity?

Even if he doesn't feel the same anymore, I still want him to know how I feel.

I didn't fight for him, for us, before, so it's time I started doing it now.

Chapter Forty-Eight

I park at the curb outside Slater's house, behind a black BMW, marveling at the changes I can already see. He's completely renovated the outside of the house, and it's freshly painted with a brand-new porch and wraparound deck. The front yard has been landscaped, and while it's low maintenance, and there aren't many colorful shrubs or flowers, it still looks pretty.

I get out of my car and lock it, wiping my sweaty palms down the front of my jeans as I approach the house. I debated messaging him to let him know I was on my way over but decided against it. I don't want to give him any opportunity to back out. I need to say what I came here to say before I drive myself crazy going over and over it in my head.

I press the bell, nervously brushing my hair back off my face as I wait for him. The door swings open, and a tall, slim, stunning brunette answers it with a smile. All my bravado disappears in a split second. "Hello." Her voice is soft, and her accent is from out of town. "Can I help you?"

Bile coats my mouth, and I feel like puking, but I return her smile with a shaky one of my own. "I was looking for Slater, but I should've called before dropping by." I turn on my heel. "I'll come back another time."

I don't even give her the chance to respond before hightailing it out of there. A heavy pressure settles on my chest, and my stomach has dropped to my toes. An anguished lump rests at the back of my throat, and I feel like crying.

Slater has clearly moved on, and that's why he was so hesitant about letting me back into his life. He's probably told his girlfriend all about me and he's trying to keep me away from her.

I fumble in my purse for my keys, cursing when they slip through my fingers, landing on the ground. As I bend down to pick them up, I commence a silent inner chant. *Don't you dare cry, Gabby James. This is all your fault, and you've no one to blame but yourself.* I slide into the car, and my hands are shaking as I buckle my seat belt.

A loud thump on the side window has me jumping in fright.

"Belle! Lower the window."

Just looking at Slater, knowing that I'll never have the chance to reclaim any kind of relationship with him, breaks my heart all over again. I need to get out of here before I fall apart in front of him, but I won't be rude. I lower my window a smidgeon. "I'm sorry, Slate." I hate how my voice trembles. "I didn't realize you had company. Forgive the intrusion."

He scrutinizes my face, missing nothing. "You're here now, so you might as well come inside." He opens my door and holds out his hand. "C'mon."

I shake my head. "It's fine, Slate. I'm fine." I force my mouth into a smile. "Go back to your girlfriend. We can talk another time."

Planting his hands on top of the car, he leans in. A subtle half-smile plays on his lips. "Belle, it's not how it looks. Come inside and we'll talk now." His eyes plead with me, and my traitorous body wants to go inside, but my aching heart won't let me.

I just want to go home and sob into my pillow.

And, yes, I'm aware of how pathetic I sound.

Bite me.

"Please, Belle."

I shake my head, struggling to keep my composure. "Just forget it, Slate, okay," I whisper.

Determination creeps over his face, and he reaches in, quick as a flash, and grabs my keys. Then he slides his arms under me and lifts me out of the car, throwing me over his shoulder.

"Slate! Oh my God. What are you doing? Put me down!"

"I asked you nicely, Belle, and you still turned me down, so you should've known I'd take matters into my own hands." He shuts the door with his foot, locks the car, and tightens his hold on me as he starts walking toward the house.

"Slate, what's your girlfriend going to think!?" I hiss.

"She's not my girlfriend," he says, striding toward the house like a man on a mission.

His words are like a balm to my sore heart, but I caution myself not to celebrate prematurely. "Okay. This is ridiculous. I'm a grown-ass woman and a mother! Put me down. I'll come inside, but I'll do it on my own two feet." I attempt to wriggle out of his hold, and he brings his other hand up and slaps my ass.

I'm so stunned I'm speechless.

"Cat got your tongue, Belle?" he teases, and I pound my fists on his back.

"Slater Kellan Evans! Put. Me. Down."

He chuckles. "You sounded just like Mom there."

"I'll bet you never carried her into the house like a sack of potatoes."

"Nope, but she never gave me reason to."

"I've left the paperwork on the kitchen counter," the mystery woman says, fighting to keep the laughter from her voice. "Just sign where all the yellow tabs are and then seal it in the envelope."

Slater finally puts me down, but he wraps his arm around my back, keeping me pressed firmly against him. I'm about to protest when I realize it would be completely counter-productive. Instead, I lean my head on his chest and fist my hand in his shirt, relishing the smell and touch of him against me. If this is all I'll get, I'm going to milk every single drop of it.

"Thanks, Madilyn. I'll do that and organize a courier to come pick it up first thing."

"It's already organized," she confirms.

"You're the best. Thank you."

"It was nice meeting you, Belle," she says, and I force my face away from Slater's warm chest. He spins me around so I'm facing her. "Assuming you are the infamous Belle?" She arches an elegant brow.

"Infamous?" I squeak.

"Madilyn." Slater's voice holds considerable warning.

She grins, stepping away. "Enjoy your evening, boss. I'll talk to you tomorrow."

"Boss?" I inquire, looking up at him.

He takes my hand and escorts me into the house. "Madilyn is my assistant. She moved from Iowa to help me set up the office here."

"Oh." That thought equally elates and depresses me. "Does she have to be so hot?" I blurt instead of keeping that thought trapped inside.

He throws back his head, laughing. "Jealous, Belle?"

"No." I lie, tossing my hair over my shoulder.

"Well, your observational skills haven't improved much," he taunts with a playful grin.

"What? She's beautiful, and don't even try to tell me she isn't."

He's rolling his eyes as he guides me into the kitchen. "Yes, Madilyn's beautiful. No, we aren't fucking, nor have we ever fucked. I'll tell her husband you think his wife is hot and you're open to a threesome."

I smack his arm. "Do you have to take so much enjoyment from my humiliation?"

"Belle, admit it's funny."

"I'll admit no such thing." I pout, but I can't keep it up for long. Then I notice my surroundings and my eyes almost bug out of my head. "Holy crap, Slate! The kitchen is gorgeous and completely unrecognizable." It's all cream gloss cupboards, matching marble counters, and high-tech appliances. At the rear of the kitchen is a floor-to-ceiling glass window which opens up the back of the house, perfectly showcasing Janine's beautiful garden. He flicks a switch and the outside garden lights up. I move to the window, peering outside. "Look how big our tree has grown."

"It's flourishing," he agrees, quietly standing beside me.

"And you fitted a little gazebo too. Wow. It's beautiful." I look up at him. "Did you do all this yourself?"

"I hired contractors to build the extension, upgrade the heating, plumbing, and electric, and fit the new floors and kitchen. I spent the last of my budget on the exterior of the house, so I'm doing the rest of the work myself. It'll take a while, but I like having a project to occupy me at the end of the working day."

I spin around, taking the whole room in. "It's stunning. You've done a great job."

"Thanks, but I'm sure you didn't come here to admire the kitchen."

"No. I came to talk to you because there's some stuff I need to get off my chest."

He nods. "Okay. Let's grab some drinks and talk in the living room."

"I'll just have a water," I say when he opens the refrigerator.

He takes out a beer for himself and a water for me. "Are you hungry? Would you like something to eat?"

I shake my head. "No. I've already eaten, and I'd prefer to just get this over and done with."

He eyeballs me with amused curiosity. "That bad, huh?"

"Groveling usually is," I deadpan, following him out of the room.

The living room has also undergone a transformation. It's twice the size, and the glossy walnut floors, warm cream and copper-colored walls, and plush rug give it a rich, decadent feel. Slater sits down on one side of the brown leather couch, and I sit on the other, kicking off my shoes and pulling my knees into my chest. I wrap my arms around my legs and draw a brave breath. "I'm sorry for barging in here like this," I start. "But I was afraid if I gave you advance notice that you'd come up with some excuse."

"I probably would have," he admits, tipping the beer bottle into his mouth. I'm momentarily dazed as I watch his throat work, and even that's sexy as hell.

"Jeez, I really need to get laid."

He almost chokes, and his eyes widen as he stares at me.

"Oh, shit. I said that out loud, didn't I?"

"Yeah, and now you can't take it back." His eyes darken, and my core aches. Flashes of the past whip through my mind, and I remember it all.

His hands roaming my body.

His lips searing a hot trail across my heated skin.

The feel of him holding me close as he thrust inside me, whispering endearments and dirty shit as he claimed me over and over again.

Now I'm fully aroused, and I'm sure it's evident on my face. *Focus, Gabby. You didn't come here to jump his bones although it'd be a nice development.*

I blink a few times to clear my head. "We'll park that for the moment because I have more important things to say." I worry my lips between my teeth. "I owe you a massive apology, Slate. I have this big speech all prepared, but it'll probably come out all wrong, so please just bear with me and try not to interrupt until I'm finished."

"I'm all ears, Belle. Shoot."

My chest rises and falls. "I have never regretted anything as much as I regret our conversation over dinner that last night before you moved to Iowa. I said those things in a deliberate move to make you hate me and leave me behind." He opens his mouth to speak, but I hold up a palm. "You promised. Just let me get this out." He nods. "You were like my guardian angel those last few months we spent together. You were my rock, and I know, hands down, that I would not have got through Billy's birth or Dylan's death without you. What you didn't know back then was how much I wanted you. How crazy in love I was with you."

He looks at me like I'm swinging from the cray-cray tree. Like I couldn't possibly have felt that when I worked so hard to avoid him.

"Every minute spent with you was like a form of personal torture. I craved your touch so badly, and I hated myself for it. It felt like the worst betrayal, and guilt was my new best friend. I mean, what kind of woman buries the guy she thought was her forever guy and then instantly craves another man?" Air whooshes out of my mouth. "I threw myself into caring for Billy and tried to deny my emotions. I bottled up all my feelings over Dylan's death and our forced breakup and tried to pretend like I was okay."

"You weren't okay," he acknowledges in a low voice.

"No, I wasn't okay. When you asked me to move to Iowa, I wanted to say yes, but I was consumed with guilt for even thinking about it. And I didn't know how to be with you when I hadn't even properly grieved for Dylan yet. I didn't want you to be the one to get me through that. How could I ask you to console me when I was mourning another man? Plus, I couldn't take Billy away from Heather, so I latched on to that as the reason why it wouldn't work because I needed to convince myself. I knew if I told you that you'd find a way around it."

"I did. I had a Plan B."

"What?"

"I knew asking you to move to Iowa was a huge step that you weren't ready for. I knew you needed to be close to your family and Heather, but I had to try. I fully expected you to turn me down, and then I was going to tell you I had a second job offer, from a local firm. It wasn't as good an offer, but it was good enough. I was going to ask you to move in with me, and I'd stay here and take care of you both, but I never got the chance, because you told me you didn't want me. That you couldn't take a risk on me. That you thought I'd grow tired of waiting and fuck around on you."

I scoot closer to him on the couch. "I never knew that, and I'm sorry, but it wouldn't have made any difference. There is no way I would've let you pass up the Iowa opportunity. Not when I knew it was your dream job."

He leans toward me. "A dream job means nothing without the woman of your dreams by your side."

"I hated hurting you," I whisper, "and, in my confused state, I thought I was doing the right thing."

"You slayed me, Belle. You destroyed me. You made me believe everything we'd shared meant less to you than it did to me. I wondered if you'd always felt like that about me. If that was really how you saw me."

My heart aches. *How could I have done that to him?* "Never." I shake my head. "I've never thought that about you. My God, you were an incredible boyfriend, Slate. Those months we spent as a couple are some of the best times of my life. I hate that I made you doubt yourself, and I'm so sorry. I wish I hadn't said any of those things, and I know you would never have done anything like that. I've hated myself every single day since I lied. I wanted to call you so many times, but, at first, my counselor urged me to hold off while I was working through stuff, and then, it seemed like too much time had passed, and I figured you'd forgotten about me and moved on."

He snorts. "Yeah, that wasn't very likely."

My heart soars at the insinuation, but I plow on. "I cried myself to sleep when you left, and it was the first night I'd cried since Dylan's death. It unleashed a lot of pent-up emotion, and I was forced to deal with everything. I was a basket case. Every feeling I had buried resurfaced, and I could barely cope. Heather and Mom took over caring for Billy while I took some time to get my head straight. It took a good while to untangle my feelings. To mourn Dylan the way he deserved to be mourned. I had to get a handle on that first, and it wasn't easy, but I came out stronger and more self-aware. Especially when it came to you."

I close the gap between us and take his hand. "I know this is prob-ably too late, but I need to tell you this." Tears prick my eyes as I stare into his beautiful face. A face that's as familiar as my own. "I love you, Slate. I love you so much, and it's not anything recent. I've loved you for a very long time, probably as long as you've loved me. And I know what you're going to say. That it isn't true, because I was in love with Dylan, but I was in love with you too."

He looks dumbfounded, and more than a little incredulous, which I expected. "Fate is a fucked-up bitch, but I truly believe everything happens for a reason. I was blind to my feelings for you back then because I needed to be there for Dylan. He needed my love more than you did, and I'm glad I was there for him and that we got to share our time together."

I hope I'm not making it worse and that he's hearing what I'm trying to tell him. "What I had with Dylan was special, and he will always own a piece of my heart. What you and I have is different but no less special or precious to me. When we were together, I began to see what had always been there between us. I just hadn't wanted to see it."

I take both his hands in mine. "I believed Dylan was my forever love, but I was wrong, because it's *you*, Slate. It's always been *you*. Circumstances might have kept us apart, but I never stopped loving you. I still love you and want you." Tears fill my eyes. "I'm all in now, Slate. I'm yours if you still want me."

Chapter Forty-Nine

His gaze is drenched in emotion as he pulls me onto his lap. I go willingly, circling my arms around his neck and burying my face in his hair. His body trembles underneath me, but he still hasn't said anything. "Say something. Please."

"Do you have any idea how much I love you, Belle?" He tips his face up and we're so close it would take nothing to press my mouth to his, but I summon restraint from somewhere.

"You still love me?" I whisper, hope powering through my veins.

"Yes. You're impossible not to love. Believe me, I tried. I tried to forget you. I tried to move on, but I couldn't do it. I went on a few dates after I moved away, but none of them ever led anywhere, because I couldn't stop comparing them to you. No one came even close to measuring up. So, I stopped trying, even if I was tormented night and day by thoughts of you."

He leans his forehead on mine. "I almost picked up the phone to call you a hundred times. And every time Ryan came to visit, I had to forcibly shut my mouth to stop myself asking about you. I've been in hell these past two years without you. Even if this job opportunity hadn't come up, I would still have come home. To you."

I run my fingers up the back of his neck, and my heart is so full, buoyed up by his loving words, but something doesn't add up. "Why have you been avoiding me then?"

He eases back, staring straight into my eyes. "I'm afraid, Belle. I've lost you twice already. I don't think my heart can withstand a third time. It'll kill me."

"Baby, I'm all in." I peer deep into his eyes, praying he sees the truth of my conviction. "I'm not going anywhere. I'm madly in love with you, and I want us to spend the rest of our lives together." I can't be any blunter than that. I need to touch him, so I cup his beautiful face. "More than that, I'm ready to fight for us. Nothing or no one will ever come between us again, and that's a solemn promise."

"Do you really mean that, Belle?"

"Yes." My head bobs up and down. "And it's not just us anymore. I would never let any man into my life, into Billy's life, unless it was serious. We're a package deal."

"I get that, and it only sweetens the deal." He graces me with a brilliant smile. "I was there when Billy was born, and I've loved him from the second he arrived in this world. I would never do anything to hurt him, which is why, if we do this, we need to take it slow."

"We can do that! We can go at a snail's pace, if you like." Excitement lights up my face. "Just please give me a chance to prove I'm genuine. That my love is genuine."

He coils his hand through the back of my hair. "Don't hurt me again, Belle. Please."

It's like a sucker punch to the heart. "I promise, I won't, Slate. Just let me love you."

The air changes, and electricity crackles in the tiny gap between us. I'm acutely aware of how close we're pressed against one another when I feel him hardening underneath me. He drags his thumb across my lower lip. "It's been torturous trying to stay away from you these past couple weeks." His voice is thick with desire, his eyes dark with need.

I reposition myself so I'm straddling him, and my fingers delve into his hair. "I've felt the same, but I was trying to be patient."

He smirks. "I can guess how challenging that must've been for you."

"I'm well aware I'm not known for my patience." I grind my hips against his erection, moaning.

"Slow, Belle, remember." He presses his mouth to my neck, dusting my skin with a light layer of kisses as his hands roam up and down my back.

"Slate. That feels so good."

He runs his tongue up the side of my neck, nibbling on my earlobe, and I almost buck off his lap. A chuckle rumbles through him, and his hands slip under my shirt. His warm palms glide against my heated skin as he continues to tease my ear and neck with his tempting lips. I'm rocking against him, my core throbbing and pulsing with need. "Please, Slate," I murmur. "Please kiss me."

Holding my face in both hands, he draws me to him, his gaze roaming my face as if he can't believe I'm here. "I've dreamed about this every day we've been apart."

"Me too," I truthfully admit. "I have missed you so much."

His mouth collides with mine, and it's an explosion of mutual longing. He angles my head, deepening the kiss, and I'm floating on a cloud. I feel his kiss all the way to the tips of my toes, and he's lighting a fuse within my body. No single kiss has ever felt so complete. Has ever completed me so much. I'm whimpering into his mouth and grinding against his pelvis, grabbing his hair and running my hands over his broad shoulders and strong back.

Roping his muscular arms around my waist, he keeps me flush to his body while kissing me with everything he's got.

I'm so happy I could cry.

We kiss and kiss and kiss, barely drawing a breath, and I savor every second of being back in his arms again.

Eventually, we break apart, and I rest my head on his shoulder as he maneuvers me on his lap. He's still hard as a rock, but he's making no move to do anything about it.

"I'm horny as fuck." I nuzzle my nose against his neck.

"Me too." He thrusts his erection into me to drill the point home. "But I'm not going to make love to you today, Belle. I meant what I said. We need to take this slow. It's as much for your and Billy's protection as it is mine." I sigh, and he chuckles. "It'll be worth the wait, honey. I swear." He kisses my temple.

"I haven't had sex with anyone since you," I admit. "It's quite likely my lady parts have shriveled up and died in the meantime. Are you sure you want to wait?"

His eyes pop wide. "You didn't have sex with Dylan after we broke up?"

I shake my head. "No. We were just best friends in the period before he passed. We did kiss and cuddle sometimes, but it was never more than that. I know he was disappointed, but it quickly got to a point where he couldn't have made love to me even if either of us had wanted it."

"I know you'd said that, but I just assumed..."

"Sometimes, I feel like a real bitch for denying him that before he died. Especially because I knew his illness was behind his aggression and the cheating, but I couldn't help the way I felt. It was still a betrayal to me, and it altered the dynamic of our relationship. It wasn't possible to go back."

"You shouldn't feel guilty for that. You can't help how you felt."

I sit up straighter, pecking his lips briefly. "It was also you too. I was still in love with you, Slate. My feelings for you hadn't changed just because we were forced apart, and that was the main reason why I couldn't go there with Dylan, because that would have felt like I was cheating on you."

"We weren't together, Belle, and I wouldn't have held it against you, but I've got to admit I'm happier knowing this."

"Does it help you believe I'm sincere?"

"It does." He twirls a lock of my hair around his finger. "You removed the pink strands from your hair. I kinda liked them."

"I can get them again." I shrug.

"Belle." His voice is barely louder than a whisper. He runs the tip of his finger along my cheek. "I haven't slept with anyone since you either."

I almost fall off the couch. "But I thought you said you dated other girls?"

"I said I went on dates with other girls. Dates as in singular. I never saw any girl more than once."

"That still doesn't explain it."

"I know I could've had sex with any of those women, and a few of them were very direct in letting me know that was what they wanted, but I had zero interest. During a particularly low moment, I took a woman to a hotel room because I told myself if I had sex with someone else it would make it easier to forget you, but I couldn't go through with it. She was pissed as hell."

"I'll bet, but that makes me even happier than I already am." I hug him tight. "We both waited for each other after all."

Chapter Fifty

The next couple months are some of the happiest of my life. Slater and I are officially together, and we go on regular dates, like any normal couple. He also spends plenty of time with Billy too. Billy is completely enamored with Slate, and we have tons of fun on our family outings, but Slater refuses to stay over, and we still haven't slept together. I'm growing more and more impatient even if I understand his hesitation, to a point.

When he shows up at my door the same time as Mom one Friday evening, I'm immediately suspicious. "What's going on?"

"You didn't tell her?" Mom raises a perfectly trimmed brow at Slater.

"I wanted it to be a surprise."

Billy chooses that exact moment to come barreling down the hall, shrieking when he spots Grandma and Slater.

"What surprise?" I ask, as Slater high-fives my son.

"It wouldn't be a surprise if I told you." He smirks, scooping Billy up into his arms and tickling the shit out of him. I pout, and he chuckles. When he passes Billy over to Mom, he circles his arms around my waist, kissing the tip of my nose. "Pack a bag, Belle. We're going away for the night."

"Going where?"

"You'll see." His eyes glint wickedly.

I'm about to protest again when I realize what this means.

We'll be alone.

In a bed.

All night.

My eyes instantly light up, and I throw my arms around him and squeal. He chuckles again when I race up the stairs, two at a time. Grabbing clothes and toiletries from my room, I stuff them into a bag before hoofing it out of there mere minutes later.

Slater shoots me a lopsided grin when I skip downstairs, and he pushes off the wall, briefly pecking my lips. "I think you just won the award for the fastest bag packing ever."

"It's amazing what one can accomplish with the right motivation," I joke.

After saying goodbye to Billy and Mom, we set out in a westerly direction. We chat casually as we drive, and I'm practically bouncing in my seat, begging and pleading, but he still won't tell me where we're going. Ninety minutes later, he turns into a winding driveway, lined with towering trees, and I gasp as the old stately house comes into view. It's a newly opened boutique hotel that everyone has been raving about.

"Oh, wow. This place is magnificent," I say, twirling around in the impressive lobby. "No wonder everyone's been gushing about this place." Marble tile squelches under my feet and a stunning chandelier hangs over our heads. Chic, sweeping staircases, adorned with gold handrails and plush gold-patterned carpet, extend on either side of the reception desk.

Slater checks us in and then ushers me to the elevator which takes us to our suite. I swoon over the lavishly decorated four-poster bed before gravitating to the window like a bee to honey. The large floor-to-ceiling window overlooks the extensive grounds outside.

Several little walking trails emanate from a colorful garden in the center of the space, and the whole place has this old-world-romantic vibe that I'm loving.

Slate comes up behind me, wrapping his arms around my waist and pulling me back into his body. "Do you like it?"

"I love it." I twist my head around and kiss him softly. "Thank you for bringing me here."

We take a walk around the grounds and then stop by the quaint bar for a quick drink before getting changed for dinner. Conversation flows freely over a sumptuous five-course dinner, followed by a couple of exquisite cocktails. I'm a little tipsy as we make our way to our suite just after midnight, and my nerves are jangling with excitement at the prospect of making love with Slate all night.

I gasp as I walk into the room, marveling at the rose petals on the bed, the flickering candles softly glowing in the room, and the bottle of chilled champagne awaiting us. Tears prick my eyes. "Oh, Slate. You big ole romantic." I slide my arms around his neck, drawing his head to mine, and I kiss him deeply, pouring everything I'm feeling into each brush of my lips. "I love you." My voice rattles with emotion. "And this is perfect. You're spoiling me."

"You deserve to be spoiled, and I want to be the one to do it." He holds me close, and I rest my head on his chest, feeling the steady beat of his heart under my ear. I emit a contented sigh as I wrap my arms around him. "I love you, Belle," he whispers, and I squeeze him tighter.

After a few minutes, he takes my hand and leads me to the bathroom. The massive jacuzzi tub is full, and delicate floral scents tickle my nostrils from the scattering of rose petals resting on top of the water. Candles dotted around the opulent room provide the only light, and it's so dreamy and romantic. "Take a bath and relax," he whispers, brushing my hair aside to plant a lingering kiss on my neck.

"Will you join me?" I ask, holding my breath. He turns me around, gently cupping my cheeks, and I spot the indecision written all over his face. "I need you," I whisper, stretching up to capture his lips.

He kisses me tenderly before pulling away. "Belle." His voice is soft, pleading. "I'll take care of your needs, but tonight isn't about sex. That's not why we're here, and it's not going to happen yet."

I drop my eyes, trying to disguise the rejection from my face, but I'm not quick enough. He wraps his arms around me, holding me close. "Baby, look at me." He tilts my chin up. "I love you, and I know I'm asking a lot, but we agreed to take this slow."

"I know," I whimper. "I'm trying to be patient and respectful of your wishes, but I'm scared I'll be old and gray before you make love to me again."

"I promise that's not the case, and, believe me, I want to. I really do, but my head needs to be in the right space."

"And it's not?" This time I don't even attempt to hide the hurt from my voice.

"Don't be upset, please, Belle." He caresses my cheek. "Take a bath and then we'll talk." He hugs me to him for a couple minutes, and I'm trying to not let it get to me, but it's challenging, especially when a horrid inner voice is whispering nasty things in my ear.

I know Slater loves me.

I do.

He shows it all the time.

But I want to be desired too, and it hurts that he can't or won't make love to me yet. I'm struggling to accept it because I'm so hot for him, and I don't understand how he can keep me at arm's length, not if he feels the same way I do.

"Stop overthinking it, Belle. You're beautiful and sexy, and this isn't about you," he says, as if he has a hotline to my innermost thought. "It's about me."

He separates from me and walks out of the room, returning a minute later with a glass of champagne. "Soak in the tub, drink your champagne, and my arms will be waiting for you when you get out."

He kisses me deeply. "I love you." Then he walks out leaving me alone with my thoughts.

I step out of the bathroom, wrapped in a fluffy towel a half hour later, with an empty glass. Slate is lounging in the bed in a pair of low-slung pajama pants, and he smiles up at me, placing his cell on the bedside table. "You look gorgeous," he says, pulling the covers back and patting the space beside him. I crawl into the bed while he takes my glass and refills it. We sit with our backs against the headrest, alongside one another, sipping our champagne. Every so often, he leans over, pressing light kisses all over my face.

"Why aren't you in the right space?" I blurt, after a few minutes of silence. I'm determined to have this out now. To see what I can do to help ease his fears.

"I'm still scared, Belle. The guilt is holding me back too."

"Guilt?" My voice carries my surprise. The fear, I can understand because we've discussed that before, but this is the first time he's mentioned any guilt.

"I promised Dylan I'd look after you and Billy, and I let him down. I let you push me away, and I walked without fighting for you. I should never have done that."

"Hey." I twist around and kneel in front of him. "I'm the one to blame for that, not you. And Dylan shouldn't have put that responsibility on your shoulders, that wasn't fair. Whether we are together or not is up to *us*. It's dependent on our feelings, not on whatever twisted sense of loyalty you feel." I cup his face. "There's no point regretting it now. Things happen for a reason, and we're together now. That's all that matters."

"What if I'm not good enough, Belle?" Genuine turmoil flashes across his face. "What if I'm not a good enough father? I'm so scared of messing this up and letting Billy down." His voice cracks, along with my heart. "I would hate myself if I messed things up with us and Billy was the one who paid the ultimate price."

"Oh, Slate." My heart bleeds for him. "I understand why you feel like that, and I love you for loving my son enough to prioritize his welfare, but if everyone lived by that motto, then no one would take a chance on anything." I lace my fingers through his. "You have to have more faith in us. We're *not* going to mess this up. And you're *not* going to hurt Billy. You're already an amazing father to him, so please don't beat yourself up over this, because it kills me to hear you say this stuff."

He brings my hand to his mouth, kissing the underside of my wrist. "I do have faith in us, Belle. I do. But I can't help being cautious. A lot of it is tied up with my feelings about Mom. When I was in Iowa, I finally spoke to a therapist. I have a lot of unresolved emotion that I'm working through. Losing Mom was the hardest thing I'd dealt with up to that point, and then I lost you when we discovered the baby was Dylan's, and then I lost you again when you turned down Iowa. I can't stand to lose you a third time. To lose Billy. I wouldn't survive it, Belle." His face contorts in agony, and I can't deny the truth when he's being so brutally honest with me. "A part of me knows it's irrational to worry so much, but I can't help it. I'm trying to deal with those fears, but you need to give me a bit more time." He kisses me quickly. "This isn't about me not loving you enough. It's about me loving you too much."

I lean forward and hug him, blinking back tears. I'm partly responsible for the things he's feeling, and I don't want to push him too hard, but him holding a part of himself back from me hurts so much. I want to make love to him. To feel more deeply connected, and I think it would help. But if he needs to be on the same page, before we take that step, then I can't force him, no matter how much I think we both need it.

At least I understand it more clearly now, and my earlier rejected feelings fade away. When we reunited, I promised I'd try to be more patient and understanding, and I'm not about to renege on my word. I can wait, and I know it will be worth it.

Chapter Fifty-One

Things settle back into the usual pattern after we return from our night away, and I work hard to push my own needs aside and to let Slater know that I'm happy to let him dictate the pace. Gradually, I feel a subtle shift in the air, and I sense he's happier and less troubled by concerns, but he still hasn't initiated sex. Things are progressing, and we make out like bandits any chance we can get. We also enjoy regular oral sex, and I can't say he isn't looking after my needs, but he still seems reluctant to bridge that final gap.

We've just shared a wonderful Thanksgiving with my family, and it was everything I hoped it would be. Except I'm still horny and frustrated, and I've decided it's time to take matters into my own hands. I believe Slate is in the right place now. He just needs a helping hand to see it.

"Holy fuck," Slater exclaims as I twirl in front of him.

"You like?"

"Like?" His pupils dilate and he stalks toward me like a hunter hellbent on capturing his prey. My ovaries start a happy dance when he hauls me to him, his hands instantly grabbing my ass. "I fucking love it, but you do realize I won't be letting you out of my sight dressed like this? Not even to go to the bathroom."

"I have no issue with that." It's what I was planning when I spent a fortune on this black lace minidress and the matching Gucci shoes. The dress has a bustier top with a lace panel overlay that stretches to my collarbone and down my arms. The back dips into a low V, barely covering my ass.

Slater slips his hand under the dress, running his fingers over my bare cheeks. I'm already soaked underneath my thong, and when he grinds his obvious erection against me, I see stars. "Mom has Billy till tomorrow, so you can spend the night," I rasp against his mouth.

"Hmm." He nibbles a path along my neck and up to my ear. "We'll see."

My ardor instantly deflates, and rejection churns like acid in my gut, but I'm not going down without a battle, so I mask my disappointment and pull him out the front door.

We're celebrating Alice's birthday tonight, and all the gang is here by the time we arrive at the club. Terri is pregnant again, so she's not drinking, but the rest of us are in flying form.

"If it isn't the troublesome twosome!" Austin thumps Slater and Ryan on the back before grabbing them into a bear hug.

"Dude, you came!" Ryan is ecstatic to see his old wingman.

"Wouldn't have missed it. It's been too long."

Then he spots me, emitting a low whistle as he rakes his gaze over me. "Fuck me. You look incredible, Gabby." He presses a lingering kiss to my cheek, and I can't help smirking. Austin is a notorious flirt, and he just might be able to help me out.

"I could say the same for you." I deliberately eye him from head to toe. "You look great, Austin."

Slater growls, tossing Austin a look loaded with caution as he pulls me into his arms. "Hands off my woman, Powers, or you'll be getting reacquainted with my fists."

"Possessive as ever, Evans. Good to see some things haven't changed." He winks at me, and I snort when Slater hisses at him.

"Come dance with me, babe." I grab Slater's hand. "You can release your inner Neanderthal Man on the dance floor."

"I'll knock him the fuck out if he looks at you like that again," Slater claims as we start dancing.

"You're sexy as hell when you're jealous." I press my body against his and shimmy up and down. "Forget about Austin, and let's show everyone I'm yours." If there's one thing Slater Evans never backs down from, it's a challenge. We dance provocatively, grinding and thrusting against one another, lips and hands exploring. We ravish one another's mouths when the music slows down, clinging to each other as if we can't get close enough. I'm so turned on I'm close to begging him to take me to the restroom and fuck me. I'm considering it when he whispers in my ear, "Do you want to get out of here?"

I eyeball him. "Are you saying what I hope you're saying?"

He slams his mouth to mine, kissing me fiercely. "What do you think?"

I squeal, and he chuckles. "I think I've tortured us both enough."

"Let's go then!" He laughs at my enthusiasm as I drag him over to the table, and we offer up brief goodbyes to everyone before making a hasty retreat.

"C'mere, baby." He bundles me up in his arms as we wait outside for the taxi. "I know what you did back there, and that was downright sneaky."

"Moi?" I feign innocence. "I'm sure I don't know what you mean." I fail to smother my grin.

He slaps my ass firmly. "Sure, you don't, you little tease." He nips at my bottom lip before claiming my mouth in a searing hot kiss.

"You're not mad, are you?" I inquire, pulling back to examine his face for any telltale signs. "Maybe it was wrong of me to flirt with him, but you needed a little push, babe, and you know I have zero interest in Austin or any other man. You are all I see. All I need." I slide my hands up his delectable chest. "I'm crazy, madly, deeply in love and lust with you, and I need to feel you inside me, babe. It's time. I don't want to wait any longer."

"It's been as hard for me as it's been for you, Belle."

"Hardy, har," I joke, slipping my hand down and palming the evidence of his arousal.

He shakes his head, smiling. "You're incorrigible." He kisses the tip of my nose. "But it's one of the things I love most about you." He clasps my face in both his hands. "I just wanted us to be sure, Belle. Because this is a big step, and there's no going back.

"Baby, I know." I peck his lips briefly. "I wish I had a way of letting you into my heart so you could feel everything I feel for you, and then there'd be no fear, but I get it. You need to work through your feelings. But we both want this, and it's right to move our relationship forward. We can still take it a step at a time, but don't fight this any longer. Please."

He presses his forehead to mine. "I wish I could show you my heart too so you can see how deep my love runs, to know it's not about me not loving you."

I place my palm over his beating heart. "I don't need to see it to know. You show me every day and in every way." I choke back my tears. "Billy and I are so incredibly, unbelievably lucky to have you in our lives.

"I'm a lucky son of a bitch too, I know that. And I'm trying to make sure nothing comes between us this time. I'm trying to work through the last of my fears and finally let go of them. I just need a little more time." He hugs me tightly. "But I'm ready to take this step with you, because I want to shower you with love and worship your body until the sun comes up."

Amen to that. "I love the sound of that, and I love you for caring enough to do this the right way." I rest my head on his chest, listening to the steady beat of his heart. "This is our time, Slate," I whisper. "I just know it is."

"Do you mind if we go back to my place?" he asks a couple minutes later as the taxi draws up.

"No, of course not. I just want you to make love to me. I couldn't care less where it happens, as long as it happens!"

"God, I'm stupid in love with you," he says, grabbing the back of my head and pulling my mouth to his. "I can't wait to slide inside you."

We're all over one another in the back of the car. I'm straddling his waist and rocking against him as he demolishes my mouth, his tongue tangling wickedly with mine as his hands wander to the promised land. Moans and gasps fill the air as we share the same frenzied need.

"No fucking in my taxi," the grumpy driver says, and I burst into a round of uncontrollable giggling.

Slater moves me off his lap, gathering me into his side. "Behave, Belle," he teases with a devilish glint in his eye as his hand slips between my thighs.

We burst into the house in the dark, and Slater shoves me up against the wall. He fumbles with the hem of my dress, pushing it up to my hips, and then he cups my pussy over my black, lacy thong. "I really want to make slow, sweet love to you, but if I don't get inside you right now, I'm gonna explode."

"I'm not complaining," I pant, already riding his hand.

He pushes my thong aside, sliding two fingers inside me. "Fuck, you're drenched, Belle."

"It's been two and half years since I last had sex, what did you expect?"

He rips my thong, and the scattered material falls to the ground. Cool air wafts over my exposed skin. "I'm going to fuck that sassy mouth after I fuck your pussy," he promises, and my core pulses with renewed need. He grabs a condom from his wallet while I'm frantically tugging at his jeans, desperate to free him. He moves my hands away, popping the rest of the buttons and pushing his boxers and jeans down his legs to his knees.

My chest is heaving and my pussy dripping when he brushes his thumb across the bead of precum resting on the tip of his cock and then pushes it into my mouth. My core is quivering as I lick the salty flavor off his skin, sucking his thumb with gusto. "Fuck, that's hot."

I release his hand so he can sheathe himself, licking my lips in anticipation. He is rock hard, his cock bobbing against his stomach, as he pierces me with a dark look full of promise. I almost come on the spot. Yanking my leg up, he opens me to him, positioning his cock at my entrance. He peers deep into my eyes. His gaze is flooded with desire and love, and I'm overwhelmed with emotion. I'm so in love with this man, and I don't think he understands how far reaching my feelings go. "I love you and I want you. So much, Belle. But I need to ask this one final time. Are you sure you want to do this now?"

"Slate. I love you profoundly, deeply, until the ends of time." I peck his lips. "But if you don't fuck me right now, I'm going to scream so loud I'll rouse the neighbors."

He slams into me, and I cry out as he fills me inch by inch. "You're so tight. Oh fuck, Belle. That feels so good." He moves slowly until he's fully seated, and his muscles tense while he holds himself still, letting me acclimate to the feel of him inside me again. "You okay?"

"I'm good, babe." I kiss him fiercely. "I'm more than good. I'm home." He rubs his thumb across my mouth, his face awash with emotion. "Don't hold back. Go for it. Show me you're all mine."

He needs no further encouragement, and he ruts into me like a wild animal, thrusting over and over while his tongue plunders my mouth and his lips leave mine swollen. My back rubs against the wall as he fucks me, and my body purrs, fully alive for the first time in years.

Without warning, he pulls out, flipping me around. "Hands flat on the wall, Belle," he instructs, nudging my legs apart. I push my ass up in the air, granting him full access to my pussy, and he slams into me again, pounding me with unrestrained need. My orgasm is building, scaling new heights, when he slides his hand around, pressing his thumb to my clit and starts rubbing. I scream as my climax powers through me, and then he's joining me, roaring his release as I continue to clench around him.

When we've both come down from our high, he turns me around, hugging me against his chest. "I love you, Belle. I love you so completely. No other woman has ever made me feel the way you do."

"You're my everything," I say, snuggling into his chest. "You and Billy complete me."

He carries me upstairs and lays me down gently on the bed. After cleaning me up with a warm cloth, he strips me out of my dress before tossing his shirt and climbing under the covers with me. Pulling me to him, he kisses me tenderly. "I never want to be without you again."

"You never will be. I'm in this for life."

"I need to make love to you now." He crawls on top of me, pushing his cock against me so I can feel how hard he is again. "I'm so hard for you, Gabby. All the damn time. Holding back has killed me too, but I wanted us both in the right place."

I trail my hands up his chiseled abs and chest. "I'm not angry, Slate. I know why you did it, and it only makes me love you more, but there's no holding back now."

"Agreed." He flattens his cock against my stomach, and I moan. "This time I'm taking it slow because I want to worship and love every inch of your beautiful body." His mouth descends on mine, and his kisses are passionate and drenched in his love. His lips leave a trail from my mouth down my neck and to my breasts. He flicks my nipples with his tongue and fondles my sensitive flesh. Then he takes turns sucking the hardened tips into his mouth as his hands roam the curves of my body.

When he finally lowers his head between my thighs, I'm so turned on I come in less than thirty seconds. He looks up at me, winking, and the sight of his glistening lips sends a new wave of tingles shooting through me. "I'm on the pill," I tell him as he reaches for another condom. "We don't need that."

"Thank fuck." He slides inside me in one confident, slow move, and I arch my back off the bed. Then he makes slow love to me, worshiping every inch of my body with his mouth, his tongue, his hands, and his cock, and I've never felt more cherished or more loved.

We fall asleep wrapped around one another, and a deep sense of contentment washes over me.

He wakes me the next morning with breakfast in bed, and I'm deliciously achy all over. After we've eaten, and cleaned our teeth, we engage in round three, and it's every bit as tender as his lovemaking last night. We lie, sated and sweaty, in one another's arms after, just enjoying being together. "Can I ask you something?" I say, looking up at him.

"Anything. You know that." He squeezes my waist.

"Will you move in with us?"

He turns rigidly still in my arms, and I worry I moved too fast. I'm just so happy. We've committed to one another, and it feels like the next logical step. I know he still has fears, and I'm determined to help him through them.

He props up on his elbow, staring down into my face. "I want that, Belle, honestly, I do, but we're only back together a few months, and I'm not going anywhere. I don't think there's any need to rush."

I can't keep the hurt off my face. "We've known each other practically our whole lives, and we love each other. Billy already adores the ground you walk on. I want to go to sleep beside you every night and wake up beside you every morning. I don't need more time to know I want and need you full time in my life."

His face contorts, and I brush my fingers over the worry lines furrowing his brow. "What else is holding you back?" I stare into his eyes. "Be honest with me."

"I know you love me, Belle. I don't doubt that, but I still feel like I'm second best. I wasn't your first choice, Dylan was, and there's still a part of me that believes I'm only the backup plan, and it hurts. You planned your whole future around Dylan. Not me."

My heart pains me so much in this moment, and all the bad decisions I've made return to haunt me. "I hate you feel like that, and nothing could be further from the truth. It was never a competition between you. It was just different loves at different times. It doesn't mean I love you any less or any more than I loved him."

"I can't help thinking if he was still here that you'd be with him, and I know how terrible that sounds. Believe me, I know how petty and futile it is to be envious of a guy who lost his life, but it's how I feel. I can't force myself to feel otherwise."

"I can understand, to an extent. You were a witness to my relationship with Dylan. I know how hard that must've been, but if he was alive, I would still be with you. I would still choose you."

"You can't say that for sure."

I sit up. "I can, but it's also pointless arguing that point because he isn't here. We are. Billy is. And that's where our future lies." I rest my hands on his chest, trying to ignore the stabbing pain in my chest. "What can I do to make you see you're the only one?"

"Just give it a little more time. I'm nearly there."

"And then you'll move in with us?"

He winces. "I can't move into that house, Belle. I'm sorry, but I can't live in a house that Dylan purchased for you. I know how petty that sounds." He sighs. "But I don't want to walk around being reminded of the guy who was always your number one."

Fuck. This is worse than I thought. I thought he had conquered all his fears and overcome his guilt, but this is a whole other ball game. I had no idea he was feeling like this, and it kills me. How can I convince Slate that he matters every bit as much? That my love for him is as strong as the love I shared with Dylan? Words are not going to be enough, so I'll just have to show him through my actions. I'll continue being patient, and I'll keep fighting, every day, until he has all the proof he needs to know *he's* my number one.

Chapter Fifty-Two

"**A**re you that excited you can't eat?" Slater asks with a teasing smile as he watches me toy with the food on my plate.

"You nailed it, babe," I lie, pushing away my half-eaten plate. My messed-up appetite is less about excitement over the impending concert and more to do with nerves over what I'm planning to do.

It's been six months since Slater dropped the bomb about feeling second best, and I've done everything in my power to show him that's not the truth, but he hasn't mentioned us moving in together since, and I've been too afraid to bring it up.

On the surface, everything is perfect. We are blissfully happy and head over heels in love. We have regular hot sex, and we can't keep our hands off one another, just like the first time we were together. He treats me like a princess, and he adores the ground Billy walks on.

A few months ago, Billy called Slater Daddy for the first time. It was a bittersweet moment, for Slater and me, and we both cried. It's only natural Billy would draw that conclusion, because in most every way, that is what Slater has become to him. The obvious joy on Slater's face was wonderful to see, but I couldn't help feeling a pang of sorrow because of Dylan. But I got over it, like I do with every little milestone Billy passes. Dylan isn't here to bear witness to any of those things, and I have to accept that.

I'm lucky my son has an exceptional father figure in his life. On occasion, Slater expresses concerns, and it hurts me that he doubts himself sometimes. But I understand where it's coming from. Slater grew up without a father, and he worries he didn't have an example to learn from. I remind him he had my dad and that he's a natural anyway.

I believe he's a better father *because* of the fact he grew up without one. He wants to ensure Billy misses out on nothing, so he probably overcompensates a bit. Not that Billy minds in the slightest. Slater is amazing with him, and I fall more deeply in love with him every time I see him with our son. It's nothing short of miraculous.

But I want us to be a proper family. I want us to live together and to share the same last name. I want to grow Slater's babies in my tummy. I want the whole shebang, and I know he does too, but there's still this sliver of doubt loitering in his mind, and I've wracked my head for months trying to figure out how to get through to him.

Until Slater handed me the perfect opportunity.

He knows I'm a big Shawn Lucas fan. That I never miss any of his concerts. It turns out he worked with an intern in the Iowa office whose girlfriend is best friends with Dakota Gray, Shawn's girlfriend. Not only did Slater get us excellent seats near the front, and VIP backstage passes, but he also scored us an invite to the after-party and the promise of hanging out with Shawn in person. I screamed the house down when he told me, and later that night, the idea came to me.

Now, I think I must've been insane to come up with this plan. And I'm queasy at the thought of following through. But it's all set in motion now. I can't back out.

When Slater wasn't looking, I borrowed his cell and called Jake— the intern. When I explained, he was totally onboard. He spoke to his girlfriend, Daisy, and she lined up the call with Dakota. I was nervous as fuck speaking with Shawn's girlfriend, but she's a total sweetheart, and she put me at ease straightaway. She gushed over my plan, telling me Shawn would too, and she somehow got him to agree, and now I'm here.

About to puke all over this restaurant because I'm more nervous than I've ever been my entire life.

We finish our meal, or at least Slater does, and head to the arena for the concert. Our seats are epic, and I'm grateful because being able to see him will help settle my nerves.

I nearly give myself whiplash checking the time on my cell every five minutes, and I know Slater is wondering what the hell is up with me tonight. I'm lying back against his chest, swaying to the music, trying to enjoy the show, but nothing can distract me from what I'm about to do. I go over it in my head, repeating the words, because I'm terrified I'm going to get up there and go blank.

I've thought very carefully about what I want to say, and how I want to say it. I'm only going to get one chance to do this right.

I tell Slater I need the bathroom, and I rush to the side entrance where Dakota told me to go. She is one of Shawn's official dancers, so she's not able to greet me personally. Shawn's assistant is waiting for me instead, as prearranged. She guides me to the side of the stage and instructs me to wait there. I'm shaking like a leaf, more terrified than I've ever been in my entire life, and I can't even enjoy the fact I'm getting a close-up view of the show.

When Shawn finishes singing his smash hit, "Midnight Dancer," Dakota slips off the stage, smiling as she skips toward me. "I'm so happy to finally meet you," she enthuses, giving me a quick hug.

"Me, too. Thank you again for organizing this. I really appreciate it." I'm thankful my voice sounds okay, even if I'm quaking inside. Shawn is currently warming up the crowd, and I wet my dry lips, cautioning my racing heart to calm the fuck down.

"This is so exciting!!" Dakota's eyes shine with excitement, and she's practically bouncing on the spot. "What's going through your head right now?" she inquires, glancing over her shoulder as she keeps an eye on proceedings on the stage.

"I'm wondering why I thought it was a good idea to go for dinner before the show when I'm about to be reacquainted with my meal any second now." I'm also wondering if I'm missing a few brain cells because how the fuck did I think I could stand up here in front of all these people and profess my undying love?

My knees almost buckle underneath me, and I'm shaking all over. The adrenaline surge and flurry of butterflies keeping company in my chest are so intense I wonder if this is what it feels like right before one has a coronary.

She hugs me again. "I think you're incredibly brave and this is one of the most romantic things I've ever heard."

The crowd roars and Shawn beckons me with a wave of his fingers. "Let's give this pretty lady a big round of applause," he hollers, "and help her do this." The crowd goes wild at his words. I close my eyes and take a deep breath, reminding myself of why I'm doing this. One of Mom's favorite sayings is "go big or go home," so I'm going all out.

Slate's beautiful face swims in front of my eyes, helping to ground me.

I can do this.

I can do this for him.

Because I want him to understand he's my everything.

"You're going to kill it," Dakota whispers, recognizing my terror and trying to reassure me. She keeps a firm hold on my hand as we walk out on the stage, toward Shawn.

"What if he says no?" I whisper, my voice laced with panic.

"You won't know if you don't ask. Keep the faith." She squeezes my hand, and her touch keeps me moving even if my feet are urging me to get the fuck out of Dodge. I scan the vast auditorium. The lights are blinding, and the noise of the crowd is deafening, but I can scarcely hear over the pounding of my heart and the rush of blood in my ears.

Shawn wraps me up in a big hug. "Knock it out of the park, Gabby. We're rooting for you," he whispers.

My nerves must be bad if I'm barely conscious of the fact one of the biggest popstars in the world, and one of my idols, just hugged me and whispered in my ear and all I can think about is Slater and how I really don't want to mess this up.

Shawn passes the mic to me. I clear my throat and pull my big girl panties on. For some reason, Dylan pops into my mind. Almost like he's here, watching over proceedings and cheering me on.

"Hey, Wilmington. Are you all enjoying the show?" My voice is a little shaky, but it booms out over the stadium and the crowd cheers, which actually helps ease my nerves. It also helps that I can't really see them because the overhead lights are all switched on, and they are ridiculously bright. That is an immense relief.

"My name is Gabrielle James although most people call me Gabby. My boyfriend calls me Belle. Hey, Slate!" I wave in the direction of our seats, wondering if Shawn's assistant and bodyguard have reached him yet. They are going to bring him onstage for the end. "Yes, this is really me up here and, no, I'm not crazy although some might argue that's debatable."

The crowd laughs with me, and I turn my head slightly, so they know I'm addressing them. "I'm here today because I have a story to tell and something important to say to my boyfriend, and Shawn was gracious enough to let me do this." I smile at my idol, swooning a little when he smiles back. Shawn has his arm around Dakota, and I can tell by their mutual expressions they are genuinely loving this.

"I hope you can forgive me for hijacking the stage, and I apologize in advance for the profanities, but this isn't the kind of story I can tell without cussing a bit. Sorry, Mom. Please don't disown me."

The crowd chuckles, and I forge on. "While I'll try to keep this brief, I need to give you some context." The crowd has grown quiet, and I can tell they're intrigued and dying to hear what this is all about. "This is a story about two amazing guys and two great loves." I bite back my nerves, silently encouraging myself to go on. "When I was ten, I met a boy named Dylan Woods."

A few murmurs ring out, and I'm not surprised. Dylan was a mini-celebrity in his own right, for a period of time, and I figure at least some people here have heard of him.

"I fell for him pretty much immediately, and we became best friends. A few years later, he became my boyfriend and the center of my world. We were young, but we knew we had this insane connection and that we were destined to be together forever. We made all kinds of plans, and I never doubted the future because I believed in our love."

The crowd is listening intently, and my nervousness has transformed to something different. Now, I'm itching to tell this story. "Then this bitch named fate intervened, and this bastard named cancer happened, and Dylan was taken from me. Less than two days after our son was born."

This is the part that is still so hard to say out loud, and I have to pause for a moment to collect myself. I blink my tears away. "I was devastated after he died, but my son helped keep me sane. And he wasn't the only one."

I look over in Slater's direction, and my heart swells with love for him. "I said at the start that this is a story of two loves, and I haven't told you about Slater Evans. Slater is my brother's best friend, and I've known him since I was a little kid. Growing up, Slate was always around, and our histories are as entangled as mine and Dylan's. What I didn't know back then was that Slate was in love with me."

The crowd is hanging on my every word, and it spurs me on. "I was so wrapped up in Dylan that I didn't realize what was right under my nose. A few months before Dylan's cancer was diagnosed, we broke up, and it was messy. Slate became my rock, my confidante, my best friend. Gradually, I realized he was so much more than that, and we fell into this heady, passionate relationship that had me questioning everything I'd ever thought I knew about myself. When Dylan became ill and I discovered I was having his baby, Slate selflessly stepped aside, pushing his own feelings away to allow me to do what he knew I had to do. But he was still there for me, and when I needed him, when my son needed him, he stepped up to the plate without question."

I walk closer to the front of the stage. "Because the way Slate loves is a thing of beauty. When he gives his heart, he gives it completely. His love lifted me up when I couldn't find my feet. His love propelled me forward when I couldn't find the strength to go on. Time and time again, he shoved his own feelings and needs aside in favor of mine. He is, without doubt, the most selfless, giving, compassionate, intelligent man I know, and I'm so blessed to have known him for most of my life. He's a far better person than I am, and I hurt him in ways I wish I could take back."

The crowd starts hollering, and I turn around, watching Slate approach with a smile on his face. When he reaches me, he immediately takes my free hand and squeezes it. "Everyone, this is Slate. As you can see, in addition to being a stellar human being, he's also really fucking hot." The crowd roars their approval, and Slate shakes his head, chuckling.

I realize I'm actually enjoying this now. There's no doubt, being up here has brought out the hidden showgirl in me.

"Right now, Slate is wondering what the ever-loving fuck I'm doing up here, so I better get to the punchline." I draw a deep breath and face him. "I know I hurt you and that you're holding a part of yourself back as a protective mechanism. I can't fault you for that. I also know you've constantly felt under Dylan's shadow. That you feel second best. I've tried to explain how I feel so you understand how wrong you are, but I've failed thus far. So, I decided to stand up here tonight, in front of all these amazing people, to tell you how much I love you." He squeezes my hand, and his eyes turn glassy. "How much I've *always* loved you. Just because I didn't realize it back then doesn't make it untrue."

The crowd is so quiet you wouldn't even know there are over twenty thousand people in this arena.

"I have loved you for longer than I even knew Dylan. And it's never been a competition for me. I feel blessed to have experienced what it's like to be loved so completely by two different men at two different times in my life. You could never be second best, Slate, because your love shines too bright to be overshadowed. The way you love me, the way you love our son, is unique and unrivaled, and every morning when I wake, I pinch myself to confirm it's real. I'm so happy you've given me a second chance because I can't imagine my life without you in it. I know you're scared to invest your whole heart, but I'm not scared to guarantee that for the both of us."

My mouth feels dry as I get to the bottom line. I glance at Shawn and Dakota, and they encourage me with their expressions and their smiles.

"Dylan owned my past, but you own my present and my future, Slate, if you'll have me." I drop to one knee, and my heart is thumping wildly in my chest. A chorus of shocked gasps echo around the stadium. Recognition dawns on Slater's face. "I will never love anyone the way I love you, and Billy already loves you every bit as much. Marry me, Slater Evans, and cement my status as the happiest girl in the world."

He grips my forearms and lifts me to my feet. Then his arms sweep around me, and his lips crash down on mine. This kiss is the kiss to end all kisses. A kiss worthy of an Oscar. A kiss that I won't ever forget, one I will cherish forever. His touch is full of every emotion he's feeling. The crowd is going wild, hollering and whooping, and my heart is careering around my chest. Slater keeps a firm hold of me as he finally breaks the kiss. We're both panting, and tears glisten in his eyes.

"You are crazy, Belle, but I wouldn't have you any other way. Nothing would make me prouder than to call you my wife. I can't even get mad at you for stealing my line." He pecks my lips. "So, yes, babe. A million times yes."

I fist my hand in the air. "He said yes!" I shout into the mic, and the crowd is going insane. Shawn and Dakota approach, hugging us one at a time.

"If you hadn't said yes, I just might have," Dakota quips, smiling at Slate. "Damn, girl, you nailed it!" She hugs me again.

"Congratulations. We're both really happy for you," Shawn says. "Thank you so much for letting us be a part of something this special. You blew me away, Gabby." He bundles his girlfriend in his arms. "You're a lucky man, Slater. It's not every guy who finds a girl with bigger balls than him."

We all laugh at that.

"Thank you so much for letting me do this," I tell him, clinging to Slate. "I'm sorry I monopolized so much of your show."

"Are you kidding, Gabby? You had the crowd eating out of your hand. They'll be talking about this for a long time to come."

Slater and I wave to the crowd before exiting the stage hand in hand. As soon as we're backstage, Slater pulls me into his arms. "I hope you're not planning a long engagement," he whispers. "Because I can't wait to call you Mrs. Evans."

Epilogue

Four months later

I stare at my reflection in the mirror, blinking at the vision in white. I chose a vintage Vera Wang, and it fits me like a glove. It's a high-necked, lace, fitted gown with a very low back that fans out in a fishtail style. My hair is pinned up loosely with strands framing my face, and my makeup is natural and flawless. I look like a princess, and my heart is full to bursting point, but my emotions are veering all over the place, and I'm trying to get a grasp on them.

In all my years of imagining my wedding day, I never imagined I would feel so many differing emotions. I'm unbelievably happy—that's a given—the nervousness too. But sorrow was not an emotion I expected to feel on my special day. I'm determined to process these feelings now so when I walk up that aisle I'm the happy, glowing bride Slater expects and deserves.

A knock at the door rouses me from my troubled inner monologue. I turn around as Mom slips into the room, her eyes instantly welling. "Oh, Gabrielle. You're so beautiful." She puts her bag on the chair, pulling me into her arms. "I'm so proud and so happy for you." She smiles through her tears. "But I know what's put that veil of sadness over this happy occasion, and I have something I think will help."

She removes a tablet from her purse, handing it to me.

My brows knit together. "What is it?"

"You need to be sitting down for this." She pulls me to a chair, sitting down beside me. "Dylan asked me to give you this recording on your wedding day."

I'm glad she had the foresight to make me sit, because I almost take a tumble as it is. Tears sting my eyes, and I cover my mouth. "Mom, I don't think I can watch that."

"I thought you'd say that, and, I'll be honest, I loved Dylan as much as I love my own sons, but there was no way I was giving this to you today without understanding what his message contained."

"You already looked at it."

"Yes. I hope you're not angry with me."

I shake my head. "I'm not. Not at all."

"This will help, but if you don't want to watch it, I understand too."

I'm quiet for a few minutes as I mull it over in my head. If I don't watch it, I'm going to be preoccupied all day wondering what he said. I can't do that to Slater. I *won't* do that to Slater. He deserves every part of me today. "I want to watch it."

"Good girl." She pats my back, handing me a pack of tissues. "Do you want me to stay?"

I shake my head again. "No, I'd like to watch it alone."

"I'll be right outside if you need me."

She quietly exits the room, and I press the play button before I change my mind.

The image loads, and pain lances me across the chest. My lip wobbles as I cast eyes on Dylan. Looking at him after all this time is hard. Even more so because I can see how very ill he was when he made this. When he was dying, I almost didn't see the ravages caused by his cancer, because I'd grown accustomed to it, and I was able to look behind it, to see the boy I knew. But, now, I can see it all too clearly, and my heart hurts all over again.

I hit the pause button, and sobs burst free of my soul. Huge, wracking sobs fill the room, and I know I'm messing up my makeup, but I need to purge this today. To be free of this sadness before I give my heart to another man. After a few minutes, the sobs subside, and I find the courage to press play.

"Hey, Dimples. If you're watching this, it means today is an important day. It means my baby's getting married." His eyes fill with tears. "I could've written you another card, but today's too special to treat it otherwise. Besides, the things I have to say need to be said while you're looking at my face. Granted, I'm not as ruggedly handsome as I once was." I snort-laugh as tears roll down my face. "But I know you love me just the same."

I do, Dylan. I do. A part of me will always love you.

"I'm going to ask you to do a few things for me today. First rule is no tears. We can't have you walking up that aisle with panda eyes." I smile, dabbing at my eyes, wishing I could tell him he's too late. "I want nothing to take from this joyous occasion, because it's a celebration and you should be nothing but happy. I didn't ask Lucy to give you this message to make you sad on your wedding day. I asked her to deliver this because I want you to know how happy I am that you're getting married. I'm really happy for you and Slater. At least, I hope it's Slater you're marrying although it's totally fine if it isn't him once the guy waiting for you in that church is worthy of your love and devotion."

I'm staring at the screen in amazement.

"But I have a strong feeling it's Slater, and that makes my heart sing." He chuckles, or at least he tries to, but it comes out like more of a coughing, spluttering sound. "Would you have ever thought you'd hear those words coming from my mouth?" he teases before his expression turns serious. "Slater Evans has loved you as long as I have, and he's the only one I trust to love and cherish you the way I would have. I also have it on good authority that he'll make an excellent father for Billy, and I have faith he'll raise our son right."

Tears continue to leak out of the corners of my eyes even though I swipe them away, but they keep coming.

"All I want is for both of you to be happy. To move on and live full lives. For your house to be chock full of love and laughter and for Billy to be surrounded by siblings. By now, I'm guessing you've realized what an amazing mom you are, Gabby. Don't waste that gift. Have lots of babies, Dimples. Love them all with that big heart of yours."

Now I'm sobbing again, but my tears are intermingled with joy and a sense of relief. Placing my hand on the screen, I run my finger across his face, remembering how good a man Dylan was. He couldn't have known exactly how much his blessing means to me. Or perhaps he did realize it, and that's why he was insistent on this message.

"My biggest fear in leaving you is that you'll cling to the past and not let go. It's okay to remember and miss what we had, but I don't want you to miss out on living in the process, because you've got a lot of living to do, Gabby, and I need you to promise you'll live life to the fullest. If my illness has taught us anything, it's that life is too precious to waste even a second with regrets."

He sits up straighter, putting his face right into the camera. "After months of being consumed with anger, I've finally accepted my fate. And it *is* fate. Close your mouth and stop gaping at the screen."

I clamp my lips shut, shaking my head, laughing and crying at the same time. He knew me so well.

"Things happen for a reason, babe. We found each other when we were incredibly young, but there was never any doubt in my mind that you were my soul mate. I truly believe we found each other as kids for a reason—so I could experience what it's like to love and be loved so completely in return. The joy and happiness we found in one another over our nine years together is more than a lot of people experience in an entire lifetime. You came into my life to make mine complete, Gabby. To give me that lifetime's experience in a shorter timeframe. I believe that wholeheartedly, and it's how I've made my peace with this."

He slumps back on the bed, and his breathing is labored, his chest heaving up and down as he stares at the screen. Clearly, this was both emotionally and physically draining for him.

"I have no regrets, and you shouldn't either. Especially not today. If you were feeling nostalgic and it was making you sad, don't go there. You look beautiful, by the way." He's grinning. "I know because I'm there with you. I'm always with you." He pauses to draw a breath.

"I may not believe in a God, but I believe in an afterlife, and I'm here waiting for you and for Billy. I hope I don't see you both for a very long time. When we meet again, I can't wait to hear all about your life. So, dry your tears, babe. Yes, I know you're crying even though I asked you not to." He blows me a kiss. "Go out there and make that man your husband and live a long and happy life knowing you have my blessing and my good wishes and that I want nothing but great things for you."

He sits up again, reaching out with his hand. "Go make me proud, Dimples. Give Billy a big kiss from me, and never forget how much I love you both."

The screen turns black, and I bury my face in my hands, sobbing, purging the last of the sadness from my heart and my soul. Mom pads softly into the room, smoothing a hand up and down my back. After a few minutes, I look up at her with tears dribbling down my chin. "Perhaps you should've given me that before I got my hair and makeup done."

We both crack up laughing, and I grab a clean tissue, mopping up the remnants of my cryfest.

"Was I wrong to give it to you?"

"No." I shake my head and clutch her hand. "Definitely not. I needed to hear that, and I needed to let go. I'm okay now." I give her a reassuring smile. "Well, except for my panda eyes." I grin as I stand, and she pulls me into a hug.

"I love you, Gabrielle."

"I love you too, Mom."

"I know you're going to be incredibly happy because that man out there loves you so very much."

"I love him very much too." I ease out of her arms. "I'm so lucky I got to love and be loved by two amazing men."

"You are, sweetie, but it doesn't surprise me because you're pretty darn amazing."

"You're my mother. You have to think that."

She laughs. "It doesn't make it untrue."

I roll my eyes, but I'm smiling. "Can you send the hairdresser and makeup artist back in. I don't want to keep my man waiting."

"Don't let me trip, Dad," I murmur as we start our slow procession up the aisle.

"I'll never let you fall, Buttercup. Not as long as there's breath left in my body."

I grip his arm tighter. "I know, Dad. Thank you for being an amazing father. Today and every other day of my life."

I think it's true what they say about weddings. That it brings every emotion to the surface and helps you realize how lucky you are to be loved by so many people. As I glance around the church, at the smiling faces of our family and friends, I acknowledge the truth of my thoughts.

My eyes turn to my son, and I'm crying again. He's our ringbearer today, and he's walking in front of me. He turned three a couple months back, and he's such a big boy now. He glances over his shoulder, as if he's privy to my inner thoughts, shooting me a big, goofy grin. He gets more like Dylan with every passing day, and my heart soars with love every time I look at him.

We're nearing the top of the aisle, and I let my eyes feast on my intended. We lock eyes instantly, and I stop breathing. Slater looks so handsome in his tux, but it's the unflinching adoration and unmistakable love in his gaze that derails me.

We don't lose eye contact as Dad hands me over to my man. The instant my hand is in Slater's, I feel at home. "You look so beautiful," he whispers, leaning over to kiss my cheek. "Like a goddess."

"You look beautiful too, and I love you so very much." I can't keep the smile off my face as I peer into his glistening brown eyes.

The priest welcomes everyone, and the service proceeds. I hold Slater's hand the entire time, and we can't stop grinning at one another. It's almost surreal. That we've made it to this point when there were times I thought I'd lost him forever.

Most of the words ghost over my head, because I'm so lost in my gorgeous, strong, compassionate man, until it's time to recite our vows.

We face one another, holding hands, our eyes glued to each other. My heart is complete as I promise to love and cherish Slater every day of my life. I can't hold my tears back as he professes his love for me before the congregation and slips his ring on my finger. A round of enthusiastic applause and raucous whooping breaks out when the priest announces we are husband and wife. Slater's joy is obvious in his passionate kiss, and I wrap my arms around his neck, high on love and the thought that he is mine and I am his forever and ever.

"Daddy Slater?"

We break apart at the sound of Billy's cute little voice. He's looking up at Slate with so much awe on his face. "Does this mean you're my real daddy now?" Slater lifts him, keeping him on one side of his body while he wraps his arm around me on the other side. I circle my arm around my son, overjoyed to finally be a proper family, even if his question still plucks at my heartstrings. But I'm over my sadness and nothing can diminish the joy and happiness of finally having the family unit I've craved. "I will always be your daddy, Billy, and I will be here for you every second of every day that you need me. But Daddy Dylan will always be your daddy too, watching over you from heaven and making sure you're safe."

"Wow. I'm really lucky I have two awesome daddies."

I almost choke over the lump in my throat. "Yes, you are, sweetie. We're both so lucky." Slate and I dot kisses all over Billy's face before Ryan coaxes him out of our arms, so the ceremony can conclude. He looks so handsome in his tux too; all my brothers do. I glance briefly at my bridesmaids, making sure Myndi is okay. I know this day is hard for her, and I love her so much for putting aside her own feelings to be here for me.

After the church, we travel to our new house, where the wedding reception is being held, by chauffeur-driven limo. Billy is sitting in between us, in the car, holding both our hands, with a huge, happy smile on his face. "Can I sleep in my new room tonight, Mommy?"

I kiss the top of his head. "Yes, little munchkin. You get to sleep in your new room tonight."

Since Slate and I bought the house three months ago, Billy has been chomping at the bit to move in. But we wanted to carry out some renovations first, and Slater wanted to do things the traditional way, waiting until we were married before officially moving in. We're not even staying here tonight. We're staying in a suite at a top hotel close to the airport. My parents are babysitting Billy, and they'll bring him to meet us in the morning. Neither of us wanted to go off on a honeymoon and leave him behind, so the three of us are going on a vacation-slash-honeymoon. It will be our first family vacation abroad, and I think I'm more excited than our son.

"Yay, yay, yay." Billy is bouncing up and down, overjoyed at the prospect of sleeping in his new Marvel-themed bedroom. Slate insisted on doing all the work in his room and our master suite himself, and he's done an amazing job.

Slate watches Billy jumping around with emotion etched all over his face. He leans over Billy's head to kiss me. "I love you, Mrs. Evans. Thank you for giving me this amazing life."

When Forever Changes

"Right back at ya, Mr. Evans." I peck his lips. "I'm so happy I get to share the rest of my life with you."

The driveway is already overflowing with cars when we arrive. We've hired catering staff for the day and they are ready to greet us, offering us both a glass of champagne. A red carpet stretches around the side of the house, bringing people to the marquee that's been set up in our vast backyard.

Once Slate and I decided we wanted to buy someplace new to start our married life, we wasted no time house hunting. It was this beautifully landscaped garden that ultimately led to our decision to buy this house even if the interiors needed some work.

I knew living in the house Dylan bought was a stretch too far for Slater, and I had already come to terms with moving out. I refused to sell it though. I want to keep it for Billy until he comes of age. Perhaps he'll want to raise his own family there some day. We considered moving into Slater's house—his mom's old home—but that would've only been a temporary stopgap. It's not a large family home and considering we both want plenty of kids it would only suit us in the short term. So, after discussing it at length, we decided we'd buy something together. I have more than enough money to buy it outright, but I knew Slater would never go for it. I was sad when he put his Mom's house on the market, but I understand his need to do this on equal terms, and I didn't attempt to stop him.

All has worked out well in the end, and we're happy with our decision.

The scent of jasmine tickles my nostrils as we walk into the lavishly decorated marquee. Laini, the wedding planner, has outdone herself. Circular tables dressed in shades of gold and cream occupy one side of the space. Beautiful bouquets, filled with blooms of cream, gold, and lilac are stunning centerpieces on all the tables. The girl we hired to play the harp is entertaining our family and friends as they make their way into the tent. At the top of the room is a stage and a dance floor for later. Waiters and waitresses canvass the room offering beverages and canapes.

"Congratulations." Caleb is the first to greet us with Terri by his side. She's cradling their sleeping, four-month-old son in her arms, and my heart melts looking at him.

To say I'm broody is an understatement.

Ryder and Billy grin at one another as they make a beeline for the dance floor, and I can't help smiling. They are as close as brothers, and I'm happy they have one another.

Slater slides his arm around my shoulders. "Thanks, brother."

Caleb slaps him on the back and leans in to kiss my cheek. "You look stunning, Gabby. Far too good for Evans."

"Don't I know it," Slater says, rolling with it. "I'm not ever going to forget." He presses a kiss to my temple and I beam up at him.

"This is so beautiful, you guys." Terri looks around with a hint of envy. "I'm sorry we got married in a hotel now. Having it at home is much more special."

"We were fortunate we could make it happen, but your wedding was fantastic too," I reassure her.

"I'm sorry I missed it," Slater says. Terri and Caleb got married a year after Dylan passed, and it was while Slater was still living in Iowa. He was invited, naturally, but chose not to come because of me.

I'm so glad those lonely, single days are behind us.

Caleb looks over my shoulder, frowning a little. "I hope they're not going to make a scene."

We all turn and look. Ryan and Myndi are exchanging what looks like heated words in the far corner.

"Do you think we should intervene?" I ask my husband.

"Allow me." He kisses me softly on the lips before walking to the warring couple.

My nieces-slash-flower girls rush into the marquee, heading straight for the dance floor to join their cousins. Dean and Alice make their way over to us, laughing as the girls race through the room.

"Congrats, Gabby." Dean pulls me into a hug. "I hope you, Slater, and Billy are very happy."

"Thanks, big bro." I squeeze him tight. "And thanks for letting me borrow the two little princesses for the day."

Dean snorts, jerking his head up. "I don't know about that. Look."

Mia has her gorgeous lilac dress hitched up to her knees as she prances around the dance floor chasing a clearly terrified Ryder. Tia sits on the middle of the floor, in a most unladylike position, rummaging through the party bag we gave her, with her dress in a million creases. Billy looks on like girls are some weird alien creatures, and I can't control my laughter.

While everyone is preoccupied watching the kids, I ditch my champagne in the plant pot behind me.

"You'll have to lock those two up when they get to their teens," Alice jokes with Dean before pulling me in for a hug. "The boys will be lining up outside the front door."

"Over my dead body," Dean hisses. "My daughters aren't dating till they're at least eighteen."

I roll my eyes. "Good luck with that plan."

"I approve," Slater says, circling his arms around me from behind and pulling me into him. "If we're lucky enough to have any daughters, I'll be right there with you, bruh."

"This isn't the dark ages, and there's no need to act like such cavemen." I roll my eyes.

"We're well aware of what century it is, Belle. Why the hell do you think we want to keep the girls away from boys? We know exactly the kind of naughty thoughts running through boys' heads."

"Do tell," Ryan says, swiping a beer from a passing waiter as he joins us. "What kind of naughty thoughts were you having about Gabby when you were just a boy?"

Alice and Terri giggle, and Slater groans. "If I told you, I'd have to leave the country," he quips.

"I'll bet." Ryan smirks. "I remember your dirty mouth, Evans. You're lucky I haven't beat your ass before now."

"Only because you know you wouldn't win."

Ryan puffs out his chest. "I can take you any day and you know it."

"You two sound like some of the punks in my class," Terri says, popping a canape in her mouth. "You almost make me miss them."

Just then, I spot Laini hovering nearby trying to get my attention. I wave her over, and she offers us congratulations before ushering everyone to the gazebo area for the wedding photos.

The sun is starting to set in the sky when the band commences playing. Slater enfolds me in his arms as we share our first dance as man and wife. Christina Perri's "A Thousand Years" is another one of my all-time favorites, and it happens to be a song Slater connects with too, so the choice was easy. The words convey our history and the depth and strength of our love, and it's one of the most romantic songs I've ever heard.

It couldn't be more perfect.

This whole day couldn't be any more perfect.

This man—my husband, my soul mate, the man who has loved me from boyhood, the man who completes me in every way, the man who brings a smile to my face just by existing—couldn't be more perfect. I'm crying and laughing and full of so much elation as we sing the words to each other. Slater spins me around before pulling me in closer for the more intense parts. He fuses our mouths, and I'm lost in his kiss and the moment, knowing I've found my eternal love, the man who will share my life and be by my side until I take my last breath.

It's an exhilarating feeling, and as we dance, surrounded by family and friends, by our adorable son and our nieces and nephews, sharing this wonderful occasion with all those who are near and dear to us, I know I'll cherish this day for the rest of my life.

It's after midnight before we make it out of the house and into our wedding car, en route to the hotel where we're spending the night, and I can't keep the secret inside me anymore.

I've been bursting to tell him all day, but I wanted to wait until we were alone, and this is the first opportunity I've had.

"I want to give you your present now, dearest, darling husband."

Slater smirks, eyeing the driver in front. "What, right here?"

I smack his arm. "Not that kind of present." I shoot him a wicked grin. "I'm saving that for when we get to the hotel." Watching to ensure the driver isn't looking, I pull the skirt of my dress up and flash my garter and suspenders at him.

"Holy fucking shit." He pulls me to him. "You're a real temptress, Mrs. Evans, and you'll pay for that."

"I'm holding you to that promise, Mr. Evans."

He discreetly places my hand on his hard cock. "So am I." He kisses me tenderly. "Little tease," he murmurs, nibbling on my lower lip.

"Hey, stop distracting me. I haven't given you your present yet." A massive grin spreads across my mouth as I pull the little wrapped package from my purse and hand it to him.

He slants me a lopsided grin as he shakes the box. "What is it?"

I roll my eyes. "Open it and see!"

He tears at the wrapping, opens the box, and gasps. His wide eyes flit to mine, and they're already glistening with tears. "Is this real?" he whispers, holding up the little booty.

I take his other hand, placing it over my stomach. "It's real. We're having a baby."

He pulls me to him, circling his arms around me and raining kisses on my face. "Just when I thought I couldn't love you anymore." He's openly crying now, and it's one of the things I love about him. He's never afraid of vulnerability or of showing his true emotions. "You have made me so happy today, Belle. I wished for this life with you, and now we're living it. I'm so in love with you. I love you so much; more than I can ever convey."

"Right back at you, Slate." I rest my head on his shoulder. "Thank you for letting me back in. For letting me prove how much I love you."

"Thank you for going to so much trouble to reassure me."

"That's what true love is." I lift my head to look at him. "It's not being afraid to fight for the person you love, and never giving up even when all seems lost."

And it's about realizing that sometimes love changes and takes a new direction. It doesn't replace the love that came before or diminish its importance. It's about rebuilding the foundations and understanding that sometimes love can throw you curveballs that seem like it's the end of the world.

When it's only the beginning.

When Forever Changes

If you need to talk to someone regarding cancer, please call the American Cancer Society's cancer helpline at 800-227-2345 or the National Cancer Institute at 1-800-4-CANCER

If you need to talk to someone regarding brain cancer, please call the National Brain Tumor Society at 617-924-9997

If you live outside the United States, please contact your local support services.

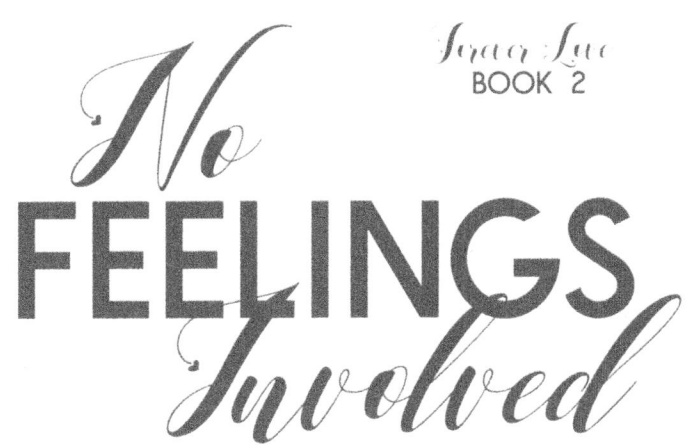

Forever Love
BOOK 2

No FEELINGS *Involved*

USA TODAY BESTSELLING AUTHOR
SIOBHAN DAVIS

Can this skeptical player let down his guard long enough to let love into his life, or is this forbidden romance a train wreck in the making?

Ryan James doesn't believe in love.

It's a truth he learned early in life.

A truth he carried with him into adulthood. He broke his golden rule one time, but Myndi trampled all over his heart, cementing his belief that love is a lie and not worth the effort.

Now he's returned to his cynical views and promiscuous lifestyle, racking up more notches on his bedpost than he can count.

Until Summer Petersen comes crashing into his world, threatening to knock down his walls with her tempting body and sunny, sweet personality.

Summer is determined to lose her V-card before she starts freshman year of college, and the hot, older guy with the cute dimples, dazzling smile, and rippling biceps is just the man for the job. Ryan doesn't take much persuading, and he rocks her world, giving her a night to remember.

When they walk away, there's an unspoken agreement it was a one-time thing. Ryan doesn't do feelings, and Summer doesn't want to be tied down at eighteen.

But when she moves into her brother Austin's apartment, she's shocked to discover her new roomie is the guy who recently popped her cherry.

Ryan can't believe he slept with Austin's baby sister, and if he finds out, he'll literally kill him. Keeping their hook up a secret is nonnegotiable. Keeping his thoughts, and his hands, off Summer, less so. Because the longer he's around her, the more he finds himself catching feelings for the gorgeous brunette.

Summer doesn't want to care for her older brother's best friend, but Ryan makes her feel things she's never felt before, and she's slowly falling under his spell.

Embarking on an illicit affair behind Austin's back has train wreck written all over it, but provided they keep their feelings in check, they can end this before he ever finds out.

It's not like either of them is in love.

Right?

Chapter One
Summer

"We should've worn bikinis," my bestie Hannah jokes, plucking at the lacy tank top clinging to her chest like a second skin, as we navigate our way through the throngs of people toward the bar. The popular Newark bar-slash-club is teeming with people, loud music pumping from speakers as the Indie band on stage works the crowd like pros.

"That would've been one guaranteed way of achieving my goal," I shout in her ear with a grin. "Why didn't I think of that?"

"You seriously think you'll have any issue finding a hookup in here?" Jordan—Hannah's boyfriend—inquires, quirking a brow as he glances around the room. "You could wear a sack and easily find someone to rid you of that pesky V-card."

Hannah thumps her boyfriend in the upper arm. "Don't be so flippant. Summer has standards, and the guy needs to meet the criteria."

"What criteria?" he asks, shoving his way to the bar and propping his elbows on the grimy countertop.

I scoot up alongside him, with Hannah on my other side. "He needs to be older and know what he's doing. I haven't waited this long to give it up in a sweaty encounter with some drunken frat boy who needs a compass to locate my clit."

Jordan smothers a laugh as the bartender approaches. He casts a skeptical glance over us, but the magical bands around our wrists, and the line of thirsty customers, are enough to convince the overworked bartender to let his suspicions over our age go, and he accepts Jordan's order of three beers without question.

That hundred bucks I spent on a fake ID is already paying dividends.

With beers in hand, we navigate our way around the other side of the bar where it's not so packed.

"Damn, why does it have to be so hot," Hannah moans, fanning her face with her hands.

"We won't stay long," I promise, patting her arm. "Once I find my prey, I won't be hanging around." My eyes flash with intent as I take a sip of my beer, scanning the talent in the room.

Jordan rolls his eyes. "You're something else, Summer."

I shrug, smiling back at him. "You know what I'm like when I set my mind to something."

"Pigheaded," Hannah quips, smirking as she brings the bottle to her mouth.

"Determined," I correct her.

"You know I can call Justin, and he'd come to the city in a heartbeat for you," Jordan says. "He'd help you out for sure."

"I love Justin. You know I do, but only as a friend. It'd be weird having sex with him. I value his friendship too much to risk it."

Justin is Jordan's best friend from Bridgeville, our hometown. When Hannah and Jordan started going out in freshman year of high school, Justin and I kissed a few times. I know Hannah and Jordan would have loved for us to become a couple too, but I realized, almost immediately, that Justin and I would be much better off as friends. Still, that hasn't stopped my bestie and her boyfriend from trying to play matchmaker over the years.

But you can't force chemistry.

It's either there or it isn't.

"Are you sure you'd rather do it with a random?" Hannah asks, for like the millionth time.

"We can't all be as lucky as you." I clink my bottle against hers, smiling warmly at Jordan, while I continue to check out the guys in our vicinity. "And you didn't have three overprotective big brothers cock-blocking you at every turn."

"True dat." Jordan scrubs a hand over his stubbly chin. "Charlie had every fucking guy terrified to even ask you out."

"Hence why I'm still a virgin starting college."

"It's not that unusual, Sum," Hannah says. "I'm just worried you're going into this without thinking it through."

"I don't need to think it through," I confirm, my eyes homing in on the heaving dance floor with interest. "I'm ready. I want to have sex, and I want it to be a night to remember. That wouldn't have happened with any of the guys back home. I want to find some hot, older guy to rock my world and ensure I'll never forget the night I lost my virginity. And I want to walk away in the morning with no regrets and zero plans to see him again."

I extend my hands into the air, swaying my hips in time to the music. "I'm finally free, Han. Free to do anything I want. Be anyone I want. The last thing I want to do is hold off for a boyfriend and tie myself down freshman year of college. No offense to you two, but I want to spread my wings before settling down."

"None taken," Hannah says with affection. "If you're sure, then you should go for it."

"I'm glad you approve," I say, putting my beer down and handing hers to Jordan. "Because you're dancing with me."

I tug the hem of my short black minidress down, smoothing a hand over the front to remove the wrinkles. It's a simple dress, but it's well made, and it hugs my delicate curves in all the right places. I've always been a believer that less is more which is why I'm not wearing too much makeup and I've got my pink Converse on my feet instead of the red stilettos Hannah favored.

"C'mon." Hannah gives Jordan a quick kiss before looping her arm through mine. "Let's get this show on the road."

We push our way into the middle of the dance floor and move in time to the music. I toss my long, dark, wavy hair over my shoulder, shimmying my hips back and forth and losing myself to the rhythmic beats. I have no clue who the band is, but they're awesome, and it's not long before I've forgotten all about guys and I'm letting the music carry me away. My eyes are closed, and I'm swaying my hips with my hands roaming my body, absorbing the melody and lyrics, feeling the music all the way through to my bones, when Hannah nudges me in the side.

"Hottie alert dead ahead," she shouts in my ear. "He hasn't taken his eyes off you in the last five minutes."

I jerk my eyes open, looking straight in front of me, and my gaze instantly locks on the guy in question. He's standing at the front area of the bar in a small circle of guys and girls. But he's not paying any attention to the surrounding conversation. He's blatantly staring at me, not even attempting to disguise his interest.

He's smoking hot, and the way he's devouring me on sight has my body tingling all over.

"I think my ovaries just exploded," Hannah hollers over the loud music, flattening a hand over her chest as her eyes drink him in.

"Mine too," I murmur, readily agreeing as I confidently return his inquiring gaze. His biceps flex as he brings a bottle of beer to his mouth, and I watch in fascination as his throat works while he drinks. Watching him swallow is one of the sexiest things I've ever witnessed, and my panties are already wet, my core aching in a way I haven't felt in forever.

He doesn't take his eyes off me as he drinks, and his intense stare sends a shiver coursing through me. His long, slim fingers grip the bottle with ease, and now I'm imagining his big hands exploring every inch of my body. Setting his beer down on the bar, he runs a hand through his dirty-blond hair, muscles rolling in his arm with the motion.

No Feelings Involved

Hannah and I are captivated, watching him as if we've never seen a hot guy before. And I know it's obvious as fuck. Because we're standing in the middle of the dance floor, motionless, with our jaws trailing the ground, bits of drool clinging to the corners of our mouths. The guy's voluptuous lips twitch at the corner, and I curl my fingers at him in a "come hither" gesture. His smile expands as he walks toward us, and a shot of liquid lust pools in my core.

"Holy fucking hotness," Hannah exclaims, and I couldn't agree more.

I hold his gaze as he walks this way, unashamedly ogling him, making sure he knows I return his interest. With the way his shirt clings to his broad shoulders and toned chest, it's clear this guy works out, and I'm betting he has a body made for sin.

Check box number one.

While I'm not the greatest judge of age, he's definitely no frat boy, and he exudes confidence and maturity that confirms he's older.

Check box number two.

He's weaving his way through the masses, and I swear I hear a collective swoon from the largely female crowd. A few girls make grabs for him, but his focus is singular, and locked on me. He's already making me feel hugely desired, and I'm seriously turned on, and we haven't even spoken yet.

Check box number three.

His cocky swagger is like an aphrodisiac as he stalks toward me, quickly eating up the distance with his long strides. I can't tell the color of his eyes yet, but he's sexy and good-looking, and he sure looks like he knows how to use his equipment.

Check. Check. Check.

I throw out my mental checklist, already knowing this guy fits the bill.

I keep a heated smile on my face as he approaches, my heart beating excitedly behind my rib cage.

He stands directly in front of me, towering over my five-foot-six-inch frame, like some Greek Adonis. "I'm Ryan," he says, in a rich deep voice that does funny things to my insides. "And you're beautiful."

His gorgeous, big blue eyes suck me in, and a shiver runs through me.

It's hard not to gawk.

This guy is seriously gorgeous.

Dark cobalt eyes framed by a thick layer of long lashes. Chiseled jawline with just the right amount of stubble peppering his chin and cheeks. Strong nose. Kissable lips. And that hair. My hands curl into fists as I fight the craving to drag my fingers through the dark blond strands to see if they feel as silky as they look.

Snapping out of my daze, I extend my hand. "I'm smitten, and you're sexy as hell."

His chest rumbles as he chuckles, taking my offered hand and bringing it to his lips. My knees buckle when he presses a kiss to my knuckles, delicious tremors ricocheting all over my body. "Dance with me?" he asks, moving behind me before I've even replied. His arm wraps around my waist, and he pulls me flush against his lean, hard body. I place my hands over his, loving the feel of his skin against mine.

My body's on fire as we move in sync to the music, and it's not from the dense heat in the room.

Remembering Hannah, I look around, but she's disappeared. I glance over my shoulder, at the place where we left Jordan, breathing a sigh of relief when I notice her draped around her boyfriend.

Ryan pushes my hair aside, nuzzling into my neck, and a little moan escapes my lips. "You feel so good pressed up against me," he whispers, grazing his lips along the column of my neck, his body moving fluidly against mine as we dance a provocative dance.

I arch my head back, granting him more access. "Don't stop," I plead. "I want more."

His body shakes with silent laughter as his mouth turns more urgent. He presses hot, wet kisses up and down my neck, nibbling on my earlobe, as his hands begin to softly explore. His fingers brush against my sides, moving up and down my body. My movements become harder, and I push my ass back into his groin, gasping as I feel the hard length of his erection pressing into me.

We're grinding against one another in a way that's hugely obvious, and my body is humming and purring, my arousal elevated to "don't give a fuck if I'm in public dirty dancing with some hot, random stranger" mode. My heart is soaring in my chest, my pulse throbbing in my neck. I haven't done anything like this before, and the exhilaration is addictive. Sure, I've made out with guys, blown guys, and let a few go down on me, but it was all closeted, in quick, drunken fumbles at parties.

My brothers would freak the hell out if they could see me now, but that acknowledgment only pours more fuel on the flames.

I have spent my entire life in the quiet little town of Bridgeville.

A place I'm proud to call home.

A place I love wholeheartedly.

But it's insular and suffocating at the best of times. I couldn't sneeze around town without someone finding out about it. I'm unbelievably excited to be starting UD in a few weeks, for a variety of reasons but especially because of the freedom it offers. I love my parents and my brothers to the moon and back, and I'm so damn lucky I have them watching out for me, but their smothering protectiveness has clipped my wings, and now it's time to let them soar.

I have so many ambitions. So many plans. And I can't wait to begin this new phase of my life.

Ryan's hand subtly grazes the side of my breast, and my core throbs painfully. We're pressed tight against one another, with no gap between us, his enticing body melded against my spine, and I want more.

I want all of him.

I don't care that I don't know him.

That we've barely exchanged any words.

This is exactly how I want it to be.

One hot illicit night with a stranger.

A memory to cling to when I'm old and gray.

It's clear this isn't his first rodeo, and I'm under no illusion. His moves are practiced and assured.

He does this a lot, but I honestly don't care.

Reaching my arm back, I cup the nape of his neck, angling my head around as I pull his face down to mine. Our lips collide in a searing-hot kiss I feel all the way to the tips of my toes. He takes over, his mouth gliding with skill against mine. Keeping his lips locked on mine, he repositions me with a gentle touch until my front is pressed against his. He leans down, and I stretch up, my arms circling his neck as his arms wrap around my waist. His tongue licks the seam of my mouth, requesting entry, and I open freely for him. Stars explode behind my closed eyelids as his tongue plunders my mouth, licking me all over, and I whimper against his lips, pulling him tighter.

He grabs hold of my ass, prodding his erection into my pelvis, and then my hands are exploring, roaming the ripped planes of his muscular back down to his delectable ass. We're panting and groaning, and I'm ready to combust when he pulls back, peering down at me with lust in his eyes. "Want to get out of here?"

I nod, barely able to string a coherent sentence together.

He presses his lips to mine in a tender kiss that's completely at odds with the way we were just ravishing one another. "Fuck, you're so sexy. I can't remember the last time I was this horny."

His words shouldn't thrill me, but they do. "Try forever, in my case," I honestly admit.

His mouth twists into a devilish smile as he leans in closer. "You have gorgeous legs," he whispers into my ear, sweeping his fingers up the side of my thigh, and my legs almost go out from under me. "And now I'm imagining them wrapped around my neck."

My core throbs in a way it's never throbbed before, and butterflies scatter in my chest at the thought I might get what I'd hoped for. Ryan is all man, and the thoughts of him moving over and in me has me in a nervous-excited space. "That can be arranged," I tell him in a breathy voice, hoping he doesn't see through my façade. I doubt he'd be as keen if he knew how inexperienced I am.

"Your place or mine?" he inquires, taking my hand in his much larger one.

"Mine." I had already agreed to this with Jordan and Hannah in advance. They want me to be safe, and close by, in case anything happens. "I'm staying at the Regency for the weekend."

"You're an out of towner?" he asks, looking happy at that news.

"Yes," I semi-lie. While I'm technically an outsider now, I won't be come August when classes start. But he doesn't need to know that. The less we know about one another, the better. "Is that a problem?" I inquire, already guessing it's not.

"Nope." He plants a hard kiss on my mouth. "Quite the opposite." He waggles his brows.

"You want no attachments. Got it."

His eyes drill into mine. "If that's a problem for you—"

"It's not," I rush to reassure him. "Not at all. I'm only interested in one night. I'm not interested in forming any attachment either."

"Cool." He tugs me forward, assertively forging a path through the crowd.

Curious by nature, I ask, "Do you do this a lot?" as we exit the dance floor.

"Define a lot." I can hear the smirk in his tone.

Maybe I should be offended or disgusted, but I'm not. All I can think is this guy will have mad skills, and he couldn't be any more perfect. He's not interested in making small talk for hours to charm me into his bed. He's direct about what he wants, and that speaks to me on a base level. We're both on the same page, and I want to lose my virginity to him. We're attracted to one another, and I can tell this will be a purely physical encounter.

It's exactly what I'm looking for—mind-blowing sex with a random stranger.

One night.

No expectations.

No strings.

No ties.

"There's no such thing," I cheekily retort. "And I couldn't care less."

He spins me around as we reach the edge of the dance floor. "You genuinely mean that." I nod. "That's really fucking refreshing," he adds, caressing my cheek. "I'll give you a night to remember." His voice drips with promise, and my core pulses in response. "I'll worship you like a queen." As he lowers his mouth to mine, kissing me deeply and unhurriedly, I don't doubt him for a second.

Chapter Two
Ryan

"You sure you want to do this?" the guy—Jordan, I think she said his name was—asks her for the umpteenth time as we pile into the elevator. He's getting on my very last nerve. It's not like I don't get it.

He's protective of his friend in the same way I'm protective of my sister Gabby, and I have huge respect for him for it. But *I* know where to draw a line. This guy hasn't stopped the whole ride back to the hotel. Now, we're finally on the home stretch, and he has to go there again.

"Han. Please. Take him into your room, and fuck his brains out so his mind stops churning," the hot little thing at my side says. She darts in, kissing his cheek. "Stop, Jordan. You're not my brother. And I've got this."

"Like I said in the Uber, you can trust me to look after her. She's safe with me," I reiterate.

And you have a photo of my driver's license, I mentally add, rolling my eyes as I recall his aggressive request and the way he scowled at my ID. I'm guessing it's to do with the obvious age gap, but who the fuck cares. We're both consenting adults, and that's all that matters.

Hannah hauls Jordan away, finally leaving us in peace.

My hookup takes her key card out of her purse, unlocking the door. "I'm sorry about that," she says as we walk into her hotel room. "He's a little overprotective."

"A little?" I quirk a brow. "I'm protective over my sister, and he makes me look like a pussy in comparison."

"Enough about Jordy." She slides her palms up my chest. "I want to get tonight back on track."

"Sounds good." I grab her waist, reeling her into my body as my lips descend on hers. There's nothing tender about this kiss or the way she's arching her tight, hot little body into me. The peaks of her nipples are taut through the material of her dress, turning the hard-on in my pants into a solid wall of muscle that begs to drive inside her.

I lift her up, and she automatically wraps her gorgeous legs around my waist. My palm slips under the hem of the ridiculously short dress she's wearing, meeting smooth, bare flesh and my cock jerks in anticipation. I wasn't lying when I told her I haven't been this horny in ages. This girl has seriously turned me on, and I can't wait to get her writhing underneath me.

Placing her down flat on the bed, I hover over her on my knees. "Are you sure this is what you want?" I ask her again, because a guy can never ask too many times.

"Hundo P," she confirms in a breathy tone, betraying evidence of her age.

Back at the bar, I had given no consideration to her age until I got up closer. Despite the band around her wrist suggesting she was twenty-one or older, I guessed she was younger. Before we left, I asked her outright, almost changing my mind when she confirmed she was only eighteen.

At twenty-six, I'm a good bit older, and I rarely go for women who are that young. But there's just something about her. And she's obviously as into this as I am, so where's the harm? It'll be one night of fun, and then we'll never see each other again. I don't see it as an issue.

She sits up, stroking my cock through my jeans, and any last-minute reservations fly out the window. I rip my shirt up over my head, fighting a knowing grin as her jaw slackens at the sight of my naked chest. "Fuck. Me," she blurts, her eyes mentally caressing me.

"I fully intend to, sweetheart." I stretch around to unzip her dress. "Take it off," I command as I stand, quickly getting rid of my jeans and shoes. She stands up on the bed, shimmying the dress down her hips and kicking it away. My cock throbs, precum leaking out of the tip, as I drink her in. She's so sexy standing in front of me in a black lace thong and matching bra, with her hands on her slim hips, shooting me dark, seductive looks. But there's also an innocence about her that's endearing.

As soon as the thought pops into my head, another unwelcome one does. I want to ignore it, but I can't. I crawl onto the bed in just my boxers and pull her down onto my lap. "You have done this before, right?"

"Of course," she squeaks, and I instantly know it's a lie.

"Fuck." I lift her off me, rubbing my hands down my face. "I know that's a lie, and I can't do this. I'm sorry." I lean over the end of the bed, reaching for my jeans.

"Because you don't fuck virgins, or some other reason?" she asks, hurt lacing her tone.

I cup her face. "Because your first time shouldn't be like this." I peer into her beautiful blue eyes, wishing I could be selfish enough to forego doing the right thing. "You won't ever get your first time back, and it should be with someone you love."

She straddles my lap before I can stop her, resting her hands on my shoulder. "Was yours?"

"Fuck, no," I admit before I think to lie. "And I've regretted it ever since."

"Why?" Genuine curiosity is etched across her face. "Because you didn't love her, or it wasn't any good?"

"Both, although I'm just as much to blame as she was. I didn't have a fucking clue how to pleasure a woman back then."

A triumphant glimmer appears in her eyes. "And that's exactly why I want to do this with you. Why I set out to lose my V-card tonight to an older guy."

My eyes almost bug out of my head. "You had this planned?"

She nods before frowning. "Well, not with you, because you were the one who approached me. But, yes, I wanted to do the deed tonight. I'm only in the city for the weekend, and I don't want to waste the perfect opportunity."

She runs her fingers along the fine hairs at the nape of my neck, and fuck, if I don't feel it in every part of me. This girl's touch affects me in a way I haven't felt in years.

That's another good reason to get the fuck out of here, but I'm stalling, because she intrigues me.

And my cock's still stiff as a brick, and he's a greedy motherfucker who doesn't understand what it means to have a moral code.

I shouldn't be contemplating this, but I know, deep down, that I haven't completely ruled it out. "Why now? And why a stranger?" I inquire, smoothing a hand up and down her spine. Her skin is like silk under my callused fingers which isn't helping my cause.

"Because I'm ready. I want to have sex. I want to explore that side of myself that's undiscovered. If I'd found someone back home I'd wanted to have sex with, then I wouldn't be a virgin, but there's been no one, and I..." She trails off, her brow furrowing as she tries to find the right words. Her brow smooths out, and she smiles at me, digging her fingers into my hair as she speaks.

"I want it to be memorable. Most all my friends said it was a non-event, and I don't want that. I want to remember tonight for years to come. I know I could find someone to hook up with when I start college, but I don't want to give it away to some guy with fumbling hands and a lack of regard for my needs."

Her confidence is super sexy, and I work hard to swallow my lustful growl.

"I want it to be with someone who knows what he's doing," she continues. "Someone who will make it enjoyable for me. Someone who will ensure it's a pleasant memory." She kisses me sweetly. "Someone like you."

She sits back on her heels, examining my face carefully. "But I won't beg for it either." She straightens her spine, drilling me with a determined look. "I'm eighteen, and I know what I want. There's nothing wrong with you and me being together like this, but if you can't get past the fact I'm young and inexperienced, then it's best we end this right now."

"I get why your friend was so protective now," I murmur, resting my hand gently on her hip.

"Jordy and Hannah are the best, and I love them for worrying about me, but this is my decision, and they ultimately respect that." Her eyes penetrate mine. "I have given this a lot of consideration, and I know what I want. I want to have sex with you." She leans in and kisses me deeply before pulling back, her face flushed, her lips slightly swollen. "So, what's it to be? Will you fuck me?"

Her eyes glimmer with challenge and determination, but I detect the vulnerability she's working hard to disguise. Rejecting her would hurt her, and I don't want to dent her confidence or cause her any pain.

She wants this.

I want this.

And I *will* make it good for her.

I can give her what she wants, and we'll both walk out of here happy and sated.

Gripping her hips, I pull her body in tight against mine. "No. I will not fuck you." She opens her mouth to respond, but I place my fingers over her lips, silencing her. "I will make love to you, because that's the way it should be when it's your first time." Taking her wrist, I plant a tender kiss to her skin, loving how she shivers at my touch. "I'll ask you one final time. And whatever way you answer is fine." I kiss her wrist again, never taking my eyes off her. "Are you sure you want to do this with me?"

She nods her head enthusiastically. "Yes. I want you to make love to me. I'm even more sure now." Reaching around, she unclasps her bra, quickly tossing it aside, baring her naked chest.

My eyes lock on her tits, and my cock throbs behind my boxers. They're small, but a decent handful, and perfectly formed with pert rose-colored nipples. I'm already salivating, my body desperate to be inside her. "You're so beautiful." I kiss her lips before lowering my head to her left nipple, gently sucking it into my mouth. Her skin is so soft and pliable, her small bud tightening the minute my mouth suctions on it. I tenderly knead her other breast, enjoying the little moans she emits as her hips rock against me. I trail my nose along the delicate skin of her exposed neck before I devour her mouth with all the pent-up need mushrooming inside me.

Flipping us around, I place her flat on the bed, resting her head on top of the pillows. I kiss her for a few minutes until she's moaning and writhing underneath me, and then I work my way down her body, kissing, sucking, licking, and caressing every inch of her beautiful skin before lowering my mouth to her pussy, inhaling her intoxicating scent.

"Please," she whimpers, bucking her hips up as I rub my nose along her slit through the thin lacy material.

Hooking my thumbs in the side of her thong, I slide it down her legs and off her body. I stand, my eyes drinking in her gorgeous nakedness as I kick off my boxers and grab a couple condoms. My dick pulses as she feasts on it with her eyes, licking her lips as her eyelids darken with lust. I crawl up over her body, tossing the condoms on the bedside table. "You are fucking gorgeous, and I'm feeling very honored," I admit over her lips as I keep my body propped up by my elbows.

"Well, thanks, but could you stop talking now and get in me already?" She quirks a brow as she grabs hold of my ass, pulling me down on top of her.

I chuckle before brushing my lips against hers. "So impatient." I shake my head, grinning. "I need to make sure you're ready. Trust me to do this the right way."

She wraps her legs around my waist, angling her hips up into me, and I groan as my cock presses against her silky, warm flesh. "Trust me, I'm ready. If I was any wetter, we'd both be drowning."

A laugh bursts free of me. "Are you always this direct?"

"Always." She smiles as her hands absentmindedly caress the cheeks of my ass, causing precum to leak from the tip of my cock. "In my family, we have a rule we always speak our minds." She shrugs. "And no one lets an argument or emotions fester. I've grown up with straight talking, and I don't know any other way to be."

In a lot of ways, I could say the same of my family. Except for the festering part, but I shove those thoughts aside before they distract me. "I like that." I slide down her body, watching her eyes roll back in her head as I kiss my way along her hot flesh. "I like you."

"I like you too," she pants. "But I'd like you a lot more if you got to it."

I chuckle against her stomach as I move lower. Pushing her legs aside, I sink to the apex of her thighs, licking my lips in anticipation. "Has anyone ever gone down on you before?" I ask as I line my mouth up with her glistening pussy.

"Yes. I'm a virgin, but I'm not completely inexperienced."

I scowl at her response, not liking the thought of anyone touching any part of her, before I realize how hypocritical my thoughts are. "Well, buckle down, honey, because no one has eaten you like this." Before she can reply, I plant my mouth against her inviting pussy and ravish her with my tongue and my lips.

She is absolutely drenched, yet when I push a finger inside her she's so tight I almost change my mind. But my dick won't let me. And I don't want to disappoint the gorgeous girl moaning and squirming on the bed.

Slowly, I work my finger in and out until I feel her loosen up, and then I add another one. When her moans ratchet up, and she's arching her back off the bed, I suction my mouth over her clit and suck hard as my fingers continue to pump in and out of her, going faster and faster until she detonates, shattering under my touch in a way that sends my heart soaring. I watch her as my fingers and mouth continue to milk her climax, and the look of sheer bliss on her face almost has me coming on the spot.

When her body relaxes, I move up to kiss her before grabbing a condom.

"Let me." She takes it from my hands, rolling it down over my aching cock. "You're huge," she exclaims, a look of concern washing over her face for the first time. "Are you sure that thing'll fit in me?"

I work hard to smother a smile. "It'll fit and I'll take it slow. I promise." Gently, I push her down, lowering my body carefully against hers. I kiss her long and hard, peppering her face and neck with kisses while skimming my hands over her body, caressing her lush curves.

Her body is toned yet supple, and I could touch her all day long and never tire. I dip my finger inside her once more to check she's ready. Then I line up my cock and slowly inch inside her, keeping my face locked on hers the whole time. "If you want me to stop, you only have to ask." I stall as a glimmer of pain flashes in her eyes. "It will hurt a little at first," I confirm so she knows what to expect.

"I'm good," she rasps. "Don't stop. Just go slow."

It takes colossal willpower to hold myself back, but I do, because I don't want to hurt her. When I feel myself pushing through the tight ridge, I stop, watching her expression carefully. "You okay?"

"Keep going," she says through gritted teeth, and I push on until I'm fully seated inside her.

The feeling is indescribable.

Her walls hug my cock, and I know I won't last long. I move really slowly as I kiss her, my hands caressing her breasts while I carefully plunge in and out of her. Gradually, I feel her softening, and she moves instinctively against me.

"Faster," she pants, digging her fingers into the cheeks of my ass and tightening her legs around my waist.

I rock into her faster, still holding back, all the time kissing and worshiping her body. When I feel her gripping me tighter and her body tenses up with impending climax, I lose my restraint, pumping into her more rapidly, allowing myself to let go. She orgasms a split second before I do, and our joint mutual groaning and heavy breathing fills the air. My skin is slick with sweat as I pump my hips two final times before collapsing on the bed, pulling her with me, keeping our bodies fused together.

Pushing damp tendrils of hair back off her glowing face, I peer deep into her eyes. "Are you all right?" I examine every inch of her face to gauge her mood. "Was that okay?"

"I'm just perfect." Her smile is radiant as she beams at me. "And it was more than okay. That was amazing. Now I understand what all the fuss is about."

I cup her face and press a tender kiss to her lips. "That was incredible. Thank you."

Her arms encircle my neck, and she pushes her delectable tits into my chest. Her eyes sparkle with mischief as she grins at me. "How soon can you be ready to go again?"

My cock instantly hardens at her words, and I push my hips into hers, ensuring she feels what she's doing to me. "How soon is too soon?"

In a flash, she's straddling me, her long hair cascading down her back as she rocks on top of me in a seductive pose that cranks my lust to a new all-time high. "No such thing as too soon," she purrs, grinding down on my cock, and I can't contain my grin as I grab a fresh condom from the bedside table.

Chapter Three
Summer

"Two-bed places will be scarce at this late stage," my brother Charlie says on Sunday evening as we tuck into the sumptuous pot roast dinner Mom made.

"I'm confident we'll find something," I reply, in between mouthfuls of gorgeous beef, not overly worried, even if our apartment-hunting expedition this weekend was unsuccessful.

Jordan's last-minute decision to join Hannah and me at the University of Delaware has messed up our plans. Before, us girls were happy to share a dorm room, but now, we're apartment hunting off campus so we can all live together.

"I'm sure Austin will let you stay with him if you can't find a place," Mom says, adding another dollop of creamy mashed potatoes to my plate.

I almost choke on the lump of beef in my mouth. "I'm sure Austin does not want me cramping his style," I splutter.

"Or cramping yours," Charlie teases with a wink, and I discharge a "shut the fuck up" look in his direction.

"Besides, he doesn't have room for all three of us."

"I don't know why you think it's a good idea to move in with a couple anyway," Charlie says, pushing his empty plate away and rubbing his flat stomach. "That was awesome, Mom. Thanks."

Mom removes his empty plate, messing up his dark hair, before leaning in to kiss his cheek.

"They're my best friends. And I don't want to share with a stranger."

A knowing smile slips over my mouth at the mention of the word *stranger* as my mind instantly conjures up images of Friday night and my tangle between the sheets with a hot, sexy stranger. My body tingles all over, and my core aches, reminding me I'm still sore after our marathon sex session. I never knew I could contort my body into so many positions or that I could orgasm so many times, especially as a complete novice, but Ryan worked my body like a pro, and I was putty in his skillful hands. We didn't catch a wink of sleep all night, and we couldn't get enough of one another. He was so gentle and considerate, and I really couldn't have chosen a better guy to do the deed with.

It was, hands down, the most amazing night of my life.

"Why are you grinning like a crazy person?" Charlie asks, his blue eyes narrowing suspiciously. My youngest brother graduated from UD recently with a degree in agriculture and natural resources, so he's well attuned to college life, and I'm guessing he understands this past weekend was about more than just apartment hunting.

"I'm just happy. Is there a law against that?" I retort, offering him my sweetest smile.

"Uh-huh." He eyeballs me with intensity. "Maybe you *should* stay with Austin."

"Don't start." I roll my eyes. "You need to quit the protective big brother shit. That might've worked when I was still in high school, but I'm eighteen and starting college soon. You, Austin, and Marc don't get to pull that crap on me anymore."

"That's what I'm afraid of." He scrubs his hand across the thin layer of stubble on his chin. "College guys are horny fucking bastards,

Sum. You need to watch yourself. Especially with those frat boys. They are total fucking manwhores."

"Charles Benjamin Petersen." Mom admonishes Charlie with a slap to the back of the head. "I will not tolerate that foul language at the dinner table."

"Aw, come on, Ma." He rubs the back of his head. "I'm only looking out for my baby sister." He accepts a cup of steaming hot coffee from her with an innocent smile plastered upon his face.

"You can look out for your sister without resorting to cussing," Dad says, finally lifting his head from his newspaper. "No disrespecting your momma."

"Sorry, Mom." Charlie looks sheepish, and I grin, pleased it focuses the conversation on my brother and not his statement.

But the reprieve doesn't last long.

"Your brother has a point though," Mom adds, pinning me with her serious face as she takes my half-eaten plate away and hands me a coffee. I groan, mentally preparing myself for it. "I know you're on the pill, but make sure you always use a condom. *Always*. Trust none of those boys, no matter what loving endearments they whisper in your ear."

Charlie spits coffee all over the table, and Dad turns pale. "Jeez, Mom. You shouldn't be encouraging that sh—stuff."

"Give it a rest." I roll my eyes again as I mop up the mess he made with a paper towel. "It's not like I'm going to sleep my way through campus or anything close to it."

Although I plan on indulging my newly discovered sexual appetite whenever I feel like it, it doesn't mean I won't be safe. I'm not completely reckless. But now I've gotten a taste for sex, there's no holding me back.

"What about young Justin?" Dad muses, putting his paper down and giving me his full, undivided attention. "I always thought he was sweet on you. You should date him."

My eyes almost bug out of my head remembering all the times Dad sent less than friendly vibes in Justin's direction any time he dropped by our farmhouse. "Justin's a friend, Dad. Besides, he has a full ride to Oregon State, and he'll be thousands of miles away from me."

"Exactly my point." He wiggles his eyebrows, and his tan, weather-beaten brow creases with the motion.

"Benny." Mom shakes her head, strands of reddish-brown hair tumbling around her face with the motion. "Summer can date who ever she pleases, and you'll just have to get used to it." Her tone brooks no argument, and I'm glad to have at least one member of my family on my side. "She's not your little princess anymore."

"I'll always be your princess, Daddy," I refute, getting up and pressing a kiss atop his head, noticing more gray hairs among the dark strands. "Having sex with boys won't change that."

This time, it's Dad's turn to choke on his coffee.

"I'm calling Austin," Charlie cuts in, removing his cell from the pocket of his jeans to phone my eldest brother. "If you room with him, he can at least vet the guys first."

I snatch the cell from his hand before he can make the call. "If you're trying to deliberately piss me off, you're doing a stand-up job." I faux glare at my brother. "For the last time, I am *not* staying with Austin. I'm perfectly capable of vetting guys myself, but thanks a bunch for the vote of confidence."

"I literally cannot wait to get out of here," I grumble to Hannah an hour later, flopping down on her bed. "You should've heard the crap coming out of Dad's and Charlie's mouths. Their attitudes are like something from the Dark Ages."

"Charlie's just spent four years fucking his way around UD, so he's probably right to worry," she unhelpfully adds.

"I don't know if that's true, but if it is, then he's a total hypocrite. Of all my brothers, he's usually the one I can count on to have my back, but he put Austin and Marc to shame today. It's not as if I'm planning on riding the entire male campus. It's ridiculous."

She nudges me in the side, grinning. "Imagine the hissy fit he'd throw if he knew about Friday night."

Rolling onto my stomach beside her, I laugh. "Oh, my god. He'd blow a gasket. They all would." I prop my head up with my hand, facing her. "It's just as well I won't ever see Ryan again. It's safer for him that way," I quip.

"I don't know how you can do that."

"Do what?"

"Have an incredible night of amazing sex with an awesome guy and just walk away knowing you'll never set eyes on him again. Aren't you even the tiniest bit tempted to hook up with him again?"

"Nope," I instantly reply, popping the P. "It was a onetime deal, and we're both happy with that even if I have been replaying every second of my time with him on a continual loop in my head." I roll onto my back, smiling up at the ceiling like the cat that got the cream. "He was truly something else."

"You know Jordy still has a copy of his driver's license on his cell. If you want to contact him, I can get his name and address for you."

I shake my head. "Tell him to delete it. I won't be contacting Ryan again. As hot as he is, and as incredible as the sex was, I don't want to be tied down, and I very much doubt he's interested in dating a college freshman. In fact, I got the distinct impression he doesn't date, but he clearly hooks up. *A lot.* Because he had all the right moves."

There's a dreamy quality to my voice, like every time I think of him. And I want to retain that feel-good factor. Attempting something more could ruin all the good memories I have of him, that night, and handing over my V-card.

Hannah copies my move, and we lie side by side on her bed, both staring up at the ceiling. "I'm so glad your first time was a good experience. You were right to wait and do it like you did."

"I have no regrets," I honestly admit, turning my head to look at her. "My only fear is he's set an impossibly high standard now. That no college guy will ever measure up."

"You could have fun testing that theory out," Hannah suggests, smiling wickedly.

"That I can," I agree, with a matching smile.

August can't come quick enough.

"So, I hear someone's no longer in possession of her V-card," Justin says with a cheeky grin on Friday night as we sit on the bed of Jordy's truck at the side of the field.

"If your bestie wasn't so busy groping my bestie, I'd punch him in the nuts for telling you that." Not that I specifically asked Jordan to keep it private, but it was an unspoken rule.

"I won't tell another soul. I was just teasing."

I dangle my legs off the edge of the truck as I take another sip of my warm beer. Out on the field below us, the party is in full swing. "It's cool. I'll be out of here in a few weeks, and I give zero fucks after I'm gone."

"You say that like you plan on never coming back home."

I shrug. "I'll be back. The rents would never let me get away without regular visits, but I don't plan on settling back here after I graduate. I want to go traveling for a year or two, and then I'll probably move permanently to the city if I can get a teaching job somewhere close by."

"You have it all worked out."

I snort. "Hardly." I nudge his shoulder. "I have a rough plan for my life, but I'm deliberately keeping it loose so I can take advantage of any amazing opportunities that come my way. This feels like the start of something epic, and I never want to lose that feeling."

"I admire you so much, Sum. You haven't changed since you were a kid, and you're still the same sweet, adventurous girl I remember."

Thinking back to last weekend, I'm wondering how sweet he'd think I was if he knew the things I let Ryan do to me. "Knock it off, dude." I elbow him in the ribs. "If anyone has his head screwed on right, it's you. You've always wanted to play ball in college and join the NFL, and you're on track to achieve your goals." I smile up at him. "I. Admire. You."

"Promise me you'll keep in touch. I'll really miss you." His voice softens, and I lift my eyes to meet his piercing green ones.

"Aw, are you getting all sentimental on me, Juju?" I joke, using the pet name I gave him when we started high school.

"I am, Sunshine." He raises my pet name with one of his own making. We exchange identical grins. "I've spent years dreaming of playing college football, and I'm fucking ecstatic about playing for the Beavers. But I'm feeling a little nostalgic these last few weeks, and one part of me hates that everything's changing."

He shrugs, and, for a split second, he looks so sad. Wanting to take that look off his face, I scoot over right beside him, wrap my arm around his back, and snuggle into his side. "That's only natural," I say to appease him, because I'm feeling zero nostalgia at the prospect of moving away for college. But I'm only moving to Newark, which is under two hours away. I can come home anytime I feel homesick. Maybe I'd feel differently if I was moving clear across the country like Justin is. "I'm sure you'll be fine once you adjust. You'll be too busy with classes, football, and hooking up with hot college chicks to feel homesick or lonely," I add in a jokey tone, trying to lighten the moment.

"Yeah, probably," he agrees, wrapping both arms around me, and holding me close. We're not usually this touchy-feely, but I'm sensing Justin needs this now, and there's nothing wrong with two old friends hugging one another. We're both quiet, silently watching the party rage on in the distance while trying to ignore the moans and groans coming from the front of the truck.

"Sum," Justin says after a few beats, tilting my chin up with his finger. I look into his eyes, confused when I see his expression. "Do you ever wonder what would've happened if we'd kept dating?"

Calling the few kisses we shared back in the early days dating is a stretch, but I'm not about to split hairs with him. "Not really," I truthfully admit.

"Why didn't we?" he whispers as his eyes drift to my mouth.

I gulp over the sudden lump of nervousness wedged in my throat. "Because we weren't feeling it," I remind him.

"Maybe the timing wasn't right," he whispers, his eyes searching mine for permission as he lowers his head toward me.

I should pull back, because starting something with one of my best friends just before we separate for college is not a good idea, but there's a part of me that's curious to see if Justin's kiss will ignite my blood the way Ryan's kiss did.

The curious part wins, and, as Justin moves in for the kill, I offer no resistance, letting him kiss me.

Chapter Four
Ryan

"Are you sure you're okay with this, man?" Austin asks me for the umpteenth time, as we carry the new mattress into the spare guest bedroom.

"It's cool. She's your sister. We can hardly leave her stranded with no place to stay." We drop the mattress down onto the bedframe, walking back out to our living area.

We only moved into this apartment five months ago, just as we celebrated one year in business.

Although it's early days, the state-of-the-art gym we own and run together is doing better than expected, and our membership is growing exponentially as word of mouth increases.

Being ahead of our five-year plan so early in the game is encouraging, and we're both excited for the future. It's a shit-ton of hard work, and neither of us has much downtime which is one reason why I don't mind that Austin's baby sister Summer is moving in with us for a while. This place is empty often, and it's not like I'll see that much of her, anyway.

"Hopefully, a place will free up in one of the freshman dorms and this is only a short-term thing," Austin adds, grabbing a couple bottles of water from the refrigerator and tossing one to me.

"I'm back!" Miley calls out as the front door slams. Her face lights up as she rounds the corner and sees her boyfriend. "I got the cutest bed set for your sister," she says, placing her shopping bags on the kitchen counter before waltzing into Austin's open arms.

It's actually kinda funny to see him like this. I met Austin freshman year of UD, and we instantly clicked. We moved into a house off campus with my best buddy Slater and another mutual friend, Michael, during our sophomore year, and we all lived together until we graduated.

It's fair to say all of us enjoyed the college life until Michael had to move back home to care for his sick dad, Slate fell for my sister Gabby, and I ended up dating her best friend Myndi. Austin was the only single one in the house for a couple years, and he made the most of it. It was around that time we resorted to calling him Powers in a nod to Austin Powers, the legendary manwhore extraordinaire.

When I want to piss Austin off, I call him Powers in front of Miley, and it never fails to rile him up.

In all the time I've known him, he's never had a steady girlfriend. Until now. The instant we hired Miley to work the front desk at the gym, I knew my buddy was smitten. It didn't take him long to convince her to go out with him, and they've been together four months now, and it's getting more serious by the day. I'm happy for him although I've lost my wingman, and sometimes it's difficult being around them because it reminds me of what I had with Myndi.

As usually happens, my mood dips to the floor as soon as thoughts of my ex enter my mind, and I work hard to consciously evict her from my head. Thinking of that shit doesn't do me any good.

"I'll dress her bed and finish the room," Miley says, pecking Austin on the lips one final time. "I hope she likes it."

"She'll love it, babe." Austin can't resist kissing his girl again. "Summer's very laid-back, and she'll be delighted you went to so much trouble for her."

"I'm so excited to meet her," Miley adds, bouncing on her feet, her loose blonde curls swaying with the motion. "Having another girl around here regularly will be nice." Planting her hands on her shapely hips, she drills me with a pointed look, her warm brown eyes chastising me. "Instead of dealing with the rotating line of females out of your bedroom."

I shrug, casting a grin her way. "Can't help it if the ladies want to sample my goods. Who am I to deprive the lovely ladies of Newark of the opportunity of a lifetime?"

She rolls her eyes. "I swear, your ego gets bigger every time we talk."

"Just stating the facts."

"Yeah, about that." Austin rubs the back of his neck, looking a little sheepish as his blue eyes follow his girlfriend out of the room. "Could you dial things back while Summer's here? She's only eighteen and way too impressionable. Those assholes on campus will be all over her. I have my work cut out trying to protect her as it is. Last thing I need is her seeing your revolving door of hookups and getting ideas."

Mention of her being eighteen brings me back to my hookup from last month. I don't even know her name, but she left a lasting impression. For reasons unknown, I haven't been able to shake her from my mind. And I've had zero interest in screwing any woman since which is most unlike me.

When I close my eyes in bed, I replay every second of that incredible night we spent together, and I can almost feel her pliant, warm body underneath me.

Almost smell the sweet scent of her perfume.

Almost hear the exquisite sounds she made as she came apart in my arms.

The fact she trusted me enough to give me her virginity blows my mind. And while I know I rocked her world, there's no denying she rocked mine too. There was nothing about the experience that was in any way uncomfortable. It felt as natural as breathing, and that

Siobhan Davis

unnerves me. No sexual encounter has ever affected me as much, and my preoccupation with it, with *her*, has raised alarm bells I haven't heard in years.

I'm glad we parted ways without exchanging contact details, because I have a feeling that girl would've been dangerous for my heart.

Austin flicks his fingers in my face, dragging me out of my mind. "Earth to James. Where'd you go, man?"

"What were you saying?"

"Can you go easy on the hookups while Sum's here?"

"In case you hadn't noticed, I haven't been hooking up that much lately anyway, so it's cool." I clamp my hand on his shoulder. "I'd do anything for Gabby, so I get it."

"That's another thing," he adds, looking awkward. "You can't hit on her. She's off-limits to you."

I'm surprised he's gone there. He should know he doesn't need to articulate it. But now he has, I'm going there too. "Pity *you* didn't get that memo when my sister was living with us." I pin him with a knowing look.

"I only kissed Gabby one time. It was nothing. And she's happily married now, so no harm done." He shoots me a wolfish look, and I decide to mess with him.

"So, I can kiss Summer, and you'd be fine with that?"

"Hell to the no!" He glares at me. "If you put your mouth, or any part of your anatomy, anywhere near my sister, I will throw you off the roof of this building." He crosses his arms over his chest, narrowing his eyes in warning. "Don't think I'm joking. I mean it, James. She's too innocent, too fucking young, for you. Keep your hands to yourself."

I chuckle. "You're too easy to wind up, Powers. Relax. I won't touch your little sister. Scout's honor." I salute him, and he flips me the bird, just as my cell vibrates in my pocket. I grin as I spot the caller. "Speak of the devil," I tell my sister as I answer her call. "Powers and I were just talking about you."

504

"So that's why my ears are burning," Gabby quips down the line.

"Powers was just reminiscing about what a fantastic kisser you are."

Austin flips me the bird again, shouting into my cell. "Your brother is an asshole."

Gabby laughs. "Tell him I agree, and why has it taken him so long to work that one out?"

"I'll tell him no such thing." I prop my butt on the back of the couch and cross my feet at the ankles. "So, what's up?"

"We're having dinner here on Sunday, and we want you, Austin, and Miley to come."

"I don't know if we can get away, Tornado. The gym is getting busier by the day."

"I'm glad to hear it's going well, but I'd never have invested in your new business if I knew it meant I'd hardly get to see you. We miss you. Especially Billy and Daisy. We haven't seen you in ages. Can you not get someone to cover for a few hours?"

Her pleading tone works as an effective guilt trip. It *has* been ages since I've caught up with Slate and my sister, and I miss my nephew and little niece.

"The whole fam will be here, and everyone's dying to see you," she continues, adding more guilt on the pile. "*Please*, Ryan. Just come for a couple hours." Gabby and I have always been super close, and, while I have a great relationship with my two older brothers too, I've always had a special bond with my only sister. I struggle to say no to her. "Okay, I'll work something out." Her contented sigh trickles down the line. "Hang on a sec. Let me talk to Austin."

I put my cell down to address my buddy. "Gabby and Slate have invited us to their place for dinner on Sunday. We can get Derrick to cover, right?"

While Austin and I manage the business on a rotational basis between us, Derrick is one of the personal trainers we employed from the start and the only other guy we trust to look after stuff in our absence. He's filled in a few times when we've both had outside plans, and he knows the ropes.

"Sure. I'll message him now. Tell Gabby we'll be there."

I lift my cell to my ear. "You hear that?"

"Yep. I'm so happy you guys are coming, and tell Miley not to bring anything but herself this time."

"Austin's sister Summer might come too. She's moving in with us for a while."

"The more, the merrier, and I look forward to meeting her." We shoot the shit for another few minutes, and I end the call when the doorbell chimes.

Miley comes racing out of the guest bedroom. "I'll get it!" she squeals, rushing past Austin toward the front door like she's on skates.

"Wow. Enthusiastic much?" I say to Austin, re-pocketing my cell.

He grins, running a hand through his short brown hair. "If you think Miley's excitable, wait until you meet Summer. I have a feeling those two will hit it off."

"You're really selling it, dude," I deadpan, wondering exactly what I've agreed to. Excited chatter drifts toward us, and Austin grins wider. I know he's happy she will be staying with us, and I can't fault him for that. His family is close knit, like mine, and from the way he's spoken about his only sister over the years, I know he loves her in the same way I love Gabby.

Pushing off the couch, I straighten up, plastering a welcoming smile on my mouth as the girls round the corner and come into view.

All the blood drains from my face when I lock eyes with Austin's beautiful sister.

Fuck my life.

This cannot be happening.

Summer's familiar blue gaze widens in shock for a split second before she hurriedly composes herself. Austin sweeps her up into his arms, oblivious to the sudden tension in the air and the furious beating of my heart.

Out of all the girls in this city, I had to sleep with the one girl completely off-limits. Austin will literally kill me if he finds out I had sex with his baby sister. Worse, that I took her virginity.

Summer stares, bug-eyed, at me over his shoulder as he hugs her, clearly as shocked as I am.

"Don't say a word," I mouth to her. At least not until I've had time to talk to her alone and we can work out what the hell we're going to do.

"Well, duh," she mouths back, rolling her eyes, and my lips twitch at the corners.

"Let me look at you," Austin says, shucking out of her embrace and holding her at arm's length. "You look different," he adds. "But I can't put my finger on what it is."

My eyes subtly glance over her. She has her dark hair tied back in some kind of messy bun, which only serves to highlight her stunning face. Her skin is devoid of makeup, and it's flawless with a light dusting of freckles across her nose and upper cheeks. Her eyes are big and bright, and it's cheesy as fuck to say this, but she glows.

She exudes warmth and vitality, and the first impression I had of her wasn't wrong. She's so comfortable in her skin, betraying maturity that belies her age. I can't imagine anything fazing this girl, and what you see is what you get. There is no pretense or falseness about her, and it's refreshingly different.

No wonder I've struggled to forget her.

She's wearing a tank top under an open blue-and-pink checkered button-down shirt and minuscule jeans shorts. My eyes are glued to her long, lean, bare legs, and my cock twitches as visions of our hookup resurrect in my mind's eye. I'm picturing how her legs were wrapped around my neck as I plunged deep inside her, and I still remember how silky smooth her skin felt under my hands as I traced my fingers up and down her legs while I fucked her.

My cock is now straining against the front of my jeans, and I'm terrified Powers will notice. *Down, boy*, I caution, forcing the image of a naked Summer from my mind. I think of the most mundane things while willing my hard-on to deflate.

"What's different?" Austin asks her again with a slight frown. "Did you do something with your hair?"

She shakes her head, fighting a grin. I think I understand why she appears different to her brother, and I rub a tense spot between my brows as I consider the clusterfuck my life has just become.

A massive smile graces Summer's lush mouth as she grins at her brother. "I'm all grown up now, Austin." She flicks a subtle glance in my direction. "In every sense of the word. Maybe you're finally noticing that."

Chapter Five

Summer

"**Y**ou better not be saying what I think you're saying," my overbearing big brother spews, his handsome face turning an unflattering shade of red.

"I am, and you'll get over it." I offer him a sweet smile, trying to ignore the fact my heart is trying to beat a path out of my chest.

I cannot believe the guy I gave my virginity to is standing right over there.

And I have no clue who he is to my brother.

He looks scared shitless at the direction our conversation has taken, but he shouldn't worry. There's no way in hell I'm telling my brother what went down between us. I won't have Ryan's murder on my conscience.

Austin splutters, for once lost for words. Miley loops her arm through mine, winking conspiratorially at me. I've known her for all of five seconds, and I already know I'll love her. Although, I suspected I would. The girl who tamed my big brother is clearly someone special.

"Aren't you going to introduce me?" I ask Austin, quirking a brow as I motion toward the spot where a mute Ryan is standing.

"Uh, yeah." Austin scrubs the back of his neck, and I stifle a laugh. My veiled confession has really thrown him for a loop. I swear he still looks at me like I'm five sometimes.

In some ways, I'm not as close to Austin as I am to Marc and Charlie purely because of the eight-year age gap. Austin left for college when I was ten, and though he visited regularly, he missed out on most of my childhood. In other ways, my relationship with him feels closer, more natural, and more akin to friends than siblings.

Unless it comes to the subject of boys.

Then he's every bit as smothering as my other two brothers.

"This is my buddy James. Say hi to your new roomie."

New roomie? Oh, hell to the no. Someone please pinch me. This cannot be real. *He's* Austin's roommate, friend, and business partner? I don't understand. The world spins for a split second, and I'm confused. Did Ryan lie about his name that night in the club?

"Nice to meet you, Summer," Ryan, James, whatever the hell his name is, says, stepping toward me and extending his hand.

"Likewise." I drill him with a penetrating look as I grip his large palm firmly. Fuck, he's even more gorgeous in the light of day, and my memory has not done him justice at all.

His dark denims hug his muscular thighs like a second skin, and his tight T-shirt highlights his ripped arms and chest to perfection. He returns my intense gaze with one of his own as we shake hands, and desire coils low in my belly. Delicious tingles whip up my arm once we make skin-to-skin contact, almost like I've been electrocuted.

His eyes darken momentarily, letting me know he felt it too.

Interesting. I'd supposed my reaction to him that night was one-sided because it was all so new. Now, I'm wondering if there isn't more to our chemistry. Not that I want to explore it. The fact he's my new roomie is an added complication I don't need.

"Where's your stuff?" Austin asks, his brow creasing as he looks to where my hand is still joined with Ryan's.

I let go and dig my car keys out of my pocket. "In the trunk of my car. Have at it, big bro." I waggle my brows at him, dropping the keys in his palm, and Miley giggles.

"I'll help," Ryan offers, and the guys leave as I allow Miley to escort me to my new bedroom.

"I hope you like it," she says, nervously opening the door. "I painted it, and the guys assembled all the furniture." She waves her arms around the room. "But if you don't like anything, we can return it to the store, and you can pick replacements. We can even repaint it."

The room is much larger than I was expecting with muted gray walls and a big window, which lets in lots of light. The focal point is a king-size bed covered in a pristine white comforter. A pale pink velvet quilt and an abundance of gray and pink fluffy cushions elevate it from something simple to something elegant. Two framed prints in complementary colors hang on the wall behind the bed, and two white bedside tables rest on either side. One has a small pink lamp atop it, and the other has a potted plant. A desk and overhead shelving unit on the right-hand side of the room will come in handy once classes start. The only other furniture in the room is a three-door fitted closet off on the left.

"This is amazing." I spin around to Miley, flinging my arms around her. "I love it, and I wouldn't change a single thing. Thank you so much." She hugs me back with the same enthusiasm, and I'm thinking maybe living with my brother won't be as bad as I expected, provided Miley's around.

"Told ya," Austin says, smirking at Ryan as they enter the room, depositing my bags and boxes on the floor.

"Told him what?" I inquire.

"That you two would hit it off." Austin pulls Miley into his arms, kissing the top of her blonde head, and my heart swoons.

"If you love her, it stands to reason I'd love her too." I smile at my brother, so happy to see him happy.

He doesn't even flinch at the mention of the 'L' word.

Wow.

My brother really is head over heels for this girl.

"And how could I not after Miley did all this for me?" I cast a glance around the room. "I believe you both helped too. You didn't have to go to so much trouble, but thanks so much. I really appreciate it."

"I think I might have to ditch you in favor of your sister," Miley jokes, squeezing Austin at the waist.

"I wouldn't blame you if you did," Austin instantly replies, pulling me into his other side. "She's pretty fucking awesome."

I laugh, and my eyes meet Ryan's as he hangs back in the doorway with a strange smile on his face. He notices me watching him and he snaps out of it, pinning his gaze on my brother. "Do you want to go out for lunch or eat in?"

"Sum?" Austin eyeballs me. "What do you want to do?"

"I've got to unpack," I explain. "But you guys should go out. I'll grab something later." I could use the time to clear the fog from my brain and try to wrap my head around the fact the guy I gave my virginity to is my new roommate for the next few months.

"Why don't we grab lunch from the deli place around the corner, and then we can all eat here?" Miley suggests, earning herself a kiss from my brother.

"Sounds like a plan," he agrees, taking her hand. "We'll go, and doofus here can put the coffee on." He nudges Ryan in the ribs as he passes by. Ryan stares at me for a minute before following the loving couple out of my bedroom.

Blowing air out of my mouth, I shake my head in disbelief, tossing a bag on my bed. Removing items of clothing, I hang them up in the closet or fold them neatly into the accompanying drawers, while I contemplate the curveball thrown at me.

"Can we talk?" Ryan asks in his deep voice, startling me.

I jump about ten feet in the air, dropping the sweater in my hand. "Don't sneak up on me like that!"

"Your door was open. I was hardly being covert." He ambles into the room with his hands buried in the pockets of his jeans as I quickly shove the sweater into my closet.

"You can't tell him. Like ever," I blurt, plopping onto the bed and patting the space beside me.

"Well, I'm glad we're on the same page. I value breathing," he teases, sitting down beside me.

"As do I," I agree, and he chuckles. "But, seriously, Austin can never know. You've no idea how overprotective he is of me or perhaps you do. Maybe now you realize why I was still a virgin."

"Trust me, I have no desire to ever tell him. He would never forgive me." He looks down at the floor, clenching and unclenching his fists, and I frown. When he looks up at me, remorse is written all over his face. "If I'd known who you were, I'd never have gone through with it."

"Don't do that," I groan, shaking my head. "Don't say you regret it and stomp all over my happy memory."

"I'm not saying I regret it." His features soften, and it would be so easy to get lost in his baby blues. "I don't regret it. Not at all." He cups my face, and my heart races around my chest. I feel his touch all the way through to the tips of my toes. "I could never regret such an amazing night, but I've broken the bro code, and Austin would be furious if he found out. He made me promise to keep my hands off you, but I didn't realize I'd already messed everything up." He worries his lower lip between his teeth, and I have a sudden, almost uncontrollable urge to nip at his lip. I sit on my hands to quell the craving. "Why didn't you mention you were going to college here?"

I arch a brow. "We didn't exactly share personal details other than intimate body parts." My core pulses in remembrance, and I squeeze my thighs together, hoping he doesn't notice.

"True." He grins, and his eyes sparkle, and I get lost in their hypnotic depths. He peers into my eyes, and electricity crackles in the space between us. All the tiny hairs lift on my arms and my mouth is suddenly dry. A muscle clenches in his jaw as he continues to stare at me, and my chest is heaving the longer he looks at me. He's so unbelievably gorgeous, and I don't know how I'm expected to live here with him and keep my hands to myself. He blinks in fast succession, looking up at the ceiling, and it breaks whatever spell we were under. "Austin will never speak to me again if he finds out, and I wouldn't blame him. You're his little sister. If—"

"You didn't know. We didn't know," I rush to reassure him, fighting the urge to reach out and touch him. "Why'd you say your name was Ryan, anyway?"

He looks perplexed. "Because that's my name."

"I thought your name was James?"

His lips kick up at the corner. "My name is Ryan James, but your brother always calls me James."

I nod a couple times. "Ah, now it makes sense. I've heard Austin talk about you for years, but he has always called you James. Not that it really matters. Even if I knew you were Ryan, I would still never have made the connection in a million years. What are the chances, huh?"

"I know, and it's not like it matters. We can't change what happened." He drags a hand through his dirty-blond hair before pinning me with earnest eyes. "But nothing else can happen between us. It was a strictly onetime thing, and you're way too young for me even if you seem older."

"Agreed," I say, ignoring the little stabby pain in my heart. "I never expected to see you again, and I was cool with that. I don't want things to be awkward while I'm living here, so I can forget about it if you can."

He stands, nodding. "Perfect. I'm glad we had this talk." He opens and closes his mouth in quick succession, and I wonder what he's holding back. After a couple beats, he slants me a friendly smile as he backs out of the room. "I'll let you continue your unpacking."

"So, Summer," Miley says, placing her elbows on top of the table. "Do you have a boyfriend?"

"Nope. I want to enjoy the full college experience, and a boyfriend would only get in the way."

"Oh, wow, okay." She emits a tinkling laugh.

"Do I even want to know what the full college experience entails?" Austin asks, ramming the last piece of his sandwich into his mouth.

"Shouldn't you know? Or has it been that long since you graduated you've forgotten?" I push a loose strand of hair back off my face while I perform a mental countdown in my head.

"Don't fucking push me, Sum," Austin warns, and I hadn't even counted to two before he reacted predictably.

I lean back in my chair. "Oh, relax. I doubt I'll be even half as wild as you were."

"Even half would be disastrous," Ryan adds, fighting a smile. "Let's just say your brother made the most of his college experience and leave it at that." He shifts in his chair, and his thigh brushes against mine, heating my body upon contact. Our eyes meet for an infinitesimal moment, a spark igniting in the tiny space between us, until he pulls his leg back and turns his head around.

"Yes, please," Miley cuts in. "It's not like I'm keen to hear old war stories either."

"Babe." Austin slings his arm around her shoulders. "That was the past. You know I only have eyes for you now."

Ryan makes a gagging sound while I sort of melt into a puddle. I would never have thought Austin had it in him to be so romantic, but it's lovely to see.

"Shut your face, dude," Austin says, elbowing his buddy in the ribs. "I still remember how gaga you were for Myndi, and you spouted worse shit, believe me."

The smile instantly wipes off Ryan's face, and his chair screeches in protest as he shoves it back, standing abruptly. Without saying a word, he stacks our empty plates before taking them to the sink.

"Shit, man. I'm sorry," Austin says. "I know better than to mention the she-devil."

I'm dying of curiosity here, but I bite my tongue to stop my probing questions because I can see how tense Ryan is at the mere mention of this girl, whoever she is.

"It's fine," Ryan says through gritted teeth as he rinses the plates before placing them in the dishwasher.

"So, does anyone know of any drama groups in the area?" I ask, deliberately changing the subject in the hope it'll defuse the tension in the air.

"Not by name," Miley says, "but there are a bunch around Newark, and I believe there's a theater company started by students in the college."

"I remember hearing something about that," I say. "I'll check it out next week."

"You act?" Miley asks.

I nod. "I've been a member of the local drama group back home since I was twelve, but it's only a hobby, really. I thought it might be fun to get involved in something new while I'm in college."

"Won't that interfere with your weekend plans?" Austin asks.

"What weekend plans?" I frown. "Is there something you know that I don't?"

"Won't you be flying out to watch the Beavers' games? There's a lot of talk about Justin online. He's definitely on the NFL watch list."

"Who's Justin?" Ryan asks, scowling a little as he retakes his seat alongside me.

"Summer's new boyfriend," Austin unhelpfully supplies, deliberately winding me up.

"He's not my boyfriend. He's just a good friend."

"Charlie said you were dating him."

I roll my eyes. "Charlie's got a big mouth, and he loves to stir shit. He was just trying to wind you up in the hope you'd tighten the leash on me."

"So, Charlie didn't catch you giving Justin head in his truck last weekend?"

"Austin!" Miley pinches his muscly arm, a look of abject horror on her face. "Oh, my god. You can't say stuff like that to your sister!"

I reach over and pat her hand. "In our house, no topic is off-limits. Trust me, before you pay the fam a visit, you'll want to leave your morals and your embarrassment at the front door. You never know what'll pop out of their mouths, so don't say I didn't warn you."

"Nice attempt at deflection." Austin smirks, and I flip him the bird.

"Oh, whatever." I sigh. No point in denying it. Although I'd rather yank my toenails off with tweezers than have this conversation in front of Ryan, Austin will just keep badgering me if I don't fess up. "That was me, but it doesn't mean I'm dating Justin. I'm not. We messed around the last few weeks, but it wasn't anything serious. He's in Oregon, and I'm here. I have zero interest in doing the long-distance thing."

"So why even bother?"

I don't want to explain to my brother how we sort of fell into it. I didn't stop to question it. When he kissed me that night at the field, I wanted to see if being with another guy would feel different after experiencing sex for the first time. And while Justin didn't set my body on fire the way Ryan did, he definitely set my heart rate pulsing, and I enjoyed spending time with him these last few weeks. If we hadn't been moving away for college, who knows what might've happened, but we are, and I won't waste any time thinking about what could've been. I didn't have sex with him, although it tempted me, but I knew if we'd taken it that far it might alter our friendship, and I value it too much to risk it.

"Why exactly do you care?" I ask.

"I'm just looking out for you."

"Trust me, you've nothing to worry about with Justin, and if you're done grilling me, I'd like to get back to my unpacking." I give

Miley and my brother a kiss on the cheek each. "Thanks for lunch." Turning to face Ryan, I say. "And thanks for cleaning up."

"No problem." His jaw is taut as he forces a smile, and as I walk back to my room, I can't help wondering if he's pissed over Justin or if it was mention of that Myndi girl that soured his mood.

Chapter Six
Ryan

"**D**ude, are you listening?" Derrick asks from the doorway to my office, snapping me out of my head. Since Summer moved in with us yesterday, I've been hugely distracted, and not in a good way. "What hours do you want me to cover on Sunday?" he repeats.

"From one until closing."

"Cool, and thanks. The extra money will come in handy with the wedding. Clara will bankrupt me before we've even made it down the aisle," he semi-jokes. Having briefly met his fiancée, I'd say he's not too far off the mark. She gives new meaning to Bridezilla. Rather him than me. I shudder at the thought.

"No problem, and if you want additional shifts, just let me know. It might be nice for Austin and me to take a bit of a breather from time to time."

"Awesome, thanks, boss."

"Derrick, your four p.m. is here," Miley says, appearing at his back.

"I'm outta here. Later." He jogs off down the corridor, while Miley lingers in the room.

"Austin called. He's stuck in traffic on his way back from the meeting at the PR firm. He asked if you'd look after Summer and her friends."

Fucking great. Just what I need. *How the hell am I going to evict this girl from my mind if I can't get away from her?*

I had a hard time sleeping last night knowing she was in the room next door.

Hard being the operative word.

Even jerking off twice in the shower this morning has done nothing to dampen the semi I seem to be permanently sporting around her. "Of course," I tell Miley. "Let me know when they arrive."

"Oh, they're here already. I showed them to the locker room and told them you'd meet them in the reception area."

"Okay. Thanks, Miley."

She smiles before closing the door on her way out. I rest my head on my arms on top of the desk, groaning. *What the fuck have I gotten myself into?*

When I feel sufficiently calm, I walk to the lobby to greet Summer and her friends.

I'm not surprised to see the same couple from the night we met waiting with her. Austin mentioned they were her best friends, and they're essentially the reason Summer's rooming with us. They couldn't locate any available two-bedroom apartments within their budget, and the one-bed place they found wasn't big enough for all three. So, according to Powers, Summer insisted Hannah and Jordan take the place while she'd wait for a spot in the dorms to open, living with us in the meantime.

"Hello again," I mumble as I reach them, keeping an eye on Miley as she chats to a client from behind the front desk.

"Hey, Ryan." Hannah smirks, waggling her fingers at me. "It's great to see you again."

"Thanks for stepping in for Austin," Summer adds, smiling up at me. "But if you're too busy, we can wait for my brother."

No Feelings Involved

I work hard to keep my gaze focused on her face, but it's challenging. She's wearing a sports bra top and yoga pants that leave little to the imagination. Her tits silently beckon me, and my fingers itch with a craving to touch her. With her firm, tan midriff on full display and those long, slender legs encased in a clingy black fabric, she's like my every wet dream. My cock hardens under my training shorts, and I discreetly adjust myself before anyone notices.

"I second that suggestion," Jordan says, eyeing me warily, and I wonder what the hell his problem is.

"I can spare time." I deliberately ignore his sullen tone and expression, jerking my head to one side. "C'mon. I'll give you the grand tour."

"This doesn't look like any gym I've seen before," Summer says when I show them into the main CrossFit training area.

"That's because it isn't." I smile with pride. "This is our CrossFit area, which is only one part of the overall facility. CrossFit is a training program that builds strength and conditioning through varied and challenging workouts with a heavy emphasis on nutrition and diet. As you can see, we use minimal equipment," I say, pointing at the frames which several clients are using.

"You don't have weights?" Jordan grumbles, pouting like a pussy.

"We do, just not in this section of the gym. Follow me." I walk toward the door at the far end of the room, explaining as we go.

"The vision Austin and I had for this gym was a state-of-the-art facility which offers a wide variety of programs to suit different needs at a reasonable price point."

I hold open the door, allowing the girls to pass through to the corridor. "Keep walking to the end, and go into the door on your left," I instruct, taking up the rear. It takes colossal willpower to avoid ogling Summer's shapely ass, but I feel Jordan's eyes like laser beams searing into my back. Dude really doesn't like me.

We enter the main gymnasium. "As you can see, we offer a traditional workout area too with all the usual weights and ellipticals." I point over our heads. "If you look up there, you'll see one of our trained consultants conducting a spin class. That section is reserved for our classes. We have a full daily schedule including Zumba, yoga, cardio, tai chi, and we also offer personal one-to-one training sessions."

"Wow." Summer spins around, her head whipping from side to side, taking it all in. "This place is very impressive. You should be proud of what you've both achieved."

"Thank you. We are, and we've worked hard for it."

"You play hard too, I bet," Jordan says, butting into the conversation.

"You have a problem with me, buddy?" I fold my arms over my chest and stare neutrally at him. This is my domain, and if he gives me shit, he'll find his ass out on the sidewalk, pronto.

"Jordy," Hannah hisses under her breath.

"Let him say what's on his mind."

"Guys like you make me sick," he spits out, his hands clenching at his sides. "You'd think at your age you'd be past the manwhore stage, but I guess some people just never grow up."

"Jordan, you are way out of line here," Summer calmly says. "Ryan has done nothing wrong, and if anyone needs to grow up, it's you. We were two consenting adults, and it was a onetime thing. The only one making a big deal out of this is you."

"You didn't see him ogling your ass on the way over here. It's fucking disrespectful." He glares at me, and I really don't get this guy. *What the fuck concern is it of his if I stare at Summer's ass? What am I missing here?*

"You were ogling my ass?" Summer asks, fixing her gaze on me. Her mouth pulls into a lopsided grin, and she doesn't look in any way pissed.

"It was right there in my face." I shrug, smirking. "Can't blame a guy for looking." Especially when I know what said ass looks like without clothes on.

"I think Austin might have something to say about that," the douche barks.

No Feelings Involved

All good humor disappears as I step up to him. I'm at least a good three inches taller, and a heck of a lot wider, than him. He's a stupid fucker if he thinks he can challenge me, especially in my place of business. "Are you threatening me?"

"Just stay away from her. You shouldn't have touched her. Aren't there any women your own age you can hit on?"

"What happened between Summer and me is nobody's business but our own. I get that you don't like me, and I couldn't give a flying fuck, but I thought Summer was your friend, and she deserves a lot more respect from *you*."

"Ryan is right," Summer says, stepping in between us and forcing me to take a step back. "You've got to let this go. I don't interfere in your love life, and I expect the same in return. If you value my friendship, you'll tell none of my brothers. It has nothing to do with them or you."

"And what about Justin? Doesn't he have a right to know?"

Ah, now I'm getting it. He's acting the big man on behalf of his friend.

"No." Summer shakes her head and stands her ground. "I'm not dating Justin, and I've made no promise or commitment to him, nor has he. I'm a free agent, and I can do what or *who* I want. I really don't want to fall out with you over this, but you've got to drop it."

"Summer. Come on. You've got to know how Justin feels about you. He's my best friend, and you expect me to say nothing when this douche is trying to get in your pants again?"

What the actual fuck? I admit I stared at her ass for longer than I should have, but I haven't given him, or her, any sign I'm planning on hitting on her again. Summer is as off-limits as girls go.

"You obviously don't understand the concept of a one-night stand," I say, working hard to keep my tone professional. "Or the fact she's my best friend and business partner's little sister. What happened between us is in the past, and I'm really struggling to see how this is any of your concern. I stared at her ass for all of ten seconds which doesn't equate to hitting on her."

"I have a pretty spectacular ass," Summer says, wiggling her butt and winking. "I'd stare at my butt too, if it was possible."

I don't understand how she's keeping such a cool head. If he was one of my supposed friends, I'd be tearing strips off him, but she's laughing and cracking jokes to ease the tension.

"You don't have any boxing classes scheduled now, do you?" Hannah asks, shooting daggers at her boyfriend.

"Not something we offer."

"Well, do you have anything to hit because my fist is dying to punch the alien being who has invaded my boyfriend's body, and I'd rather not mess up his pretty face."

I like this girl, and I'm glad Summer has at least one decent friend. "We have pads and you could do bag work if you like?"

"Babe." Jordan moves to his girlfriend's side, but she holds up her hand, keeping him at bay.

"Don't babe me. I'm crazy mad at you right now. Have you forgotten Sum is only in this position because she selflessly stepped aside so we could live together? Something I'm sorely regretting right now."

He scrubs his hands up and down his cheeks before exhaling loudly. "I'm sorry, babe."

"I'm not the one you should apologize to." Hannah plants her hands on her hips, challenging her boyfriend with a heated stare.

Jordan looks like he swallowed something nasty as he turns to face Summer. "Sorry, Sum. You know it's only because I care."

"I know, Jordy, but you've got to let this go."

"I will." He kisses her on the cheek, narrowing his eyes at me while neither of the girls are looking.

What a tool.

"You owe Ryan an apology too," Summer says as he moves to return to his girlfriend.

A muscle clenches in his jaw as he swings his gaze around. "Sorry, man," he clips out, sounding utterly unapologetic.

I could call him on it, but I'm sick of this juvenile bullshit, so I let it go. "No problem. Forget about it."

"Where's Summer?" Austin asks, stalking into my office a half hour later and flopping down into a chair.

"She's working out on the main floor with Hannah and that asshole Jordan."

Austin chuckles. "What did the little punk do?"

"Try breathing," I mutter, not wanting to elaborate.

"He's always been a mouthpiece, but he's harmless."

"I'll take your word for it. How did the meeting go?"

"Great, although you should've been there. We'll have to appoint a manager. We can't keep splitting stuff up and working all the hours we have been."

"I know, but we can't afford to appoint someone permanently yet. Business is doing well but not that well." I lean back in my chair, locking my hands behind my head.

"Maybe we should look for some venture capital. The figures look good, and with our expansion plans, it's a good prospect for an investor."

"I'm not keen to bring in someone else. Not unless we really have to. We're lucky with Gabby as an investor because she has zero interest in getting involved in the business, but if we go external, we'll be answerable to someone else, and I like the way things are now." Gabby's ex was a tech genius, and he left her a bunch of money after he passed. She has more than she needs, especially considering the great job Slater has, so she was happy to invest in our fledgling business.

"I'm grateful to your sister, and we both know we wouldn't be here today without her support but—" He leans forward, wetting his lips.

"But what?"

"I want to have a life outside these four walls. I want to have time to take my girlfriend to dinner or go away with her for a weekend."

I sit up straighter. "We both knew what we were getting into when we started this business. You can't turn around after barely eighteen months and say you've changed your mind."

"I haven't changed my mind. I just want more work-life balance."

"And you think I don't?" I get up and come around the front of the desk, resting my butt on the edge. "I know the hours are a killer, but it won't be forever. Every startup business is like this, and we're already ahead of the curve. We can't take our foot off the pedal now. This is the time to work even harder." I eyeball him, because I need to know if he's still with me on this. "It won't be forever, and we'll get to reap the benefits in a few years."

Air whooshes out of his mouth as he nods. "I know, man. I don't want to give you the impression I'm having doubts because I'm not. This has already exceeded my wildest dreams, and working with you has been great. It's just—"

"You're in love, and you want to spend more time with your woman," I supply.

"Yeah, I do."

"I'm happy for you, bro. And, look, if you want to take Miley away for a dirty weekend, I'll work something out. Just tell me when, and I'll come up with a plan."

"I can't up and leave you to manage by yourself."

"Quit with the martyrdom. Make your plans and I'll work around it. I'll see if I can come up with some options that will allow us to take a step back more regularly."

Chapter Seven
Summer

"I'm paying as soon as I get a job," I tell my brother as I complete the last of the paperwork confirming my gym membership. Austin insists on waiving the membership fee, and while I love that he wants to do that for me—and it's nice of him to offer Jordan and Hannah a twenty percent discount too—his business is still new, and I doubt they can afford to just give memberships out for free or at discounted rates. Jordan and Hannah have passed anyway, as they can use the sports facilities on campus for free, but they appreciated the gesture.

"Don't sweat it, Sum. You can make it up to us by helping keep the apartment clean and cooking the odd dinner."

"Deal." I stretch up and kiss my brother's cheek. "Love you, and I'm grateful for all you're doing to help me out." I didn't want to move in with my brother. Didn't want to rely on him when I'm reveling in my newfound freedom. But now I'm here, I'm finding I'm not all that unhappy about it. I refuse to believe my hot, sex god roomie has anything to do with my change in attitude, and I'm happy to languish in denial.

Austin wraps his strong arms around me, squeezing me tight. "I love having you around. I feel like I was never really there for you growing up. I like we'll get to spend time together now."

"Me too," I say, but the words are muffled against his warm chest.

"Aw, you two are so sweet," Miley says, coming around the desk with a wide smile on her face. "It makes me wish I had a big brother."

"Big brothers are the best," I agree. "Do you have any siblings?" I ask, easing out of Austin's arms.

"Only one older sister. She lives in London, so I don't see that much of her." Her smile fades, and I feel for her. I don't know how I'd cope if I didn't have my family close by. They mean everything even if they drive me to distraction often.

"I'm going to head home for a few hours," Ryan says, coming up behind us, and speaking directly to my brother. "I'll be back at nine to relieve you," he adds, dangling his car keys between his fingers.

"Can you take Summer with you?" Austin asks before turning to face me. "Unless you have other plans?"

Jordan and Hannah have already left, and I made no other plans. "Nope. A ride would be great."

A cheeky grin appears on Ryan's gorgeous mouth, and I think I know where his mind has gone. "Perv," I mouth at him over Austin's shoulder as we hug goodbye. I give Miley a hug too, and then I wave at my brother and his girlfriend as I join Ryan and we exit the building.

It's still bright out, and glorious sunshine beats down on us, prompting me to lift my face up to the sky. I adore the sensation of the warm sun on my skin, and it reminds me of copious summers spent outside on the farm, attending to chores and messing around in the woods and by the small stream at the back of our property.

I follow Ryan out into the parking lot, trying not to notice how the muscles in his back and arms ripple invitingly as he moves. And I'm definitely not checking out his toned ass or remembering what his butt cheeks felt like in my hands as I urged him to bury himself deeper inside me. Desire coils low in my belly, and my mouth suddenly feels as dry as the Sahara Desert.

"Liking what you see?" he asks over his shoulder, smirking at my blatant drooling. I open my mouth to reply truthfully when he groans, holding up one large palm. "Forget I said that, and definitely don't answer." He holds the door open for me, his face pulled into a tight grimace.

"Okay?" My brow puckers as I pull myself up into the car. My arm brushes against his as I slide into the passenger seat, sending a rake of shivers all over my body. I've never had any guy affect me so potently, and the feeling is off-putting. Ryan shuts my door and jogs over to his side, jumping into the car and starting the engine. "Nice wheels," I remark as he fiddles with the air conditioning.

"She's a beauty all right. Technically, it belongs to the business, so your brother and I share it." He backs out of the parking garage and into the busy rush hour traffic.

"Do you mind if I put music on?"

"Knock yourself out." He pushes a few buttons on his iPhone which is hooked up to the sound system in the car. "There you go."

I scroll through songs until I find one that reminds me of senior year of high school. I fight a smirk as I press the play button, instantly knowing Ryan will hate this choice.

Predictably, his brows climb to his hairline as the song starts. "'California Gurls'? Seriously?"

I'm jumping around on the seat, making robotic movements with my arms, as I bop my head to the catchy beat. "I fucking love this song. We did a spoof version of *Pitch Perfect* for our senior year play, and I was Katy Perry in our rendition of this song." I put my hands up in the air, dancing around like a crazy person as I belt out the lyrics. Ryan watches me with clear amusement, and it's just as well the traffic has come to a virtual standstill because he's paying scant attention to the road.

When the song ends, he shakes his head, chuckling with the biggest grin on his face. "I would've paid good money to see that show."

"I got a standing ovation I'll have you know," I mock pout, poking him in the ribs.

"I'm sure you did. You're a fantastic singer although the jury's out on your dancing," he teases, moving the car forward as the traffic eases.

"I've got moves," I protest.

"I know you do," he blurts before cussing under his breath.

"Let me guess," I say, arching a brow, "forget you said that too?"

"So, are you studying drama?" he asks after a couple beats of awkward silence, purposely ignoring my question.

"Nah, drama's only a hobby. I want to be a teacher, so I'm majoring in early childhood education."

"Is that something you've always wanted to do?"

"Pretty much." I pull my legs up into my chest, resting my face sideways on my knees. "I was one of those freaky kids who loved school, and I adore children, so it seems natural to want to work in that environment. I feel like I can relate to them, and the thought of playing a nurturing role, helping kids develop and grow and learn, makes me feel all warm and fuzzy inside."

"That's great, Summer. I wish I'd had that focus at your age. I didn't have a clue what I wanted to do when I started UD, and it's only the last couple years I found something I was passionate about. You're ahead of the curve, in so many ways."

I almost blush at his compliment, and a heady warmth invades my chest. "Were you a business major like Austin?"

He nods as he maneuvers the SUV around the corner in the apartment's direction. "Yeah. Not that I had any burning ambition to work in business, but it seemed like a good idea at the time and it's served me well now."

"How come you didn't study something sports related?" I ask, because it's clear that's where his passion lies, along with Austin's.

"I wasn't as into sports back then. I liked to run, but I didn't see it as something I'd want to pursue as a career," he admits, "but I can't really complain. I'm where I am now thanks to my passion for sports and the business degree I earned. Sometimes, although you might feel lost and aimless, you're on the right path even when you don't realize it." He enters the parking lot of the building, swinging into the designated space.

"That's profound."

He kills the engine, staring blankly at the windshield, and his voice is strangely numb-sounding when he speaks. "So many times, I've thought my life was going in a certain direction only for something to derail it, but I finally feel like I'm in the right place and that all the shit I went through happened for a reason. To lead me to this point."

"What shit?" I blurt before I can question the wisdom.

He visibly shakes himself out of whatever place his mind had wandered to, forcing a fake smile on his face as he opens his door. "It's nothing. It's in the past, exactly where I want it to be."

I'm still pondering his words as I slowly unbuckle my seat belt. My door swings open, and Ryan gently holds me at the waist, helping me down. My heart rate speeds up at his touch, and my body tingles all over. Little goose bumps sprout on my arms, and I'm acutely aware of his proximity. He looms over me and heat rolls off his body in hypnotic waves, almost knocking me off my feet.

He has so much *presence*.

And he's so masculine in a way that both thrills and scares me.

All the other guys I've been with—Justin included—seem so boyish when compared with this man. Visions of his large hands roaming my body, as he explored every inch of my bare skin, surges, unhelpfully, to the forefront of my mind, and I'm hot all over.

"Hey, are you okay?" He holds onto my elbow, attempting to steady me, but his touch knocks me even further off-kilter, doing little to ease my temporary lack of balance. "You're not dizzy after your workout, are you?"

I snort. "Hardly. Calling it a workout is a huge stretch of the imagination." I wasn't even exerting myself, yet I still found myself breathless. I shuck out of his hold, feeling like a stranger in my body, and not liking it one bit.

"You obviously exercise regularly," he says, his eyes quickly scanning my body before a familiar scowl paints his lips.

"Not in a gym." I lift my arm, flexing my biceps. "These muscles are thanks to farm work, but it's clearly no match for working out with weights and machines because I was virtually dead after fifteen minutes on that stepper."

He chuckles, ushering me across the parking lot toward the elevator. "I can schedule a session with one of our personal trainers, if you like. They can devise a training plan that will help you build muscle strength and stamina."

"That would be cool," I agree, stepping into the elevator alongside him.

"I'll grab a quick shower," I say when we enter the apartment, conscious I smell like moldy ten-day-old socks. "And then I'll fix dinner."

Ryan tosses his keys on the counter, shrugging off his hoodie and flinging it on the back of a stool. "You don't have to make dinner. I can fix something myself."

I roll my eyes. "Don't be ridiculous. It hardly makes sense for both of us to cook separately, and I want to earn my keep."

"I won't argue if you insist," he complies with a wink, sauntering toward his bedroom.

I'm walking toward the bathroom a couple minutes later, wrapped in my fluffy bathrobe, when I hear the shower start up in his bedroom. I'm surprised Ryan wangled the master suite out from under Austin, but I'm grateful because it means I'm only sharing the main bathroom with my brother, and I won't risk bumping into the guy I gave my V-card to in a minuscule towel.

As I stand under the stream of warm water, I can't help thinking of Ryan standing naked in his shower only a few meters away, and my body grows hot and needy as my mind's eye conjures up his image. I try to dismiss the visual, as I do every time it surfaces in my mind, but I'm a lost cause.

Before I know it, my hand is gliding down over my stomach, and my fingers are caressing my swollen clit as I close my eyes and revisit the night I lost my virginity.

I come seconds later, leaning against the tiled wall as wave after wave of powerful bliss rockets through me. My chest is heaving, and my legs are shaking, as I turn off the water and step out. Wrapping a towel around my body, and another one around my head, I swipe my hand across the steam coating the bathroom mirror, staring at my flushed reflection.

Before I met Ryan, my plans had been to come to UD with no ties or expectations other than to enjoy my freshman year of college and to enjoy my single status once I was no longer under my brothers' watchful eyes. But, already, I feel my resolve wavering, and I don't like it.

I don't want this guy to get under my skin.

I don't want to feel a growing attachment toward him.

I don't want his touch to ignite the lustful fuel flowing through my veins.

I don't want to picture him fucking me when I'm getting myself off.

Hannah and Jordan's lumpy couch is looking more and more appealing by the minute. I sigh, wondering why it's proving so hard to shake this guy from my thoughts.

It was only sex, I remind myself. A hot hookup. An amazing one-night stand and a clear onetime thing. Perhaps, because it's so new, and he's the only one I've had sex with, it's natural I feel some kind of connection with him. It doesn't mean I have feelings for him other than an ongoing desire to jump his bones again.

I'm drawn to him because of the sex, I conclude, nodding at my reflection in the mirror as I lie to myself, buoyed up by the fresh thoughts skating through my mind.

There's an easy cure for this ailment.

A surefire way to get Ryan out from under my skin.

I need to have sex with someone else.

Chapter Eight
Ryan

Summer isn't around when I step into the kitchen, so I set about making dinner for both of us. I have the chicken and veg cooking in the skillet and the noodles bubbling in the pan when she finally emerges from her bedroom, dressed in tight yoga pants and a loose shirt.

"I would do that." She leans in and sniffs the steam rising from the stove. Her delicate floral scent wafts through the air, and her perfume, combined with the curve of her ass in those pants, stirs my lust, reminding my libido that it's still in full working order. "That smells yummy, and I'm starving." Her tummy rumbles at that exact moment as if to prove a point.

"It'll be about ten minutes." I flip the ingredients in the skillet with a practiced twist of my wrist. "Help yourself to a drink. Miley has wine coolers you can steal or there's beer too," I say before remembering she's underage, and I'm not sure if Austin would approve of me offering her alcohol. "Forget I said that. Grab two bottles of water."

She rolls her eyes, smirking as she opens the refrigerator. I try my best not to ogle her gorgeous ass in her form-fitting yoga pants as she bends over. "I'm going to suggest they use that statement as your epitaph," she teases. "And I'm eighteen, not eight. I've been drinking since I was fifteen. I know how to handle myself, so I'll have a beer. Thanks."

She tosses a bottle of water at me so fast I almost don't catch it. I watch as she closes the refrigerator with her hip before popping the top on a beer, arching her head back as she takes a sip. Her throat works elegantly as she slowly drinks, and it shouldn't be such a turn-on, but I'm fucked if it isn't. My cock thickens in my shorts, and I discreetly adjust myself before she notices.

This is becoming a regular occurrence in her presence, which is hugely disconcerting.

I can't be lusting after her.

It's wrong on a million different levels.

But try telling that to my greedy hormones.

She's only been here a little over twenty-four hours, and I'm almost permanently hard. I seriously need to get laid. Maybe then I'll be able to evict her from my thoughts.

"I'll be back," she says, striding out of the kitchen like a woman on a mission. I hear her messing around with the TV, but I keep my focus on making dinner while silently cautioning my dick to get with the program.

"Can you lower the heat on that and come with me," she asks, a couple minutes later. I glance at her, my curiosity instantly piqued when I spot the mischievous expression on her face and the long blue wig she's sporting on her head. "I have something to show you."

Intrigued, I turn off the heat on the stove before trailing her into the living room. "What the hell is that?" I point at the image frozen on the TV screen.

"You said you would've paid good money to see me, so let's see if that's true." A giddy smile transforms her entire face as she presses play on her phone and the recording streams on the screen.

Summer is wearing the same long blue wig in the video, along with the most indecent outfit I've ever seen. My jaw drops to the floor as my libido fully reawakens at the sight of her in those tiny sparkly blue shorts and outrageous bra top. The fake cupcakes jutting out from her bra jiggle around as she sings and dances to "California Gurls" on the screen. My cock is saluting her at full mast now, and damn, does she look good up on that stage. She exudes confidence and sexiness, and she's having the time of her life.

I'm so distracted by the screen I haven't realized she's performing the routine alongside the TV until she's halfway through. It draws my eyes to her, and I lose all interest in the video as she expertly performs the dance moves right there in front of me. She sways her hips from side to side, rolling her stomach back and forth as she flings her arms up and out. When she dips down and wiggles her chest, I almost come in my boxers. My throat is dry, and my heart is racing around my rib cage like it's barreling around a competitive track.

I remember watching Katy Perry in the video for this song, and Summer has nailed all of her cheeky facial expressions and her sultry moves. When it gets to the part where Katy sprayed stuff from these tubes glued to her tits, Summer fakes the movement with a comical look on her face, and a hysterical laugh bubbles up my throat. I let it loose, because pretending I'm amused is better than admitting how fucking aroused I am right now.

Rapturous applause breaks out on the screen accompanied by catcalls and a few shouted, obscene proposals.

"Well?" Summer is slightly breathless, her cheeks stained red, as she faces me with her hands on her hips. On the screen, she's blowing kisses to the audience, and then she turns and wiggles her butt at the crowd.

My knees almost go out from under me as I crack up laughing, and once I start, I can't stop. I'm doubled over, clutching my stomach, in almost physical pain, as tears peel out of my eyes.

At first, she fake pouts, pretending to stomp her foot in anger before she joins me in my laughter. Both of us are roaring laughing, with tears streaming from our eyes, and it helps release some of the sexual tension I've been holding onto since that night.

I'm wiping tears from my eyes as she shuts down the feed and disconnects her cell from the TV. "Fuck, Summer. You're one crazy chick. I can't believe you got up there on stage like that." I shake my head, still chuckling.

"I was pretty nervous that night," she admits. "I knew my dad and brothers would flip, but when I got up there, I lost myself to the music, and it was fun." Her face glows as she reminisces.

"You were amazing, but if you were my sister, I'd have totally fucking lost the plot when those assholes spouted that shit."

"Please don't mention the war. Austin and Charlie almost came to blows with these two guys in the row behind them. My dad and my uncle had to separate them." She giggles. "Fun times."

"Something tells me you enjoy getting a rise out of your brothers," I tease as I head back into the kitchen to rescue dinner with her trailing hot on my heels.

"They deserve it," she says, removing plates and silverware from the cupboards. "I could barely pee without them breathing down my neck. Their overprotectiveness is legendary."

"You're their baby sister. What do you expect?" I heap food onto both our plates, carrying them over to the dining table. We usually sit at the counter to eat but the table is more comfortable.

"Not to be suffocated unfairly," she retorts, sliding into the chair across from me.

"You sound just like my sister Gabby. She used to say the same about me and my brothers."

"I can't wait to meet her," she says, rolling noodles around her fork. "Austin said she's married to your other friend Slater and they have a little boy and girl?"

I nod, chewing my food quickly before replying. "Yeah. Billy is four and Daisy is just five months old. I feel bad because I've had little time to visit lately."

"I'm sure your sister understands. Running your own business is a twenty-four-seven commitment. I've seen it with the farm. You're always on the go."

"I think it's getting to your brother," I admit, recalling our earlier conversation. "He wants to take Miley away for the weekend, but finding cover for both of them is an issue."

She chews her food slowly, looking lost in thought. Then her eyes come to life, and she leans across the table. "He should take her to London to see her sister! I could cover the front desk, so that only leaves you to find one additional pair of hands to help."

"You'd do that?"

She looks at me like I've grown ten heads. "Sure. He's my brother, and if he's stressed, I want to help. It's not rocket science, right? I pick things up quick, and I could spend a few evenings after classes with Miley so she could train me."

I shouldn't agree to any plan which involves spending more time with her, but I'm eagerly nodding before my brain has had time to catch up, and I can't find it within myself to be unhappy about it either.

"Just a tiny bite, please?" Austin pleads with his sister from the passenger seat of our SUV as we make the road trip to Lewes on Sunday afternoon.

"You'd swear I never feed you," Miley grumbles from the back seat.

"You are not getting a *crumb* of this apple pie," Summer chastises her brother from her position alongside his girlfriend. "It's a present for Gabby."

"She won't mind if there's a slice or two missing, and you have the apple jelly too."

"Not happening, asshole," Summer confirms with finality. "And you shouldn't ruin your appetite before dinner."

"Are you eighteen or eighty?" Austin teases, sticking his tongue out at his sister.

"Says the guy who's acting like he's five." I can feel Summer rolling her eyes at him, and I snicker.

"Glad to see you're in a better mood," he says. "She must've been some lay."

"Shut the fuck up." I take my eye off the road for a split second to glare at him. I do *not* want to have this conversation around his sister.

"So, you're back to your manwhore ways?" Miley inquires, lifting a brow.

"I hate that word," Summer pipes up, and I swallow the sudden lump in my throat. Our eyes meet in the mirror, and my heart rate accelerates at the mischievous smile on her face. "If Ryan meets a random stranger in a club, there's an obvious attraction, and they're both into it, then why shouldn't he go back to her hotel for sex? And how does that make him a manwhore?"

Holy fucking shit.

Bile travels up my throat as I risk a glance at Austin before drilling Summer with a subtle "what the fuck" look through the mirror. *What the hell is she playing at?* I know Austin thinks she's just referring to the girl I met last night, but it's too close to the truth for comfort. Distracted, I fudge the gear stick, and the car lurches forward, jostling our bodies with the motion. "Sorry," I mumble, trying to get a grip.

Austin opens his mouth to say something, but Summer hasn't finished. "If I told you I got laid last night too, would that mean you'd call me out on my slutty ways?" she adds, and I almost crash the car at her statement.

"Who was he?" Austin growls, shooting me a slightly worried look before swiveling in his seat and narrowing his eyes at his sister.

"Oh, don't get your panties in a bunch, Powers. It was hypothetical. I hate the way society labels men and women in touch with their sexuality. If people are single, the sex is consensual, and they want to explore different partners, why does that automatically mean they're a manwhore or a player or a slut?"

Steam is practically billowing out of Austin's ears. I don't know if it's her casual use of his nickname or her liberal views that has him on edge, but he's a grenade waiting to explode.

"Summer," he grits out, rubbing a spot between his brows. "I don't know what you've been doing or who you've been talking to, but that is not an acceptable attitude for an eighteen-year-old freshman to have."

"She's an adult, Austin," Miley says, leaning forward in her seat. "And Summer was just expressing an opinion. You need to lighten up."

"Maybe *you* need to get laid more often, and you might not be so tense," Summer bravely says.

"Summer."

Austin's tone carries considerable warning, and I don't want us arriving at Gabby and Slate's place with tension lingering in the air, so I intervene. "For the record, I didn't get laid last night." It had been my intention, and the gorgeous brunette glued to my side at the club had made it clear she was up for it, but I wasn't feeling it, and I rushed out of her apartment, spewing apologies as I left her semi-naked and wanting. "I'm in a good mood because I'm spending time with my family, so can we just focus on having a nice dinner instead of goading one another over sex?"

The conversation turns casual after that, thank fuck, and in next to no time, I'm pulling into the driveway of Gabby and Slater's house.

"Wow, nice place," Summer says, sliding out of the back seat before reaching in to remove her purse, the pie, and the homemade jelly.

"Here. Let me take that." I hold out my hand for the pie, but she places her purse in my palm instead.

"Thanks!" She waggles her brows, grinning, before making a beeline for the front door.

I'm mumbling under my breath as I use the key fob to lock the car, trailing behind the girls as we walk toward the house. Austin chuckles at my dilemma, and I'd flip him the bird if my hands weren't otherwise occupied holding Summer's purse. "Shut it, ass face."

"She has you wrapped around her little finger already, and she's not even living with us a week."

"She's kind of hard to say no to." And that's a fucking understatement.

"She's a little minx, but she has a heart of pure gold." He scratches the back of his neck in an obvious tell. "You don't think she was serious back in the car, do you?"

We're veering into dangerous territory, and I want to get the fuck out of Dodge as fast as I can. "She's not a little girl anymore, Austin. She's beautiful and spirited, and she'll get attention. You'll just have to deal with it." I sigh as I watch the front door swing open. "I'm sure you haven't forgotten the shit we got up to our freshman year. You can't expect her to act like an angel when you were the devil incarnate," I joke.

"The thought of any fucker putting his hands on her makes my blood boil." His hands clench into fists at his sides, and an icy shiver tiptoes up my spine. "I know it's hypocritical as fuck, but I pray she doesn't run into any guys like us. I think I could adjust to a boyfriend, but a string of random fucks?" He shakes his head, a deep frown creasing his brow. "Not a chance in hell."

I wet my dry lips, hoping he doesn't notice the beads of sweat forming on my brow. I'm glad we had this chat because it helps remind me she's off-limits. Austin would lose the plot if he found out I took her virginity or that I can't get her out of my fucking head ever since. This is a timely reminder and one I need to heed because I've too much invested in our friendship to risk it.

"You have a stunning home," Summer is saying to Gabby in the hallway when I step foot inside the house.

"Bro." Slate welcomes me with a slap to the back. "Good to see you. You too, man," he adds, nodding at Austin.

"We must arrange a few beers soon," Austin suggests. "After Miley and I get back from London," he adds in a low tone.

Slate raises a brow. "What's in London?"

"Miley's sister, and I'm planning a surprise trip so keep that to yourself."

"Uncle Ryan!" Billy's high-pitched screech cuts through Slater's response and I bend down as my adorable nephew comes charging down the hallway.

"Billy!" My mom calls to him from the end of the hallway. "Walk, don't run!" She flaps her hands in the air in consternation.

Paying her no heed, Billy flings himself into my arms, and I bundle the little dude up, cherishing the feel of his small body against me. "I missed you," he says, tightening his arms around my neck, and my heart swells with love.

"I missed you too, buddy." I stand, keeping him in my arms. "So, so much." I kiss the top of his head before messing up his dark hair.

He twists around in my arms, coming face to face with Summer, and his eyes pop wide. "You're pretty," he tells her, his cheeks reddening a little.

I can't disagree with him.

Summer is wearing a simple white sundress, flat gold sandals and minimal makeup, with her hair hanging in loose curls down her back, and I've never seen a woman look more gorgeous. Every time she looks in my direction, she steals my breath away.

"Thank you. And you're so handsome I think I'll run away with you." When she smiles at him, her entire face lights up, and I swear the little guy swoons, right along with me.

"I'd run away with you," the little charmer supplies, nodding eagerly as he opens his arms to go to her.

Summer scoops him up, and he clings to her like he's afraid she'll vanish if he doesn't hold her tight enough. "You smell pretty too," he adds, nuzzling his nose into her hair.

Gabby laughs, and Slater slides his arm around her waist as they smile at their son.

"What have they been putting in the water around here?" I joke, leaning in to kiss my sister on the cheek. "Or have you been sending the little dude to Casanova classes on the sly?"

"I think he's just inherited some of your traits," Gabby quips, yanking me into a bone-crushing hug. "I missed you, little big bro." She squeezes me so hard it's a wonder I can still breathe.

"Missed you too, Tornado." I kiss the top of her blonde head before holding her at arm's length. "You look fantastic." She truly does. There's no evidence she only gave birth a few months ago, and she's practically glowing. I may have had concerns when she and Slater first dated, but I can't deny how amazing they are together and how great it is to see her happy after all the heartache she experienced.

"Thanks. I'd like to say the same, but you look like shit." She brushes her hand over the five days' worth of growth on my chin, rubbing her thumb along the bruising shadows under my eyes. "Are you getting any sleep?"

"I'm sleeping and eating and shitting." She swats my arm, scowling at my crude language, and I pull her into a gentle headlock, like old times. "Stop fussing. I'm fine," I say, messing up her hair.

She punches me in the gut, and I'm momentarily winded as she escapes my clutches, straightening up and brushing tangled strands of long blonde hair from her face.

"No hitting, Mommy," Billy chastises, wagging his finger at Gabby, and we all crack up laughing. He's still wrapped around Summer like a koala, showing no signs of giving her up.

"You want to give Summer a break there, dude?" I suggest, opening my arms for him.

"She's mine." He circles his arms tighter around her neck, glaring at me, and another round of laughter breaks out.

"Wow. I'd hate to see what he's like when he's older if he's this possessive already," Austin jokes.

"I'm betting he'd still have nothing on you, Marc, and Charlie," Summer is quick to reply.

"Girl, I think we have lots to talk about," Gabby says, prying Billy out of Summer's arms and putting his feet on the ground. "Why don't you rejoin your cousins outside?" she suggests, kissing his cheek. "I'm sure Uncle Ryan will play basketball with you."

His little hand wraps around mine, and he looks up at me eagerly. "C'mon." He leads the way. "I'll let you be on my team."

"Duty calls." I wink at Summer as we pass, and she waves us both off.

"It's okay, Uncle Ryan," Billy says when we're out of earshot.

"What's okay, buddy?"

"If you want the pretty girl to be yours."

My mouth drops to the floor as I stare at my nephew, slack jawed.

"You can look after her until I'm old enough to marry her," he adds with a level of supreme confidence that only comes with youth. "But promise you'll treat her like a princess because my daddy says every boy should treat every girl like that." And with those parting words of wisdom, he drags me outside with my jaw trailing the ground behind me.

Chapter Nine
Summer

"That was delicious," I proclaim, beaming at Gabby with a full stomach. "Thank you so much."

"I'm glad you enjoyed it, and we're thrilled you could join us today. You're welcome to visit anytime." Her happy smile is genuine, and she looks so like Ryan when she smiles. They share the same blue eyes, blonde hair, quick wit, and charming personality.

"I appreciate that," I say, raising my voice. The kids are racing around the table having grown bored with sitting down a long time ago. I smile as I watch them giggle and shriek.

Ryan's eldest brother Dean is here with his fiancée, Alice, and his two twin daughters from a previous marriage. Mia and Tia are seven and most definitely the leaders of the pack. Ryan's other brother Caleb is here with his wife Terri. They have Ryder, who's basically the same age as Billy, and their seventeen-month-old son, Roman. Ryan's mom and dad, Lucy and Paul, complete the guest list, and they've all been friendly and welcoming.

"Okay." Gabby stands, talking in a commanding voice. "Who wants ice cream?" The kids all squeal in delight, skipping and jumping after Gabby as she walks into the kitchen. I gather up plates and follow her in. After depositing the dirty dinnerware in the dishwasher, I help her with the ice cream, and then we bring the kids outside, settling them on the picnic bench. Billy takes hold of my hand, refusing to let me go until Gabby bribes him into releasing me. I kiss his cheek, promising I'll come out and play after we've eaten dessert.

"He's really taken a shine to you," she says as we work side by side serving up apple pie and cheesecake for the adults.

"He's adorable. I wasn't joking when I said I'd run away with him. You must be so proud."

"I am. He's a great kid." Her eyes glisten proudly. "They both are."

"I hope Daisy wakes soon. I'm dying to meet her."

Gabby glances at the clock. "She's having a power nap today, but she had a turbulent night, so I'm not surprised."

"You must be exhausted."

"It comes with the territory." She shrugs. "We live in a perpetual state of sleep deprivation, but I wouldn't swap my life for the world." A sad, nostalgic look sweeps across her features momentarily.

Miley and Lucy appear in the kitchen then, and together, we return to the dining room, handing out dessert before reclaiming our seats.

"This apple pie is to die for," Paul, Ryan's dad, says a few minutes later. "Ryan said you made it yourself from apples grown on your family farm?"

I nod. "Yes, and the apple jelly too."

"You know, we've had Austin over to dinner plenty of times, and I don't think I've ever asked him much about the farm," Lucy says. "I thought it was a cattle farm?"

"It used to be," Austin responds before I can. "But Dad had to diversify over the years."

"We grow a variety of vegetables, fruits, and flowers," I continue. "And we sell the produce locally online and via the farmer's market in Milton. Although the focus is on beef and duck, the farm wouldn't be profitable without the other side of the business."

"You seem very knowledgeable," Lucy adds. "Do you plan on working on the farm after college?"

I shake my head. "Definitely not. That's my brother Charlie's forte. He recently returned home to work on the farm after getting his agricultural degree."

"Summer wants to be a teacher," Ryan confirms. "When she's not performing Katy Perry songs on stage, that is." We share a conspiratorial grin.

"How the hell do you know about that?" Austin asks, quirking a brow.

"Summer put on an impromptu show the other day." Ryan smirks at the memory.

"She what?" Austin splutters, almost choking on his pie. "You better not have been prancing around the apartment in that excuse for a costume."

"Oh, for the love of all things holy, keep your hair on. I wasn't wearing the costume." His shoulders visibly relax, and I can't stop myself from pushing his buttons. "Although I would have if I'd thought to bring it with me. Ryan deserved the authentic experience." I shouldn't wind Austin up but he's making it too easy.

My brother is lost for words, and I'm struggling to contain a grin when Ryan sticks the knife in. "She played me the video from the show though, and damn, that was some costume."

"Why the hell would you show him that?" Austin asks, getting worked up and now he's just pissing me off. However, we're guests in Gabby's home, and I don't want to bring tension to the table, so I work hard to offset my annoyance.

"We were talking about it in the car on our way back from the gym, and I thought it'd be funny to show him."

"Do I look like I'm laughing?" Austin growls, and I notice Miley clamping her hand down on his thigh under the table in warning.

"This is priceless," Slater says, showcasing a mad grin. "I never thought I'd see the day where Austin would be all loved up or act like he has the biggest stick up his ass, and now I've witnessed both. Today's a good day." He rubs his hands together, as Gabby swats the back of his head.

"Don't tease our guests. It's not hospitable."

Slater snorts. "We're talking about Powers."

Austin flips him the bird just as the baby monitor emits a loud wail. Slater stands, but Gabby tugs on his arm. "I'll go. Summer wants to meet Daisy."

I hop up out of my seat with no further encouragement, practically skipping out of the room after Gabby.

"Hello, my little princess," Gabby murmurs as we pad carefully into the baby's room.

A nightlight rotates a smattering of tiny stars across the ceiling in the dimly lit space. Daisy cries, kicking her legs out and reaching her arms up to her momma. Gabby holds her close to her chest, gently rocking her. "Would you mind switching on that lamp?" she whispers, gesturing at the dresser off to the side of the crib.

I switch it on, and the room comes into clearer view. "Wow. This is a beautiful room." It's painted in a pale shade of green with matching white wooden furniture. One wall has large daisies floating across it as if they were blowing in the breeze, and the wall at the back of the crib spells out Daisy's name in large white foam lettering. Fitted shelves hold tons of cuddly toys and family photos, including a cute one of Billy holding his baby sister in his arms.

Gabby watches me looking at it as she changes her baby's diaper. "That was minutes after Daisy was born," she explains. "Billy was so excited to meet his sister, but it completely overwhelmed him when the time came to see her."

"I can tell from his expression." I run my finger along the frame, my heart full as I take in the wide-eyed shell-shocked stare on her son's face.

"He loves her so much," Gabby admits, tickling her daughter as she dresses her.

No Feelings Involved

I return to her side, smiling at the gorgeous little blonde princess. She's gurgling and kicking out her legs, and I want to bundle her up into my arms. "It'd be hard not to. She's beautiful, Gabby." I place my finger in the baby's hand, and her tiny fingers latch on. "She looks so much like you with her blonde hair where Billy is dark-haired like Slater."

Gabby smiles quietly at me as she lifts her daughter up. "Would you like to feed her?"

"Oh, yes, please." My grin is wide. "I didn't want to be rude, but I'm dying to hold her."

"C'mon then. Let's go down to the living room, and I'll get you set up."

I'm seated on the brown leather couch, while Gabby has gone to the kitchen to fetch a bottle, cradling her gorgeous daughter in my arms. Sounds of conversation and laughter trickle in from the kitchen as the rest of the adults enjoy an after-dinner coffee. Daisy gurgles, and I can't stop peppering her face with little kisses. I'm rewarded with the biggest smile, and my heart seriously melts.

I can't wait until my brothers settle down and pop out little Petersens. I know Mom's dying for some grandkids too. I'm betting they will subject Austin and Miley to lots of teasing about weddings and babies when my brother finally plucks up the courage to bring her home.

Even though she's hungry, little Daisy is impeccably well-behaved, giggling as I blow raspberries on her chest.

"You have mesmerized both my children," Gabby says with a smile as she steps into the room. "Are you sure you aren't Mary Poppins in disguise?"

I laugh as I prop the baby up higher on my shoulder, accepting the warm bottle from Gabby and bringing the nipple to Daisy's mouth. All the years of babysitting the neighbor's kids means I'm well accustomed to babies. Daisy latches on instantly, sucking greedily on the bottle, and I run my finger along her soft cheek as I smile at her. "I wish. How cool would it be to fly over the city via umbrella?"

"It might be a bit cold and wet," she jokes with me.

"It'd be worth it though." I coo at Daisy as I gently snuggle into her while she feeds. "I'm happy to babysit if you ever need a sitter."

"You might be sorry you offered," she quips.

"Not at all. Honestly, if I can help, I'd be happy to."

"That's sweet of you. Thanks." She sits back farther in the couch, casting a glance at the large family photo, of her with Slater and the kids, hanging over the mantelpiece, an automatic smile cresting upon her face. "Date nights are rare these days, but if we have something to go to, usually my parents babysit, or sometimes Dean and Alice if they don't have the twins with them." She folds her hands in her lap. "Ryan used to babysit Billy a lot when he was a baby, but he's way too busy now with the gym, and I'd only feel like I was imposing."

"I'm sure he wouldn't mind once he could arrange cover."

"I know he wouldn't," she agrees, her eyes drifting to the photo on the side wall. Her expression turns nostalgic, and I stare at the man locked in an intimate pose with Gabby, trying to keep the curiosity out of my eyes, but I'm a naturally nosy person so it's difficult.

"That's Dylan," Gabby volunteers. "Billy's father."

"I didn't want to pry, but I was wondering. I'm sorry," I add, realizing my faux pas upstairs. "I shouldn't have presumed anything about Billy and Slater."

"It's okay. Slater gets that a lot when he takes Billy out, and it's a natural assumption."

"Does Billy see Dylan often?"

"Dylan passed shortly after Billy was born," Gabby quietly admits, and I feel awful for opening this topic of conversation.

"Oh, my god. I'm so sorry. I'm too nosy for my own good."

Gabby pats my arm, smiling. "It's fine. We don't shy away from talking about Dylan. Billy knows all about him, and he loves bragging he has two daddies, one of whom is an angel looking after him from heaven."

Her smile is radiant and full of love and pride for her son. She looks up at the picture again, and my eyes follow suit. It's a beautiful photo but tinged with sadness now I know the history behind it. They are both sitting on the floor, and Dylan has his arms wrapped around Gabby's baby bump from behind. She's leaning back into his chest, staring up at him, and he's meeting her eyes, the look of love and adoration transparent in his gaze.

"He was my first love," Gabby continues explaining, "and I thought we'd be together forever, but fate had other plans." She wipes a lone tear aside. "I will always love Dylan, and I love that I have a piece of him in Billy, but Slater is the love of my life, and he has made me so incredibly happy. He adopted Billy, and he treats him as if he's his own flesh and blood, and don't even get me started on how he is with this little one." She squeezes her daughter's toes. "I'm lucky to have him, and I love the life we share."

Slater appears at that exact moment, as if he's in perfect tune with his wife. From the expression on his handsome face, I'm guessing he heard the tail end of our conversation. "I love you," he tells her, not fazed at the fact I'm right here. Sitting down, he slides his wife onto his lap, wrapping his bulky arms around her. I've been watching the way they are together, and it's obvious they are very much in love.

Someday, I hope to have what they have. When I've lived my life to the fullest and I'm ready to settle down and start a family.

"We're so very lucky," Slater says, kissing his wife on the cheek, as he talks. "After the things we've experienced, we never take a single day for granted."

"I love that," I truthfully admit, draping Daisy over my shoulder after she's finished her bottle. I gently rub her back, and she emits a loud burp almost instantaneously. "It's how I want to live my life. With no regrets. Grasping every opportunity to live life to the fullest because you never know what's lying in wait around the corner. It's part of the reason I want to go traveling after college before I settle into my career. There is such a vast world out there, and I want to explore it."

I carry Daisy over my shoulder, continuing to rub her back as I wander back into the kitchen, letting Gabby and Slater have some precious alone time. Miley and Lucy have been busy cleaning up the kitchen, and some of the others have meandered outside to watch over the kids, while Ryan, Austin, and Paul are still sitting around the kitchen table drinking coffee.

"You look right at home there, Summer," Paul says when he spies me.

"I adore babies, and this one is precious." I sit down, turning her around in my arms, still holding her close.

"Stop hogging the precious one," Ryan jokes, holding out his arms. "Hand the cutie over." I carefully deposit his niece into his arms and our fingers brush. As usual, delicious tremors ricochet up and down my arms from the contact, and from the way Ryan jerks a little, I can tell he's definitely feeling it too.

The back door swings open rather forcefully, and a little ball of energy barrels through. "Pretty girl," Billy says, raising a smile to my lips. "Can you play basketball with me?"

"Her name is Summer," Ryan reminds him.

"I know." Billy pouts, comically folding his arms across his small chest. "But Daddy Slater calls Mommy beautiful, so why can't I call Summer pretty?"

I extend my hand toward him and he links his small fingers in mine. "I don't mind if you call me pretty girl once I'm allowed to play ball."

"You can play anything of mine. Anything." He looks so sincere, and my heart melts again. Seriously, these kids are making me feel broody in a way I've never felt before. Which is crazy because I'd never consider having a child at my age. I definitely want kids, a whole host of them, but when I'm much older and I'm at a place in my life where I can devote my full attention to them.

"Wow, Sum." Austin says. "You're hooking them young these days."

"Age is only a number," I toss out. "I'm sorely tempted to kidnap your sister's kids and never give them back," I admit, eyeballing Ryan.

"I can't say I blame you because they're gorgeous kids, but you're wearing rose-tinted glasses. Kids are a shit-ton of work. Come babysit them overnight sometime, and I bet you'll be eating your words," he says, nuzzling his nose into Daisy's neck. She giggles nonstop, and he's fascinated by her. There's something magical about watching a big, burly guy cradling a cute baby in his arms, and my ovaries swoon as Ryan continues to lavish affection on his niece.

Billy tugs me outside, and I spend twenty minutes running around the backyard with all the kids playing ball. I haven't had this much fun in ages. They really are a great bunch of kids and such a lovely family. My parents would get on famously with Ryan's.

I stop to take a breather, heading back inside to grab a bottle of water. The sound of angry voices greets me as I step into the kitchen.

Ryan is standing in the middle of the kitchen with a face like thunder. Gabby has a worried expression on her face as she stares up at Slater, pleading with her eyes for him to do something. The only other people in the kitchen are a strange man and woman who weren't there before.

The man is standing protectively behind the woman, his arm resting on her shoulder as he whispers in her ear. She's stunning with shoulder-length wavy reddish-brown hair and expressive green eyes. "I'm sorry, Ryan," she whispers. "I didn't know you'd be here."

His gaze lowers to her swollen belly, and a flash of pain glimmers in his eyes before he conceals it. "Whatever, Myndi. It's not like I care." But as he looks up at her, challenging her to disagree, it's blatantly obvious he cares, and a sharp pain spreads across my chest at the realization.

Chapter Ten
Ryan

I can't fucking believe this. This is like my every worst nightmare rolled into one. It's been over two years since Myndi and I broke up, and I'm still pissed over the way she treated me. Seeing her again brings a host of repressed emotions to the surface, and I'm not in the mood to revisit my past.

She moved to Australia shortly after all that shit went down, and except for Gabby and Slate's wedding last year, I haven't had to face her since then.

I knew she was in a new relationship, and I couldn't give two fucks about the stuck-up jerk in the blazer and button-down shirt glowering at me. She's welcome to her nerdy doctor boyfriend, but seeing her like this is akin to a slap in the face and I'm ill-equipped to deal with the host of conflicting emotions running through me.

She looks up at her boyfriend, and they communicate silently with their eyes.

I remember a time when we used to do that.

A time when I thought maybe, just maybe, I was wrong about love and marriage.

But I wasn't wrong.

Siobhan Davis

I'd gotten it right all along.

He nods, and she turns back around to face me. Remorse and pity emanate from her in spades, and I fucking hate that. I want nothing from her.

Especially not her pity.

And her remorse is too fucking late.

"Can we talk in private?" she asks, beseeching me with her eyes.

"We've nothing to talk about." I cross my arms over my chest, trying my best to avoid looking at her swollen belly.

"We both know that's not true."

"You had plenty of time to talk before you emigrated to Australia, and I seem to recall the only words you had for me were harsh ones. I'm not in the mood for a repeat."

"I was in the wrong," she admits, reaching her hand out.

I flinch, stepping back from her touch, almost tripping over Summer. I didn't realize she'd come back inside, and I hate she's a witness to this. I grab onto her elbow to stop her from falling. "Sorry. I didn't see you there."

"It's fine." Her soft smile is laced with concern, and fuck, if that doesn't thaw the new layer of ice around my heart.

"Is this your girlfriend?" Myndi asks, her tone hopeful as she pins Summer with an eager smile.

"She's mine," Billy cuts in, strolling into the room like he owns it. "But I told Uncle Ryan she could be his until I'm old enough to marry her. He promised to treat her like a princess," he tacks on the end, like that totally justifies it.

"Oh, jeez." Gabby bites down on her lower lip to stop from laughing. "I think you need to have a word with our son," she murmurs to Slate, and Slate promptly brings Billy out of the room for a man-to-man chat.

Myndi's gaze bounces from me to Summer, and she looks awkward as hell. I really don't give a shit if she's embarrassed, but I won't disrespect Summer. "Not that I owe you any explanation, but Summer is Austin's sister. She's living with us at the moment."

558

"Oh. I'm sorry for jumping to conclusions." She offers Summer her hand. "It's nice to meet you. Ryan and I used to date in college, and I lived in the house with him and your brother for a while. I see the resemblance now."

I harrumph, and Myndi's baby daddy looks like he wants to rip my head from my shoulders.

I'd like to see him try.

"Please don't remind me," Summer says. "Most of the time I try to forget we're related."

Myndi laughs, and it rubs me the wrong way. I can't stomach being in her presence any longer. The ghosts of the past are choking the life out of me every second I'm around her. "I'm going outside. It'd be nice if you left by the time I return," I spit out, as Gabby gasps.

"I'm so sorry. He's—" I don't hear the rest of Gabby's apology as I storm outside.

"Hey, man. You okay?" My brother Caleb approaches me with caution, because they all know how crazy that woman makes me.

"I'll be fine once I don't have to look at her face." Caleb shares a loaded look with my other brother Dean. "And no, before you ask me for the thousandth time, I don't want to talk about it. Why the fuck is she here, anyway?"

"Gabby didn't know they were coming," Dean coolly states. "You know she'd never ambush you like that. I'm not even sure if Gabby knew Myndi was pregnant."

"They're best friends. Of course, she knew," I bark, venting my frustration in the wrong direction.

"Don't fucking take it out on Gabby, Ryan," Caleb snaps back. "She lost her best friend in all this, and she's never once blamed you for that."

"Because it wasn't my fucking fault!" I yell.

"Keep your voice down," Dean cautions. "There are kids around."

I attempt to rein in my anger, but I'm too wound up. Air whooshes out of my mouth as I drag my hands through my hair.

"Fuck." I chew on the inside of my mouth. "Seeing her again just brings so much shit to the surface, and it's not something I enjoy thinking about."

"I get it," Dean says, nodding as he squeezes my shoulder.

Dean is the only one who knows everything that went down with Myndi. I wanted to confide in Slate, but I couldn't ask him to keep it a secret from my sister, and if her best friend didn't tell her the truth, then I wasn't bringing them into it either.

"And I understand," he continues. "Every time I have a confrontation with Annie, I'm in a foul mood for days after."

Annie is Dean's ex-wife, my nieces' mother, and a Class-A bitch. It doesn't matter that she's apparently happily re-married; she still loves trying to wind my brother up any chance she gets.

The door opens behind me, and our parents join us. Great. Just what I need. "You okay, son?" Dad asks, looking me directly in the eye.

"I'm fine," I lie, tension tightening my jaw and twisting in my gut.

"Maybe you should talk to her," Mom softly suggests. "It might help if you unburdened whatev—"

"Seriously, Mom? You're in no position to lecture me on this," I snap. Shaking my head, I harrumph at the audacity of that woman to interfere, given her track record and when she hasn't a clue about the situation with my ex.

"What exactly does that mean?" she asks with a frown, sharing a troubled glance with my Dad.

"Nothing." I push past her. "Forget it. I'm going for a walk to cool off. I'll catch you later."

I veer left, away from the yard where the kids are playing ball.

Slate and Gabby purchased this house primarily for the lavish gardens. It stretches over two acres, and they have all the outdoor space they could ever need. I walk for five minutes until I come to the small covered seating area nestled between leafy trees and flowering shrubs. Plonking my butt down on the love seat, I cradle my head in my hands, wondering why I keep letting that woman get to me.

Why I enabled those cruel words she spoke to dig so deep into my heart, damaging it beyond repair.

Why I ever believed I was destined for love and marriage and the kind of family life my best friend shares with my sister.

"Hey."

I pick my head up as Summer's sweet voice rings out.

She shoves a bottle of beer at me. "Thought you could use this. Miley says she's good to drive us back."

My fingers curl around the cold glass, tingling where my skin comes into contact with her hand. "Thanks." I whip the bottle away as if her touch is toxic.

It might as well be.

For the first time in over two years, I've met someone who threatens these steel walls I've built around my heart, and I don't fucking like it one bit.

I don't want to feel the things I'm feeling for this girl, and I'm terrified it goes beyond lust.

I made a promise to myself when things turned to shit with Myndi.

A promise I wouldn't let myself fall again, and I won't break it. Not even for someone as gorgeous and sweet as Summer.

"I'm not great company right now. You should head back." I don't even look at her as I attempt to dismiss her.

In true Summer fashion, she ignores me, dropping onto the seat beside me. "I like it out here, and we don't have to talk. I'm good with silence."

We sip our beers, rocking back and forth on the seat, in amicable silence, and the irony isn't lost on me.

After a while, she sets her empty bottle down on the ground and clears her throat. "You know, I believe people come in and out of our lives at different times to teach us something. Maybe it's something about ourselves. Maybe it's something about the world. But I think every experience helps shape us. Helps prepare us for the future. Even the bad stuff. Even the stuff that seems like it might break us."

I twist around to face her. "You want to know what I think?" She nods eagerly. "I think that's the biggest crock of shit I've ever heard," I spit out, still riled up. "That you're way too young and naïve to know what you're talking about. And I doubt you've faced any bad shit in your life." I'm being a jackass, but I'm too pissed to tone it down.

She purses her lips, staring calmly at me while she contemplates how to reply. "You're right. About it all, except the crock of shit. You might not share my beliefs, but that doesn't give you the right to be rude about my opinions. Yes, I haven't had to face many obstacles in my life. I know I'm luckier than most. But just because I have limited personal experience doesn't mean I'm wrong."

I pick at the label on my beer, mulling her words over, as she stands. Panic is instant. "I'm sorry. Don't go," I blurt before I've had time to rethink it. "I didn't mean to disrespect you or your beliefs. It's just hard for me to look objectively at it when my experiences have tainted my opinions."

"I understand, and you're forgiven," she says, running her hands over the bark of a large, old, oak tree.

"Just like that, huh?" I inquire, climbing to my feet.

She spins around, her dress swirling around her thighs with the motion, reminding me of the ballerina on the top of the music box Gabby had as a kid. She used to watch that little ballerina rotate for hours at a time, forcing the rest of us to suffer that sickly sweet melody repeatedly. "I don't bear grudges. Life's too short."

"I hope you never change, Summer," I truthfully say, shoving my hands in the pockets of my jeans to ignore the urge to touch her. "There aren't many like you in the world."

She beams at me, dropping a curtsy that's cute as hell. "Why, thank you, kind sir." She turns back around to the tree, straining her neck to look up. "I have an idea." There's a devilish glint in her eye as she looks over her shoulder at me. "Let's climb this tree."

I stare at her blankly for a few seconds, sure I must've heard that wrong. But she's already on the move, expertly placing her feet on the bark, and pulling her torso up as she climbs.

"Why?"

"Because it'll be fun." She says this like my question was preposterous.

"You've done this before," I remark, watching her scale the tree with skill. I place my hands on the bark, deciding I may as well join her in crazy town.

"Well, duh." She looks down at me, laughing. "I grew up on a farm with an orchard and a small forest. Climbing is practically my middle name." Her eyes shimmer with excitement and adventure, and I force my gaze away as she climbs higher, flashing her panties at me. I concentrate on climbing the tree and not looking up, but it takes mammoth self-control. I must be as crazy as she is to even contemplate this. It's been years since I did anything on the spur of the moment, and the feeling of exhilaration is just what I need to distract my troubled mind.

She's light on her feet, her body flexible, as she climbs higher and higher, while my heavier limbs struggle to keep pace with her. Eventually, I catch up, and I sit on the thick branch directly across from her. She has her hands planted on either side of her, her legs dangling over the edge, as she swings them back and forth with no fear.

"I tried to persuade my parents to let me live in the woods at the back of our property after I watched *The Hunger Games*," she tells me without invitation. "I wanted to be like Katniss. Minus the killing part, obviously." She grins at me. "I was convinced I could survive out there, blanketed in Mother Nature's arms, and I could fend for myself."

"What happened?"

"My parents agreed to let me spend one night outside, and I barely lasted four hours." She giggles. "Although that was Marc and Charlie's fault because they snuck into the woods once it was dark and started throwing things and making noises, and I got spooked so I ran all the way back to the house leaving my tent and my bag behind." She rolls her eyes. "It's a wonder I still speak to any of my brothers given the stuff they pulled on me growing up."

"It's a rite of passage. Gabby can tell you about all the shit Slate, my brothers and I pulled on her over the years."

She smiles. "I wouldn't have it any other way, because then it'd mean they don't care."

Silence engulfs us, and I scan the land down below and in the distance. "It's peaceful up here."

"It is," she agrees. "I love it, and you can see so much."

I lean back against the trunk of the tree, swinging my legs up onto the branch. "Myndi accused me of cheating on her," I admit, suddenly wanting to talk to Summer about it although I'm not brave enough to tell her everything.

"And did you?" she asks in a curious tone devoid of malice or accusation.

"No. I would never do that. *Never.*" Not after what I witnessed as a kid.

Cheating is a major deal breaker for me.

I rub a tense spot between my brows. "If I had ever felt like that, like I wanted to be with someone else, I would've ended things with her before betraying her trust. She knew how I felt about cheating, but she still wouldn't accept that I was innocent."

"Why did she believe you'd cheated on her?"

A pain slices across my chest as I revisit one of the most painful times in my life. "Because this bitch manipulated the situation one night when I was out at a club without Myndi. Catching me completely off guard, she pulled me into a kiss, and her friend recorded it in the seconds before I realized what was happening and pushed her off me. I was so fucking mad, especially when I discovered she posted it on social media within minutes, tagging my girlfriend, ensuring she'd see it and jump to the wrong conclusion."

I pull my knees up to my chest, staring out at the darkening sky. "Myndi had already decided before I even got home to explain. She knew that bitch had been chasing after me for months. Knew I'd been continuously turning her down, but she didn't want to hear my version of events, choosing to believe that photo instead."

I gulp over the lump in my throat. "I understood her initial reaction because the photo was pretty damning, and Myndi's ex had cheated on her, so she had understandable trust issues. But the difference between her and me is that if it'd happened in reverse, I would've given her the benefit of the doubt because *I* trusted *her*. I'd never given her any reason to doubt my loyalty, yet she immediately believed the worst. I thought she'd cool down the next day, but she didn't. She refused to believe me, some other shit went down she blamed me for too, and that was it for me."

"That sucks, and I'm sorry it happened to you."

"Well, I'm not," I honestly admit. "Because it proved that we never would've made it as a couple. It was better to find that out before I'd invested any more of my time in a relationship that was going nowhere."

"Is that why you don't date anymore?"

"Who told you I don't date?"

"I kinda guessed that first night we met, and Miley confirmed it."

Fucking Miley and her big mouth. Not that it matters. It's good that Summer knows this in case she's harboring any silly notions of her and me.

"I didn't date before Myndi, and I haven't dated after her, and that's what I prefer. I enjoy casual hookups when I need to fuck, and I make sure the girl knows it's only a onetime thing. That it's only sex. A pure physical release and nothing more."

"And you haven't grown tired of it? You don't feel lonely?" Again, her questions are inquisitive, not critical in the slightest. It's so easy to talk to her. To be honest with her. Because she genuinely doesn't judge.

"Nope." It's not a lie if I'm deluding myself. "This way, there are no complications." I swing my legs back around, looking her straight in the eye. "No feelings involved. That's exactly the way I like it."

Chapter Eleven
Summer

I can tell he's convinced himself he believes it, but deep down, he knows it's not the truth, and that makes me sad for him, because he's so closed off, so guarded, so unwilling to open his heart again that he might miss out on the greatest love of his life. Of course, I don't voice those opinions, because he'd just chalk it up to my innocence and inexperience again, and I don't want him thinking I'm hitting on him either, so I keep those thoughts to myself.

But I feel for him. I truly do. I have no plans to tie myself to a guy, but my heart is wide-open, and if love finds me, I won't turn it away.

I'll embrace it.

Jump off the cliff with gusto, allowing myself to free fall, trusting that I'll land safely. Yes, I might be damaged or broken when I hit solid ground, but I know I'll survive.

Ryan would never leave the platform, missing out on the entire experience, and I hurt for all those lost opportunities he's most likely already foregone.

"We should get down," he says, dragging me out of my head. "It's getting dark and we need to head back to the city."

"Okay." I make a move, but he shakes his head.

"Let me go first."

I don't argue, letting him descend first and giving him a head start before I climb down. A gentle breeze blows around me as I descend, still lost in thought, and I'm a little distracted.

I'm about twenty feet off the ground when I lose my footing. It happens so fast, and it's so unexpected, that I do the one thing you should never do—panic. My hands grapple at the tree trunk, my fingers desperately trying to hold on even as I feel myself falling.

"Fuck! Summer!" Ryan shouts from somewhere below me.

I close my eyes, humming under my breath as I go into that Zen place in my head, preparing for the inevitable hard landing. It's not as if this is the first time I've fallen out of a tree. I have a history of broken bones to prove it, so I'm expecting the worst.

But it doesn't happen. Instead, I land in a pair of strong, warm arms, and relief washes over me. With my eyes still shut, I wrap my arms around Ryan's neck, resting my head on his broad chest, inhaling his potently masculine scent.

Might as well take advantage of the opportunity while I can.

Being held by him again is nice. His heart is beating frantically under my ear, mirroring the pounding organ in my chest.

"You scared the shit out of me," he exclaims, his voice gruff. "You're lucky I'd reached the ground, or you could've been seriously injured."

My eyes flicker open, and I lift my head, peering into his piercing blue eyes. "Thank you for saving me."

He makes no move to put my feet on the ground, and I raise no objection. My heart is thumping wildly, doing cartwheels and somer-saults behind my rib cage as we stare at one another. Something inde-cipherable passes in the tiny space between us, and despite my previous protestations, I know I want him. I'm only fooling myself by pretending otherwise.

I want him so badly I could cry.

I need to feel his lips on mine again.

To savor the feel of his tongue as it sweeps inside my mouth.

To burn from the fiery tingles scorching a path across my skin in all the places where he touches me.

His chest rises, his pupils darken, and I imagine his mind has gone to the same blissful place mine has. My tongue darts out to moisten my dry lips, and his eyes follow the motion. "You shouldn't thank me," he half-whispers, his eyes still glued to my mouth.

"Why not?" I whisper back, circling my arms more firmly around his neck as he holds me closer to his chest.

"Because I'm about to do something I shouldn't." He lowers his head, lining our mouths up, and his warm breath fans over my face. "Now is the time to say no if you don't want this," he whispers across my lips.

Determination flows through me, and I bridge the tiny gap between us, pressing my lips to his.

Our mouths glide effortlessly together. Once, twice, three times. Just a barely there kiss each time. A fleeting meeting of lips.

But it's everything.

Everything.

I feel his touch everywhere as if he's kissing me all over my body. *How the hell can a few feather-soft kisses make me feel so damn much?*

He angles his head, moving his lips more precisely over mine as the kiss deepens, and I eagerly open my mouth, ready to welcome his tongue when my brother pours ice water over our moment.

"Summer! James!" Austin hollers, his voice way too close for comfort. We rip our mouths apart, and I wriggle out of his hold as he quickly puts me down. I move away from him, and one infinitesimal second later, my annoying, cock-blocking brother is right up in my face. "There you are."

"Yes. Here we are." I smother my frustration as adrenaline courses through my body and my core aches with need. My heart pounds against my chest as I consider how close we came to being discovered.

Holy shit.

If Austin had arrived and found me wrapped up in Ryan's arms, kissing him, there would've been hell to pay.

Talk about a close call.

"It's time to go," he says. "I don't want Miley driving back in the pitch-dark."

"We're ready." Ryan's voice sends shivers cascading up and down my spine, but I purposely don't look at him, and he's keeping his distance from me too. "Let's go."

"And he hasn't mentioned it all week?" Hannah asks, on Friday at lunchtime, as we share a table in the campus cafeteria. This is the only day of the week where our different schedules enable us to have lunch together.

My first week as a college freshman is just about over, and I lived to tell the tale. Truth be told, I'm loving all my classes, and I've made friends with a bunch of guys and girls who share some of the same electives, so things are good.

"Not a word. In fact, I've hardly seen him. If I didn't know how busy he was with the gym, I'd say he's avoiding me." Even though I spent two nights this week training with Miley, Ryan still evaded contact with me.

"How do you feel about the kiss now?" she inquires. I had called Hannah the minute I got back to my room Sunday night and told her everything.

Ryan was quiet and distant in the back seat of the car as we drove to Newark from his sister's house, pretending to sleep most of the journey, but I knew from his breathing he was awake.

I shrug. "Whatever. It's not that big of a deal. Austin interrupted before we were properly kissing. It won't happen again, and that's probably for the best."

"Probably?"

"I mean it *is* for the best." I stab a piece of chicken, popping it in my mouth. "Nothing can come of this attraction between us. I know it. He knows it," I add, once I've chewed my food.

"Well then, we're going to that frat party tonight. You need to find another pair of hot lips to distract you."

"You won't hear me complaining, sister."

***

"Who else is going to the frat party tonight?" Austin asks as we eat dinner alone at the apartment later that day.

"Hannah and Jordan and a bunch of people from class," I confirm, shoveling a forkful of pasta in my mouth.

"Be careful. Some of those frat boys are complete assholes with no agenda except fucking as many girls as they can. Don't leave your drink unattended, and don't go off with someone you don't know."

"I know how to take care of myself, Austin. You've got to quit this shit. I know you mean well, and I appreciate that you care, but you've got to stop treating me like a little girl. I'm an adult now, and I can fend for myself."

"I want nothing to happen to you. And I want to protect you from assholes who might break your heart. Is that so wrong?" He places his silverware down to take a sip of his water.

I reach across the table, curling my hand around his. "I love how protective you are, but there are some things you can't and shouldn't protect me from."

I bite down on my lip, carefully considering my next words. "I need to make mistakes, Austin. Because it's all part of the learning process. Part of growing up and discovering who I am and who I want to be. I'm not planning on falling in love or getting my heart broken, but if it happens, I'll embrace it fully. And if anyone is doing the protecting after that, it'll be me. I'll be the one protecting my heart until I'm ready to give it away again."

My brother smiles at me. "You always had such a wise head on your shoulders, yet you're so innocent and excitable at the same time.

I hope you know how special you are, Sum. You'll make some guy so fucking lucky someday."

He looks down at his plate, toying with his food, looking contemplative. "It goes against my nature to say this, but I'll stop. Or, at least, I'll try to. I respect your wishes once you promise you'll do your utmost to stay safe."

"I have no desire to be utterly reckless."

He scowls. "That's hardly a reassuring statement."

"Austin, you've just got to trust me, and know that if I need anything, you'll be the first one I come to. I promise."

He sighs, nodding. "Okay. And for the record, I do trust you. It's those dicks on campus I don't trust."

I'm finishing curling my hair when my cell pings with an incoming text from Hannah letting me know they are on the way up in the elevator. Unplugging the curling iron, I apply a light layer of lip gloss before casting one final glance over myself in the mirror.

It's my first frat party, and I don't know what the usual dress code is, so I'm playing it relatively safe tonight. My ripped jeans, stiletto heels, and black lace-trimmed tank top scream sexy without looking like I've tried too hard. Grabbing my gray leather jacket and a silk scarf from my bed, I pull them on and then tip my head upside down, loosening out the waves in my hair so they flow naturally down my back.

Satisfied with my appearance, I exit my bedroom just as the doorbell chimes, almost colliding with Ryan in the hallway.

"Shit, sorry. You okay?" He grips my elbow to keep me from falling, and his touch electrifies me.

Like always.

"I'm fine." I shuck out of his hold, offering him a brief smile.

His eyes rake up and down my body like a sultry caress, and butterflies scatter in my chest. He's only wearing plain sweats and a tee, and his feet are bare, but he looks totally hot. This guy could wear a sack, and I'd still want to bang him. The air is fraught with the usual tension, but neither of us makes a move to separate.

I'm acutely aware of how close we're standing to one another, and the chiming of the door for the second time, but I can't drag my gaze away from him, and it appears he's the same. His eyes drink me in, his gaze caressing me with intent, and he may as well be undressing me for the way it makes me feel.

When Ryan focuses his singular attention on me, it's intense and all-consuming, and it's difficult to remember how to even breathe.

"You look..." he says before backtracking. "You're going out?"

I nod, as the doorbell rings again, finally snapping me out of my trance. "Yep. Heading to my first frat party, and I need to answer the door before Hannah busts her way through it."

I walk as quick as my heels allow, swinging the door open as Hannah has her finger poised over the doorbell. "About damn time," she says, pushing past me. "I desperately need to pee." She runs off in the direction of the bathroom, and I step aside.

"Come on in," I say to Jordan and the two guys standing behind him.

I lead them into the living room when I hear Ryan tinkering about in the kitchen. I'd rather avoid another confrontation between him and Jordy. There's still no love lost between them. "Summer, this is Dalton and Sean," Jordan says, introducing his friends.

"Hey." I smile. "Good to meet you."

"Trust me, the pleasure is all mine," the taller, dark-haired guy says taking my hand and planting a kiss on the back. "I'm Dalton."

"I'm Sean," the second guy says, nudging his friend out of the way and stealing my hand. "And you're fucking hot."

A snort resonates from the doorway, and I glance over to where Ryan is propped against the doorjamb, eyeing the guys warily. Crappity crap. Things are about to go south.

"Who are you?" Sean asks, the same time Dalton says, "Got something to say, buddy?"

"He's the douche I was telling you about," Jordan pipes up, and I glare at him. I will beat his stupid ass if he told them the story of how I lost my virginity.

"Relax," he whispers in my ear. "I didn't tell them everything. I just warned them he might be here."

"You're really begging for an ass kicking," Ryan says, sauntering into the room with a nonchalant look on his face.

"Do I look like I care?" Jordan retorts, squaring up to him.

"What's going on?" Hannah asks, arriving into the room with impeccable timing.

"Nothing," I say, grabbing Jordan and shoving him toward his girlfriend. "Let's go."

"Lead the way, babe," Dalton says, draping his arm around my shoulder without invitation.

Tossing his arm off, I purposely ignore Ryan as I walk toward the door.

"Summer. Wait a sec," Ryan says just as I'm about to step foot out into the hallway.

"I'll meet you at the elevator bank," I tell the others, beseeching Han with my eyes. Taking the cue, she drags Jordan and the guys away as I turn around to face Ryan.

"If you're planning on lecturing me, save your breath," I say before he's opened his mouth. I fold my arms across my chest, daring him to challenge me.

His Adam's apple bobs in his throat as he fixes those gorgeous blue eyes on me. "Are you sure you want to go out with them? Those guys seem like dicks."

I shrug. "Maybe, but I don't see how it's any of your business." I'm not being rude, just stating a fact.

He's quiet for a few beats, and then he exhales loudly. "You're right, it isn't." A muscle pops in his jaw. "Have a good night." With a brief nod, he goes into the apartment, slamming the door, leaving me staring at the wooden frame, wondering what the hell is going on between us.

Chapter Twelve
Ryan

"We're going to head, man," Austin says, clapping me on the back. Miley is tucked under his left arm, smiling up at him like he hung the moon.

"I think I'll stay." I gesture with my eyes, capturing the bartender's attention. "I'll have another." I point at my almost empty beer.

"Thought as much." Austin grins, his eyes darting to the curvy brunette pressed into my side. "Later, bro."

Miley kisses my cheek, whispering in my ear. "You are so much better than this."

Her words piss me off, and I scowl at her, ignoring the warning look Austin shoots my way.

The brunette maneuvers herself into the space between me and the counter, pushing her ample tits into my chest. "How about we go back to my place?" she purrs, setting her hands on my shoulders and leaning in close.

"I'm not interested." I gently remove her hands from my body.

"What?" She plants her hands on her hips, narrowing her eyes at me. "But we've been flirting for the last hour."

"No. You've been flirting. I've just been sitting here listening to you blabber on."

Her cheeks inflame, and her nostrils flare. I'm being an asshole, and it's not her fault I'm in a fucking shitty mood and taking it out on her. "Look, Sasha."

"My name's Sandy, asshole."

"Sandy. I'm sorry. You're beautiful and great company, and at any other time, I would be up for going home with you, but I've had a crappy week, and I'm just not in the mood."

Her features soften. "Do you want to talk about it?" she asks, and now I feel even worse. Because I just want her to leave me the fuck alone. I don't want to talk to anyone. I want to drown my frustrations in my beer and anesthetize my brain so the images of Summer fucking that douche Dalton leave my mind. My head is a melting pot of confusion, thanks to Summer and Myndi fucking with my sanity. I certainly don't need to add another female to the mix, no matter how much a physical release might help.

"No, but I appreciate you asking. You should go. I'm lousy company tonight, and you deserve so much better."

She grabs her jacket and purse, surveying me with keen eyes. "Whoever the woman is, I hope she realizes how lucky she is." She kisses my cheek. "Take care, Ryan, and don't get too drunk."

Pity I didn't heed her warning. I'm in the taxi on the way back to the apartment, and I'm seeing double and triple of everything. But my head is too foggy to fixate on Summer, so it's mission accomplished.

I stumble into the apartment, heading straight to the kitchen where I down a couple bottles of water with a few pain pills as a precautionary measure.

Against my better judgment, I knock on Summer's bedroom door, telling myself I just want to check she got home safe. Austin is staying at Miley's again, and I promised him I'd look out for her when he's not here, so it's not like I'm doing anything wrong. Her room is dark, with no light seeping out from under the door, which indicates she's either asleep or not home yet. My vision is blurry as I check the time on my watch, but I decipher it's just past two a.m. Risking it, I gently open her door, cursing when I spot the empty room and her unmade bed.

My jaw locks tight as I head into my bedroom, stripping my clothes off and walking naked into my bathroom. I turn the shower on and step under the cold stream of water, needing the icy shock to help sober me up.

It's not unheard of for frat parties to go on until all hours. Hell, I remember coming home a couple times at eight and nine in the morning, but this is Summer we're talking about, and I don't like thinking of her out there somewhere, alone and drunk and vulnerable.

I'm considering options as the cold water batters my body like a thousand tiny knives penetrating my skin. But it works as an effective sobering agent, and my head is a lot clearer when I finally step out, shivering and shaking as I wrap a towel around my hips and another one around my shoulders.

I grab two more bottles of water and make a strong cup of coffee before retreating to my bedroom again. I turn on the TV, pulling a pair of sweats on as I prop myself up on the bed to wait for her. I'm giving her until three a.m., and if she isn't home by then, I'm calling her.

It's now three forty, and she's answered none of my calls or texts, and I'm going out of my mind with worry. I've just decided to head out in search of her when the front door crashes open, and the sound of footsteps in the living room confirms she's home.

I walk with urgency out of my room, my heart careening around my chest when I find her lying on her side on the couch, passed out, with Jordan and Sean looming over her.

"What the actual fuck?" I growl, storming toward them. "What the fuck did you do to her?"

"Sus drunkkkk," Hannah slurs, and I whip my head around, discovering her sprawled across the lounge chair.

"No one did anything to her," Jordan snaps, sounding coherent.

"I'd never let anything happen to Hannah or Summer. I only had two beers, and she was by my side all night except for the times she was sucking face with my buddy here." Jordan smirks, elbowing Sean in the ribs as a muscle ticks in his jaw.

"I think I'm in love," Sean slurs, crouching down beside Summer. He reaches out to brush hair back off her face, and I'm done.

Yanking him up by the shirt, I pull him away from her, shoving him toward the door. "Get the fuck out of my apartment, and don't come back."

"Someone sounds jealous," Jordan taunts, and I'm this close to punching the annoying punk. I know he's doing it to wind me up, but I'm a ball of pent-up-frustration, and it won't take much to snap.

"Yeah, *Dad*," the other asshole says, shucking out of my hold and swaying on his feet. He's completely wasted. "It's obvious you've got a boner for her. Too bad you're too old."

Now I really want to punch something. Preferably his annoying, ugly head, but I doubt I'll win any brownie points with Summer if I go around beating up her friends.

"Get him out of here," I tell Jordan. "You and Hannah can stay if you want to wait for an Uber, but he leaves now."

"We're going." Jordan scoops Hannah up into his arms, before glowering at me. "Keep your hands off Summer," he warns.

"Mind your own fucking business," I snap. As if I'd take advantage of any girl in that situation.

"This *is* my business. She's Justin's girl, and I promised him I'd look after her."

"Who the fuck is Justin?" Sean asks, frowning.

"Not now." Jordan dismisses him, eyeballing me like I'm scum of the earth. "You had your fun with her. Now let her be. She doesn't belong to you, and it's pathetic how obvious you are around her."

"Get the fuck out," I demand, losing the last semblance of my patience. "In case that isn't clear enough for you, you're not welcome here again."

"Fuck you, man."

Refusing to be dragged into any more of this juvenile bullshit, I ignore him, closing the door after them with relief. When I return to the living room, Summer is quietly moaning on the couch. "Summer?" I kneel beside her, sweeping hair back off her face as she slowly opens her eyes.

"Ryan," she mumbles, reaching out for me. "Don't feel so hot." She reeks of beer and cigarettes, and from the way her eyes are rolling around her head, I'd say she's drank more than her body weight tonight.

"Do you need the bathroom?" I ask as she gags.

She nods and I lift her into my arms, racing toward the bathroom.

I position her on her knees in front of the toilet, removing her jacket just before she retches. Grabbing a hair tie off the counter, I gently pull her hair into a messy ponytail, rubbing her shoulders as she pukes.

When she's expelled everything in her stomach, she slumps sideways, resting her back against the tub, moaning and clutching her head. "I've got the spinnies," she slurs. "Can't see straight."

A chuckle escapes my mouth as I bend down and wipe her mouth with a towel. "Stay put." I run into the kitchen and grab a bottle of water and some pills. When I return, she's lying on her side on the cold tile floor. "Shit." I gently shake her shoulders. "Summer. Wake up."

"Wha?" She groans, swatting her hands at me. "Go away. Sleeping." She's even fucking adorable when she's all messy and drunk. I prop her upright. "Open your eyes. I need you to take this."

She opens her eyes, staring unfocused at me. Lifting her hand, she traces her fingers across my cheek. "You're beautiful, you know that?"

"Isn't that supposed to be my line?" I tease, opening her mouth and bringing the bottle to her mouth. "Drink."

She downs it like a trooper, letting me open her mouth and place the pills inside. Her eyes never leave mine, and they're clearer and less tired looking now. "I can't stop thinking about you," she admits, keeping her eyes trained on mine. "I think that could be a problem."

"Tell me about it," I say, helping her stand up. She sways unsteadily, but I've got my arm wrapped firmly around her back and I won't let her fall. "You're too tempting for your own good, Summer."

"I like you," she murmurs, resting her head on my shoulder. "I like you more than I should."

She'll be so embarrassed tomorrow when she finds out she said all this. However, I doubt she'll remember. Which is why I give her the same honesty in return.

"I know, Summer. Believe me, I feel the same way."

"You do?" She tries to circle her arms around my neck, but they flop back to her side, and I chuckle again.

"I think this is a conversation for another day. You need to get to bed and sleep this off." Glancing down, I notice the puke on her shirt and the end strands of her hair. "But you need to shower first." There's no way she can stand up by herself, so I place her back on the ground while I start the shower and gather a towel and toiletries. I test the water, ensuring it's lukewarm before I kneel beside her, gently removing her clothes.

I try not to look as I strip her even though I know every square inch of her body intimately. I leave her in her panties and kick my sweats off so I'm only in my boxers. Then I lift her into the shower, placing her directly under the spray of water with her back pressed up against my chest. She shrieks as the stream of water beats down on her, but I keep my arm wrapped around her waist, telling her she's okay and I've got this.

I take my time washing her. Gently rubbing the cloth up and down her arms, over her tummy, across her breasts, and down over her shoulders and back. I'm painfully hard, even though I'm trying my best to be good here, but Summer only has to look at me to turn me on.

The little whimpers and moans of pleasure leaving her mouth aren't helping either. When my fingers massage the shampoo into her hair, I almost come on the spot as she gasps and writhes against me, rubbing her ass against my erection, confirming she's as horny as me. Thoughts of pinning her to the wall, and fucking her from behind, invade my mind, torturing me with visions of something I want but can never have. And even if I could, I would never do that now. Not when she's so drunk and incapable of thinking clearly.

"Oh, god, Ryan." She moans, slinging her arm back and around my neck. "I'm so horny. Fuck me. Please."

Kill. Me. Now.

It takes enormous willpower to turn her down especially when she slides her hand between our bodies, palming my hard dick. I want nothing more than to let her drop to her knees and suck me off, but I won't disrespect her. She's not in her right mind to make such a call.

I remove her hand, keeping a hold of her as I reach over and turn the shower off. "You're drunk, Summer, and you need to sleep this off."

"No," she pouts, twisting around, so she's facing me. Her nipples are hard peaks jutting into my chest, fueling the arousal coursing through my body. "I need to sleep with you." She stretches up to kiss me, and I twist my head to the side so her lips press against my cheek.

"It's not happening, babe." I lift her out and swaddle her in a towel before slipping one around my hips. I tug my wet boxers off underneath the towel before urging her to do the same.

"You take them off me," she challenges with a glint in her eye.

"I can't touch you there."

"Why not? You did before?"

"Summer. Please. Just remove your panties. You can't get in bed with them on."

Her eyes flare. "Fine." She deliberately drops the towel, hooking her thumbs into the side of her panties and pulling them down her legs. She sways, and I hold her elbows to steady her as she removes the last item of clothing. I keep my eyes fixated on her face despite the almost overwhelming urge to lower my gaze to her gorgeous tits.

When she kicks the panties away, I swaddle her in the towel and carry her into her room. I place her down carefully on the bed, gently patting her skin dry. Her eyes roll back and forth, and she's close to passing out again.

Removing her sleep shorts and tank from under her pillow, I help put them on her before grabbing the hairdryer from her bedside table and sitting up behind her on the bed. I dry her hair as she leans back against my chest, and it's one of the most intimate moments of my life. Her eyes flutter open and closed, and she holds onto my arm, her soft touch and unspoken trust reaching places deep inside me.

When her hair is dry, I help her into the bed, tugging the covers up under her chin. "Sleep well," I whisper, as she clings to the last vestiges of consciousness.

I straighten up and her arm darts out, brushing my leg. "Don't go," she whispers in a sleep-drenched voice. "Stay with me."

"I wish I could," I whisper, brushing strands of silky hair back off her face as she finally succumbs to slumber. "I want to so very much, but I can't." I wait another couple minutes, making sure she's fast asleep before I slip out of her room. I snatch another bottle of water and a couple pills and leave them by her bed before returning to my room where I toss and turn in a restless sleep for the remainder of the night.

I drag my weary ass out of bed at eleven a.m. the following morning, yawning as I walk into the kitchen.

Summer's bedroom door is still closed, and there's no sign of life out here, so I figure she's still sleeping. We don't have to be at the gym until three, so we have a few hours to relax before our shifts start. She's covering the front desk alone today as a kind of dummy run before next weekend when Miley and Austin are in London. They're away from Thursday night until Tuesday afternoon, and Summer, Derrick, and I are filling in for them.

I make a pot of coffee, deciding to call my sister before I make breakfast. "I'm so glad you called," Gabby says when she answers. "I've wanted to call you all week, but Slate said to give you time. I'm sorry about Sunday, Ryan. I swear I didn't know she was dropping by."

The anguish and guilt in my sister's tone are like a punch in the gut. I never wanted her to get caught in the crossfire, let alone ruin her friendship with her best friend, but that's exactly what happened when Myndi and I broke up and I feel awful about that. "It's okay, Tornado. I know you didn't know, and I don't blame you. I'm the one who should apologize to you for ruining your dinner party."

"You ruined nothing, Ryan. We had a nice time. At least until that point."

"Why is she here?"

There's a pregnant pause before Gabby replies. "Her and Will are engaged, and they wanted to come back home before the baby is born," she quietly confirms, and I hate the little stab of pain that accompanies her words. "They have both secured jobs at the hospital."

I say nothing for a while. "All I ask is that you don't invite her over when I'm there."

"I'll keep my distance from her, Ryan. You're my brother. You come first."

Her loyalty warms my frozen bones. "I love you, Gabby. So fucking much, but you've sacrificed enough for me. She was your best friend. You don't have to cut her out of your life anymore. Not because of me. Just keep us apart. Never tell me anything about her, and things will be fine."

Silence engulfs us again. "What happened, Ryan? Where did it go wrong for you two because I don't understand?"

This isn't the first time she's asked me, but I couldn't tell her back then, and I can't tell her now. "It's water under the bridge now, Tornado. She's moved on."

"But you haven't," she supplies. "I know whatever happened hurt you, and I hate seeing you like this. I want you to find your person and be happy."

"I am happy," I lie. "I don't need a woman to make me feel complete."

"Oh, Ryan." Her voice cracks, and I hate to upset my sister.

"Stop worrying, Gabby. I like my life exactly the way it is. Not all of us are destined for marriage and a family."

I once harbored those dreams. Came close to turning them into reality. Until they came crashing down around me. Now I know I'll never have that, because I'm not cut out to be a husband or a father.

Chapter Thirteen

Summer

My tongue is glued to the top of my mouth when I finally emerge from my alcohol-induced sleep coma. Beams of buttery sunshine stream into my room through the gap in the blinds, confirming it's time to get my lazy butt up out of the bed. I'm yawning as I sluggishly climb out from under my warm comforter, stretching my arms out over my head. My tummy rumbles as hunger claws at my insides.

Memories of last night resurrect in my mind while I toe on my slippers and wrap a robe around my body. I sit on the edge of the bed, brushing my hair as I piece back the events of last night. I remember how crazy the frat party was. I also remember consuming copious red cups. And dancing on top of a table with Hannah. Making out with Sean. Feeling sick in the Uber on the ride here.

Hell.

I drop the brush, cradling my head in my hands as I remember Jordan referring to me as *Justin's girl* and Ryan angrily kicking Sean and him out.

I puked.

A lot.

And Ryan took care of me.

Vague recollections of him showering with me awaken my libido, and my pussy pulses with renewed desire. I remember what I said to him and asking him to stay with me.

I suppose it could've been a lot worse.

I could've puked *on him*.

Or thrown myself at him.

Or said way worse.

Considering how smashed I was, I think I got away lightly.

As I glance at the water and pills by my bed, my heart does a funny little twist. Ryan could easily have taken advantage of me last night, but he was a perfect gentleman, and he took such good care of me.

The more I get to know him, the harder it is to deny that I crave his touch as much as I crave his company.

I pad out of my bedroom, taking a pee and brushing my teeth before wandering in the direction of the delicious aromas wafting from the kitchen. Ryan is standing at the stove, singing along to the song playing on his iPhone as he cooks something in the skillet.

"Morning." I round the island unit, making a beeline for the coffeepot.

"Fuck." He slams the skillet down on the stove. "Don't sneak up on me like that."

"Not my fault you were too busy singing to notice my arrival," I tease, pouring myself a giant mug of coffee.

He steps behind me, reaching over my head to extract two plates from the cupboard. Heat rolls off him, crashing into me, and every tiny hair on my body stands alert. My lips stall around the rim of my mug as he leans into me, setting the plates down and bracing one hand on the edge of the counter. With his other hand, he gently touches my arm. "How are you feeling today?" There's a slightly rough edge to his deep voice.

"Ugh. Okay," I splutter, as his finger brushes up and down my arm.

He's barely touching me.

It's the lightest of caresses, but it's wholly intimate, and I long to turn around and latch my mouth onto his. To wrap my legs around his waist and grind my hips against his hard-on. To yank his sweats down, push my panties aside, and direct his cock inside me. To feel him moving as one with me so I forget I exist on this planet without him.

"Good." He steps back, and I feel bereft. "I hope you're hungry and that you like omelets."

"I love them," I reply, my voice coming out a little more high-pitched than usual. I hop up onto a stool, quietly sipping my coffee as he silently works at the stove.

A few minutes later, he slides a plate with a delicious-looking tomato and ham omelet across the island unit to me. "Dive in." He takes the stool beside me, wasting no time devouring his brunch.

"This is so good," I say in between mouthfuls of the fluffy, cheesy goodness. "Thank you."

"You're welcome." He smiles at me, and my heart starts cartwheels.

It's futile ignoring what's happening between us.

I'm attracted to him.

I like his company.

I want to get to know him better.

More intimately.

There. I've finally said it. I've finally admitted it to myself, and the world is still standing.

"And thank you for looking after me last night. I really appreciate how much of a gentleman you were." I eye him directly as we speak so he can tell I'm genuine.

"It's no problem. You were pretty wasted."

"I was." He chuckles, and I frown. "What?"

"You never react how I expect you to. It would embarrass most girls, but you own that shit."

I grin, shrugging. "No point deluding myself or you. And I'm not embarrassed for speaking my mind. I meant every word."

He stalls with his fork halfway to his mouth. Now it's his turn to ask, "What?"

I flash him my most seductive smile. "I meant it when I said you were beautiful and I really liked you."

"I could say the same, but it doesn't change a thing."

"Why not?" I set my silverware down, swiveling on my stool to face him. Our legs brush, and a jolt of electricity zips through me. His leg jerks, and I know he felt it too. "You can't deny we have chemistry. I know you're attracted to me as much as I'm attracted to you."

"I'm too old for you, Summer."

I scoff. "Seriously? *That's* your objection?"

"And your brother is my best friend. He most definitely wouldn't approve."

"I'm not suggesting we run off and elope." I roll my eyes.

"What *are* you suggesting?"

I haven't really given it much thought, but I don't want to waste the opportunity either. "A friends with benefits arrangement," I blurt. His eyes pop wide, and I blabber on before he can shut me down. "Having sex has awakened a side of me I've never explored. I want to discover my likes and dislikes. To explore my sexuality with someone I trust. We're attracted to one another, and neither of us is interested in dating or a relationship, so it seems like a perfect solution."

I pat myself on the back for coming up with such an ingenious plan on the spur of the moment. Especially when I'm so hungover.

"Let me make sure I've got this straight," he says, leaning back and staring at me with an incredulous expression. "You want me to educate you about sex, behind your brother's back, but you're not interested in any relationship outside of a sexual one?"

"That's about it in a nutshell." I nervously tuck my hair behind my ears, afraid he'll turn me down because it sounds so...clinical, so impersonal, when it's put like that. "But we'd be friends. Obviously. I mean, we are friends, right?"

"I'm not sure I could just be friends with you," he says with a hint of sadness in his tone. He cups my face in his large hands, examining my face. "Agreeing to have sex behind your brother's back is a recipe for disaster. If he found out, he'd quite likely kill me."

"We'll be careful. He won't find out." I'm grasping at straws because it feels like I've already lost this battle.

His thumb presses into my lower lip, and he stares at my mouth, looking conflicted. I wait with bated breath for him to decide. When he lifts his chin to look at me, my euphoria dies as I spot the decision on his face.

"I think you're breathtaking, Summer. Truly. Inside and out. Making love to you was incredible, but I'm not the kind of man you should be mixed up with. You need to find a guy your own age. One who will respect you and treat you right." He stands, clearing away our plates. "Whatever this attraction is between us, it's got to end. Nothing else will happen. I'm sorry if that hurts you, but in time, you'll see it's for the best."

"I'm such an idiot," I tell Hannah over lunch in this dinky little café the following day. "And I'm so embarrassed. Now I'm stuck working with him, and it's awkward. We didn't speak at all in the car on the way to and from work, and at the gym, all our interactions were about professional matters. It was weird and uncomfortable, and now, I'm terrified Austin will pick up on something and read into it, which would be comical, considering nothing's going on and it never will because he only sees me as this inexperienced little kid with nothing to offer him."

"Wow. Breathe, girlfriend," Hannah says, slanting me a sympathetic look. "It's his loss. Not yours. The world is your oyster, babe, remember?"

"It's hard to hold on to grandiose notions when I'm feeling deflated."

"You'll bounce back. Jordan says Sean is crazy about you. He keeps asking for your number. You should go out with him."

"I thought Jordy is opposed to me dating other guys, or is it just Ryan he has issue with?"

She cringes a little. "It's Ryan, but that doesn't mean he won't vet any potential dates or hookups. He promised Justin he'd look out for you."

"Why? What exactly does that mean?"

She squirms in her seat. "I don't really know. Jordy's loyal, and he won't say. I get the impression Justin has plans for you when you are both finished college. I could be wrong, but I think he's relying on Jordy to ensure you find no one permanent in the meantime."

"Meanwhile, he's free to fuck around with whoever he wants with no interference?" I snap, grabbing my cell out of my bag.

"It's only a guess, Sum. Would it be so bad if he cared that much?"

"He doesn't have the right, Han! I know we were kind of dating before we left, but it was casual. We haven't even had sex, and who the hell knows where we'll be and who we'll be with in four years' time? If Justin is holding onto some romantic notion about us, then it's time I set him straight."

She nods. "I'll grab us more coffee while you make the call."

Justin answers just before I'm about to hang up, sounding groggy. "Hey, babe," he croaks. "It's good to hear from you."

We made a deal when we went our separate ways for college not to smother one another, so we've only shared a few texts in the last few weeks. Hearing his voice again is good. Still, I'm mad at him.

"What did you make Jordan promise you about me?" I spit out.

"What?" He sounds a lot less fuzzy now, and I detect the wariness in his tone.

"Jordan's acting weird. Well, weirder than usual, and I know you said something to him. I want to know what it is."

"Look, can we talk about this later? Now isn't a good time." His voice spikes with a tinge of fear.

"No. I want to talk about it now. You—"

"Come back to bed, Justin," a feminine voice says in the background halting my words.

"You are fucking unbelievable," I say before hanging up. "Ugh!!" I cradle my head in my hands.

"What'd he say?" Hannah asks, sliding back into her seat. She hands me a fresh coffee.

"Nothing. He was too distracted by the girl he was in bed with."

"Shit."

"It doesn't matter. It just proves my point."

"Are you sure? You look upset."

"Of course, I'm upset. Everyone thinks they can tell me how to run my love life, and I'm fucking sick of it. Maybe I'll become a nun and forget about sex and boys because all they do is mess with your head. This is exactly why I want no entanglements. It seems like even casual sex is more trouble than it's worth. Honestly, I give up."

"Are you all packed?" I ask Miley as I'm preparing to leave the apartment on Wednesday night. They are heading on their mini vacay tomorrow, and Austin finally let the cat out of the bag regarding their destination. Watching Miley squeal and then climb all over my brother was kind of disturbing, but at least someone's happy.

Ryan and I have been cohabiting in this awkward space all week. I'm calling the housing assignments coordinator daily, inquiring into whether a free dorm room has become available yet. Even Hannah and Jordan's floor sounds appealing at this stage.

"Yes," Miley squeaks, jumping in her seat. "I'm so excited, and I can't believe Austin arranged for me to visit my sister." Tears prick her eyes. "He's so thoughtful, and I'm so in love with him."

"Aw, that's super sweet." I grab her into a hug. "You help bring out the best in him, Miley. I've never seen my brother so happy."

"I think he's the one," she whispers, glancing over her shoulder to ensure he's not in earshot. "Or is that weird for me to admit to his sister?"

"Not weird at all." I shake my head. "And I hope it's true because I'd love to call you my sister-in-law someday."

"What are you two whispering about over there?" Austin asks with suspicion in his voice.

"Just girl stuff," I say, with a shrug. "Nothing you need to worry your pretty little head about."

"Aw, you think I'm pretty, sis?" Austin kisses the top of my head before reeling Miley into his arms.

"The prettiest," I sweetly reply. "And that's my cue to leave."

"I'll drive you," Miley says, grabbing her keys and pecking Austin on the lips.

"I can walk. It's not that far, and it's a nice evening."

"I want to drive you so I can come inside and watch. Unless that'd make you nervous?" she adds, her brow puckering.

"It wouldn't but you don't have to."

"I want to. I want to support you. And I've never been to auditions. It'll be fun."

"Well, okay then. Thanks." I really hope Austin and Miley make the distance because I can't imagine anyone better than her for my brother. She has such a pure heart, and she already feels like my sister.

The look my brother gives his girlfriend in that moment melts me into a puddle of goo on the floor. "I love you," he tells her, nuzzling his head into her neck, and happy tears pool in my eyes.

"We shouldn't be too long," I say, hugging my brother once he's finally torn himself away from his girl.

"Break a leg," Miley says, slipping into a seat in the auditorium at the theater arts company where auditions for *Romeo and Juliet* are being held. Mom always says go big or go home, so I'm auditioning for the part of Juliet, even though I probably don't have a snowball's chance in hell of getting it.

"Thanks!" I give her a quick hug before meandering backstage. The girl in charge gets me to complete some paperwork and then advises me where to stand in line.

"Hey, beautiful," a husky voice says in my ear, and I look around, startled to see Sean standing behind me. I haven't seen him since last Friday night although I know he's still pestering Jordy for my number.

"Hey yourself." My tentative smile is rimmed with suspicion. "What are you doing here?"

He shrugs. "Auditioning. Same as you."

I narrow my eyes at him. "If this is some kind of attempt to ingratiate yourself, it won't work."

He chuckles, and a mop of light-brown hair falls into his warm chocolate-colored eyes. "I don't play games, and my reasons for being here are the same as yours. I love to act. Had a part in every play in high school, and I was a member of the amateur dramatics group in my local town. I didn't even know you'd be here."

Sincerity radiates from his expression and his tone and I give him the benefit of the doubt. "Sorry for jumping to conclusions."

"It's cool." His wide smile is disarming. "But now, I really hope I get the part if it means I'll get to spend more time with you."

"Provided I get the part, and I might be pushing expectations auditioning for Juliet."

His grin expands, and my eyes pop wide. "Hang on!" I glance down at the sheet in my hand. "You're auditioning for Romeo, and they've partnered us up?"

His eyes twinkle with mirth as he waggles his brows. Leaning down, he presses his mouth to my ear. "Just as well we've already kissed. There won't be any awkwardness when we get out on that stage, and it'll give us an edge over the other audtionees"

"Always playing an angle, huh?" I tease.

He shrugs again, still smiling. "I like to win, and I'll take every advantage I can."

"A man after my own heart," I joke.

"Truer words have never been spoken." Reaching out, he tucks a few stray strands of hair behind my ear as he smiles confidently at me. "I won't be leaving here without your number either." He leans in close to my ear, and his warm breath fans over my skin. "I like you, Summer," he whispers, placing one hand on my hip. "And I'm not giving up until you agree to go out on a date with me."

Chapter Fourteen
Ryan

S ummer is quiet as I drive us to the gym on Thursday evening after dropping Miley and Austin off at the airport. I'm not surprised. It's been the pattern since our difficult conversation on Saturday. I remind myself I'm doing the right thing.

So why do I feel so lousy then?

I miss talking with her. I miss her energy and her enthusiasm, and I hate that there's so much tension between us. It's my fault it exists, and I owe it to both of us to get things back on an even keel. Clearing my throat, I glance at her briefly before speaking. "How did your audition go last night?"

Her face showcases her surprise as she turns around. She's so beautiful. So natural and unaware of how she turns heads wherever she goes, and it only adds to the appeal.

Focus, Ryan.

I silently chastise myself as I so often need to do in her presence.

If only we'd met under different circumstances.

At a different point where she's older and the age gap doesn't matter so much.

At a point where her brother is more mellow and I can talk him around.

But dreaming won't get me anywhere. I need to repeat that she's not meant for me. That I don't do relationships. Even if they're offered with no strings attached.

Try telling that to my greedy dick though.

"I think it went well, but competition is fierce." She shrugs casually, offering me a small smile. "Now it's in the hands of the gods."

"When will you find out?"

"Next week. There may be a round two, or they'll announce the main cast straightaway. I'll just have to wait and see."

"I hope you get it."

"Me too." Her knee bounces off the floor of the SUV. "But I won't stress about it. If it's meant to be, it'll happen."

We're silent the rest of the journey, but it's not an uncomfortable silence, and for that, I'm grateful.

I see little of her the rest of the day as the gym is busy, and we're both kept occupied. After the last few clients have left, she helps me lock up, and then we leave for home. Summer lets out a massive yawn as she climbs into the passenger seat.

"Tired?" I inquire, slowly backing out of the parking spot.

"A little. That was a long shift, and I had a full schedule of classes today too."

"If it's too much—"

"It's not," she rushes to reassure me, cutting me off. "I'm just getting used to my new schedule is all."

She kicks off her sneakers, lifting her legs to the dash. The car swerves as I take my eyes off the road for a split second, the lure of her long, slim legs too much to deny. Her lips kick up at the corners, and I silently curse myself for giving the game away. It's just so hard to be in her company and not stare at her. My body hasn't gotten the memo she's forbidden fruit, and every second in her presence is a battle with my self-control.

"Any word yet on a dorm room?" I blurt.

"Keen to get rid of me?" Her eyes flash knowingly as she levels a smirk my way.

"No, I..." Air expels from my mouth in a loud rush. "It's nothing personal, Summer. I just think it'd make things easier for both of us."

She sighs, and I hate that the smile slips off her face. "I know, and I'm trying, but no space has opened yet, and there's a couple of girls ahead of me on the list." She rubs a tense spot between her brows. "I can always sleep on Jordy and Han's couch for a few weeks." She pulls out her cell. "I'll message her now to make arrangements."

"Don't." I drag a hand through my hair. "I don't want you sleeping on anyone's couch." Especially not that douchebag's. I don't trust him around her. His behavior is off, and I'm wondering if there isn't more to it. "I don't want you thinking you're not welcome at our place. Because you are. This is my issue, and I'll handle it. Forget I said anything."

A big smile graces her luscious mouth, and I almost crash the car. Fuck.

Her whole face lights up when she smiles like that, and it's like getting sucker-punched in the nuts.

My vision blurs.

The world pales.

And I'm completely caught up in the moment.

"There you go again." She's fighting a laugh. "We really need to expand your vocabulary, Ryan."

The way she says my name is such a turn-on, and I realize exactly how fucking screwed up I am over this girl. I shouldn't want her. But I do. I want her so badly. And I don't know how long I can hold out before taking what I want.

"The problem isn't my vocab," I admit, pulling up to the curb outside my favorite takeout place. "It's that I continuously say shit around you I shouldn't."

"That only happens because you're trying to censure yourself. You need to just speak your mind."

"Trust me," I say, killing the engine and twisting around to face her. "If I spoke the things on my mind, I'd be in a whole new world of trouble." Before she can reply with some flirty response, I open the car door, sliding out. "I'm buying dinner. What do you want?"

Friday is a long-ass day at the gym, thanks to an arduous double shift. I desperately need to unwind, so when the staff asks if I want to join them for drinks after we're closed, I tag along. Summer is there too. Looking effortlessly pretty in a light, flowery summer dress and pink Converse. She's chatting and laughing loudly, drawing people to her without even trying. She's surrounded by a group of guys and girls, and every male member of my staff is entranced by her, none of them doing a thing to disguise it.

Not that I can blame them.

She's bewitched me too.

"She's a big hit with the clients as well," Derrick informs me, noticing the direction of my gaze, sliding a fresh beer into my hand. "You should hire her on a permanent part-time basis to cover for Miley."

"I already plan to talk to Austin about it when he returns," I truthfully admit. Even though I'm trying to create distance between us, there's no harm in hiring her because the gym is busy, and we don't get to interact that much. Summer needs a job, and we need someone flexible to cover for Miley, so it's a no-brainer.

"I think you might have to issue a memo to male members of staff though," Derrick adds with a grin. "Or else Austin will fire their asses left and right for hitting on his baby sister."

I snort. "You're not wrong. I'll definitely be having a word in a few ears."

I lose count of how many beers I drink the longer I stay rooted to my stool, growing more and more forlorn, and more envious, as I watch Summer flirting up a storm. If this was any other girl, I'd suspect she's doing it on purpose to piss me off. But I know that's not Summer's M.O. She's just being herself.

When Matthias slides his hand down her back, coming to rest dangerously low on the curve of her ass, I've reached my limit. Jumping up, I drain the rest of my beer and stalk toward them. I glare at him, pointedly fixing my gaze on his wayward hand until he gets the message, yanking it back as if electrocuted. "Let's call it a night," I tell Summer, sliding my arm protectively around her shoulders and steering her away from the fawning crowd.

"Okay," she readily agrees, waving at the rest of our staff. "See you guys tomorrow!"

I call an Uber, and we jump in, both quiet on the trip back to the apartment.

The instant I step foot in the door, I tell her goodnight and escape to my bedroom before I do something I regret.

A couple hours later, I'm still tossing fretfully in my bed, unable to switch my mind or my body off enough to go asleep. My mouth is parched, thanks to the aftereffects of drinking too many beers, so I pad out to the kitchen in my boxers to grab a drink of water. I slam to a halt when I see Summer, bent over, with her ass sticking up in the air, peering into the refrigerator. The light from the open door illuminates her stunning form, and my dick instantly turns rock hard. She's wearing a thin tank top and a flimsy thong, and her peachy ass cheeks are on full display, shattering my self-control in a nanosecond. All night I've denied the craving to touch her, and I can't resist any longer.

"Summer," I growl, stalking toward her like a predator hunting his prey.

She jerks upright, emitting a little shriek as she turns to face me. The refrigerator door closes, and I slam her up against it. My lips are on hers before she can mount any protest.

I ravish her mouth, pushing my tongue into her wet warmth as I grind my hips into hers, letting her feel what she does to me. She moans into my mouth, grabbing handfuls of my ass as she pulls me in closer. Blood thrums in my ears, and liquid lust races around my body while the devil in my ear taunts me to take her. To lay her out on the counter and fuck her senseless.

I slide my mouth along her cheek, tugging on her earlobe. "What the hell are you doing to me?" I whisper.

She palms my erection, and my dick jumps at her touch. "I think it's pretty obvious." I can hear the smile in her voice. Her tone turns breathless. "I want you to fuck me, Ryan. No second-guessing. Just do it. Right here. Right now."

A primal growl rips from the back of my throat as I lift her up. Her legs instantly wrap around my waist, and I carry her over to the counter, sitting her down.

"Fuck, that's cold." She laughs, tightening her ankles over my butt cheeks while bending down to kiss me.

My hands slip under her tank, moving up her flat stomach to palm her gorgeous tits. Her nipples instantly harden, and I roll them between my thumb and index finger as she writhes on the counter. Yanking the top off in one fluid move, I lower my mouth to her breasts, lavishing them both with attention. My hands knead her delicate flesh, and my tongue laves at the taut peaks of her nipples until she's panting and begging me for more.

"Lie back," I command, my cock straining painfully against my boxers. She obeys immediately without question, and I strip her of her panties, nudging her thighs apart, as wide as they will go, until she's spread out before me in all her glorious nakedness. "You are so incredibly beautiful," I tell her, leaning over her bare body to kiss her. "Every single part of you. Inside and out."

Her eyes shine with happiness, and I kiss her mouth tenderly. "I am so fucking hot for you." My hand moves along the curve of her body, delighting in how responsive she is to my touch as I watch her arch into my hand.

"Me too," she rasps. "I want you, Ryan. Please, I need you."

I crouch down between her thighs, positioning her legs on my shoulders. Keeping one hand on her stomach to hold her in place, I lower my head to her pussy and dive in, swiping my tongue up and down her slit, tasting her glistening skin, before pushing my tongue into her channel and devouring her like I won't ever get to do it again. With my free hand, I press down on the sensitive bundle of nerves as I pump my tongue in and out of her. My finger swirls around her clit, and she explodes on my tongue, screaming and lifting her hips up, bucking against my mouth as her climax powers through her body.

Her limbs turn boneless, her body sated, and she glances at me with a dreamy look on her face. Precum leaks out of the tip of my neglected cock, and I want nothing more than to bury myself inside her, but the child-like, wondrous, happy expression on her face brings me back to earth with a bang.

She looks so young.

So innocent.

And I feel like the worst kind of predator.

Pain slices across my chest, constricting my breathing. I stumble back, burying my face in my hands. "Fuck." *What the hell am I doing?*

"Ryan?" Her questioning tone has me lifting my head. She scrambles off the counter, coming straight at me. "No! Don't do this!" Her hands land on my bare chest, her touch like hot coals, and I jerk sideways, away from her grasp. "Look at me!" She tries to grab my face, but I dart out of her reach. "Don't you dare say this was a mistake!"

"It *was* a mistake," I snap. "I shouldn't have done that. I'm sorry."

She glares at me with her hands planted on her hips. "It *wasn't* a mistake. We are two consenting adults giving in to our attraction to one another. There is nothing wrong with that." She drops to her knees in front of me, reaching up for my cock.

I race around the other side of the counter. "Don't fucking touch me, Summer. We can't do this."

She stands, shaking her head, pinning doleful eyes on me. "I want to kill your ex for what she did to you. You can spout the age gap and my brother at me all you like, but I know the real obstacle is your fear. Fear of feeling something. Fear of opening your heart and letting someone in again. So much fear you can't even give your body what it needs."

I both hate and love how observant she is. Hate she's peeled back my layers and seen what others rarely see. Hate how vulnerable I feel in front of her even though she's the one standing completely naked. But another side of me loves she sees me so easily. That she just gets me.

Her eyes lower to my aching cock. "I told you that first night I won't beg, and I meant it. I won't get trapped in some back-and-forth drama with you. I've made my intentions clear, and I won't keep doing this." She grabs her tank and thong off the floor. "The ball's in your court, Ryan. But plan your move carefully, because the next move is your last one."

Holding her clothing clasped to her chest, she walks out of the kitchen, without uttering another word, leaving me rooted to the spot, utterly conflicted and confused.

Chapter Fifteen
Summer

"I'm sorry if I hurt you," Ryan says as we walk from the car to the gym the following morning.

"I think you're hurting yourself more," I acknowledge, propped against the wall while Ryan unlocks the door.

"True," he quietly admits. "I'm just trying to do the right thing."

That pisses me off on several levels. "The right thing for whom?"

He steps foot into the building, inputting the code to deactivate the alarm, before responding. I saunter toward the front desk, dumping my bag on the counter.

"For you," he says, coming up behind me.

I snort, shaking my head. "At least have the decency to be honest. It's not for me or even for you. You're conforming to what society has conditioned you to conform to. Or you're doing it to appease my brother. Don't pretend you're doing it for me or for you."

"Believe what you want," he snaps, a muscle clenching in his jaw. "One day, you'll thank me."

I flap my hands around, my anger increasing with every stupid word spewing from his gorgeous mouth. "Continue to wallow in your delusion if you want but I won't." We glare at one another, but the heat of arousal still simmers in the air. "Even now, you can't shield your desire for me. I won't pretend I don't want you, but I meant what I said last night. I won't play this game."

"You think this is a game?" he shouts. "I'm not playing games, Summer. I'm trying to do right by you. I'm not the one for you. I'm not the one to help you explore your sexuality. Or be anything else. Why can't you accept that?"

I prod my finger in his chest, incensed. "Maybe because you say one thing but do another!"

"Well, that won't happen again." He works hard to rein in his anger and frustration. "I give you my word. I won't lay another finger on you. I'll be on my best behavior."

"So, that's it? That's your final answer?" I'm disappointed he isn't even prepared to think about it.

He nods. "It is. This is the way it has to be."

"Fine." I slant him a fake smile, plonking down in my chair and powering up the desktop PC.

"Good." He looks at me for a few seconds, but I purposely ignore him, concentrating on logging in as I try to bring my blood pressure back down. "For what it's worth, I'm sorry it has to be like this," he adds before walking off.

"Only because you're too chickenshit to give in to what you really want," I mumble under my breath once he's out of earshot.

I spend the rest of the day avoiding him. Only talking to him when my job demands it. I eat lunch at my desk, replying to Sean's earlier text and then updating Hannah on my plans for tonight. Although the gym remains open until ten p.m. on Saturdays, it's quieter after six, and there isn't a need for someone to man the front desk, which means I get off early today.

Sean strolls through the front doors at six on the button, just as I'm powering down the computer. I took a quick bathroom break a while ago to get changed into skinny, ripped jeans and an off-the-shoulder light sweater and to touch up my makeup, so I'm ready to get the hell out of here. I toe on my heels as I smile at my approaching date. "Hey, beautiful." He produces a single red rose from behind his back, handing it to me with a shy smile that's very endearing.

"Oh, wow, thank you!" I bring the flower to my nose, inhaling the familiar scent.

"You're welcome. Ready to go?"

"Give me a minute to tell my boss I'm outta here." I turn off the computer and zip up my bag, leaving it and the rose on the counter as I walk to Ryan's office. I knock on the closed door, and he calls me in. "I wanted to let you know I'm leaving now," I say in a polite tone.

"You're seriously going out with that guy?" He gestures toward the wall of cameras behind his desk, the screen of the lobby enlarged, and I shouldn't be surprised he was watching.

"It's none of your business." I turn to leave.

"I didn't have you pegged for one of those girls."

Slowly, I turn back around. "What girls?"

"The kind who manipulates when she doesn't get her own way. I turn you down, and you instantly revert to Plan B." He shakes his head, a look of disgust forming on his face.

I am so enraged I can barely speak. I want to rip his annoying head from his shoulders, but I won't give him the argument he so desperately craves. I'm anti-drama, and I won't indulge the fury, indignation, and frustration demanding I call him out on his shitty accusation, no matter how tempting. Instead, I adopt the moral high ground. "I don't have to explain myself to you, and I'm not going to. Goodnight, *boss*."

Holding my head up high, I walk calmly out of the room, down the hallway, and back out to the lobby. Forcing a cheery smile on my face, I grab my bag and my rose and hook my arm through Sean's. "Let's ditch this joint."

***

"Thanks for walking me home and thanks for a great date," I tell Sean later that night, outside the apartment door, stifling a yawn. It's after three, and I'm officially pooped.

"I'm glad you enjoyed it," he says, moving his hand to my hip. He draws me in close. "I really want to see you again."

I cup his face. "I'd like that."

"Yeah?" Surprise is written all over his face. "I thought you'd make me work hard for date number two too."

I quietly laugh. "I had fun, and I enjoy your company, but I'm not looking to date anyone seriously, and I'm not interested in a relationship."

He kisses the tip of my nose. "Challenge accepted."

I snort. "It isn't a chall—"

My sentence is cut short when his mouth descends on my lips. We spent most of our time in the club making out, so the feel of his lips moving against mine isn't a huge surprise. It's not unwelcome either. Sean is an amazing kisser. And he's been attentive and easy to talk to all night.

Last week, I initially thought he was a player, but now I'm getting to know him better, I realize my initial assessment was incorrect. Sean is definitely boyfriend-worthy, if that's what I was looking for. He's studying computer science. He's into acting. He comes from a small town not too far from Bridgeville, and he adores his family. He's handsome and funny, and he doesn't take himself too seriously. He also gets extra brownie points for his honesty, and his direct approach is very appealing. While I'm not in the market for a boyfriend, I've decided I'm going to just go with the flow and see where this takes me.

I circle my arms around his neck, drawing him in closer, and we stay locked in our embrace, kissing and kissing, until he finally breaks us apart. "I could kiss you all night long," he whispers over my mouth. "But I'll be a gentleman and go home before my wandering hands have other ideas." He winks, and I stretch up, pecking his lips one last time.

"I think you might be one of the good guys." I kiss his cheek before grabbing my bag off the floor.

"I think I'm already falling for you." He winds his hand through my hair, drawing me into his body again. He kisses me deeply before releasing me. "Sweet dreams, beautiful. I'll message you tomorrow."

"Goodnight, Sean." I wave him off, only entering the apartment when he's disappeared from sight.

I'm smiling to myself as I enter the darkened living room, dropping my keys and bag on the chair.

"Did you fuck him?"

I scream at Ryan's unexpected question, my heart rate elevating to coronary-inducing proportions as I scan the room for him. "You fucking scared the hell out of me!" I squint in the darkness to make out his form. As my eyes adjust, I see him sitting in the recliner chair, his back rigidly stiff. He turns on the lamp at his side, and we stare at one another in silence for a few beats. His gaze drifts to my lips, and he scowls at the sight of my mouth, glistening and swollen from Sean's kisses.

"Did you?" he asks, failing to mask his fear.

"Not that it's any of your business, but no."

His shoulders visibly relax, and then he's up on his feet, stalking toward me. "Can I have a do-over?" He stands right in front of me, leaving barely any space between our bodies.

"In what way?" I narrow my eyes, urging my pounding heart to remain calm.

"You're right," he whispers, reaching out to caress my cheek with the tip of his finger. "I am scared. And scarred from my past breakup. But no one has even attempted to breach my walls. Until you came along."

"And?" I arch a brow, determined I will not make this easy for him.

"I want to stop fighting this." He gestures between us.

"What exactly are you saying?"

He takes hold of my hips, pulling me in flush with his body. "I can't make huge promises, Summer, because I don't want to commit to something and then let you down, but if your offer is still on the table, I'm in."

"Sex with no strings," I repeat, wanting to ensure we're both on the same page.

He nods. "Once we both agree we're exclusive for as long as we're sleeping together. And we have to keep this from your brother." Guilt furrows his brow as the words leave his mouth, and I know he's sacrificing a part of himself agreeing to this.

"It ends as soon as one of us wants to stop," I supply. "No bad feelings or regrets. We agree to part ways with no ill feelings."

He palms my face. "I have no issue agreeing to that."

"And you won't turn around tomorrow and change your mind?" I inquire, needing to know he's not going to mess me around anymore.

"I promise I won't. I've thought of nothing else since last night, and when you left with Sean, I was going out of my mind thinking I'd missed my chance with you." He cups the back of my neck, his gaze boring into mine. "I don't know why I'm so concerned about the age difference when it's clear you're the more mature one of the two of us." His lips kick up at the corner, and my heart swoons behind my ribcage.

I press my body into his, slipping my hands around his back and down to his delectable ass. "Not in every sense of the word," I whisper, gently rocking my hips against his so he catches my meaning.

"Perhaps we can both teach one another a few things," he whispers back, thrusting his solid erection into my lower stomach.

"When do lessons start?" I rasp in a breathy tone.

His pupils dilate and he licks his lips as his eyes drift to my mouth. "How about right now?"

I should probably tell him no. Not when I was just kissing another man outside the door. But Ryan has this hold over me, and I can't resist, so I raise no objection, shrieking as he lifts me up, urging my legs to move around his waist. I snake my arms around his neck as my legs hug his torso, and our mouths collide in a wild frenzy of lips and teeth and tongues. Sean's kisses pale into insignificance in comparison. Ryan cups my ass, keeping me upright, with my legs straddling his waist, while walking toward the hallway leading to the bedrooms.

He kisses me senseless, my head is spinning, and I'm wondering how the hell he can walk and kiss like that when he kicks open the door to his master suite, growling low at the base of his throat.

He flings me down on the bed, and then we're frantically tearing our clothes off, as if it's a race, our eyes never leaving one another as we shed our outer layers. I shunt up the bed before lowering onto my back, stretching my legs out wide in a welcoming gesture. Ryan pulls a bunch of condoms out of his drawer, tossing them on top of the bedside table. "This will be fast because I need to be inside you, baby."

"You won't hear any complaints from me," I confirm, my eyes glued to his long shaft as he fists one hand around himself and pumps his cock. I sit up, my tongue darting out to lick the bead of precum at his crown.

"Fuck," he hisses, his eyes rolling back in his head. "Lie back down, and spread your legs real wide."

I dutifully obey, and my body hums in anticipation as I watch him lower his face between my thighs. When his hot tongue touches my sensitive flesh, I emit the neediest moan, my body almost arching off the bed as intense pleasure courses through me. He licks me up and down, like I'm his favorite flavor of ice cream, and stars explode behind my eyelids. I cry out when his tongue invades my pussy, alternating between sliding inside me and swirling around my clit. My limbs are contorting in spasm-like motions, and I'm moaning like a woman possessed under his expert ministrations.

Damn, Ryan is so fucking skilled with his tongue. I know he's ruining me for life. I get the sense no other guy will ever be able to match his skills in the bedroom.

He drives his tongue in and out of me with a faster pace before pressing his thumb down firmly on my clit, and I detonate, like a thousand fireworks exploding in the nighttime sky. My body shudders and shakes as the most intense orgasm grips me. Tears of pleasure leak out of the corners of my eyes as my body convulses with blissful sensation. Ryan stays with me through it all, milking every drop of my arousal, and then he's rolling a condom on and pushing inside me.

I clench around him, hugging his cock tightly as he eases in farther. My legs go around his waist, my ankles crossing over his firm buttocks, and then he's lifting me up so I'm sitting on him as he pounds into me with fierce determination.

His mouth suctions around my nipple, and I like this position. He plunges his cock deep inside me, and his fingers dig into my hip as he rocks me back and forth. He trails a line of hot kisses up my neck before claiming my mouth in a hungry kiss. "Fuck, you feel too damn good," he whispers, nipping at my upper lip. "Your pussy is so tight." He grips my hips firmly, ramming into me, and I throw my head back, giving in to the heavenly sensation.

Without warning, he pulls me off him, flipping me over onto my belly before I can protest. "Lift your ass, baby," he demands, pressing my head down onto the bed as he pulls up my legs until I'm kneeling, nudging my thighs farther apart. Then he slams back into me from behind, thrusting in and out as he holds me in place with one hand tight on my hip.

His other fingers roam the crease of my ass, and when he presses one finger into my hole, I shatter instantly as a powerful climax consumes me. He roars out his release, pulsing inside me in short, sharp, strokes, and we're both shuddering and moaning until we're fully sated.

I collapse on the bed, my trembling knees giving way, and Ryan drops behind me, curling his sweat-slickened body around me. "You okay, sweetheart?" he whispers in my ear, as his arm encircles my waist.

"I'm wonderful," I rasp, leaning back into him with my body as I clutch onto his muscular arm. "I think I could become addicted to sex."

His body rumbles with silent laughter. "I have zero issues with that." He presses a soft kiss to that sensitive spot just behind my ear, and a shiver works its way through me.

"Your touch does the most amazing things to me." I lean my head around, stretching my neck to kiss him.

"Ditto, babe." He kisses the tip of my nose. "And I haven't even begun touching you in all the places I want to." He kisses me deeply, his tongue sweeping against mine in languid strokes as I feel him hardening against my back. "Do you need another few minutes, or are you ready to go again?" he asks, quirking a brow.

I turn around in his arms, grinning. "Do you really need to ask me that?"

He laughs as his fingers glide down my body before curling back inside me. My eyes close, and I sigh in contentment. "My body is yours to do with as you please," I murmur, fully meaning every word.

"Buckle up, baby," he says, flipping me over onto my back and hovering over me. "Because the night is only getting started."

Chapter Sixteen

Ryan

We are both struggling to keep our eyes open the next afternoon as we drag our sleep-deprived bodies from the SUV in the parking lot at the gym. We're surviving on minimal sleep, thanks to our marathon fucking session. I lost count of how many times I was inside Summer or how many orgasms I gave her last night. All I know is it was one of the best nights of my life.

She joked she was addicted to sex.

I'm terrified I'm addicted to *her*.

Glancing around to ensure the camera is angled over the other side of the lot, I reel Summer into my arms, leaning down to kiss her.

Now I've given myself permission to give in to our chemistry, I can't stop touching her. We held hands most of the journey from the apartment, and I couldn't stop looking over at her. She looks tired but happy, and I imagine it's how I look too. "I don't know how I'll get through the next nine hours without touching you," I honestly admit, hugging her.

"I'm sure we can steal a few sneaky kisses," she says, trailing her fingers along the downy hair at the base of my neck. Her touch ignites a fire in me every single time, and it's like every part of my body is hot-wired to my cock.

"Do you walk around with a permanent boner?" she asks, feeling my growing erection prodding the flesh of her stomach.

"Only since you appeared on the scene," I truthfully admit.

"That shouldn't make me proud, but it does." Her gratified grin does funny things to my insides, and I wonder how the fuck I'll avoid catching feelings.

"You should be proud, baby." I kiss her again. "It's a real talent. I only have to glance at you and I'm rock hard."

The gym is very busy for a Sunday, especially when I need to cover classes for one of our trainers who called in sick.

I'm back in my office, trying to grab a late lunch as I pore over last month's accounts, when Summer slips into the room, quickly locking the door behind her. I arch a brow in a silent question, and she hurries toward me with a naughty glint in her eye.

Rounding my desk, she stands behind me. Her small hands land on my shoulders, and a moan emits from my mouth when she kneads my tense flesh. Her velvety lips brush the bare skin at the nape of my neck as she continues massaging me, and a shiver tiptoes up and down my spine.

"I thought you looked stressed," she whispers in between peppering my neck with featherlight kisses. "But your shoulders are tied into knots, baby. You need to unwind," she adds, digging her fingers into the corded muscle on my shoulders.

"You have something in mind?" I ask, my voice thick with lust.

"I do, but I only have a ten-minute break, so I'll have to make this quick." Before I can ask, she spins me around in my chair, drops to her knees on the floor, and yanks my shorts and boxers down my thighs, freeing my hardening cock. "Sit back and enjoy, babe," she says before lowering her hot mouth over the head of my now throbbing dick. It's clear from the confident way she fists my cock at the base as she slides her mouth down my aching length she knows what she's doing.

No Feelings Involved

I close my eyes as she works me over, taking me deep into her mouth and sucking me firmly. Her lips glide up and down my cock as she quickens the pace of her hand stroking my overheated flesh. A guttural moan rips from my throat when she gently grazes her teeth along my length, and precum leaks from my crown.

Suctioning her lips more firmly, she takes me all the way to the back of her throat as she picks up her pace, bobbing up and down, and a familiar tingle builds at the base of my spine. I open my eyes, reveling in the determination on her face as she sucks me off, and that's all it takes to lose control.

The orgasm rips through me without warning, and I shoot hot spurts of semen into her mouth before I've had time to even consider withdrawing. Summer stays with me, swallowing every drop of cum, and when she peers up at me with glassy eyes, glistening lips, and a satisfied, happy smile on her face, cracks splinter in the shell encasing my heart.

Tucking my cock back into my shorts, I pull her up into my lap and kiss her slowly, tasting myself on her lips as she kisses me back with the same longing. Very quickly, the kiss transforms, and we're devouring one another, our hands wandering as an intense need takes over. My cock thickens, and I need to be inside her. "How many minutes do you have left?" I ask, trailing a line of kisses down her neck.

"About four," she pants.

"I can make that work," I say, lifting her by the hips and spreading her, belly down, over my desk. "Are you on the pill?" I ask, yanking the yoga pants and her thong down her slim legs.

"I am, and I'm clean. I haven't slept with anyone but you."

The dormant Neanderthal gene in my DNA loves to hear that, and my cock needs no further incentive. "I'm clean too," I supply, driving into her in one quick move. I fuck her hard and fast over my desk, slamming in and out of her as I pull her ass back a little so I can slide my hand around her body and play with her clit. I up the ante, rubbing her tight bud quickly to match the thrusts of my cock, until we're both climaxing in record time.

I grab tissues from my desk drawer and clean her up before helping her fix her clothes. Smoothing her hair back into her ponytail, I slowly pull her into my arms for a hug. The feel of her slim body against mine brings all my protective instincts to the surface, and I hold her tightly as I press light kisses into her hair.

My heart expands, and I'm feeling things I haven't felt in a long time.

I know I'm in serious trouble with this girl, but I can't stop now.

I don't want to stop.

She already means so much to me.

"I better head back out before someone notices," she says into my chest, and I reluctantly let her go.

"Thanks, baby." I peck her lips tenderly. "I'm definitely less stressed now," I add with a smug wink.

"Glad to be of service," she teases, squeezing the cheeks of my ass before sliding out from our embrace. "But I better get back. My boss is a real stickler for timekeeping, and he can be a bit of a prick when he wants to be."

I quirk a brow as my lips fight a smile. "Is that right?" I smack her ass as she turns around to walk toward the door. "Better not delay so." My eyes stay glued to her shapely form as she sashays toward the door, pivoting at the last second to blow me a kiss.

I'm still grinning five hours later as I exit my office en route to the lobby although the sight of that idiot Sean leaning over the front desk, mooning at Summer, instantly wipes the errant grin from my face. "We're closed," I snap.

Straightening up, he frowns at me. "I was just going." He turns to Summer. "You know how to reach me if you change your mind."

"Goodnight, Sean," she says, smiling sympathetically as she powers off the computer.

Sean narrows his eyes at me on his way out the door. A rush of relief surges through me with his departure.

"You don't need to eyeball him like you want to murder him with your bare hands," Summer says, coming up alongside me and threading her fingers in mine. "I set him straight. He knows I'm not interested in any more dates."

"Good." I let go of her hand to activate the alarm, trying to shake my jealousy free. When the building is secured, I grab hold of her hand again, leading her out to the parking lot.

"I know how important trust and loyalty is to you, Ryan," she quietly admits while we walk. "I would never promise you exclusivity and then sneak around with other guys behind your back. That's not who I am."

I slam to a halt, turning to face her. I gently cup her face. "I appreciate you reconfirming it, but I already know that, and I trust you." Truth. I know Summer isn't the type to say one thing and mean another. She's an open book, and I trust her to tell me when she wants our arrangement to end. A sharp pain stabs me in the chest at the thought of this finishing, but I ignore it, already feeling hugely conflicted over this girl.

Summer sleeps in my bedroom the next couple nights, but she's forced to return to her own room when her brother and Miley return from their London vacation, leaving me feeling lonely in my empty bed at night. She has a busy college schedule, and now that Miley is back, she's only working three short shifts a week, so we see little of one another in the weeks that pass.

On nights when Austin stays at Miley's, she's a firm fixture in my bed although we don't get much sleep. I can't keep my hands off her, and she's an eager student, readily agreeing to experiment with different positions and angles and excitedly embracing the sex toys I introduce her to.

For the first time in a long time, I'm having fun, enjoying life, and feeling happy. It's also forced me to assess how I've been living my life up to this point, and I can't deny how lonely and depressing my previous existence was.

I'm not the only one to notice the change.

"When are you going to tell me who she is?" Austin asks one morning, as we're eating breakfast together in the kitchen. Thankfully, Summer has already left for class and Miley stayed with a friend last night, so it's just the two of us alone with this awkward conversation.

"I don't know what you're talking about." I turn my back to him as I refill my coffee, trying to keep my burgeoning panic at bay.

"C'mon, man. You can't fool me. Even if I hadn't heard the sounds coming from your room the other night, I'd still know there's a woman on the scene because I can't remember when I last saw you this happy."

Fuck. I suspected Austin might have heard something when he turned up unexpectedly the other night. He'd had an argument with Miley in the middle of the night and stormed back to the apartment. Summer had been energetically riding me at the time, and neither of us had been quiet. As soon as we'd heard him, Summer had fled to the en suite to hide, only creeping back into her room once the coast sounded clear. It was a close call and a timely reminder we need to be more circumspect.

Case in point.

"It's nothing serious." I casually shrug, hating how much those words make me feel like a liar. "Just a bit of fun."

"But it's the same woman?"

I could lie. I probably should. But it doesn't feel right to, so I merely nod.

Austin slaps me on the back. "Knew it. You're falling for her."

Panic jumps up and bites me, and I rear back. "I'm not," I bark. "It's just sex, and it won't ever be anything more, so drop it."

He holds up his palms. "Woah. Relax there, buddy. I won't mention it again." His eyes dart sideways, and his face lights up. "Oh, hey, Sum. I thought you'd already left."

"I had," she says, her voice sounding a little choked, and I mentally curse under my breath. I risk a quick glance at her, spotting the hurt she's not fast enough to hide, and I know she overheard our conversation. "But I realized I forgot one of my books a couple blocks away and turned around." She hurries past us. "Don't mind me. Continue your conversation."

Austin watches her scurry away with a frown on his face. "Does she seem upset to you?"

"No," I lie.

"I'll ask Miley to check in with her later. Find out if something's up," he mumbles, looking distracted as he rinses our plates in the sink.

"I'll grab my stuff and meet you downstairs at the car," I say, needing to get rid of him so I can talk to her.

I enter Summer's room without knocking, closing the door behind me as quietly as I can. She looks up from where she's sitting on the side of her bed, wearing every emotion on her face.

"Hey." I kneel in front of her. "I'm sorry you had to hear that, but it wasn't as brutal as it sounded. I said what he needed to hear."

Tossing her long wavy hair over her shoulders, she bites down on her lower lip, peering at me with earnest eyes. "You have nothing to apologize for. We agreed it was friends with benefits, so you spoke no lie."

I take her hands in mine. "But?"

Her chest heaves as she stares at me. "It hurt hearing it spelled out like that," she honestly admits.

"Do you want to end this?" I whisper, silently praying her answer is no.

"No!" she blurts. "I don't want it to end, but I'm afraid I'm growing attached to you."

I'm already there.

I think it, but I don't say it. I've only known this girl a few months, only been sleeping with her for the past few weeks, and I'm already way too attached. But she doesn't need to know that. Whether or not I've caught feelings doesn't change the situation. I should let her go, but I need to work myself up to that.

"Are you sure you don't want to call it quits?" I ask again even as I'm cursing myself for pushing an agenda I *don't* support.

"Do you?" she whispers, and I detect the fear in her gaze.

I slowly shake my head. "While I don't enjoy all the sneaking around, I enjoy spending time with you, and this is the most fun I've had in ages. I'm not ready to end it yet."

A relieved sigh slips from her gorgeous lips. "Me either." She leans forward, resting her head on my shoulder, and I pull her down into my lap, cradling her against my chest.

"Good, because I want to take you out on a date," I blurt before I've had time to properly engage my brain.

Her eyes shimmer with excitement when she lifts her head to look at me. "I'd love that."

I kiss her quickly, my stomach churning unpleasantly as I wonder what the hell I'm doing.

My head and my heart are at war over this girl, and I have no idea who the victor will be.

Chapter Seventeen
Summer

I can see Ryan from up here on the stage, and he is *not* a happy camper. I forgot that the director said we were rehearsing the kissing scene today. Otherwise, I would've met Ryan at the restaurant instead of agreeing he'd pick me up at the theater. I could tell he wasn't pleased when he heard they had cast me as Juliet against Sean's Romeo, but he articulated zero concerns. *Why would he?* It's not like we're boyfriend and girlfriend or that we have a right to demand anything of one another.

But it's obvious Ryan doesn't like it.

That shouldn't make me happy.

But it does.

I'm hoping Sean doesn't notice Ryan's scowl and put things together, because he's been pretty relentless in his attempts to convince me to go out on a second date with him, and I think he's smelling a rat. He's determined. I'll give him that. And very persuasive when he wants to be, but I've been persistent in declining his various offers.

I couldn't tell him I was seeing someone when I initially turned him down because that's not technically true.

I'm just sleeping with Ryan.

We're not dating.

Although, increasingly, the lines are becoming blurred. The fact he's seated in the auditorium, waiting for me, further proves that.

I was surprised when Ryan suggested a date, but I didn't hesitate to agree because I adore spending time with him, and I get as much out of our conversations as I do the amazing sex.

The longer this goes on, the more attached I become, and I can't deny I'm feeling something for him. I should probably cut him loose, but I can't make myself do it. And even though I feel guilty as hell because I'm sneaking around behind my brother's and my best friend's backs, I can't deny how much of a thrill it is to be conducting a secret, illicit affair with someone as incredible as Ryan.

"Want to grab something to eat?" Sean asks when the director calls it a night.

"I already have plans, but thanks for asking."

I hate the dejected look on his face. Hate I'm responsible for it. I'd love to propose we head out another time, as friends only, but I know he'd read more into it, and I don't want to mislead him.

"You'll never say yes, will you?" he asks, resignation clear in his tone.

"Not at the moment. I'm sorry, Sean. And it's like I said. You're great. This is nothing to do with you. It's all about me and where I'm at right now."

"The pathetic thing is I believe that," he says, shuffling awkwardly on his feet.

"It's not pathetic. It *is* the truth."

"I don't understand. We had a great first date, and you were into a second one. I don't get what changed overnight?" He runs a hand along the back of his neck, imploring me with his eyes.

"I just changed my mind." I grip the strap of my bag, praying he lets things go after this. I have started dreading rehearsals because I know he'll corner me at the end.

"I wish you hadn't, but I won't push it anymore. If you ever change your mind, let me know. I'd take you out in a heartbeat."

I lean up and kiss his cheek. "You're the best. And it's fun acting with you. I think it'll be easier for both of us if we just agree to be friends."

Ryan is waiting outside the theater when I exit after everyone has gone. "Hey." Butterflies scatter in my tummy as I look up at his handsome face. His piercing blue eyes penetrate mine as he lifts his hand, brushing his fingers across my cheek, leaving a trail of fiery tingles in his wake.

"Hey, babe." Dipping his head, he claims my lips in a sweet kiss. "You were fantastic up there. A real natural."

My heart soars at his compliment, and I lace my fingers in his as we walk. "Thank you. You'll come to the opening night, right?"

Lifting our conjoined hands, he presses a kiss to my knuckles. "I wouldn't miss it for the world."

We're tucked into the back of the quaint little Italian restaurant, pressed up against one another in a cozy booth, waiting for our food to arrive. Ryan has his arm wrapped around me, and my head is resting on his shoulder.

We're as comfortable with one another as if we've been together for years.

Unspoken words linger in the space between us, and while it's not awkward, it's heavy. Despite what we both agreed at the outset, I think it's safe to say we've both caught feelings, and I'm fearful things are about to turn messy. But I don't want to be a Debbie Downer tonight. Not when Ryan has brought me to this romantic restaurant and we can be ourselves without having to duck and dive to avoid discovery. This place is off the beaten track, so we figure we're safe enough to openly embrace without fear of being spotted.

"Is this where you take all the women you're hiding?" I joke, needing to lighten the atmosphere.

"You're the first woman I've brought here," he admits, running the tip of his finger up and down my bare arm, sending a cavalcade of shivers tumbling across my sensitive skin. "I don't date, remember."

"Yet here we are." I stare deep into his eyes, instantly getting lost in them.

"Yes. Here we are." His words are a whisper spoken over my mouth before he brushes his lips briefly against mine.

"What are we doing?"

"I'm fucked if I know."

I can't resist smiling. "You make me very happy."

"You make me happy too."

The waitress arrives then with our pasta, and we're both quiet until she's left. I twirl the spaghetti around my fork, mentally debating whether to open this topic up or just let it drop. But I've never been one to shy away from speaking my mind, and I'm not about to start now.

"Can I ask you something?" I inquire in between mouthfuls of the sinfully creamy pasta.

"Of course." He shovels a forkful of lasagna in his mouth, watching me warily despite his acquiescence.

"I know you said you didn't date because of what happened with your ex, but is there more to it? Because your sister and Slater are so happy. Your parents seem to have a great marriage, and so does your brother Caleb and his wife Terri. Aren't there enough positive examples to negate the bad experience you endured?"

"Why do you want to know?" he asks, placing his fork down, looking like he's swallowed something sour.

I shrug. "Because I'm nosy. Because I care about you. Because I can't understand how some woman hasn't snared you yet. Because I want you to be happy."

"I am happy."

I prod the crease in his brow. "That scowl suggests otherwise."

"Or I was until you started this line of questioning." He sighs, shoveling more food in his mouth and slowly chewing as he contemplates something.

I wait him out, eating my pasta as he deliberates.

"The truth is," he continues after a few minutes of silence. "I've never been into relationships or commitments. I've known since I was little. I've never seen myself getting married or having kids."

I put my silverware down. "Why?"

He runs a hand nervously through his hair. "Because relationships aren't always what they seem. And trusting another person, opening yourself up fully to another person, can come back to bite you." He eyeballs me, and I see a world of hurt hiding behind his eyes. "The people you love the most have the power to inflict the worst damage, and I don't want to open myself up to that kind of pain. I let my guard down one time, and it burned me, but Myndi also did me a favor, because she made me realize I'd been right all along."

"Sometimes we have to open ourselves up to risk experiencing the greatest joy of all," I muse, my heart heavy with sadness for all he's denying himself. "I've never had my heart broken, but I know it'll happen, and I won't deny myself intermittent moments of amazing happiness for fear I'll suffer pain down the line. I'd rather experience those fleeting happy moments than miss out on them altogether."

"Maybe you're a braver person than me. Or I'm just older and more embittered."

"Or scared of feeling too much?" I repeat.

He pushes his food away, draining his beer in one go. "If you're asking this because of you and me—"

"I'm not," I rush to reassure him, regretting opening this conversation because the mood is subdued now, and that's all my fault. "I told you I'm naturally curious, but I shouldn't have started this conversation. I don't want to make you sad or uncomfortable. I just … like you." I shrug, smiling as I grip onto his arm. "And I want to know what makes you tick."

"I think you have a fair idea of what makes me tick," he says, taking my hand and placing it on his crotch. I know what he's doing, and it makes me sad, but I want to redirect this conversation too, so I let him deflect with sex.

We're both quiet on the walk back to the apartment, and I fear my prying has driven a wedge between us. A wedge I'm desperate to eliminate before Ryan decides he's had enough and calls time on our arrangement. But, typically, my brother and Miley are in the living room when we return, putting paid to my plans to use my body to bring Ryan back around.

I wait a couple hours until all is quiet in Austin's room before tiptoeing into Ryan's bedroom. He's not asleep either. Lying on his side under the comforter, he looks as troubled as I feel. He whips his head around when I slide into bed beside him. "What are you doing?" he hisses. "You can't be in here."

I push him flat on his back and straddle him. "I need to feel you inside me. I need to make this right between us again. I can be quiet."

He looks at me like I'm crazy. And I get it. I'm vocal in bed, but I'm determined to bite my tongue because I can't go asleep leaving things like this between us. I need to feel close to him.

"I very much doubt that, and you don't need to make anything right. We're fine."

"We're not." I whip my top up off my head, exposing my bare chest to him. "And it's my fault our date was ruined."

He cups the back of my head, pulling my face down close to his. "It wasn't ruined."

"I shouldn't have said anything. Sometimes I don't know when to shut my big mouth."

"Don't say that," he whispers, pressing tiny kisses to my face. "I love that about you. I never want you to be anyone but yourself. You gave me a lot to think about is all." He cups my face, peering into my eyes. "You're changing me, Summer, and that scares me a lot."

"We can be scared together, because you're changing me too."

It's as close as we've come to admitting we have feelings outside the bedroom.

"I don't want to break your heart," he whispers with pain etched across his face. "And I'm terrified that's what I'll do."

"Don't be so cocky," I tease, wanting to defuse the heaviness that seems to have surrounded us tonight. I slide off him, shucking my panties off and tugging his sleep shorts down his body. "Maybe I'll be the one breaking your heart." I straddle him, stroking his hard length a couple times, brushing the tip over my aching pussy.

"I've no doubt," he rasps, gripping my hips and lowering me onto him. "But I'm too far gone to stop this now."

"Me too," I whisper as I rock against him. "So, let's agree to go with the flow and see where this takes us. We'll deal with the fallout when it happens."

"Sum!" Hannah squeals, jumping up and down in her chair when I arrive at the stadium for the football match on Friday night. "It feels like I haven't seen you in forever," she adds, grabbing me into a hug. "And that sucks, because this isn't how I imagined our freshman year of college."

Nor me. "I'm sorry I've been so busy lately. Between classes, working at the gym, and rehearsals, I have little free time." I didn't add Ryan to the mix because Hannah doesn't know about him. I hate I'm keeping it from her, but I can't tell her, because she'll tell Jordan, and he hates Ryan. I don't trust him not to blab to my brother. So, I'd no choice but to conceal it from her, which is the first time I haven't confided in her about stuff going on in my life. Guilt presses down on my chest. "Where's Jordan?" I look all around, but there's no sign of her boyfriend.

She gulps, and tears pool in her eyes. "He bailed to hang out with Sean and Dalton although he said he'd meet us at the club later."

"What's wrong?" I clasp her hands in mine.

She swipes at the tears leaking out of her eyes, sniffing. "I'm probably overreacting."

"To what?" I lower my voice, conscious we're in a packed stadium with prying ears all around.

She bites down on her lower lip. "He's been distant the last few weeks, preferring to hang out with the guys than spend time with me and he... he seems to have gone off sex. He's always tired, or it's late or there's some crappy excuse. I"—a shuddering breath rattles her chest, and her lip wobbles—"I think he wants to break up with me."

"He changed his plans to come to UD for *you*." I rub her hands, trying to reassure her, but a niggling worry presses at the back of my mind. It's been there since I had a long phone call with Justin last month.

He'd called me back the day after I hung up on him, and we'd had an honest conversation. Justin told me he has feelings for me, but he doesn't want to be tied to a long-distance relationship while he's in college, and I was glad we were on the same page. We agreed to be friends. That we'll hang out if we're both at home in Bridgeville, but we made no commitments outside of that, and the conversation considerably eased my mind.

Except when I quizzed him about Jordan, and he claimed he hadn't asked him to do anything regarding me. So, I don't understand where all the overprotectiveness has been coming from. Why Jordan took an instant dislike to Ryan. Why he seemed more than happy not to give my cell number to Sean at the start. I'd convinced myself he was just being a good friend, because I don't want to be thinking the things I'm thinking, but given what Han's just admitted, I'm scared I might be on the right track.

"I think he's regretting it," she says on a sob. "I think he regrets not going to Oregon with Justin."

"Have you spoken to him about it?"

She shakes her head. "I'm trying to pluck up the courage to have the conversation, but I'm terrified he's going to break it off. I love him so much, and the thought he might not feel it anymore is killing me."

"Which is why you need to talk to him, Han. You're torturing yourself not knowing. It could be completely innocent, and you're worrying yourself for nothing, but you won't know unless you talk to him."

The club is jam-packed by the time we arrive. We stopped to have dinner after the game and ended up chatting for hours. It felt good to spend that time with my bestie, but unease still claws at my insides, not helped by the fact the guys are smashed already and surrounded by girls fawning all over them. Hannah's face falls when she notices, and I loop my arm in hers, pushing the girls out of the way so we can reach their side. Sean acknowledges me with a sheepish smile while chatting to a cute girl with short blonde hair. Jordan kisses Hannah on the lips before dragging me into a bear hug. "Haven't seen you in ages," he slurs, tightening his hold on me. "Missed you."

Subtly, I extricate myself from his embrace, plastering a smile on my face. "Me too. But I'm here now." I nudge him in the ribs. "Get the drinks in."

He smacks a kiss off my cheek. "Anything for you."

Hannah is crestfallen, watching his retreating form as he heads toward the bar with Sean in tow. "See what I mean now?" She wraps her arms around herself. "He looked happy to see you, but he barely glanced at me." Her lower lip wobbles, and my heart aches for her.

I hug her close. "Do you want to go?"

She shakes her head. "No way in hell am I leaving him here with all these girls hanging around."

I nod in understanding, as my cell pings in my pocket. I check it discreetly, a wide grin appearing on my face as I read the text from Ryan.

I see you, gorgeous.

Without looking obvious, I scan the club, my heart jumping wildly when I spot him with some staff from the gym at the end of the bar. Miley's blonde curls bounce around her head as she sways her hips to the beat of the music, looking like she's lost in her own world. My brother is staring at her with a love-struck expression on his face, as if she's the only one in the room, and he looks suitably distracted.

My cell pings again.

Meet me in the disabled toilet out back.

I whip my head up after reading the text, licking my lips and narrowing my eyes as I zone in on Ryan. My pulse skyrockets, and heat floods my body as he levels a provocative look my way. I cast a glance over my shoulder, ensuring Hannah isn't looking, before I look back, blowing a kiss in his direction.

"I'm just going to the bathroom. Will you be okay here until Jordan returns?" I ask Han, feeling a little guilty for ditching her in favor of a bathroom hookup.

"I'll be fine." She kisses my cheek. "Go."

I fight my way through the crowded room, pushing through the double doors out into the hallway at the back. There's a spring in my step as I skip along the passageway, climbing the stairs to the upper level where the bathrooms are. Sneaking off like this with Miley and Austin in the vicinity is risky, but the thrill of being caught only adds to the allure.

I guess I'm a bit fucked up.

An arm wraps around my waist from behind, and I lean back into a warm body, a wide grin spreading across my lips. My hair is pushed aside, and someone presses a wet kiss against my neck. All the tiny hairs on my body stand on high alert because I instantly know this isn't Ryan. Removing the arm from around me, I stumble awkwardly, staring in shock at Jordan. I hoped I was wrong about him, but it seems my instincts were correct. "What the hell are you doing?" I splutter, just as I spy Ryan coming up the stairs. With a surreptitious shake of my head, I urge him to stay back. Although the immediate scowl on his face tells me he's unhappy, he moves into the corner, staying out of sight.

"Baby," Jordan slurs, taking a step toward me. "Come back here."

I place my hands on his chest, holding him at bay. He's trashed, so it doesn't take much effort to keep him at arm's length. "Jordan, stop."

"Come on, Summer. Don't pretend like you don't feel this thing between us."

"I don't, Jordan. You're my friend, but that's it. That's all there will ever be between us."

"I don't believe you. You're just saying that because of Hannah."

"I'm glad you've remembered your girlfriend," I say, struggling to keep my voice level. "The girl who's my best friend in the entire world. The girl who loves you to the moon and back. Have you forgotten all that?!"

"I can't help how I feel," he slurs, reaching for me again.

"Stop grabbing at me, Jordy. I don't want you to touch me."

"Please, Summer. Give us a chance."

I close my eyes, swallowing over the anguished lump in my throat. "Jordan, that'll never happen. Go back to Hannah. She'll be wondering where you are."

"I don't want her. I don't love her anymore."

My eyes meet Ryan's as my heart aches for my bestie. He's respecting my wishes, holding back in the shadows, but he's primed to intervene. I stare at Jordan, wondering if I've ever really known him at all. "If that's the truth, you need to tell her because you're hurting her. She knows something isn't right, and you owe it to her to be honest. But it's nothing to do with me. I don't have those feelings for you, Jordan."

"I came here for *you*," he pleads, slouching against the wall as he pins me with doleful eyes. "I love *you*."

"I'm sorry, but I don't love you, and I never will." I fold my arms across my chest as hurt slices across his face. "You need to tell Hannah the truth. If you don't, I will. I won't have you making a fool out of her, Jordan."

I see the moment his hurt transforms to a darker emotion. He darts forward, grabbing my arm before I can duck out of his reach. "Suck me off, then. It's the least you can do."

"What?! How the hell do you figure that?" I try to wrestle out of his hold, but he digs his nails into my arm, and I sense movement from the corner.

"You blew Justin. Now it's my turn."

"Fuck you, Jordan, and get your hands off me!" I fume, still trying to wriggle out of his death grip.

Ryan's livid face comes into view as he takes a step forward at the same time the door to the men's bathroom opens and Sean steps into the hallway, his eyes narrowed in anger. "I heard every word, Jordan, and I believe Summer asked you to let her go." He crosses his arms, glaring at his friend. "This isn't cool."

"I thought we were friends," I say, sadness dripping from my tone as Jordan finally releases my arm. "But no true friend would ever treat me like this. Treat Hannah like this."

This will kill her.

I shake my head, swallowing back the bile swimming up my throat, as Sean pushes me back a little, shielding me with his body. Ryan has retreated to the corner, and I'm certain he hates staying hidden. I need to end this before he decides it doesn't matter and risks everything. "I won't tell her what you just said, but I *will* tell her the earlier stuff if you don't man up and come clean. She deserves better than this."

All the fight leaves Jordan, and he stares at me through bloodshot eyes for a couple minutes before nodding, and then he walks away with his shoulders hunched over and a dejected look on his face.

"Are you okay?" Sean asks, concern underscoring his tone.

I plant a fake smile on my face. "I'm fine. Just hurting for my friend."

He nods, as I place my hand on the door of the ladies' bathroom, indicating my intent. "Okay. I'll leave you to it. But if he hassles you again, you know where I am." He presses a kiss to my cheek before walking down the stairs.

No Feelings Involved

I can't speak over the lump in my throat as I watch Ryan stride toward me. A sob breaks loose of my chest when he silently draws me into his arms, and I cling to him as I cry, understanding this will change everything between Hannah and me. And not in a good way.

Chapter Eighteen
Ryan

Summer has been distraught since earlier, and I'm trying my best to comfort her. Even though Miley and Austin are in the apartment tonight, there's no way I could leave her to sleep on her own. She's bundled in my arms as we cuddle in bed, having finally succumbed to sleep. I sensed Jordan was harboring feelings for Summer because his behavior wasn't normal, but hearing him tell her he loved her was still a shock. I have never wanted to beat a guy as badly as I wanted to beat that douche when he told her to suck him off. He's lucky I wasn't drunk, or I doubt I'd have shown any restraint.

When this comes out, it will drive a wedge in her friendship with Hannah. She seems blind when it comes to Jordan, and I'm afraid she'll blame her best friend instead of pointing the finger squarely where it belongs—with him.

My protective instincts are in overdrive, and I want to shelter Summer from the incoming storm, but I know I can't. Feelings of helplessness add to the other turmoil in my head, further confusing me. All I know with certainty is that I'm not letting Summer go. Not when she'll need me to lean on in the difficult weeks ahead.

My alarm goes off a half hour earlier than usual, and I rouse the

Sleeping Beauty in my arms. "Baby." I press a kiss to her temple, threading my fingers through her hair. I hate to disturb her when she looks like she's in a deep sleep, but she needs to go back to her room before Austin wakes. "You need to get up."

She snuggles into my body, and I close my eyes, savoring the warmth of her skin against mine. "This sucks," she murmurs into my bare chest, and a chuckle works its way through me.

"I won't disagree. But unless you want your brother to catch you in here, you need to leave. Now."

Yawning, she sits up, rubbing sleep from her eyes. Then she turns around, leaning down to press a delicate kiss to my mouth. "Parting is such sweet sorrow," she whispers against my lips, reciting one of Juliet's most famous lines, "that I shall say goodnight till it be morrow." Her smile is adoring as she kisses me one final time before tiptoeing out of my room.

I'm in a daze watching the closed door after she's left, because it's in this moment that reality finally dawns on me.

I'm in love with her.

I'm completely head over heels for Summer Petersen.

And that means I'm totally and utterly screwed.

"Thanks for agreeing to come with me," I tell Summer later that night as we leave the gym en route for my sister's house.

"It's no problem. I told Gabby previously I was happy to babysit and getting to spend more time with you is the icing on the cake."

My heart thuds in my chest, reminding me of my early morning admission.

All day, I've been walking around on autopilot, dazed and confused, wondering what the hell I'm going to do with the realization I'm in love. I found pathetic reasons to hunt her down during the working day—anything to spend even a few precious seconds in Summer's company.

No Feelings Involved

I thought Austin was pussy-whipped with Miley, but I'm ten times worse.

I'm tempted to blurt out my feelings with the way she's looking at me, but thankfully, I still have some self-control.

"Thank you both so much," Gabby gushes as Slater tries to steer her out of the house. "I appreciate you stepping in at the last minute."

Our parents were supposed to be on babysitting duty, but Dad has a chest infection, and Gabby is worried about Daisy picking it up. She wouldn't even let Mom come alone in case she's carrying any germs. Some might say she's overreacting, but I can't fault her for the all-consuming way she loves her kids. Besides, I miss my niece and nephew, and it's nice to have this extra time with them. Although Daisy is asleep, we'll get to see her in the morning as we've already agreed to stay overnight so Gabby and Slate don't feel pressured to come home early.

"It's fine," Summer reassures her as Billy curls around her leg, gazing up at her like she's a Disney princess. "We had nothing planned, anyway."

Gabby sends me a knowing look before giving us both a hug and letting Slater drag her out the front door. Her son barely gives her a second look, because he's too enamored with my girl.

My girl.

Fuck.

We eat the dinner Gabby already prepared, and then we play a game of basketball before the light fades. "Pretty girl," Billy says, once we're back inside, batting his eyelashes at Summer. "Will you watch Avengers Finity with me?"

"Sure thing." Smiling, she raises her hand and he high fives her. "I love *Infinity War*, and I'm a big Avengers fan. The Cap is my favorite. Who's yours?"

He grabs hold of her hand, pulling her into the living room. "Iron Man is the best!" He jumps up and down. "I know! I know! Let's wear costumes!" He drags her in the opposite direction, and Summer giggles, shooting me a disarming smile.

"Go for it," I say, grinning back at her. "I'll set the movie up and make popcorn while you're gone."

I'm munching my way through the bowl of popcorn when Summer and the cute little guy return. "I'm Iron Man!" he proclaims in a gruff voice, puffing out his chest behind his costume and bounding into the room, displaying impressive arrogance like a true mini Tony Stark.

"And I'm Black Widow," Summer announces, in an assertive tone, striding into the room behind him in a figure-hugging black jumpsuit, holding two toy swords in her hands. She stands confidently beside my nephew, the two of them projecting superhero status, and I can't contain my laughter.

"You dare to laugh at me?" She quirks a brow. When Billy flips up his Iron Man mask, exchanging a devilish look with Summer, I'm on instant alert.

"What's going on?" I question with clear caution in my tone.

"Billy and I made a new rule," Summer says, winking at my nephew as a wicked smile graces her mouth. "You can only watch the movie if you're wearing a costume." She throws something at me. "You're up, champ. Go get dressed."

I inspect the flimsy red and blue silky material with trepidation, my mouth curling in disgust. "Oh, hell to the no."

"That's a bad word, Uncle Ryan," Billy says, wagging his finger at me. "Now be Spiderman, or I'll tell Mom you were cussing again."

The little blackmailing shit.

Still, I can't keep the smile off my face. There isn't much I won't do for my nephew, it seems, as I saunter out of the room with the offending costume in hand, subtly spanking Summer on the ass as I pass by her.

"What the actual fuck?" I question out loud to myself a few minutes later, all tangled up in the too-tight costume. How the fuck does Slate fit into this thing? I tug on the material, trying to stretch it out so it reaches my wrists and my ankles and isn't molded to my dick like a tight layer of foreskin. That's assuming it's Slater's because right now I'm questioning if this suit is even adult sized.

Little beads of sweat dot my brow as I finally get the damn thing on. I look in the mirror, laughing at the state of myself squeezed into the minuscule costume, deciding that Summer owes me at least a blow job for this.

The instant I step foot in the living room, shouting "I am Spiderman," because hey, when in Rome and all that shit, the room erupts in an explosion of laughter, and you'd swear there were twenty people in the room not two. Or one point five if you consider Billy's still a kid.

Summer drops to her knees, tears pouring out of her eyes, and she can't stop laughing long enough to speak. Billy is running around the room, giggling and squealing.

"Hey, it was your great idea," I say, strolling over to the couch and plopping down on it. The material scrunches up at my thighs, almost giving me a wedgie, and I squirm on the couch trying to get comfortable. Summer shrieks, almost convulsing with laughter, before jumping up and dashing out of the room. "Was it something I said?" I joke with Billy, and he giggles, snuggling up on the couch with me and snatching the popcorn.

I'm still cursing the damn costume a couple minutes later when Summer returns wearing a Wonder Woman outfit this time. If I thought the crotch of my Spiderman costume was tight before, it's nothing on how strained it is now I'm sporting the biggest boner known to man. Discreetly, I pull the throw off the back of the couch, covering my nether regions before Billy notices the giant bulge in my tighter than tight pants.

"Are you trying to kill me, woman?" I ask as Summer flops down on the other side of me. "Death by giant erection," I whisper in her ear, and she splutters, holding up a hand, trying to compose herself long enough to speak.

"Stop!" She titters, clutching her stomach as if she's in pain. "I've already had to change because I peed my pants."

I just stare at her, and she cracks up in laughter again. "You seriously peed your pants?" I inquire, fighting a bout of laughter myself.

She punches me in the arm, but it's a feeble effort, and I barely feel a twinge. "It's your fault." She looks over me, snorting with laughter. "How the hell did you even get that thing on?"

"It wasn't without challenge, trust me." I wink at her, and she rests her head on my shoulder, her light laughter warming my insides.

"You look totally fuckable in that costume," I whisper in her ear. "I want you to wear it later when you're riding me."

"Do you think that's why Gabby and Slater have so many costumes upstairs? Do they play superhero in the bedroom?" she whispers, waggling her brows suggestively as my stomach sours.

My insides shrivel at the thought, and I scowl at her. "Thanks a bunch for that lovely visual of my sister. Now, I have a renewed urge to punch my brother-in-law in the face." I know Gabby and Slate usually dress up to go trick or treating with Billy at Halloween, and I'm sticking to that story as the most logical explanation.

Otherwise, I'm likely to land one on Slate the second he steps foot in the door.

"I think it's great they have such a healthy sex life. I hope I'm lucky enough to have that when I'm married."

I scrub my hands down my face as Billy, mercifully, presses play on the movie. "Can we please stop talking about my sister's sex life," I hiss. "You're making me ill."

A serious expression washes over her face. "I guess that's how Austin would feel if he knew the things you were doing to my body," she muses, and it in no way helps my current dilemma.

Thankfully, there's no more talk of sex during the movie, and the little guy keeps us entertained spouting most of Iron Man's lines before he's even spoken them on the screen. Think Billy's a bit obsessed. His eyes droop midway through the movie, and Summer and I share a conspiratorial look.

Billy only agrees to go to bed if the pretty girl reads him a bedtime story.

No Feelings Involved

While Summer reads to him, I check on my little niece, beaming at her tiny little body, wrapped contentedly in a soft blanket in her crib. Her thumb is in her mouth, and she looks like a little angel. I bend down, placing a barely there kiss on her silky smooth cheek, my heart full of love.

Then I stand just outside Billy's door listening to Summer reading him a story, complete with animated voices and vivid expressions. As I watch her with my nephew, I can picture her with our kids, and that scary thought is enough to send me scurrying back downstairs.

I'm on my second beer when Summer reappears in the living room. I finally pried the nightmare costume off, and I'm only in sweats, with my upper torso and feet bare. My cock swells as she strides toward me with a wicked gleam in her eye. She's still wearing the red corset top, flimsy blue skirt, and gold knee-high boots, and my lust for her elevates to an all-time high when she climbs onto my lap, straddling me. "I'm not wearing any panties," she whispers, leaning down to claim my lips in a bruising kiss. I slide my hand under that excuse of a skirt, finding her wet and wanting. My fingers slide through her folds, and I pump them in and out of her while she pushes my sweats down to my hips, freeing my throbbing cock.

I grab her hips and position her strategically, and we both moan quietly as I situate myself inside her. She rocks on top of me, and I'm happy to let her set the pace. She bobs up and down on me, never losing eye contact, and my hand slips into the top of the corset top, my fingers finding a path to her hardened nipples. Her pussy hugs my cock as she continues to ride me, and my heart swells to bursting point while I hold her adoring gaze.

Her eyes shimmer with desire and something deeper, and I wonder if she's feeling it too. I move forward, claiming her lips, just as the tappity-tap of heels on the hallway floor brings me crashing down to Earth with a bang.

Our eyes pop wide, and she scrambles off me, hurriedly fixing her clothes and smoothing back her hair as I yank my sweats back up my body. I throw the blanket over us mere seconds before my sister and best friend step into the room.

Thank fuck, we hadn't switched the movie off.

"Hey." My sister's gaze bounces between me and Summer, and I pray she's not putting two and two together.

"You're home early." It's only just past eleven, and I wasn't expecting them home for at least another couple of hours.

"Yeah." She looks up at Slater with uncertainty in her eyes. "Our night was unexpectedly cut short."

I raise a brow in silent question. She gulps, knotting her hands in front of her. "Myndi's waters broke at the restaurant," she quietly adds.

"Oh, right." My chest tightens, like it always does at the mention of her name, but it's not as constricting as usual.

"That's exciting." Summer smiles at my sister, and I could kiss her for attempting to lighten the atmosphere. "I hope everything goes okay."

"Me too." Gabby chews on her lip as she scrutinizes my face with a furrowed brow. Her gaze flits to Summer, and her eyes pop out on stalks as she takes a proper look at her. "Is that my Wonder Woman costume?"

A slight blush stains Summer's cheeks, and it's the first time I've noticed even a hint of embarrassment on her face. Good to know she's not superhuman. "Yes, I hope that's okay. Billy wanted us to dress up for the movie."

Slater sends me a smug grin, and I know he's worked it out. Guess I'll be fessing up in the morning. I flip him the bird and mouth "shut the fuck up" behind the girl's backs.

"Of course," Gabby reassures her while her gaze bounces between us. It looks like she's debating with herself. Then the lines smooth out of her brow, and she says in a cheery voice, "I think I'll make coffee. Who wants some?"

Chapter Nineteen
Ryan

"What's going on with you and Summer?" Gabby asks me the following morning as we're eating breakfast in the kitchen. Summer has gone with Slater and Billy to walk Daisy in her stroller.

"What?" I splutter, almost spitting coffee all over the table.

"The room reeked of sex last night, and the telltale signs were all over both your faces," she calmly says, refilling my mug.

"Tell it straight why don'tcha, Tornado," I deadpan.

She's quiet as she reclaims her seat across from me. "Does Austin know?"

I shake my head, swallowing the thick lump in my throat. "He wouldn't approve."

"It's not his place to approve or disapprove."

"She's young."

"And you're immature." Gabby flashes me a grin. "I'd say it's a match made in heaven."

I poke my tongue out at her. "That's a little harsh, sis. I've grown up a lot the last couple years."

She slides her hand across the table, squeezing mine. "I know you have. I'm only teasing, but, honestly, I think Summer's perfect for you. She doesn't take herself too seriously, yet she's got a good head on her shoulders. And while she's young at heart, she's mature in all the ways that count."

"She is," I admit, unable to stop my big smile. "She's incredible."

Gabby's jaw slackens, and her eyes pop wide. "My god. You're in love with her."

No point lying. My sister is a persistent little minx when she wants to be, so it's easiest to come clean at the outset. I slowly nod, ignoring the nervous fluttering in my chest. "I am, but it can't go anywhere."

"Why the hell not?"

"Because I'm not destined for anything long-term."

"I'm fucking sick of hearing this bullshit, Ryan." She glares at me. "Why the hell don't you believe you're worthy of love? Why are you so against a loving home and a family like I have?"

"You know why."

"All I know is you felt this way long before Myndi screwed with your head, and I'm sick of your deflective bullshit. What made you so cynical? Especially when we had the perfect example of a loving marriage growing up!"

"Oh. please." I roll my eyes. "Don't tell me you bought into that charade."

Her eyes almost bug out of her head. "What the actual fuck, Ryan?" Realization creeps across her face. "This is something to do with Mom and Dad?" Her brow puckers in confusion.

"I'm not talking about this." I take a big gulp of my coffee, my chest burning with the knowledge I gleaned when I was seven.

"You damn well are." She glares at me again. "Our parents are as crazy in love now as they were when they met."

I snort. "It's bullshit. It always has been."

She leans across the table. "What are you talking about? Spit it out, Ryan, or I'm calling them right now."

"It's all lies!" I shout. "She cheated on him! Mom cheated on Dad!"

Gabby vehemently shakes her head. "No way, Ryan. There's no way she'd do something like that."

"I fucking saw her! All right!"

"What?!"

I rest my head in my hands, sighing. A sour taste coats the inside of my mouth as I pin my gaze on my sister and admit this for the first time. "I was seven when I saw her. I'd been out playing ball with Slate, and I came back early because I fell and cut my knee. She didn't hear me come in because she was shouting at some strange man. I edged toward the kitchen, frightened, and then I saw it. Saw them kissing." My jaw locks tight as the image replays in my mind as if I only witnessed it yesterday. It's ingrained in my mind, and I've never been able to look at Mom the same way since. I know she hates that she's not close with me like she is with Gabby, Caleb, and Dean. I hide my true feelings behind my humor, but my anger simmers beneath the mask I wear in her presence. I have come close to telling my dad on so many occasions, but I've always held back out of fear.

Gabby slouches in her chair, looking deep in thought. She sits up straighter, a knowing look replacing her troubled expression. "I bet it was Mickey Delaney."

"Who the fuck is Mickey Delaney?" I ask, wondering why that name sounds vaguely familiar. "Wait. You don't mean the quarterback who used to play with the Patriots?"

She nods. "Yeah, I think so. Mom said he had a great sporting career." She pulls out her cell phone, and I'm thoroughly confused.

"What are you doing?" I stand.

"I'm getting Mom. You need to talk to her."

"No way. I'm leaving," I say, even though I already know my sister won't allow it. If she's risking the kids picking up germs by calling Mom over here, I know she won't let this drop.

"Sit the fuck back down," she hollers, rounding the table and jabbing her finger into my chest. "You're not leaving until you hear Mom tell you the story."

"What story?"

"The story of her first love. Mickey Delaney."

Summer, Slater, and the kids arrive back at the same time Mom pulls up to the house. Daisy is fast asleep in her stroller, and Summer offers to take Billy up to his room to play so we can talk. "Are you okay?" she mouths at me, and I shrug. Not gonna lie. I have no clue what Gabby knows only she's adamant that the scene I witnessed as a kid could not have been as it seemed. Summer doesn't know what's going on, but she's picked up the tension in the air.

"I'll fill you in later," I mouth back at her before Billy hauls her up to his room.

"What's going on?" Mom asks when she arrives, clasping my face, concern radiating from the back of her eyes. "Are you sick?"

"No, Mom." Gabby pulls her into a hug, before forcing her into a chair. "Ryan needs to hear about Mickey Delaney." She sighs sadly. "He has it in his head you cheated on Dad because he saw you kissing another man in the kitchen when he was seven."

Way to just put it out there Gabby.

"Oh my god." Mom clamps a hand over her mouth, tears pooling in her eyes as she stares at me, horror-struck. "Is that what you've thought all these years?"

I fold my arms across my body. "I know what I saw. You were kissing a man who wasn't my father."

"Oh, my poor boy. This is why, isn't it?" Tears roll down her face, and a heavy weight presses down on my chest. I might not have the best relationship with my mother, but I still hate to see her cry. "This is why you keep me at arm's length. Why you never let me in." She breaks down then, sobbing, and Gabby wraps her arms around her, offering soothing words as I stare at Slater, conflicted.

"Ryan," Mom sobs over Gabby's shoulder. "I have *never* cheated on your father. *Never*. I love him more than words can express. I can explain what you saw." She swipes at her tears, and Gabby releases her, sitting in the chair beside her.

Mom gestures for me to take the seat in front of her, and I silently sit down. I don't protest when she takes my hands in hers, leaning into me with earnest eyes. "I'm guessing you ran away after you saw that kiss?" I nod tersely. "Then you wouldn't have seen me push him away. Or heard me tell him I loved your father and I would never go back to him."

"Who was he to you?" I choke out.

"Mickey Delaney was my first love. He lived four doors away from us when I was growing up. We were childhood sweethearts, inseparable, until he got a full ride to play ball at the University of Southern California. I didn't get a scholarship to join him, and my parents couldn't afford the tuition, so I went to UD where I met and fell in love with your father. Although it was a tough decision, I broke things off with Mickey before anything started with your dad."

Her chest heaves as she implores me with her eyes. "Mickey turned up at our house one time, completely out of the blue, after years, telling me he still loved me and begging me to leave your father for him. His most recent engagement had just ended, and he told me he couldn't move on, that no one else measured up."

She stares off into space, lost in thought for a few seconds, before she redirects her attention my way. "I told him no outright, then he kissed me. It startled me for a minute, and I didn't push him away straightaway, but as soon as I realized it, I did exactly that. I told him I loved your father, and I loved our family, and I would never betray him for any man. He got the message, and he left soon after that. He apologized for kissing me, and that was the last time I ever saw him. I swear it."

She squeezes my hands. "Please say you believe me." When I don't respond immediately, tears well in her eyes again. "Call your father! He knows all about that visit. He knows that he kissed me. If you don't believe me, maybe you'll believe it from him."

"That's the truth?" I croak. "And you've never cheated on Dad?"

"No!" she cries out, tears streaming down her face again. "I love all of you too much to ever risk ruining what we have. I'm so fortunate. I know that, and I'd do nothing to jeopardize it. I've never wanted to because I'm happy in my life."

"Mom." I'm fighting tears now. I can't believe I've been under a misconception all these years. That I've judged her so unfairly. I pull her into my arms, and then we're both crying. Gabby and Slate quietly leave the kitchen, and I cling to my mom, holding her in a way I've denied myself for years. "I'm so sorry, Mom."

"No, sweetheart." Mom eases back, cupping my face. "You have nothing to apologize for. I'm sorry you had to see that. Sorry you've thought that of me all this time. All these wasted years." She sobs, and I hate I've hurt her, hurt myself, for something that was never anything to begin with. "That's why you don't believe in love or marriage?"

I nod. "I always thought it was a lie. If you could fool Dad for all those years, then I never wanted to marry. To leave myself open to that kind of betrayal. But I've been so wrong, and now I feel foolish."

She presses a kiss to my head, holding me close. "I can understand how it must've looked to a child. I wish you'd come to me or spoken to one of your siblings about it."

"I couldn't. I didn't want them to feel the way I did. To know your love wasn't true."

"Oh, Ryan." She presses kisses to my cheeks. "I love you so much, and it's always pained me that our relationship was strained. This explains everything."

"I'm sorry, Mom. I'm sorry I hurt you, and I love you too. More than I can say."

She palms my face. "Promise me you'll let go of these feelings and open your heart. I worry about you so much. I want you to find a nice girl and settle down, but you're so closed off. Don't let a misconception take something so precious away from you."

No Feelings Involved

"Will you be okay?" Gabby asks me a few hours later at the front door. Summer is already in the car waiting for me, and Mom left a half hour ago.

"I just need to process everything."

She grabs me into a hug. "I love you, little big bro, and I want you to be happy." She keeps a hold of my arms as she stares into my face. "If you love Summer, tell her, and then make things right with Austin. It's only a matter of time before he realizes because you two can't disguise the way you feel about one another. I had my suspicions before we came home last night. Austin will figure it out, if he hasn't already, and it's better if he hears it from you first."

Chapter Twenty
Summer

Ryan's been very introspective since Sunday, not that I blame him. The truth has shaken his whole belief system to its core, and he's trying to process everything. I've been quiet too, because the situation with Hannah and Jordan is hovering over me like a bad smell, and I'm on tenterhooks waiting for him to talk to her.

Everything comes to a head Friday night, and it's a clusterfuck of epic proportions as I suspected it might be.

Ryan and I have only just gotten home from the gym when a loud pounding sounds on the front door. Ryan looks up from the stove where he's cooking dinner, sharing a puzzled look with me. "I'll get it." I move toward the hallway.

"Let me." He moves protectively in front of me.

"Open the fucking door, Summer," Hannah hollers, thumping on the door with her fists.

"Fuck," I whisper.

"You have done nothing wrong," Ryan reminds me, kissing my temple.

He opens the door and Hannah barrels inside, steam practically billowing out of her ears. "How could you do this to me?" she screeches, tears pumping out of her eyes. "You know how much I love him!"

"I haven't done anything, Han," I protest, closing the door before we air our dirty laundry to the neighbors. I'm grateful Austin and Miley are working the late shift and they're not around for this confrontation.

"The hell you haven't." She shoves me, and I stumble on my feet, my heart racing. I've never endured Hannah's anger before, and her vicious hostility surprises and upsets me.

"Touch Summer one more time," Ryan says, sliding in between us, "and I'll be escorting you outside. If you're not prepared to sit and listen to what she has to say, then I think it's best you leave now and return when you're calmer."

"She stole him from me," Hannah wails.

"Summer has done no such thing. I don't know what your boyfriend has told you, but she's been a loyal friend to you for years, and you owe her the benefit of the doubt."

I touch his arm, urging him back. I'm grateful for his support, and his quick defense only makes me love him more, but this is between my bestie and me, and we need to talk alone. He eyeballs me and I silently communicate the message. He nods. "I'll be in the kitchen if you need me."

"Thank you," I mouth. Hannah follows me into the living room, whimpering the whole time. I plonk down on the recliner chair and she sits on the couch. "I'm so sorry, Hannah. I know how much you love him, and I'm shocked over all this."

"Huh." She harrumphs, pulling a tissue out of her jeans pocket. "I'm sure you are. I bet you can't wait to hook up with him."

My eyes go out on stalks. "Are you for real right now?" She glares at me. "Jordan is nothing but a friend, and I've never, ever, given him any sign I felt any differently toward him. When he approached me last weekend at the club, I told him point-blank I wasn't interested, that I didn't share his feelings. I was the one who told him he had to tell you or I would."

"Why?" she spits out.

"Why?" My tone betrays my disbelief. "Because you deserved to know the truth, and you were already torturing yourself over things you couldn't explain."

"We could've gotten through this, but you had to interfere."

My mouth opens and closes like a fish out of water. I can't believe she's twisting this around. "I seriously have no words, Han. I know you're upset, but surely, you don't mean that. Why would you want to stay with a guy if he doesn't love you anymore?" I lean forward, resting my elbows on my knees. "You deserve so much better than that, and I didn't want to see him making a fool out of you. That's why I told him to tell you."

"Oh puh-lease." She sends daggers at me. "I know exactly why you told him that. You want him for yourself, and you can't wait to get me out of the way."

I wonder if some alien being has stolen my best friend and replaced her with a poor substitute because the woman sitting across from me now is a stranger. I get that she's hurt. I'm hurt for her. But that's no excuse for accusing me of shit she knows I'd never do.

"No. I don't."

"I don't believe you."

I shake my head sadly. "Even if I had feelings for Jordan, which I don't," I categorically state, "I would never choose him over you. Not in a million years. Your friendship is worth more."

Unlike you.

The thought flies into my mind, and even though I feel mean thinking it, I can't help remembering all the ways Hannah put our friendship to one side in favor of her relationship with Jordan. It never bothered me before, but considering her fake accusations, it enrages me now.

"You've a funny way of showing it."

"Do I?" I flap my hands in the air, losing the tenuous control of my emotions. "Time and time again, you've put your relationship with him above our friendship. When he changed his plans last minute to come to UD, I stepped aside so you two could get a place together even though it meant moving in here with my brother, which was something I wasn't keen on." Not that I can regret how things have turned out because Jordan's decision indirectly led me to Ryan.

"That doesn't mean you don't want him now." She's grasping at straws, and she knows it.

"For the last time, I have no interest in Jordan. Not now. Not ever." There's only one surefire way of getting through to her, and I blurt it out before I properly think it through. "Besides, I'm seeing someone else. Someone I'm crazy about."

She snorts, sending an incredulous look my way. "Who? The Invisible Man?"

I grind my teeth to the molars. I want to tell her, but with the way she's acting, I'm not sure I can trust her to keep my confidence. "I've kept it on the down low for a reason, but it's true."

"Sure it is." She snarls at me. "If that's the best you can do, you're even more pathetic than I thought." She rakes her gaze over me in a derisory manner, and a splinter cracks my heart in two. "I don't even know what he sees in you. You're not anything special."

"That's enough." Ryan's voice is laced with anger. He plants his hands on my shoulders, giving me a reassuring squeeze. "Summer and I have been seeing one another, and I'm every bit as crazy about her."

My eyes widen in shock at his admission, but it's happy shock. I reach up, taking his hand and smiling at him.

Hannah is momentarily speechless as she stares at both of us. Then her mouth twists into a hurtful grimace. "You've been fucking him all this time, and you didn't tell me?"

"I wanted to, but Jordan hates him, and I was afraid he'd cause trouble."

Her lower lip wobbles as the truth of my statement hits home.

She stands abruptly, wrapping her arms around herself. "Jordan and I can fix this. But you need to stay away from him and stay away from me."

I rise, moving toward her. "Hannah. Please don't push me away. I'm your friend."

"You're no friend of mine." She brushes past me. "You think you know someone," she tosses over her shoulder before exiting the apartment, violently slamming the door shut behind her.

"Yeah," I whisper to myself, fighting tears. "I'm with you on that front."

Chapter Twenty-One
Ryan

S ummer was uncharacteristically quiet the rest of the weekend, and I'm sorely tempted to have a private word in Hannah's ear, but I doubt Summer would appreciate me interfering, so I leave it alone. I can't believe the nerve of that bitch to come here and throw that bullshit at Summer. *Who needs enemies with friends like that?*

Miley and Austin are at the movies Sunday night, and Derrick is covering the nighttime shift, so when we return to the apartment a little after six, I run a bath for Summer and then order takeout while she's, hopefully, relaxing. I have one of those sappy chick flicks paused on the screen when Summer materializes, bundled up in a fluffy robe with her damp hair tied into a messy bun on top of her head. A weird fluttering takes up residence in my chest as I walk to her, pulling her into my arms without hesitation.

Fuck, I'm turning into such a pussy.

But I honestly couldn't give two shits about it.

When she rests her head on my chest and sighs, I tighten my hold on her, lacing my fingers through her silken hair, wishing I could absorb her heartache and take away her pain.

Hannah is a shitty friend. I thought she might've cooled down by now and reached out to Summer to apologize for the way she treated her, but she has made no effort with her at all. If you ask me, Summer's better off without her.

The bell chimes, and I pry myself away from my girl to answer the door. I peck her lips lightly. "That's our takeout. Go sit, and I'll plate up."

When I return with our food and a couple beers, Summer is curled up on the couch, with her knees pulled into her chest, staring off into space. I set the food and drinks down on the coffee table and sit beside her. "Hey." I tilt her chin up with one finger. "She'll come around. She was just upset." I don't really believe that, but I know they've been friends since they were small kids and that her friendship means a lot to Summer, so I'm keeping my honest thoughts to myself.

"I don't know that she will, and I'm not sure I want her to."

I probe her gorgeous, sad eyes, reaching out to caress her cheek because I can't seem to go a minute without wanting to touch her. "Talk to me."

I lean back in the couch, pulling her into my side. She fists her hand in my shirt as she rests her head on my shoulder, and I could happily die right now, completely satisfied. Yup; I've most definitely traded in my Man Card. My heart elevates in my chest as I gaze adoringly at her.

Summer soothes something in me by her very presence, and I know I need to do right by her. Starting with telling her I'm in love with her and then breaking the news to her brother, if she's in agreement to make things official between us. But this isn't the time for that, so I bite my tongue as I wait for her to unburden herself, smoothing my hand up and down her back and holding her close.

"I've been doing a ton of soul searching since Friday night, and I don't think my friendship with Hannah is as close as I believed it was. It's like I had blinders on, because I didn't see how I always took second place to Jordan." She tips her head up, looking me directly in the eye. "It's not that I expected to come first all the time. Not at all. But now and then would've been nice, except she always blew me off to spend time with him, and I never stopped to question it."

"I'm sorry." I kiss her temple.

"I don't get how she can blame me for this. I've never said or done anything to lead Jordan to believe I had any romantic feelings for him, and I haven't betrayed her. Demanding he tells her the truth was my way of protecting my best friend from further pain but she has thrown even that back in my face."

She sits up straighter, leaning both her hands on my chest. "I was really upset yesterday, and, honestly, my emotions have been veering all over the place, but now, I'm just sad because I know that even if we patch things up, our friendship will never be the same. Or maybe it will be," she adds, her brows knitting together. "But that won't be enough, because I don't want a friend who isn't there for me when I need her or one who throws accusations my way when her life turns shitty."

"Just be true to yourself, Summer. Friendships are two-way streets, no different from any other relationships. There needs to be give and take and mutual trust and respect. If Hannah can't offer you that, then maybe she doesn't deserve a place in your life."

The working week is crazy, and I've barely seen Summer since Sunday night, except for brief stolen kisses as we pass each other in the apartment like ships in the night. All week, I've thought of nothing else but opening my heart and my life up to Summer, and I know I'm ready.

But I don't really know how she feels. We need to have a heart to heart to see where things are going with us. I've been texting her all day, asking if she's free after rehearsal tonight to go for dinner, but I'm growing increasingly worried when I still haven't heard from her by the time my shift is over.

I head home to get changed, and then I plan to head over to the theater company to wait for her.

I'm turning my key in the lock, listening to the shouting coming from inside with growing trepidation. Stepping into the apartment, I close the door, toss my keys on the table in the hall, and walk into the living room.

Austin is pacing the floor, fisting tufts of his hair in his hands, shouting at Summer, while she stands stock-still with tears silently rolling down her face. She's wearing sweats and a ratty T-shirt, her face devoid of makeup, with her hair in a messy ponytail. She looks paler than normal, and something is clearly wrong. Miley is tugging on Austin's elbow, whispering in his ear, concern etched all over her face.

"What's going on?" I ask, stepping into the room.

Summer's lower lip wobbles as she looks at me with blatant fear in her eyes.

"Shall you tell him, or will I?" Austin yells, and Summer flinches at the harsh tone of his voice.

I instinctively move to Summer's side, wondering if he's figured out what's going on with us. "Stop shouting at her," I say, working hard to keep my voice calm.

"Don't tell me what to do with *my* sister!" Austin snaps, glaring at me.

"Austin." Miley's tone is firm. "Stop this. Your sister is upset enough as it is. All you're doing is making things worse. You need to calm down."

"I can't fucking calm down!" he screams. "And I'm upset too! She's eighteen years old, and this'll ruin her entire life!"

"That's not true," Summer says, sniffling as she wraps her arms around her shivering body.

Discreetly, I place my hand on her lower back. "Is someone going to tell me what's going on?" I'm guessing Austin hasn't figured it out as all my limbs are still intact, but I have no idea why he's so riled up.

"Some asshole has knocked her up!" he admits through gritted teeth, and I sway on my feet as my ears ring and my eyesight blurs.

"What?" My eyes dart to Summer's in shock. Her silent tears transform to full-blown sobs as she looks at me with these big, apologetic eyes. "You're pregnant," I whisper. "Seriously?"

"These things don't lie," Austin says, shoving something into my hand. Blinking to clear my foggy head, I stare at the three pregnancy tests with the clear blue line confirming she's pregnant. "Imagine coming home to find those on your little sister's bedside table," he fumes.

My mind is bouncing off the walls as panic joins the bile swimming up my throat. I know this baby is mine, but why didn't she tell me? What the fuck are we going to do now?

"She won't tell me who the father is." Steam is practically billowing out of Austin's ears, but I don't blame him. I remember how shocked I was when I discovered Gabby was pregnant at nineteen, and I almost punched Dylan's lights out.

I snap out of my daze, preparing to man up and tell him the truth when Summer pinches my arm, pinning me with anguished eyes as she answers her brother. "It's none of your business."

And that was so not the thing to say to him in the moment. "The fucking hell it isn't!" He paces again. "If it's one of those obnoxious, jumped-up frat boys, I will lose my fucking shit. I mean it, Summer."

"Austin, please calm down." Miley pleads, trying to grab her boyfriend and stall his frantic pacing.

"How the hell can I be calm?" Tears prick his eyes, and his voice cracks. "She's my little sister, and some asshole did this to her. She hasn't even begun to live her life." He shakes his head sadly, swiping at errant tears, and I feel like the biggest shithead.

"A baby isn't the end of the world, Austin," Summer quietly says. "You know I adore kids."

"Adoring kids and raising one at your age isn't the same thing, and you know it! What about UD? And all your travel plans?"

"I can still do what I want. I'll just have to make adjustments and maybe push the time line out." She's shuffling nervously on her feet, avoiding looking at me as she talks in a soft but determined voice, and I know she's trying to put a brave face on it, but her fear is still palpable. I don't know how long she's known about it, but I'm guessing she only found out today because the girl I know, and love, wouldn't keep this hidden from me. I couldn't get a hold of her today, and I figure this is why. She was at home, by herself, trying to process this.

She doesn't even know I'm in love with her.

Or that I was planning on asking her to be my girlfriend for real.

Who knows what thoughts were going through her mind?

I may be confused and terrified too, but she needs me, and I won't let her down.

I'm done hiding.

Sliding my arm fully around her waist, I pull her securely into my side. Then I turn to my best friend and business partner with a fierce look on my face. "I'm the father. It's my baby."

Austin just stares at me in obvious shock. It's like one of those cinematic moments. You know, where the screen seems to focus in on a scene and the surrounding environment fades out. Until an explosion happens, and everything comes back into focus in a nanosecond.

This is exactly like that because Austin just stares at me, and you could hear a pin drop in the room for a few seconds until an animalistic growl rips from the back of his throat, and he lunges at me, punching me square in the face.

Summer screams.

Miley shouts.

And I stagger back, a little dizzy, pressing my fingers to the trickle of blood leaking out of my throbbing nose.

Austin comes at me again, landing a punch in my gut and winding me so bad I drop to my knees, struggling to catch a breath. "You fucking asshole!" he roars, slamming his fist into the side of my head this time. "I told you to keep your filthy hands off her!" My head jerks sideways, and I stretch my hand out to stop myself from falling flat on the ground. My head is spinning, and my breathing still hasn't returned to normal, but I deflect his next hit as Miley yanks on his arm, trying to pull him away from me.

Summer crouches down in front of me, crying. "I'm sorry."

"Don't fucking say sorry to him!" Austin yells, wrestling to get free of Miley's hold. "He took advantage of you, and now you're paying the price!"

I see the switch flick in Summer. Jumping up, she dries her eyes, storming over to her brother, pushing her face up in his. "Ryan did *not* take advantage of me! He tried to do the right thing. He kept pushing me away, but I pushed back harder every time until he caved." She fists hers hands on her hips. "Our relationship is one hundred percent consensual."

I stagger to my feet. "I love her," I tell him, hating that she's hearing this for the first time like this. "And while I'm shocked about the baby, because I didn't know, I won't leave her to deal with this alone." I turn my head to Summer. "I'll be with you every step of the way, if that's what you want."

"You love me?" is her wide-eyed response.

I ignore Austin and Miley, focusing on the only person in this room who matters. Or, the only two people who matter, I correct myself, as my eyes lower to her flat stomach. "Come here." I hold out my hand for her to walk to me because I'm afraid to move a muscle in case Austin goes for me again.

She walks toward me with fresh tears in her eyes. I reel her into my arms, kissing her forehead. "I love you so much. I was going to tell you tonight, and if you agreed, I was planning on speaking to your brother after that."

"I love you too," she whispers through her tears, and a hint of a smile ghosts over her lips. "I only found out about the baby this morning. I don't even know how far along I am. I was planning on telling you tonight, but Austin went into my room while I was in the shower, discovered the tests I'd stupidly left out in plain sight, and then this whole shit show started."

I urge her head toward my chest, and she obliges, circling her arms around my waist. I hold her tight, pressing kisses into her hair. "It'll be okay. I know we have a lot to talk about, but we're in this together, right?"

She sniffles, nodding her head, and hugging me tighter.

I risk a look at her brother. The anger has not left his face, and he's glaring at me like he wants to rip my torso apart with his bare hands and remove all the vital organs from my body until I'm no longer breathing. "I know you're pissed but—"

"Don't even talk to me right now, James. I mean it. I can't stand to look at your face."

"I'll look after her. I'll love her and the baby and make sure they want for nothing."

Austin snorts. "*Maybe* your intentions are honest, but you have no fucking clue how to be there for any girl let alone a baby. At the first sign of trouble, you'll run a million miles away."

"That's not fucking fair," I spit out.

"Isn't it?" He arches a brow. "Look what happened with Myndi and how much of a basket case you've been since then."

"This is not the same thing, and Summer means the world to me."

"Doesn't mean you'll stick around for her."

I rub a tense spot between my brows, eager to end this conversation because he's pushing buttons I don't want pushed. "You know what, I don't have to explain myself to you." I straighten up, keeping a firm hold on Summer. "Summer and I have things to discuss in private."

Austin opens his mouth to say something, but Summer pins him with a look the devil himself would be proud of. "I think you've said enough for one night, Austin." Then she sighs, and her features relax a little. "I know you love me and you're just worried, but you've got to step away from this and let me and Ryan figure it out." She moves to his side, tentatively opening her arms for a hug.

He pulls her into his arms, squeezing his eyes closed as he hugs her close. "I'm sorry for shouting, but this has come out of left field."

Opening his eyes, he bores a hole in the side of my skull as he speaks to his sister. "This is not what I wanted for you, Summer." He pauses for a couple beats. "Ryan is not who I'd choose for you," he cruelly adds, digging the knife in further. "I hope you know what you're doing."

Chapter Twenty-Two
Summer

"Are you feeling okay," Ryan asks once we've sequestered ourselves in his bedroom, away from the wrath of my brother. "Have you been sick or anything, because you look a little pale?" He leans his back against the headrest, opening his arms for me.

I crawl into his embrace, instantly feeling less agitated as his strong arms go around me. "I've been sick a few times this week," I admit. "At first, I thought it was just a passing bug, but this morning, the sickness was terrible. I couldn't stop throwing up, and it was only then I realized my period was a couple days late. I went to the pharmacy and grabbed some tests and, well, you know the rest."

"It's my fault. I should've insisted we use condoms, but it felt so good to be inside you with nothing between us."

I cradle his face in my hands. "We both agreed, and I'm on the pill, so it should've been safe. I don't know how this even happened." A little burst of laughter emits from my mouth. "I'm like one of those naïve virgins you read about in books. A few months after popping my cherry, I end up knocked up." I shake my head, because it almost feels fictional even though I know that's not true. No form of contraceptive is one hundred percent reliable, and we should've been taking extra precautions. It's not like I'm the first eighteen-year-old to ever get pregnant.

"Don't say that." He kisses me softly. "You're nothing like that."

Although I don't want to, I shuck out of his arms, sitting up beside him. I can't have a serious conversation while I'm sprawled on top of him. "Can we get serious?" He nods, threading his fingers through mine. "How do you really feel about this?"

His chest heaves, and he scrubs his free hand back and forth over the scruff on his chin as he considers my question. Then he turns on his side, still keeping our hands connected, and peers directly into my eyes, letting me see everything he's feeling. "I think I'm still in shock, but I'm not unhappy about it. I love you, Summer, and I want to plan a future with you. I'd already decided that before I heard the baby news." He smiles, but it's a little off. "But I won't lie and say I'm not scared, because I'm terrified what your brother just said out there is true. I've only had one serious relationship in my life, and that ended up a complete mess. I want to care for you and the baby, but I've never done this before. I want to be who you need me to be, but I'm scared of failing you."

His honesty and vulnerability are exactly what I need to hear, and I'm so glad he was truthful. I press my lips to the corner of his mouth. "I love you, Ryan James, and I already love this baby." I take his hand, placing it over the smooth planes of my stomach. "While I didn't plan on having kids this young, I can't be unhappy about it. It's a little baby." My grin expands. "A little miracle from heaven. A little piece of you and a little piece of me." Tears well in my eyes, but this time they're happy tears. "As long as you are with me in this, we'll figure it out as we go. That's all I ask of you, Ryan. Just be with me. Work through the highs and lows with me."

He rubs his hand back and forth across my stomach. "I can do that."

I sense he's holding back. "Please say what's on your mind."

He looks up at me, gulping. "You're so young, Summer. I can't help feeling selfish for wanting you, and now, everything you dreamed of for your future has changed in an instant, and I feel responsible for that."

"Stop." I press a kiss to his lips. "We made this baby together. You didn't force me into anything, and plans can be adapted."

"I'll take on the bulk of the childcare so you can continue with your studies," he says, still rubbing my belly. "Derrick has already taken on more managerial responsibility, so him and Austin can manage the daytime between them, and I can cover at night once you get home from school."

"I can drop the theater and cut out a couple of optional electives," I add, excitement mingling with the blood flowing in my veins. "And I'm sure my mom will help as much as she can."

Ryan's face turns a sickly shade of green, and I can't help giggling.

"Oh, boy. I'd totally forgotten about telling my family. If you think that was bad with Austin..." Oh shit. He has no idea what he's in for with Dad and my other brothers. He pulls out his cell. "What are you doing?"

"Looking for a store in Newark that sells full body armor."

"Good thinking," I immediately agree, giggling again, because there's no denying he'll need it.

We make the drive to Bridgeville early Sunday morning and I have never seen Ryan look so nervous. His knee jerks off the floor the entire trip, and he's gripping the steering wheel so tight it's a wonder he has any blood flowing to his fingers.

"You're sure Austin has said nothing to them?" he asks me as we breach the town perimeter.

"He promised he hasn't said a word. He knows he owes me for the way he reacted last week." I pat his hand. "Try not to worry. I already told Mom you were my boyfriend, so at least that's not a shock, and I should be able to get her on our side quick. She'll help me protect you."

"Not funny, Summer," he grits out as little beads of sweat form on his brow.

"At least they already know you," I supply, trying to help ease his anxiety. "That helps."

He snorts. "I'm not sure if that's a good thing or a bad thing."

"It's a good thing," I reassure him. "They know you're a good guy."

He looks skeptical. "I hope you're right."

Ryan looks like he's about to vomit as he pulls the SUV to a halt outside my parent's farmhouse. I fix my off-the-shoulder sweater, slip on my heels, and slick gloss on my lips. I tried harder with my appearance today, deliberately wearing more makeup than usual and wearing a smart sweater with skinny jeans and heels. Ryan's not the only one who's nervous, and looking good helps my confidence. Plus, I wanted to convey maturity with my look, so I avoided my usual Converse and casual clothes.

Ryan opens my door, helping me out. I place my hands on his shoulders and stretch up to kiss him. "I love you, and no matter what happens here today, it's you, me, and the baby that matters. They're bound to be shocked, but I know my family, and they'll support us. It might take a little while to process, but they'll be okay with this. Trust me."

He rests his forehead on mine. "I do, baby. I really do. I just don't want to mess anything up. I want them to see I'll love and protect you both. That I won't let you down."

I press my body into his, angling my head and pulling his mouth to mine for a slower, longer, deeper kiss.

"Ahem." A loud throat clearing has us pulling away, and I look up at my brother Charlie, meeting his scowl with a wide grin.

"Big brother, Charlie. How are you?" I go on an immediate charm offensive as I walk up the steps toward him. Ryan grabs the gifts for my parents from the back seat, following behind me.

No Feelings Involved

"Seriously, Summer?" Charlie grumbles as he pulls me into a bear hug. "I know I warned you off the horny frat boys, but he's almost old enough to be your dad."

"Don't talk crap, man," Ryan retorts, narrowing his eyes at my brother. "I was only eight when she was born."

"Not a medical improbability," Charlie argues, and I jump in before this thing escalates.

"Don't be an old fuddy-duddy." I thump him in the arm. "Age is irrelevant. I'm an adult. Ryan's an adult." I snake my arm around Ryan's waist. "We love each other, and there's no law that says we can't be in a relationship."

Charlie's jaw hangs open, and his eyes pop wide at the mention of love. I close his mouth with a carefully placed finger under his chin while ushering Ryan into the house. "That fish out of water look is *not* attractive on you."

"Is that my princess?" Dad calls out as our footsteps echo along the hardwood floors.

"Hey, Daddy." I bound into the kitchen, wrapping my arms around my dad from behind.

"Hello again, Ryan," Mom says, welcoming him with a warm smile.

"It's nice to see you again, Mrs. Petersen," Ryan politely replies, handing her the large box of chocolates from that expensive hand-made place she loves. "These are for you."

"You shouldn't have." She kisses his cheek, accepting the gift. "My lips thank you. My hips not so much," she teases, setting the box down on the counter and looping her arm through his.

"And this is for you, sir," Ryan says, looking my father square in the eye as he hands over the gift-slash-bribe.

Dad pulls his glasses down from his head, inspecting the label on the special edition bottle of whiskey Ryan picked up for him. "Very nice, son." He pats Ryan on the shoulder. "We'll sample that after dinner," he adds with a wink.

Ryan grimaces. "I'll take a rain check. I'm driving."

"I can drive back," I say with a shrug.

"Only if it's not late. I don't want you driving in the dark."

My heart swells with love like it has all week as Ryan fussed over me, running me nightly baths, driving me to and from classes and the theater, cooking me dinner. He even got up earlier than necessary to fix me a proper breakfast. And he came with me to the Ob-gyn, where my pregnancy was officially confirmed, asking questions while I sat there in a bit of a daze.

Mom smiles at me, and I grin back just as my other brother Marc steps into the kitchen. "Marky Mark!" I rush to my brother, throwing myself into his arms. "I didn't know you'd be here!"

"I flew home for the weekend, especially to see you," he says, enveloping me in his arms. "It's been too long, Sum."

It's been months since we were together. Marc recently got a promotion at the investment banking firm he works for in New York, and he's been working flat out with hardly any free time.

"I'm glad you're here." I slip out of his arms, casting a glance over my shoulder at Ryan. He's sweating bullets, and I feel for him. I grab his hand, pulling him over to Marc as he's the only one in the family he hasn't met before. "This is my boyfriend, Ryan." Marc's expression is carefully impassive as he gives Ryan the once-over. "Be nice to him," I plead. "He's important."

Marc quirks a brow in question, amusement teasing the corners of his mouth.

"They're in *love*," Charlie cuts in, teasing, as he swipes a bread roll from the basket in the center of the table.

"Well, I think it's wonderful," Mom says, pulling out a chair for Ryan. "And Austin's known Ryan a long time, so he's hardly a stranger."

Ryan helps me into the seat before claiming another chair beside me. Mom just beams at him like he hung the stars in the night sky. I had a feeling she'd be easy to win over, but I'm still not entirely sure how she'll take the baby news. Even though it might not be a good idea, we're waiting until after we've eaten to tell them about my pregnancy.

Hopefully, everyone will keep their food down.

"Speaking of Austin, why isn't he here?" Marc asks.

"He's working," Ryan supplies. "We rarely get to take time off at the same time." It's not a lie, per se, but the truth is, Austin has barely spoken to Ryan all week and things are tense at home and at their co-owned place of work.

Ryan has tried talking to him, but he refuses to listen to a word he has to say. The tension is unbearable, and I've tried talking to Austin too, but he's furious with Ryan, and nothing I say makes a difference. Miley asked me to back down, telling me she's working on bringing him around. I have faith she can succeed where we've failed.

She has been amazingly supportive since the news broke, and nonjudgmental, and it only makes me love her more. If Austin doesn't marry her, I might just turn gay for her.

"Hmm." Charlie bites off the crust of his roll, slowly chewing as he watches me and Ryan. "What does Austin think of your relationship?"

Ryan's shoulders stiffen, and I reach for his hand, squeezing it in what I hope is a comforting gesture. "Austin's being a complete ass," I honestly admit. "Although that's partly our fault because we didn't tell him we were seeing one another until it got serious."

"It's my fault," Ryan cuts in. "I should've told him from the outset."

"Austin can blow smoke up my ass," Mom declares, and my body rumbles with laughter as Ryan gawps at her. "I haven't set eyes on his girl yet, and they're together seven months!" she exclaims. "He's in no position to criticize." She squeezes Ryan's shoulders. "Don't you worry about my stubborn eldest son. He'll calm down soon. He just doesn't enjoy being kept in the dark about anything."

"Truth," I add, nodding. "We planned this surprise party for his sixteenth birthday, and he got so mad," I tell Ryan, chuckling. "All he did was grumble all night we hadn't invited the right people, hadn't ordered the right food. Yada yada." I grab two rolls from the basket, handing one to Ryan.

"And it was all for the sake of complaining," Mom agrees, setting a plate piled high with food in front of Ryan. "Because he loved every minute of that party. He just hated the fact he knew nothing about it beforehand."

Thankfully, the conversation moves off us, and my brothers don't grill Ryan *too* much, while we all tuck into the gorgeous dinner Mom prepared, and it's going better than I expected. However, Ryan is still stiff as a brick beside me, and now we've finished eating, I want to get this over and done with.

I squeeze his hand, and he squeezes back, and we look at one another, silently communicating with our eyes. We argued on the way here over who would be the one to announce our news.

Ryan wanted to do it.

He feels it's his responsibility.

But this is my family, and I want to be the one to tell them.

We eventually compromised, agreeing I'd tell my family today, and he'll break the news to the rest of his family next weekend when we are at his parents' house for dinner.

We already told Gabby and Slater, because we needed advice on what to ask at our Ob-gyn appointment, and Ryan's sister was the perfect person to confide in. They were wonderful too, and very supportive, offering their congratulations and help in whatever way they can.

I clear my throat. "So, I have news I'd like to share." My gaze roams the table. Charlie's eyes have already narrowed in suspicion, but the rest of them look curious.

Rip the Band-Aid, Summer.

This is even harder than I imagined, and I gulp over the clump of nerves clogging my throat. Ryan squeezes my hand again, sliding his free arm around my shoulders in a blatant show of support. "I'm pregnant," I blurt before my nerve fails me.

"Oh, my fucking god." That's Charlie. "I knew it!" He all but growls at Ryan.

"Are you suddenly psychic?" I question, raising a brow.

"I wish," he snaps. "Then I could've predicted this and warned Austin to keep this douche away from you."

"He's not a douche! And I won't sit here and listen to you hating on him. We have done nothing wrong!"

"Except forget to use condoms it seems," Charlie continues.

"I'm on the damn pill!" I yell as Ryan pulls me closer into his side. "And unplanned accidental pregnancies happen to lots of women!"

"You're still a kid!" Charlie bites back.

Tears stab my eyes as my brother pins Ryan with a hateful expression. "Stop it! Just stop." Tears leak out of my eyes, and a dense weight settles on my chest.

"I know you're upset," Ryan says, ignoring protocol and pulling me down onto his lap. His arms wrap around me, taking the edge off my anxiety. "But you have no right to speak to your sister like that. If you won't keep a civil tongue, we'll be leaving because I'm not having Summer upset. The stress isn't good for her or the baby."

"What are your intentions toward my daughter, Mr. James?" Dad asks, leaning his elbows on the table. Clear shock is visible on his weather-beaten face, and I lose control of my tenuous emotions. I hate thinking I've disappointed him.

I bury my face in Ryan's neck, trying to stifle my sobs. Damn pregnancy hormones already have me in an emotional tailspin.

"I love Summer, and I plan to raise this child with her. I've already looked around for an apartment for the three of us, and my work situation is flexible, so I'll be able to mind the baby while Summer continues her undergraduate program. The gym is doing well, and I can provide for both of them." He straightens his spine. "I assure you I'm going nowhere."

"What about long-term?" Dad asks.

"We're not together that long, but I already know Summer is the woman I want to spend the rest of my life with," he says, earning a shocked gasp from me. We haven't once discussed marriage, and I can't say it's crossed my mind because I'm still trying to come to terms with the baby bomb.

He drops a loving kiss to the top of my head. "But Summer is young, and I don't want to clip her wings, so your daughter will call the shots. I'm happy to go along with whatever she wants because I just want her to be happy."

I completely break down then, sobbing hysterical, happy tears.

"Sweetheart." Concern is laced in Ryan's tone as he gently lifts my head up. "Don't cry."

"Happy tears," I mumble, sniveling as I wipe my hand across my snotty nose and under my red eyes.

"Attractive, Sum," Marc says, speaking up for the first time. "It must be love if Ryan is still here," he quips, and I appreciate he's trying to reduce the thick tension in the air.

Ryan hands me a tissue from the supply he's started keeping in his jeans pocket for this very reason. "Your sister is always beautiful to me, inside and out. She's the most amazing person I've ever had the privilege to know."

That sets me off again, and everyone looks at me with a hefty dose of concern. I bat my hands in the air, half laughing, half crying. "It's just my hormones. Ignore me."

Silence descends for a few beats, and I stare at Ryan, trying to gauge his mood. He looks more relaxed now we have distributed the news.

"Very well," Dad says, reaching across and shaking Ryan's hand. "All I ask is that you take care of my daughter and our grandchild and you've assured me you will." His voice sounds a little choked and I'm struggling to hold my tears at bay again.

Seriously, pregnancy hormones are no joke.

"How far along are you?" Mom asks, genuine concern stretched across her face.

"The doctor thinks about four weeks," Ryan answers when he

spots my trembling lower lip. "Although we won't know for sure until our hospital appointment."

"So, a May or June baby then, most likely," Mom muses. "That timing is great. You'll just be finishing freshman year, and if you like, you can come home for the summer, or the first few weeks, at least."

"Thanks, Mom. We haven't thought that far ahead yet, but we appreciate the offer."

"Anything you need, honey. You only have to ask."

"Let's all join hands around the campfire and sing *Kumbaya*, why don't we," Charlie grits out. "And pretend that it's fucking fine that my eighteen-year-old sister got knocked up by a pedo."

"That is enough, Charles," Mom demands, her jaw tightening. "You will apologize to Ryan for that comment."

"The hell I will." He stands abruptly, slamming his chair back, and it knocks to the ground. Rounding the table, he looks down at me. "This shouldn't have happened to you, Summer. You had such big plans."

"A baby is God's blessing," Mom says, trying to be helpful, but it's the worst thing to tell Charlie.

"A baby will ruin her fucking life, Mom!"

"My sister had a baby at nineteen," Ryan supplies, and I'm in awe of how calmly he's speaking after the horrible comment my brother just made. "She discovered her boyfriend was dying at the same time. I remember feeling similar things, but the truth is, my nephew Billy is the best thing to happen to my sister, and our family wouldn't be the same without him. I get that this is a shock. It's not what I would've wanted for Summer either, but I won't sit here and say I'm unhappy because I know Summer will make a fantastic mother. A smart woman once told me things happen for a reason, and I fully buy into that now."

I remember telling him that, not realizing how prophetic it would be. And, as Ryan smiles at me—a sincere, confident, happy smile—I see the truth of his statement written all over his face.

Chapter Twenty-Three

Ryan

"I thought Austin was the biggest drama queen in your family," I joke as we make the trip back home later that evening, "but Charlie is a piece of work." He stormed off after my comment about Gabby and didn't return, not even to say goodbye to his pregnant sister. I feel bad for Summer that two of her three brothers are acting like idiots. Like I said, I understand it, to a point. But you only need to look at her to see how emotional she is. Surely, they could set aside their feelings about me to support their little sister? That's what I did, when I was in their shoes, and I processed everything in the background in my own time.

"Honestly, Charlie's always been prone to dramatics, so his reaction isn't that unexpected. He'll stew for a few days and then snap out of his head, call me, and beg for forgiveness. It's Austin I'm most disappointed with, because he's still keeping you at arm's length."

"It's only been a week. It'll all work out." I say what she needs to hear because she's been under enough stress today, but I don't know if Austin will ever forgive me.

Another couple weeks pass by, and Austin is still cold-shouldering me. It's making working together an absolute misery, and I've decided we're having it out today whether he likes it or not. I can't continue like this. If he won't meet me halfway, we need to have a serious discussion over what to do with our business. Whether he buys me out or I buy him out. I don't want it to come to that, but I'm not prepared to put up with this stress every day for the rest of my life, and business partners can't run a company together if they're barely talking.

I call him to my office on the pretext of reviewing the new marketing plan the PR firm emailed over. He's wearing the same intolerant look that's been on his face for the last three weeks when he drops into the chair in front of my desk, folding his arms sternly across his chest. I get up and lock the door so we're not interrupted. He straightens up, eyeing me warily, instantly realizing I've hijacked this meeting.

"I want to talk about Summer."

"Well, I don't," he predictably barks back.

"You've made that perfectly clear. But the longer this goes unsaid, the more it hurts Summer. And this is *really* hurting her, Austin. She's crying most every night because we're not speaking. We need to work this out because we both love her."

He grinds his teeth, flashing me a dark look. "I asked one thing of you, James. One goddamned thing. Not to lay a finger on her, and you just couldn't help yourself," he snarls.

I lean forward with my elbows on the desk, slanting him an earnest look. "I tried to stay away from her, I swear it. And I did at the start, but I couldn't stop myself from falling for her. Your sister is an amazing person and so easy to love."

"How do I know you won't let her down?" he asks, crossing one leg over his knee.

"Because I give you my word. I'm in this for the long haul, Austin, and I told your father that." His brows climb to his hairline.

"I'd marry Summer tomorrow, but I'm respectful of her age and her dreams, and I've already told her she's setting the agenda."

He taps his fingers on the arm of the chair. "Do you mean that? You want to marry her?"

"I do." I wet my dry lips. "Although I haven't mentioned it to her, as I don't want to freak her out, and she's enough on her plate." I stare absently at the wall as I work out how to best explain it. I eyeball Austin. "When I was with Myndi, I thought I was in love, but I know now it wasn't real love because the way I feel about your sister, after only a couple months, is ten thousand times more than I felt for my ex."

I get up, walk around, and prop my butt against the edge of the desk, shooting him an earnest look. "I'm so fucking sorry I didn't tell you sooner. There were good reasons, but I still should've told you."

"I get so mad every time I think about you two sneaking around and lying behind my back." His nostrils flare. "And I can't even think about that night I heard her in your room. I'll have nightmares for the rest of my life." A shudder works its way through him, and he squeezes his eyes tight.

"I can relate. I've heard Slate with Gabby occasionally, and it turns me into a raging bull. Every damn time, I want to drag his ass out and beat him bloody."

Austin's eyes blink open, and his lips twitch. "Man, you've no idea how many ways I've imagined killing you."

"Wow. Thanks for that, buddy."

He sighs, dragging a hand through his hair. "Look, I know I've been stubborn about this."

That's putting it mildly.

"But the betrayal stung, you know. And I'm worried about Summer. This is a lot of responsibility on her young shoulders."

"She's tougher and stronger than you and Charlie seem to think." I'm getting fed up of their bullshit in that regard.

"I know. I just don't want to see her life getting derailed."

"If you talk to her, you'll see she doesn't feel like that. We've discussed this at length. Summer was born to be a mom. She's amazing with kids, and she'll be a natural. I'll do my utmost to give her everything her heart desires."

Austin stares at me, and then he stands, slapping me on the back in an unexpected move. "See you do."

"Are we good?"

He nods. "Yeah, and, look, I'm sorry for the things I said about you. That was a low blow, and I take it back."

"What about the ass kicking I let you give me?" I inquire, raising a brow.

"Let, my ass," he mumbles, and I give him that one. "Fucked if I'm ever apologizing for that. You deserved it, and you know it."

"I'm so happy you and Austin made up. My heart is singing a symphony," Summer croons later that night when we're lying in bed.

"You know what part of my body's rocking a symphony, babe?" I angle my hips into her side, stabbing her with my erection.

"You are almost as insatiable as me," she jokes, instantly whipping her nightie up over her head.

I slide my hands up her stomach, cupping her fuller breasts. "There's no almost about it. Fuck, babe. I love your bigger tits. If this is what you're like at seven weeks pregnant they'll be like giant melons by the time you're ready to deliver the little munchkin." I nuzzle my face into her breasts, loving the feel of her smooth, silky skin against the stubble on my chin.

"I knew you only wanted me for my body." She smirks as she climbs on top of me, lowering herself perfectly over my hard length.

We both groan, but before she moves, I flip her underneath me, leaning down to suck on her lower lip. "I want to make love to you."

"Show me what you got, stud," she says, pushing her hips up as her hands claw at my bare ass. "But don't go too slow. I need it hard."

"Your wish is my command." I alternate between driving into her in long, slow, seductive strokes and slapping her with my cock as I slam in and out at a vicious pace. Sweat glides down my back as I lift her legs up over my shoulder when she urges me to go faster and harder. I pound into her, quickly losing control, loving the feel of her insides tightly gripping my cock, and the way she tilts her hips up to meet my every thrust.

I gently cover her mouth with my hand when her orgasm hits, stifling her loud moans. After I've released inside her, we both collapse in a sweaty heap of tangled limbs. "Baby, you really need to learn to be quieter. At least until Austin moves out properly, because he's already imagining ways to murder me. Your cries of pleasure are not helping my cause."

"Well, stop fucking me so thoroughly then," she says, matter-of-factly. "It was nice of him to let us take this place," she adds, quickly changing the subject.

"He spends most of his time at Miley's anyway, but, yeah, it saves us having to look for another place." We've already decided we're converting Austin's bedroom into the nursery, and Summer has been scouring Pinterest looking at boards and color schemes and other shit.

"Ryan."

I jerk my head to the side at the noticeable change in her tone, instantly on alert. "Yeah?"

"Are you happy?"

Such a basic question, but if you'd asked me before I met Summer the answer would've been complicated. But not now. Now the answer is simple. I wrap my arms around her, kissing her deeply. "I'm happier than I've ever been. I love you." I slide my lips down her body, stopping to kiss her belly. "And I love you too, little munchkin."

I should've known my happiness would be short-lived.

"This is a fucking nightmare," I tell Austin when we finally get a minute alone. For the last few hours, we've been locked in our conference room at the gym with the local cops and our attorney. They have arrested one of our trainers, Matthias, on suspicion of sexually assaulting a female client, on the premises, one night late last week. We're co-operating as best we can.

"You think he did it?" Austin asks, as we stroll down the hallway toward our adjoining offices.

"I've had to speak to him a couple times about being too 'handsy' with some clients, not that that means he's guilty." I rub a tense spot between my brows. "I don't know."

"I thought they were dating, and I have a feeling there's more to this than meets the eye."

"Maybe. Still doesn't change things. We need to discuss how to handle it. We don't want our female clients thinking they're unsafe here."

"We'll have to fire him," Austin says, in sync with my train of thought, following me into my office.

"I know." I grab my cell off my desk where I'd left it. "Which'll suck if he's innocent." I punch in my code and the sight of dozens of missed calls and texts from Summer and Miley has alarm bells blaring in my ears. "Fuck."

"What?" Austin picks up on the anxiety in my tone, as I speed dial Summer.

"I have a bunch of missed calls from your sister and your girl-friend." Austin races out of the room before I've even finished my statement, returning a few seconds later with his cell in hand, while I listen to Summer's automated response.

I swipe my finger over the last text from Miley, and all the blood drains from my face.

"We need to get to the hospital," Austin says, with his cell pressed to his ear, but I'm already one step ahead of him, keys in hand, grabbing my jacket from the back of my chair.

I toss the keys to him. "You drive. I'm likely to crash." I call Derrick while we're dashing from the building, explaining it's a medical emergency, asking him to offer our apologies to the men waiting for us in the conference room and to manage the gym in our absence.

"Do your messages say anything specific?" I ask Austin as we climb into the SUV.

"No. Just that Summer was in the hospital and you needed to get there ASAP." He wastes no time flooring it out of the parking lot.

I cradle my head in my hands as he drives, offering prayers even though I haven't prayed since I was a kid. I have a horrible feeling history is repeating itself, and my stomach churns so violently I think I might puke. Summer's only eight weeks pregnant, and we haven't even seen our baby on the ultrasound. Just hearing his or her little heartbeat at the Ob-gyn's office that time was enough to cement my love for my unborn child. If anything happens to Summer or our little munchkin, I'll die.

"Hang in there, man." Austin lands a hand briefly on my back. "We don't know what it is yet, and Summer will need us to be strong."

Neither of us articulate our thoughts, but I know we're both thinking the same thing.

We race through the hospital corridors toward the maternity section, and Miley jumps up to greet us the second we burst through the double doors. She runs toward Austin, sobbing, and something inherent dies inside me. I slam to a halt, air whooshing through my ears, my heart pounding in my chest. Miley flings herself into Austin's arms, tears pumping out of her eyes.

"Miley," I croak. "Is Summer—" I lose my voice, and my chest heaves painfully.

"She's okay," Miley sobs. "But she lost the baby."

I stagger backward, my spine slamming into the wall, but I barely feel it. The most intense pressure weighs down on my chest, and I'm struggling to breathe. I squeeze my eyes shut, trying to hold my tears in, but I'm fighting a losing battle, and tears roll down my face as the enormity of the situation hits me full force.

Austin grabs me to him, his shoulders shaking with emotion. My mind churns, my emotions veering all over the place. The pain in my heart is unbearable.

This is all my fault. I knew at the outset; I would hurt Summer, but I still selfishly claimed her.

She'll probably hate me now.

Although I'll take it.

I'll take all the pain if it means she comes out of this intact.

Chapter Twenty-Four

Summer

The door creaks as it opens, and Ryan enters the room. His eyes are bloodshot and red-rimmed, and he looks how I feel. "Ryan!" I cry, sitting up in the bed and opening my arms for him. He enfolds me in his strong embrace, and the dam breaks.

I was trying to be brave, fighting tears as Miley burst out crying when the doctor confirmed I'd had a miscarriage. But I can't hold it in any longer, and I sob on Ryan's shoulder, soaking his shirt. His body shudders under my embrace, and I'm not surprised when I pull back and see his damp cheeks. "Our baby is gone," I wail, and the pain in my heart is so intense I wonder if this is what it feels like right before you have a heart attack.

"I'm so sorry, sweetheart." Ryan cradles me in his arms. "I'm so, so, sorry I let you down."

"I was so scared," I whisper, sobbing as tears continue to pour from my eyes. "I called you nonstop, but when I couldn't reach you or Austin, I called Miley. She hadn't left for her folks' place yet, so she came straight to campus and brought me here." Thanksgiving is only a few days away, and Miley was planning on spending it with her parents.

"Thank god, she was there for you, and I'll never forgive myself that you went through this alone. We had an emergency at the gym, and we were locked in meetings all morning. I'd stupidly left my cell in my office." He squeezes me tight, pressing a fierce kiss to my temple. "I'm sorry, Summer. I'm so incredibly sorry."

"It's okay." I run my fingers through his hair. "It's not your fault." Spasms cramp my stomach, and I wince, drawing deep breaths.

"What's wrong?" Ryan's entire body has tensed up.

"Cramping," I pant, breathing heavily, trying my best to ignore the slicing pain twisting my insides into painful knots. I draw long breaths, in and out, just like the nurse showed me. "Doctor said it's normal," I add, watching the layer of panic intensify on his face. The pain passes a couple minutes later although I know it's only a temporary reprieve. "I'm fine now." I cup one side of his face, hating to see him hurting so much.

A muscle clenches in his jaw. "What happened? And what did the doctor say?"

"I went to the bathroom after my first class because I had terrible cramps, and it worried me. When I noticed blood on my panties, I completely panicked, and I couldn't stop shaking and crying. It took three attempts to place the first call to you my fingers were trembling so badly."

I curl my fingers into his hair, biting down on my lower lip. Gently, he removes my teeth before it breaks skin.

"When I got here, they hooked me up to an ultrasound, and I knew instantly the baby was gone because I couldn't hear his heartbeat." Sobs overtake me again, and I collapse into Ryan's chest, fisting his shirt as piercing cries ring out in the sterile room. He rubs a hand up and down my back until my cries die out. I'm exhausted, clinging to him, in a weird alert-dazed state. My voice is monotone as I continue explaining. "The doctor said, unfortunately, lots of women experience miscarriages with their first pregnancy. I'm going into surgery soon to have a D and C so they can remove..." I burst out crying again, unable to verbalize it.

"Fuck, Summer. I'm so sorry." Ryan is crying again too. I know because I feel his wet tears hitting the side of my forehead.

The doctor chooses that moment to enter the room, offering us sympathetic looks. Ryan introduces himself, still keeping me locked in his embrace. "Is there any internal damage to Summer?" he asks with concern etched across his face. "She'll be able to have more kids, right?"

The doctor clutches the clipboard in his hand to his chest. "There's no internal damage, and Summer will most likely have no issue conceiving or bringing a pregnancy to full term in the future. In situations like this, we always run a set of routine tests to determine there are no genetic defaults or issues. Ninety-nine percent of the time, we find no explanation. The rate of miscarriage is much higher with first-time pregnancies."

He tilts his head to the side. "I know that's not much comfort, but provided nothing shows up in the tests, you should have normal pregnancies in the future," he says before advising that a nursing team will be with me shortly to bring me to the operating room. "I'm sorry for your loss," he adds before exiting the room.

Ryan and I cling wordlessly to one another until it's time for me to go to surgery. He kisses me on the lips before I leave promising he'll be here waiting when I get out.

The days after are some of the hardest of my life. I'm sad, and I can't stop crying. I can barely summon the strength to get out of bed. I've never felt this way before, and I don't know how to handle it. Both our families rally around, dropping by to offer support, but, honestly, I just want to be alone with Ryan. To mourn our loss together.

Austin and Derrick take control of the gym, ensuring Ryan is always with me. The doctor advised me to stay home and rest for at least three days, and I'm under strict instructions not to do anything strenuous. So, we spend our days cuddling on the couch watching back-to-back movies or binge-watching the latest Netflix shows.

After my crying jaunt in the hospital, and those first couple days back home, I'm unbelievably numb now. Maybe I cried myself out. Used up eighteen years' worth of tears in one go.

Now, I feel empty inside.

Hollow in more ways than one.

Without even realizing it, my hand keeps gravitating to my barren stomach. When I notice Ryan noticing, and the familiar anguish washing over his face, I remove my hand, but it keeps happening, like an invisible force wants to remind me of my loss at every conceivable moment.

Both of us lie awake for hours at night, pretending to one another that we're asleep as we suffer in silence. We haven't had sex. The doctor advised abstaining for a few days, but I have zero desire to have sex, anyway. It's as if my life force died the instant my baby's did.

The news reaches Hannah, and she drops by laden down with flowers and apologies. I'm grateful she's extended an olive branch but too numb to do more than acknowledge her gesture.

I can't fault Ryan for how well he's cared for me these past few days, but when the day comes for him to return to work, I silently admit to feeling relieved.

Things are... different between us.

I don't know how other couples deal with traumatic events, but we're struggling to find the right words to communicate. I don't want to keep talking about it, because it's too painful, but going on with our lives and having casual conversations about mundane things seems like an insult to our little munchkin's memory.

The grief only intensifies after we hold a small memorial service in the graveyard back home. We have no remains to bury, but we installed a little headstone and had a priest say a few prayers. Both our families attended, but I was numb during the whole thing, and my body felt like a block of ice in Ryan's arms.

We all go back to our farmhouse after the service, and I'm not surprised to see my parents getting on so well with Ryan's parents—both sets of grandparents bonding over their loss.

"Can I talk to you for a minute?" Charlie asks, looming over me as I sit on the couch, tucked under Ryan's protective arm.

"Sure." My voice is devoid of emotion.

"In private." His eyes dart to Ryan.

"Whatever you want to say to Summer will be said in front of me or not at all," Ryan says, holding me tighter to his side. "I won't have you upsetting her."

"That's the last thing I want," Charlie meekly replies. "And you can come. I guess you need to hear it too."

We go upstairs to my old bedroom. I sit on the bed with Ryan beside me. Charlie crouches down in front of me. "I owe you a big apology," he says, reaching out and taking my hands. "I'm so sorry for all the hurtful things I said the day you told us about your pregnancy. I planned to come to the city to apologize, because I knew I was out of line, but I never had time to before..."

"Before I lost the baby," I confirm.

"I'm so sorry, Summer."

"Are you?" I question, but there's no malice in my tone. You'd have to feel something to invoke such strong emotion, and I feel dead inside. "You didn't want me to have this baby, anyway."

"Of course, I'm sorry! And I didn't want for this to happen." Air expels from his mouth in frustration. "I don't blame you for thinking that, but I hate you're hurting. I'm so sorry you lost your baby. I genuinely am." He stands, offering his hand to Ryan. "And I'm sorry I was so judgmental. I never should've said the things I said."

"Forget about it," Ryan says, accepting his handshake.

"I forgive you," I whisper to my brother, because I don't want to be estranged from him any longer.

Life is too short.

I've just learned that lesson the hard way.

I lean my head on Ryan's shoulder, suddenly drained. He doesn't hesitate to hold me tight, and I siphon some of his warmth and his strength hoping it'll help get me through the weeks, and months ahead.

Time ceases to have much meaning. I get up, eat breakfast, go to my classes and rehearsal, do my shifts at the gym, and attend study sessions in the library, jam-packing my day so I collapse into bed at night, exhausted, hoping tonight will be the night I stop dreaming about things that have been stolen from me. But no matter how far I push myself, nothing works. I still toss and turn most nights, snatching an hour's sleep here and there, but it's never enough.

I'm yawning as I stand in front of the mirror staring at my pallid reflection. I look like shit. There are massive bags under my eyes, my lips are dry and cracked, and my skin lacks vitality. I'm like a shell of a person, and I know I can't continue like this.

"Are you okay?" Ryan asks from his position in the doorway. He's holding onto the top of the door, offering a nice view of his impressive biceps and chest, and an inkling of desire stirs in my loins for the first time in weeks.

"I think we'll be adding that to your epitaph too," I joke, in reference to how many times he asks me that question. I pad toward him in my towel, beads of moisture still clinging to my skin from the shower, and I rest my head on his chest, circling my arms around his waist. "I'm tired of feeling sad all the time," I admit, and it's the first real honesty I've given him since the day in the hospital. I have struggled to talk to him about my feelings which is most unlike me, but then I've never dealt with anything like this before. He's shut himself off as well, and I realize, in this moment, that I don't want to lose him too.

"Me too," he quietly says, enfolding his massive arms around me.

"Let's take the day off," I suggest, looking up at him with pleading eyes. "Let's make love and then go out and do something together."

He weaves his fingers through my hair, slanting me an apologetic look. "I can show up late, but I can't take the full day off. We're firing Matthias today and our attorney is attending the meeting. It's important I'm there." My heart sinks when I recognize he has no clue of the importance of the date. "I'm sorry, baby. What about tomorrow? We can spend the day together before we both head home for the Christmas break."

"Sure." I plaster a fake smile on my face and wriggle out of his grasp, but he hauls me back instantly.

"We can still go back to bed for a couple hours." His eyes darken with lust as his hand climbs up my bare thigh, his fingers sweeping across my pussy. The look he pins me with is hot as fuck, but the urge has already deserted me, blanketed by a fresh layer of sadness.

"I can't miss two days of classes," I lie, reaching up to peck his lips. "Rain check later tonight?" I uphold my cheery expression, feeling like pure shit when a dejected look appears on his face.

"No problem, babe." He moves past me, switching the shower on. "Have a good day."

Chapter Twenty-Five
Ryan

"**F**uck, fuck, fuck!" I exclaim, banging my head against the wall when it finally clicks with me.

"What the hell, man?" Austin asks, his brow furrowing.

"Summer asked me to take the day off today, and I'm a dumbass because I didn't realize why until now." Austin looks as confused as me. "It's one month today since we lost the baby," I explain.

"Shit."

I'm sick to my stomach. "I can't believe I forgot. I feel like a complete shit."

"Hey, don't be too hard on yourself, man." Austin clamps a hand on my shoulder. "I know this has been rough for you too."

A lump the size of a bus wedges in my throat, as I nod. I'm trying so hard to stay strong for Summer, but I'm cut up on the inside too. Everything I never realized I wanted was in arm's reach until it was snatched away. Guilt churns with sorrow in my gut every day, and it's a miracle I can get out of bed most mornings.

There's no handbook when something like this happens, and I

feel like I'm drowning in a pool of failure. Summer and I grow more distant every day. Sure, she sleeps in my arms, but she may as well be invisible. I hate that her light has faded, and I feel wholly responsible. I want to erase her sadness and openly love her, but I'm struggling with the how. We haven't had sex, or shared intimacy other than hugs or kisses, since she miscarried, and I miss feeling close to her. I don't know if I should be the one to initiate it or just wait until she's ready. So, I take care of her in other ways, hoping it demonstrates how much I still love her.

It elated me this morning when she suggested we make love, but her subsequent rejection tore more strips off my fragile heart. Now I know why she reconsidered.

Before we lost the baby, Summer would've told me outright the significance of today. But that's another closeness we've lost. We don't talk like we used to, and I'm scared I'm losing her.

Maybe she's no longer interested.

I hate even thinking this, but the truth is there's nothing tying her to me now.

Perhaps she's realized that.

Perhaps she's realized that she'd rather be with a guy her own age. Someone with considerably less baggage.

But I don't know, because we haven't properly talked since the miscarriage.

Partly that's my fault, because of the crippling guilt.

"Hey, where'd you go?" Austin asks, pinning me with worried eyes.

"I need to make it up to her," I say, plonking my butt in the seat and lifting the phone. "I think I have just enough time to organize it."

A few hours later, I'm standing outside the theater waiting for Summer to exit the building. I couldn't stomach watching her rehearse with Sean, so I'd rather stay out here in the biting cold than watch his hands, or his lips, anywhere near her.

She doesn't know I'm here. I spent the late afternoon lining things up. I've booked us a table at the little Italian we've grown fond of, and I hve a simple bouquet of lilies waiting for her in the car. I thought we could visit the graveyard, but they've already closed, so I'll offer to take her this weekend instead, if she wants to go.

I pat the envelope in my inside coat pocket, allowing a sliver of hope to build inside me. I'm hoping the surprise trip to Venice will bring color to my girl's cheeks again. I think the time away will do us the world of good.

We need to live our lives again.

We'll never forget our little munchkin, but we can't wallow in grief forever.

Summer wants to travel, and she's never been out of the U.S. so I'm hoping this trip will set our relationship on a new path and remind her of all she's got to look forward to. I've also found a great grief counselor who specializes in counseling couples who've lost children, and I hope she'll agree to go to a few sessions with me, because it's fair to say we need help. The counselor was my sister's idea, and I'm glad I called her earlier.

I rub my hands together, tugging the collar of my coat up higher as the door to the theater opens and people spill out. Summer is last out, and her loud peals of laughter tickle my eardrums from here. She's with Sean, and she's doubled over, in convulsions of laughter. Didn't realize he was such a comedian, my snarly inner voice spits, as my insides contort painfully.

I'd give anything to be the one to make her laugh, but the truth is, it's been weeks since I've seen her face light up like that.

There have been zero smiles around me.

Jealousy and anger batter me from all sides as I watch them laughing and chatting, lingering by the door, reluctant to leave.

It's the slap in the face I needed.

The reality check I've been fighting every second from the instant she came into my life.

Summer should be with someone like Sean.

Someone the same age with no cares or responsibilities.

Someone who can make her forget her grief.

Not someone who reminds her of it every minute of the day.

I've been deluding myself into thinking we could turn this around.

We can't. I see that now.

She hasn't spotted me yet, so I tuck my chin down, keeping my head low, and hightail it out of there.

We spend Christmas break at home with our respective families, and the time apart helps cement my belief I'm right to end this now before I hurt her anymore. My family notices I'm withdrawn, and they try to coax me into talking, but I don't want to discuss it with anyone. I know what I have to do, and once we return to the city, I set about sticking to my guns.

I'm pacing the living room waiting for Summer to return home from classes, just anxious to get this over with now. I've practiced what I want to say. I don't want to lie to her, but if I tell her the truth, I'm afraid she'll try to talk me out of it.

I'm even more afraid that she'll agree with me.

So, I know what I need to say to make this happen.

She'll probably hate me. Austin most definitely will. But, hopefully, in time, he'll realize I loved her enough to set her free.

"Fuck, it's cold out there," Summer says, bounding into the apartment, bundled up in a puffy jacket, woolly hat, and scarf, looking adorably cute. I want to grab her into my arms and never let her go. But I can't. For once, I need to act selflessly and let her live the life she deserves.

"Why don't you take a shower to warm up, and I'll have some hot chocolate ready when you get out?" I suggest, not wanting to jump straight into this the second she gets home.

"That sounds perfect," she agrees, approaching me with a little gleam in her eye. Quick as a flash, she cups my face, welding her ice-cold hands to my skin.

I jerk back out of her reach, my skin tingling as a shiver works its way through me. "Fucking hell, Summer. Your hands are like blocks of ice."

She giggles, and I want to change my mind. There's no doubt she's turned a corner recently. Showing me glimpses of the girl I fell in love with. It hasn't escaped my notice it's happened while we've largely been apart.

Which is why breaking up with her is the right thing.

"Go shower." I kiss her forehead even though I want to kiss her lips, heading toward the kitchen to make hot chocolate before I do something stupid.

Like drag her to the bedroom.

Or revert to selfish mode and kick my plan to the curb.

"Ohmigawd, this is so good," Summer says, moaning in a way that has my dick twitching in my boxers. "I nominate you chief hot chocolate maker," she proclaims, closing her eyes and groaning as she sips on the chocolaty goodness.

My dick now salutes her at full mast, and I subtly adjust myself in my jeans before she notices.

We flippantly watch TV as she sips her hot chocolate. With her makeup-free face, hair scraped back in a tight ponytail, and the slouchy sweater, pajama pants, and fluffy socks combo she's sporting, she looks every bit the young, innocent girl she should be. I hate that her involvement with me has dulled the edges off her shine. But she'll bounce back, when she has the freedom to spread her wings. When I'm no longer blocking the light.

I can't delay this anymore.

Turning off the TV, I turn to face her, taking her hands in mine, hoping she can't feel how badly I'm trembling. "We need to talk."

"Annndddd nothing good ever comes of starting a conversation like that," she jokes, her lips tugging up until she sees the sober expression on my face. "Oh." Her smile disappears, her eyes growing wide. "Oh." Tears well in her eyes, and I already hate myself.

"You know how special you are to me, Summer. I wanted so

699

badly for things to work out between us, but they're not. Things have been strained between us ever since we lost the baby and—" This is the hard part. The part that will devastate her. But I have to say it, because she needs to let me go. "I think it happened for a reason. To prove that we're not right for one another after all. That there's someone better out there for you than me."

"You can't honestly believe that," she whispers as a tear creeps out of the corner of one eye.

I'm suffocating inside.

Drowning in my own lies.

Yet I push on.

"I do. You're the one that taught me to believe in that, and don't say you don't believe it now because it's been your mantra right from the start."

"You misunderstand," she says, yanking her hands from my grip and swiping angrily at the tears sliding down her face. "I still believe things happen for a reason. You think I haven't thought of this in the weeks since we lost our child? Haven't raged at God, if there is one, asking him why he took something so precious from us? Why he took away something I never even realized I wanted that badly until it was dangled under my nose?" Her voice cracks, and I sit on my hands to stop myself from pulling her into my arms.

Our inner musings were so similar. What a shame we couldn't talk to one another about it.

"I've done all that soul searching, and I have made my peace with it." She leans into me, and the floral scent of her shower gel swirls around me, almost choking me with renewed pain. "The time wasn't right. That's all," she says, rubbing her finger back and forth across the locket I gave her for Christmas. "I firmly believe our time will come again, maybe when we're in the right place to start a family." She cups my face. "I'm sorry I've been so shut off. That I've given you no attention. It doesn't mean I don't love you, because I do. There aren't adequate words to describe how very much."

It's so typical of Summer to assume all the blame, but I won't let her. She has done nothing wrong. I'm the one that's made all the mistakes, right from the start. "Don't," I croak, unable to hear anymore, removing her hands from mine. "Don't make this any harder than it already is."

Her lip wobbles, and her face falls, as she realizes I'm deadly serious. My heart is fracturing behind my rib cage, and I need to get this done and get out of here before I cave.

"Why?" she whispers.

I harden my heart and force the words from my mouth. "I'm just not feeling it anymore. I'm so sorry."

Her chest heaves, and she licks her lips, fighting to keep her composure. Neither of us speak for a few minutes, and it's the worst form of torture. "Okay," she quietly says. "The agreement was we'd end it when one of us wasn't into it anymore, and I'll uphold our deal."

That deal was thrown out the window a long time ago, but if that's how she needs to handle it, I won't disagree.

I stand, pulling the duffel bag I previously packed out from behind the couch. "I've checked into a hotel. You're welcome to stay here until a dorm room becomes available. I'll cover the rent and utilities and lodge money into your bank account to cover groceries."

"I don't want your money, and I don't want to stay here. I'll go," she says, springing up from the couch with fire in her eyes.

"No way." I fold my arms and stare her out. "We may not be together anymore, but I still care about you, and you are *not leaving*. I've made this decision, so it's only right I'm the one to go."

"This is your apartment, Ryan!"

"Don't fight me on this." I sling the bag over my shoulder. "It's yours for as long as you need it."

Because I'm a glutton for punishment, I take her in my arms for a goodbye hug, holding onto her firmly before she can pull away. "I'm so sorry, Summer," I whisper in her ear. "But you'll be fine."

As I walk away from her without another word, with pain

burning a hole straight through my heart, I remind myself I'm doing this for her.

So, she can have the life she deserves.

Find someone worthy of her.

Someone who doesn't ruin everything he touches.

Chapter Twenty-Six
Ryan

Four Months Later

My fingers clutch the pen, hovering over the paperwork as I experience last-minute doubts about signing on the dotted line. Dropping the pen, I lean back in my chair, rubbing my hands down my face. I know making this official is the right thing to do, but I'm still reluctant to sign. Even though I haven't spoken to Summer since the day I broke her heart and mine, at least here I'm comforted by the knowledge I'm breathing the same air as her.

No one knows this, but I hung out around campus and the theater company in the weeks following our split, desperate to just see her beautiful face. She quit working at the gym and moved out of the apartment almost immediately, cutting herself out of my life.

I almost went crazy without her.

Hence why I sought her out.

I made sure she never saw me. Sticking to hiding behind corners and watching her from the shadows. Until I realized my behavior was borderline stalking, and I forced myself to go cold turkey.

But, at least here in Newark, I know she's within reach if I ever grow a pair of balls and acknowledge that I made the worst decision of my life the day I walked away from her. If I ever find the courage to fix it.

With that thought swirling through my mind, I snatch the pen up and sign my messy scrawl on the new contract paperwork. Moving to manage our new gym in Dover is the right move. It was that or let Austin buy me out of the business because we can't continue to work side by side when we barely talk anymore.

I knew when I ended things so callously with Summer that Austin would never forgive me. And he hasn't. I cannot fault him for it. I deserve the animosity he's shown me these past few months. I deserve to have lost one of the best friendships I've ever had. Because I promised him I'd take care of his little sister, and in his eyes, I abandoned her to her grief too soon after she lost our baby.

I want to come clean with him. To tell him I did it for her. To set her free. To admit that I'm heartbroken and lonely and so, so lost without her in my life.

But if I do that, he might just understand, might try to talk me around, and he might just convince me.

No, removing myself from Newark, from the temptation of having Summer so close, is the right thing to do.

Stuffing the paperwork back in the envelope, I leave it on my empty desk, grabbing the box with my belongings, and walk out the door telling no one goodbye.

I've only been at the Dover gym a week when Austin pays me an unexpected visit. "What's up?" I ask, closing the door to my office after he steps inside. We're both tense, standing across from one another, neither making a move to sit down.

"Look." He rubs a hand along the back of his neck. "I hate how things were left between us, and I want to talk to you about Summer."

"Is she okay? Has something happened?" I blurt, terror caging my heart in a vise grip.

"Calm down. She's fine. It's nothing like that."

"What then?" I fold my arms across my torso, my shoulders still rigid with stress.

"Let's sit." Austin walks to the small leather couch in the corner of the room, and I trail behind him.

We sit down, and I brace my arms on my thighs, waiting him out. I don't have to wait long. "I want to level with you," he says. "No bullshit. Just cards on the table." I nod, encouraging him to go on. "You've been utterly miserable since you broke up with her. She's putting a brave face on, but I know she's hurting too. I was so fucking angry with you I didn't realize it at first. But having some distance this past week gave me time to think about things, and it doesn't add up."

He stares at me, really stares at me, as if he can see into my messed-up head. "Why did you break up with Summer? And don't feed me the same bull you fed her."

To tell the truth or continue the lie? I lean back, sighing. May as well come clean. Maybe we'll be able to salvage our friendship from the ashes. "Because I believed letting her go was in her best interests. She was so sad all the time, and it was my fault. I felt like I was holding her back. Stopping her from fulfilling her dreams. I never want to be that selfish."

"Do you still love her?"

Pain rattles my chest and my heart aches for the girl I lost. "More than ever," I quietly admit.

He twists around, eyeballing me. "Then fight for her, goddamn it."

"What?" I splutter, sure I must be hearing things.

"Don't let her go, or you'll end up regretting it."

I arch a brow, wondering if I've wandered into some alternate realm. "I'm not who you'd choose for her, so why would you tell me to do that?"

"You *are* who I choose for her. You two were good together, and you made her happy. It's not your fault she lost the baby."

Well, I guess we'll just have to agree to disagree on that. "It's probably too late," I say, looking down at the ground.

"It's not, but if you leave it much longer, it could well be."

I jerk my head back up. "Why d'you say that?"

"That punk Justin is sniffing around. He's asked her to transfer to Oregon State next year to be with him. He's a big deal to the Beavers, and I know he'll make it happen."

"So, you just want me to get back with Summer to stop her from moving across the country?" I surmise, anger bristling under my skin.

"Fuck, no!" Austin sits up straighter, scrubbing a hand over his chin. "Truth is, I've been a shitty friend and a shitty brother. You might as well add a hypocrite to the mix. My background with chicks wasn't any cleaner than yours, but I still gave you crap. And—" He blows air out of his mouth. "And I'm so fucking sorry, man. Sorry for being a sanctimonious, stubborn prick. If I wasn't all up in my head, I would've realized the truth earlier, because you're good people, James. I've always known that." He clamps his hand on my shoulder. "You're also my best friend, and I miss you. I'm sorry I fucked up. That I wasn't there for you more. But I'm here now, and I'm telling you to get your shit together and go get your girl." He drills me with a dark look. "Before that punk ass swoops in and steals her away from you."

"Okay, I've had enough," Slater says, slamming his beer bottle down on the table and powering off the TV.

"Hey, I was watching the game," I protest, even though I can barely concentrate on anything after my talk with Austin earlier.

"No, you fucking weren't." He glares at me. "You were staring at the screen, but you weren't watching a second of the game. You were lost in your own head again. Like you've been every single time I've seen you since you broke up with Summer, and I'm done with the bullshit." He leans forward on his elbows. "You have Gabby worried sick about you, and, honestly, you're freaking me out too. I've never seen you like this. Not even after Myndi."

"Because I've never loved and lost *the one* before," I blurt.

"Finally." He rolls his eyes to the ceiling.

"Finally, what?" I snap.

"Finally, some show of honest emotion."

I flip him the bird. "Screw you, asshole. We can't all be perfect and have the perfect fucking life."

"Sometimes, I seriously want to beat the shit out of you in the hope it'll knock sense into that thick skull of yours."

"Wow. You're really rolling out the hospitality."

The Dover move happened fast, and I haven't had time to find a place to live yet, so I'm staying with Slate and Gabby for a few weeks until I find my feet. After living in the apartment on my own for months, it's been nice surrounded by noise and people again.

"We should've had this conversation months ago. Hell, years ago." He moves over to the couch, dropping down beside me. "I, no, *we*, can't sit back and watch you self-destruct anymore. You need to talk about all the shit you keep locked up in your head. If you won't talk to me, at least talk to your sister. It's killing me seeing how upset she is for you."

"You don't play fair." I pout.

"I'll use whatever advantage I can, but it's no lie. We're worried, and I'm not accepting the bullshit anymore. I'm your best buddy. Fuck, we're basically brothers. You used to tell me everything. Now you shut me out, and I don't know what the fuck I did to deserve it."

"Slate, it's never been about anything you've done. If I tell you the truth, you'll definitely want to beat the shit out of me."

"I think you want to tell me. I think you need to for your sanity." He lays a hand on my shoulder. "You're the closest I have to a

707

brother, Ryan, and I'd never judge you. You've been there for me. Let me be here for you."

"We're really going there? Doing the heavy shit?"

He nods, grinning. "It's been a while."

"We'll need more beer for this. Lots more beer." I waggle my empty bottle at him.

"I'll be back."

"And Slate?" I call out after him, looking over my shoulder. "Make sure Gabby isn't around. She can't hear this."

I settle back in my seat, closing my eyes as I wait for his return. He's right, not that I'll admit that out loud. But I need to purge this from my soul. And I want his advice on Summer. I don't want to lose her. Not if there's a chance she still has feelings for me. But I'm crippled, plagued by guilt and taunted by selfish thoughts, and I'm driving myself demented with all the back and forth.

Perhaps Slate can help me make sense of my head. Help me figure out where I go from here.

"The coast is clear," he says, when he re-enters the room with an ice bucket and a bunch of beers.

We pop the lid on a couple bottles, a comfortable silence descending for a few minutes. "I still love Summer, and I miss her so damn much. Every day I go without seeing her, another little piece of me dies," I admit, finding this easier to divulge than I expected.

"I know how that feels, and it sucks. Big time," Slate agrees.

"I remember telling you you were an idiot for letting Gabby go when she was pregnant because you believed it was the right thing for her, and I've basically done the exact same thing."

He doesn't hesitate. "Idiot." Slate fights a smile, and I flip him the bird again.

"I'm no good for her, man."

"Why?"

"Because I'm a total fuckup in relationships, and she lost the baby because of me." Although it almost killed me to break up with her, and it's killing me all over again, every day I wake up without her in my life, I'd do it all again if it's the best way of protecting her. Of letting her live a full and happy life.

"Dude." Slate's brow creases. "You can't honestly believe you're responsible for her losing the baby. It isn't anyone's fault. Miscarriages happen, and there isn't anything you could've done to prevent it."

"She was stressed, and mostly, that was because of me. Because Austin and Charlie didn't approve."

"Did the doctor say stress caused her miscarriage?" Slate demands in an angry tone.

I shrug, and that only angers him more. "Why the fuck do you do this to yourself? It's not your fault," he roars.

"Keep your fucking voice down, or this conversation's over!"

"Why are you shouldering the blame? Why?"

"Because it's not my first rodeo."

His eyes narrow. "Explain that."

I rub my throbbing temples, sighing. "The day everything turned to shit with Myndi, the day that bitch kissed me and posted it online, was also the day I discovered Myndi was pregnant with my baby."

Slater's jaw drops to the floor, and I don't think I've ever seen him so shocked. He urges me on with his eyes.

"I hadn't known. She was hysterical, crying and shouting, beating her fists at me. She refused to believe I was innocent, and she already had her bags packed. She went to her sister's place the next day, telling me she needed space. I wanted to give it to her, but she'd just dropped a bomb, and my head was a fucking mess."

"Why didn't you say anything?"

"You and Gabby were planning your wedding, and I didn't want my sister to get caught in the crossfire. I was still hoping Myndi and I could work things out."

"But you didn't. What happened?"

"I'd been sending her daily texts, and she was sending me back hate-filled replies. After ten days of that shit, I'd had enough, so I went to her sister's house, demanding she speak to me." I rub at the sudden tightness in my chest. "She was so angry and still worked up. Maybe it was pregnancy hormones, or her ex, Travis, ruined her faith in men, I don't know, but she was screaming and shouting at me, pushing me around, refusing to listen to the truth. And something snapped in me then. I gave up. I told her we were done, but I wanted to be involved with the pregnancy, and I'd help raise the baby."

I stare at the ceiling, hating to be reliving this, but feeling a little lighter at the same time. "Her sister threw me out of the house, saying I was stressing Myndi out and it wasn't good for the baby." I exhale heavily. "I went home and licked my wounds for a couple weeks, debating what to do."

I eyeball Slate before I admit this next bit 'cause he's gonna be pissed I went to my brother instead of him—even if he knows it makes sense because my eldest brother is a respected attorney. "I went to Dean and told him everything. I needed to know what my rights were, what I could legally do, because Myndi was refusing to answer my calls or texts, and I knew she was shutting me out."

Slate's jaw tightens, but he says nothing, just waits patiently for me to continue.

"A few days later, I got a text, a *fucking text*," I spit out, "from Myndi's sister saying she'd lost the baby. I was upset and angry, because she'd shut me out. She was already home from the hospital and everything."

A shuddering breath leaves my body. "I should've waited until I'd calmed down before charging over there, but you know how much of a hothead I used to be."

"Used to be?" Slate teases, and the faintest hint of a grin appears on my lips.

"It was, hands down, the most god-awful conversation I've ever had in my life. I won't rehash it all, but the gist of it was she told me, point-blank, that it was my fault she'd lost the baby. Because I cheated on her and then broke up with her, and the stress of it led to her miscarriage."

"What the actual fuck?" Slate snaps, his features contorting into an angry scowl. "The nerve of that bitch!"

"As long as I live, I'll never forget that conversation," I quietly admit, rubbing my tense jaw. "I live with the guilt of it every day. And then, basically, the same thing happened with Summer, and it was at that point I really believed it."

I eyeball my best buddy. "I'm not the guy who gets the girl and the family. I'm the guy that messes everything up. The guy who ruins relationships. That's who I am, and it's why I walked away from Summer even knowing she's the only one for me."

The pain in my chest intensifies to the point I can barely breathe. "I have no interest in anyone else. I can't even look at another woman. All I ever see is Summer, but she'll never be mine, and I'm trying to come to terms with that."

I'm returning from walking Daisy in her stroller the following morning when I notice the strange car in the driveway. Slate greets me at the door, helping lift the stroller inside. "She's asleep," I whisper, so he knows to be quiet.

"I had nothing to do with this," he cryptically says, and my brow puckers in confusion.

"To do with what?" I whisper.

Just then, Gabby appears behind her husband, reaching for my hand and tugging me forward. "I overheard your conversation last night," she admits before thumping me in the arm. Unlike Summer's feeble attempts, my sister knows how to throw a punch and hurt.

"Ow."

"That's for not telling me," she says with tears in her eyes. Without warning, she throws herself into my arms. "I'm so sorry you went through that, Ryan, and it's not your fault. Either situation." She looks up at me, tears streaming down her face. "I hate you've believed that for years. I'm so fucking pissed at Myndi for treating you like that."

"And that's why I never told you or Slate. I didn't want to come between your friendship."

"You're my brother. I love you, and I always want to be the shoulder you lean on. I need you to promise that you'll never shut me out again. I hate the thought you were dealing with that on your own."

She's sobbing, and I hate seeing her cry. I wrap her up in my arms, kissing the top of her head. "I promise I won't keep stuff from you again, Tornado."

Sniffling, she straightens up, taking my hand and dragging me toward the living room. "Good. Now, just remember that, and don't be mad." She shoves me into the room on my own, pulling the door closed behind her.

Myndi stands in front of the fireplace, staring at me, her eyes red from crying, her skin damp with tears.

My guard goes up automatically. "Why are you here?" I glance around the room, wondering where her baby is. Gabby let it slip the other night she'd given birth to a little girl. But there's only the two of us here, so she must've left the baby at home with her fiancé.

"Gabby called and told me what you said."

"And?" That still doesn't explain her presence.

"It wasn't your fault, Ryan," she says, nervously approaching me. "I've wanted to apologize to you for years, but you never let me speak."

"What does it matter now?"

"It matters because you've pushed that girl away because of me!"

I harrumph. "Don't flatter yourself, Myndi. Summer and me breaking up had nothing to do with you."

"It has everything to do with me, and you know it." She gets braver, moving directly in front of me. "I said horrible, hateful things to you after we broke up, Ryan, and you didn't deserve it. I don't want to offer excuses, but I felt betrayed, and I was heartbroken and hormonal, scared and angry, and it was easiest to lash out at you than admit I was the one in the wrong. That I was the reason we broke up, because of my trust issues. It was never anything you did."

"I never cheated on you, Myndi."

"I know." Her eyes well up, and her gaze pleads with me. "You were an amazing boyfriend, Ryan, and I hate how we ended. You don't suck at relationships. You're at your best when you're in love. Although, I sense what we had doesn't even come close to what you share with Summer."

"It doesn't," I say, because there's still a small part of me that wants to inflict hurt in the way she did.

"I'm thrilled to hear that," she says, and my eyes pop wide at the genuine expression on her face. "I've hated myself over what I did to you. Gabby doesn't speak of you often, but I knew you'd reverted to your old ways, and I feared it was all my fault. You're an amazing person, Ryan, and I want you to experience the joy and happiness I have in my life, because no one deserves it more than you. You have a big heart, and you shouldn't deprive the world of it."

Tentatively, she reaches out, touching my arm. "I'm so sorry for the hurtful way I pushed you away. For doubting you. For hiding the pregnancy and miscarriage from you. It's unforgiveable. You should've been there, and I deprived you of that."

Big, fat tears roll down her cheeks. "But most of all, I'm sorry for saying it was your fault. I was stressed, yes, but that was all my doing. You were telling me the truth, and I refused to believe it. That's on me. Not you." She squeezes my arm. "It was so wrong of me to blame you. I'm sure the stress wasn't good for me, but it's not the reason I lost our baby. It's never been your fault and I hate I planted that thought in your head. That it grew roots."

Her features soften. "I'm heartbroken that you and Summer lost your child. I cried when Gabby told me. No one should have to endure that twice. My heart aches for you both."

I swipe at the errant tear that escapes my eye. "Thank you for saying that."

"Do you love her, Ryan?"

I should tell her to fuck off and mind her own business, but she's reached out to mend bridges, and I want to make my peace with this.

I'm sick of hating her.

Of feeling so guilty all the damn time.

It ends now.

"I love her so much it physically hurts."

"Then fight for her!" That old Myndi feistiness rises to the surface. "Don't do what I did. Don't push her away. Especially not out of some misguided notion I stupidly planted in your brain. I know I only met Summer briefly, but I knew by looking at her she was perfect for you. It's why I didn't hesitate when I asked if she was your girlfriend. You both looked like you fit together. Gabby gushes buckets about her, and that's the stamp of approval if I ever heard it. No one is ever good enough for her little big bro," she says, her smile expanding. "So, if Gabby is on Team Summer, then I know you've found a good one."

In a surprising move, she grabs me into a hug.

Even more surprising, I let her.

"Be happy, Ryan. That's all I want for you. You deserve it. If Summer is your happiness, don't lose her. Win back your girl."

Chapter Twenty-Seven
Summer

I wipe my sweaty brow as I return from the dance floor, grabbing the bottle of water from Hannah's outstretched hand, guzzling it back like I'll die if I don't rehydrate immediately. The club is packed with students on one last hooray before final exams start. I've been studying up a storm, and I'm confident I'm adequately prepared, so when a bunch of our classmates organized tonight, I jumped at the chance to go out after months spent in virtual hibernation.

"That guy is so checking you out," Hannah hollers in my ear.

"I'm not interested," I say without even looking in the direction she's pointing.

"You can't stay celibate forever."

"I have three words for you." I tip the empty bottle up, opening my mouth and trying to suck down the last few droplets of water. I pin my bestie with a smug look. "Pot. Kettle. Black."

"So original," Hannah drawls, slinging her arm over my shoulder. "I'm thinking about turning gay. You up for it, sister?"

I shake my head. "I'm strictly hetero, but you should go for it. That chick in the corner has been staring at your butt all night."

"What?" Hannah shrieks, her hands landing on her butt as she slings wide eyes over her shoulder.

"I'm just joking. Not about the gay thing though. I'd support you no matter what. You know that."

Marc came out over Christmas, confirming he's in a relationship with a man. My parents were pretty much floored, but when I thought about it, I wasn't all that surprised. Not that it makes any difference. I love my brother no matter who he loves. I just want him to be happy, and if being with another man does that for him, then I'm behind him one hundred percent.

Her eyes tear up, and she yanks me into a bone-crushing hug. "I know that. And I'm so glad you forgave me. You're an awesome human being, Summer May Petersen. The absolute best."

After Ryan broke up with me, I felt lost and alone until Hannah rode to the rescue. We hashed things out, and she apologized for the way she treated me. We got everything off our chests, worked through our issues, and came out with a stronger friendship at the end.

I don't doubt she has my back now and vice versa.

She kicked Jordan to the curb, and we both moved into a dorm together.

Neither one of us has been with a guy since then. We're both waiting to heal our hearts. Although, to be honest, I don't know that any guy will ever measure up to the guy I lost.

"Have you heard from Justin?" she asks, dragging me with her to the bar.

I shake my head. "Not since I turned him down." Justin surprised me at spring break by turning up on my doorstep and begging me to transfer to Oregon State to be with him. Seems college life isn't all it's cracked up to be, and he was apparently missing me. Hearing what had happened with Ryan, and the miscarriage, freaked him out because he realized he could lose me. He wanted us to give things a proper go which isn't something we could do while separated by thousands of miles.

I was half-tempted, because everywhere I go in Newark, I look over my shoulder for Ryan. Silly, I know, but for a while there, I kept imagining I saw him. Perhaps it was my mind playing tricks on me or my heart just refuses to let him go. I've picked up the phone to call him so many times, but I never follow through. I went out on a limb for Ryan James before, and if there's ever any chance of us getting back together; he has to initiate it this time.

Hannah says I'm an eternal optimist, and maybe she's right.

Or I just believe in true love. I know that's what I shared with Ryan.

I've been seeing a therapist. I know, shock, horror. First time in my life I've had to see a shrink. But I've recently turned nineteen, and I feel like I should win some award for only having to seek one out now. She's helped me work through my feelings. The aftermath of my miscarriage is a bit of a fog as I ghosted through my life for a while there. If it wasn't for Ryan, I'm not sure I'd have found the will to even attempt to function.

Instead of talking to him, I internalized everything, shutting him out. I gave no consideration to his feelings, and I feel horrible about that now. But I wasn't being deliberately selfish. I just couldn't see past my own grief.

My head is clearer now, and I think that stuff he fed me the day he broke up with me was a crock of shit. I think he said what he knew would work. That I'd accept it and not fight for our relationship. I'm sick I fell for it. But not enough to grovel at his feet to take me back.

If we are meant to be, we'll find our way back to one another. I still firmly believe in my mantra, and that's how I've gotten on with things since our split. I wouldn't call it living life to the fullest, but I've gotten a lot of my spark back.

I can't give my heart away again.

Not when Ryan still owns every piece.

Not until I know he doesn't want it for real.

"Are you sure you did the right thing turning him down?" Hannah asks as she battles her way through to the bar, yanking me out of my inner monologue.

"Yes. I don't love Justin. Moving to be closer to him wouldn't have made a blind bit of difference. I still love Ryan. Whether he loves me back doesn't change how I feel."

It's opening night at the theater, and a rush of butterflies has taken up residence in my stomach as I stand at the side of the stage with Sean, ready for the show to start. "You nervous?" he whispers.

"Definitely," I whisper back. "You?" I arch a brow.

"A little, but I like that I am. The day I don't feel nervous is the day I've become complacent, and complacency is never a good thing."

Sean and I have become great friends, and he was a wonderful support in those early weeks after my breakup. He's been happily dating Evangeline for the past six months and there's nothing but friendship between us now, but I'm cool with that.

I beam up at him. "I love that, and it's so true."

The music starts, and we're called into position behind the curtain. "Break a leg," Sean whispers, kissing my cheek.

"You too!"

The nervous fluttering in my belly subsides after a few scenes, and I'm thoroughly enjoying myself now. However, I can't stop sneaking surreptitious looks at the audience, wondering if he's out there somewhere. Which is silly. Because Ryan won't show. It's been months since I've seen him, and if he didn't show up to Austin and Miley's engagement party last week, he will hardly show up here. I hate that my breakup affected Austin and Ryan's friendship, but Miley said they are recently back on speaking terms, and working their issues out, which makes me happy.

My family is in the third row, and they give me a standing ovation when the play ends. Austin and Charlie let rip with loud whistles, and the biggest grin is planted on my face. The rapturous applause is ear-shattering, and when the whole auditorium stands to applaud, a surge of pride floods my chest. Sean and I hug, both on a complete high, and I'll miss rehearsing with him.

We have a couple more shows to put on, then there's a couple weeks before exams start, and then I'm heading back home for the summer.

I still haven't decided about Venice. The day I moved into our dorm, a letter arrived from Ryan with the tickets, explaining he'd purchased them before we split. He beseeched me to take the trip. To finally breach the skies over the US, and though I really want to go, going without him doesn't appeal. But the tickets expire at the end of the year, and during summer break is the best time to go, so I'll have to make my mind up soon.

I'm due to meet my family at a local restaurant to celebrate, but I'm still stuck at the theater, trying to get away from the party atmosphere backstage and the well-wishers. At last, the building empties out, and I wave goodbye to the final few stragglers as I make my way outside to wait for my Uber.

"Summer."

Goose bumps sprout up and down my arms, and butterflies scatter in my chest at the sound of his deep, dulcet tones.

He came! My heart rejoices as I spin around toward his voice.

Ryan steps out of the shadows, smiling as he walks toward me. He's wearing a black button-down shirt, rolled up to his elbows, high-lighting his strong, tan arms. A glint of silver from the watch I gave him as a Christmas gift flashes in the darkness, warming my heart. I drink him in as he advances, trying not to ogle the way the dark denims hug his muscular thighs, or the way his shirt stretches across his defined chest and abs. His hair is a little shorter, but a few strands of dirty-blond hair still sweep across his brow. His piercing blue eyes penetrate mine as he draws to a stop directly in front of me.

Tears glisten, unbidden, in my eyes, as I stretch my neck up to look at him. God, how I've missed him. I shove my hands in the pockets of my light jacket, resisting the urge to touch him.

Electricity crackles in the space between us as we stare silently at one another.

No measure of time apart will ever dilute the love I feel for this man.

"You look beautiful," he says, pinning me with a panty-melting smile.

"Thank you." I drag my lip between my teeth. "Did you see the show?"

He nods. "Told you I wouldn't miss it for the world." He reaches out, brushing his thumb along my cheek, eliciting a trail of fiery shivers. "You were magnificent. You belong on that stage, Summer."

My heart rejoices at his words, and his tender touch. "How've you been?"

"Lonely," he instantly replies, dropping his hand, and I feel like crying. "Missing you like crazy."

"Yeah?"

"Yes." He runs a hand nervously through his hair. "I know I've just ambushed you, but could we go someplace to talk? I have so much I need to tell you."

"My family's waiting for me at Gallagher's. Maybe another time?"

"Tomorrow then? I could pick you up first thing, and we could go for breakfast somewhere?"

"I've got a study session in the library in the morning. Exams are close." I shrug apologetically. "But I don't have plans for tomorrow night," I add as my Uber pulls up to the curb.

"Okay, great. I'll come pick you up."

"Okay, thanks."

Awkward silence descends, and I hate it, but that's the way it has to be until I hear what he has to say. "Okay, bye." I wiggle my fingers at him as I open the door to the car.

"Good night, Summer. I'll see you tomorrow."

His sultry voice does funny things to my insides and I'm a quivering mess as I slide in the backseat of the car, staring at Ryan through the window as we drive by.

"There's our Juliet!" My dad's loud voice carries over the noisy restaurant, and I swear heads turn in my direction.

"You say that like I've just stepped off a Broadway stage not the stage of a college theater company," I tease, hugging my dad from behind.

"You might as well have," Miley says, jumping up and squealing as she hugs me. "You were amazing. Like, you're seriously talented, Summer."

"Thank you. That's sweet of you to say."

"She clearly is," Charlie says. "That kiss seemed so real I almost believed it."

I slap the back of his head. "Stop stirring shit. Sean has a girlfriend, and we're strictly friends."

"If you say so." He waggles his brows, stuffing a piece of bread roll in his mouth. Hopefully, that'll shut him up for a few seconds.

"Well done, Summer." Austin pulls me into a hug. "I'm proud of you."

"Same here. I'm so glad I got vacation time to come. I would've kicked myself if I missed it," Marc interjects, waiting his turn for a hug.

"Thanks for coming," I say, stepping into his open arms. "Both of you." I smile over his shoulder at his partner, Eric, delighted Marc brought him to meet the family.

The dynamic at the table should be interesting.

"What the fuck are you doing here?" Charlie barks, glaring at someone over my shoulder. I don't need to turn around to know it's Ryan. And it's not my brother's hostile reaction either. I think Ryan could step into any room, in any place, in any country, and I'd know he was there. I'll always feel an invisible pull toward him.

"I didn't come to cause trouble," Ryan says, approaching the table cautiously. I notice Austin grinning, giving Ryan a none-too-subtle thumbs-up. Guess the bromance is back on. Slowly, I turn around, surprise evident on my face. "I'm sorry," he says to me. "I just can't wait until tomorrow. I figured your family should probably hear what I have to say too."

"What the fuck is he talking about, Summer?" Charlie demands, putting himself all up in my face.

People at the tables closest to us perk their ears and tilt their heads up.

"Everyone, sit down," Mom hisses. "Let's not make a scene in public." She calls a passing waitress over, asking her to bring one more chair for Ryan.

He sits down beside me, and I look around the table at the silent, mostly stony faces of my family, thinking Ryan has monster balls for following me here. "Are you sure you want to do this now?" I whisper in his ear.

Reaching under the table, he covers my hand with his and squeezes, nodding at the same time. He clears his throat, twisting his body so he's looking me directly in the eye. "I lied to you."

It's a good opening line, ensuring he has my full attention. "About what?"

"I didn't want to break up with you, but I truly believed I was doing the right thing for you."

Charlie snorts, and I level him with a warning look. Mom clamps a hand down on his thigh, and I trust her to keep him in line.

Ryan ignores everyone but me, keeping his eyes locked only on mine. I sway a little in my seat. He always had the ability to melt me on the spot, and when he focuses his sole attention on me? I'm a goner.

"I've done a lot of soul searching. Talked with a therapist. And I've realized that I let what other people think of me affect my actions. Especially when it comes to you. I knew the age gap concerned your family, and it's why I held back initially. It's also one reason I ended things with you in January." His hold on my hand tightens. "I was afraid being with me was holding you back. That you'd be better off with someone your own age. Someone who didn't come with the baggage I have. I thought the best way to prove my love was to set you free."

"That—" I can't not say something, but he shushes me with a carefully placed finger to my lips. I clench my jaw to stop myself from sucking his finger into my mouth like I want to. It's one thing I know he likes. One way I used to turn him on.

However, I doubt my brothers, or my dad, would appreciate seeing that.

"Please, sweetheart. Let me get this out." His Adam's apple bobs in his throat, and it shows how truly nervous he is.

"I won't interrupt. Go on," I urge.

"I felt like I failed you when you lost the baby. Because I wasn't there, and I knew you were under a lot of stress, and I blamed myself for that."

It's so hard to stay quiet. To hear the torment in his voice and do nothing to reassure him. But I promised I wouldn't interrupt, so I start a mental checklist of all the things I want to say to him later.

"I also blamed myself for my inability to comfort you appropriately in the aftermath. I wanted so much to help you, but I didn't know how, and I was hurting. It was my little munchkin too," he whispers, tears filling his eyes. My fingers automatically curl around the locket I never take off. Ryan gave it to me for Christmas and it has the initials S, LM, and R intertwined in three interconnecting hearts. I don't even remove it to shower, and during the long months of our separation, it has given me some measure of solace.

"You have always been so vibrant," he continues, "so full of life, and you weren't in those weeks. I hated myself for what I'd done to you. It felt like I dulled your light, and I never wanted to do that." Emotion slashes across his face, and I want to hug him so badly.

So, I do.

Screw my family and what they think.

I fling my arms around him, resting my head on his chest, listening to the wild thumping of his heart. We cling to one another, and no one at the table utters a word. Ryan pulls back a few minutes later, still keeping his arms loosely around my back, and I keep my hands planted on his waist. "I made a mistake, Summer."

He caresses my cheek, his eyes burning brightly. "I love you. I have always loved you. I never stopped. Not for a second. If you still feel anything for me, I'm begging you for another chance. Let me prove to you we belong together. Let me love you the way you deserve, and I promise you won't regret it."

I don't realize I'm crying until tears drop off the edge of my chin, trickling down my neck. Some girls wouldn't back down, even in the face of such a romantic declaration, making the guy work harder to win back her love.

But I'm not like other girls.

I have always marched to my own beat.

And I won't torment either of us any longer.

"Ryan," I choke out, my throat clogged with so much emotion. I cup his face. "I've loved you from the minute I met you, and my feelings have never changed. I still love you every bit as much. Maybe more after you risked the lion's den to pour out your heart," I tease, giggling. "You don't need to beg for another chance. I want that too." I take his hand, placing it on my chest, in the place where my heart beats in sync with his. "My heart still belongs to you. You own every part like you own me body and soul."

We move at the same time, our lips meeting in a tender kiss suffused with every emotion we're feeling. Vaguely, I hear the restaurant break out in a round of applause, and I wouldn't be surprised if a video popped up online at some point later.

But I don't care about anyone else.

All I care about is the man kissing me like I'm the only oxygen he needs. As we cling to one another, kissing like we're in our own little cocoon, I know I was right to believe in our love.

I had faith we'd find our way back to one another, and now we have.

Epilogue 1

Ryan

Three years later

"I'm so proud of you, baby." I pocket my keys and wrap my arms around Summer from behind. She tosses her graduation cap onto the counter, leaning back against me.

"I can't believe I've graduated." Her voice is giddy with excitement as she turns around, circling her arms around my neck. "And I can't believe we're going traveling in two days!" Her squeal of joy does twisty things to my insides. I love seeing her so happy.

"Believe it, babe." I kiss the tip of her nose, surveying the boxes littering our apartment and the half-packed suitcases open on the living room floor. We bought this place when we got back together, and we're renting it out for the next year while we're overseas. "It's happening."

"You're the absolute best boyfriend in the whole wide world," she says, pressing her hot body into me. "And I'm the luckiest girl on the planet."

"Hey." I swat her ass. "Stop stealing my lines."

Her eyes fill up. "I love you, Ryan. Thank you for making all my dreams come true."

This girl.

She gets me in the feels every damn time.

"Waking up with you every day by my side is a dream come true for me. I'd do anything for you, Summer. I want you to be happy."

I remember the dark days, when we lost the baby, and the way her light dimmed. I've made it my mission since then to ensure her light shines brightly. We'll never forget our little munchkin, and not a day goes by where our little angel in heaven isn't on my mind. But life has to go on. And I look forward to giving Summer plenty more babies. But she's only twenty-two, and even though I'm feeling broody as my thirtieth birthday approaches, I can wait a little longer before taking our relationship to the next stage.

She hugs me close, and her heart beats strongly against my chest. "I never thought it was possible to feel so happy," she whispers into my ear, her warm breath tickling me and stirring my desire. "I know it's because I get to share my life with you."

I hold her tight, knowing I will never let her go. She's mine. For now and always. "Ditto, babe." I kiss her deeply, and every kiss is like the first time we kissed. Even after years together, I still lust after her so much. "Why don't you take a shower while I put the champagne on ice?" I suggest.

"Only if you join me." She looks up at me through hooded eyes that blatantly transmit her longing.

"I thought that's a given." I smirk, swatting her butt and shoving her toward our master bedroom. "I won't be long."

I set the champagne in a bucket of ice, grab two glasses from the cupboard, and remove the chocolate-covered strawberries from the refrigerator before walking toward our room, shedding my clothes as I go.

Steam swirls around the en suite bathroom, masking my view of my girl, but I can hear her. Singing to herself like she usually does in the shower. Summer has a fabulous voice, and I could listen to her sweet tones all day long.

I slide the door open and join her, pulling her back into my chest and brushing her wet hair to one side so I can kiss her neck. She stops singing, and a little whimper emits from her mouth as I press my hard cock against her ass while my hand slides around to her stomach, my fingers inching lower.

She's filled out a little more, sporting shapely curves in all the right places, and it only makes me love her body even more. "You still turn me on so much, Summer," I rasp, nipping at her earlobe as my fingers sweep over her pussy.

"Same for me, babe," she murmurs, angling her head so she can kiss me. My tongue plunges into her mouth the same time I slide two fingers inside her, and her pleasurable moan has precum leaking from the tip of my cock.

We continue kissing, our tongues dancing wildly as our desire elevates, while I pump my fingers in and out of her, using my thumb to swirl circles around her clit. I know when she's close, because she bites down on my lip, her breathing is ragged, and she's riding my hand with wild abandon. "Come for me, babe," I say, pinching her clit, and she detonates in my arms, screaming out my name as she orgasms.

She reaches around, takes hold of my aching cock, and starts leisurely stroking it from root to tip, just how I like it. But I'm impatient today. I just want to be inside her. "Hands on the wall and ass in the air, baby," I command, moving us both a little more directly under the water.

Summer places her hands on the tile wall and tilts her peach of an ass up. I rub my fingers from her pussy up along the crack of her ass and she sucks in a sharp breath. "This is gonna be hard and fast, baby, because I can't wait a second longer." Gripping her hips, I position my cock at her entrance and ease inside her. This is one of my most favorite things. Taking my time inching into her, feeling her walls grip my cock, her hips jerking with need, as she demands I give her all of me.

As soon as I'm fully seated, I slowly pull out and then slam back into her, over and over, hitting the top of her pussy with my cock, ensuring she feels every part of me. Releasing one hand from her hip, I move it down to her clit, rubbing her swollen nub as I ramp up the pace of my thrusting, pounding in and out of her as warm water cascades over both of us.

My orgasm hits out of nowhere, tingling sensations darting up my spine as my balls tighten up, and I release inside her, shouting her name as we fall apart together.

After, I bundle her up in a towel and carry her into our bedroom where we make love and drink champagne until the early hours.

The next year is, hands down, the best year of my life. We planned our itinerary carefully, and it paid off as we travel between continents enjoying the best of different cultures.

We visit the pyramids in Egypt, the Colosseum in Rome, the Eiffel Tower in Paris, go up on the London Eye, and kiss the Blarney Stone in Ireland on the first leg of our journey. We can't resist returning to Venice, enjoying another romantic sojourn in the historic city. Venice will always have a special place in our hearts because it was our first foreign trip together, and it's the city where we fell in love with one another all over again.

From there, we travel to Asia, visiting the bustling city of Hong Kong, walking the Great Wall of China, and the Cu Chi tunnels in Vietnam, gawping in awe at the Borobudur Temple in Indonesia, and sampling the wonderful cuisine in Thailand.

In between exploring, I do a couple hours work a day, managing the business finances, acquisitions, and expansion plans and working on our new franchise business model while Austin holds the fort back home. We have weekly conference calls to discuss key decisions, and the business is going from strength to strength. We now have ten gyms in Delaware and Philadelphia, and with our franchise plans, we have the ambition to grow it to fifty locations within the next five years.

I'm lucky I run a business that allows me to take a year off and that I have a business partner who loves his sister so much he was willing to take on the bulk of the responsibility while I'm traveling. I had returned the favor, somewhat, when Miley and Austin had their first child last year, running things single-handedly while he took three months off to be with his new family.

When Summer and I got back together, Austin and Miley agreed to take over the Dover gym while I moved back to managing the original Newark one so I could be close to Summer while she finished her studies at UD. Now, we have managers running each location, and Austin and I recently set up a small operations office in Milford.

When we return from our year abroad, we plan to sell the apartment and buy a house in Lewes, and I'll work out of the operations office while spending time on the road traveling to the various gyms.

But I need to make things official first, and I can't wait any longer. I've been dying to make Summer my wife for years, but she was too young, and the timing wasn't right.

Eight months into our trip, we relocate to Australia, and I propose to Summer on the steps outside the Sydney Opera House. I'm a basket of nerves, but she says yes before I've even finished speaking, flinging herself at me with tears of joy rolling down her face.

We spend three months touring Australia and New Zealand before flying to South America on the last leg of our trip. Hiking the Inca trail to Machu Picchu was at the top of Summer's list, and we kept the best for last.

By the time we return home, we're exhausted but happy, and I'm looking forward to starting this next stage of our lives.

"Now, don't be mad," I say to Summer as we exit our flight, heading into the airport terminal. "But I have a surprise."

"What kind of surprise?" she asks, hooking her hand in mine.

"I sold our apartment and bought us a house."

She slams to a halt, her mouth trailing the ground. "What the what?"

I pull her into my arms, walking us over to the side of the hallway, out of the way of the throngs rushing through the airport. "I wanted us to come back to a fresh start, so I've been looking for houses online, and I found a few that looked promising. Austin helped me sell the apartment, meeting the realtor and sending me the paperwork to sign, and Gabby and Slate helped me find the new place. It's in Lewes, like we discussed. I paid a deposit, but I haven't completed the paperwork yet in case you don't like it." I peer into her eyes. "Are you mad?"

"I haven't decided," she says, her lips fighting a smile. "I'll reserve judgment until I see the place."

"I freaking love it!" Summer exclaims, twirling around on the wide lawn at the rear of the property. We have our own apple orchard, a small vegetable patch, and pretty flowerbeds. It comes equipped with a small children's playground. The house itself is a modern build, and it's in walk-in condition although I know Summer will want to put her own stamp on it. With four bedrooms, four bathrooms, a study, a dining room, a large living room, and a massive homey kitchen, it's the ideal family home. I had a good feeling about it when I first saw it listed online, and Gabby and Slate loved it when they visited.

If we go ahead with the purchase, we'll only be five minutes from their place and only twenty minutes from Austin and Miley.

Summer jumps into my arms, wrapping her legs around my waist. She peppers kisses all over my face. "It's absolutely perfect, and I am definitely not mad. Thank you, babe." She plants an excitable kiss on my lips, and it quickly grows heated.

A throat clearing reminds me we're not alone, and I reluctantly place my fiancée's feet back on the ground.

No Feelings Involved

"Does that mean you want to go ahead with the purchase?" Mrs. Johnson, the realtor selling the property, inquires with a warm smile.

"Absolutely," Summer says, clapping her hands before she leans into my side, clinging to my arm.

I circle my arm around Summer's back as I face Mrs. Johnson. "How quickly can we close the deal and move in?"

Epilogue 2

Summer

Six years later

"It's time to sing Happy Birthday to Harper," I holler out the kitchen window, where everyone is congregating to enjoy the glorious summer sunshine. Our youngest is two today and both families are here to help us celebrate.

We're a lively bunch now with more kids than I can count. Gabby and Slate's eldest son Billy is fourteen and getting more grown up by the day. He towers over Gabby and me, and he's already pushing six feet. Daisy is ten, and they also have Jayden who's eight and Olivia who's six. Caleb and Terri's two are fourteen and twelve, respectively. Ryan's eldest nieces, Mia and Tia, are turning eighteen soon, but neither of them is here today as they are on a cruise with their mother and her third husband. Dean is here with his wife Alice though. They found out after they got married, and were struggling to conceive, that Alice can't have children, which was a huge blow to them, but they got through it, and they love having their nieces and nephews to stay, especially now Dean's girls are grown up and heading to college in New York in September.

On my side, Miley and Austin are here with their two kids. Landon is almost eight and Lillian is five. Marc and Eric couldn't come because of work commitments, as they both still live in New York, but they mailed an extravagant gift for Harper, which she loved. Charlie is here with his wife, Evita, and their twin four-year-old sons. Charlie is running the farm full-time on his own since my dad passed away three years ago. He had a massive heart attack, and it was a huge shock. We were all so upset because it was sudden, and we never got a chance to say goodbye.

Mom still hasn't gotten over it, and I don't know if she ever will. I cast a glance over my shoulder, watching her chatting with Miley, noticing how much she seems to have aged since Dad died. They spent almost forty-five years together, and they were soul mates in every sense of the word, so it's really hit her hard.

We've offered Mom the opportunity to come live here if she wants. We got permission to build a small two-bed bungalow on the grounds of our property, so she'd have her own space. She turned us down, citing her inability to leave the farmhouse, and I understand it. She spent her entire married life there, and all her memories are tied to that house. Still, she knows the offer is there should she ever want to avail of it.

"The cake monster is here!!!!" Brayden proclaims, bursting through the door into the kitchen. He's our eldest. He's five, and he was a honeymoon baby. Ryan and I got married a couple months after we came home, settling for a small ceremony with family and a few close friends.

I discovered I was pregnant the day the local elementary school offered me a teaching position, but, thankfully, they were good about it. I still teach there although it's only on a part-time basis as I want to be around for my kids as much as possible in their early years.

We're incredibly lucky Ryan and Austin's business is doing so well. They have fifty gyms now in eight states with sixty percent franchised and forty percent directly owned. I'm very proud of them, and it's given us a very comfortable lifestyle. I don't have to work at all, but I like the few hours I do three days a week, and it helps me keep my identity outside of my important role in the house.

"Calm down, Bray," Ryan says, chuckling as our son races around the kitchen with his cousins, screaming and shouting. He's closest to Olivia and Lillian, which isn't surprising because they're all the same age and they've grown up together.

Austin and Slate wrangle the kids into chairs, and Harper bangs on the table with her plastic spoon, gurgling and laughing and trying to wriggle out of her highchair.

While Brayden is dark like me, Harper is the spitting image of her dad with her blonde hair and big blue eyes. She will definitely break hearts one day. Although she may look like her dad, her personality is all me. She's into all kinds of mischief, she loves singing and dancing, and she never stops babbling, having an amazing vocabulary for someone so young.

Slater is already teasing Ryan over what a handful she'll be in her teenage years. They are lucky with Billy. He's mature for his age, and he doesn't give them too much to worry about. At least, not yet.

Brayden is the opposite. He looks like me but has more of Ryan's personality. He's so adorable with his little sister, and so protective, just like his dad.

"Say cheese," Lucy, my mother-in-law says, ushering everyone around the table for a group photo. Since my father-in-law, Paul, retired last year, they have both taken up new hobbies, and she's glued to her Nikon like you wouldn't believe. They now spend half the year in Florida, but they returned last month to spend the summer in Delaware.

"Cheezzz," Harper says, clapping her hands and bouncing so enthusiastically in her chair I worry she'll bounce right out.

"No more Coke for her," Ryan whispers in my ear as we pose for the photo.

"Don't be ridiculous." I shake my head. "I wouldn't give a two-year-old Coke." He bites down on his lip, averting his eyes, his guilty expression giving the game away. "Ryan! Seriously?"

"It's her birthday, and I only gave her a teeny drop."

I roll my eyes, but I can't stay mad at him, because he's such an amazing father and very hands-on. The kids adore him. I joke it's like having three kids because he sometimes acts like he has the maturity of a three-year-old, but I wouldn't change him for the world. I find it ironic I'm the strict one and he's the big softie.

Ryan starts everyone off singing Happy Birthday, and I record the moment on my iPhone, zooming in on Harper's delighted little face as she sings along, not yet knowing all the words and oblivious to the fact it's her we're singing the song for. She blows out her candles, and we cut the cake, enjoying five minutes of peace while the kids stuff their faces.

After we've cleaned up the kitchen, we ask Billy to keep an eye on the little ones outside in the backyard while we usher the adults to the living room. Ryan refills wine glasses before sitting in the last vacant seat, pulling me down onto his lap. "We have news," I say, unable to keep it in any longer.

"Oh, shit," Charlie splutters. "Hearing those words coming from your mouth still sends the fear of god into me."

"No ageist remarks," I warn him, patting Ryan's chest. "My old man still gets testy."

"Less of the old," Ryan retorts, squeezing my waist. Pinning my brother with a smug look, he adds. "And Groucho Marx said you're only as old as the woman you feel so I'll be eternally youthful."

"We might be related by marriage now," Charlie replies with an equally smug expression. "But I can still beat your ass."

"Okay, enough, you two." Charlie and Ryan have this twisted relationship where they constantly banter and wind one another up, but it's amicable all the same. However, I know if I don't put a stop to this now, they'll derail our announcement.

"Sorry, babe." Ryan pecks my lips, and smiling, I lean my head on his shoulder. He places his hands carefully on my stomach, a wide grin stretching across his face as he skims his eyes over our family. "We're pregnant again. Baby's due in six months."

No Feelings Involved

The room erupts in a cacophony of congratulations, and I'm manhandled by each person as I'm pulled into happy hugs.

There was a time I worried I wouldn't be able to get pregnant. When I fell pregnant so easily with Brayden, I was ecstatic but terrified too. Every twinge, every pain, sent me running to the doctor's office, afraid something was wrong. Ryan was the same. He'd told me what happened with Myndi when we got back together, and while he let go of his guilt and self-blame a long time ago, old fears resurfaced when I was pregnant, and he was every bit as worried as I was.

But we worried for nothing, because both my pregnancies were easy sailing, and I'm determined to be uber relaxed this time.

I run my fingers over the locket at the base of my throat, always remembering our little angel in heaven. Ryan had Brayden's initial engraved on it after he was born, and the same after Harper arrived, so I know he'll do the same with this new little one. Brayden knows he has a sibling in heaven, and we took him with us on our annual graveyard visit this year. Harper is too young to understand, but we'll tell her when she's old enough.

"You okay?" Ryan asks, pulling me back down onto his lap.

I plant my hands on his shoulder, pressing a featherlight kiss to his lips. "I'm perfect. I was just thinking about our little one in heaven," I truthfully admit.

"Me too." He runs his finger over mine on the locket, staring deep into my eyes. "I love you so much, Summer. Thank you for this amazing life."

"You don't have to thank me. We were meant to be, Ryan. It's always been written in the stars."

"I'm glad you broke through my walls and obliterated my concerns. If I hadn't opened my heart, hadn't let myself feel all the things I was feeling for you, I would've missed out on all of this."

My heart is full of love for this man. "It worked both ways, babe. You showed me something I didn't realize I was looking for, and you showed me how to love. You're the best husband and the best father. But above everything, you're my best friend."

Our relationship has taught me many things, but the most important lesson learned is that you should never close yourself off to love. Love comes in many guises, and forms. People will have opinions. Some supportive. Some not so much. All that matters are the two people in the relationship. Whether others approve doesn't matter as long as you're in it together.

We're lucky both our families came around.

I've gotten to live my dreams with my dream man by my side.

It doesn't get any better than this.

Inseparable is another one of my angsty and emotional standalone romances and it is available now in e-book, audiobook, and paperback formats. FREE to read in Kindle Unlimited.

Subscribe to my newsletter to keep updated with all my new releases and sales. Type this link into your browser: http://eepurl.com/dl4l5v

Acknowledgments

I'm proud of every single novel I've written, but *When Forever Changes* is a book I'm especially proud of because I've poured my heart and soul into this project. I've spent months living with these characters, feeling *everything* they felt and living with this as if it was something I was actually going through myself. I'm emotionally and physically drained, especially because I couldn't read over this without crying in several places, *every single time.* After writing the first part of the epilogue, I had to go downstairs to seek out a hug from my husband. My eldest son (he was seventeen at the time) was concerned when he saw me sobbing until he discovered I was crying over fictional characters I had created, and then he looked at me like I was crazy, haha. But having these emotional moments is huge for me, because it means I've delved deep and wrung every last drop of emotion I can from a scene. I'm feeling a huge sense of achievement to have executed this book in a way I believe does the story justice.

Gabby's story has been in my head all year, and I was itching to write it by the time I sat down to start it. When this idea first came to me, I couldn't stop thinking about what I would have done if I was Gabby, if I was faced with such heartbreaking situations at quite a young age. I felt a deep connection with Gabby, and I hope the emotion I was feeling has transferred to the pages. When I wrote the acknowledgments for *Inseparable*, I said if I'd done my job correctly then you, dear reader, should have felt all the feels. That sentiment applies here too. I hope you've experienced the whole gamut of emotions reading this but that ultimately you are happy because

Gabby, Slater, and Billy are in a really good place in their lives when we say goodbye.

When I was growing up, in a small town in Ireland, cancer was quite prevalent, but it seemed to diminish for a certain period of time only to return in recent years worse than ever. At any one time, I always know at least a handful of people with cancer. It has touched my family on several occasions, and someone very close to me is battling cancer right now. My youngest son was devastated earlier this year when one of his friend's fathers passed away very suddenly from cancer that was only diagnosed at the later stages, and it brought it all home again.

I think it's quite conceivable that most everyone reading this book has been impacted by cancer in some way, so I hope I have portrayed Dylan's situation, and the emotions surrounding his condition, appropriately and realistically and that I haven't upset anyone too much. I undertook a huge amount of research to authentically portray the things Dylan underwent, but if I misrepresented anything please forgive me.

I have to thank a few people who helped get this book published. My wonderful editor Kelly Hartigan who is extremely talented at what she does and a dream to work with. To Robin Harper for creating one of my all-time favorite covers, and thanks also to Sara Eirew for the gorgeous photo. I couldn't do any of this without the support of my wonderful team – my sister/manager Ciara Turley, my PA Zsuzsanna, critique partner Jennifer Gibson, my publicist Sarah Ferguson and her team at Social Butterfly PR, my husband and Hollianne Sullivan. MASSIVE thanks to my amazing beta readers. Thanks to my team who beta read this book: Jennifer Gibson, Sinead Davis, Deirdre Reidy, Dana Lardner, Danielle Smoot, and Karla Carroll. Thanks also to my ARC team, street team, and bloggers/bookstagrammers/booktokers around the world who help spread the word about my books. Much love to Siobhan's Squad on Facebook and to all my READERS the world over. I never imagined I could have this career, and it's all thanks to people like you who took a chance on one of my books, so, from the bottom of my heart, THANK YOU!

The Indie author community is an amazing community, and I'm blessed to have so many author friends around the world. Thank you all for your support and your friendship.

My husband and my two sons are my entire world, and I couldn't do this without them. Love you Trev, Cian, and Callum.

Don't forget to subscribe to my newsletter or follow me on Facebook to stay up to date with planned new releases. I love hearing from my readers so feel free to drop me an email anytime – siobhan@siobhandavis.com

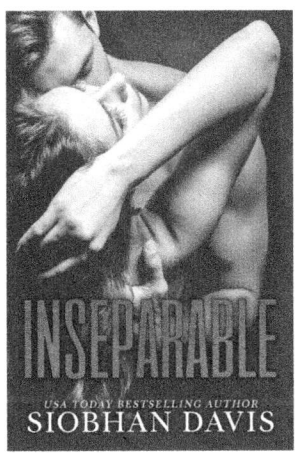

A gritty, angsty, friends-to-lovers standalone romance from USA Today bestselling author Siobhan Davis.

A childhood promise. An unbreakable bond. One tragic event that shatters everything.

It all started with the boys next door...

Devin and Ayden were my best friends. We were practically joined at the hip since age two. When we were kids, we thought we were invincible, inseparable, that nothing or no one could come between us.

But we were wrong.

Everything turned to crap our senior year of high school.

Devin was turning into a clone of his deadbeat lowlife father—fighting, getting wasted, and screwing his way through every girl in town. I'd been hiding a secret crush on him for years. Afraid to tell him how I felt in case I ruined everything. So, I kept quiet and slowly watched him self-destruct with a constant ache in my heart.

Where Devin was all brooding darkness, Ayden was the shining light. Our star quarterback with the bright future whom everyone loved. But something wasn't right. He was so guarded, and he wouldn't let me in.

When Devin publicly shamed me, Ayden took my side, and our awesome-threesome bond was severed. The split was devastating. The heartbreak inevitable.

Ayden and I moved on with our lives, but the pain never lessened, and Devin was never far from our thoughts.

Until it all came to a head in college, and one eventful night changed everything.

Now, I've lost the two people who matter more to me than life itself. Nothing will ever be the same again.

Inseparable is available now in e-book, audiobook, and paperback formats.

About the Author

Siobhan Davis is a USA Today, Wall Street Journal, and Amazon Top 10 bestselling romance author. **Siobhan** writes emotionally intense stories with swoon-worthy romance, complex characters, and tons of unexpected plot twists and turns that will have you flipping the pages beyond bedtime! She has sold over 1.5 million books, and her titles are translated into several languages.

Prior to becoming a full-time writer, Siobhan forged a successful corporate career in human resource management.

She lives in the Garden County of Ireland with her husband and two sons.

You can connect with Siobhan in the following ways:

Website: www.siobhandavis.com
Facebook: AuthorSiobhanDavis
Instagram: @siobhandavisauthor
Tiktok: @siobhandavisauthor
Email: siobhan@siobhandavis.com

Books by Siobhan Davis

KENNEDY BOYS SERIES

Upper Young Adult/New Adult Contemporary Romance

Finding Kyler

Losing Kyler

Keeping Kyler

The Irish Getaway

Loving Kalvin

Saving Brad

Seducing Kaden

Forgiving Keven

Summer in Nantucket

Releasing Keanu

Adoring Keaton

Reforming Kent

Moonlight in Massachusetts

STAND-ALONES

New Adult Contemporary Romance

Inseparable

Incognito

When Forever Changes

No Feelings Involved

Second Chances Box Set

Still Falling for You

Holding on to Forever

Always Meant to Be

Vengeance of a Mafia Queen

Reverse Harem Contemporary Romance

Surviving Amber Springs

Dirty Crazy Bad*

MAZZONE MAFIA SERIES

Dark Mafia Romance

Condemned to Love

Forbidden to Love

Scared to Love

THE ACCARDI TWINS DUET

Dark Mafia Romance

CKONY (The Accardi Twins #1)*

CKONY (The Accardi Twins #2)*

RYDEVILLE ELITE SERIES

Dark High School Romance

Cruel Intentions

Twisted Betrayal

Sweet Retribution

Charlie

Jackson

Sawyer

*The Hate I Feel^*

*Drew^*

THE SAINTHOOD (BOYS OF LOWELL HIGH)

Dark HS Reverse Harem Romance

Resurrection

Rebellion

Reign

Revere

The Sainthood: The Complete Series

ALL OF ME DUET

Angsty New Adult Romance

Say I'm The One

Let Me Love You

Hold Me Close

ALINTHIA SERIES

Upper YA/NA Paranormal Romance/Reverse Harem

The Lost Savior

The Secret Heir

The Warrior Princess

The Chosen One

*The Rightful Queen^*

TRUE CALLING SERIES

Young Adult Science Fiction/Dystopian Romance

True Calling

Lovestruck

Beyond Reach

Light of a Thousand Stars

Destiny Rising

Short Story Collection

True Calling Series Collection

SAVEN SERIES

Young Adult Science Fiction/Paranormal Romance

Saven Deception

Logan

Saven Disclosure

Saven Denial

Saven Defiance

Axton

Saven Deliverance

Saven: The Complete Series

*Coming 2022

^Release date to be confirmed

Visit www.siobhandavis.com for all future release dates. Please note release dates are subject to change based on reader demand and the author's schedule. Subscribing to the author's newsletter or following her on Facebook is the best way to stay updated with planned new releases.

Made in the USA
Monee, IL
06 April 2025

15269579R00413